A COUNTRY SUCH AS THIS

Books by James Webb

A COUNTRY SUCH AS THIS
A SENSE OF HONOR
FIELDS OF FIRE

A COUNTRY SUCH AS THIS

By James Webb

Doubleday & Company, Inc., Garden City, New York 1983

Grateful acknowledgment is made to the publishers of the
following copyrighted material to be reprinted in
A Country Such As This:

"Settin' the Woods on Fire" by Fred Rose & Ed. G. Nelson.
© Copyright 1952, renewed 1980 by Milene Music, Inc.
Used by permission of the publisher. All rights reserved.

"This Land Is Your Land" by Woody Guthrie. TRO—© Copyright
1956, 1958, and 1970 Ludlow Music, Inc., New York, N.Y. Used
by permission.

DESIGNED BY LAURENCE ALEXANDER

Library of Congress Cataloging in Publication Data

Webb, James H.
    A country such as this.

    I. Title.
PS3573.E1955C68   1983   813'.54
ISBN: 0-385-18010-1
Library of Congress Catalog Card Number 82-45969
Copyright © 1983 James Webb

To my father, who taught me the stuff of leadership,
and how to fight.
And to my mother, who taught me sacrifice,
and how to love.

ACKNOWLEDGMENTS

Many people have been both kind and helpful to me in the writing of this book. I thank them all, and particularly the following.

In the publishing industry: my editor, Kate Medina, who has been uncannily attuned to the book's aspirations; Betty Prashker, who worked with me to conceive it; my agent, Sterling Lord, who as his clients know is more than an agent, and his assistant Beth Thompson.

For the aviation and prisoner of war portions of the book: Dr. D. C. Allard of the Office of Naval History, for his assistance in my research; Colonel Fred Kiley, USAF, perhaps the greatest repository of knowledge regarding the POW experience of Americans in Vietnam; and the following individuals who shared their time and emotions with me in interviews:

Captain Ken Coskey, USN (Ret.), five years a POW, for naval flight school and the POW experience.

Rear Admiral Byron Fuller, USN (Ret.), six years a POW, his wife Mary Anne, and their children Peggy and Captain Robert Fuller, USMC, for the POW experience at home and in Vietnam.

Colonel Murphy Neal Jones, USAF (Ret.), nearly seven years a POW, whose chronology as a POW formed the basis for Red Lesczynski's in this book.

Captain Zeb Knott, USN (Ret.), five air combat tours in Vietnam and former Boss of the Blue Angels, for the Blue Angels and air combat over Vietnam.

Captain Red McDaniel, USN (Ret.), six years a POW, who has written of his own experiences in his book *Scars and Stripes*.

Commander Dick Schram, USN, Vietnam combat veteran and former member of the Blue Angels, for the Blue Angels.

Bonnie Singleton, wife of Colonel Jerry Singleton, USAF, seven and a half years a POW, for the POW experience at home.

Vice Admiral James B. Stockdale, USN (Ret.), seven and a half years a POW, and his wife Sybil, for the POW experience at home and in Vietnam.

Commander Bill Wheat, USN (Ret.), Vietnam combat veteran and former Boss of the Blue Angels, for naval flight school and the Blue Angels.

For the Marine Corps activities in Korea: Peter Braestrup, Colonel Bill Holmberg, USMC (Ret.), whose exploits provided the basis for Judd Smith's combat experiences, and Colonel William Riley, USMC, all of whom served as Marine platoon commanders in Korea.

For the Marine Barracks and White House escort portions: Majors Terry Murray, Dave Sanaszak, and Doc O'Connor, all USMC, of Marine Barracks, Washington, D.C.

For the FBI chapters: Robin Montgomery, a fellow Marine in Vietnam, now with the FBI.

For the Ford City, Pennsylvania sections: The people of Ford City, particularly the Krukar family, including my wife, JoAnn, her mother, Annie, and her father, John Krukar. *Polska Nietska Niewa.*

For the southwest Virginia episodes: My friend Jim Taylor, and my cousins, particularly Buck and Jewell Jones of Gate City, Virginia, whose blood and history I proudly share.

And, as always, my family, JoAnn, Amy, and Jimmy, for enduring my obsession with this book.

CONTENTS

AUTHOR'S NOTE

In a novel with the historical and cultural sweep of *A Country Such As This*, it is sometimes necessary to rely on literary license in order to ensure continuity of plot and characters. Consequently, actual historical chronology has been slightly altered on occasion. For instance, Queen Elizabeth II did not visit President Eisenhower in Washington, D.C., until 1957, although her visit in this novel takes place in 1954. As another example, Red Lesczynski is allowed to finish his flight training in a shorter time period than was normal, and the ship on which he deployed, the U.S.S. *Princeton,* had actually deployed a few months before the time period in the novel. Other than with such minor alterations that were themselves not essential to the historical movement of our country, the chronology of this novel is faithful to actual events.

A number of nonfictional characters also appear in this book, often at locales that do in fact exist. The author wishes to emphasize that, except for individuals who are clearly indicated by their own names, all characters in this novel are fictional.

A COUNTRY SUCH AS THIS

Part One

BLOOD BROTHERS

PROLOGUE

They were to be three men gathered in triumph.
That had been the formula.
But it would not happen.

HE BEGAN BY VISITING Arlington Cemetery. He followed Sheridan Avenue through a sea of markers, around a woodsy bend and to the bottom of a hill. He stopped near a small drinking fountain, and walked down a grassy row past eight other stones until he reached it. He tried a soliloquy as he silently confronted the grave, attempting to find meaning in the etched letters that proclaimed name and birth and death. It didn't come off.

So he got back into the car, and drove east. He would go to the other place. He had to do that, anyway. It had been a promise, consecrated by blood. You could foul the world in many ways, he thought, and maybe you were even supposed to. But failing to honor your word was different. You defiled yourself, not the world, and you did so indelibly.

The sign on Memorial Bridge said *Welcome to Washington.* The far riverbank unveiled parks and monuments, and the green prayer rug of a Mall. That loosened him up; it always had. These were the symbols of his country on the other side of the bridge, and they caused his emotions to burst in the air above Washington like Fourth of July fireworks. They conjured up a many-headed mood, like the confusing mix of love and anger and insecurity a child feels when he sees his parents quarrel.

He could see the Jefferson Memorial's global roof and the square, columned Lincoln Memorial and then the Washington Monument piercing the summer smog, a bayonet. Far down the Mall the Capitol Dome glimmered sedately, and on the edges of that long green lawn, nearer to him, the old buildings of the Smithsonian Institution spoke to him of accomplishment, and heritage. Further upriver, he caught a corner of the Kennedy Center and the Watergate apartments, where the amateurish burglary of a political headquarters began a torturous process that drove a President out of office.

Metaphors, all of them. Rorschachs on the Potomac. They once had left him invigorated, bristling with pride. They still did some of that, but now they also reminded him that he was weary. It was June 1976, and the country was approaching its two hundredth birthday on the edge of a decade of defeat—the defeat of war, the defeat of a President and his minions, and most of all the defeat of confidence, the shattering of the very nucleus of what it had always meant when one thought of the word "American."

The ugly buildings began, modern architecture, square boxes and long glass windows messing up the far edge of the Mall. He turned onto Independence Avenue and was suddenly at a stop sign in front of the Rayburn House Office Building, and then was passing it. The Capitol building was near him on the left, awesome and serene, the temple of his culture, Broadway and Sunday school gathered under the same dome. Passing it, he remembered what Sam Rayburn used to say about running the country, that any jackass could kick a barn door down, but only a carpenter could build one, and he found himself shaking his head, like a disgusted football fan watching a lousy game. He marveled again at how few carpenters there had been in American politics during the past twenty years. And how many jackasses.

He drove through the city. It changed once he left Capitol Hill, growing ugly and hopeless. This was his country, too: Black people gathered on porch steps and at street corners, watching him with an energy or anger that was dormant at that moment, latent and unfocused. Trash was on the streets and in the yards and the air smelled heavy and wet, faintly alive, as if all of them had spat on the sidewalk at the same time in their apathy or disgust, and the hot sun had boiled the water and the odor out of the spittle and the warm June breeze had nudged it around the buildings and the cars, picking up dust and fumes until the air was heavy with it, spit and dust and fumes but mainly spit. He felt a new emotion rise inside him. It was not guilt, but rather the other side of it; a relief that he was not among the little brick boxes of tenements, down in the garbage and the weeds, staring out with dark angry eyes and gathering spittle on the top of his tongue.

The John Hanson Highway began. A quarter of a century before, the city had ended abruptly at the highway, but as he looked through the tree lines he realized that now it was following him into the countryside. It was insidious, the city. It grew like a fairy ring in the grass, killing off its center and moving ever outward in a circle.

Eventually he saw the sign. *Annapolis, 12 miles.* He crossed a little bridge, over the back waters of the South River. The river was murky and banked by reeds. Black folk fished at its edges, reaching over the reeds with long cane poles. And then another sign: *Historical District, Next Right.* It charged him, because in a sense he was a part of that history, but also because it made him remember. He had always used this road coming back.

He drove over another little bridge. The water underneath was clean and the homes that dotted the banks had wooden docks and small boats and looked quaint and lush, and their vision was a warm hand that stroked the wrinkles off his brow. Straight ahead were the peaks of the Maryland State House and the governor's mansion, and then off to his left was the opaque turquoise of the Naval Academy's chapel dome. He remembered the first time he had seen the dome on his return from a summer at sea, how excited he had been even as he protested his worldliness, because upon seeing it he was officially an upperclassman. For that moment as he stared at it, waiting for a light to change, the unexplainable joyous exultation of his youth was fresh and real again.

The dome was larger than the Capitol Dome in Washington. Not really, but in his mind and remembrance it would always be so. And there were 489 panes of glass in the chapel windows. There had always been 489 panes of glass in the chapel windows, and two anchors out front, and an inscription on the doors that said, *"Non sibi, sed patriae." Not self, but country.* All that would never change, and so he would always be young when he confronted it.

He drove through Church Circle and State Circle and stopped for a moment at the Farmer's National Bank. He withdrew the safety deposit bag from the bank, and eighty-seven dollars that remained in the savings account. The brick streets tickled his tires, vibrating the car. Then he was at the waterfront. The sun was dappled in a thousand little bowls of waves that he knew were filled with silt and jellyfish. Along the dockside was a mix of old and new; people everywhere, moving in and out of bars and restaurants and little shops, cars thick along the narrow roads. Beyond, he could see the Severn River and the large antennae of the Communications Station on its opposite bank, and then the endless Chesapeake Bay with a thousand sailboats dotting it, and finally the thin frail strands of the Bay Bridge, far on the horizon.

He was not ready to go into the bar. It was not really the same bar —before it had been Mario's, and you could get a bacon and tomato sandwich for a quarter. But now it was the Old Town Tavern, Established 1776. Bicentennial pretentiousness had joined with the spreading fairy ring, and Annapolis was a Washington playground. But that wasn't the real reason he hesitated.

He drove onto the academy grounds. As he left the packed gaiety of the waterfront, the tourists and sailing folk with their colorful bathing suits and bleached hair and fifty-thousand-dollar playthings in the water, the memories began to focus. He parked the car inside the academy gate and walked along a flat, wide field that had been dredged up from the river. He reached the seawall and the whole emotion became exact, and finally he understood it. The suction that had begun twelve miles out had pulled him into the vacuum of his past, until the years engulfed him.

He walked the seawall. The smells embraced him, a perfume of seaweed and salt and ambergris. He gazed out where thousands of people were working their boats and drinking their drinks and he thought, as he used to do so often before, that they were having fun, and he was not having fun. That was the distinction, the gossamer he had been reaching for in town. Annapolis would never be fun; it would always be business, serious business. He had come there in the afterwash of a great war and had left in the middle of another one, and all the time he was preparing. Annapolis to him was loneliness; a continual yanking at his innards, a catching in his throat as he missed friends and women and life.

He was alone now, and he was walking. It seemed he had been always alone, always walking, so in his mind it might have been years before, and he thought easily about the rest of it. It all mingled together. At one moment, watching the heavy gray buildings across a wide field to his left where he had spent four years preparing, he was young again, walking lonely and preparing. Then without a conscious decision, he was himself, on the other side of it all, looking back. He passed a few midshipmen, and they did not look young, nor did he feel old. He played games with himself. It was easy to do. He was there, at that moment, judging it, noting the changes, and then at the next moment he was a plebe, seeing it for the first time, trying to understand what was happening to his life.

All the while he was remembering four years inside those unforgiving walls, when time had stood strangely still, momentous events occurring and he reading about them and commenting on them, but powerless to do anything about them, even the ugly war that had broken out in 1950, during the summer after his third year. And then, with the abruptness of birth, he had tumbled out of the womb and he was struggling merely to live, to keep his head above water, unconscious of the reality that those struggles were part of a force that was making the world turn. The flotsam that had kept him from drowning had always been values. He had gained his values in many places, but he had clarified them here. It was his one great satisfaction, that he had honored them. Not always, but whenever he could. And not that they had taken him along the roads that had been promised those years before.

That had been the surprising thing about the past twenty-five years. And yet, looking back, it had also been inevitable. Life was not supposed to be simple, but at least it was going to be predictable, like the problems he had solved in class. Here was the situation, there was the data, and he had memorized the formula. You plugged in the data, and the answers fell out at the bottom of the equation. That was going to be life; plug and chug. They all had the formula—duty, honor, country. The data would merely happen. And the answer would be great things, and happiness.

He walked the Big Tour, nearly three miles, past Luce Hall and Bancroft Hall and then over to the classroom areas, Mahan and Maury and Sampson and Isherwood Halls, still avoiding the new buildings, the testimonials to advanced academics which mildly irritated him, not because of their testimonials but because of their newness. And then finally he was ready.

How silly. How inevitable. It would be a reunion of one.

Inside the Old Town Tavern, which was doing a booming Bicentennial business, a young woman just out of high school led him back to a corner table, eyeing the safety deposit bag with skepticism. It was lush and dark inside. The waitress was wearing a short, full black skirt, a white blouse with a bow tie, and a triangular Revolutionary War hat. She handed him a menu, which he declined. When she began to protest about the rules of the Old Town Tavern, Established 1776, he bribed her with a five-dollar tip taken out of the eighty-seven-dollar bank account. He sat quietly in the corner then, unpacking the bag, trying to be inconspicuous among the other guests. He laid the contents on the table.

The Time Machine.

A set of stars, for an admiral or general. A bottle of Scotch, Johnny Walker Red. And an envelope containing a poem.

He opened the Scotch, hesitated for a moment, and then took a pull straight from the bottle. It was rather like Holy Communion. he thought, feeling the whiskey burn down the back of his throat and splash into an empty stomach. He opened the envelope.

It wasn't a bad poem.

> There are gains for all our losses,
> There are balms for all our pains,
> But when youth, the dream, departs,
> It takes something from our hearts
> And it never comes again.

He missed them, then, just as fully as he missed his youth. Annapolis was filled with reminders that had been there before, and yet they had been the dominant memory as he stared at buildings and monuments. They had burst out of this placenta with him, and it was all going to work, but now it was down to him. They had believed, as had he. They had wanted it, all of it—to make the country go, to love and be loved, and someday to die in peace. They had gotten some of it.

They had shared his last moments of innocence. Not innocence from sin, but from life: success, failure, sorrow, joy, denial, gratification, it didn't matter. It all changed you, scarred you up in different ways. So they were special, partners on the other side of a cannibalistic, devouring life-warp.

He stared at the oddments of the Time Machine and they again became boy-men who shared his deepest secrets and especially his dreams. There was only one thing to do, really, and he would do it in their honor, a somewhat silly gesture, perhaps akin to what he knew the Japanese did at their Shinto shrines, when they left a departed friend's favorite cigarette or *sake* so that his spirit might partake of it.

He would celebrate them. Yes, that was a proper homage. He would not grieve; grieving was for cowards. He would get gloriously drunk. He would sing and dance, maybe even puke on the floor. He would remember all their joys and pains. Because that was the sum of a good life, anyway—having the courage to celebrate.

CHAPTER ONE

Friday, June 1, 1951

SHE WORE A DARK BLUE, ankle-length dress. She had nice teeth, when you could get her to smile and reveal them. Her blond hair was parted on the left side and brushed tight against her scalp, no tease, no puff, straight until it reached the bottom of her neck, where it piled in curls against her upper shoulders. *So tell me,* thought Judd Smith, thinking of the advertisements, *is this a girl with natural curl, or does she have a TONI?*

"Waitress! Sweet little honey-haired nymph, goddess of morning, who carries the very *soul* of this country in her womb, just as the soul of Greece rode in Helen's eyes . . ."

She stood cross-armed in front of Smith, her head cynically cocked to one side, breasts pressing against the fabric of her uniform. She was stocky, world-wise and twenty-eight, and what she had been carrying to Smith's table for two hours was not the Soul of America, but beer, from the eternally splashing spigots of Mario's Bar. She shrugged. "You want another round, or what?"

Smith stared fondly at her as he lay back in his chair, sprawled in a sea of white that was his Marine Corps dress uniform. His gray eyes had a Scottish highlander's bounce, peering out from behind a square, freckled face. He was a blend of Indian and Celt, and the face showed it: light brown, wavy hair over high cheeks and a narrow Algonquian nose, thin lips that were capable of stifling all emotion if the mood called for sobriety. Just now they were parted in a devil's grin, as one of his wide hands caressed her thigh behind the knee. "Actually, I'd like to make love to you."

She laughed quickly, shifting her leg and scanning the other tables to see if anyone had overheard, then shook her head slowly, flattered but still sardonic. "You wouldn't know what to do with it if you had it dropped in your lap, kid."

"No, actually, I'm quite a package. You ought to check me out." Smith tapped his brand-new second lieutenant's bars. "Don't let these fool you, doll. I was in the Fleet for two years before they locked me up over there in the Marble Monastery." His bright eyes were teasing and his hand found her leg again. He sat forward, momentarily caught up in his own words, the thought of making love to this clone of a Saxon barmaid not even having entered his head until he had spoken the words and heard her response. "You look pretty lonely, you know." She shook her head, still faintly flattered, but now tapping on her order form as if to demand that he get back to her business. He squeezed her leg. "Actually—"

Joe Dingenfelder and Red Lesczynski were laughing at him, jibing him, telling him to leave the poor tired woman alone. Anything was funny after six beers, even Judd Smith's predictable attempts to bed every woman who moved slowly enough to be spoken to. He stared at them with false irritation, and his slow drawl became a sudden command, "Will you two please shut the hell up?" He turned back to the waitress. "Actually, we'd like a razor blade."

"A *razor blade?* What do you think this is, a drugstore?" Another table called for her. She ran a hand through her carefully bleached hair, contemplating Smith. She liked him, he could tell. Women usually did. He was clean-featured, well-built, and courteous, with a smile that could make even the coldest old spinster remember prom night. "Would a steak knife do?" She shook her head suddenly, as if to clear it. "What am I saying? What are you guys up to, anyway?"

"We're going to cut our wrists." Lesczynski and Dingenfelder started laughing again, and she scurried off to the other table. Smith called after her. "No, we really are!" He turned back to his friends, grimacing. "You maggots."

Joe Dingenfelder toyed with the cigar Smith had foisted on him, and wiped an ash from his bright green cashmere sportcoat. The coat was a graduation gift from his physician father, and Dingenfelder, known for his fastidiousness, inspected it continually in the bar's dim light. He had slender, pianist's hands, and his long fingers had indeed found their greatest solace on the keyboard of a Steinway, even during the demanding years at Annapolis. Dingenfelder watched Smith grab his beer and toss down half of it, and he laughed at his wild man of a friend, his chocolate eyes softening his face into an almost apologetic docility.

"Don't you know alcohol kills brain cells, Judd? It's been scientifically proven. We've probably killed a million brain cells this afternoon. And they don't regenerate, either."

Smith snorted. "Any goddamn brain cell that can't live through a

good drunk deserves to die, Dingie. You're doing yourself a favor, getting rid of all them nonhacking, underachieving ones. I'm working on
improving your efficiency, there, Einstein."

Dingenfelder continued to laugh. It was funny. Everything was
funny. He shook his head helplessly, looking toward Red Lesczynski.
"How are we ever going to get along without the guiding light of Judsonia Shelby Smith?"

Smith burped, staring after the waitress. "You actually think you're
getting rid of me? Hey, Dingenfelder. Hold onto your wallet, boy. You
never know when I'll show up on your doorstep."

Dingenfelder nodded knowingly. "Drunk and diseased."

"Screwed, blued, and tattooed. Not to mention broke. But what are
friends for, right, Dingie?"

"Whatever you say, Judd. You bought the last round." Joe Dingenfelder pulled hesitantly on his cigar, gazing queasily around the dark
cave of a bar that they had not even been allowed to enter until a few
hours before, when they had thrown away all the confinements and
abstentions of midshipman life in one collective toss of their caps into
the air. They were finally graduates and commissioned officers and
able at last, among other wonderful things, to drink publicly in Annapolis. It was all unfamiliar to Dingenfelder—the bar, the beer, even
the cigar—but he hung on gamely to this mandatory anthem of good-
bye. Even if the combination of the three now made his stomach
churn.

Red Lesczynski had picked up Joe's nausea. "Watch out, Judd.
Tchaikovsky's going to flash all over his new sports coat."

"Damn it, I am not!"

"Dingenfelder, you're a case." Smith had finished his beer, and was
looking for the waitress again.

Red Lesczynski slapped the table with a heavy hand, his pink features glowing with good humor and excitement. He looked enormous
in his white ensign's uniform, as if he would soon burst out of it at the
chest and collar. The glasses on the table bounced at his casual movement. "I've been saying for four years that Dingie's going to be late
for his own graduation, and this morning I turned around at
0800 and he was still in the rack."

"Was I late? Huh?"

Red Lesczynski jutted a thumb toward Dingenfelder, shaking his
head. "The only guy in the class of '51 who forgot to bring his second
lieutenant's bars to graduation."

Dingenfelder shrugged, his mind off his nausea, that little smile crossing his face again. "I'll be a first lieutenant by the time I finish grad school, anyway. So who needs second lieutenant's bars?" He stroked his new sports coat fondly. "They don't look good on civvies."

Smith grunted. "Goddamn Air Force. Businessmen in uniform. Here we are in the middle of a war, and they send Dingie-Lingie off to grad school."

"Eat your heart out, dirt ball."

"Are you kidding me? School is jail. I've done my time."

They grew silent then, immersed in the effects of the beer, contemplating separate futures.

In a month, after graduation leave, Smith would report to Quantico for Marine officers basic training, and would then go to Korea. Lesczynski would soon report to Pensacola, to earn his Navy pilot's wings. And in September, after temporary duty in the Pentagon, Dingenfelder would pursue a master's degree in Aeronautical Engineering at MIT. It was conceivable that they might not see each other again for years.

Joe Dingenfelder broke the silence, peering at Lesczynski with open envy. "You'd better be careful leaving Sophie alone in this town, Red. With 725 brand-new officers out on the make, you might never see her again."

"Get serious. That girl would bleed and die for Red." Judd Smith shook his head. "Never seen anything like it. I'd undertake the bonds of matrimony my own goddamn self if I ever found a woman like that. You don't deserve her, Red. I tried to tell her that, but she thinks just because she grew up with you she knows you better than me and Dingie, and you know that's a bunch of crap."

Lesczynski smiled blandly in the dark, self-conscious about discussing that part of his life. It was the very center of his existence, and it was private. He found himself rubbing his face, trying to penetrate the alcohol-induced numbness with stubby fingers. "I want to meet the woman who catches you, hillbilly. I'll be the first to offer her my condolences."

"Here she comes now. Shh." Smith's face took on a warm intensity as the stocky waitress approached once again, holding a steak knife in one hand and peering at them with a combative hesitance. He threw both hands into the air, as if to embrace her. "You came back! I knew you would. I want you to know I haven't even looked at another woman the whole time you've been gone."

"Lucky me. All right, gents. If you cause any trouble with this knife I'll call the cops." She peered at Judd Smith from the corner of one eye, a look that acknowledged him as someone just as knowing as she in all the offbeat ways of life, ways that she also knew viscerally the other two would never comprehend. "I'm only doing this because we love each other, honey. You know, there's something about a man in uniform. As long as it's not one of them goddamn middy suits."

"I *knew* you'd fall for me. It just takes time." Smith reached out to put a hand on her full hip and she casually slapped it away. Dingenfelder and Lesczynski laughed, and Judd took the knife from her hand instead. "Great. Now we'll need another round of beer, my love, so I can calm the nerves of these unsteady beasts."

"Just don't forget." She raised a finger in warning. "I'm not fooling about calling the cops."

"Hey, this is *Mario's!* Would I do anything to spoil the reputation of such a fine establishment?" She sauntered away, swinging her hips for Smith as if in heat. He turned to the others and slapped the knife against the palm of one hand, again and again, grinning.

"This is dumb, Judd." Red Lesczynski seemed more embarrassed than afraid, his eyes flitting around at the other tables in the packed bar. My friend, thought Judd Smith, staring into pale blue, laughing eyes, you will always have a boy's face. The floppy ears, the wavy shock of flame-red hair, the uncomplicated, innocent energy that lifts your eyebrows and makes smile-wrinkles in your cheeks. Your face will take on the bags and wrinkles of experience, but it will never be old.

Smith dismissed the others in the bar with a jerk of his head. "The hell with everybody else. They've got their own problems. Now, how good a friend are you, Red? Huh? Would you bleed for a friend?"

"For a *reason* I would. If you were in trouble, you know I would. But not just for the hell of it. Come on, Judd, I'm twenty-two years old."

"So what?" Smith continued to tap the knife, still grinning. The waitress set down three more beers and playfully let her hand rest on Smith's neck for an instant before she walked away. He called quickly after her, "I love you, you know that." Then he focused in on Red Lesczynski again. "You goddamn Polacks can be so stupid. What do you need for a reason, anyway, a horde of Chinese attacking me? This is the best reason in the world, Red. This is the way of the warrior. If you'll mix your blood with me, then we're one people. Whatever happens to you, happens to me."

"You've been reading too many comic books," Joe Dingenfelder interrupted, appearing even more queasy from the beer and cigars. He watched the steak knife bounce on the flat of Smith's palm, again and again, and allowed one thin hand to reach inside his coat and hold his stomach. "Anyway, not with that knife. Oh, come on, Judd. What if I cut a vein or something?"

"This isn't comic-book stuff, this is for real. The Indians used to do it when they accepted whites as fellow warriors. If you'll mix your blood with mine, we're brothers. And if we're brothers, your battles are mine, your enemies are mine." Smith dropped his lyrical near-mimicry and tossed the knife onto the center of the cluttered table. "Come on, guys. Y'all are getting yourselves a pretty good deal."

"If this is such a good deal, why did the Indians lose?" Red Lesczynski was weakening, though; it was apparent in the way he studied the knife with resignation. He looked up and examined Smith's determined face, then sighed. It was inevitable. Finally, he picked up the knife.

Joe Dingenfelder's eyes grew round. Smith smacked him on the shoulder, startling him. "Take off your coat, Dingie." Dingenfelder slowly removed his coat and carefully folded it, watching Smith and Lesczynski both reveal muscled forearms as they raised the sleeves of their dress-white uniforms. Smith pushed empty beer glasses and ashtrays to the far side of their little circular table, and laid his forearm on the cleared portion, wrist up. "Put all three arms together, here, and give me the knife." Joe Dingenfelder was delaying, nervously fumbling with his shirt button. "Come on, Dingie, it won't hurt."

The three forearms lay side by side, Lesczynski's from across the table and Dingenfelder's next to Smith's. The three clenched fists belonged to men from three different worlds, bonded by a four-year military regimen, yet destined for separate lives that would interweave only by accident in the coming decades.

Red Lesczynski's thick arm dwarfed the other two, made large by a continuous weightlifting program that he had begun in grade school. His meaty hand and fat fingers would guide the stick of a fighter aircraft with the same dedication and consistency that had given him, day by day, exercise by exercise, the muscled arm.

Joe Dingenfelder's thin forearm and the delicate hands that had trembled through boxing classes and other unnatural demands, that even now twitched, near panic, under Smith's raised knife, spoke of an artistic and intellectual power that would someday go beyond mere piloting. Dingenfelder was a creator, a genius awaiting recognition.

And finally the instigator's own lean, muscled shaft of bone and skin, with its thin wrist and wide, hard fist, the hands of a working-man, a farmer or a trucker, who had by some accident ended up at the United States Naval Academy and who by some other accident would soon go to war in Korea as a Marine. Judd Smith was an impon-derable, a collection of aggressions and energies turned loose from the steep ridges of southwest Virginia when he had enlisted in the Marine Corps at the close of World War II, sent to the academy prep school by the Marines when his recruit tests revealed a mind whose depths were completely untapped. The wide hands had indeed driven trucks and farmed. What future awaited him, beyond a war, was unknown.

Without warning Smith lowered the knife and quickly sliced all three wrists, blood immediately streaming and flowing onto the table top. Joe Dingenfelder yelped and cradled his arm, then became afraid he would drip blood onto his new trousers and put his arm back onto the table top, his narrow face querulous.

Smith smashed his wrist onto Dingenfelder's, standing as he did so, his face alive with delight. A glass crashed to the floor. He screamed as his wrist connected with Dingenfelder's. *"Brother!"* He then held his bleeding wrist out to Red Lesczynski, who had grabbed a napkin and was holding it above the cut, protecting the white of his uniform. Their two wrists met, forming a cross in the air, and they both yelled it together, *"Brother!"* Dingenfelder had begun to smile hesitantly then, and held his arm in the air, meeting Lesczynski's. *"Brother!"*

The waitress had trundled across from the bar when the glass broke. She dropped several napkins onto the table and chided the three laughing men as they leaned back in their chairs, half-drunk and yet sated by their act, this full affirmation of kinship.

"Well, you weren't kidding, were you? You're damn lucky you didn't break any more glasses. You guys. No more beer for you, or you'll be cutting each other's throats, never mind arms."

Smith reached absently out to pat her on the hip and laughed when his arm was slapped away. "Now, honey, don't get mad."

"Well, you can forget about *that*, and I mean it."

"You'll be back. They all come back." She sidled off after having left the bill on the table.

Judd Smith watched the others for what seemed like a long time.

All three held napkins to their wrists. Their silence emanated a mood that was on the brink of both joy and embarrassment. "So, that's it. My blood is your blood. Your blood is my blood." He grinned, feeling a little foolish. "Anyway, Indians don't forget these things."

Joe Dingenfelder eyed him almost shyly, his face lit with a small smile. "So, how does it feel, having Jewish blood?"

Smith laughed, shaking his head. "I'll tell you, Dingie, I think it's already getting to me. I'm even starting to like that coat."

* * *

It had grown dark outside. They dawdled in front of Mario's, making small talk, not knowing how to end it. A warm, humid breeze blew in off the Chesapeake Bay. The intermittent glow of distant lights washed over them, from boats in the narrow harbor and cars turning along the waterfront. They stood uneasily, basking in a rare, evanescent mix of innocence and fear, as if it were the moment before first jumping into an open, thrashing sea, or being shot into outer space.

Red Lesczynski searched the faces of his friends. "You guys sure you can't come to the wedding? You know they love you in Ford City." He laughed softly, considering Judd Smith. "Come on, Judd. You've never seen a Polish wedding, have you? I'll even fix you up with that girl Anna again. She *liked* you."

"I wish I could, Polack. But like the man said, I've got miles to go." Judd Smith stared at the dirty sidewalk, and then back up at Red Lesczynski. They both knew that was untrue, that he really had nowhere in particular to go, at least not until his Marine Corps training started. Smith shrugged, unmasked by Lesczynski's knowing look, and toyed with his Marine Corps cap, finally putting it on. "This is just the best place to say good-bye, that's all. And this is where we'll have our reunion. You guys agree, right? Twenty-five years. We'll drink the Scotch and count each other's wrinkles and tell lies. Just the three of us. No excuse, unless you're dead." He grasped Joe Dingenfelder's shoulder. "Dingie, you took care of the Time Machine and the money, right?"

Dingenfelder sighed with exasperation. It was the tenth time Judd Smith had asked him. "Yes, Judd. The Farmer's National Bank. It's in our joint names. Two hundred ten dollars in savings, seven dollars to be withdrawn annually to pay for the safety deposit bag. Interest compounded semiannually at 2 percent, over twenty-five years. It should cover it. In fact, we should have enough left over to pay for a dinner."

"Listen to that. Our very own Jewish banker."

"I've never made fun of the fact that you're dumb. Don't knock the fact that I'm smart."

"What was in the envelope, Dingie?" Judd Smith was grinning, mildly taunting Joe Dingenfelder. "Come on, now. I toss in booze, Red throws in admiral's stars, you put in a mystery envelope. Don't be cute. You can tell us."

"It's a poem, that's all. Come back in twenty-five years, Judd, and I'll read it to you." Dingenfelder smiled gently, suddenly softening at the thought of actually leaving. "Don't get killed over there, Judd. I really worry about you, you know."

Red Lesczynski grabbed both of them in his powerful arms for one last moment. It was time to leave. They were getting too sentimental, and besides, he had to go meet Sophie. "Let's just all be careful, okay? Can we promise each other that? It's a rough life, all this."

"Come on, Red, you're a better man than that." Judd Smith searched Red Lesczynski's eyes from a foot away, his chin high, his own face squinched into a dare. "Careful people are boring as hell. Let's promise each other we'll be brave."

CHAPTER TWO

I

SOPHIE HAD INSISTED ON taking the bus back, even though he was driving and even though it was only seven hours, so that everyone would know they didn't spend the night along the way. That was just the way you did it, or to be more precise, that was the way you showed that you *didn't*. *Red,* she had insisted in that small, lilting logical voice, *Red, what if the car broke down on the way and we had to spend the night at a hotel or something, or if we even came in the next morning because of it? You know what everybody would be saying. And we've made it this far, lasted this long, so why take a chance on something like that?*

So he drove back alone from Annapolis, journeying further and further inland, past Breezewood and then into the western Pennsylvania mountains toward Pittsburgh, and finally cutting north along narrow roads through coal towns and factory towns with their small, cluttered business districts and heavy black air like low clouds from the smokestacks. Red Lesczynski was coming home. It was his fate in life always to be coming home, but never again to live there, to have left his home in order to preserve his place in the community. It made his trips more precious. Coming home was his best reward for having forever left. He was Ford City, Pennsylvania's ambassador to America.

His new Buick rode smoothly. He loved to drive. It was the next best thing to flying. He guided it easily on the narrow concrete. The Buick was a dream. It had Dynaflow, torque tube drive, an F-263 Fireball engine, a push bar forefront ("smart style and unsurpassed protection," the advertisement had promised), white glow instruments, four wheel coil springing, dual ventilation, and self-energizing hydraulic brakes.

Not bad, for the sixth son of a foundry worker. No, sir. The Navy wasn't bad at all.

His excitement increased with every mile, until by the time his Buick raced easily up the ridge behind Ford City, he was so elated that he was singing. It was late afternoon. He stopped the car on top

of the high ridge that they called Ford Cliffs and he caught Ford City
in the pink of a distant sundown, just in time to say good night.

The Pittsburgh Plate Glass factory dominated his vision, a half mile
of narrow, same buildings that stretched out in the valley below him
like a box of dominoes placed end to end, paralleling the ridge. The
factory was sandwiched between an uncurving length of the Allegheny River on the far side, and ribbons of railroad tracks on the side
nearer to him, toward the town. The tracks were cluttered with freight
cars that were being loaded with plate glass even at this hour, for
Pittsburgh Plate worked around the clock. Closer still was the town,
wide and thin as the factory itself, filling the space between the factory and the steep ridge on which he sat. Its square box houses and
their exact plats of company-town yards were seven streets deep, and
a hundred wide.

Red Lesczynski watched all of that, the layers of river and factory
and railroad tracks and town, but it was the churches that kept him
singing. They said it all as they reached above the boredom of the
cracker box homes. They jutted into the air with the severe stone architecture of the Germans. They hunched under the onion bulbs of
the Ukranians. They boasted the gaudy, unapologetic turquoise of the
Poles. They stood complacently behind the frugal, plain bricks of the
Irish. And mixed among them were the others, gathering places for
Italians and Syrians, Slovaks and Jews. Ford City, factory town. Ford
City, immigrant town.

Nearly six thousand people were nestled in between the river and
the ridge, most of them having straggled in, family by family, over
those two decades of unparalleled immigration that bracketed the
turn of the century. Eastern Europeans dominated the town. They
were called "hunkies" by the others, a label that had begun decades
before because of the handkerchief-like babushkas that their women
wore.

Ford City was not idyllic. It was not even comfortable. Its families
were welded to the factory in an often unhappy symbiosis, so dependent on the well-being of the plate glass industry and the whims of
management that the very small-town isolation they loved was at the
same time their greatest threat. But it was home.

Hey, you hunky town, you layer cake of dreams!

Lesczynski drove down the ridge and through narrow streets past
yards and gardens and people calmly taking in the evening on their
porches. A few dozen others sat on benches in the small town park.

Old John Ford had donated the park sixty years before, to the town that bore his name. His "grateful workers" had in return paid from their salaries for a bronze statue of Captain Ford at the end of the park closest to the factory. So now, forty years after his death, John Ford still stared placidly from his concrete pedestal, behind a rusting, creaking gate, toward the center of the world he had created.

The Pittsburgh Plate Glass Company. In 1887 Ford had selected this tract of bottomland next to the Allegheny River for a new plant. It was not only his interest, as he indicated at the time, to create an industry close to raw materials and transportation, but to "carve out a worker's community, a new settlement to provide men with a livelihood, a home, and all social services." Lean and rawboned Southerners of the textile belt might have nodded in instant recognition of such rhetoric, rasping with the brown lung: what you mean is, a mill town. Soot-faced mountain dwellers further south in Pennsylvania, and further still in Kentucky and West Virginia, might have grunted their assent, coughing from the black lung: what you mean is, a company town. Broad-backed steelworkers from the hills and valleys that traced the Allegheny all the way to Pittsburgh would have blinked through eyes parched into sandpaper from the foundry fires: what the man means is, a factory town.

But no matter. It was home, and Red Lesczynski loved it. *Ford City*. It housed his family, it cradled his values, it called to him from the far recesses of his spirit whenever he needed just that extra little piece of pride, *Hey, hunky town, this one is for you!*

He stopped his new car in front of his home and Frank Zbikowski looked up from his chair on the porch next door and his eyebrows raised in something that resembled triumph and before Red Lesczynski could open the car door Zbikowski had done it for him, and then the old man was pounding him on the back and shoulders, tattooed arms moving in front of Red's face like comic strips.

"Is that you, Red? Hey, the Navy's in town! I was just telling the wife, you know, about that time last fall when I heard you on the radio in that Army-Navy game and they gave you the game ball. It felt like I was there myself!"

* * *

The football recruiters liked hunky boys. They were tough and they would cut their hearts out and lay them on the table for the right coach. So the recruiter followed Red Lesczynski through all the little

coal and steel towns during his senior year, watching him break skulls with a steady Slavic ferocity on the playing field and watching him retreat into a shy, hesitant formalism during their interviews off the field, watching the bright glow in his ice-blue eyes when ships and airplanes entered the discussion, and, finally, watching with a knowing satisfaction when the muscled youth signed his letter of intent in the small, cluttered living room of his family home.

That was November 1946, the first time Red Lesczynski realized the irony that he would have to leave Ford City in order to preserve his place there. He signed the letter, knowing it was in many ways a warrant of voluntary banishment from family and community, but watching with an overwhelming exultation as the recruiter drove off and his mother and grandmother dashed excitedly out the door, old Baba stopping for a quick moment to pick up her shawl. He lost track of them as they walked down the narrow little streets, past the German Catholic church and the Slovak Catholic church and the Russian Orthodox church and the Polish Catholic church with its bright-blue roof, even striding purposefully past the Dago Catholic church and the funny, spireless building where the boring Presbyterians came in to pray. He knew that at every church, indeed at every house where tired factory workers raked thin leaves or their wives retrieved half-frozen clothes off clotheslines stretched from porches to nearby trees, his mother and Baba would deliberately stop, offering inane introductories about the coming snows, the coming holidays, the probable strikes at the factory, waiting for their chance, the slightest little interrogatory about family or future. He could clearly visualize his mother going coy, cuddling into her sweater, and Baba smiling, pulling her shawl around her and nodding, her face like a nun's, framed by a gray babushka, the shriveled, hunchbacked old grandmother finally raising a small, gnarled fist and proclaiming with a shriek that a half-century before had been trained by calling hogs on the flat plains of southern Poland,

"Hey, my Stasu, he go Annapolis, learn be boat captain, be *REAL AMERICAN!*"

And he finally knew that he had been ostracized by their very love when his father and older brothers took him to the Falcon Club that night. In the club, the red and white flag of Poland covering the wall that faced the door, amid cheers that pierced the pall of the factory and the gloom of a country smashed by Germany, destroyed by a war, and swallowed by the Russians little more than a year before, a crowd

of thick, knowing men embraced him, pushed beer down his virgin lips, mussed his wavy shock of fire-red hair, pounded on his back with meaty hands, then issued him notice with eyes that already knew he had begun a journey that would take him forever away from their club and his blood. Many had bled for their new country, this United States, and in a way for Poland, as recently as a year before. They had known war and they had known officers, in the manner that they had always known the factory and known foremen.

"God. Damn. Officers," one beery worker jested to his father as he pressed another drink into the boy's uncertain hands. "The next thing, we'll hear he's a Republican, too."

And in the kitchen with his mother when he returned home, Sophie, the only woman he had ever known, almost a sister on summer swims along the river and sledding outings down the ridge's icebound winter roads, childhood friend, homecoming queen, waiting maiden, afraid of this place called Annapolis that would rob her of her teenage bridehood, of four years of children, of, perhaps, her future. But it would not. She would come with him, when the time came. The world would be too large and impossible for him if she did not. In the small living room, under the drone of the radio's protective noise as the other eight family members snored one floor above, Red Lesczynski cupped a bare breast in his large hand and swore his eternal devotion.

So he went away for four years or forever and he gave Annapolis and football his best Ford City hunky shot, and with every play, even in the awesome stadium in Philadelphia, a hundred thousand voices cheering, cameras rolling, national radio broadcasting his efforts against Army and Notre Dame, back in the very first twitching of toe and ankle that drove him forward into a tackle, was the impulse that had started that terrifying and exhilarating night when he knew he must leave his family and community in order to remain a part of them. Waiting for a command on the drill field or for an opponent's ball to snap, he could feel those words as if his people were all standing just behind him, elbowing, pointing, nodding with proud electric eyes, their exclamations drifting into his eardrums like shots of adrenalin,

My boy Stasu, hey he go Annapolis . . .

＊　＊　＊

"Are you ready, Red?"

"I've been ready for four years."

"You're supposed to be nervous."

"Why? This isn't exactly like going to the dentist, Pete." Lesczynski peered into the mirror, taking his eyes off the high collar of his Navy dress-white jacket and smiling placidly at his older brother. "Take it easy. There's nothing to get excited about."

Pete checked his watch. The white coat he had rented from Bedner's danced away from him at the waist, unable to adjust to the mass of torso that began just under his shoulders. His white carnation boutonniere was dangling dangerously to one side, as if ready to jump to the safety of the floor. His wide, fleshy face peered uncertainly at the watch as he calculated the time remaining before Mass. "Twenty minutes."

Lesczynski finished his collar. "We'll be early."

Pete shook his head, frustrated with the easiness of his task as best man. He was remembering his own wedding two years before, when Junior, the brother immediately older than he and thus his best man in the family tradition, had been driven to fits by Pete's anxieties. Junior often teased Pete that he almost had to get married in his place, Pete had been so late and befuddled. But Pete had not experienced his younger brother's four years of regimens and ceremonies. A nine o'clock nuptial Mass blended into all the other obligations of the past four years, and could just as well have been a meal formation.

Lesczynski smiled again at his older brother, putting a protective arm around his heavy shoulder. "Don't worry, Pete. I'll tell them you had to dress me."

"They'll never believe that. You didn't even get drunk at your own bachelor party. You're not even hung over." Pete said it as an accusation.

"Sophie wouldn't like it. That's no way to start a marriage."

"Sophie wouldn't like it? That's no way to start a marriage? Sophie doesn't have to like it! That's the way all marriages are started!" Pete frowned, his own baggy eyes floating in small bowls of tomato soup that had nothing to do with his work in the foundry. Pete obviously felt that Red's sobriety was an indication of his own failure as best man, even though he had drunk manfully himself in the previous night's celebrations.

Lesczynski inspected himself one last time in the mirror. His three medals, two for marksmanship and the other the National Defense Medal, were perfectly centered over his pocket. His ensign's shoulder-boards had been brushed with a whisk broom to remove all lint, and their gold braid gleamed above his thick shoulders as if he were a Cossack general. The gold buttons along the front of his jacket were in place, with the eagle emblem on each of them straight up. He smiled broadly, at peace with himself, and glanced for one last time around the small bedroom he and Pete and Junior had shared through their childhood. The Virgin Mary was on one wall. Jesus hung from the cross on another. And Franklin D. Roosevelt, that third element of the hunky trinity, smiled benignly from another, just above the bed in which Lesczynski had dreamed for so many years of being what he now was and doing what he was about to do. Nervous? Pete had to be crazy to think he would be nervous.

"Good-bye, room. Good-bye, house. Good-bye, Mum and Pop." He grabbed Pete by his thick neck. They squeezed through the small door as if the two of them made a crowd. "Come on, Pete. We'll walk slow. This is the greatest day of my life. I want to take it all in, all the flowers, all the clouds, all the people. I'm a sponge today, Pete. I'm going to catch it all."

Pete smiled uncertainly, pulling at his ill-fitting rented coat and shaking his head. "The other brothers, they got normal weddings. Me, I got a guy who wants to smell the flowers instead of hold his head." Pete shrugged resignedly, pushing his gorilla of a younger brother through the kitchen door. "Come on, sponge. Go smell flowers." He sighed, throwing heavy hands into the warm June air. "So who says I deserve this?"

There was more to soak up than Red Lesczynski had ever dreamed. The crowd began near the German Catholic church, three full blocks from the Polish church where the nuptial mass was being held. They lined the streets, the curious and the well-wishers, the friends and the others who had merely been lifted from the grinding isolation, the feeling of separateness, by turning on a radio once a year for three years in a row and hearing "Tackle by Lesczynski" again and again. He walked awkwardly down the middle of the street and waved, at the same time embarrassed and enthralled. More than a thousand people, 20 percent of the entire town, had filled the church and the nearby streets.

Pete grunted, adjusting his boutonniere as they reached the church steps and giving his hung-over head a small squeeze. "Gee, Red. All these years we've known each other. Why didn't you tell me you were famous?"

It was so overwhelming that it became a blur. Five hundred people jammed the church, men of all ages in their only suits, women with their little hats and visorlike lace veils, white gloves covering callused hands, the old widows in their perennial places in the back pews, dressed in black, heads covered in their best babushkas, the wedding an excuse to pray one more important time before Deliverance and to peer out from their boring last days into the future and their past. A long white runway filled the center aisle, pure as the April snow, pure as Sophie, and he stood at the front of the church and watched her walk it, slow and sure, filled with a cat's awareness, as if she were indeed on stage. She paused at the Virgin Mary and left a bouquet and crossed herself, a gesture of her purity, and joined him forever with a tight grasp of his hand. She even winked and smiled to him, ignoring the priest for a quick moment, completely unafraid. That was Sophie, that was Red. What was there to fear in getting married?

Afterward there was breakfast in the basement of the church, the mothers weeping, the fathers somber, all the men dressed in the same ill-fitting white coats as Pete (a banner day for Bedner's clothing store), each with a boutonniere, the women with corsages (a cause for rejoicing at Arner's Flower Store). Baba boasted a brightly flowered silk babushka, her very finest, and had even bought new glasses from Dr. Siegel, who offered a Special Wedding Discount. They retired quickly to Sophie's house for a private reception, and respite. The real celebration would begin at five o'clock that afternoon, inside the Falcon Club.

* * *

May God bring you joy, they all told her. For some it was a wish that God bring her what they had found in wifedom and motherhood, for others it was a secret hope that she might find what they had not. They called to her on the streets as she and Red walked from her house to the Falcon Club. They came up to her and kissed her or embraced her. Tina Wojzciewoski, who normally reserved such grandeur for the Fourth of July, had gotten drunk and tossed a hundred firecrackers into her backyard as they passed, then performed a staggering, waving dance in the yard for them as dozens on the street laughed. *We're only getting married,* thought Sophie again and again, but she had seen too many weddings to believe that. Marriage was a signal of rebirth for them, an affirmation, an embracing of their own eternity. And the ceremonies were also a diversion.

The Women's Auxiliary of the Falcon Club had cooked all week. The Bingo tables in the club had been covered with pink butcher paper, the color of the bridesmaid's dresses, and one long line of tables was a cornocupia of Polish delight: *Holupki*, rolled ham, *roski*, large pickles, *pirogi*, fried chicken, homemade bread, poppy-seed rolls, nut rolls, waffles doused with powdered sugar, potato and ten other kinds of salads. As the guests poured in, Bertha Bohoskey and Marie Chervanek marched tensely behind the tables, wearing house-dresses and white nursing shoes and aprons. Bertha's hairy legs bulged with muscles and clots of varicose veins. The club would be packed with five hundred ravenous people, and it was their nerve-wracking mission to content them all.

On another table was the wedding cake, iced the same pink as the butcher paper and the bridesmaids' dresses, and beyond that was an empty table that quickly was cluttered with brightly wrapped presents. They began to pack the hall, the men again in their only suits and the women wearing bright colors and taffeta, chokers and pearls, new pairs of seamed stockings, and soon the presents were being carefully placed on the floor, underneath the precarious stacks that had filled the table.

Sophie stood in the reception line, smiling and hugging and talking, gradually beginning to feel hot and weak inside her full and heavy gown but determined that she too would absorb every moment and file it away for slower times. Red stood next to her, in many ways such a physical contrast that she often wondered how they could have shared the same ethnic blood. He was pink-skinned, compared to her tawny yellow. He was huge, large-boned and naturally strong, as if that frame had been designed to carry ox carts on its back, while she was almost slight, though firmly muscled. *He goes out where I go in,* she thought, watching him with an admiration that bordered on worship. He is up where I am down, he is hard where I am soft. She clutched his hand, knowing where it was without having to look, at the same time smiling and hugging the latest old foundry worker in his pinched suit who had watched her grow from a tow-headed little girl and wanted to wish her well. But he is warm where I am warm.

Red had brought Baba up to stand with him. The wizened old woman wore a black wool dress and her prized silk babushka. She had new black tie-up shoes and she clutched her oversized purse against her chest, just underneath the large cross she always wore to church. Her hair was pulled back in a bun and she wore no makeup. She was just a worn-out old woman who had never really found her place out-side of Poland, but watching Red squeeze her, Sophie felt instinctively that he would never stop loving her, Sophie, if he kept on loving Baba like that. Baba was so special to him, and that said it all. Baba had never once in his life called him Red, or even Stan, the American per-version of his full name, Stanislaus. It was always Stasu. *My boy Stasu.* Even now she had a wrinkled arm around his trim waist and was babbling to a guest in the receiving line in broken English about her Stasu. Baba was the anchor. Forgetting her would set them all adrift.

The bar served whiskey or beer. For most of the men, it was whis-key *and* beer as they casually dropped shots of whiskey into their beer glasses. The guests filed past the food tables, devouring Bertha Bohos-key's and Marie Chervanek's creations with the completeness of an army of locusts, and proceeded to the long, presently pink Bingo tables, delicately carrying paper plates to avoid spilling food on their best clothes. The army of people who had packed the red-walled Bingo and dance room of the Falcon Club to unbelievable capacity fell silently into their food, like a fight crowd in between rounds.

Then, slowly, as the beer and the whiskey and the food set in, there came a tinking sound, a spoon against a water glass, and then an-other, and in a few moments the whole hall echoed with the sound, in unison, tink tink tink, and behind it laughs and catcalls. "Come on, Red!" .

So he grinned and stood and she felt him lift her from her chair as if he were picking up a child. He grabbed her at the elbows and took her off the floor and kissed her full on the mouth, the crowd now applauding and screaming its delight, and he had no sooner eased her back into her chair when the tinks came again, tink tink tink, so she surprised them all by standing up herself and grabbing a floppy ear in each hand and kissing him for a very long time as he sat, stunned at first, his hands by his sides, and then embraced her and then, finally, stood again himself, lifting her up again. It was almost too filled with passion and delight for the old-country Catholic audience, which whooped and applauded, but did not tink their glasses again.

On a stage covered with silver and red wallpaper, three fat, tired-looking men, who worked during the week in the factory, set up stools and began tuning their instruments, speaking in hushed tones to each other. The men among the guests quickly broke down the Bingo tables as the women did away with the paper plates and trash, and in

minutes an accordion backed with a drum and a saxophone burst out
with a lively polka. They danced in an explosion of gaiety, women and
men, women with each other, women with children, children separate
and together, around and around while men tossed red powder from
buckets to the floor, as if fertilizing a garden.

"Ladies and gentlemen. Ladies and gentlemen, excuse me." The accordion player called to them several times and finally the shouts and
laughter halted as they turned toward the stage. "We would like to
play all night, and maybe we *will* play all night, but you know that
Red and Sophie probably got better things to do." The old accordion
player's clown face, with its large, bulbous red nose and the eye
sockets that seemed to crease all the way into his ears, beamed with a
self-satisfied grin as the crowd whooped and whistled at his little joke.
"And as you all know, and most of you damn well remember, there
comes a time when a girl has to say good-bye, and go become a
woman. So will you please clear the floor? Sophie and her bridesmaids
are going to line up over here. Mrs. Bohoskey, can you bring the whiskey and the cake, and we'll have the *Este Nasa*."

Sophie stood at the end of the line, next to Linda Melnick, her best
friend through school and her maid of honor. In a tradition that had
begun centuries before, in another country and probably under the
pre-Christian rigors of Slavic formality, the bridal dance required that
she say good-bye to everyone who had come to the wedding by dancing with them, one at a time. And in a more recent twist, no doubt
brought on by the near-poverty that seemed also to be a Slavic tradition, each guest who danced with her dropped a small bit of money
into the maid of honor's apron, creating a dowry of sorts that would
help Sophie's father pay for the wedding.

She was already exhausted. She had Red to think of once they left
the reception and drove off to the Coach and Four Motel in Kittanning for their first night of love. But she watched the hundreds of children and women and men form in a line and she felt like weeping, so
deep was her thanks that she had such friends. On they came, one at a
time, dropping dollars that might have gone for shoes or perhaps a
movie into Linda's apron, and on Sophie danced, around and around
to the upbeat, driving music from the stage, hundreds and hundreds
of times around the dance floor until she became numb to it, as if she
were running a marathon. The men would drop their dollars and take
a shot glass of whiskey and toss it, then reel her around the floor, each

one trying to outdo the other. The women and children would dance, and when they finished would take a piece of cake. And Sophie danced, dry in the throat, light of head, her heart pumping the final ounces of adrenalin that her system could provide.

Finally, after what seemed like hours, she had danced with everyone. Her father approached her then, his dark eyes deep and translucent, and held her gently with his rough worker's hands. He was a small, barrel-chested man, and she could feel his firm muscles as he squeezed her for a too-long second after they finished their turn around the floor. Her mother followed, in the tradition. They reeled together around the floor self-consciously, and then returned to Linda and the others. Breathing rapidly from the dancing, her mother slowly took the bridal veil off Sophie's head.

"My baby." Her mother began to cry and so did Sophie. Red came up for the final turn around the floor, the crowd now screaming and applauding, and she left her girlhood in her mother's hands with the veil.

As they finished, Red lifted her easily and carried her toward the stairs. He would have had to, anyway, even if it were not part of the tradition. She was completely drained. Linda had tied her apron into a knot, the money inside, and tossed it into Sophie's lap as Red carried her away. Red even raised one hand, effortlessly carrying her with the other, and waved good-bye. In the dark of the stairway he squeezed her against him and kissed her, sucking tears from her cheeks.

"Is anything wrong, Sophie?"

"People cry when they're happy, too, you know."

Outside the Falcon Club people battered them with rice as they dashed toward Red's Buick. Pete stood next to the car and opened the door for Sophie, grinning with self-satisfaction as he patted Red's shoulder hard, the way they used to do in high school.

He slammed Sophie's door. "At least I was able to screw your car up for you. It wasn't a total loss."

Red stared at the marked-up car with the crepe paper dangling all over it and the tin cans tied from the rear bumper. People continued to pelt him with rice. He hit Pete's shoulder the same way Pete had hit him. "You did great, Pete. Are you drunk again?"

"Hell, yes, I'm drunk again. Why aren't you drunk again? Hey, Red—" Pete eyed him slyly. "Do you know how to do it?"

Red was halfway to his own car door. He halted, and stared quizzically at his brother. "Do what?"

Pete shrugged, angling his head toward Sophie, who was trying gamely to keep smiling as she waved at the people who still stood in front of the club. "You know . . . *Do* it."

"Aw, Pete." They might have been ten years old again, Pete the big brother and Red the embarrassed innocent. "You shouldn't talk like that." He slammed the car door and drove off into Forever, tin cans rattling the road until even the Syrian homes down the street turned on their lights from curiosity.

* * *

From Pittsburgh they drove south, through the hills and factory smells of West Virginia, a state raped and ignored by the nation whose furnaces it feeds. They bit off the southwestern tip of Virginia, passing within a thirty-minute drive of Judd Smith's mountain home although not realizing it, because Judd Smith didn't go home much anymore. They rumbled slowly over narrow, curving roads as they traversed the western sections of North and South Carolina, Sophie now wearing a halter top and shorts, watching the countryside with wide eyes and occasionally taking in the square, voluptuous muscles of her new husband as he drove hour after hour, as comfortable behind the wheel as he was anywhere, even in her arms. The insides of her thighs were still warm from him, slightly sore as she crossed her legs. She remembered someone having told her a long time ago, perhaps in a hushed, schoolgirl conversation or maybe in one of the thousand books she devoured while waiting for him to graduate and marry her, that once a woman has been loved the right way she will never, ever feel the same about herself or her body again, and that was the way she felt even as the stretched skin of her womb whispered in pain, because she remembered the rest of it, the whole four days of it.

In Georgia the soil went brick-red and the roadside was cluttered with small, desolate little cottages with patched roofs and gardens at the side, the porches filled with ill-dressed families, alternately white and black, who sat silently and stared with opaque faces at Red's new car as they fanned themselves from the dank, oppressive heat. There seemed to be no difference in the way most of them lived, white or black. The difference was at the gas stations, where they used different bathrooms and drank from different water fountains, and in their attitudes. The whites were falsely loud, deliberately offensive when they noticed the Pennsylvania tags. They reminded her of Judd Smith. The blacks were falsely docile, careful not to stare at her heavy breasts or her slim, bare legs. They reminded her of cowed Doberman pinschers. In Alabama both parts of the disparity were worse. There was anger, even cruelty in the air.

Just outside Pensacola the soil went white from sand and the road was immersed in a sea of scrubby pines, cabbage palms, and thick, gnarly shade trees that looked something like oak trees but weren't. The grass in the yards of the little houses had a shabby look because of the sandy soil. Homes and cars displayed the quick decay that the salt air of a southern sea town perpetrates on all objects, peeling paint and growing quick, huge scabs of rust. Black mammies waited for buses on street corners, on their way to maid jobs. Sophie wiped sweat from her hairline and neck and felt an unease growing inside her, an undirected fear, like a roll of greasy nausea. What was this place to which Red rejoiced in taking her, with its rust and heat and cruelty? Why must she leave her home?

Then the road ended and the Gulf of Mexico burst before her, calm and blue, washing gently on beaches of salt-white sand that stretched as far as she could see, and all was forgiven, anything was possible.

"Oh, Red, look! Isn't it beautiful! Come on, stop the car. Let's go into the water. Please? I've never seen the ocean before!"

They ran together along the beach, she in her shorts and halter, he in a pair of tan working slacks, mindless of the sand and salt water that soon covered both of them. Finally they stood laughing, thigh-deep in the water itself, splashing each other like schoolchildren.

She giggled, defending herself from a warm curtain of water. "Red, stop it! Oh, we're a mess. How can you report in like this?"

Lesczynski began to stare south and west, far into the distance, his face excited and intent. Water dripped from his nose and chin and she saw that she had lost him for that moment, and followed his gaze, immediately becoming enveloped by a sudden knowledge, a jealousy. A few miles away, two SNJ Texan trainers were taking off from Chevalier Field, practicing formation flying. Up they went, small specks, and then they curved off over the sea. In a few minutes, two more went up and away. He touched her shoulder, still staring after his dream, as if he had just caught sight of the most beautiful woman in the world. Finally he shook his head with joy, and embraced her right there in the water, cars along the parkway behind them honking at their frolic.

"I just can't believe they're actually going to *pay* me to do that!"

He drove her through the good parts of Pensacola then, and it became exciting, an exotic foreign seaport. First settled by the Spanish in 1559, it was the oldest community in the United States. Because of its natural harbor, the city was an attractive site for naval powers, and for centuries Pensacolans had traded flags like some towns trade merchant goods. Red told her that more battles had been fought over the small port than in any other place in the country. She could see it in the architecture and in the names, a blend of British and French, Spanish and Indian and American.

The stucco and tile roofs of Spain mixed with old frame houses that could have come from anywhere. Barrancas Avenue crossed Main Street, Cervantes intersected with Palafox. Across from the Spanish-flavored building that was city hall, in a little park on Intendencia Street, was a monument dedicated to someone named Chipley who had been a Confederate hero in the Civil War.

But old Spain dominated, perhaps because it was the most foreign, the most antique, the most irretrievable, and when Red Lesczynski ceremoniously stopped the car in front of the high stucco of the San Carlos Hotel, Sophie fell in love with it.

"Are we really staying *here?*"

"Just for tonight." He grinned, salt stains running in little rivulets along the hollows of his cheeks. "I mean, it isn't exactly the Coach and Four, but what the hell, this isn't Kittanning, either."

"Oh, my!" Mosaic marble floors, marble posts in the lobby that ran all the way to a twenty-foot ceiling where old four-blade fans slowly turned, thick red carpets, and a high dome above the lobby itself, decorated with colored glass like one might find in a church. A marble stairway with polished brass railings went up to a mezzanine. Other guests stared curiously at them as they stood in the middle of the lobby, dripping water from their clothes. They were half dressed by hotel standards, and overwhelmed by the old hotel's opulence.

Later, in the small hotel room, she jumped naked on the bed as if it were a trampoline, her large breasts bouncing, her dark hair flying, her wide-cheeked Slavic face a child's.

"Come on to bed, Red. Come on, you big fighter pilot. Make me a baby right now. Oh, I think I'm going to like the Navy after all."

That was just Sophie's style, and she did have style. She rarely held back anything; not an opinion, not an emotion, not an impression. Her large brown inquisitive eyes stared like a happy child's into shop and car windows as she and Red walked along the streets of Pensacola, over to other tables as they dined in the hotel's elegant restaurant, even directly into her husband's as the waiter stolidly awaited their dinner order.

"Hey, Red. Before I order, tell me something: can we *really* afford this?"

She flaunted her lack of worldliness and culture like some women flaunt their jewelry. Sophie Lesczynski knew what she wanted from the world, and she had it, right across the table from her as the waiter allowed his eyes a small roll toward the ceiling. She would make a home, grow a family in her very own belly, go along for this ride they called Navy life, and the rest of the world would simply fall into place.

And, my God, she thought, smirking back to Lesczynski as he shook his head at her deliberate *faux pas,* when Red starts drawing flight pay we'll be making more than three hundred dollars a month. And the Navy will give us quarters. That's more than Dad makes right now, and Red's only twenty-two. Of course we can afford this. We're *rich.*

The next morning he awoke automatically at dawn, in one of those obsessed, removed trances that made her know he was thinking about those same airplanes he had watched the day before on the beach as if they were indeed a competing love, a mistress. He showered and put on his service dress-khaki uniform, inspecting himself time and again in the mirror, and by eight o'clock had her up and fed and packed and in the car, heading toward the Naval Air Station to report aboard.

She took it all in: the sailors in their dungarees and white bell-bottom uniforms, the winding roads through pine and scrub, the planes that seemed ever to circle and dive like swallows, scattered through the air for miles on all sides, the naval aviation cadets who marched in their midshipman uniforms from building to building, the square, austere buildings themselves. So this is it, she mused to herself, waiting in the front seat of the car as Red went from office to office, getting his orders signed and applying for housing. *This is your life, Sophie Lesczynski.*

He spent ten minutes warning her that the quarters they had drawn were supposed to be terrible, but they weren't terrible. In fact, they were better than the Ford City home of her girlhood, and they were incomparably better than what she had seen driving through West Virginia and Virginia and the Carolinas and Georgia and Alabama.

Terrible was a variable. It depended on one's frame of reference. Two bedrooms, a living room and dining room, a small kitchen, government issue furniture, even a yard, and the utilities were paid. Uncle Sam was a regular philanthropist compared to old John Ford.

II

"Hey, Sophie."

"Well, hi, Louise. How's the baby?"

Louise Maxwell held the right side of her bulging stomach. She had brought her new General Electric indoor-outdoor portable radio onto the concrete step of the porch that adjoined her quarters with Sophie's, and was lazily enduring the hot Florida autumn as Johnny Ray tore the air with a ballad about loneliness and loss. She motioned for Sophie to join her on the step, shaking her head and dripping her words like slow sorghum, her Mississippi drawl making her sound as if she cleaned out the inside of her mouth with her tongue every time she spoke a word.

"I rolled over last night and he kicked the living *tar* out of me. It's a boy, I know that. Boys kick more, that's what my mama says. And I'd say he darn well wants *out*." She sat forward on the step, elbows on her knees, running long, delicate fingers through her blond Lilt permanent. "And that makes two of us. It's too *hot* to be sitting here with nine yards of fat all over my body." Louise brightened, elbowing Sophie as she sat down next to her. "Jimmy says when the baby's born, we're going to have a watermelon feast, right here in the front yard. Watermelon and beer. I don't know *why* I crave watermelon the way I have over the past few weeks. Jimmy says I must have a nigger in the woodpile."

"*Louise.*"

"Sorry. You're so nice, sometimes I forget you're a Yankee."

Sophie giggled, then examined Louise with bemused eyes. "You've just got to learn not to say things like that, Louise. You'll hurt Jimmy's career. The Navy's got all kinds in it."

"Well, Jimmy said it about *me*, not about somebody else." Louise rubbed her stomach, and then the small of her back through her print maternity blouse. The October sun raised beads of sweat in the hollows underneath her eyes and along her neckline. "What you all don't understand is, some of my best friends really *are* niggers. Niggers are just different, that's all. What's wrong with that?"

"You shouldn't call them that, if they're your friends. I don't think they'd appreciate it." Sophie eyed her mischievously. "I'll bet you call me a dumb Polack behind my back. Do you tell Polack jokes about me?"

"You're not a dumb Polack. You're the happy Polack, that's what I call you. But you're still a Polack, Sophie, you can't get around that."

"So what should I call you?"

Louise smiled brightly, as if she had been waiting to make her joke. "Like Jimmy says, you can call me anything you want, as long as you smile when you say it."

Aircraft droned on the fringes of their vision, student pilots performing stalls and loops and turns, in various stages of instruction. Louise nodded toward the sky. "So, which one is yours? If you can see one that's upside down, that's probably Jimmy. He's in acrobatics today."

"Red's got his A-19 today." Sophie stared pensively toward Whiting Field's northern airfield. "If he makes it, he can solo on his next flight, and he's only been flying six weeks. I'm so proud of him. Louise, I'm pregnant." Sophie dropped the news as if she had said, "There's a cloud in the sky," or "You have a stain on your housedress," not even taking her eyes away from their searching gaze.

"*What?* Hey, Sophie, that's great!" Louise tried to catch Sophie's eyes. "At least I *think* it is. How does Red feel about it?"

"I haven't told him yet. I don't want to break his concentration." Sophie touched her friend on a knee, smiling at her. "Don't say anything, okay? I'll tell him after he solos."

*   *   *

This boy can fly. He had heard Lieutenant Myers mutter it to Lieutenant Commander Bullock after Red's A-18 check ride, Myers performing a "guest instructor" chore, certifying that Lesczynski was ready to move on to his solo, the switch of instructors for the key check ride something of a safety measure by the Navy, to countermand any possibility that the regular instructor was either too easy on a man, or less than thorough in every aspect. But there had been no need to worry about that. Lesczynski was burning a hole through flight training. He had received "above average" marks on almost every flight, a rarity. The Navy was anxious to get good pilots to the fleet, for Korean War service, and Lesczynski was only too happy to comply.

3

Lieutenant Commander Bullock was a wiry little Texan who had downed eight Japanese aircraft during World War II, participating in the battles of Midway and the Philippine Sea, or as the naval aviators termed it, the Marianas Turkey Shoot, since they had shot 346 Japanese planes from the sky in just a few hours. His sunburned face had the texture of creased leather. When he was not flying, he chain-smoked Camel cigarettes, right down to a half-inch nub as if they were still precious wartime commodities. His favorite verb, noun, adjective, and adverb was "fuck." But Bullock and Lesczynski developed an immediate rapport that bordered on passionate mutual admiration. Each knew the other man loved flying down to the marrow in his bones, lived for it, dreamed of it, brought it home inside his mind just as businessmen drag home bulging briefcases.

In his nearly four months at Pensacola, Lesczynski had gone through preflight school, which for academy and ROTC graduates was a condensed version of the course the regular officer candidates studied, and had already amassed more than twenty hours of detailed one-on-one cockpit time with Bullock, in what was termed basic training. After he soloed, he would go on to precision flying, acrobatics, gunnery, dive bombing, cross country flying, and, finally, the carrier qualifications that distinguished naval aviators from all others. With luck, after that he would enter advanced training as a future jet fighter pilot, which would require some four months of fighter training in Kingsville, Texas, and then jet training back at Whiting Field, flying the little TV-2. If everything worked out perfectly, he would deploy to Korea as an F-9 pilot, flying the same plane in combat that the elite Blue Angels flight demonstration squadron had been flying around the country until the war broke out and they formed the VF-191, the first F-9 squadron in the Navy. The F-9 was a hot little plane. It was capable of 515 knots, with a rate of climb of almost nine thousand feet a minute, and it could carry six 250-pound bombs off the deck of an aircraft carrier. It was a true pilot's dream in 1951.

But a Korean deployment was a long way off; eight months to a year, at best. For now Red Lesczynski had to master basic skills, and the SNJ Texan.

"Take it on over to Pace, Mr. Lesczynski."

Bullock growled it casually, and Lesczynski knew what was coming. He had handled the whole flight himself. He had taken the plane up, navigated from field to field, shot touch and go landings at Whiting and Saufley fields, stalled it, taken it for spins, and otherwise shown the gruff, demanding Bullock that he could go it alone. Pace Field was a square mile of grass north of Pensacola, and it was traditional for instructors to allow students to make a first, unofficial solo attempt from its solitude.

He approached Pace, and Bullock growled again through his headset. "Land it, and taxi it around."

He brought it in, dropping the landing gear at one hundred and thirty knots, lowering his flaps at one hundred knots during the final approach, touching down gracefully, tail-first in the naval aviator fashion, in order someday to catch the landing wire on a carrier, and hit the deck at a perfect sixty knots. Flying was a study of thoroughness, of concentration, that was not unlike the complete attention to detail and one's surroundings that football required. It was not a new attitude for Lesczynski to learn, only new knowledge.

"Taxi it over there. Okay, put the brakes on." Bullock hopped out of the plane like a spry little leprechaun, screaming over the loud engine. "Take three landings and come back and pick me up." He walked over and sat on the grass, grinning, and lit a Camel.

Turn into the wind, lock the tail wheel, open the throttle, and away you go. He was up, on his own, almost a soloist. He could come back down and pick up Bullock and Bullock would take the plane home, a courtesy to a successful student. And the next one, the *next one*, would be all his.

*   *   *

I've got a baby inside me, Red Lesczynski, down in there growing brains and a spinal cord right now, and you don't even know it. You're pushing a plane around the sky and I'm giving you your eternity. I heard the car door slam and in five seconds you're going to walk in that door and I'm going to tell you, solo or no solo. You're going to be a papa.

He walked into the little living room, dressed in the one-piece flying suit that she found so undeniably sensuous, and hugged her. "So how did your day go?"

She patted him on the back and paced slowly around the room, a half-smile on her face, her hands behind her as if she were a child holding back a secret. "Well, Louise and I and Sara Detweiler did the old forts today. We did Fort Barrancas and Fort San Carlos and Fort Pickens and that old hospital. Do you know the hospital? They say they built those high brick walls to keep the mosquitoes out so the patients wouldn't get yellow fever. I guess they thought that mosquitoes couldn't fly very high. Do you believe that, Red?"

"No. I don't believe anybody was that stupid. Then again, maybe they were. We're probably doing something just as stupid right now that people will be laughing at in a hundred years. Is that all you did?" He had gone to the refrigerator and fetched a beer, and was sitting in the stark, carpetless living room on a government issue chair.

"It takes a long time to do that, Red. Fort Pickens is quite a drive. Louise is going crazy, in her ninth month and all. She wants to have a watermelon party. She says—" Sophie squinched up her nose and giggled. "She says Jimmy teases her that she has a nigger in the woodpile. What does that mean, Red?"

He leaned back in the chair, watching her, a warm smile creasing his face. "It means Jimmy Maxwell is a good guy, but people are going to be calling him a bigot."

"Oh, I know that. But what does the expression mean? Does it mean he's teasing her about being part colored?"

"It's supposed to be a friendly insult. Is Sara still hot for that lieutenant instructor?"

"Red!"

"Well, I think that's terrible."

"She's just having a hard time, Red. We're trying to help her."

"Is that what you call it? A hard time? She marries a guy and comes down to Pensacola and immediately starts seeing someone else. Bruce is so turned around he's ready to bilge out of flight school."

"She's not that much worse than Judd Smith."

"Judd isn't married, Sophie. There's a difference."

"We're working her through it, Red. You've got to be patient in these things. Not everybody can have a *loving, dedicated, beautiful Polack* waiting for them when they come home." She laughed, and dropped herself onto his lap. "Uh, Red—"

"You spilled my beer. And you didn't even ask me how my flight went."

"Well, I already know how your flight went." She stood up and mimicked him, curling one small hand into a fist and leaning forward, her eyebrows furled as she waved the fist in front of her face. "*You knocked their socks off!*"

He sat sprawled in the chair, his head back, laughing toward the ceiling. "See? You're already taking me for granted."

Now she was Baba, hunched over, pointing a knowing finger. "Hey, my Stasu, he go be plane captain, fight Korea!" Then she returned to his lap, resuming her normal tones. "Okay, how'd you do?"

"I knocked their socks off."

"Boring, boring." She kissed him on the forehead, then on an earlobe, then on the lips. *I'm going to tell him. He'll do all right on his solo anyway and I need to share it with him. Half of it is him. But will he resent it if it gets in his mind? I should wait until after. But I need to tell him.* "Uh, Red—"

"Uh, Red. Uh, Red." He kissed her back. "What are you trying to tell me, except that you forgot to make dinner?"

It was true. In her nervousness, she had completely forgotten dinner. She cocked her head, raising her eyebrows. "That was it. How did you know?"

"I can read your mind like a book, Sophie."

* * *

"Good morning, Mr. Lesczynski. Gonna take it out yourself today, huh?"

"Hi, Ron. Yeah, it's the big day."

The plane captain was a sailor about his age, a pleasant little Italian from Pittsburgh named Cimaglia. He and Lesczynski had developed a pattern of easy banter about home over the weeks they had known each other. "They had an early snow in Pittsburgh last weekend. Did you hear about that?"

"No. In *October?*"

"Yeah, it's gonna be a bad winter." Cimaglia smiled. "That's another reason why you can't beat Navy duty, at least around here."

"Still seeing that little blonde?"

"Well, let's see, the quote was, 'I don't know if my fiancé would like to share me, now that he's home from the war.'" Cimaglia shrugged, laughing, and Lesczynski joined him.

"All right, let's do it." Lesczynski grew immediately serious, walking toward the aircraft as if it were for that moment an opponent in a fight. The little SNJ Texan always reminded him of a bumblebee, with its fat nose and stocky fuselage. In fact, when the sky was filled with them, Lesczynski often found himself thinking of Pensacola as a giant beehive. The SNJ, which was only twenty-eight feet long and yet had a wingspan of forty-two feet and a height of twelve feet, had been the standard trainer for both the Army Air Corps (redesignated the Air Force in 1947) and the Navy since the late 1930s. It cost just over twenty thousand dollars a copy, could take off from a standstill in nine hundred feet, cruised at one hundred and sixty knots, and was one of the safest planes in the world to stall, spin, roll, dive, and invert. Even as Red Lesczynski approached his trainer, Army observers were peering out of the same plane in Korea, dodging ground fire as they pinpointed enemy positions.

He tossed his parachute onto the rear edge of the left wing, imitating Lieutenant Commander Bullock's casualness, and began a walkaround of the aircraft, accompanied by Cimaglia. Thoroughness and suspicion were the bywords of an aviator. It did not matter how many times an item had been checked; the ritual of checking and crosschecking, repeated over the years until it became habit, separated live aviators from foolish dead ones. *You only have to mess up once.* That was Bullock's byword.

The gas cap was on the wing. He unscrewed it and stuck his finger into the hole, feeling liquid. He peered down the wingtip to check for damage, and checked the wing itself for telltale ripples that would indicate overstress from recent acrobatic maneuvers. He checked the wheels for hydraulic leaks and air. He peered inside the cowling behind the propeller for leaks and loose wires. He looked down both sides of the fuselage for stress wrinkles, then played with the rudders and elevators to see if there were any constrictions. Finally, as if he had been doing it all his life, he nodded to Cimaglia in the same manner as a connoisseur approves a fine wine.

"She'll do."

He donned his parachute and climbed into the forward cockpit. Cimaglia strapped him into the pilot's seat and then stood by the plane with a hand-held fire extinguisher as Lesczynski went through more checks and cross-checks inside the little cockpit. He fired the propellor from inside, continuing his checks, and Cimaglia backed away, awaiting further word. Lesczynski took a secret, deep breath and picked up the hand-held microphone.

"South Whiting tower, this is Willie Baker five-eleven, request permission for taxi, over."

"Roger, Willie Baker, this is tower, you are clear for taxi."

"Roger, five-eleven out."

Lesczynski grinned widely, his blood pumping as it used to do just before the opening kickoff of a football game. He raised both hands to Cimaglia, heels together, thumbs out, and moved them apart. Cimaglia grinned back, showing two fists together to indicate that Lesczynski should hold the brakes, and then pulled the chocks from in front of the wheels. He held the chocks up to Lesczynski like trophy bass, his fists closing again and then opening, telling Lesczynski to release the brakes. The little Italian guided Lesczynski onto the runway, pointing to one wheel, Lesczynski braking it, turning the plane. Finally he pointed both hands toward the runway: Go get it, Big Red.

Lesczynski moved down the runway in snaking "S" turns, the front of the SNJ so high that its pilot could not see directly over it when taxiing. The aircraft was no longer an enemy. It roared loudly and responded to his slightest twitches and he was in its heart, no he *was* its heart, as much a part of it as the engine itself. He picked up the microphone again.

"Tower, this is Willie Baker five-eleven, request permission to take the duty for takeoff."

"Roger, five-eleven, you're cleared to take off from Runway three-six."

Check the lap belt, tighten and lock the shoulder harness, turn into the wind and lock the tail wheel, check the mixture control, the generator main line switch, the fuel pressure, put your wing flaps up, pour on the throttle, and away you go. The tail lifted up and the plane followed it and Red Lesczynski was the Red Baron, the Polish Falcon, in the air by himself for more than an hour of touch and gos, spins and stalls, crossfield navigating and experimentation. It was freedom in the cockpit, a sense of total removal from all except that which he controlled. *I was born to do this,* he rejoiced, staring down at verdant green patches of earth cut by dull gray roads where mere mortals drove sluggish cars, at the white beaches and the blue translucent sea. Somewhere back in that Slavic blood there really was a falcon.

She watched him from the window as he marched slowly up the front walk, showing no emotion, his flight suit grabbing at his shoulders and his thighs. She knew he had done it but he so rarely showed his feelings over such things in public that he was unreadable. He opened the door and stared at her with an expressionless face, his pale eyes skylike behind cheeks and a wide, straight mouth that neither smiled nor frowned. Then he closed the door behind him and threw his fist into the air and screamed, "I did it!"

She jumped up and down with him in the stark room, screaming herself, "That's great, that's great!" Then suddenly she was yelling, "I'm pregnant I'm pregnant I'm pregnant!"

He stopped and grabbed her small shoulders, trying to hold her still as she continued to bob up and down, her eyebrows raised and her mouth in a wide, toothy grin. "You *are?*"

"Yeah, yeah! We're going to have a baby, Red!"

"When did you find out?"

"Three weeks ago! Yeah, yeah!"

"*Three weeks ago?* Aw, Sophie, you shouldn't keep things like that from me. Why didn't you tell me?"

She stopped jumping and stood still, looking up at him like an abashed child. "I was afraid I'd mess up your solo."

"Are you kidding?" Lesczynski shook his head, smiling bemusedly. "I just missed three weeks of my baby!"

"Well, I can tell you, nothing much happened." She grinned brightly. "I'll bring you up to date, if you want."

"Hey, we've got to celebrate. Let's take the Maxwells to Trader Jon's after dinner, what do you say?"

"Do you think Louise can still fit through the door?"

* * *

The dark street in front of Trader Jon's raunchy loud museum of a bar was lined with new cars. A half-block away from the bar's stained, weatherbeaten front the thumping music, heavy with drums, dominated an otherwise silent street.

Jimmy Maxwell held his head as they slammed the car doors and started toward the bar. "He's got that nigger band in there again. It sounds like a damn juke joint."

Sophie nudged Red hard, as if demanding that he respond. Lesczynski sighed over to his Mississippian friend, a man he had come to admire and respect over the months he had known him. Jimmy Maxwell was an erect, bright product of the Naval ROTC Unit at Ole Miss, where he had been a standout hurdler on the track team, as well as commanding the ROTC unit itself. Maxwell had served a year aboard a destroyer out of Norfolk, then applied for flight school when the Korean War broke out. He, too, was an aspiring fighter pilot.

Sophie nudged Red again. As they opened the door, Lesczynski patted Maxwell on the back. "Personally, Jimmy, I like nigger music. In fact, I even like *Negroes!*"

"Well, so do I. I think everybody should own at least one."

"No-o-o-o! That's bad, Jimmy."

The music hit them like a blast of heavy wind. On a stage in the back of the cavernous bar, standing in front of the four-piece band, three Rubenesque, half-naked women danced and undulated, their arms seeming to cut little swaths through the heavy smoke. Off to the side, a small dance floor was packed with young, short-haired men and various arrays of women, wives and easy lays rubbing shoulders, bouncing to the same music. The walls of the bar were covered from floor to ceiling with signed pictures of well-known aviators, fighter aces, members of the prestigious Blue Angels, and various admirals, all of whom had at one time or another tipped a beer with Trader Jon. Dangling from the ceiling throughout the bar, like the Spanish moss that hung from the trees outside, were models of classic military aircraft from all over the world, German Fokkers mixed with American Grummans and Japanese Zeros.

Trader Jon worked behind the bar, dressed in his own uniform, a pair of dirty Bermuda shorts and tennis shoes, replete with deliberately mismatched socks, a baseball cap, and a T-shirt. No one had ever seen Trader Jon wear two socks of the same color. He was a thick-shouldered, barrel-chested man with the face of a fighter and the heavy arms of a longshoreman. He had come to Pensacola from New York in 1941, opening up his bar at a time when the Naval Air Training Command began matriculating twenty-five hundred new aviators a month, in contrast to the few hundred a year they had been training before World War II. His bar had become a shrine. It was said that at one time or another Trader Jon had served a brew to almost every naval aviator in the fleet. He served as a father confessor to many young aviators, as well as a no-interest bridge-loan department when bank accounts ran empty before payday.

Lesczynski ushered Sophie into one of the barber chairs that stood in a row in front of the bar, and sat on the arm. "Hey, Trader, it's a big day! I soloed and Sophie's pregnant!"

Trader Jon slammed a beer in front of Lesczynski. "On me. For the solo." He nodded toward Sophie. "She shouldn't drink if she's pregnant. No hard stuff, anyway."

"Shouldn't drink?" Jimmy Maxwell eyed Louise's bulky frame.

"What do you want, a pickled kid? She should drink beer." He nodded toward Louise. "She's ready to drop, you know." He studied her face, and then her bulging stomach. "I'd say a week."

Sophie giggled, her eyes warming to him. "I didn't know you were an obstetrician, Trader Jon."

"Only in my spare time. Hey, this is a modern place. We offer all services. Tony, over there, is a psychologist."

Red Lesczynski played briefly with a model of an old biplane above his head, then sauntered slowly along the edge of the wall, studying the signed pictures of men who had given naval aviation its cherished tradition. *I can do anything that any man on this wall has done,* he mused, his lips suddenly tight with determination. *I can do it all, fly anything, meet any other pilot in the world one-on-one and drop him in a ball of flame. I can, I can . . .*

He sat down at the bar again, one arm around Sophie. Trader Jon set another beer in front of him. He pointed a thick finger at Trader Jon. His eyes were like knives and his teeth bare. "I'm going to *make* your wall, Trader! You just wait."

* * *

Six months away from home. Or maybe always.

Time became measured by the slow realization that it would never change, this feeling of uprootedness and loss. And a baby would be born into it. A sadness murmured in her womb with every tiny movement of her child.

Sophie stared forlornly at the little Christmas tree, her small hands resting on a stomach that was beginning to swell quite noticeably. Her back was against the couch, her head pushed into the middle of its rear cushion, so that her chin rested on her upper chest. She looked like a child who had a stomachache after eating too much holiday dinner.

"Oh, Red, I'm so lonely." In December Ford City went cold and ugly, a cruel gray blanketing the ridges and the factory and the little boxes of homes, matching the metallic grimness of the sky. But Christmas was a time of church bazaars and family gatherings, of wandering sons and daughters finding their way home, of bright colors and happy music. Pensacola, with its frenetic training programs and perpetual transients, was a frigid place to spend a first Christmas away from home, despite the greenery outside. And even the Maxwells were gone, Jimmy having reported to Corpus Christi, Texas, in November for fighter training.

"Come on, Sophie." He sat next to her, handing her a cup of lukewarm eggnog and squeezing her around the shoulder. "Cheer up. We'll have dinner and open presents and maybe we'll call home. How would that be?"

"Oh, I—" She made an attempt at a bright smile, her chin still on her chest, and then she was crying. "I don't *like* this, Red. I mean, I'm so proud of you and I know it means so much, but, I mean, we're never going to go home again, are we? Not both of us together. We don't have a home anymore." She was sobbing, wriggling as he tried to kiss her. "We *don't*, Red." Her head was buried in his chest now, soaking his sweater with tears. "The military doesn't allow you to have one. Next week you're going to do your carrier landings and then we're going to Corpus Christi and then it will be back here in Pensacola and after that, well, after that I guess you're going to Korea and after that it will be someplace else and it will *always* be someplace else, Red, *always* a new place and new people. I want to see my mom and dad and go to church with the people I grew up with. I want Linda Melnick to talk to me about being pregnant and I want Dr. Kotzky to pat me on the shoulder and tell me to keep my weight down. I want to make your dinner and watch you come home from PPG and drop your lunch pail on the table and turn on the radio and catch the Pirates game. It just isn't fair."

"Aw, Sophie, come on, now." He gently rocked her. "It doesn't do any good to think about that. We've got a piece of home here. That'll just have to do. And the rest will take care of itself. Come on."

He took her hand and led her to the Christmas tree, and in the Slavic tradition they knelt before it prior to eating the Christmas Eve dinner. Sophie wept softly as he folded his hands and bowed his head. "Thank you, Lord, for giving us this life and each other. Please bless our families, and our child, and bless this food which we take in Your name. Amen." They both crossed themselves and walked slowly to the table. Three places were set, again in the tradition, in the event someone came unexpectedly for dinner. Slavic legend held that Christ sometimes came for Christmas Eve dinner in the form of a beggar, and no one was ever turned away from even the poorest table on Christmas Eve.

They sat at the stark government issue table, around one corner of it, the silence punctuated by Sophie's occasional sniffs as she fought back her tears. At home, her whole family, eight children with their wives and husbands and babies, were joyfully following the same routine, renewing their love and their family bonds. Red took a walnut and cracked it, tasting the meat inside and smiling gamely as he gave Sophie a piece. The meat was sweet.

"See? It's going to be a good year."

He then picked up an *oplatki* wafer, which her mother had sent in a Christmas package, dipping it in honey, and took a bite, after which he dispensed a bite to Sophie, priestlike as he held it before her. "Merry Christmas."

"Merry Christmas."

She had made lentil soup and *popaki,* a traditional fish dish, the batter comprised of leftover dough from the *roski* and poppy-seed rolls she had made days before. They ate quietly, and then she was crying again, embarrassed but unable to control it anymore.

"Sophie, please, come on, now."

"I'm sorry, Red, really."

"I love you."

"I know you love me, and I love you or I wouldn't be down here in this, this *place,* waiting. That's all I've been doing for four and a half years, and I don't know what I'm waiting for, really. I'm just always going to be waiting. I'm sorry." She blotted her eyes with her napkin. "I'm being pretty ridiculous."

"Let's open presents."

She dropped the napkin and looked at him with a small, playful rebuke. "You can only open one. The others have to wait until after Mass, remember?"

"There isn't any midnight Mass here."

"Ohhh—" He thought she would cry again. "All right. Then I guess we can put the baby in the manger now, too." Her mother had also sent her a small plastic replica of the manger scene. At home, Baby Jesus wouldn't go into His place until after midnight.

There were cards and presents from both Joe Dingenfelder and Judd Smith. Lesczynski grinned widely, reading them to her. "Listen to this, Sophie. It's Dingenfelder. 'Like all good Bostonians I am in the business of falling in love properly. Her name is Dorothy and she goes to Radcliffe, although she will insist to you that she attends Harvard. She wants to be a lawyer and she thinks she can keep me from marrying her. Hope you are happy. I hear Judd is cleaning up at Basic School, but we all knew he'd be Commandant of the Marine Corps someday, didn't we?'"

Sophie smiled wanly, sitting on the floor next to the Christmas tree, her gaze far away. "He's so sweet. What's in the package?"

Lesczynski unwrapped it, and laughed. "Two MIT sweatshirts, and a note: 'Maybe you expected cashmere coats?'" He tossed the sweatshirts to her, and opened Judd Smith's card. "'Dear Polacks: Happy you're going to have a kid. Somehow I didn't think Red would be able to figure it all out this fast. I'm on my way to the war sometime after the New Year, probably early February. What can I say? It ain't World War II but then again it beats supervising trash details at Camp Pendleton. I enclose the first present you'll receive for the boy. I know it will be a boy because men who keep women happy have boys, and if I know one thing about Red, Sophie, he'll break his ass to keep you happy.'" Lesczynski peered secretly over the card at Sophie. She reached out and stroked his leg.

"Isn't that a silly thing to say, Red? I mean, he means well and all, but I hate to think I'm the product of someone who wasn't kept happy."

"That's just Judd. He found a present for a boy and had to make up a reason. He doesn't mean anything."

"So, what is it?"

Lesczynski opened the package, a slow expectant grin growing on his face. "A blue blanket, and, and—" His head moved side to side and he laughed, from the stomach.

"Well, what is it, Red?"

He held it out to her. "A *jock strap*, size extra-small!" He continued to laugh, still shaking his head. "Judd Smith, you are unbelievable."

She laughed, too, then fell silent, remembering. "You know, behind all that, Judd is really a Teddy bear. He'll make someone quite a husband, Red."

Lesczynski dropped the jockey strap to the floor and reached for another present. "The woman who hooks into Judsonia Smith had better be ready to do battle."

CHAPTER THREE

JUDD SMITH SAUNTERED INTO the Come On Inn, all spiffed up in his Marine Corps greens, thinking to have lunch. He felt great. *Yeah, I feel so good,* he had just teased old Asa Hodges at the hardware store, *that I just about need to take pills for it.* Then two steps inside the doorway he stared into the face of Buford Coulter, which was gathered into such a grimace of hate that it was obvious that Coulter was contemplating killing him. And Smith froze as quickly as if that vitriolic gaze had turned him into a cigar-store Marine.

His was not an idle fear. There were men in Bear Mountain County, not the least of whom at that moment was Buford Coulter, who would kill you over the smallest issue of dignity. There were places in Bear Mountain County where even the sheriff refused to go. And that might include the Come On Inn, for as long as it took Buford Coulter to ventilate his murderous rage.

All Buford Coulter would have needed before pounding Judd Smith's head down inside his shoulders was the slightest hint of a reason. Such as, for instance, Judd saying hello. Or, for that matter, Judd forgetting to say hello. Or, possibly, Judd's failing an attempt to justify entering the restaurant where Buford Coulter's new, young wife worked behind the counter. Or, for that matter, Judd's not even attempting to justify why he had dared to enter the restaurant where his former wife (although he did not claim her as such, and in fact refused to acknowledge that he had been married even under the greatest duress), now Buford Coulter's bride, served customers. Watching the heavy-chested truck driver's curled lips and the huge, fat hands that squeezed a soda can like it was cardboard, Smith began to wonder seriously whether he was going to live long enough to accord the Chinese troops in Korea the honor of shooting him dead.

It had been a wholly innocent act. He had no idea that Alma, a long-ago recipient of his teenage passions, was working in the only restaurant in Bear Mountain Gap, Virginia. He had merely come into town for a final walk-around in his uniform before heading out in two days for Camp Pendleton, California, and then to Korea. It was a mountaineer tradition to come to town and show off the uniform. It had been a morning of backslaps and handshakes, full recompense for the ignominious way in which he had skulked off on a clanking, odorous bus almost seven years before, largely because of this same sultry little piece of muscle and boobs who now stared delightedly at the coming bloodbath from behind the counter. In fact, the morning had been so rewarding, such a switch from the way these people had once so openly viewed him, that he had decided to spend the afternoon in town, too. But he was hungry, so he had marched on over to the Come On Inn for a quick sandwich. And that, as Judd Smith was fond of taunting other people, had been his first mistake.

Coulter tossed the crumpled soda can to the floor. Alma picked it up and trashed it, even before it had stopped rolling around. The dozen or so other customers had grown silent, and were now watching the confrontation with tense curiosity. Smith knew that he was in a losing situation, no matter what happened. If he beat Coulter with his hands, the large mountaineer would come at him with a knife. If he beat him with a knife, Coulter would find a gun. If he beat him with a gun, Coulter's family would never forget it, and Judd Smith could count on facing off with one of them and then another for the rest of his life, and it would in all likelihood not be a very long life, at that.

That was the way of the mountains. Dignity killed more people than wars or car wrecks, either one.

And all for what? Coulter simply needed to stake out his territory, to be publicly reminded that, although Judd Smith had once owned Alma Ferell's body with a completeness that was in fact a marriage, no matter what Judd Smith chose to call it, and although Judd Smith had run from that responsibility, indeed divorced it, Buford Coulter now owned it, lock, stock, and barrel, to hell with this educated asshole who wore lieutenant's bars on a Marine Corps uniform.

Judd Smith stood motionless, watching Coulter smolder and fume. He needed a few seconds to think about this. Smiling slightly to mask his fear, he reached into an inside pocket and pulled out a Lucky Strike. He always smoked Lucky Strikes. If you wanted a treat instead of a treatment, you smoked Old Golds. If you wanted to guard against throat scratch, you smoked Pall Malls. If you Believed in Yourself, you called for Philip Morris. If you were a Discriminating Person, you bought Herbert Tareytons. If you smelled 'em, smoked 'em, and compared 'em, you went for Chesterfields. But Lucky Strike Green had

Gone to War, and Judd Smith was going to war, so it had to be Luckies.

He didn't get it lit. Buford Coulter's chair screeched across the linoleum and the big man began to stand, signaling the beginning of Judd Smith's destruction, and there was only one thing to do. Smith hated worse than anything in the world to bite his tongue, but it was that or die, and he had already decided to save dying for Korea. He gave off his famous Judd Smith grin, shrugged with his best attempt at nonchalance, and walked directly up to Coulter. Then he grabbed Coulter's hand and pumped it as if they were old friends.

"I heard yesterday that you and Alma tied the knot, Buford, and I just wanted to come on in here and tell you that I hope y'all have yourselves the greatest hookup God ever laid eyes on. Yes, sir, I'm real proud to know y'all are together." Then he strode with deliberate calm out the door, coolly lighting his cigarette, thanking that same God that he was a half-block down the street before Buford Coulter had recovered.

And Buford didn't even follow him. Smith breathed a sigh of relief, climbing into his new, candy-apple-red Packard with its whitewalls and chrome reverse rims—a graduation present to himself—and drove off toward home. He was done with town. Once every seven years or so would do it.

* * *

They had remembered him in town, all right: *that there used to be the screw-loosingest boy. Loopy as a bullbat and mean as a snake. But now look at him. That's what happens with them midnight babies.*

One morning during the cold winter of 1927 Ida Smith began labor with her third child and her husband, now familiar with the routine, went out on a horse, picking his way down icy dirt roads and then back again, bringing the midwife. All afternoon and into the evening the midwife worked with Ida Smith, coaxing and pushing and clutching her and finally pulling and there was blood on the bedroom floor and Judd Smith howling. The midwife wiped the baby and then her brow and checked the clock and finally shook her head. She watched the small baby who even then seemed to be mischievously scrutinizing his surroundings from behind deep, smoky eyes, slowly eyeing bed and walls and father as if he were measuring the minute of his birth against some unknown but very clear referent.

"Sister Smith," the midwife had exclaimed (for she was of the church and saved, just as Ida Smith herself), "you got yourself a midnight baby. That'll be a wild one, sure enough. Now, you know what you got to do."

And Ida Smith indeed knew. She and the midwife both were the unwitting inheritors of ancient Gaelic superstition, passed down from mother to daughter, midwife to friend, for centuries. Midnight babies were regarded as different, even peculiar. They would be wild. They might well show a brilliance as they grew older. But you couldn't separate it out, it all went together: Peculiar, wild, brilliant.

So Ida Smith did her best to moderate it, never rocking his cradle when it was empty, putting a knife inside it for the first week to keep away bad spirits, never speaking his name aloud in the house until Preacher Cosgrove baptized him, even handing the preacher the name on a piece of paper rather than telling him. And in spite of all of these precautions, or perhaps because of the expectations they created, Judd Smith became a genuine, 100 percent All-American Midnight Baby, wearing his wildness in Bear Mountain as if it were a harelip.

Trouble became his own domain, just as some boys take to fixing cars. Judd Smith could get into trouble with anyone, over anything. His parents never let him miss a Sunday church service, and some Sundays he could even make the preacher mad, just by sitting in a pew and grinning at him. His daddy used to boast perversely that Judd Smith couldn't sit by himself in an empty room for an hour without doing something that would cause a knock on their door and an unbelieving complaint from somebody down the road. It was expected of him. It was the way he was supposed to be.

And his daddy tried them all, leather straps and willow branches, ax handles and even an occasional fist, but it hardly did more than dent Judd Smith's forgiving smile, for he was not a mean-boned boy, he was simply ornery. *It's all right, Pa*, the small smile would ordain. *I know you got it to do.* So after a while, even that stopped.

And then Judd Smith had discovered that pleasure stick between his legs, and what went on the other end of it. He was fourteen. There was no holding him back after that, not even any more raising him. The warm smile and the daring nature grew vibrant and irascible. He was a hunter, a good one, and he learned to hunt for that, too. Until he caught onto Alma Ferell. Then before you knew it he was married, and pretty soon after that he was gone.

Judd Smith was not exactly a liar. In fact, he had a very profound
sense of ethics. The problem was, they were personal. When it came
time to put Judd Smith into the right little box as good or bad, right or
wrong, believer or disbeliever, the boxes didn't fit. A piece of him always hung out; a moral here, a personal interpretation there, and the
way he dealt with his arguable marriage with Alma Ferell was nothing more than ethics as usual for Judd Smith.

He had indeed married Alma Ferell in 1945, when he was eighteen
and she had just turned fifteen. She had missed her period twice, and
those wonderful breasts had swollen even more, and Judd Smith, having taken her virginity and violated her on numerous other occasions,
dutifully marched her down the aisle to the gentle beat that the tapping of her daddy's shotgun made on the church floor. A month later,
she began menstruating again, and Judd Smith immediately declared
the deal to be off. Vows to God be damned. Image in the community
be damned. Daddy's shotgun be damned, damned, damned. There not
only was nothing honorable in marrying a woman who had only
thought she was pregnant, there was a great deal of self-mockery in it,
as well. Besides, if it was honorable and ethical for him to step forward and marry a girl he had impregnated, thus openly admitting he
had violated church law by fornicating before marriage, wouldn't it be
just as honorable and ethical for her father to accept that such fornication did not create a child and thus did not lock Judd Smith into a
childhood marriage? Either way, Smith reasoned, church law was violated, one way by fornication, the other by a false wedding vow.

So he had finally concluded that, if the child had not existed, then
neither had the marriage, since the one had been the basis for the
other. This might have been the subject of debate among church
scholars, but Judd Smith just didn't give a hang whether the church
liked it or not. It hadn't been a marriage, and that was the truth and
they could shove it.

At the same time, the Ferell family and the other people in Bear
Mountain County took a decidedly dim view of Smith's decision to sin-
gle-handedly annul his marriage. *Who growed that boy, anyhow? If
God didn't want him to get married, He wouldn't have made Alma
miss her period. And just look at what he done. Had himself a nice little girl who was pure crazy about him, then embarrassed her and her
family like that. That boy's got a cold streak inside him, sure enough.*

That had been May 1945. The Germans were stomp-down beat. Iwo
Jima was secure. Okinawa was winding up, and the great American

war machine was pausing, catching its breath, waiting to make a leap onto the Japanese mainland. It was going to be the biggest battle of the war, aside from the Russian Front. The Americans expected 2 million casualties, more than double the number for the entire war up to that point, Europe and the Pacific combined. They were going to kill Japs on the beaches, shoot them out of trees, root them from deep caves. Judd Smith wanted to be there, just as his brothers had been at Anzio and Leyte Gulf, just as his great-grandfather had been at the Battle of the Wilderness, just as his more distant ancestors had been at King's Mountain. Then right in the middle of recruit training, before he'd even had a chance to sit on a ship and ponder his gory future, some wiseass dropped an atom bomb, and then another, and Judd Smith was again trapped, this time inside a uniform, an infantryman with no one to shoot at.

His company commander had been amazed at his intelligence test scores from boot camp, particularly since Smith had left school after the tenth grade. He had given Smith another test, this time for a high school equivalency degree, and then another one, for the Naval Academy prep school. In a few months, Smith found himself at Bainbridge, studying the sort of mathematics and sciences that would be required of him at the Naval Academy. In a year, he was admitted.

And every step of the way, from the first paper he had signed in order to enlist, Smith had to put, in writing, his own version of the truth. QUESTION: ARE YOU NOW, OR HAVE YOU EVER BEEN, MARRIED? Answer: No. At the end of every leave period at the Naval Academy, the midshipmen were required to fill out a "Marriage Form," asking the same question. Each time, Smith answered the same way. If it had been discovered that, in the county courthouse of Bear Mountain County, Virginia, there existed documents attesting to the marriage of one Judsonia Shelby Smith to Alma Lynne Ferell, no amount of equivocation would have kept the U. S. Naval Academy from dismissing Smith for an honor violation; that is, a repeated lie.

Sometimes Smith would think of that terrifying month he had spent as Alma Ferell's banner of respectability, and he would shudder with a secret mix of shame and self-righteousness.

Come on, now, you call *that* a marriage?

* * *

The mountains in winter reminded him of a plucked pheasant, those rich colors of summer and autumn gone, giving way to dull patches of gray and brown, like the cold and prickly skin of a shot bird. He drove winding dirt roads outside of the small town, his car struggling up slopes and skidding on patches of ice. Little boxes of homes gathered near the roadway, small footbridges laid across rushing streams, the mountains behind them jutting up like tidal waves. The county government had placed a sign and a large garbage bin at one turn. The sign read "DEPOSIT TRASH IN BIN." Predictably, many of the local people had taken to dumping their trash underneath the sign, just in case the government was getting the wrong idea about who was in charge.

He followed four more miles of dirt roads, winding along the valley floor, every now and then climbing a steep slope as he progressed from hollow to hollow. Finally he made a left turn and drove along a road so narrow that the tips of winter branches from the trees on either side played scraping melodies across his roof. Smith Hollow lay dead ahead, his family's home for more than a hundred years.

The hollow widened out and the family house sat across another cold, swift stream. His mother was at the stream bank, reaching into the small springhouse, their equivalent of a refrigerator, for a jar of milk. She stood when she heard a car, then waved to him as he eased over the creaking wooden bridge. He parked in front of the smokehouse, just down from a gray, unpainted barn where new calves lowed and stirred, and walked with a deliberate military stiffness toward his mother, smoothing out the wrinkles in his uniform. She and his father were beside themselves with wonderment at his recent good fortune. He was the only one of four boys and two girls to have even finished high school, and here he was an officer.

"Hey, Ma! Your bad boy's home!"

"Well, I'll be." She smiled with a soft edge that came from an almost disbelieving pride, and shook her head as if he had just told her a story of wild adventure. *My little midnight baby. Look at that.* "You get on over here and let me give you a big old bear hug, Judsonia." He might have been gone a week or a decade. The welcome was always the same. She took it when she could get it, Ida Smith, and Judd gave it when he showed up. Which wasn't often.

"Let me help you with that milk, Ma."

She clutched it to her print housedress, shivering from the cold and heading toward the small frame home. "Now, don't you do a thing to that uniform, Judd Smith! This old dress, it doesn't matter."

The next morning he rose before dawn and helped his father water and feed the cattle. The old man was half-stooped, wiry and gray. It occurred to Judd Smith as he helped him work that his father seemed almost lost inside his bulky coveralls and coat, as if he had shriveled up like a prune as he aged. His teeth were brown from chewing to-bacco and scattered from inadequate care. In all, he looked a decade older than his fifty-two years. But he was still as strong as his son, and more cantankerous than his wildest bull.

"*Git on!*" He kicked his way into both of the cattle barns, causing calves and cattle alike to low and scatter before him. He would pull fifty-pound bales of hay from the loft and casually drop them down to Judd as if they were pillows. He was not a fairy-tale farmer, old Ransom Smith. His animals were not friends any more than the insides of automobile engines were friends to a mechanic. He walked among them as if they were pitiful beggars, roughly lifting the tails of young calves to check their asses for the scours, spitting tobacco and mumbling about the cost of the sulfur pills it took to cure the oozing infections. His cattle would be somebody else's dinner in a year, anyway.

He had a mountaineer's scorn for verbosity. He let Judd's mother do most of the talking, unless it was on matters of discipline or men's talk, such as hunting or the farm. When the last bale of hay was spread, he looked sideways at his son, measuring his own blood in a way that seemed to indicate that he was pleased with the eternity he had passed down in this particular little conduit. Then he spat once and angled his head toward the steep hill behind their house.

"Reckon you can still climb that?"

"I do believe I can."

"Hit ain't easy in the ice."

"Well, I'll catch you if you fall, then." The old man liked that. He had never gotten away from the secret belief that his boys had grown up softer than he, and particularly this half-wild seed who had run away in disgrace and come back like a king, with college and officer's bars all rolled into one.

They followed a worn cattle trail up the steep hill, tacking this way and that across it, passing ancient boulders and avoiding cow dung and ice. Judd reached down and casually picked up a small black arrowhead, putting it into his pocket. The old man kept a collection. He had hundreds of them. Some of them dated back twenty thousand years. These rough hills had been a common hunting ground for Cherokee and Shawnee, Saponi and Tutelo, as well as other tribes. Many of the first settlers, Judd Smith's family included, had mixed their blood with the Indian. Part of himself had shot that arrowhead. Climbing the hill with the sharp flint cold against his thigh, Judd Smith felt the Indian in him listening for the stirring of a deer in the nearby brush.

From the top of the hill in the crisp clear air of this February morning Judd could see forever. Somewhere to the south, along the ocean of mountains that rolled and pitched and yawed, clinging to winter mists in their little hollows, Virginia ceased and Tennessee began. He never had figured out exactly where, although he had tried on many lazy summer mornings as a boy.

His father wasn't even breathing hard. They sat together on a large rock and pondered the mountains, not speaking, the old man occasionally spitting a dark stream of tobacco juice off to one side. Judd knew there was a reason they had climbed the hill. It was to this same rock that his father had brought him for the few "man talks" he had received as a boy, just as his father's father had brought the old man up the hill decades before. Judd and his brothers had laughingly named the spot Man Talk Rock back then. His father spat again. Judd lit a Lucky Strike and waited.

"Did they train you good, Judd?"

"If they trained me any better, Pa, they'd just have to make me a damn general." The old man laughed, but with eyes that studied the far mountains rather than his son. Judd slowly realized his father was upset, perhaps afraid. It was hard to picture this flinty sharp old arrowhead of a man afraid. "I'll tell you, Pa, they been training me for five years. Can you figure that? Four years at the academy and then another six months at infantry officer's school, and that don't count the training at boot camp and prep school."

"Well, I figured they had." The old man spat again, still staring off into the mountains. "That was some kind of a graduation." Judd had sent them pictures. "All them boats and uniforms." He brought his eyes back to his son's face, studying it judiciously, and then slowly reached inside his coat, pulling out a long, thin bundle wrapped in a rag. He handed it to Judd. "This here is for you."

Judd took it and slowly unwrapped it. Inside a handmade leather sheath sewn tightly with rawhide was a finely polished hunting knife. Judd removed the knife from the sheath and allowed a bare hand to trace the four-inch blade. It took a thin slice from his index finger.

"Ouch."

"Hit's a sharp one, boy." His father watched with obvious pride. "I balanced it out so you could throw it."

"You made this, Pa?"

"Hit ain't much." The gray pockets of the old man's unshaved face creased with a smile. "I figured you might have some use for a good knife over there."

"It's a beauty." His father had packed strips of hard leather end on end like a stack of quarters to make the handle, and had contoured them to fit the curves in a man's grip. Judd tried to make a joke. "Well, I'm going to keep this with me the whole time, Pa. But I hope I don't get close enough to have to stick somebody with it."

The old man shook his head, dusting his trousers to knock the cold out of them, and started to walk back down the hill. "Knowing you, Judd Smith, you'll be getting a lot of work out of that old knife."

* * *

The 17th Replacement Draft formed at Camp Pendleton, California, in February 1952, for cold-weather training at a place called Pickel Meadows in the Sierra Nevada Mountains, and shipment to Korea. The 17th was a special airlift replacement, filled primarily with infantry lieutenants needed to command rifle platoons of the ravaged 1st Marine Division, something of an "air-mail special delivery" approach to war, while most other officers and men journeyed for a month aboard ship.

Camp Pickel was perfunctory. The men mulled around in the middle of a snowstorm, demonstrating to themselves that they could indeed function in freezing weather, getting used to "Mickey Mouse" insulated boots and floppy hats and fumbling with weapons through heavy, mitten-like gloves. It seemed to him that they were merely demonstrating that they knew what it felt like to be cold. The four-day training cycle was cut to two days, ironically enough because it was snowing too hard.

Back at Pendleton, they were given a three-day liberty, the last fond gift of the Corps before they went to war.

"Come on, Judsonia. Let's get the hell out of this place." Donny Stuart and Al Dieter, two of his carousing friends from his first days at Quantico, stood impatiently over his cot. Dieter was booting Smith's rump through the underside of the canvas bed. He rolled over and peered at them, watching their grins and inspecting their immaculate uniforms. Stuart had mashed his pisscutter cap low over his eyebrows, and was waving toward the Quonset hut's door.

"Seventy-one hours and thirty-seven minutes, and counting. Come on, Smith, get your ass in gear. It's going to be a long time before you see a round-eyed woman again."

"You guys go ahead." Smith lay back, his hands behind his head, staring solemnly up at them. "I've got some things I need to do."

Dieter elbowed Stuart. "He's found himself a honey right here in Oceanside."

Stuart shook his head. "Nah. He hasn't had time. Hey, Smitty, listen. You need to get out of this place. Come on to Los Angeles with us. I got a car and everything."

Smith sat up, swinging his feet around until they touched the concrete slab of a floor. He picked up two letters from the top of his seabag, fondled them, and then handed them to Stuart. "Mail these for me, will you?"

"You can write letters in Korea, Smith, but you can't go to Hollywood in Korea. Do you know what I'm saying?"

"You remember I was telling you about Lesczynski, one of my roommates?" Smith's voice was almost incredulous as he continued, ignoring the two men. "I can't believe the guy is going to be a *daddy*, in just a few months. And this guy Dingenfelder, the—"

"Albert Einstein of the Air Force." Dieter nodded his head, hurrying Smith along as he peered at his own watch.

"Yeah. Well, he's at MIT, spending his days at the Wright Brothers' tunnel, studying the effects of something or another on wing structure."

"So what?" Stuart was unimpressed, his freckled face in an impatient scowl.

"So what am I doing?"

"You're coming to L.A. with us." Dieter reached down and muscled Smith out of his cot.

Smith mildly resisted them, standing in his boxer shorts on the cement floor and laughing. "Come on, Dieter. You know what I mean." He paused, shaking Dieter off, and sat back onto his cot. "I think I need to get married."

"*What?*" Dieter and Stuart nudged each other, Dieter finally putting an almost fatherly arm on Smith's shoulder. "You poor turkey, I think the pressure's getting to you." He reconsidered, slyly angling his head and winking to Stuart. "I'll tell you what, Judd. Come to L.A. with us, and we'll find you a bride, I guarantee. A movie star!"

"You don't know anybody in L.A."

"What the hell difference does that make? You know they just hang around the corner of Hollywood and Vine, waiting for good-looking Marines on their way to war."

"You've been watching too many movies, fool. The only thing you're going to bring back is the clap from the skivvy house you and a hundred other guys end up in. No, thanks. Not this time. Just buy me a bottle of booze, okay?"

Stuart brightened. "Jack in the Black."

"You got it, Tennessee." Smith handed his friend a ten-dollar bill, a small price, just then, to regain his peace.

During the winter months in southern California the warm air rising from the sea pulls the cooler land air out onto the water, drawing the distant desert's hot dry daytime breeze over the coastal areas in a current known as the Santa Ana winds. The bald, round hills of Camp Pendleton are warm and brown in winter, a perfect place to test your endurance.

And Smith ran, hour upon hour, all three days, as his friends held their gallows' feasts in San Diego and Los Angeles. He didn't care. For all his frequent frolic, Judd Smith was in his heart a loner. When he had finished boot camp six years before, he had gone into a tattoo shop and had an eagle inked into his upper shoulder, to him a symbol of his singularness. *Eagles don't fly in flocks.* There were times to party and there were times to retreat inside, to define one's self and to put a life that soon might end into order.

It had begun to bother him, in these final frenetic days of preparation, that he had never asked himself why he even wanted to go to war. None of his compatriots had ever once mentioned it aloud. The war was there, and they were all going to it, in a way riding the emotional afterwash of World War II.

The war itself was in a stalemate. The big battles, Inchon and Chosin Reservoir, had ended a year before. Opposing forces now faced each other like two angry crowds along the 38th Parallel, awaiting a negotiated cease-fire. Judd Smith had followed the political decisions closely. He had rooted for General Douglas MacArthur when the general returned home to adulation for having refused to let President Truman make battlefield decisions. He believed in what MacArthur

4

had said about "the great threat in what is presently called communism, the imperialistic tendency or the lust of power that squeezes out every one of the freedoms which we value so greatly." Smith simply had never really considered why he, personally, had been working so hard to gain the right to stand in front of a gun and have it go off in his face. It had all been safely abstract until the last few days, a controllable fantasy. But now it was as if he had been chasing the biggest, baddest bear in the woods, dreaming of bagging it, and then suddenly come upon it and began wondering, just as the paw came forward and the claw ripped off his head, *Why the hell did I ever want to go hunt bears, anyway?*

I am doing this for many reasons, but the overriding one in this: because I am Judd Smith, and I am powerless in my blood and soul to do anything else. I am Judd Smith, prisoner of my history. I am Judd Smith, on the way to war. I am Judd Smith, pushing against that mountain, climbing uphill to the truest Man Talk Rock.

* * *

They took a packed train to San Francisco, and boarded a three-decked seaplane called a MARS at the naval facility at Treasure Island. In Hawaii, they broke into smaller groups and loaded into C-54 transports, spending restless, agitated nights on Guam and at the Yokosuka naval base in Japan. Finally they landed in Korea, at a base simply termed "K-50," on the southeast part of the peninsula.

K-50 was the transient center for Marines entering and leaving the war. Judd Smith stepped out of the plane and his lungs immediately filled with a heavy chunk of icy air that made him choke and cough. He stared past four dilapidated mess tents, low-slung in the snow like broken old mares, and saw a collection of perhaps a hundred men waiting to leave Korea on the C-54's return flight to Japan. They were huddled around fifty-five-gallon drums, trying to keep warm. Their cold-weather gear was torn and faded. They stared at the new arrivals with empty, vacuous eyes, their faces burned deep red by the cold, their eyes themselves sunken as if retreating from it.

They emanated nothing, that was the only thing he could think of as he watched them, *nothing*. Not happiness or misery or anger or relief, not anything. They seemed neither happy nor unhappy to see the new lieutenants. Many of these men had fought in the Chosin Reservoir breakout of a year before, and had beaten back the communist offensive of the previous April. They had then endured a battle for position that eventually became a brutal war of attrition, not unlike the trench warfare of World War I. They appeared to have no feeling for what they had done. They gave no indication that they cared one way or the other about what Judd Smith was about to do. They seemed, thought Smith, as he walked near them on his way to a supply tent, as if they did not really comprehend that there was anything left on the other side of the plane ride they were about to take, other than winter and war.

Boot, insulated, rubber, pr. Cap, field, cotton, M1951. Drawers, winter, M50. Glove inserts, wool, pr. Glove shells, leather, pr. Hood, parka, field, M1951. Jacket, shell, field, M1951. Laces, shoe pac, 72", pr. Liner, jacket, field, M1951. Liner, trouser, field, M1951. Mitten shells, trigger finger, type 1. Mittens, inserts, trigger finger, M1948. Shirt, flannel, green. Socks, wool, cushion sole, 3 pr. Trouser suspenders, M50, pr. Trousers, shell, field, M1951. Undershirt, winter, M50.

He drew mounds of gear, and signed a myriad of forms. He found himself laughing. Paperwork! Did Hannibal require his men to sign for gear? Did Genghis Khan, who had rampaged very near where the 1st Marine Division was now emplaced? Field transport pack. Canteens. Steel helmet with fiber lining. Gas mask. Entrenching tool. Mess kit. Compass. .45-caliber pistol. And, for the truck run to the division rear, an M-1 rifle, since the 17th Replacement Draft was to function as its own security for the convoy to the front.

It took four hours for the convoy to reach division headquarters, near the 38th Parallel. After the convoy had been on the road for two hours, the men standing like frozen statues in open-bedded trucks, Judd Smith felt certain he might soon go mad from the cold. The temperature was perhaps twenty below zero, but the wind and the movement of the truck created a wind chill that was closer to eighty below. Smith watched the gray countryside with its desolate, demolished towns, the sweeping valleys and sharp mountains blanketed with snow, the sky that was itself heavy with dark ice, and passed through a claustrophobia so deep that he would have screamed aloud if his friends from Quantico had not stood next to him in the truck bed.

The cold surrounded him, teasing tears out of his eyes and then freezing them on his cheeks. It was numbing parts of him, burning other parts, and freezing still other parts. There was nothing he could do to stop it, and that, more than the cold itself, was the reason for his half-hour of mad, fearful desperation. The cold came to symbolize his loss of control over his very life, his dependence on fate. *I'm like a cow being pushed wild-eyed down a slaughter chute,* he thought again and again. He finally controlled his hysteria by ignoring it, pushing it away, and then he understood the numb stares of the men on the air strip at K-50. The purging of all emotion had become their refuge from insanity.

The new replacements processed methodically through the stages that brought them closer to battle, from division to regiment to battalion, staying a night at each headquarters. Friends fell away to other jobs. He and Stuart were able to stay together through their assignment to the 2nd Battalion of the 1st Marine Regiment, but parted at company level. Soon he was alone, heading in a jeep toward a sector of the front lines manned by Echo Company.

Chinese artillery fell behind him with brittle crumps as he was driven up steep, pocked roads to the company sector, and he knew he was finally inside the battle area. At the company command post, a weary-looking first lieutenant, his face burned red from the biting wind, gave Judd Smith the first smile he had been awarded in Korea, standing and grabbing his hand. It was a smile of relief, of sudden reprieve.

"New meat!" That was how First Lieutenant George Armbrister, United States Marine Corps Reserve, had greeted Judd Smith. New meat. *Now, will somebody get me the hell out of here?*

Armbrister then paced in front of a sandbag bunker built into a trench line, a sort of cave, littered with ammunition boxes and C-ration cans and mummy sleeping bags. A trash fire smoldered just down from him, three men silently huddled around it, emotionless and worn as tramps in a railyard.

"You can have your pick," said Armbrister. "My weapons platoon and a rifle platoon both need officers." It was a test, in a way, a precatory forgiveness if Judd Smith lacked the courage or desire or perhaps the madness necessary to lead a rifle platoon, which was incomparably more dangerous than supervising the defensive positions of a weapons platoon.

The main reason Smith did it was Armbrister himself. It had been a forgiveness but it had also been a dare. And for this one moment, Judd Smith felt superior to the worn and beaten Armbrister. The cavalier smile returned, his cheeks suddenly cracking from the cold as he grinned at Armbrister. A *weapons* platoon? Come on. "I would *dearly love* to lead a rifle platoon. So where's my lines?"

The lieutenant he was to relieve had already left, on the jeep that had brought him. The platoon was in the hands of a fat, veiny-nosed master gunnery sergeant who appeared on the verge either of a heart attack or a nervous breakdown, or maybe both. The master gunnery sergeant made it clear to Smith within ten minutes that he had fought in the Big War, that he had stayed in the Reserves in order to supplement his income and his ego, that he had forgotten everything he had ever known about the Marine Corps in the intervening years before he had been rudely called up to fight in the Great Shithole of Korea, that he was too old and worn to fight and too scared to remain with a line platoon, and that he badly needed a drink.

Judd Smith resolved to get rid of the man at his first opportunity, and replace him with a young, aggressive sergeant. He stood listening to the litany of lament, slapping himself from the biting cold, and finally searched the trenches for a trash fire. "How do you get *warm* around here?"

The master gunnery sergeant shook his huge square head morosely, an indication of overwhelming helplessness. "You wait until spring."

CHAPTER FOUR

WAITING WAS SOPHIE LESCZYNSKI's thing. It was a remarkable enterprise. If she concentrated hard enough on it, almost any travesty was bearable. She could reach beyond the misery that was today, either attempting to ignore it, or making jokes about it when she had to face it square in the mirror of her consciousness, and put off the pain by maintaining, over and over, that it didn't matter, it was temporary, and if she could just wait long enough it would all get better.

She didn't even have to lower her expectations if she was waiting. She simply altered her timetable. For four years she had played the game while he was at Annapolis, working in the reference section at the Armstrong County library (a temporary roost), reading a thousand books, writing him every day except for the glorious few she would see him over Thanksgiving and Christmas and Easter, and the whole three weeks he would be home in the summer. When the academy was done it would be different. She would have him in the evenings and on the weekends, see him and talk with him as she did for the first ten years she knew him.

But when she was given that luxury she realized it was nothing more than a tantalizing little morsel, one tiny candy kiss. She followed him to Pensacola and made his meals and kept his home and bedded him, gladly and often, and slowly she comprehended that he was going away again, that he loved her and wanted to be with her but that he also loved what he called his honor, worshiped that wild goose of a calling that demanded that he forsake her and all the other things he said he loved in order to fly fast planes laden with bombs off the flat surface of a warship. It didn't make a lot of sense. It was not quite rejection, but it would have been had not his love for her been so very palpable. It was simply disappointment, and when she worked her way through it she ended up saying to herself yet another time, *when he gets back it will be wonderful, it will be heaven, all I have to do is prepare myself for waiting and then endure.*

And in the meantime she looked inward, to the growing frontier of her own stomach. That would hold her. The baby would wait with her and grow with her and yearn with her. And it would be like having half of him there going through all of the loneliness with her, too.

She went with him to Corpus Christi, Texas, just after Christmas and made their home in a tiny off-base apartment as he progressed through fighter training. He knocked their socks off, as he always laughingly put it, taking the F-6F through familiarization, gunnery, navigation, and cross country flights, and finally the second round of carrier qualifications that earned him the coveted gold wings of a naval aviator. She went with him back to Pensacola where he was a member of one of the last classes to become jet-qualified at Whiting Field before they moved the course to Texas, he flying the TV-2, which was actually an Air Force plane called the F-80 Shooting Star.

She grew heavy and slow with child as he grew cocksure. He completed a syllabus on the F-9F Panther, his dream plane, getting in seventeen hours of cockpit time before receiving his orders to report to Miramar, California, to join squadron VF-193, which would deploy for Korea in August 1952. He grew a flaming red moustache and talked with his hands when he spoke of flying, his thick palms twirling through the air and his wide blue eyes following them. At times, she found herself actually forgiving him for his enthusiasm, then feeling a sad sort of shame over her jealousy. It wasn't right for her to want all of him. And, just think, in seven or eight months, he would be back, filled with stories, more relaxed with himself, and then it would be over. Until the next time.

One hot, windless Pensacola May night she rose from their bed to urinate for the fifth or sixth time in as many hours and as she got to her feet she felt warm liquid inside her thighs. She stood next to the bed, staring at Red's sprawled, comfortably sleeping frame, and her first thought was not to wake him, not to interrupt his rest for what might end up being hours of pacing and sitting. Then for some reason his eyes opened and he stared curiously back at her.

"Are you all right, Sophie?"

"I think my water just broke."

"Oh, my God!" He jumped from the bed, immediately awake, and was dressed within a minute. In two minutes more they were sitting in the car, she with her hands folded in front of her swollen stomach, a night bag at her feet, all the time thinking, *Isn't military training nice? See how quickly he was able to take charge!*

At the hospital they put her in a dark room with four other moaning soon-to-be mothers and once she was on a roller bed they shot her with something that made her sleepy. They wouldn't let Red come back to be with her. When she asked for him they told her it wouldn't be right to crowd the room with husbands. She lay alone, feeling the tremors of her child as it fought to break apart her pelvis, wanting Red, wanting the child, but feeling somehow abandoned as she waited for a doctor she had never met to perform an act she had never experienced in a room filled only with other strangers.

When they finally wheeled her into the delivery room they strapped her onto a table with her legs apart as if she were some sort of hobbled animal, employing a casual violence that terrified her, at the same time informing her that there was nothing to be worried about as someone hit her with a needle that made her lower parts grow numb. They were telling her to push and she pushed and puked for what seemed like hours, they themselves also pressing against her nakedness, squeezing the contours of her soft young skin as one might knead a bowl of dough. This strange young man who was not Dr. Kotzky stood between her legs with a pair of forceps, huddled and intent with concentration, reminding her somehow of a barber as he concentrated on that one spot with his weapon.

Finally he reached in and pulled, hard, so hard she wondered how he had escaped decapitating her child, and she felt an emptiness inside her, even through the numbness. She heard her placenta plop into a metal bowl underneath the table and she watched with an almost shivering anticipation that had overwhelmed the drugs and numbness as the doctor snipped the umbilical cord and clipped the baby's navel with what looked like a small clothespin.

"It's a boy."

Her first thought was to wonder whether Judd Smith had really known, and whether he maybe really did have a way about such things, perhaps a sort of hillbilly wisdom. Before she could even ponder it the nurse carried the tiny little mass of weeping, jerky movement over for her to see. He was still covered with a wet, milky coat. He was so beautiful, so round and pink with a fat little *dupa* and a healthy howl, and she clutched him to her, feeling that she had been born for this, the passing on of life. She cried, overcome with exhaustion and unmitigated joy. *See what I did, hey? My little Polski.* The nurse was smiling through her mask, Sophie could tell.

"He's a big feller. I'll bet he goes nine pounds."

"Can you show him to my husband?"

The nurse read her tag again and strode out into the hallway beyond the door. "Less — KIN — ski!"

It seemed appropriate, in this uncaring factory of a room. They couldn't even get the name right. The nurse called two more times, *"Less – KIN – ski, Less – KIN – ski,"* and Sophie heard his quick steps as he jogged up from the waiting area. "It's a boy."

"Can I see my wife?"

"At two o'clock this afternoon you can. Visiting hours."

"He's going to have red hair, just like me."

"So what did you expect, a little Indonesian?" She giggled at Red as he stood awkwardly over her bed, both hands in front of him, clutching his cap. She looked somehow *flowery* to him as he stared into her small, pretty face with her dark hair pulled back into a bun and her tawny skin still faintly flushed from her morning's ordeal. As if she had blossomed, he thought, deciding. She touched his hand. "He'll probably want to fly airplanes, too. That'll be my luck. I can see it, twenty years from now, Lesczynski and Lesczynski, one half of the Blue Angels, talking to each other with their hands about spins and barrel rolls." She watched him with suddenly sensuous eyes, a small grin creeping over her face. "We have to wait six weeks, you know. I'm so sore I can't even cross my legs. Do you think you can wait six weeks, Red? I don't."

"Sophie!" Six feet away, on the other side of a drawn curtain, another young officer was sitting on a bed next to his wife, and Lesczynski squinched his face as he nodded his head toward them. "Come on."

"Huh, Red?" She reached out and tugged him by his belt, bringing him to within a few inches of her face. "Huh?" She was laughing now, seeing that he was indeed becoming aroused, and finally she released him and lay back on her pillow, her warm eyes and flushed face and pixie grin intact.

He was grinning back, their small exchange having become a comfortable secret. "No, I probably can't."

"So what are we going to name him, Red? You've got to decide."

"Joseph Judsonia Lesczynski." Lesczynski said it as if it were a formal, undebatable pronouncement. "Joseph for Dingenfelder, Judsonia for Smith, Lesczynski for me."

"Judd might get jealous, taking second place."

"The kid was born in the South, how can he complain? We'll call him 'J.J.,' how's that?"

"'Tackle by J.J. Lescznyski.' It has a ring to it, I guess." She shook her head with a faint ironic bemusement. "I never thought I'd have a kid named Judsonia, I must admit."

"That's what happens when you become a 'real American,' Sophie."

"Oh? Well, as long as you don't want to name our daughter Betty Crocker, I guess I can live with it."

* * *

Red Lesczynski made his final training runs with Air Group 19 aboard the U.S.S. *Princeton* in early July 1952. Soon they would deploy to waters off Korea. The squadrons of twenty-four F-4U Corsairs, thirty-six AD Skyraiders, and twenty-four F-9F Panthers spent several days in carrier takeoffs and landings, getting the feel of the ship and of each other.

The *Princeton* was one of the later versions of the *Essex* class carrier that had been so indispensable during World War II air operations at sea. Commissioned in late 1945, the *Princeton* had missed that war, but had deployed twice already to Korean waters, where four heavy carriers operated continuously. Lesczynski wanted to take his F-9F into battle against Chinese MiGs, but the Air Force had snatched that role in Korea. Navy aircraft were primarily engaged in supply interdiction missions, and only occasionally in air-to-air engagements or close air support of ground troops. Interdiction was not glamorous business, but it was hard work. Navy and Marine aircraft had dropped almost as much ordnance over Korea as all American aircraft had dropped in all of World War II. Department of Defense analysts were projecting that, should the war continue until 1953, American interdiction bombing in Korea would exceed World War II figures by as much as a hundred thousand tons. The little single-engine AD Skyraider could now carry as much bomb tonnage as the B-17 Superfortress of World War II fame.

The *Princeton* was as long as three football fields, and weighed thirty-three thousand tons with a full load. In addition to the ninety aircraft, she sported a dozen five-inch guns, five dozen 40-millimeter antiaircraft guns, four dozen 20-millimeter quadruple mount antiaircraft weapons, and a crew of twenty-five hundred men. The massive, straight-deck carrier held several million gallons of ship and aircraft fuel in its hull, as well as a thousand tons of ordnance, and could travel at thirty-three knots.

Shipboard life conjured up a joyousness in Red Lesczynski, and with it a residue of guilt. He liked to watch the open sea break and crash around him with its black square menacing blocks of waves. He liked the abrasion and demands of a continuous operating environment, and the easy fraternity of men gathered around a mission. The spirit of goodwill among the officers and sailors was almost primitive in its simplicity, with talk of wartime operations and oriental liberty ports. He liked the feel of the H-8 hydraulic catapult as it literally shot him and his aircraft over the bow of the churning carrier, leaving him to his own good graces to pull the plane into the air. He experienced a depth of concentration and satisfaction when landing his jet onto the carrier that was impossible to articulate. His communication with the landing signal officer was almost psychic as he raced toward the matchbox that bounced upon the sea, dropping the plane onto an arresting wire and feeling it jerk him to a halt, all in the space of only a few seconds.

Then he would go down narrow, dim passageways and cold metal ladders until he reached the small stateroom he shared with another pilot. He would enter the room and quickly survey its two bunkbeds, two desks, and a sink, and Sophie would be smiling brightly at him from a picture on the desk and he would feel himself become awash in a kind of loneliness that bordered on grief. It was not merely last year and it would not be just for today. It had been for five years and it would last for their entire young adulthood. *What kind of a man am I,* he would sometimes wonder, *who can find joy in something that keeps me away?*

❋   ❋   ❋

"Well, I'll write you every day." How many times had she already said that, and here they were only twenty-three?

"I'll write you, too, Sophie." He tried to tickle J.J.'s fat chin and the baby slobbered on his finger. "You take care of your mum, you hear?"

They stood on the long San Diego pier in a gray morning mist, the two brows of the carrier crowded with families saying a last good-bye. Small children ran among the clusters of uniformed men and wives and babies, calling to each other, invariably running back to tug on a father's leg and say one final almost-forgotten particle of farewell.

"I'll worry about you driving. Don't pick up any hitchhikers."

"It's all right, Red." She shook her head, smiling almost sadly. "Here you are, going off to Korea, and you're worrying about me driving to Ford City. Besides, Louise and I are caravaning all the way to Memphis. Ford City is about a day away. We'll be fine." She shook her head again. "I can't believe the luck, with you and Jimmy in the same squadron. Keep him out of trouble, will you?"

"He's a big boy. If he can just stop using the word 'nigger' he'll be fine. Sophie—"

"Do you think you'll be able to see Judd?"

"Are you kidding? He's in the trenches. Sophie—"

She interrupted again, as if he would not be able to leave her if they could only continue talking. "Well, maybe he could get some time off and meet you on liberty in Japan."

"No, the Marines don't quite work that way." He stroked his young son's wisps of red hair, and then placed his hand on her cheek. "Aw, Sophie. This could really get old."

She was suddenly squeezing him, crying, the three of them in a tight ball of arms. J.J.'s slobber was wet on his neck. He started crying, too.

"I don't want you to go, Red. I just really don't, I'm sorry. I don't *like* this."

It mixed inside him, the excitement and the sorrow, and he was too paralyzed to speak. Finally he choked something out, regaining some composure as he felt the occasional stares of other officers and men. "Maybe they'll end the war soon, and bring us back early."

She sniffed, releasing him, smoothing down the collar of his khaki uniform and patting the gold aviator's wings that meant so much to him. Almost as much as she did. Could that really be true? "Maybe. But I don't think they will, do you, Red?"

CHAPTER FIVE

"You know, Lieutenant, this is the *craziest* goddamn war. I don't think I could make up a war and have it be any crazier. Nope. I don't."

Sergeant Francis Thomas Canavan leaned forward in the chest-high trench, his helmet on the back of his head, his elbows resting casually on the dirt parapet in front of him as if it were a backyard fence at home. He was shirtless underneath his flak jacket. A C-ration Pall Mall dangled from the corner of his mouth. A newly arrived letter from his mother stuck out from the hip pocket of his dusty uniform. He gazed sardonically from their mountain outpost, looking directly at the enemy. There the bastards were, clearly visible in the day, a hundred little ants that were actually Chinese soldiers milling around in their own trenches less than a mile away. And there they had been, for a year, except for periodic surges or retreats that usually changed the texture of the front by perhaps a few hundred yards at a time. "So, what kind of a war *is* this, anyway? Huh, Lieutenant?"

Judd Smith chuckled, standing next to Canavan. "World War I."

Down the trench line someone screamed, "Fire in the hole!" and a 20-millimeter single-shot machine gun barked off a round in the direction of the enemy. Someone else yelled, "He's down!" and Frank Canavan knew also to get down. Casually scratching the shamrock tattoo on his tanned left shoulder and tossing his cigarette out of the trench, Canavan sat right where he was as three 82-millimeter mortars plinked out from the Chinese trenches, plink plink plink, and in twenty seconds impacted across the outpost, the three explosions throwing up dust and debris, but not causing any casualties. From far behind the outpost, along the American lines, came the metallic twang of artillery counterbattery fire, followed by heavy crumps along the Chinese lines as the rounds impacted. The ritual was complete: insult, retort, rebuttal, and riposte. It would be quiet again for a while.

Canavan shook his head as he slowly regained his feet, wiping loose earth from his pointy nose and fleshy, laughing cheeks. His blue eyes danced on his dirty face. His thin mouth was curled into an amused, searching grin, as if asking Judd Smith if he didn't see the humor in the very absurdity of it all. Canavan gestured again to Smith, his hands wide and open, as if pleading. "I would like, just for the once of it, to simply *fight* the bastards! I mean all of us against all of them, and then it's over." His voice carried the lilt of South Boston, the greatest Marine Corps enclave north of the Mason-Dixon line, another reason why Judd Smith listened to and admired his young platoon sergeant. Canavan had a brother, two cousins, and a dozen friends serving in Korea.

Canavan had been Smith's platoon sergeant for four months. He was invaluable. He knew how to supervise men. He knew his job, from laying mines to calling artillery to supervising rations. He was young. And he was not afraid. Canavan perfunctorily knocked the dust off his trousers. Then he lit another Pall Mall and peered north and west again, across miles of scrub and pine. "Can you imagine setting into trenches on Iwo Jima and trading with the Japs day after day, month after month? They should let us get this bit of a war over with, don't you think, Lieutenant?"

"Well, I personally wouldn't be too quick about going after the Chinese Army with our little old Marine division, Sarge."

Canavan stared at Judd Smith as if he were committing heresy.

That was the Marine Corps, Smith thought again, watching his platoon sergeant's insistent face. They steeped you in so much mythology during training that you ended up believing you could do the impossible. And sometimes, just to reinforce the fairy tale, you did, as when the 1st Marine Division broke out from the Chosin Reservoir in the winter of 1950, saying it was merely "attacking in another direction" after being surrounded by the Chinese Army. Its men not only fought their way out of the encirclement, but carried their wounded and even their dead back with them.

But that had been a breakout, not an attack. "Iwo Jima wasn't on the southern tip of the world's biggest people factory, Sarge. Remember the Frozen Chosin? If we went out after those Chinese bastards, they'd put so many people on the Korean peninsula that it would break off and fall into the ocean."

Canavan thought it over. "Well, now *that's* not a bad idea."

Smith lit a Lucky, his eyes searching for more movement from the Chinese position. "Nope. This is it. We've already won this war, Canavan. Don't let any of the crap you hear tell you different. We got back what they took when they started, and we showed them they can't go around grabbing real estate. That's a *win*. It's just a different kind of a win from World War II. But we've got all we can handle, right here. I just wish the damn politicians would stop drinking tea and come up with a cease-fire."

Canavan remained unconvinced. "Ah, Lieutenant. We've kicked their asses every time we've met them head-on."

"So, don't press your luck! What do you want to die for, spite? This goddamn war is *over*. They just haven't figured out how to stop it yet. It's going to end right here where we're sitting, give or take a few miles, so we may as well just let it happen."

The Chinese mortar tinked again and both Canavan and Smith immediately crouched back down inside the trench. The round exploded harmlessly once more and Smith grunted. "The snipers must have killed them a Chink. That one was payback." He elbowed Canavan as they stood up again. "What's a billion minus one, Sarge?"

"A billion minus one? Come on, Lieutenant, is this a joke?"

"Yeah, and we're the punch line. Because that's how many goddamn Chinese are on the other end of this hill."

* * *

Taedok-san dominated the terrain of the 1st Marine Division's central sector, its dark green pinnacle the highest elevation for miles, rising out of a flat plain that extended for perhaps two thousand yards in front of the American main line of resistance. The era of fire and maneuver in the Korean War had faded into history, and in the late spring of 1952 the Marine Corps units had been moved westward, to straddle the vital corridor that ran from Panmunjom to Seoul. Panmunjom itself, the site of the intermittent truce talks attempting to end the war, was only five miles from the Marine lines. The Imjin River snaked along a mile behind their positions and parallel to them, making both retreat and reinforcements difficult. Two first-rate Chinese units, the 65th and 63rd CCF Armies, faced the Marines to their front, fielding fifteen infantry battalions, ten organic artillery battalions with guns ranging from 75 to 155 millimeters, and an armored division as well. The Marines were outnumbered by more than two to one, and the Chinese had the capability of drawing on a bewildering manpower pool to reinforce their troops. The corridor seemed designed by Buddha for screaming, pillaging hordes, and Genghis Khan, among others, had left just such a legacy.

The Marines dug in and the Chinese dug in and the reason that Sergeant Frank Canavan was so convinced that he was fighting in the craziest war imaginable was that, by the time the Chinese posted and emplaced their outposts in front of their main lines, and by the time the Marines did likewise, these sizable, well-armed garrisons were almost within one hand-grenade toss of each other. The Chinese controlled Taedok-san, but the Marines owned a piece of it, too, and Judd Smith now sat with a reinforced platoon of little more than a hundred men on a forward outpost that was closer to the Chinese lines than it was to his own. In fact, his trench lines, dug months or years before by one side or the other, actually connected with the Chinese lines.

So they would sit on their hill, which provided the only American view around the dominating heights of Taedok-san, and watch the goings-on along the Chinese lines, occasionally sniping and directing artillery onto Chinese movements. And the Chinese would do the same, peering from Taedok-san down onto them and over to the Marine front, attempting to blow away anything that moved.

The new sector had been a welcome change at first. The Marines had relieved a Korean division on the lines, and although the Koreans had not been known for their fighting ability, they had made a workable truce, of sorts, with both the Chinese and the elements. The Korean bunkers were superb. In the tradition of Korean houses themselves, the exhaust pipes from their little stoves ran underneath the bunkers, heating the floors. Winter on the fighting lines had not been as cruel to the Koreans as it had to the Marines. More importantly, the Koreans, who faced an eternity of living on the tip of what Judd Smith called "the world's greatest people factory," had worked out a veritable nonwar in their sector, shooting only when they had to, patrolling only for defensive security, being careful to avoid antagonizing the Chinese. It had become clear that the war would be decided at the truce talks, not on the battlefield. Even under the best of peace conditions, the Koreans would be in bunkers along this line for decades, and conceivably generations. It made no sense to them to provoke their own deaths.

But the Marines, in the words of Judd Smith himself, took over the sector "like a bunch of ants at a jelly convention," sending out combat patrols, reworking defenses, dispatching artillery barrages on targets of opportunity—in short, fighting. The Chinese had a slogan for everything, and they had one for the Marines: *They fight as if they had no family.*

The Chinese hadn't helped matters. As the Marines were setting in

along the steep ridges, the Chinese erected loudspeakers and welcomed them to their new positions. "Captain Credo, did you know
your wife back in Peoria, on West Alpine Street, is seeing another
man? How does that make you feel, Captain, to know you have been
brought over to Korea to die while another man enjoys your wife?"

The artillery exchanges, which often resembled private arguments
more than battles, began early.

And then came the outpost wars; bitter, brutal fights in front of the
two main battle lines, as if they were spectator matches for the enter-
tainment of the masses of other soldiers stretched along both sides of
the battle area. Reinforced platoons such as Judd Smith's would assault and gain a piece of ridge or a hill, either dig or reoccupy deep
trenches and bunkers, and then await the inevitable Chinese assault
that would in the end solve nothing. The outposts had names, which
became the names of the battles: Samoa, Siberia, Bunker Hill, Reno,
Vegas, Carson.

There were military justifications for the bloodlettings that caused
these pieces of high ground to change hands so often: better mortar
positions, better observation, the denial of mortar positions and observation to the enemy. But Judd Smith sensed quickly that the real
reasons were political. The two armies were like tired fighters dancing
at a distance in the late rounds, searching and probing, looking for
one small weakness that could be exploited. The politicians were like
anxious judges, sitting at ringside. Judd Smith's and the other platoons
that traded slaughter with similar-sized Chinese units were nothing
more than tentative jabs, thrown out by the high command. It was
delicate, tense at the negotiating tables. A wrong or foolish move
along the outposts could provide just enough momentum for one side
or the other to press an advantage, and win its final negotiating points.

* * *

Summer came. It had a resort tinge to it. The abandoned paddies
that covered the valley floor filled with runoff water and went all
green, and Judd Smith grew a suntan over the frostbite scars on his
face and hands. The world on the outposts was the same; the enemy
artillery and mortars an irritant, like rainsqualls, men living in hand-
dug caves along the hillside, cooking their C-ration meals on little
three-legged mountain stoves, lounging and sleeping by day in the
dirt on top of ponchos, standing watch in their fighting bunkers by
night. The Chinese prowled and probed in the dark and the rats

rustled around discarded tins at the edges of the perimeter, twitching barbed wire and rolling cans, until the men could no longer tell the rats from the Chinks and threw grenades at every movement. The days wore on them. Some were wounded and some died and all of them waited for the end of it.

But at Panmunjom it apparently was not the same, although no one knew the cause of it, and so one afternoon the word came over the radio from Captain Singleton, the company commander, to abandon the Taedok-san outpost that midnight. Something about an intercepted piece of intelligence, indicating a large Chinese attack. Come off the hill, said Captain Singleton. Orders from the general himself. And tomorrow, after the Chinese attack the empty hill and go home empty-handed, you can go back.

Sergeant Canavan had laughed mightily upon hearing that. "Oh, so the Chinese are going to find the outpost empty, the only observation post that can see around Taedok-san, and then snap their fingers and say the hell with it? In all due respect, sir, I'll bet the officer who figured this out ain't going to come back up the hill with us tomorrow."

No bet. At midnight they quietly moved down the hill. They carried their weapons in one hand, and Willie Peter bags filled with ammunition and supplies slung over the other shoulder. They had even taken down the faded and torn American flag that Canavan had erected at the high point of the hill. They marched across a thousand yards of no-man's-land back to the forward edge of the main lines, each of them thinking more about the prospect of having to retake the outpost the next morning than about abandoning it in the dark. As they walked they could hear mines detonating on the forward slope of the outpost, signaling the Chinese attack. Once back inside the friendly lines they sat next to the fighting bunkers and watched Marine artillery blast the hill with barrage after barrage, but Judd Smith and his platoon knew that the bunkers and the trench lines they had so carefully repaired could easily absorb such damage.

At seven o'clock the next morning, the word came down from the battalion headquarters to return to the hill for outpost duty. It surprised no one, not Captain Singleton or Judd Smith or Sergeant Canavan or Private Wintzjwrynski, the platoon messenger, or probably even the goddamn politician or officer who had dreamed the whole thing up, that they never made it near the hill. A few hundred feet

from the bottom of it the Chinese opened fire from their newly reinforced Judd Smith Special bunkers, undamaged despite all of the artillery, and Chinese mortars bracketed the platoon in the open field. Sergeant Canavan went down, as did several others. Judd Smith's only
recourse was to call his own artillery barrage onto his former outpost,
and to retreat back to the Marine lines. It would require at least a battalion if they wanted to retake Giveaway Hill, and they didn't have a
battalion to spare.

Back inside the friendly lines, Judd Smith checked other casualties
and then went over to Canavan, who was lying on a stretcher. A piece
of shrapnel from the Chinese artillery had torn a hole in Canavan's
side. Doc Marone, the platoon corpsman, was wrapping Canavan's
chest. The cocky sergeant, who wrote home every day, reached into
his hip pocket and handed Smith an envelope.

"I knew this was going to happen, sir. I could see it coming last
night. Here, sir. For my mother."

Smith took the letter. Doc Marone gave him a secret nod, indicating
that Canavan was not in danger of losing his life. Canavan shook his
head, watching Doc Marone finish up the bandage. "Send it if I . . . if
I . . ."

"Well, you're just about a dumb shit, Canavan, did you know that?"
Smith sat down next to him. "I'm going to write your mother and tell
her that."

"*God damn it, I am not!*" Canavan's bright eyes went afire in anger,
and Doc Marone had to hold him to the ground. "Lieutenant, if you
write that, I'll come back from the dead and kick your fucking ass! My
mother will show that letter all over the neighborhood, she will . . ."

"Then you better not die, Sarge."

In a half-hour a little Bell HLT-4 helicopter buzzed in from a rear
hospital area, and they loaded Canavan and another man into the two
external pods that extended from the bulbous fiberglass canopy. In another half-hour he would be in surgery. During World War II, a scant
seven years before, Sergeant Canavan might well have died from loss
of blood, but in Korea, he could conceivably be well enough to return
to his platoon within a month.

Sergeant Canavan was pale as they strapped him into the pod, the
helicopter blade whirring above him like a large fan. His blue eyes
still burned into Judd Smith, though, and he even managed to call as
they began to cover him with the fiberglass protective roof. "Lieuten-

ant, you will write no goddamn letters to my mother, sir, do you hear me?"

"You've got three weeks to get back here, Canavan, or I'm spilling the beans."

＊　＊　＊

The Chinese were quick to take advantage of their new outpost on Giveaway Hill. As the weeks passed, the enemy patiently burrowed and dug, inching their units by night toward the Marines, until the once-tranquil paddies where the Korean *Idi Wae* boys used to saunter on their resupply patrols to the outpost were themselves behind the Chinese lines. In some places, less than five hundred yards separated the Chinese front lines from the Marines. Taedok-san, which dominated the valley and rolling hills just as Mount Fuji dominates Japan's Kanto Plain, was now more than two thousand meters to the Chinese rear.

"Come on in, Judd. Sit down. Cigarette? Well, how's it going on the MLR these days?"

He knew it was going to be bad as soon as Colonel Stevas called him Judd. He had been associated with the Marine Corps and the Navy for seven years, and no senior officer had ever called him Judd. It was always "Mr. Smith," or "Lieutenant Smith." And now here was his battalion commander, a hard-bitten old ex-sergeant who had commanded a company on Tarawa, loving him up like he was a buddy instead of some little puke second lieutenant who just happened to know the terrain of the Chinese lines backward and forward, mostly because he used to operate on it before the command or the politicians gave it away. He sat down slowly, eyeing Colonel Stevas as if the wiry old terrier might jump across his field desk and take a hunk out of his ass if he moved too fast.

"Thank you, sir." He took out a C-ration Lucky Strike and lit it, sitting at a wary near-attention. He drew deeply and flicked the ash, waiting, not caring to engage the colonel in trivialities, instead merely staring at his cigarette and thinking, *Lucky lucky lucky, Lucky Strike and lucky me.* Finally he looked back up at Colonel Stevas, daring the battalion commander to get on with it. *All right,* he thought, his senses tight and clear, awaiting his fate. *The envelope please. And the answer is, Judd Smith will die in . . .* No answer yet. *Where, Colonel? Come on, be a sport and end the suspense.*

Colonel Stevas apparently decided that he had been a good guy long enough. He grew gruff, his high voice barking at Judd, all business. "We need to take some prisoners."

Oh, really, thought Judd Smith, suddenly feeling flippant. Well, why don't I just walk over to the Chinese lines and capture you a few? Then he realized that the colonel was going to order him to do just that.

Stevas abruptly stood, and pondered the map on his wall. "We got Chinese coming out of the ying yang. Everywhere we look, everything we do, we end up bumping into goddamn Chinese. I even got goddamn Chinese bouncing around in my *dreams,* Lieutenant." He whacked the map with the back of his hand, turning to face Smith. "It's pretty clear they're up to something. They just walked out of the truce talks again, too. The High Command thinks they're getting ready for a last, big offensive, to see how much ground they can take, and then try for a cease-fire."

He turned back to the map again. "If they push us off this string of hills, there's nowhere we can regroup on this side of the river, and I don't know how the hell we'd get to the other side under fire, either. Jesus, we'd all get shot or drown, one or the other. But that's not the goddamn problem. Hell, everybody's got to die sooner or later. Do you know what that would do, Lieutenant? You got any *idea* what that would mean?"

"Well, yes, sir, I—"

The colonel wasn't looking for an answer. He was almost shouting now. "Can't you see the newspapers? The Chinese rout the Marines and push to the river and then stroll back into the truce talks with a leg up, pissing in everybody's faces. That would be the war, Lieutenant, the whole goddamn stinking war!"

Colonel Stevas sat back down, quickly rubbing a lined face that reminded Judd Smith of the dry, wrinkled heads on the apple dolls that were so popular in the mountains near his home. "So, we've got to get the jump on the bastards. And in order to do that we need some prisoners, so we can interrogate them and find out just what the hell they're up to."

Stevas looked at Judd Smith as if he were only now discovering his presence. His leathery face was a rainbow of emotions, first appearing harsh, dominated by the same almost exuberant pugnacity that he had displayed in front of the map, and then seeming almost kindly, as if he were standing over Judd Smith's grave, fondly eulogizing his un-bounded courage and devotion.

"They say you know that terrain out there better than anybody in the battalion. All right, Lieutenant. I want you to pull a night raid, and I want you to come back with some goddamn Chinese soldiers. *Live* ones."

In the afternoon they had a final rehearsal on the other side of a long ridge five hundred yards behind the Marine lines, dropping off half of the platoon into its "catcher's mitt" position, moving quickly for another four hundred yards, and then pivoting, weapons before them in the assault, and charging back toward the stationary unit. Smith had chosen one end of a Chinese outpost on a low ridge line in front of Taedok-san. He knew the ridge and the fields around it, as did most of his platoon. There would be an old trench line behind the outpost, and that would be the key terrain feature in the dark. They would reach the trench line, do a column left movement along it, and then do a left flank and simply assault the Chinese from the rear and drive them out of their fighting positions into the catcher's mitt.

Nothing to it, right, Colonel?

Watching his men stumble over the rough terrain, even in the day-light, Smith began to feel the same mad, uncontrollable claus-trophobia that the cold had brought him six months before as he bounced on an open-bedded truck toward the front. This wasn't going to work. The Chinese weren't stupid. *I am going to die.*

The warm summer sun began to fall and both the Protestant and Catholic chaplains came down from battalion headquarters and held services, almost every man in his platoon attending, even the irascible, paganistic Wintzjwrynski taking Communion, and Judd Smith found himself praying, over and over, *please, God, please, God,* not even knowing what to ask for, really, just trying to trust. Then a fat, preten-tious Army intelligence officer walked among them, passing out ether vials wrapped up in cushion-sole socks, telling them that they should put their prisoners to sleep. The thought of pressing a sock against a Chinese soldier's face while the bastard had a rifle and grenades and a knife was so ludicrous that the platoon began laughing, first at the officer and then at each other, practicing technique. *Now, hold still, Chink. This won't take long.* It grew dark and they began camouflag-ing one another, drawing on faces and hands with the pasty black and green sticks as if they were children using crayons. Again they teased each other, and then a few of them broke out into a rendition of Al Jolson, getting down on one knee and singing "Mammy," as if they were dressed for a high school play.

They finally formed behind the bunkers of the main lines, their dark column stretching out like a twitching, many-headed snake. Judd Smith walked among them, checking weapons and grenades and camouflage, all of them sober and quiet now, deep inside their individual fears. Wintzjwrynski accompanied Smith, his messenger, but more like a bodyguard or perhaps a shadow. Ski whispered a dozen times to various friends, "We're in a bundle of shit and you know it," until it became a litany, the code word for the patrol.

Captain Singleton came to the head of the column to wish them luck, and Judd Smith found himself snarling, captured by his anger, "We're going to get *slaughtered*, Captain."

The captain was a good man, a friend. "I'm sorry, Judd. This wasn't my idea."

"Write that to my mother."

A rifle squad from the company defending that sector of the lines led them through a secret path in the maze of barbed wire, to its outer reaches, and then they followed an old road for a hundred yards, finally turning onto a brief trail they had cut through the brush the night before. The trail gave them their azimuth toward the Chinese outpost. From then on Judd Smith had no control. He walked inside the column, blindly following the point fire team with the others, clutching his carbine and stumbling through a rice field pocked and torn by artillery, a no-man's-land that a month before had been Marine territory.

The mud sucked at their boots. Men stumbled and fell in the dark. The enemy outpost was a hulking, knobby shadow to their front and then to their left and finally, amazingly, to their rear. It did not exist, because if it existed, then this was really happening, and it was too ludicrous, mused Judd Smith, to be real. *Please, God.* He was simply walking, pulled along by a vacuum, dripping nervous sweat from his fingers until his weapon was a slippery mess.

The column halted, and they knelt in the weeds. It was so quiet that the whiny breathing of Wintzjwrynski from three feet behind him was a dragon's roar. In the distance, as empty and hollow as a memory, he could hear men speaking low and easy, soldiers relaxing into the night. Metal clunked metal. He could not see them, but the Chinese were very near.

Then some fool fired his weapon. Some *American* fool. It erupted into the night like a sudden scream at a funeral; morbid, piercing, suicidal. One shot, that was all, but it made Judd Smith want to flee, to call the whole thing off, to vomit. But he couldn't even quit. They were a few feet from the enemy, and hundreds of yards from their own. The ball game was over. The essential ingredient of a raid was surprise, and now there was no surprise.

They were thirty dead men now, parboiled in the juices of fear, crouching at the edge of their graves. And there was only one possibility of surviving. He whispered, but it seemed to him a scream. *"Move it out! Hurry up!"*

They hurriedly made their left turn, stumbling in the dark, following the trench line. Then in a millisecond, the time it takes to lift one foot into the air, the whole world exploded in light and noise. A Chinese machine gun fired the length of the trench line and Judd Smith's point team was firing back and everywhere there were flashes from grenades and rifles and the agonizing screams of men blown apart. He found himself running down the trench toward the machine gun, thinking of his trapped men, screaming, mindless in his fear and fury, commenting absently to himself that this was not really happening as a bullet ricocheted off one elbow and another pierced his boot. His own men crouched inside the trench line as bullets and tracers from other weapons interlaced over their heads, preferring the murderous machine gun in their fear, even though every burst ripped their entire flank.

This is just a bad dream, just a dream. Several grenades impacted near the flashing muzzle of the gun and finally it grew silent.

"Move it out!" There was no control, only thirty men fighting their own little wars of survival. A green parachute flare burst over the black earth, casting dying men in a sickly haze for three seconds, their faces drawn in unbelieving fear. It was an indication that prisoners had been taken by someone, somewhere in the mess, that the raid could now be termed a success. They jogged screaming and shooting back toward the "catcher's mitt," wanting out of it, pulling wounded men along with them, and somewhere a few were pulling prisoners.

Then they tumbled into a second trench like cartoon characters dropping off the edge of a cliff. No one had known about the second trench. The Chinese had built it in the dark over the few weeks they had owned the territory in front of Taedok-san.

They fell on top of dozens of startled Chinese. The trench was filled with the sickening, urgent sounds of death-dealing blows, scattered, individual wars drawing screams and blood. Judd Smith ran toward what had once been the front of the column, again trying to gain some control and move his men out. To his right, a Chinese bunker opened up, as large as the downstairs of his family home, and Chinese soldiers chattered and scurried, more surprised than he. He emptied his carbine into the bunker and a half dozen of them ran toward him, their arms in the air, surrendering. He didn't know what to do with them. He pushed them into the trench line, toward the center of the assault force.

After fifteen minutes of barroom brawling, they took that tiny portion of the trench. From what Smith could tell, he had seven men operational when the trench grew quiet. His right forearm was dripping blood like a slow faucet, and his boot was sloshing with it. The Chinese were reacting, moving a counterattack toward the trench. He could hear their rifle fire as they approached. The trench itself was honeycombed with large bunkers. He started pushing his men out of the trench, tossing the wounded ones over the side also. There was no sense in trying to assault to the catcher's mitt. They would have to go back the way they came.

They had more prisoners than they had Marines. The prisoners caught on to this as Smith and the others tried to work their way out of the trench line, and began fighting with the Marines, beating them with their hands and trying to take their weapons. The Chinese counterattack was getting nearer.

I am going to die.

He found himself growling like a rabid dog, the knife his father had so religiously honed and sharpened for him cutting throat after throat, piercing chests, men shuddering under his stabs, some fleeing, crawling off into the dark unknown. He didn't care where they went or if they were dead. He simply wanted them to leave him alone, to get the hell away and let him live. The Appalachian cowhide of his knife was soaked with oriental blood.

If I know you, Judd Smith, you're going to get a lot of work out of that old knife.

They kept three docile, whimpering Chinese. The remnants of his platoon, perhaps half of what he had started with, began inching their way back toward the Marine lines, hiding, leapfrogging, dragging their wounded. The counterattack was pursuing them. Muzzle flashes and grenades came ever closer. He actually thought they were out of it, though. They were more than halfway back. Then without warning something heavy and loud detonated near his right hip and spun him to the ground.

He gasped in the dark, his eyes wide and his throat emitting an involuntary whine. He had a hole in his stomach; a big one. He could feel where the explosion had dug. He allowed his fingers to play around the edges of the wound, then withdrew them in terror, instead raising his head and peering intensely across the foot of black air toward his hip. He could not see the hole. His lower abdomen felt like it was emptying onto the ground. He had gone immediately cold and weak. The rest of it faded away; the screams, the explosions, other people. This was it, it really was going to happen, death was creeping up on him as he lay on the hard ground. A wet and comfortable peace was overwhelming him, drawing him away.

"Come on, Lieutenant." Doc Marone knelt over him, searching through his torn uniform pieces for the wound.

"I'm dying, Doc. Tell Sergeant Haney he's in charge."

A weak voice drifted over to him from the clump of battered men. "I'm dying too, sir."

Please, God. Please, God, I'm not ready, I promise . . . I promise . . .

He was sinking. He could feel himself leave his body, beginning at the toes, until it was as if he were floating cool and comfortable on a viscous sea, weightless, affixed to his body only at the head, a Voice or maybe his own mind soothing him, assuring him,

Come on over, Judd, just let go, one little gossamer will end it

And there was no pain on that side, no anger or even death, only this floating peaceful freedom and the Voice or his mind telling him to join it,

Come on over, Judd, just say yes

Please, God

He could see them struggling over his used-to-be, the mangled parts that were no longer appended to him and therefore no longer hurt, and it would be so easy, so comfortable, and it would be all over, no pain, no guilt, only this serene freedom that called to him,

Just say yes

No

Say yes

Please, God, no no no

Doc Marone had slapped two syringes of serum albumin into him, one in each outspread arm as he lay there in the dirt, and wrapped his guts back inside him with wide bandages, around and around, and the pressure that resembled his stomach lining somehow told him he would live. And then he could again hear the rifles firing and men screaming and they were helping him up, all of him back inside this mangled form that cried to him in pain, that would never stop hurting or remembering.

"Right here, Lieutenant." Wintzjwrynski picked him up and put one arm over a shoulder, and the remnant of platoon began hobbling back toward the lines again.

"*Third Platoon! Where the hell is Third Platoon!*"

At first he thought he was hallucinating. Jogging out from the main lines, with Chinese tracers marking his progress, Francis Thomas Canavan was embarking on a one-man rescue mission. Canavan came sliding in under a burst of fire as if he had stolen a base, and peered at Smith.

"You all right, Lieutenant?"

"Are you kidding?"

"Well, goddamn if this isn't the biggest pile of shit I've ever seen."

Judd Smith managed a weak, fading grin. "What the hell are you doing out here?"

"I heard about the raid in the hospital. You didn't think I'd miss this one, did you, sir? What can I do?"

"Sarge, we got people scattered all over the place. Go find 'em."

Canavan took five ragged volunteers and went out after the other casualties, the team's progress marked by bursts of rifle fire and grenades. Smith could hear him calling to wounded men, gathering them like a mother hen. *I'm going to write his mother about this.*

The fire fight had turned into a full-fledged battle, as artillery exchanges alternated from the Marine lines to the hills surrounding the Chinese outpost. Smith and the others limped slowly back through the reminiscent innocence of the little trail they had cut the night before, then onto the old road, then finally to the lines, where stretcher bearers awaited them with fervent, unbelieving stares.

It would never be the same. Nothing would ever be the same after having caught such a close glimpse of both his primitivity and his eternity. It was as though he had bracketed the bounds of human possibility in those few hours, reached into the darkest corner of his insides and found the cave man that could allow him to murder with a growling delight, then searched into the black sky, far above the tracers and the stars, and seen beyond his own death, all the way to God. Mere twentieth-century mortality would never again be even mildly interesting.

He vaguely remembered Captain Singleton walking beside his stretcher before he passed out, telling him that every man on the raid had been either killed or wounded. Then the captain mentioned, with some embarrassment, that the colonel was sorry about the casualties, but pleased with the raid. They had captured a Chinese officer who was jabbering like a bluejay.

CHAPTER SIX

"Judd?"

Red Lesczynski checked the name on the patient's chart at the end of the narrow hospital bed, then peered back at the bed's occupant. Judd Smith lay calm as a corpse, sheets up to his chest, his naked arms flat and still on top of the covers. A broad shaft of Japanese sunlight warmed him, glowing on a sleeping face that was as smooth and placid as a child's, mottled from the frostbite of six months before, stubbled from its need of a shave. The sunlight illuminated thin arms, one bandaged thickly at the elbow, the other strapped down, playing host to an intravenous tube that ran up to a bottle that hung over the bed. On the shoulder of the bandaged arm, the left one, a tattooed eagle peered down toward the wound, its beak open and its talons out, readying to land on an unseen prey.

The tattoo was the only reason Red Lesczynski could be sure that the sleeping man before him was his former roommate. The sight of this pallid, wasted figure lying deep in a drugged slumber caused Lesczynski to shake his head again and again, overpowered by the enormity of what Judd Smith had survived. He was remembering the last time he and Smith and Dingenfelder had sat together in that odorous Annapolis bar, drinking to the future and brotherhood. *Be brave.* What a big deal it had been to strike their wrists with a steak knife, and actually draw blood!

He absently checked the small, fading scar on his right wrist, feeling somewhat embarrassed at his own health.

"Hey, Polack. We've got to stop meeting like this. It could get serious." Smith's eyes had opened, the only part of him that moved. His words seemed forced from somewhere deep inside him, quiet and flat. His thin lips parted in a welcoming smile. "So how's the kid? I told you it was going to be a boy."

Lesczynski stumbled over his own tongue, not knowing how to begin. Smith still smiled at him. "What's the matter, you never seen a member of the walking dead before? Goddamn squid. So, tell me. Does the jock strap fit J.J. yet? With a name like—" Smith winced, trying to force more words out past a pain that was throbbing through the sudden tightness of his face. "Do me a favor, Red."

"Sure, Judd. What?"

"Pick up the conversation for a while. You're a goddamn bore."

Lesczynski found himself laughing softly, and moved to the head of the bed, standing just next to Judd Smith. His hand brushed Smith's forehead, gentle as a kiss. "You're an asshole, Smith."

"Speaking of assholes," Smith's voice had that flat, fading calm again. Sweat dripped from his hairline, down along the sideburns and trickled into an ear. "You know what a colostomy is, Red?"

"No."

"Pull the covers back. Give yourself a treat." Lesczynski slowly peeled away the sheets, wincing as he saw Smith's tightly wrapped midsection and the plastic bag that had been surgically affixed to his lower right waist, where doctors had brought out a piece of his colon in order to allow the rest of his insides to heal. Oozing brown matter stained the inside of the bag. "Goddamn Chinks tore me a new asshole, Red." Smith's eyes half-closed. He was getting tired again. "Yup. Be the first guy on your block to fart around a corner."

"Did you—did you *lose* your asshole, Judd?"

"Nah. They'll hook me back up in a couple weeks, that's what the nurse says. Did you see Lieutenant Summers, Red? Hey, I think she's in love with me. I can tell by the way she shaves me."

"Well, it's pretty clear you didn't lose your pecker."

"No, but they shoved a catheter up it." Smith attempted another smile. "Don't ever get a hard-on with a catheter in you, Red. They stick this thing up your pecker and then blow a balloon up inside your bladder so it won't fall out. It's a real treat. My dad wrote me a letter." Smith's eyes shifted slightly, an exertion, staring at the table next to his bed. "Longest letter he ever wrote in his life. Nurse Summers read it to me. You know what he said? You don't have to read it, I can remember it all. He said, 'I told your ma when I honed up that old knife that you be puttin' it to work. I thank the Lord I give it to you. Get your insides well and come on home to visit.' That's a mouthful for my old man."

"You're a real hero, Judd." There was respect and awe in Red's voice. "Is it true you're up for the Medal of Honor?"

"I'm not a hero. I don't even know what that means anymore. I was just trying to keep on living." Smith said it with the same flat calm that he had used throughout their conversation, devoid of either bitterness or false modesty. "Eight men killed, twenty-two wounded, the colonel got his prisoner and I got me a colostomy. Red, I saw myself die. I really did. I'm not kidding, man, I was one cunt hair away, one breath and It kept saying, 'Come on over, Judd.' It wasn't that bad. It was peaceful, like falling asleep. But it was scary, maybe 'cause it was new. You only do it all the way once, so who knows? I lost the old man's knife. I feel bad about that. Some Chink's wearing it for a souvenir. You never told me what the hell you're doing here." Smith was exhausted, his face now wet and pale.

"I'm in on the *Princeton*. We're going on-station in three days. I'm flying F-9s, Sophie's back in Ford City, she got the letter about you and wrote me, and I found you. So here I am. *Damn*, Judd, it's been a hell of a year and a half, hasn't it?"

Smith didn't hear him. He was asleep again.

*   *   *

Red Lesczynski was a closet intellectual. He had discovered during his third year at the Naval Academy that he could not stop reading. It had been embarrassing at first, causing taunts from other football players and from fellow midshipmen, most of whom were engineers and regarded nontechnical reading as a sure sign of a soft mind. But try as he might, he could not deliver himself of the habit. His was an untrained, but devouring mind. He read *Sports Illustrated*. He read Kant and Schopenhauer. He read Bat Man comic books. He actually made it through every page of Parrington's *Main Currents in American Thought*, and even took notes.

He had read a dozen books about Japan as the *Princeton* made its way across the Pacific. He was fascinated with Japan, hooked on its mix of energy and obeisance, its combination of modernity and antiquity, its ability not only to survive defeat but to come back from it, adjust and actually grow. It had taken him all of about thirty seconds to confirm this compulsion, as the *Princeton* slowly eased through the straits at Hamakanaya, entering the mouth of Tokyo Bay on its way to the Yokosuka naval base.

Japan had embraced him like a lover as he stood at parade rest with the crew of sailors and airmen lining the decks in the Navy's traditional "quarters" formation and for the first time absorbing her sights and smells. On the edges of the harbor and inside the little canals that fed into it, hundreds of old barges, which during the war had hauled coal, lumber, and food, now housed homeless Japanese families. Dirty laundry flapped like naval pennants on ropes that lined the decks of the barges. The odors of harbor sewage and ferment mixed with the water-livers' cooking fires and danced on the morning breeze, all the way up to the hangar deck where Lesczynski stood, enraptured by their strangeness. Children waved to the sailors, but few others even so much as raised their eyes as the gigantic warship passed. Its wake, even in the snail's crawl that it employed on its way to docking, rocked their homes as if they were small cradles, but it didn't matter. American warships with their gray guns and stiff sailors and lapping waves had been a fact of life for seven years.

Beyond the water-livers was a dense mass of people, the largest concentration on earth, which stretched northward through Yokosuka and Zushi and Kamakura and Yokohama, Japan's greatest port city, past Kawasaki to Tokyo itself. Tokyo alone had been the home of 7 million people before the war, and 4 million had still clung to its utter rubble at the war's end, many living in ditches and boxes. With American help the city had come back quickly, and soon would regain its prewar population. The mainland was teeming. Red Lesczynski studied the impoverished water-livers, cooking and playing and smoking on their old boats, and it occurred to him that perhaps they had been pushed off the land in the same manner that foam spills out of a full beer glass, the energy from within having forced the lesser elements over the rim.

Later, after having watched painfully as Judd Smith drifted away on a morphine cloud during his visit, Lesczynski took the *densha*, or local train, into Tokyo. The large cities actually seemed to be collections of little towns, their squares in front of the train stations replete with waist-high water troughs and single gas pumps and old-fashioned mailboxes. Rickshaws pulled by thin, knobby men dominated the streets, along with bicycles. Americans were the most frequent passengers on the rickshaws, while the Japanese dominated the bicycles. Soldiers walked with Japanese women, many of them dressed in skirts and bobby socks, an almost embarrassing caricature of what they believed American women might have worn, had they been present. The older women and the others who wore the graceful, yet baggy kimonos with the *obi* band around their waists appeared to him somehow more beautiful, more elegant, more appropriate.

At every new station it seemed that the same announcer whined the same collection of indecipherable instructions from his platform microphone, and the population of the coach doubled. Small, poorly dressed Japanese crowded into the *densha*, at times actually climbing through the windows, others daring to stand astride the couplings themselves, a foot on each car. Inside, they pressed against each other with what Lesczynski could only conceive as a gentle ferocity. There was precious little space on the Japanese rail system in 1952, despite the early efforts of the Eighth Army's Third Military Railway Service and the continuing priority that the government itself placed on mass transit. Thousands of railroad cars had been destroyed by American bombing during the war, automobiles had been foregone by industry in favor of tanks and aircraft, and millions of Japanese needed to travel.

The train brought him all the way to Chiyoda, at the center of Tokyo. He rented his own rickshaw, feeling guilty as a self-deprecating, ragged little man half his size and weight pulled him around the city on a bicycle rigged to the carriage. Lesczynski watched wide-eyed as they bounced along the Ginza Strip, Tokyo's Fifth Avenue, tiny dark stores and stalls crowded together alongside large renovated buildings that a few years before had been burned to their very husks by the fire bombs of the American Twentieth Air Force. The gnarled little man indicated through sign language that Red should go into Takahashi's department store, where he bought Sophie an elegant oriental fan for the equivalent of a dollar. A fawn-eyed salesgirl told him in practiced English that Japanese customers could actually arrange a marriage through the services of the store, and then purchase the whole wedding ceremony, walking out of Takahashi's sworn to the bonds of matrimony. She giggled every few sentences when she talked, and kept putting a hand over her mouth. Japanese girls were cute and innocent, and Red Lesczynski was a king.

Heavy wet perfume filled the air, a smog of sorts but not entirely offensive. Lesczynski thought he could see it in a pink haze that clung to the late afternoon sunlight, a thin nimbus of dust, smoke, and strange, exciting pollen that sat over the cluttered landscape of Tokyo like a colored-glass lid. They passed the Imperial Palace, 250 acres of ancient, delicate pines and mysterious stone surrounded by a moat, protected by forbidding gates. Now and then Japanese, most of them old and all of them dressed in the traditional way with the clumsy wooden *geta* shoes, paused in their travels and bowed deeply in the direction of the Emperor, who a few years before had been their very God but now, supposedly, was nothing more than a mere symbol. An

American soldier passed by with a Japanese woman on his arm. She ignored the bowing figures, caught up in what to Lesczynski seemed a conscious gaiety. Two other soldiers waved to him, arm in arm, obviously drunk, singing as if they had first discovered the verse that had become a tiresome, small insult, to the tune of "London Bridge":

> *Mushi mushi ano-nae,*
> *Ano-nae, ano-nae,*
> *Mushi mushi ano-nae,*
> *Ah, so, desuka!*

The old man pedaled past the Meiji Shrine and the Shinjuku National Garden, and then as dusk approached he crossed a street called the Yasukuni Dori and halted near another shrine. It covered several blocks, and each entrance was marked by large stone *torii* and proud lion-dogs.

The old man nodded. His dark face smiled, but his eyes sagged. "Yasukuni Shrine, *ne?*"

A steady stream of Japanese passed through the grounds, bowing at the shrine itself, and their solemn faces and quiet strides caused a mix of fascination and apprehension in Lesczynski. The souls of Japanese soldiers who had fallen in battle were memorialized in this Shinto shrine. Its seventy-foot bronze gate, the traditional two high posts crossed by two others at its top, was the largest bronze *torii* in Japan. Lesczynski knew that in every village, a smaller shrine was dedicated for the same purpose. At Yasukuni, the Japanese soldiers who had fallen in all of the wars since the country's unification were revered by their countrymen, their souls feeding into the soul of the nation itself, until the very enormity of their losses created an actual source of strength. For decades, ladies of the court had carefully inscribed the names of departed warriors on scrolls inside the small building. They were all there, captured in the intricate oriental word-pictures, those who had been killed in the ten civil wars from 1869 to 1877, in the Sino-Japanese War of 1894–95, the Russo-Japanese War of 1904–5, in World War I, in the first Manchurian War of 1931–32, and in the second Manchurian War, which eventually became World War II. This last war alone had added 2 million names to the scrolls at Yasukuni, five times the number of American dead from a country half as large.

There was sadness in the faces of those who bowed deeply to the dead at Yasukuni. There was loss. There was pride. But there was something else: a vestige of *Bushido,* decided Red Lesczynski as he watched the continuous trickle of men and women of all ages. Douglas MacArthur had taken the Japanese out of uniform during the Occupation, disbanded the military machine that had once claimed almost every young male citizen, even placed a clause in the new constitution outlawing not only war but any military behavior beyond pure self-defense. But *Bushido,* the way of the warrior, seemed as alive as the memories of the millions of lost souls. *Bushido* was bravery, it was loyalty, it was the spirit that could take the smiling, apologetic little businessman of 1935 and make him one of the world's fiercest and most terrifying warriors. During his military service the Japanese soldier had heard the word daily, sometimes hourly. At home his family had practiced its own version. *Bushido* meant self-sacrifice, it meant all Japanese citizens pouring their energy into the national will, draining themselves, going without food and shelter. It meant such loyalty to the Emperor and to superiors that death was to be preferred to capture. It created the banzai charges on Guadalcanal and Saipan and Iwo Jima. It allowed the repressed little businessman to turn into a crazed beast as he raped and burned through China and the Philippines. It gave strength. It shaped an uncompromising personal and national direction. It somehow nourished a mix of cruelty and fanaticism.

The little man was still smiling when Red Lesczynski returned to the rickshaw. For some reason, the smile made him uncomfortable. He paid the man his fee and set off afoot.

* * *

"Herro. You are surprise I speak your ranguage. Yes? No?"

Is this a put-on? thought Lesczynski. Come on, no one *really* says things like that. "I don't know." He chuckled quietly, caught off guard, watching the beaming, stocky man of about his age who had suddenly appeared before him with a deep bow and a broad grin. The man was short and very muscular, his bushy eyebrows and wide face somewhere down around Lesczynski's armpit. Unsure of protocol, Lesczynski returned the man's bow.

"You know Go?" The man gestured to the wide warehouse of a room where hundreds of intent, somber-faced men knelt or sat in pairs before square boards that resembled chessboards, little white and black buttons scattered with seeming randomness across them. Lesczynski had wandered inside the room because he was captured by the cultural paradox of the men themselves, rather than the game. The curious, serene figures were alternately dressed in Western suits and kimonos, some smoking cigarettes and others drawing on their little Japanese *kiseru* pipes.

"So that's what this is." The little man seemed delighted that Lesczynski had responded so honestly. He was almost childlike in his emotions, not completely to be believed and yet so seemingly earnest and anxious to be liked and understood. Lesczynski found himself grinning back, in sudden good spirits. "*Go* where?"

"Ah, is just a game. This is Kakashima Go Club. Is a very good game. You never try Go?" The little man went on without requiring that Lesczynski go through the embarrassment of answering negatively. "It would not be a hard game for Americans to learn. Is a game of strategy, same as war, many battles on the same board. You can fight five battles, you know, like in the war." He was still grinning with a smile that bordered on innocence. "Japanese take many years to learn Go. Americans, it would not be hard. General MacArthur, he would be best Go player in the whole world!" The little man held out a small, rock-hard hand, bowing again, never losing his wide smile. "I am Yukichi Kosaka and very pleased that I know you and practice my English with you. Okay?"

Lesczynski laughed again, liking the young Japanese man instantly. "I'm Red Lesczynski." He bowed again also. "Pleased to meet you, too."

Kosaka experimented with Lesczynski's name, rolling into a Japanese adaptation, losing the "l" as he did with most words. "Ah, Renshki-san." He gestured to Lesczynski's aviator's wings as they found an empty table near the doorway. "You are Navy pilot. American Navy pilots are *ichi ban*, the best in eternity. I must tell you I am so honored to meet a Navy pilot. I always want to meet a Navy pilot. My brother was killed by a Navy pilot but that was in the war and I am so happy that we are friends." They had found a table and knelt across from each other. The men on either side of them glanced with surprise at Lesczynski's hulking, uniformed frame attempting to kneel on the small *futon* cushion before the Go board, then smiled politely to him, nodding, and returned to their game.

"Your brother was killed in the war?"

"I have three brothers in the war." Kosaka still smiled brightly, devoid of outward bitterness. Lesczynski could not decide whether the bulky little Japanese man's smooth face was a mask, or the accepting and transformed visage of a completely conquered foe. "One brother fight in Manchuria and come home. One brother fight on Saipan, he die. One brother, he was a Navy pilot, too! Ah, yes! He was killed by American Navy pilot in, how you say, Midway Island battle." Kosaka scrutinized Lesczynski for a quick second. "You fight Midway Island?"

Lesczynski felt on the one hand hesitant to fall into a discussion of the recent war, and on the other embarrassed at his lack of experience. "No, I was only about thirteen when Midway was fought." He paused, thinking. "But I remember it."

"You were thirteen! Ah, I was thirteen Midway Island! You now twenty-three? Ah, so!" Kosaka seemed deeply pleased.

"So, how do you play this game, Yukichi? It looks kind of like a cross between chess and checkers."

Kosaka again appeared pleased, this time because Lesczynski had addressed him by his first name, but he did not seem anxious to play. He put both palms up into the air, a gesture of casual helplessness. "Oh, you would not want to play this game. It would be a boring game for Americans. Japanese, they study the game for many years. Did you know Japanese study Go for more than one thousand years, and Chinese for two thousand years before them? Oh yes! You know in America you have service academies? In Japan for three hundred years we had Go academy, from the time of Shogun Tokugawa Scyasu. But Americans, they could be bored or learn Go in a few hours, especially General MacArthur."

It became clear to Lesczynski that Kosaka was attempting, in a somewhat delicate way, to tell him that he did not want to play Go because it would be too embarrassing to beat his new American friend. Lesczynski found this sort of indirectness both touching and amusing, and smiled widely. "I'll tell you what. We won't play a game. Just talk me through the rules, and maybe you could show me some of the moves."

"Ah, so." Kosaka was visibly relieved. "Is a very simple game. To win, you must only surround more sections of the board than your opponent." Kosaka pointed toward the yellow wood playing board, marked off into grids by thin, black lacquer lines. "We begin with empty board, and take turns, one stone at a time."

Lesczynski looked over at other boards around the room. "Can I jump your stones?"

"Oh no. Once a stone is in position it must stay." Kosaka noticed that Lesczynski was watching one old man trying not to act gleeful as he removed several of his opponent's stones. "If you surround my stones it is a *tori,* you can capture them. But you must do it by placing more stones on the board, not by jumping." Kosaka smiled brightly, a gesture of camaraderie. "Same as landing armies on an island, yes?" He gestured to different parts of the board, rolling off the names of World War II battles. "See, you can put Guadalcanal over here and Tarawa here and the Marianas here and the Philippines over here, down here Java, and fight them at the same time! Oh yes! This is an easy game for Americans."

Kosaka then went through ten minutes of minor instructions, the basic ground rules of the game, leaving Lesczynski bewildered by terminology and procedure. His mind was filled with Japanese terms and their intricate applications, *atari* and *kiri* and *tsunagi, shicho* and *me* and *kake-me, nakade* and *seki* and *ko.*

It occurred to him as he watched Kosaka outlining the very rudiments of a game refined by millennia of deep intellectual effort that he was at the same time seeing with fresh clarity the strength of Japanese culture itself. Kosaka had mentioned in passing that virtually every successful Japanese played Go from his childhood. It was a panoramic game demanding deep thought, as intricate as their written language, requiring enormous attention to detail and planning. A man concentrating on one aspect of the board, one battle if you would, could lose the game by failing to anticipate the methodical buildup of his opponent in another corner. On the other hand, if a battle appeared to be lost, the player was supposed to abandon his stones immediately in that area and pursue the battle elsewhere. In the terminology, the stones were dead. *Like on Truk,* thought Lesczynski remembering Japanese strategy in the recent Pacific War. *And Guadalcanal. And . . .* The demands of chess, which Lesczynski played avidly, seemed small and medieval by comparison. An early loss of a key piece in chess was usually enough to signal defeat, while even a severe loss early in a Go game, according to Kosaka, might allow an advantage in another section of the board.

Finally he raised a hand, stopping the patient drone of Kosaka in midsentence. "I can't absorb any more! I promise you, I'll buy a game and try to learn it. Maybe when my ship comes off the line from Korea and I'm in Yokosuka again I'll come back and we can try to play."

Kosaka brightened as if this were the ultimate compliment. It was almost too much, this continual delight. "Oh yes! I would be so very happy to play with you and practice to speak more English. You will learn this game maybe in a few days."

"I doubt it." Lesczynski leaned back, grinning. His legs were feeling cramped from having knelt for so long. Perhaps kneeling has something to do with their patience as well, he mused. "So tell me, Yukichi, how did you learn to speak such good English?"

"Oh, I am not very good at English." Kosaka was again flattered. "You know, before the war English was part of school. Oh yes! So I study before the war. And then after the war I went back to school and I study more English, and now I talk to many Americans. And I have been to America. Oh yes! I work for Toyota Motors. You know Toyota?"

Lesczynski searched his mind. "No. What kind of motors?"

"We make cars, trucks, buses. I went to America two years ago, only for a short wonderful time, and am part of a team to study American cars. Toyota Motors has largest automobile factory in Asia, in Aichi prefecture, on other side of Yokosuka. We have made cars, trucks, and buses since 1937, except for late in the war when we made airplane parts. I am very proud to be a part of Toyota. I will work all of my life for Toyota. We have more than two thousand employees, and each year we grow. Next year we build maybe seven thousand trucks, six thousand *Toyopet* trucks—small trucks—maybe four thousand cars."

"The Japanese Ford, huh?"

"Oh, we make very good cars. Maybe not as good as American cars. Maybe someday we will make cars as good as American cars."

"You said you went back to school after the war. Were you in the Army, Yukichi?"

Kosaka nodded. His eyes dared a moment of cautious pride. "I did nothing. When I turn fifteen I went to the Army. Our leaders told us the Americans would attack us, rape our women and torture babies. The Americans were supposed to be big and have red hair, like you." Kosaka was almost awash in his hope that Lesczynski would not misunderstand him. "But not to say you would do that. And I was trained for the invasion." His eyes found the ceiling. He was remembering. "We had twenty-two divisions waiting to die for the Emperor. Then the war was over and General MacArthur came to Yokohama after he landed at Atsugi. It was the first day for the Americans and we had heard about General MacArthur. The Emperor had come onto the radio—the Japanese people had never heard his voice before!—and he told the Japanese people that we must 'endure the unendurable, suffer the insufferable.' And I was on the streets as a soldier when General MacArthur drove from Atsugi to Yokohama! Oh yes! We stood just off the road in our ranks, all along the way, maybe thirty thousand soldiers on the road. It was okay to keep the bayonets on our weapons, that was how brave General MacArthur was even on his first day! He rode by in an old charcoal burner car, he was almost alone! And we could not even look at him. It would have been disrespect. We turned away from him the same way we would turn our faces from the Emperor. General MacArthur is a great man. Do you like what your President has done to the general?"

It was the first direct question Kosaka had asked Lesczynski that in any way indicated a questioning of Americans or their policy Lesczynski was unsure whether Kosaka was interested in a substantive reply, or for that matter could absorb the details of American politics after having grown up inside such a directed, authoritarian structure. Finally he merely grinned. "No. It was not a smart thing to do." He checked his watch, and stretched his arms, almost knocking over a small old man kneeling at a table to his right. "Very sorry." He made a quick, kneeling bow, and the man did likewise. Then he turned back to Kosaka.

"Yukichi, this has really been fun. But I have to start figuring out how to get back to my ship."

"You go Korea soon?"

"Three days."

Kosaka stood and walked with him toward the door. "If you are not busy it would make me very happy if you would be honored guest at my house before you go."

Red Lesczynski bowed, shaking Kosaka's hand, for the first time wondering what the others in the quiet club had thought of his huge frame and flaring red moustache and loud, resonant voice. "That'd be great."

Kosaka gave him painstaking directions, then they shook hands again. Lesczynski waved to him as he left the club. "*Sayonara.*"

Kosaka waved back "Good-bye."

*   *   *

Lesczynski left the dirt road and walked across the tiny south garden filled with rocks and little bushes, small succulents and spears that seemed to be either onions or daffodils. Kosaka was waiting for him at the entrance of his home, standing in the open space where he had slid aside his *amado* storm door. Kosaka was smiling, bowing again and again, his hands together in front of his waist. He was dressed in a flowing black kimono instead of the Western clothes he had worn at the Go club and at first Lesczynski was not sure he had found the right house in his meanderings through a maze of similar little frame boxes. But he recognized the wide forehead and thick eyebrows, and the little gold bridge over a bottom front tooth, and of course the man seemed so delighted to see Lesczynski that it had to be Kosaka.

"Ah, I am so very happy that you are not busy and come to visit my home, Renshki-san."

Lesczynski stepped up onto the narrow porch that ran the length of the house, bowing and shaking Kosaka's hand, then took off his shoes and followed Kosaka inside. The main room of the house was perhaps the size of a small bedroom in an American home, and had fine wooden screens for walls. The ceiling was so low that Lesczynski lowered his head once inside the room. On the far wall, a screen with delicate wooden grillwork gave the impression of a window. Woven tatami mats covered the immaculate floor. The room was sparsely decorated, two *futon* cushions having been placed in front of an alcove against one wall, where a beautiful and understated paper flower arrangement mushroomed out of a ceramic vase. A painting of a Japanese country scene hung above the vase, old fir trees and a rising sun, and above the door itself was something that resembled a wide banner, with Japanese writing on it. Between the two cushions was a low table and next to it was a ceramic pot painted with flowers, three pieces of charcoal taking the nip out of the autumn air. The little hibachi was the only heating system in the house. Next to one cushion was a small, square smoking tray, holding a *kiseru* pipe, a bowl of tobacco, and an ashtray.

"This is my wife, Kaori."

A slim, rather plain woman dressed in a brightly striped kimono with an *obi* around her waist bowed slowly, her eyes avoiding Lesczynski's. She wore her hair up on top of her head, making her thin face appear very long. She carried a round tray with a ceramic teapot and two cups, and when Lesczynski and Kosaka knelt across from each other on the cushions, she moved noiselessly to the table, kneeling in front of it and pouring them both tea, and then retreated back to the doorway, where she knelt on the tatami mat itself, without a cushion, removing herself from their presence. She did not look at them as they spoke.

Lesczynski watched her quiet, servile movements and suddenly missed Sophie and J.J. with a depth that caused him to shake his head slowly. What right had he to delve into exotica while she pushed their child through the same old streets of home? And if Kosaka had just entered their house, Sophie would have asked a dozen questions by now, and told several jokes while bringing refreshments. He smiled softly to Kosaka. "Does your wife speak English?"

"Oh, some." Kosaka seemed to think it was irrelevant.

"Does she like what General MacArthur did when he gave women equal rights in the new constitution?"

"Oh yes! She is very happy to have equal rights. General MacArthur was very wise to give equal rights." Kosaka sipped his tea and slowly lit his pipe. "She is so happy to vote and when I bring my paycheck home I give it to my wife and she manages the house." Kosaka grinned. "She gives me my money to spend. She is very wise with money. Do you know what that is above the door?" Kosaka answered quickly, in order to prevent Lesczynski the embarrassment of having to think he had been challenged by the question. "Japanese houses have *gaiku* above the door. It is the saying of a famous person. My *gaiku* is dedicated to General MacArthur. It says, 'The energy of the Japanese race will enable the country to lift itself once more into a position of dignity.' General MacArthur is a great man and my wife is so happy to be given equal rights."

Lesczynski sipped his tea, trying to suppress his amusement at Kosaka's insistence about his wife's happiness. She had not so much as lifted her eyes during the entire discussion. "From what I hear, you're very lucky to have a home of your own, Yukichi."

"Oh yes. It is wonderful to work Toyota. When I first marry I stay with my family, grandmother, mother, father, two brother and one brother's wife, and my sister, all in small house like this house. You know, Japan lose maybe 3 million homes to the fire bombs, most here in eastern prefectures—Tokyo, Kanagawa, maybe Osaka." Kosaka's eyes went toward the ceiling again, as they had when he had described the coming of MacArthur in the Go club two days before. "I remember March 1945, the night bombers, making big 'X' through Tokyo, the whole city burning like one side of the sun! One hundred thousand people dead in one night, more than Nagasaki when the Americans dropped atomic bomb! And then again in June, and again in August, hundreds of bombers covering the night sky and the city burning until there are no more homes." Kosaka puffed on his pipe, his head bowing with a quick nod toward Lesczynski. "This was the fate of the Japanese people for making war and I am happy to now be friends. But it was very hard to find a home."

Kosaka glanced toward his wife, a small smile lighting his face, making his eyes dance. "My wife and my sister fight before. My sister Kozuko, she is, how you say—gramor girl."

"Grammar girl?"

"Gramor girl." Kosaka painted imaginary lipstick on with a finger, and pretended to stare into a mirror, primping. From her perch next to the door, Kaori put one hand over her mouth, smiling and blushing with embarrassment at her husband's antics, the first indication Lesczynski had that she was even paying attention to their conversation. It was evident that she understood much of what they were saying.

"Ah, *glamor* girl!" Lesczynski laughed, finishing his tea. Before he had set the cup back into its saucer, Kaori was next to the table, on her knees, smiling shyly and waiting to pour more tea. She actually grinned as she poured the tea, still blushing, but retreated without having looked Lesczynski in the eyes.

"Yes." Kosaka shook his head, as if the situation were hopeless. "You know, at the end of the war, General MacArthur gave us *demokrashi.* There was much discussion in our neighborhood societies about what this would mean for the young people. The neighborhood society decided that the young must participate in cultural meetings, to practice social dancing and English and discuss this *demokrashi.* My sister Kozuko went to the meetings and she talked some but she became the best social dancer. She is very pretty. So then when we come home there were always young boys outside the house or in the doorway to see her. And now she paints her face and fingernails and toenails in the manner of an American woman and wears American dresses and goes to dancing halls at night." He raised a hand, again careful not to offend Lesczynski. "Not to say American women should not paint toes. Only that my mother and Kaori, my wife, have difficult time with my sister Kozuko, who is a beautiful and tragic young gramor girl, and is better for my marriage not to be in the same house."

Kaori had giggled aloud in the middle of the explanation, her hand still over her mouth. Lesczynski began to realize that Kosaka's demure young wife was participating at perhaps the most subtle and yet powerful level imaginable: she was the quiet critic, who would absorb every iota of conversation and most likely go through it with her husband, subject by subject, once Lesczynski departed. From Kosaka's quick glance, it was apparent that his wife's intruding giggle was a comment on his almost comical lack of tact when attempting to hide his displeasure over his sister's "Americanization."

"So," Kosaka pressed on, determined to undo his embarrassment. "You enjoy your fighting Korea?"

Red Lesczynski twirled the ends of his moustache, caught off guard, and pondered Kosaka, wondering if there had been a deliberate double entendre in the question or whether it was merely confused English. "Someone has to fight the communists. Maybe someday the Japanese will be strong enough to help us fight, but your Navy now has ten thousand men and a hundred twenty-five ships, the largest about the size of a small destroyer. Our Navy has more than eight hundred thousand men, not including the Marine Corps, and three thousand ships. It's sort of ironic, isn't it, Yukichi, that my country fought yours and now is fighting to defend you?"

Kosaka seemed mildly wounded by the insinuation. "The Japanese people have had enough of war and are very grateful to the Americans for defending us from the Korean and Chinese communists. We are a weak nation now, and America taught us peace."

"I didn't mean to offend you. To answer your question, I don't think many Americans enjoy fighting Korea. It is said that a young man loves the excitement of fighting until he sees the results."

"Ah, so." Kosaka sucked on his *kiseru* pipe, nodding his head, impressed by Lesczynski's thoughtful reply. He nodded again, this time a form of command to Kaori, who brought a package over to the table and quietly departed. Kosaka held the package out to Lesczynski and smiled once again. "This is a gift from my heart to my honored guest that I am so happy to know."

Lesczynski opened it carefully, preserving the delicately designed wrapping paper. It was a small Go game. "Thanks, Yukichi. I will study this game when I'm at sea, and the next time I'm in port we can play."

"I would be most happy to meet with you again and be friends."

"Do you read English?"

"Oh yes!"

"Then I'll write you a letter and let you know when I'll be in port."

They both rose, and as Lesczynski exited the small house, fitting back into his shoes, he bowed deeply to Kosaka and his wife. "You are kind and thoughtful people."

Kaori smiled graciously, turning her head slightly. Kosaka bowed and grasped Lesczynski's hand. "I know you will fly well in Korea and win many battles in the tradition of American naval aviators and I am honored that you are my friend."

* * *

Here he came, the bastard, all whole with his thick legs pushing along the floor and his bulky arms swinging as if he were marching, that flaming gash of a moustache making him look like some kind of cavalier out after Roundheads, swashbuckling, grinning, his pale eyes widening at the sight of Judd Smith not only awake but half-sitting in his prison of a hospital bed. And here Judd Smith lay, manacled by the tubes running into him and out of him, by his inability even to lie on his side. Sweet Nurse Summers. She had cranked him up so his kidneys could drain into the catheter.

"You make me sick, Lesczynski."

"Looks like the Chinks did a pretty good job of that already."

"Oh, shut the hell up. Stop grinning, will you? What's so goddamn funny about a ward full of cripples?"

"Well, you're all full of piss and vinegar again. How come you're in such a good mood, Judsonia?"

"Because I like it here, what do you think?" Smith grimaced, turning his head from side to side, almost his only luxury of movement. "Christ, can you believe I've been in Japan for a month and I haven't laid me one *josan?* I'll never live this down, Lesczynski." His face softened, the thin mouth taking on a small, almost conspiratorial smile. "Hey, I'm sorry about the other day, Red. I was really out of it. I'm glad you came to see me, man. I know what it means to have to break away from a good piece of ass."

"*Judd,* that's not—"

"Ah, you don't have to bullshit me, Red. I won't let Sophie know. It just happens when a man goes Asian, you know what I mean? And the married guys are worse half the time than the single ones."

"*Smith, I have not been with a Japanese woman!*" Lesczynski's face a foot before his reminded Judd Smith of the pictures he had seen of emotionally charged German soldiers in the attack on Stalingrad, all meaty and spade-nosed and bright-eyed, the mouth set in determination, pushing fleshy cheeks into bulges at the corners. Smith stared calmly back, speaking with a soft taunt.

"Then why are you so pissed off that I said it?"

"I ought to pull your IV tube right out of your arm. No, I ought to yank on that catheter, that's what I ought to do."

"That's it. Pick on a poor fucking cripple, you goddamn Polack *josan*-screwing bully. Nobody comes in here grinning like you were unless they just got laid, so don't try to cover it up by threatening to pull out my pecker."

"Good God." Lesczynski actually stomped a foot on the ground in his exasperation. "You goddamn, *ignorant,* one-track hillbilly!" His face worked into an involuntary snarl and he again came very close to Smith, leaning over the bed.

Smith met his gaze stubbornly, his own face now tight and unsmiling. "If you make any kind of a move on me I'm calling Nurse Summers and having you arrested."

"Kiss my ass, Smith!" Lesczynski turned abruptly from the bed and began walking away, catching the surprised stares of several other patients in the ward.

Smith called after him. "Hey, Polack! Goddamn it, *Red!*" Lesczynski stopped and slowly turned around, fists clenched, peering at Smith with hurt and anger. "Come on back over here, Red. Come on, now. Huh? Come here." Lesczynski walked so slowly back toward the bed that it appeared a shuffle. "Come on!"

"What?"

"Just kidding."

"What do you mean, just kidding?"

Smith chuckled softly, his gray eyes moving around the ward and then back to Lesczynski's reddened face. "I mean I was just kidding. Every now and then I need a little excitement, you know what I mean? Hey, you try laying here day in and day out, listening to people scream and watching them throw up and bleed and stuff like that. It gets boring after a while. And I know that *right outside* this goddamn hospital a guy can get laid. Hey, man. I know you wouldn't do that, but I haven't been laid since *January!*" Smith chuckled again, shaking his head with bemusement at his former roommate. "You wouldn't really have pulled my catheter out, now, would you, Red? That would have been low."

Lesczynski had gone from a tight, red-faced rigidity, his large hands in balls of fists, to a head-shaking, smiling ease. He laughed. "Aw,

Judd, you know me better than that. I'd have just left, and waited until you got all well, and then I'd have thrown you up into a tree."

"You think you're that tough? Shit." Smith was clearly enjoying the pugnacity of their conversation. "You come after me you better bring the whole goddamn football team to help you."

"Tough guy. Right now a little old lady with a dull pair of scissors could do you in."

"Lieutenant Smith? Is everything all right?" A deep, slow southern drawl, decidedly female, came from behind Lesczynski.

"No, ma'am." Smith smiled to the small pixie of a woman. "This man has been threatening to pull out my catheter. I don't even know how he got into the ward."

She seemed used to Smith's antics. She laughed, measuring him, and then examined Lesczynski. "Is that what all the commotion was about a few minutes ago?"

Smith answered again. "Yes, ma'am, Lieutenant Summers. I was telling him how you and I were in love and all and he said, 'Judd, never fall in love with a Navy nurse, because there's always another catheter just around the horizon.' Can you imagine that? Well, anyway, I threatened his life, you know, in defense of our relationship and all, and—"

She winked to Lesczynski. "He runs in cycles, but I always dread it when he wakes up." She then turned back to Smith. "Lieutenant Smith, if you cause any more ruckus, *I'll* pull on your catheter. I swear to God, sometimes I think you need a baby-sitter." She walked on down the ward.

"Yeah, poor lady, I think she loves me, Red. I just feel terrible that I can't attend to her needs. So, when do you ship out?"

"Tomorrow."

"The big ROK, eh? Gonna get yourself a MiG, wing-wipe?"

"Don't I wish." Lesczynski made a sour face. "No, the Air Force is up in MiG country. We're *interdicting.* That means we'll be blowing away bridges and trucks and power plants. Not very sexy, I'm afraid. The Skyraiders are getting all the close air support, too. All in all, it should be a pretty routine tour, Judd." Lesczynski grinned ironically. "No MiGs, no colostomies, no Medal of Honor."

"Well, write my name on one of your bombs. 'Dear Chink: Doing fine, hope this tears you a new asshole, love Judd Smith.' And forget about any Medal of Honor. I'm not going to get that goddamn thing. I don't even want it. What the hell do they do to you after they give you the Medal of Honor, except take pot shots at you and make you sell War Bonds?" Smith stared up at the ceiling, imploring the angels of his fate. "I just want my pecker back, in good working order!"

"Is that all you can think about?"

"Just about. I'm *horny*, Lesczynski! Christ on a crutch." Smith seemed to calm down, growing ponderous, his eyebrows furled. "I think I'm going to get married."

"Got anybody in mind?"

Smith seemingly ignored the question, his eyes distant and his face serious. "Just think. If I'd been killed, I wouldn't have left any kids or anything. Judd Smith would have been wiped off the face of the earth!"

"That's a hell of a reason to want to get married."

"What do you know about it? You've already got your eternity, right there in Sophie's arms in Ford City."

Lesczynski sighed. "You may as well do it, then. Dingenfelder's ready to, any day now."

"Damn Dingie." Judd Smith raised his bandaged left arm, the eagle on his shoulder dancing, then rested it again. "He'll have to tell his grandkids he sat out the great Korean War in the Wright Brothers wind tunnel at MIT."

CHAPTER SEVEN

WHEN HER MIND BEGAN WORKING furiously and her anger started up,
Dorothy Edelson had a way of lighting a fresh cigarette and then
furiously tapping it, her blue eyes watching the lit end until it hung
off the rest of the cigarette, ready to fall into the ashtray. Then she
would gently push the cigarette against the loose tip, saving it, and
draw slowly, finally staring at her opponent. It was an unconscious device, an undemanding distraction that allowed her to collect her
thoughts and energies before attacking. Joe Dingenfelder had noticed
this tendency after having dated Dorothy only a few times, and had
used it thereafter as a device to prepare himself for her coming bursts
of blistering argument.

Just now Dorothy was in the tapping stage, staring intently at the
ashtray as Lee Schulman and Frank Hughes and Joe were discussing
Korea. She slowly twirled a portion of her dark hair with her other
hand, preparing to erupt with a logic he had learned either to acknowledge or humor, but never fight. She always won the fights, it
seemed. He never admitted it aloud, but he knew that she was
tougher than he was, and in fact that was secretly a part of her attraction.

The jukebox barked behind them, playing "How Much Is That
Doggie in the Window." The lounge of the Massachusetts Institute of
Technology's Graduate House was filled with conversations that often
had the intellectual density of the very textbooks from which the students read. Lee Schulman had also seen Dorothy explode before, and
he cut his lecture short, seeking safer ground. He turned to Dingenfelder, smiling facetiously, with a small deference to the academy
graduate's military background.

"I was reading in the *Voo Doo* joke page today, and there was a
story about this little hillbilly who enlists in the Marines and goes to
the dentist for the first time, you know, and he gets into the chair and
sees all the equipment, and he asks the dentist, 'Are you a Yankee?'
and the dentist holds the drill and says, 'Yes,' and then the hillbilly
turns to the dentist's assistant, and he says, 'Are you a Yankee?' and

the assistant holds the plate of tools and nods, 'Yes,' and the hillbilly swallows hard and says, 'Well, what do you know? Ah'm a Yankee, too.'"

Schulman laughed heartily, pleased with the smiling reaction from around the table. He adjusted heavy dark-rimmed glasses with small hands and then nodded to Dingenfelder. "Is that about like your friend?"

"Judd Smith? No." Dingenfelder gave off a small, remembering chuckle, filled with bemused affection. "No, Judd Smith would walk into the room and say, 'Are either of y'all Yankees?' and when they both nodded, he'd pick up one of the tools himself and say, 'Well, the first one of you that makes a wrong move is gonna be whistling "Dixie" with this thing shoved up his you-know-what sideways.'"

"Oh, for God's sake." Dorothy pressed the cigarette against the dangling coal and both Dingenfelder and Schulman inched slightly away from the table, Schulman clearing his throat and picking up his coffee cup, Dingenfelder feeling his eyes grow slightly larger, awaiting the outburst. She drew deeply on the cigarette and Frank Hughes stood abruptly, walking toward the jukebox, his heavy frame lumbering away with his shoulders hunched, as if in retreat.

"Get back here, Hughes." Dingenfelder reached for Hughes' belt and missed. "You've got to endure this, too."

"Endure what?" Debby Mink, Dorothy's roommate at Radcliffe, gazed at them with an angelic innocence, a pose that forever kept men unbalanced when they later became exposed to her unyielding ability at argument. She and Dorothy were partners on the debate team, and had learned well the technique of mixing sexuality with logic. She stretched slowly, her well-shaped breasts pressing against her sweater, and as the three men moonfully caressed her chest with their eyes she dropped her indictment with honey sweet, alto words. "We're the ones who've been enduring, boys. If the Korean War is such a great big deal, why are you sitting here in graduate school, letting people like this Judd Smith fight it?"

Dorothy moved in, as a right cross follows a jab in a boxing match. She had mustered her facts and she put both elbows on the table, her little hands throwing straight gestures this way and that, her high-pitched voice like knife thrusts as she talked. "Well, the truest statement is that your friends, no matter how brave or tough or funny they are, have been wasting their time and maybe their lives, and you know it and so does our government. I mean, consider the facts, for

God's sake! As early as 1947 the Joint Chiefs of Staff themselves
claimed that our country had no strategic interest in Korea. *None!*
Even this dunderhead *Eisenhower* signed that memorandum! And
Truman, two years before the war started, said that an attack by either side on the other wouldn't bring us into the war. And George
Marshall advised against strengthening the South Korean military
when he was Secretary of State, because he was afraid they'd attack
the *North* if they got too strong! And even the goddamned *Republicans* fought every appropriation for South Korea before the war! Have
you ever read any of this? Have your friends, who are so gallantly and
stupidly sailing off to be killed? A month before the war started, the
chairman of the Senate Foreign Relations Committee said that Russia
herself could take over South Korea and the United States probably
wouldn't intervene. And of course, Secretary of State Acheson rather
conveniently forgot to include South Korea in America's 'line of defense' when he was speaking before the National Press Club not long
before North Korea invaded. So, tell me, what happened in the time it
took North Korea to invade after his speech that made South Korea
suddenly so important that your friends should have to go and die
there?"

"You're so cute when you get mad, Dorothy." Dingenfelder smiled,
and patted her on the back. She drew on her cigarette again, shaking
her head with exasperation.

"I'll tell you what happened." Frank Hughes had returned and sat
heavily back into his chair. "The communists took over China, that's
what happened. And it made Asia a whole new ball game."

"Oh, posh. They took over China in 1949. Surely even Harry Truman would have found out about it by 1950, Frank." Dorothy shuddered, putting out her cigarette. "And now this smiling idiot Eisenhower, who needed a war to get him from lieutenant colonel to
general, is actually going to be President. And this madman,
McCarthy, is going to have free rein to call anyone who doesn't just
love fascists a commie. Oh, I just can't believe the American people
are such sheep." She raised her eyebrows, studying Dingenfelder's soft
spaniel eyes. "If you want to get excited about something, *Dingie*"—
she only called him Dingie when she wanted to taunt him—"try worrying about the 3 million Jews who need to get out of Eastern Europe.
They've been through *hell.* I know, I was there when it started."

"One shouldn't preclude the other, Dorothy. We're the strongest
country in the free world. In fact, we're the *hope* of the world. That

may sound corny, but it isn't, it's real." Hughes shrugged off Dorothy's penetrating stare. "Joe's friends are helping in Korea. Others are helping in Europe. Joe and I are helping through our studies here."

Dorothy smirked, rolling her eyes as she reached for another cigarette. "The mental moles of MIT, caught up in the 'Experimental and Theoretical Investigation of Large-scale Atmospheric Turbulence,' and other such studies designed to save the world."

"Well, they are, you know. Look at Joe. He's going to—"

"Investigate gravity anomalies, or something like that."

Dingenfelder took on an almost wounded look, forcing a smile. He didn't like to argue with Dorothy, but sometimes she made it hard to stay out of her debates. "Come on, Dorothy. I'm pretty proud of my thesis. I'm doing something that could help put a man on the moon someday. You shouldn't knock that. People are different, that's all. You're no more comfortable talking about wall shear stress distributions and schlieren observations and boundary layer velocity profiles than I am about talking politics. But that shouldn't make either of us stupid or irresponsible, should it?"

"We should solve the problems on earth before we look for other ones on the moon. Who needs to know what's on the moon, for God's sake? I don't care whether it's dust or green cheese—or a big ball of pus, for that matter."

"You know, I think Dorothy would argue about anything." Shulman shook his head, grinning hopelessly at Dingenfelder. "She just loves to argue, that's all. You'd better let her go to law school, Joe, or she'll be debating you morning, noon, and night for the rest of your life."

"Dorothy can do whatever she wants, I don't care."

"I'm not sure it would matter if you *did*. But you're right about the rest. Dorothy is damn well going to do whatever she wants."

* * *

Beware the woman by her father loved and by the world betrayed.

In the summer and fall there were trips to the Cape and visits with friends to the lush and fertile playgrounds of Martha's Vineyard, as well as weekends at her family's retreat at the eastern end of Long Island, near Sag Harbor. Over winter holidays they would travel, down south to Miami or up into New Hampshire or Maine for skiing. In the interim, weekend visits to New York City provided all the cultural fascinations one might desire, from plays to fine food. Dorothy Edelson was used to opulence, to motion, to doing and getting what she damn well wanted.

Yet in her very center, at the place she went to every night just before she nodded off to sleep, was an almost childlike murmur of resentment, of perpetual, irresolvable disappointment, a sense that, no matter how much she acquired or experienced in her life, it would always be unfulfilled and even slightly soiled. For all of her conscious logic, Dorothy proceeded from an amorphous ball of hate and fear, fueled by a five-year-old's vision of shocked and suddenly impoverished people huddled on a wet, fuel-slick desk, clinging together for sustenance, happy to be escaping a horror that had only begun to act itself out, yet guilty at leaving others behind to die in concentration camps and mass exterminations.

They had ruined everything, the Nazis, conjured up a mix of rage and impotence and guilt in the people who survived their attempts at genocide, *you stood by while 6 million died.* Fighting back, however late, was the answer. Like a mother who locks her remaining children inside the house after one has suffered a tragic accident, it was incumbent on the survivors to somehow atone through acts of political concern. Israel was the answer.

And most importantly, the Nazis had taken away her life, the one she had missed and dreamed of as a child in her first days in New York City, the one she had been born into, the one she deserved to experience. They had taken her father's business, a bicycle factory in Vienna, and with it the right to grow up among the tall buildings and electric trams and art galleries, the right to enjoy a European inheritance that her whole family lamented in a way that some mourn lost loved ones. *Come back, Vienna, come back you Europe before the dragon.* But like a loved one it was forever gone, charred and destroyed in the flames of a war in which Dorothy and her friends and relatives were somehow viewed to be as much catalysts as victims.

Her father had come to New York with a small bit of his wealth and all of his skills, and shifted to foodstuffs. In five short years he owned a string of delicatessens, and in ten had regained his former financial status. But it was all a plastic imitation, a compensation for what had really mattered. At night he would drink *schnaps* and talk in low, rounded syllables filled with a quiet astonishment about his life in Vienna, about courting her mother, about the Nazis. And when she went to bed, and searched her memories and emotions down deep inside where only she could go, she always found the same empty, heartsick little lament.

Her father loved her, pampered her, tried to make it up to her, and the more she loved her father the more she hated what had happened to him, the more she vowed to try and do something about it. It was impossible to resolve, as impossible as bringing someone back from the dead, but it was possible to somehow reach into the tragedy and bring out a handful of momentum, a ball of anger, a book of principles.

And, yes, to fight back. The Nazis were gone but they weren't really, not all the way, and they never would be. Their spirit hid away like a dormant infection in the moist, dark side of the human soul, the side that fostered tribal passion, exclusive religious belief, leader worship, and love of war. Any sudden, jarring event could reinvigorate the bacteria, pushing the infection back into the bloodstream of the world.

Not from Germany, at least not for decades. Nor from the rest of Europe, mindless as that continent's endless bloodletting seemed. But from the United States. No other country had such a combination of racism and fundamentalist religious sects. No other country so celebrated war, as if its dreadful leavings were a cause for joy. No other country claimed violence as a national ethos; frontier violence, war violence, swaggering, fistfight violence, football violence, fast-car violence.

Nigger-killing, electric-chair violence. In her sophomore year at Radcliffe she had become active on campus in the Willie McGee Defense Fund. McGee, a Mississippi Negro, had been convicted of raping a white woman in 1945. He had confessed to raping the woman after having held her and her baby at knife point, yes. But Dorothy knew what a confession was worth under the terror of a Nazi regime, and she had heard the stories about police brutality in Mississippi. The confession was accepted. Willie was sentenced to death. No white man had ever been put to death in Mississippi for rape. The Willie McGee Defense Fund had moved in to help, sending a young woman attorney named Bella Abzug down from New York, and a man named John Coe in from Florida. Willie was tried three times, and found guilty each time. The national media claimed the communists were using his case to discredit the United States. The NAACP pulled away from Willie's case, but Dorothy understood that as well; in a racist society, they were covering their tracks to survive, trying to avoid a commie label.

Willie was put to death. *Life* magazine ran an article celebrating it, under the headnote, "A Mississippi rapist with a slender chance to escape death is 'aided' by the Reds and gets the chair."

And there it was in a nutshell; racial hatred and commie-baiting, the two great ingredients of fascism "Tail gunner Joe" McCarthy and his minions had scared away responsible criticism, too. Dorothy's political idol during college was an Englishman, Aneurin Bevan, the so-called "bad boy of British politics." Bevan, one of ten children of a coal miner, saw postwar America as the greatest menace to the world, with its racism and its economy that fed itself off the plates of starving people everywhere. Dorothy knew that many people in the United States sympathized with "Nye" Bevan's views, but had been frightened into silence.

The United States had been in its soul a good and gracious country. It had saved her life, and she loved it for that. But she also felt that it had become warped by World War II, entranced with its power. She would help push it back to goodness; that would be her life.

Then Joe Dingenfelder had to come along and screw things up.

He was so infuriatingly patient, so easy to get along with, that sometimes his very easiness created a swell of anger in her. She did not want to get married, and sometimes she found herself standing in front of the mirror in her dormitory room, inspecting her small, heart-shaped face with its slightly overlarge nose and too small, circular mouth, the blue eyes deep but not alluring, searching for a reason that Joe Dingenfelder found her attractive. Her breasts were small, her hips a bit too wide, her voice already hard-edged from her love of debate. *I'm not a woman*, she would think, examining herself with a small displeasure, a sense of trepidation over Dingenfelder's attentions. *I mean, not feminine.* There was just enough attractiveness that she could use it effectively with an old judge in a debating competition, a raising of the eyebrows and a fetching smile, but there was not enough for this quiet, moon-eyed scientist with a penchant for classical music to be pursuing her like this. *And there is too much to do, too much to be done. I don't want to be married and locked away.*

But it nagged at her that there might never be another man with the kindness and sense of understanding that he displayed. She knew that she was spoiled and given to histrionics, and in a way it was a form of selfishness to decide to marry Dingenfelder, and she recognized that. Life, after all, was in making the best deal possible, everywhere, every way. She was becoming known for having driven suitors away after a few dates. Part of it was her refusal to demur to less intelligent men, and there was no need to do that with Dingenfelder, who simply refused to argue about matters in her arena. Part of it was a subconscious need to stay independent, to wrap her emotions inside an armor so that she could not be hurt, and Dingenfelder had obviated that fear by making it clear that she held the emotional cards. If anything, she would hurt him.

She had never given herself to a man until Joe Dingenfelder patiently and gently walked her through the minefield of her sexuality, unwrapping the fears and repressions that had begun in those cold and terrifying days of her childhood when all the world seemed bent on destroying her. It was not morality that had held her back before, but rather a sense that she would lose control. She did not feel that with Dingenfelder, who took her only as far as she desired to go. The first time he pressed his lips between her thighs she had undulated with passion for several seconds, beside herself with pleasure, and then had watched horrified, as if from another room, as a voice from within her stomach screamed, again and again, uncontrollably and without words, until Joe was next to her, a hand over her mouth, whispering into her ear that she must stop it before the downstairs occupants called the police, please stop it, but still she had screamed and he was slapping her face with one hand, the other still over her mouth, his eyes in an agonized squint in the dark room, as if he were watching a ghoul. And then, suddenly, she had stopped screaming, again without making a decision, and wept for a few minutes, her head turned away from him, and then had gone to sleep. The next morning she had refused to talk about it, and he had not insisted. Nor did he ever kiss her there again.

But I do not want to get married, and I especially do not want to marry a military man.

She hated military uniforms; they clothed men whose job it was to kill people. She had never seen Joe in a uniform, yet when she was with him the military was as near as her past, and just as volatile. She could not conceive of marrying anyone who would want to dedicate his life to waging death, even in the abstract sense of scientifically perfecting the aerodynamics of flight, when the mission of the flight would be to drop atomic bombs. She could accept, rationally, that such people were necessary in an ordered world. But so were jail guards, and she couldn't imagine spending her life around prisons, either.

And he promised, that was the key. He had his military obligation to work off once he graduated. Four years, for the academy education. Another two, for the time spent at MIT on Air Force funds. Six years. Could she really take six years of it?

Harvard Law School had accepted her for the next year's entering class. Marrying Joe Dingenfelder meant abandoning that, and instead traveling with him like a camp follower, a displaced person (how she hated that term), to the unknown reaches of a new and potentially hostile country. Flight training in Texas and Mississippi. *Mississippi!* Joe might have said hell itself. Willie McGee burned to a frizzle in an electric chair, crosses on Jewish and Negro lawns, hate and murder and discontent. And then a duty assignment in any of a dozen states, all of which seemed remote and just as threatening.

And yet, what a kind and sensuous man, what a chance to have a life that might almost be characterized as pleasant. She wanted to be in love; she just didn't think it would really happen, not all the way, not forever. And if it didn't, after she had fully tried, she would have opened herself up in a way that would cut her feelings forever dead. Arguing with people was safer. You didn't expect them to like you when you were picking them apart.

*　*　*

He had his own apartment just off the MIT campus, made possible by his second lieutenant's pay, supplemented by an occasional boost from his father. His father had also sent him his Steinway, and the living room of the apartment was dominated by the deep mahogany grand piano. He was really very good; no, he was more than very good, he was genuinely talented, and one of her greatest pleasures was having him play for her, just for her.

She called to him from the small kitchen, where she was putting together her most elaborate meal, one of perhaps three that she had learned to prepare, stuffed chicken and creamed broccoli and wild rice, with a custard dessert. He had chosen a Volnay Burgundy to go with it, defying the orthodoxy which proclaimed that white wines went with fowl. He had good taste in wines; that was another reason. "Oh, Joe, play some Bartók for me. Piano Concerto Number One?"

It was as if she had put a coin into a symphonic jukebox. His delicate fingers commanded elegant sounds out of the Steinway, first the heavy, slow notes from the low end of the keyboard that somehow always reminded her of the deep and ominous soul of Eastern Europe, and then the light, dancing energy of the whole instrument itself. It was almost astonishing, his brilliant quick fingers and the music they contrived, up and down the keyboard, alternately loud, filled with an authority that his quiet voice belied, then soft, as gentle as his hands upon her body.

The chicken was in the oven. The broccoli was turned on "simmer." The rice boiled slowly, as wild rice must. His blood and emotions pulsed poetry into his fingers, his head moving sideways and sometimes bobbing, his hands at one end and then the other of the keyboard, almost in a trance as Bartók came alive.

Her own hands were on his shoulders, a touch, filled with hesitance, that slowly grew stronger until her fingers were massaging his neck. He continued to play and she embraced him, a small bare breast against his cheek. He stopped then and turned on the stool and she gathered his head like a baby's into her chest, cradling it, kissing the top of it, and he ran his hands along her young skin, noting with a flash of humor and ecstacy that her clothes made a trail from the door of the kitchen to the very foot of his stool.

She laughed, deep inside her throat, and squeezed his head again. "Can you love me like you do that?"

Part Two

THAT YONDER SHINING LIGHT

CHAPTER EIGHT

I

Judd smith *looked* like a young Hun with his shaved head and angular features and the trim, dress-blue uniform, draped with gold brocade and gleaming with medals. He stood on the sidewalk in front of the Center House, where the bachelor officers of Marine Barracks, Washington, D.C., lived, waiting for Lieutenant Donny Stuart to join him.

Finally Stuart ambled down the Center House steps, fitting his white dress cap above his ears. He checked his watch and teased Smith.

"Kind of anxious to get on over with the big shots tonight, aren't you, Judd boy?"

"Hey, man! This is the *Queen*. Give me a break."

"You like it too much, Smith." Stuart, Judd's friend since before Korea, angled his head toward the home of the Commandant of the Marine Corps, which dominated the parade ground of the barracks with a quiet power. The commandant's house was the oldest continually standing building in Washington. The British had spared it during the War of 1812 when burning the rest of the city, as a tribute to the Marines who had faced them to a standstill in the Battle of Bladensburg.

"Yes, sir, old Judd boy can't wait to move into the Big House. Can't stand just being a little old platoon commander, marching pretty in dress parades and standing guard at Camp David. Can't wait till they make him commandant, either. Got to get his jollies messing around with the heavyweights."

"Stuart, if you don't shut up I'm going to sharpen your toes and pound you into the ground like a tent peg."

They began walking toward a waiting bus, which would take them to the White House for their volunteer duty as social aides. It was a collateral benefit to duty at the barracks. Smith and Stuart spent as many as three nights a week at the President's evening functions.

Smith nudged Stuart as they boarded the bus. "Besides, I don't see *you* staying back at the barracks."

* * *

"Yes, sir," announced Judd Smith as he sat in the President's theater with dozens of other social aides, "the Queen of England, and that's no bullshit."

"Lieutenant Smith, that sort of language is completely inappropriate for the White House, don't you think?"

Smith folded his arms, watching Captain Richard C. Cooper III's face through squinting eyelids after he allowed his eyes to settle, for a deliberate moment, on Cooper's chest. It was empty of either decorations or campaign ribbons. Cooper, a West Pointer slightly older than Judd, was now an Air Force supply officer. Cooper had fought the Korean War from a desk in the Pentagon. He was a sycophant who would make his way up to general by becoming "invaluable" in a series of staff jobs. "Why don't you go back over to the Pentagon and hold your general's hand, Cooper? And kiss my ass on the way out the door."

"Come on, Judd." Donny Stuart nudged him, whispering. "Try to act like a gentleman, for once. Just pretend, okay?"

"Aw, I can't help it." Smith responded loud enough that his words turned Cooper's large ears red. "Phonies piss me the hell off."

Major von Suskil, the senior social aide, walked into the theater to give them their briefing before the state dinner began. President Eisenhower was indeed hosting Queen Elizabeth of England, along with more than a hundred dignitaries. It was Queen Elizabeth's first visit to the United States. More than a million people had lined the streets of Washington that afternoon as President Eisenhower and the Queen slowly drove the four-mile route from the Washington National Airport to the White House in Eisenhower's black bubble-top Lincoln. Equerries, aides, ambassadors, and senators had filled the White House corridors for hours, until the sight of even the most important politicians seemed almost boring. It was grand to be a part of it, no matter how cynical Judd Smith tried to remain.

Major von Suskil stood in front of the screen, erect in his Army dress blues. They reminded Smith of the old cavalry uniforms, gold brocade hanging from a shoulder and gold braid on his sleeves and along the sides of his trousers, his chest gleaming with medals earned in two wars. Von Suskil went through the routine procedures once again. He had been briefed by both the President's social and military aides, down to the most intricate detail. He read off special assign-

ments from a checklist, mentioning such positions as announcing aides
and sector aides, the setup aide and whispering aides. Heads bobbed
in the small theater, familiar with the assignments. They had all been
through the drill numerous times before. Eisenhower had been an international figure for many years. Heads of state from the world over
wished to visit him. And he and Mamie liked to entertain.

Von Suskil finished the briefing. He checked his watch. "In place
time, 1900 hours. That's four minutes, gentlemen. Be sharp. The whole
world will be watching."

"Ain't it weird what people will do and call it fun, Donny?"

At the north portico of the White House Queen Elizabeth and
Prince Philip had arrived and been escorted upstairs to the Yellow
Oval Room for a private predinner visit with the President and
Mamie. On the south side, a level below the north portico, the cool
night air began to stir with the churn of automobile engines and the
slamming of car doors. As if following a cue, dignitaries and their
wives or dates began filling the Diplomatic Reception Room just after
seven o'clock, checking their coats and handing their invitations to civilian White House ushers, who ensured that they were valid and then
turned them over to the military social aide. The military social aide
then handed the cards, names up, to the military escorts, including
Smith, Stuart, and the now electrically smiling Richard C. Cooper III.
Cooper was watching the arriving guests with the shrewd, hungry
eyes of a vulture.

"Ambassador and Mrs. Battaglia of Italy." Judd Smith took the
cards from the military social aide and offered his arm to the ambassador's wife, a round-faced, heavy woman wrapped up in swaddles of
pink silk. They walked slowly through the foyer, where the Marine
Corps Band serenaded the arriving guests with light symphonic gaiety, and headed toward the East Room, where the President would
later receive his guests. The ambassador, a doddering old man who
stank of cigars, trailed behind. Smith made a few attempts at light
conversation, as suggested by his superiors, but drew almost no response from the ambassador's wife, who searched in front of her toward the East Room for important people.

"Ambassador and Mrs. Battaglia of Italy." Smith handed the cards,
again names up, to the announcing aide, who walked to a microphone
and announced their arrival in the East Room with an exact monotone. The announcing aide then gave the cards to another escort, who

brought them to one of three sectors of the East Room, according to a number code on their invitation. Sector assignments were designed to spread out the talent, so to speak, in the large ballroom, rather than having it collect around the door in anticipation of the President.

Smith marched back through the foyer, consciously erect, somewhat cynical behind the courteous smiles and deferential nods he gave to passing guests, fascinated by the fairy tale grandeur and at the same time secretly ashamed that it so attracted him. It wasn't real, all this, and even if it was, he wasn't really a part of it. He was an ornament, a little windup doll, a device to impress and enthrall, like a flagpole or a painting or one of the trombones in the band. I'm an Old South nigger, he thought suddenly, smiling and nodding to Ambassador somebody or other. Yes, massa. Smilin' over here, massa. Pickin' it up over here, massa. Whooee. My mind's *right*, massa.

But hey, you know, I mean the *Queen* and all. When I write the old man and tell him about this he'll just sit down and have himself a stroke.

Back in the Diplomatic Reception Room, waiting for his arm in escort, was that night's dinner prize. He usually made a game of it, trying to decide which of the female guests would draw the greatest number of old geezer diplomats toward their final heart attacks. It wasn't a very hard game, but it helped him preserve his proper distance, to treat those he escorted as if he were actually viewing them from a window or on a screen.

She stood before a square, tough-looking man with dark bushy eyebrows and white hair. Judd thought he recognized the man from some newspaper or magazine story. She had blond hair and a wide mouth that showed all of her teeth when she smiled, and it seemed she liked to smile, as if someone had rubbed Vaseline on her teeth and she wanted to keep her lips off them. But that was all right. Her blond hair piled in waves along her shoulders and her face had a classical, sharp featured togetherness to it, as if it had been designed, every piece having been consciously fit to blend with the other, rather than being a genetic accident of the womb. The contrast between the frail blond beauty of the woman, who appeared to be in her early twenties, and the scowling gray of the man, who was at least sixty, was as if Smith were watching her rest daintily against the rugged bark of an old tree.

Yeah, some old bastards have all the luck.

"Senator Jackson Clay of Virginia, and his daughter Julia."

Daughter? Well, *hey . . .*

Suddenly Captain Richard C. Cooper III was elbowing in front of him, reaching for the guest cards. "I'll take those, *Lieutenant* Smith."

Quickly, and with an adeptness that was imperceptible to anyone beyond their immediate vision, Judd Smith reached up with his left hand and grabbed Cooper at the back of his collar, pulling down hard do that he choked him and straightened him up, stopping him in mid-stride. He smiled to Cooper, his face threatening and only inches away, holding an imitation of Cooper's own sycophantic grin. "Oh, that's all right, Captain. I can handle it." He took the tickets and extended his arm. "Miss Clay?"

Her smile lit her whole delicate little face and warmed her wide blue eyes and she *curtsied,* goddamn it, she actually curtsied! "Lead on, fine sir." She took his arm. "This hand, so nobly won."

Senator Clay snorted, his eyes alert and constantly moving, yet somehow appearing tired behind his fleshy, muscular face. "Don't mind my daughter, Lieutenant. She was born in the wrong century."

She was weightless on his arm and yet she was really there, with the presence, say, of a memory, a nostalgic one. She was the creature in the film you could fall in love with and suffer over, but had to abandon in the must and trash of the movie house when she rode off into the sunset at the film's end. The gentle waves of music from the Marine Band now washed against him with a mocking reality, *I am a trombone, over here, massa,* and yet he found himself wishing that he could perform this simple chore, this supposedly meaningless, ornamental task, all night.

She examined the rows of medals on his chest. "They look like merit badges. Are you a hero, Lieutenant?"

"Well, he's got the number-two merit badge, honey." Senator Clay had taken in Smith's decorations at one glance. "I'm real proud of you, Lieutenant."

"You told me that in your letter, sir."

"I wrote you a letter? You a Virginian, son? What's your name?"

"Judd Smith, sir."

The senator pondered it. His daughter gave Judd a small wink, as if to share a moment of secret admiration for her father's memory. The East Room was only twenty short steps away. It would all end too soon. Senator Clay spat his words out, his head shaking from side to side as he spoke, as if flinging them. "Well, by God, I do remember.

Judsonia Smith, from down in southwest Virginia. That's a hard-won Navy Cross, son! You deserve a Medal of Honor! Julie girl, you don't realize what you got on your arm, now! Well, by God . . ." Senator Clay had seemingly run out of words. He took Smith's white-gloved hand and shook it hard as they reached the East Room. "Well, by God, I'm proud to meet you."

"Thank you, sir." Smith handed the cards reluctantly to the announcing aide, and smiled wanly to Julie. "Nice to meet you, too."

"Are you allowed to dance? I mean, after dinner?"

His whole body buzzed as he fell inside her blue eyes. "Well, I'll just make it a point to. I mean, if that's what you're asking."

"You come on over to where we are when the dancing starts, son." Senator Clay patted him on his shoulder with a thick, heavy hand. "You'll be doing me a favor. I'm just a tired old man. I could never keep up with her."

"So you can dance, then?" She smiled her invitation one more time, that classical face tilted to one side. "I mean, as a favor to *Daddy* and all?"

At seven-thirty a joint color guard led by a Marine captain formed at the bottom of the elegant grand staircase and marched up to place in the hallway above as the captain reported to the President inside the Yellow Oval Room. In minutes he reappeared and two men, a soldier and a Marine, entered the room and returned with the American flag and the Presidential colors, which had flanked the fireplace. They all formed at the top of the stairway then, the President and the Queen and Prince Philip with Mamie, and the color guard marched down the staircase, leading them to the East Room. Queen Elizabeth was wearing a full floor-length gown with what appeared to be large flowers on it, her young shoulders bare in the October night. She wore white gloves that went up past her elbows, and the purple sash and crown of her royalty. Over his black tie and tails President Eisenhower wore the ribbon and medal of Britain's Order of Merit, which had been given him by Elizabeth's father, King George VI, following World War II. Mamie had changed her mind at the last minute, and wore a rather simple olive-green evening gown instead of the peony red silk gown she had earlier announced she would wear. Prince Philip's uniform was arrayed with a bedazzling collection of ribbons and sashes, in the tradition of European royalty. They stopped for a quick moment at the bottom of the stairway for the bevy of photographers who were covering the occasion, Ike smiling with grandfatherly good humor, the Queen demure beside him, and then marched toward the East Room behind the color guard.

"Ladies and Gentlemen, the President of the United States and Elizabeth, Queen of England."

The guests stood at attention as the band played "Hail to the Chief" and then gathered in a receiving line under the huge crystal chandeliers of the East Room, across from its famous old standing portrait of George Washington. The "setup aide" introduced each guest to the Chief of Protocol, who in turn introduced the visitor to the President. The President introduced the person to the Queen, who passed him or her down the line to Prince Philip, who finally introduced the person to Mamie. Two "whispering aides" stood behind Mamie and Prince Philip, quietly repeating the names of the people in front of them, lest they had missed the original introduction. Just off the end of the line, a "pulloff aide" hovered, ready to escort any guest who lingered in the reception line out into the cavernous boundaries of the East Room.

The remainder of the military aides waited outside the East Room, "toeing the carpet" as they formed a military honor guard along the eighty-seven-foot Cross Hall that connected the East Room with the State Dining Room. When all of the guests had passed through the receiving line, President Eisenhower and the Queen strolled along the corridor, followed by Mamie and Prince Philip, leading the entourage to dinner past the stoic, uniformed men who stood at an attention that would have rivaled the Buckingham Palace Guards.

Judd Smith caught a glimpse of the Queen as she passed before him. She appeared from behind the potted tree on his right, and then passed close enough for him to have reached out and touched her. Hot damn, the *Queen*, he reminded himself again. But the blond girl's wide-eyed, toothy smile still mixed in his mind with his own sense of who he was not—*are you allowed to dance?*—and the Queen of England seemed now diminished, an ambulatory creature from somebody's wax museum, of some historical relevance but unreal. She was still in the movie. Julie Clay had stepped out from the screen.

As the entourage followed Ike and the Queen toward the State Dining Room, Julie Clay paused briefly with her father, smiling at Judd Smith and raising a fragile arm, holding it in front of him and pointing a long pianist's finger, as if she were a schoolteacher. She started to say something, then paused as if she were examining a portrait, liking what she saw, and then finally waved, he all the while having to stand at a rigid attention. "You look nice."

Yeah, that's what she said. *You look nice*. Well, *hey*.

* * *

"Who's the girl, Judd? The one who stopped in front of you?" Donny Stuart munched on a piece of bread, awaiting the steward who would serve his meat. The aides were gathered around an ornately set table in the comfort of the White House Mess, having their own fine meal as the President and his guests dined more extravagantly above them.

"That, Tennessee, is the woman I'm going to marry."

Stuart for some reason checked his watch as he smiled. "Well, let's see. This is October 24, 1954. I've known you for about three and a half years now, and you've been in love, by my count, maybe twenty times in that period, even though you were in Korea for eight months of it and in the hospital for a year." He lifted his head. "You're sure, now, Judsonia? I mean, this is really it?"

Smith took a piece of rare beef from a porcelain serving tray held in front of him by an old black steward. The somber, intent old man held the meat platter as if he were offering up the Queen's crown itself, leaning over, his fingers all the way underneath the tray, cradling it. Judd wondered absently if the steward had been put out to pasture from the Big Room upstairs. "Thanks." He turned and smiled at Stuart. "Hey, I'm in love, really in love. She's even from Virginia."

"Wait a minute. I'm from down there in Roane County, Tennessee, with all them Great Smoky Mountains and stud horses, but that doesn't mean I'm from Tennessee like Estes Kefauver is from Tennessee, no matter what he says every time he wants to get elected. And you're from a whole different Virginia than Senator Clay's sweet young daughter, boy. Don't you ever forget that. What is Clay, some kind of Richmond lawyer?"

The President's guests sat around a huge, horseshoe-shaped table in the State Dining Room, among masses of yellow chrysanthemums interspersed with tall yellow candles and vines of smilax. Each place setting held four gold forks, two pearl-handled knives, and a gold spoon, from President James Monroe's flatware collection. "The President's House" was engraved on each utensil. They drank out of crystal water goblets, and were given four crystal wineglasses apiece, one for each serving. The white bone china, Mamie's contribution to the White House, was edged in coin gold and emblazoned with the President's seal. A small group of Army violinists known as "The Strolling Strings" wandered among them as they dined on chilled pineapple, cream of almond soup, broiled filet of English sole, roast Long Island duckling, and frozen Nesselrode cream with brandied sauce.

Julie Clay sat next to British Foreign Secretary Sir Anthony Eden, who, her father had warned her, would be preoccupied with the recent Russian attentions in the Middle East, and an official from the French Embassy, a man with an unpronounceable last name who was so intent on peering down her dress that at one point he almost fell into her lap when she turned to speak to him after Secretary Eden drifted off into one of his Soviet-induced trances.

And all the while she thought of Judd Smith. He was so vibrant, almost electric in his mannerisms. She was charmed that he would fight Cooper so visibly to take her arm. And even Daddy had been enamored with him. Daddy was normally restrained and cynical among so-called "heroes" and men of state. It was almost comical to watch him with this Judsonia Smith. What a silly name, actually! But Virginians were known for silly names, even in the better families. It was in many cases a way of passing down two or more strong family names. In others, blacks and mountain people primarily, it seemed to be a case of having so many children that they ended up picking names out of the sky. Her father had once received a letter from the mother of twins named Early and Later Oakley, and they had been white. Judsonia wasn't too bad; at least it wasn't completely *embarrassing*.

At the head of the table, President Eisenhower rose, surveying them all with that quiet, smiling presence that had made him so beloved. Her father was one of the crustiest and most insistent of the unreconstructed Southern Democrats. He was fond of proclaiming that there were only two things in life he could guarantee he would never do: sleep with another man or vote for a Republican. But she often wondered whether Daddy himself hadn't voted for Eisenhower, although he adamantly denied it. He certainly hadn't liked Stevenson's cerebral and arrogant manner, and had made that plain when Stevenson campaigned in Virginia. And he and Eisenhower seemed to hit it off so well when they conversed. And what better proof than this invitation to dine with the Queen?

Ike raised his glass. "Your Majesty, Your Royal Highness, my friends: there have been a few times in my life when I have wished that the gift of eloquence might have been conferred upon me. This evening is one of those times. More than this, I know that each guest at this table fervently prayed that I could have had that gift, because through me each of us would like to say what we know is in America's heart: Welcome to our distinguished royal couple that have come to us to this country . . ."

Oh, that was so Eisenhower, the shy smile and the deference that made his audience pull for him rather than intellectually confront him. Ike was going on about the two great wars and the courage of the British matching the courage that Americans had shown since the early settlement days, talking about how the great days were not over, and the struggle of the free world working together against the forces of atheism and dictatorship.

". . . And at the bottom of it, the example of Britain, marching forward, carrying the flag of unity and cooperation, will be the keynote to that great successful future that will be ours, that will belong to our children and our grandchildren. Ladies and gentlemen, will you please rise with me and drink a toast to the Queen."

They all rose together, almost joyously. "To the Queen!"

The Queen stood then and peered at them with that protected warmth that had become her trademark. Next to Julie Clay, Foreign Secretary Eden came alive, straightening in his chair, his neck straining and his tired eyes reaching for her face, as if he wished to be recognized at that moment also. He was an elegant man, Eden, a hero of World War I who had lost two brothers and a son to war. The Queen spoke quietly, almost hesitantly, of the joined histories of the two countries, of the future, of a new age of exploration in the world of human knowledge and technology. Julie was faintly disappointed that she didn't mention Eden. Glancing at Eisenhower, the Queen concluded, "Fifteen years ago my father, at the White House on just such an occasion as this, proposed the toast which I will also propose tonight. I pray that the ancient ties of friendship between the people of the United States and of my peoples may long endure, and I wish you, Mr. President, every possible health and happiness."

There! It was done, and the dinner was finally over. Julie Clay felt herself grow light with excitement. The guests were collecting menus, matchbooks, and place cards for souvenirs, and were heading for the Red, Blue, and Green rooms for coffee and liqueurs. After that they would return to the East Room, where Judd Smith had escorted her and her father earlier, for a selection of songs from the President's friend and favorite entertainer, Fred Waring. Then the President and the Queen would retire, and the East Room would at last be cleared for dancing.

"Over here, son!"

Senator Clay waved an arm at Judd Smith from across the large room. The Waring Songsters had given the Queen a chorus of Americana, from "Zip-a-Dee-Doo-Dah" and "Over the Rainbow," to the President's favorite song, "The Battle Hymn of the Republic." Eisenhower had smiled like a child when many of the guests joined in the singing of "The Battle Hymn," and Judd Smith had watched with interest and a shared feeling of ostracism as Senator Clay and his daughter had sat silently on their padded chairs, chins held high, refusing to participate. "The Battle Hymn" was as offensive to Southerners as "Dixie" was to many Northerners, a symbol not only of their loss in the Civil War but also of the humiliation and frequent cruelties displayed by Northerners during the occupation and reconstruction periods afterward.

Smith walked toward them across the ornate room. It was a foreign jungle with its heavy wooden ornaments on its gray walls and its powerful, exotically dressed inhabitants. His Marine Corps cordovan shoes clicked on the polished, inlaid wooden floors and he thought, *Are you allowed to dance? Do they let the monkeys out of the cages?* But this was perhaps the most entrancing, alluring moment of his life. *Me. Does she really want me to be a part of this? Hey!*

"You looked just like a statue out there in the hall. Did I embarrass you?" She smiled evenly, holding out a milk-white hand and taking his with a grip that was at once delicate and firm.

"You can't embarrass statues, didn't you know that? That's the secret." He grinned, throwing caution away like some old chipped arrowhead on the way to Man Talk Rock. "If you'd come any closer, I'd have grabbed you, I swear I would have."

"You *wouldn't* have!" She laughed. "That's probably just what Daddy would say, did you know that?"

Senator Clay eyed Judd with a look that somehow said he was an equal. "You probably would have. And it would have served her right, too."

She was weightless in his arms as they danced, properly distant, her chin high and her smiling face fixed on his. It was that part of the Clark Gable movie where the violins played and the heroine said

something truly appropriate, sending the love-dipped arrow into Mr.
Gable's heart. And wouldn't you know it; the violins played. She tilted
her head slightly to one side. "That was so, so *flattering* when you
grabbed that captain by the neck and pushed him out of the way.
Will you get in trouble?"

"Hell, I don't care."

"You *don't?*" Her eyebrows raised and she took on the appearance of
a conspirator, a partner in some mischievous prank.

"What are they going to do, tell me I can't play nigger at the White
House anymore?" He smiled softly as he spoke, daring to press her
small breasts against him for one quick second. "Just think, if I hadn't
done it I'd be over there stacking somebody else's chairs against the
wall."

She grew properly coy. She liked to tilt her head, he could tell.
"Some people will do anything to get out of work."

"That must be it. I just really hate to stack chairs, do you know
what I mean?"

"Can you take me home?" Her left hand rather languorously
touched the back of his neck and she smiled almost triumphantly at his
stunned expression. "Daddy's not going to last very much longer.
Mama's sick, and he promised her he'd be back early. That's how I got
to come to the dinner. I've never been glad to see Mama sick, but tonight I guess I am. So can you take me home?"

He cleared his throat, gazing quickly at the edge of the dance floor,
where Senator Clay was amiably chatting with two other men and
their wives. "What would your dad say to that?"

She eyed him with another conspiratorial smile. "Oh, he already
said it would be all right."

II

"I do believe in God. At least, a part of me does. The other part of
me wants to *be* God. It's almost the same thing, really."

She sat across from him, listening intently in the dark of the Old
Ebbitt Grill, her long hands clasped under her little pointed chin in
unabashed admiration. Trophies and memorabilia covered the walls
from the visits of famous politicians and generals that spanned more
than a generation, the mahogany bar itself and the old bear on one
wall dating back to before the Civil War.

"Do you really think it's the same thing? I think it should be the op-

posite. If you believe in God you want to be humble before Him, to
recognize the power He has over every aspect of the world, not to
compete with Him."

She looked mildly confused, as if she were waiting to be taught by a
college professor, or perhaps was simply under a duty to make conversation. Her blond hair was braided and pinned up over her ears,
reminding him of a crown, and a deep red sweater struck a rich contrast with her pale, luminescent skin. She was really beautiful, he
thought again, unable to shake his amazement at himself for having
not only attracted her but holding her rapt attention for four full
months. And she did everything with the exactness of the highly cul-
tured; her nails, her jewelry, the decor of her apartment. Even the
questions she continually asked him were laid before him like
polished silver, always perceptive but at the same time seemingly designed as an encouragement that he display his intellect. In fact, he
had never really been sure that he even possessed an intellect until
Julie Clay had opened up his processes with those delicate, affec-
tionate little questions. She was a female Socrates in her own way, the
other side of challenge, a nurturer even in her examination of the
mind.

Next to them, at a table one elbow away in the dark room, two civil
servants cozied up for after-work drinks, their nearness making Judd
Smith uneasy about speaking freely. Behind them, four German tourists discussed their day of sight-seeing, heavy Teutonic words crashing
through his mind-set. Scattered throughout the restaurant were couples like Judd and Julie, dressed for the theater or some other night
activity.

Finally he shrugged, leaning over the table and speaking softly, embarrassed at his newfound sophistry. "I was raised a Baptist. I haven't
ever been a very good one, I'll admit. Even when I was a kid my old
man would have to beat the religion into me. When I did something
wrong it was the Ten Commandments along with the leather strap:
'Thou shalt not bear false witness, *whack!'* And in a way that's playing
God when you do that. But a Baptist is responsible for developing his
own relationship with God, one on one. You don't even really have to
go to church if you're a Baptist. Your own mind is your church. Well,
a weak person might look at God and say, 'God, You're so strong and
almighty, and I'm such a disaster, take me where I'm supposed to go
and tell me what I'm supposed to do, it's all in Your hands.' That's all
right, I won't make a judgment on that. But a strong person might just

say, 'God, the world worships You because You're the epitome of *power,* You have all the answers and You know where the world needs to be heading, and You can punish those who don't know the way. So, what I'm going to do is try to emulate You. I'm going to go out there and be strong and try to force my will, which is in many ways my understanding of Your will, on this world, at least as I come into contact with it in my daily life. I'm going to be like You, and people will come to me for strength.' "

"That isn't very Christian, Judd." She sipped white wine, her blue eyes admiring. "You must believe in the Old Testament God, fire and brimstone and all that. What ever happened to 'the meek shall inherit the earth'?"

"Whoever said *that* was a goddamn meek."

She sat back and laughed, as if he were hopeless. "Oh, Judd. What am I going to do with you?"

"Marry me." The Germans behind him threw a bunch of words onto their table as if they were hideous insults. The civil servant next to him had the woman's hand inside his. He had a wedding ring on; she did not. Judd Smith shrugged off Julie Clay's silence, leaning toward her. "Since you asked, that is." He mechanically lit a cigarette, watching her. She was biting her lower lip and smiling, as if contemplating married life with Judsonia Shelby Smith, hillbilly, Marine, and partner of Jehovah. He pointed a finger at her face. "Have you ever felt fear?"

"Fear?" Her eyebrows furrowed and she came forward, as if the word itself caused her to need his protection. "I suppose. I mean, we've all been afraid at one time or another."

"When? When were you afraid? I mean, *really* afraid?"

"Well . . ." Her eyes rested on an older couple who were walking toward the exit, bundled in expensive coats. The lady wore chinchilla. They stared straight ahead and did not speak as they walked, as if they were either very bored, or did not wish to be recognized in such a place. The door opened and they left the restaurant. Finally she responded. "Well, when I was twelve I was out on the Chesapeake Bay on a sailboat with some of my daddy's friends and we were caught in a bad storm. We had to take the sails down and the waves beat at us and I thought the boat was going to tip. I was afraid. I'd even say I was *really* afraid. I thought we all were going to drown."

"But how many things would have had to happen before you drowned?"

"I don't understand."

"The storm would have had to get worse. The boat would have had to tip over. In fact, it would have had to sink. Whatever flotation device you were clinging to would have had to sink, too. And whoever was in charge of finding you would have had to have lost their way."

"I still don't understand, Judd."

"Every one of those possibilities was a layer against real fear, that's all. Have you ever felt *certain,* beyond all hope, that you were going to die? Have you ever been in the belly of the whale, Julie Clay?"

"No, I guess I haven't."

"Then you've never felt real fear."

"All right." She angled her head—the angled head was her trademark, her way of silent rebuke. Her eyebrows raised, as if she were uncaring, and she sipped her wine again. "The senator's daughter has never been truly afraid. Is there a point?"

"Yeah, there is. I can never communicate to you what that felt like. Never. If someone has never had a stomachache and you have a stomachache, they can only imagine what it feels like. You can tell them it hurts over here, and it makes pressure down here, but for them it's vicarious."

"Well, that's all true, Judd, but why do I need to have been afraid?"

"You don't need to have been afraid. I'm just telling you that when I was in the belly of the whale I talked to God. I don't tell many people that, because they think it's crazy. But if you haven't been in the belly of the whale, don't say it's crazy."

"So, did God talk back? Did the two of you have a nice chat? What did He say, that you two should be partners?"

"Give me a break, will you? It wasn't as simple as that. And I'll admit I was delirious. I was one breath away from dying, Julie. All I had to do was say yes, and I was dead. I told Him I wasn't ready. I was fading off and it was easy, but it was scary. I scratched the edge of death, and God let me live for a while longer."

"Twice-born, like the Christ child?" It was clear that she did not fully comprehend him.

"No, just touched by the hand of God." He shrugged, embarrassed. "So part of me is humbled by His power to do that, and I pray. And part of me wants to share that power, and I go crazy."

"You're really deep, Judd. Most people miss that." She looked at him as if she wanted to make love to him, although he knew that however much she might desire him, however deep her urges, she would not, at least not without a wedding ring on her finger.

He checked his watch. "Well, I won't tell anybody if you won't. Hey, we're going to miss the play, if we don't get going." He took her coat from the hook above their table and helped her into it. "*My Fair Lady*, huh? Is it any good?"

She kissed him delicately on the chin, then took his arm. "Let's put it this way, you Bear Mountain roughneck. I think you'll get a kick out of Eliza Doolittle."

"Why, has she got nice legs?"

"Judd! She is a person who discovers cultural qualities that were suppressed through her childhood." Julie Clay sighed, as if exasperated. "And I just told you how deep you were!"

"Well, don't put me in a box, Julie." He suppressed a grin as they walked out of the Old Ebbitt into the bitter February wind, his eyes slowly moving from her toes up past her trim, almost frail frame to her own uncomprehending smile. "Maybe I ought to rephrase that . . ."

*　*　*

Spring 1955 came on the edge of a warm rain and with it there were cherry blossoms along the Tidal Basin, a pink, perfumed ocean of them, and he walked among them with Julie Clay and proclaimed happily to himself *I am learning how to be normal*. Parade season started and on Wednesdays just at sunset the Marines would march on the field inside the brick walls of Marine Barracks, Eighth and Eye, the finest marching units in the world, to the brisk music of the Marine Band, John Philip Sousa's pride, the President's Own. The commandant's house cast a shadow on the barracks parade field, and Judd would stand at a perfect attention in front of his platoon and weigh the wondrous possibility of someday becoming commandant against the chance to have a normal existence. Then on random Fridays his name would be announced and suddenly he would embark with his platoon to Camp David for a weekend of mountain isolation, his own plans being canceled without so much as an hour's warning, and his anger at being a pawn to the whims of the political process, even if it was to protect the President, overrode his pride.

In the real world the Brooklyn Dodgers were going to take it all the way, for the first time ever. Marciano had recently knocked out Ezzard Charles and then done the same to Don Cockell, leaving him bloodied in the ninth. Blacks in Washington were going to school with whites, also a first, and whites were busily packing for the suburbs.

The city had been one-third black when he arrived, and would soon have a black majority. In the space of the year he had spent at the barracks, during which the Supreme Court had ordered massive integration, the streets had emptied of young white families, only their pauperous old parents remaining in the little row house homes. Blacks were dining in restaurants along with whites, too, and staying in hotels. Julie thought it wrong, against the teaching of the Bible. Her father believed it to be a malicious interference by the federal government into the rights of states and localities, and often said so on the Senate floor. Judd Smith was fond of infuriating both of them by wondering aloud whether Senator Clay didn't mind their getting so close, as long as they didn't get too rich, or whether he didn't mind their getting rich, as long as they didn't get too close.

Joe Dingenfelder had married some Harvard broad, then washed out of flight school and was teaching at a Technical Command at Scott Field in Illinois. The Harvard broad, or whatever that school was that they went to and pretended it was Harvard, was pregnant. Smith had met her once, over a drink when Dingenfelder was on his way from New York to Illinois a year before. She hadn't looked to him like she was the kind who would get pregnant; too high strung, almost ferocious. He had a theory about women like her: they usually secreted a chemical that killed off sperm. Smith couldn't remember her name. He didn't like her. She'd made it clear that she didn't exactly love him, either. Her first words had been something like, "So this is the immortal Judd Smith. Are you going to bore us with war stories?" Oh well. Dingie always went for those intellectual types. Tough tomatoes, and all that.

Red Lesczynski was finally finished with his sea duty, and would report to the Naval Academy for a tour later in the summer. Sophie was pregnant with number three, having had a daughter in early 1954. Smith had written them that he wondered if their relationship was slipping, Sophie having had a girl and all. Lesczynski kept writing that Judd needed to read up on the Japanese. He seemed either obsessed by them, or anxious to display his oriental knowledge. Smith wrote back that the Japs were already beaten.

In the evenings at the Center House, he and Donny Stuart had long talks over beer about why Judd Smith was thinking of leaving the Corps. Stuart thought Judd foolish. He was convinced that Smith would be a general, and possibly even the commandant. That had been Judd's greatest dream four short years before, but now it seemed behind him, too great a price in years of overseas assignments without Julie near him.

And there wouldn't be another war. Not that he wanted one: every morning he crawled from his bed and touched the hollow, slick moonlike scar in his lower abdomen with the same hesitance that had caused his fingers to play around its wet edges when it had been fresh, and felt the same roll of heavy angry fear of that night, now incredibly almost three years in his past, and thanked his old partner of a God that he had stolen life just as a wild daring base runner steals home—by an inch. But he couldn't have justified the abandonment to himself if he was doing it in the face of further fear.

I, Judsonia Shelby Smith, First Lieutenant, United States Marine Corps, do hereby resign my commission . . .

In the summer there were band concerts on the steps of the Capitol, and others at the Water Gate, near the Lincoln Memorial. In the evenings one of the service bands would perform from a float on the river and he and Julie would sit on terraced steps, looking out toward the placid, rolling hills of Arlington Cemetery across the brown Potomac, the almost Roman architecture of Memorial Bridge to their left, and he would think, *does anyone really deserve to live as calmly, as surrealistically, as this?* On the weekends they went to the theater or to parties, not the raucous brawls of the bachelor Marine Corps but the sedate, heavy-drinking receptions of the powerful. Senator Clay adored him, fawned over him like a true son, told tales of his heroism and his rude beginnings as if Judd were Davy Crockett reincarnated, heir to history.

But Senator Clay had plans for him. He would go to law school, of course, the University of Virginia, of course. After that he would serve a clerkship with either the federal circuit court in Richmond, or the state supreme court. It could all be arranged. And after that there would be a few years with one of the "right" law firms, either one of the large international firms in Washington, or one of the state-oriented firms in Richmond. All along the way he would meet the right people, and in ten years he would be material for Congress, at the least. Senator Clay was getting tired. His only son was studying to become a dentist. Judd Smith had the military record, the humble beginnings that voters embrace, the statuesque looks, and the ability to

turn a phrase humorously, no matter who he was talking to. With just
the right chemistry between Judd Smith and the Virginia Democratic
party, he might even be heir to Senator Clay's own seat.

None of this was openly discussed, of course. It was all innuendo, or
specific encouragements on smaller points. Senator Clay had broken
the ice for him at the University of Virginia Law School, his own alma
mater. Senator Clay had already introduced him to several business
and professional friends who were judges or successful attorneys. Senator Clay, this garrulous, well-meaning bear of a man who clearly was
more motivated by his desire to see his daughter enjoy life as she understood it than by any conscious search for a successor in his own
image, had almost smothered Judd Smith with his kindnesses and his
far-reaching plans.

It just had to stop, that was all. *I don't play the whore to any man,
in any way.*

                              *   *   *

The 2200 sat on a quiet, winding street just off Kalorama Circle.
Large, leafy trees that seemed to date back to the Civil War created a
cool shade in the building's large rooms, even in the blistering heat of
August. Down a green, sloping hill was the tree-filled beauty of Rock
Creek Parkway. Just north were the sprawling grounds of the Na-
tional Zoo.

The 2200 had six apartments, two on each floor. In addition to Senator Clay it housed a Supreme Court justice, an internationally syndi-
cated newspaper columnist, a lobbyist for the milk industry, the art-
loving widow of a philanthropist, and an attorney who had served as
Assistant Secretary of State under Truman. Despite the senator's
warmth and assurances, every time Judd Smith walked its halls he felt
like an interloper, as if he should be escorting guests to various apartments rather than presenting himself. *Pickin' it up over here, boss.
Judd Smith, droppin' it here, boss.*

"Evening, Mr. Smith."

"Evening, Ignatius." Smith nodded to the rotund, slow-talking black
man with the sallow face who doubled as doorman and security guard
at The 2200. Ignatius had a clever way of smiling and shuffling for
most people who entered the high-ceilinged old apartment complex,
but he dropped the act for Judd Smith. They both knew that all the
formalities and courtesies, the parties and the cocktail receptions,

were really for people other than themselves. Neither belonged, and they embraced each other's ostracism.

"You really going through with this, now?" Ignatius could ask it because Ignatius had no right to know, no use for the answer.

"Aw, man, I dunno." Judd Smith tugged at the collar of his tuxedo, the first he had ever worn, and stopped for a while at Ignatius' desk, so hesitant to push the elevator button that he viewed the round white piece of plastic as one might secretly glare at a tormentor. "What you think, Ignatius?" Smith leaned over and provided a match for the old man's stubby cigar. "Sometimes you bite the honey, sometimes you bite the bee, know what I mean?"

"Got you a handful, sure enough." Ignatius leaned back in his metal chair, grinning good-naturedly. "Yeah, I be knowing little Julie since she wasn't high as this desk, here, and she always such a sweet thing. But the man that marries that better be putting filet mignon on the table of a night." Ignatius watched him with steady, measuring eyes. "And he better be bigger than her daddy. I do believe that man would *kill* for his child."

"I'm not afraid of any man."

"Oh, I know you not. And I believe the senator, he knows you not, too. Yessir, brother, you rightly got a chance in this. You got a chance." Ignatius relented as Judd Smith pressed the elevator button, summoning the slow, small prewar Otis and manually opening the outer door. "Don't worry 'bout it anyway, Mr. Smith. Won't change it. And you a lucky man."

"Ju-u-u-udd. Oh, you look so nice I feel like holdin' onto you all night, sugar. Come on in. Everybody else is here."

Hugs and kisses at the door, a ritual he could never get used to. Julie's mother was a faded violet, a small, slight woman who had smiled and drunk away her beauty, a quiet alcoholic who was often "sick" when the senator appeared at public gatherings, and who bore her sickness with what Judd Smith could only perceive as courage, no matter that she did not have the psychological means to stop the slow suicide of the bottle. Years of nightly receptions and weekend galas, Sunday brunches in Georgetown and Kalorama that began with stiff bloody marys or screwdrivers, weekday wine lunches with other wives, obligatory communal drunkenness; it had crept up on her alcoholic tolerance until she was suddenly peering at the world from behind a smiling, opaque daze. And of course the family did not talk about it, never publicly admitted it.

He walked through the entranceway, past two small rooms, and then entered the living room. Ten-foot ceilings, hardwood oak floors laid in the old, artistic way, concentric rectangles built around a center piece four inches wide and two feet long, Persian rugs and antique colonial furniture, the high-back chairs and sofas that might have been pilfered right out of Monticello—it was hard for him to perceive that people actually *lived* like this. And they had another residence, their true "home," in Goochland County just outside of Richmond. Fingering his rented tuxedo and walking across the room to first shake the senator's hand, Judd Smith found himself for that moment feeling like a traitor, as if he were somehow betraying his blood.

Senator Clay grinned widely, inspecting Smith with a quick sweep of his eyes. He was seeing himself, and he liked it. "What'll you have, son?"

They were drinking sherry. "I'll just take a beer, sir."

A quick, measuring pause, then a slap on the shoulder. "Atta boy."

Stonewall Jackson peered down from just above the fireplace. He was Jackson Clay's great-uncle, something like that. Julie walked in from the dining room, her hair piled on top of her head in a way that reminded him of Grace Kelly. She wore something yellow and silky and long. The diamond ring that her grandmother had worn, which the family had decided would be her engagement ring, shone like an ornate museum piece on her left hand. She walked up and kissed him and he quickly wondered what his father would say if he saw her at that moment. The old man would probably slap himself in the jaw and laugh in pure disbelief. *Judd Smith, you going off after a moonbeam, boy!* The thought pulsed into him and then passed, all with the intensity and quickness of a beat of strobe light.

"Well, there you are, Judd. What took you so long?"

Names and faces, smiles and tuxedoes, black waiters offering catered food. They were family members, close friends, twenty of the most important people in Julie Clay's life. Standing in the center of the room and unofficially receiving them, couple by couple, Julie at his side, Judd Smith felt a small, mocking creature crawling up his spine, standing on his shoulder, whispering into his ear. *Where are your people, Judd Smith? What part of this is yours? What part of your goddamn LIFE is going to be yours?*

It had been creeping up on him but now it confronted him, in one of those rare, pristine moments that showed him a clear look into his own future. He did not like what he saw, and the part that he did not like was his own self. He loved her, perhaps hopelessly. He loved her frail beauty and her eagerness to draw him out. He loved the child in her, the part that still believed in chivalry and chastity. He loved all of that much more than this leap she was providing him into a life that other people owned, that he did not desire. But he doubted that she loved him enough to take him without the baggage.

"Judd, do you feel all right?"

"I'm fine, honey. I've just got to go to the bathroom. I'll be right back."

He had to get out of the room. He was suddenly awash in an incurable sadness, a knowledge that he was destined, perhaps for the rest of his life, to feel incomplete. He could have Julie Clay and lose himself, or he could keep himself and lose Julie Clay. The demarcation was clear. Its impact was not only hopeless; it corrupted his spirit. Standing in the bathroom and staring at an antique washing pitcher as he attempted to urinate, Judd Smith felt very old, as if he had passed through an emotional warp and realized for the first time that life had gotten the best of him, for good.

But if she loves me, if she really loves me . . .

They were gathered around the long mahogany dining table. Senator Clay was standing at its head, one hand in his pocket, the small sherry glass in the other hand as out of place as if he were holding a lily. He was talking to Julie's brother about where they were going to live when Judd began law school in September. The wedding date was three weeks away. It was all going to happen very quickly, and then it would be irretrievable, as if Judd were riding on a small skiff at the edges of a whirlpool. He just didn't know if he could fight it once it started.

The waiters began to serve the food, delicate roast round of beef, buttered beans, baked potatoes. Someone next to him, a lady whom he had met but could not fix as to husband or position, was asking him what kind of law he hoped to practice. *What kind of law.* He found himself mumbling, feeling at first like a pathetic, fearful little mouse,

"I'm not going to law school."

"What did you say, Judd?" Senator Clay had heard and was staring at him from the other end of the table, his thick dark brows furled and his mouth pursed forward, as if the words had caused him to want to spit.

They came out more easily the second time. "I'm not going to law school."

The table was silent. Forks clinked against the china. They all stared at their plates. No one was smiling. It was Julie's turn, then. "You're not?"

It was absolutely strong this time, from a voice that knew it did not belong and was no longer going to try. "Nope."

"Oh, my."

He felt nauseous, even heartsick, as her hurt, disbelieving stare floated across the table to him on the edges of her lilting words. But it was his only chance. "I'm just not ready for more school. I'd go crazy sitting in a classroom for three years. Maybe later. I'm sorry, Julie, I just can't do it right now."

More silence, as if they were embarrassed at his very presence, as if he had deliberately set them up for such a disappointment. Forks clinked. Seconds were served. The senator squinched his eyes and mouth again. His voice had the growling incredulity that he normally reserved when he damned preposterous opponents on the Senate floor. "So, what are you proposing to do?"

"I think I'd like to be an FBI agent." He had never fully considered it, but it was the first hard thought that hit his mind. He had a lot of Marine friends in the FBI. They liked it. And he had to sound certain of something, or he would look like a fool.

"The *FBI?*" Julie appeared heartsick. "Oh, Judd. I don't know about this."

CHAPTER NINE

I

"GOOD-BYE, HONEY."

Joe Dingenfelder kissed his wife as they stood on the little concrete doorstep of their home, a pedestal above their tiny yard of powdery dust and dry, matted grass. It had never been much of a yard, but the August drought had baked the water out of everything alive; his yard, the sea of corn that covered most of the terrain outside of the base like froth, even the animals that walked ever more slowly and shrank, dehydrated, into their own skins. As they stood on the front doorstep a neighbor's dog, an ugly boxer with its tail recently cut and flies buzzing around the bloodied stump, walked listlessly down the sidewalk, its rear legs somewhat faster than its front ones, making it yaw sideways every few steps, as if it were dizzy. The dog wore a rabies muzzle. It was a base regulation. It made the dog look as if it were a mad, slow, disoriented escapee from a dog racing track.

Joe rubbed Dorothy's shoulder, then patted her growing stomach in an effort to coax a smile from her. Doing no good, he began walking toward his car, raising one slim arm and waving to her. "Have a nice day, okay? And try to stay off your feet."

It was All-American, classic Midwest, perfectly fitting for an Air Force captain stationed in the Illinois farm belt. Kiss the wife good-bye at the front door, keep her barefoot and pregnant. He rather liked the image, even though he knew it was false. He didn't push it, either, because he knew that if he pushed it with Dorothy, it would surely disappear, and so might she.

But she did seem to like being pregnant. He smiled softly, climbing into his 1955 Thunderbird, now almost a year old. He loved the car. It had a gleaming yellow exterior and a black interior, with real leather bucket seats and a four on the floor. Not that she openly *showed him* she liked it; that wasn't Dorothy. Dorothy needed to be able to complain, that was all. She complained, he showed her he appreciated her. That was the relationship. It was like a tennis match.

It was the other things. Dingenfelder drove into the main gate at

Scott Field, returning the stiff salute of the air policeman at the gate, the salute bringing him a deep, visceral pride. He turned left along the base road, following a string of cars past miles of open runways and hangars on his way to the Technical School. She liked sex more. Her narrow cucumbers of breasts had swollen into cantaloupes, and she seemed pleased with them, anxious that he notice and fondle them. She had grown somehow sultry. She was more of a woman. It was almost as if she had proven something to herself by carrying a child.

What she did not like was the Air Force. Joe Dingenfelder was enjoying his duty with the operating forces, more than he had ever imagined he would. He liked his job, and the people, and especially the feeling of dignity and respect that attended his officer status. It filled a lifelong void in him, a feeling of unworthiness, and yet Dorothy rebelled against such satisfaction, threatened by it. It was a good thing, he thought again as he parked the car, that she would soon have a child. Surely a baby would settle down her emotions.

He slammed the car door, walking toward the large concrete and metal building of the Technical School, still smiling as he contemplated her new set of moods. She may even end up liking motherhood more than she likes to argue, he thought humorously, entering the building.

*　*　*

Crash. She casually tossed his cereal bowl to the floor. *Crash*. She dropped his coffee cup. *Crash*. There went the saucer.

"There," she said aloud to no one, in fact to the whole world as she allowed herself a moment of satisfaction. "The goddamn dishes are done. All right?"

Have a nice day, honey. Try to stay off of your feet. Aaaaahh! She clutched her swollen stomach as she paced like a caged lioness inside the small kitchen, back and forth over broken glass and dribbles of milk, Kellogg's Corn Flakes grinding into the linoleum. Aaaahh! She moved into the tiny living room and paced there for a while, side to side, tracking the soggy corn flakes onto the eight-by-ten area rug they had bought in Belleville. Finally she simply said it, loud and self-righteous.

"*Aaaahh!*"

Her little hands moved from her stomach up into the air, two balls of fists as she pranced aimlessly about the room. She was possessed, occupied by another spirit, an alien creature that had begun to grow, unwelcome, in her womb. Soon it would grow larger, then larger still, then break off her like an amoeba splitting in two and it would dominate her, control her. It was not as if she would not love it when it was born, but rather that she did not want to face that very reality. She *would* love it. That was the trap.

She had made a few attempts at first to rid herself of it; deliberately falling hard on the stairs, secretly pounding on her stomach, douching herself extra hard and long. She had hoped fervently for an accident, just a medium-hard fender-bender that would dislodge the demon, exorcise the spirit. She didn't want to be a mother. She didn't even know *how*. Her own mother had died when she was ten, and had been sickly before that, never recovering from her flight from Austria. Motherhood to Dorothy was some vague remembrance of speaking softly and kissing a mournful, shadowed face in a dark room.

But Joe was so incredibly, infuriatingly *patient*, so easy to deal with. His quiet excitement made her doubly guilty, first for her resentment at the pregnancy and again because she could not feel his anticipation. At times she hated him for being so easy to love, as if it were a conscious deception. But she did love him, and that was what love really was, after all: a trap.

If he would just treat me worse, I could leave, goddamn him. Without pushing her an inch, he had even caused her to join the Officers' Wives' Club, and write its monthly newsletters. She was even becoming a mainstay in the club, popular with the other wives for her intellect and biting wit, simply because he wasn't enough of a man to tell her that she had a duty to participate. The other wives didn't pick up an ounce of her frustration; she owed Joe that much. But if he'd only order her to do more, she could justify quitting that, too. What a simpleton he was, sometimes!

She had to get out of the house. She decided to check the corn. It was her morning ritual.

The cornfields began just at the edge of their housing unit. The housing units were named for the munificent congressman and senators who had sponsored the bills that appropriated the money. She and Joe lived in Lanham emergency war housing. Across the street, inside the wire fences of Scott Field itself, workmen were busily constructing a Wherry Unit. At other bases, Senator Capehart was getting into the act, and would soon leave his legacy of military homes. She was supposed to feel grateful. It made her feel owned.

The Lanham housing section, called Paeglow, had eight white tene-
ment-like apartments in each building. They were two stories high.
Little sidewalks in front of them went down to a Paeglow road. The
long, rectangular blocks of ugliness were not themselves on roads, but
rather were packed into treeless fields that a few years before had
grown corn, so that the very mailing address intoned government
ownership. She and Joe lived at Quarters 1404-E. That was the way
her father and friends wrote to her, Quarters 1404-E, Scott Air Force
Base, Illinois, as if she were an inmate.

Everyone had children. She didn't know how many Paeglow units
stood near her; there were at least twenty, each with eight apartments
and each apartment with an average of three or more children. The
men had come home from the war and married and made babies and
gone to war again and come back and made more babies. She could
sit on her front porch on any given day, especially if it was warm, and
watch three hundred children mull through the development, on
swings and bikes or simply playing among themselves.

On the end unit of Quarters 1404, one woman locked her four kids
outside every morning during the summer, letting them in only for
lunch and at the end of the day. She was from Tennessee, and had red
hair. She said she read the Bible during the day and couldn't be dis-
turbed. She had her children down to a complete system of minimal
interference. If her three-year-old wet his pants, which he did with a
nervous regularity, he took his clothes off and neatly folded them, his
little Buster Brown shoes on top of the sodden pile, and delivered
them to his mother. One summer afternoon Dorothy had watched him
stop while playing in a ditch and completely disrobe, very carefully
folding his wet clothes as a dozen other children taunted him. Then
he marched naked across the small field in front of the house and
knocked on the door. His mother did not answer. In a few minutes he
was screaming, enraged, banging on the door, his pale little buttocks
already beginning to go pink from the sun. Suddenly he was throwing
his clothes, kicking dirt with bare feet. He went around to the back of
the tenement and angrily tore his mother's wash off the line, all the
while screaming and crying. Finally she let him in, probably (Dorothy
surmised) to spank him for dirtying the laundry. The next day he had
watery yellow boils on his back from the sun, two of them as large as
Dorothy's hand. Dorothy was sure that this peculiar combination of
compliance and rebellion would cause the little boy to grow up to be

a madman, filled with explosive violence. She avoided his mother after that.

She began walking along the edge of the field. It was less than a hundred feet from her front porch. She had never before seen corn up close and she had never seen a tractor work. In the spring the farmer had turned the black, Mississippi River basin soil and planted his crop and the earth had a crisp, dank promise to it and it had excited her. Every day after that she had walked to the edge of the field to examine the progress of the plants. Without admitting it, she had enjoyed watching the burst of seed, the little grasslike shoots, then the heavy rich rows of green stalks that soon grew higher than her head. The ears grew right out of the stalks, stretching the skin at first as if the stalk were pregnant. It was fundamental and yet complex, like sex. Yes, she had decided. Exactly like sex.

The children liked to run among the rows of corn as if it were a dense jungle and sometimes they would have fights, throwing the small, undeveloped ears at each other, and often the farmer came to visit the housing area to talk to the parents. One time he brought the county police with him. He was starting to dislike military kids. Dorothy had never spoken to a farmer before, either, and once she had conversed with him about the children in the fields, just to be able to hear him talk. He was a huge man with a swollen red face, blunt and righteous, and had no use for rhetoric. He spoke with a twang. She watched his massive pink forearms wave ruefully in the air, marking off the boundaries of his farm before the government had taken the land by eminent domain in order to build the housing development. The wrongness of it somehow thrilled her, and she savored the conversation for days.

When she hung her clothes up on the line in her backyard she could look west and see the beginning of a road. If you took the road west for thirty miles or so, you would end up in the miserable black shanties of East St. Louis, and then if you crossed a bridge over the Mississippi River you would be in St. Louis itself. Where the road met the housing section there was a little gas station. She had watched one afternoon as two men fought savagely with each other behind the station, first with fists and then with boards and garbage cans. She had clutched a wet sheet to her growing stomach and watched the whole thing. It was as gory as a bullfight. She didn't go to the gas station anymore.

It was a violent, frightening place, Middle America.

On the other side of the gas station, just off the fenced end of the air base, was a wide, empty field. On another afternoon while hanging clothes (you could see the whole world from the right clothesline, she wrote acidly to Debby Mink, who was now readying to enter her third year of law school), she had heard the scream of a jet engine and looked up from pinning a towel just in time to watch an F-86 Sabre Jet catch its tail on a telephone wire, having undershot the Scott Field runway, and break in two. The tail had bounced on the road, just missing a column of cars. The rest of the jet, including its doomed pilot, had landed over an area as large as a football field, in small bits and pieces. Search teams had combed the empty field all afternoon, trying to parcel up the remains of the pilot and his plane. Dorothy had lingered at the edge of the field, along with several others, watching the ever-present children search in the grass as if they were after four-leaf clovers rather than bits of flight suit and flesh. The search teams tried several times to chase them away, then gave up.

The children themselves were casual, even avid, about death and gore. One little four-year-old had stood beside her at the edge of the field watching the others, saying again and again, "poor Daddy, poor Daddy," as if she were talking about a rag doll that had been torn up. The girl had recognized the jet as the same type of aircraft that her father flew. Was it because they were young and did not understand, she found herself wondering, or was it because their fathers were also required to face it so casually?

It could have been Joe.

That was the bottom line, really. It could have been Joe, and it almost had been, scarcely a year before. He had done his basic at Graham Air Force Base in Florida and then his jet basic at Reese Field, in the dry wilderness near Lubbock, Texas, and he was moving from the T-33 jet trainer into those same God-awful hollow-nosed F-86s, a plane that always reminded her of the face of a person who had just been goosed. He had almost killed himself and it hadn't been his fault. The pressure system had sprung a leak in his cockpit and blown his eardrums out and the blown eardrums had given him vertigo, like a knockout punch, and he had thrown up into his oxygen mask and then breathed the vomit, oh, what a mess it was. He had blearily, dizzily, made an emergency landing, swearing he saw two perfectly identical runways and choosing one of them randomly, liking those odds better than an emergency ejection in his addled state, and it had been the right runway. The ground crew had to carry him out of the cockpit, his ears dripping blood and his chin and throat slick with vomit, and in the hospital he was actually *embarrassed,* the poor apologetic fool, as if he were somehow a failure. She had visited him in the hospital and thought, *He's not a pilot, he doesn't belong in airplanes, he's a piano player, a scientist. Piloting is for football players and motorcycle freaks.*

They had grounded him because of the vertigo and now he taught geometry at the Technical School. Imagine, she wondered again, a master's degree from the best engineering school in the world so he can teach geometry like a high school instructor. But at least he wasn't flying anymore.

She checked her watch, walking slowly along the edge of the cornfield. She had to get back into the house and clean up the broken dishes and be at the officer's club by ten o'clock. Today was Bridge Club day. The women would compliment her on her witty newsletter and be friendly, even solicitous about her pregnancy. She would enjoy their remarks and their company, all the while fighting it because enjoying it would entice her to accept it for good, and she could not let herself do that. *Six years, Joe. You promised.*

The corn was dry from the drought and from its ripened state, ready for harvest. The big, red-faced farmer would be pulling a large combine through the fields any day now, taking in his crop and preparing it for hauling to a rail depot. She looked forward to coming to the edge of the field as he harvested. Maybe he would wave to her. She decided that she would smile and wave back. He was a nice man and he had been wronged by his government. And after all, her house was on his land.

❉ ❉ ❉

Colonel Henry Pattakos ran the Technical School as if it were a prison and he were the warden, the instructors guards, and the students prisoners. One wrong move by an enlisted student and his future as a crew chief was dashed, as certainly as the crushed parole hopes of a prisoner who had tried to escape, or had assaulted a guard. A failed test, too drunk during off hours, the wrong kind of traffic ticket; almost anything was grounds for sending a student back to the flight line as a mere mechanic once again. Similarly, instructors could be relieved for being three minutes late to a class, or for teaching one that Pattakos felt was below par, or for leaving their wives under suspicious circumstances. It all blended together for Pattakos; deviation, however slight, was grounds. He didn't speak in terms of logic; he dealt in grounds.

The results were both a very high degree of proficiency among the students and faculty of the Technical School and an equally high degree of paranoia as well. No one knew when old Three Fingers would put the hook into them. Almost any act during a day could be suspect. Pattakos got away with it because he turned out a good product, and because he had a demonstrated career as a superb pilot. He had flown B-17s and B-29s during World War II, C-54s in the Berlin Airlift, C-47s in Korea, and had even become jet-qualified as a lieutenant colonel.

As with so many officers who did not tolerate eccentricities among their men, Colonel Pattakos himself was a dedicated weirdo. He smoked big cigars. He grew a thick black moustache. His blue dress cap had a saddle in it, drooping down toward his ears with what the World War II pilots used to call "the fifty-mission look." The earphones in the older planes created such curves in a pilot's cap, but it took a lot of pushing and squeezing at home to make one in the modern Air Force. He had been married and divorced three times. He had hung from the rafters by his heels at the officer's club, a cherished feat of the true crazies. In fact, the prevailing wisdom at the Technical School was that Colonel Pattakos didn't tolerate deviation because he didn't want any competition.

Joe Dingenfelder mused uncertainly on all of this as he walked the dark concrete corridor from the Academics section to the commander's office. A note, a summons if you would, had been lying on his cluttered desk when he came back from teaching class. *See Colonel Pattakos ASAP.* That almost invariably meant trouble.

Dingenfelder catalogued his past week's activities as he walked, searching for deviation. He couldn't find any. He'd shined his shoes properly, taught his classes with impeccable taste and precision, even made sure he parked his car at the exact center of the parking space (one of Pattakos's little binges a few weeks before had been cars parked with tires on the lines of the space, indicating a disrespect for fellow officers who had to squeeze into the next space). But of course, that had all been reactive. Colonel Pattakos was creative. You could not prepare for his outbursts by responding to his previous diatribes.

"Get in here, Dingenfelder!" The colonel had seen him turn the corner from the hallway, and called to him from his inner office. Din-

genfelder immediately walked into the room, squared himself at the center of the colonel's desk, and saluted.

"Captain Dingenfelder, reporting as ordered, sir."

Pattakos returned the salute perfunctorily, as if he were pulling gum off of his right eyebrow. On the desk just in front of Dingenfelder was the colonel's missing finger, in a jar of formaldehyde. The colonel had made an emergency landing in a burning B-29 during World War II, and had jumped out of the aircraft as soon as it stopped moving, along with the rest of the crew. Swinging out of the door like a monkey dropping from a tree branch, Pattakos had caught his wedding ring on the curved metal at the bottom of the doorway, and as he dropped to the runway his finger, wedding ring and all, had remained in the plane. The ground crew kept trying to get him into a vehicle, and then to the emergency room of the base hospital. Colonel Pattakos refused to leave until someone tossed him his goddamned finger. At the hospital, he had insisted that they put it into a jar for him, and now he carried it wherever he went. Pattakos was fond of joking that the caught wedding ring had been grounds for his second divorce.

"Dingenfelder, you goddamn Jew, what took you so long?"

Dorothy would have freaked out, perhaps even sued after such a greeting, but Joe Dingenfelder merely smiled. Out of Pattakos' wild mouth it was a term of endearment. The colonel leaned back in his chair, relighting his nine-inch cigar, of which half had already been smoked, filling the air with a rancid, dead ash odor. Finally he spoke again, his brown Greek eyes lit with energy, puffing madly on the cigar. "I'm getting rid of you. You're a fucking waste."

"Sir?" Dingenfelder swallowed hard, leaning forward with surprise. He catalogued through his mind for a defense. Instructor of the Quarter, just last quarter. Superb fitness reports, even signed by old Three Fingers himself. Excellent relations with the students and staff. Getting *rid* of me?

"Transfer. ASAP." Pattakos was reading through an official correspondence that surely was from a higher command. "It says here they want a shitbird. Advance degree, good teaching credentials, able to get along with a diverse mix of nationalities, solid family situation." The colonel was smiling around the edges of his cigar, clearly enjoying Dingenfelder's confusion. "Sounds like they're looking for the goddamned ambassador to the fucking United Nations, doesn't it, Dingenfelder?" He laughed, rubbing a long, crooked nose. "Well, that's almost right. Captain, you're going to represent the United States as the exchange officer to the Royal Air Force Technical College, RAF Henlow, Bedfordshire, England."

"Why, that's *terrific,* sir." Dingenfelder was smiling again, somewhat abashed at having been taken in by the colonel's little joke. On the wall next to the colonel's desk was a framed picture of a man who had suffered from elephantiasis of the gonads. It appeared as if his sack had been filled with fifty gallons of liquid. He was sitting on a chair and looking mournfully down between his legs. The colonel had inscribed the picture, *THIS MAN HAS BALLS.* "At least, I think it is."

"Oh, bullshit, Dingenfelder." Colonel Pattakos suppressed a grin. "I'm just getting tired of having you around here. You haven't fucked up once. Do you realize how boring that is?" He relented, standing up and shaking Dingenfelder's hand, the cigar making a dense cloud between them. "You'll do a hell of a job over there. And don't forget, you *are* America to those people when you serve with them." The colonel grinned one last time through Greek eyes, through American eyes, through eyes that had flown in the midst of flak and ground fire, eyes that measured Joe Dingenfelder with the kind of precision and exactness that put spears on the edges of his words. "So, don't take any shit from the Limeys about who's done what to save Western civilization from the barbarians."

II

Is it now down to this? mused Dorothy Dingenfelder as their double-decker bus made its slow way from Southampton north to London. The roads were filled with the evidence of industrial lethargy: bicycles and motorbikes in an era when every American seemed to own at least one car, the cars themselves ancient black autos, most of which had been built in the 1930s. Old pillboxes still stood among bright April fields of tulips and daffodils, reminders of German air raids that had ceased more than a decade before. The towns were yet dotted with dank underground bomb shelters, their grass-covered mounds of earth bracketed by two sets of concrete stairs. Children frolicked, using them as playhouses.

Toppled, smashed buildings began to appear next to the road as they neared London, dead pocks of memories from World War II. In-

side London whole blocks were still decimated, reminding her somehow of the ruins in the Forum of Rome.

Down to this? she mused again, the phrase popping into her consciousness at odd times, uninvited, like a litany. That grand empire, on
which, as the British were fond of saying, the sun never set? An empire fairly bought, as empires go, with the blood and courage of a
naval force unsurpassed in history, an empire that had called on the
rugged sons of Britain to leave their homes for years and fight all over
the globe for "bloody England"? An empire that at one time had allowed even the simplest among the ruddy, stocky folk of Breton to
supplement their wool with silks and cashmeres, to smoke Jamaican
tobacco and drink Indian tea?

All emanating from a little island the size of Illinois. *The toughest
people in the world,* that was what the Brits had been for centuries,
reaching out and grabbing chunks of land like ripe apples off a tree,
touching every continent, every sea lane, every tone and shadow of
the human race. And then in the space of two world wars, Britain had
spent more than a million of her men in Pyrrhic battles, the best she
had, from Flanders to Hong Kong. Britain was exhausted. And the
empire was steadily falling away.

Exotic names of former holdings passed before Dorothy's eyes as
she viewed a city still ravaged by war. The demise of colonialism did
not bother her any more than it probably did her old political idol,
Nye Bevan. But it was shattering to see England still in such disrepair
in 1956. And the insistent pride of the British gave it an edge of pa-
thos. *They had won the war.* It came up again and again and here she
had been in the country only one day. But Joe's Air Force uniform
seemed to bring it out of them; the bus drivers, the dockworkers, all of
them. Germany had been rebuilt with American money. Japan was
America's stepchild; it had doubled its gross national product in five
years and would double it again in the coming five. Yet Britain had
only recently come off war rations and her cities were still strewn with
the rubble of battle. The empire was melting away. British industry
seemed exhausted, paralyzed by recalcitrant unions. And here they
were ignoring all that and instead insisting, clinging to the memory as
if it were a life raft: *They had won the war.*

She was weary of it already, this dreadful European insistence on
playing out history, on freezing into roles and postures dictated by
events that had happened decades and centuries before. It was a
tangle, ominous as death itself, one that had brought about 65 million

cold corpses from war in the twentieth century alone. The eight-day
sea voyage from New York to Southampton had made it again immediate to her, summoned it from her recesses with an unprecedented
freshness; the dark, cold foreboding of her flight from it as a child, the
fearful memories suddenly as sharp as the Atlantic cold, as real as the
salt in the sea wind that hit her face while she clung to the deck railing and stared out at black, crashing waves.

Joe had talked excitedly about wanting to tour the Continent during
his leave periods from the RAF Technical College. She had at first refused, with a sudden vitriole that had stunned him. It was a means of
pushing him away, so that she might sort it all out in silence. For some
reason his mentioning it was as offensive to her as if he had asked her
to walk naked down the street. She was not ready to confront this continent that had so insistently devastated itself over and over again because of its hate and tribal passion. She no longer feared it; it was
comatose, incapable of hurting her now. But it had hurt her before,
immeasurably, irretrievably, and she was unsure whether she could yet
forgive it.

Those sorts of things didn't even faze Joe. That was why she loved
him, really. He ignored her brooding moods, her fears, and made her
confront them without even letting on that he knew she was upset.
That part of him was so beautiful.

They stayed three days in London, at an elegant old hotel filled
with white marble and shined brass and creased, smelly leather chairs
in its drawing rooms. He dragged her everywhere, childish in his excitement, pushing or carrying little Natasha, now three months old.
He knew all the museums, all the cathedrals, even the restaurants. The
musician in him wanted to experience every sensual delight and the
scientist in him had researched it thoroughly. He continually pushed
her here and there, conducting an expert's tour through a city he had
never before visited, until soon he caught her up in it, too. She saw
the pomp of Buckingham Palace and the awesome literary dignities of
St. Paul's Cathedral through his eyes, and it awoke her to majesty. He
took her to plays, arranging for a nanny at the hotel for Natasha. He
made it *fun*, and that was why she needed him, she thought again and
again. All her life, she had merely been coping, keeping up, pushing
away bad news. She hadn't really expected fun to be a part of it.

Joe spent a part of each day being briefed at the embassy and at
several military liaison detachments, and each morning she crossed
the street from the hotel, pushing an old black baby carriage through

the dense London traffic; black cars, square taxis, and yawing, red double-decker buses with their advertisements painted on the sides, and walked Natasha through Hyde Park. Natasha had a knowing look, even at three months, as if she had been born understanding that Dorothy would never be able to embrace her without feeling just a murmur of panic, mingled with a whisper of guilt. Sometimes she had to look away from the dark penetrating eyes, even when she fed the little girl her bottle. *All right. All right. I didn't want you. But you're here. You won that one; you're alive. So we're even.*

On their third day in London, Bulganin arrived from Russia for a state visit. The fat, warted animal, the other half of Khrushchev, drew protesting Free Poles from their scattered tenements throughout London. They marched right past Hyde Park, solemnly waving their banners and flags as she cowered near a small pond. Near her, young boys ignored the procession, sailing little homemade boats, and couples embraced on the spring grass as if they were alone, oblivious to the tragedy of a people murdered and eviscerated by the Germans and then the Soviets. *FREE POLAND. POLSKA NIETSKA NIEWA.*

She watched the Poles walk sturdily by in their dark coats, hundreds upon hundreds of them, wearing stoic looks on faces lined from decades of loss, and she gripped the baby carriage until her knuckles turned white and her fingers were blue. It would never end, all this European hate. It fed on its mistakes like bacteria inside a wound, alternately festering and erupting. America was alive with embryonic fascism. Europe was teeming with the lost souls of its endless wars. *And where do I belong, where do I fit in?*

For the first time she admitted it, pushing the baby carriage and watching the faces of people who had forever lost their country march before her.

I am an American. Patched and peeled in London.

*   *   *

"It's the college for the Technical Branch of the Royal Air Force."

Joe squinted as he drove, peering through the Rayban sunglasses American pilots had made famous during World War II. He had picked up his Thunderbird at Southampton. He looked odd, driving along the left side of the road with his steering wheel on the wrong side of the car. They wound north past whole cities of gray rowhouses outside of London, chimney after chimney in perfect alignment, as if they were bayonets in formation, then through Hertfordshire, on their way to Bedfordshire just above it, passing little towns with brick and stone buildings that hovered against the narrow road so that sometimes it appeared they were driving through a tunnel.

"They have a cadet squadron that's similar to college. A good number of the graduates go on to Oxford, Cambridge, and other universities for graduate work. And there are a lot of advanced courses for more senior officers, dealing with armaments, guided weapons, radar, stuff like that. We're the only Americans. They have students from Canada, South Africa, Australia, most of the NATO countries, Thailand"—he hesitated, knowing her sensitivities—"and Egypt, although it looks like the Egyptians are pulling out. It's pretty clear that Nasser's getting ready to nationalize the Suez Canal. Ever since the Brits started pulling out of Suez, Nasser's been leaning toward the Russians. The Brits are getting kicked around really bad in the Middle East, and they're mad as hell. Nasser's got Russian MiG-15s and IL-28 bombers, along with his British Meteors and Vampires. He's really been taking the Brits for a ride, and they're about ready to kick his folks out of the Technical College. No sense in training your enemies."

"Is this the famous 'wives briefing,' Captain Dingenfelder? Am I supposed to be taking notes? You'll have to hold the baby if you want that."

"Come on, Dorothy. I'm just trying to share it with you. If I don't, you're being excluded. If I do, I'm talking down to you."

She peered out of the window, watching several men working to rethatch the roof of a large brick home. It was at once quaint and frustrating, and she finally decided that she was reacting so strongly because Joe was talking politics. Who was *he* to give her a political briefing? She had spent years preparing and he hadn't known a Laborite from a Tory and here he was speaking to her as if he were a diplomat and she a dummy. "I'm sorry, Joe. I just feel like I've been thrown into a trash can for the last three years, with no end in sight. I *know* about Nasser and the Brits! I probably know as much about them as the people who briefed you at the embassy. I could give you a lecture that would leave your head spinning. And who cares?"

He was wincing, not wanting to take her on. That was the way he usually handled it—avoidance. At first the lack of conflict had been comforting, but now it was pure irritation. He just wouldn't talk these things through. "It could be fun for you, Dorothy."

"Part of it will be. But you throw that out as if I were a kid. For

God's sake, Joe, what if it was the other way around?" She watched him carefully. He kept his eyes on the road. It would never be the other way around, that was what he was thinking. He was liking all this too much, she could tell. "I'm glad you've only got three years left. I can't take any more of it." Debby Mink would finish law school in one month; that was her referent. "You're going to be teaching or whatever and mixing with all of these people. You're going to be growing. And what am I going to be doing?" She snorted. "Going to tea."

North of Hitchin the road opened up and they were suddenly in the verdant farmland of eastern England, the villages smaller and the little fields bordered by wild dogwood roses, dotted with haystacks that steamed from the past evening's rain. They hit rush-hour traffic; a column of bicycles. Above them, a little, single-engine De Havilland Chipmunk droned by, on its way to a landing at the RAF Henlow airstrip.

"Dorothy, Dorothy." His eyes had not left the road and his voice was unchanged, consciously soothing in its patient drone. "Don't be difficult, okay?"

She sighed, rocking Natasha in her arms. "Don't worry, Joe. Wifey will be good."

* * *

The front doorbell rang and Dorothy fretted for a moment as she stood before her Agamatic stove, an ornate, anthracite-powered device that had been installed in a large hearth area where her predecessors had once cooked over open fires. Anthracite was tricky, even these so-called "modern" stoves. You regulated the heat level of a burner by the amount of the hard coal fed into the stove, rather than through a knob. It had taken her eight months, but she could finally turn out a decent meal on it.

The bell rang again, with some impatience. She peered out of the kitchen window into the back courtyard, looking for a van or perhaps a delivery truck. Supermarkets had not yet hit England; food was still sold door to door. It might have been the milkman, who came every few days. Or it could have been the fishmonger, who appeared several times a week, his truck filled with fresh plaice and flounder, shrimp and prawns. It could have been the square, taciturn baker, offering scones and biscuits and Scottish bread, or the butcher on his weekly trip, or the greengrocer with his lying scales and quick verbal calculations that comprised a bill. Or the poultry man with his fat, plucked

chickens and his double-yolked eggs, or the fuel man with his truckloads of coal and coke and anthracite, which he dumped in nearby
storage sheds. But there was no truck in the long archaic driveway. So
it wasn't any of them.

Besides, it was the front door. The deliverymen almost always came
to the back door, a servile gesture that went back generations. The
constable came to the front door when he made his perfunctory visits
to assure that she, as an alien, was conducting herself properly. It
might be the constable, she thought, her insides going acrid again at
the branding word, *alien,* her mind automatically thinking of where
she had placed her alien identification card with its mug shot and all
the important criteria underneath. But the constable usually came at
night, so that he and Joe could visit over a bourbon. Bourbon was a
rarity in England. Joe could buy it at the embassy on his visits to London. The constable loved bourbon; he wouldn't come to the house in
the afternoon.

She walked the narrow corridor that connected the kitchen area to
the front of the house, passing a door that led to the basement. The
ghosts lived in the basement. Air Commodore Fitch's wife said they
were friendly ghosts. The English seemed to seriously believe in
ghosts. Dorothy really didn't believe in ghosts, but it was strange how
frequently the door opened by itself, even when she could have sworn
that she had locked it.

It might be the gypsies, or a peddler. The peddlers were vagabonds,
Omanis and Indians, who sold trinkets and jewelry. The gypsies had a
large camp near Wimpole Park, perhaps twenty miles away. They
moved frequently along the narrow Hitchin Road in front of the
house, their horse-drawn carts boxy and colorful, like a traveling car-
nival show, their children prancing alongside wearing layers of baggy
clothes, as if they were still in Eastern Europe a generation before.
Often their men would come to the door and ask for work.

She opened the door. A young airman stood at attention on the
porch, dressed in the grayish-blue of the Royal Air Force. His shoes
were shined and he carried his cap formally under one arm, as if it
were a purse. He had the scrubbed, ruddy cheeks of British youth,
and the end of his pointed nose was turning blue from the cold. He
clicked his heels slightly and made a small, stiff bow as she brought
the door fully open.

"Yes?"

"Good morning, Mrs. Dingenfelder." She finally recognized the airman. He was Group Captain Barnett's houseboy. "Mrs. Barnett sends her regards, and would like to remind you that you're expected at the Christmas Ball tonight. Twenty hundred hours." He gave another little bow.

"Well, thank you. And you can tell Mrs. Barnett that Captain Dingenfelder and I will be pleased to attend."

"Very good, ma'am." He bowed again, then put his cap back on and strode away.

She could have just telephoned, thought Dorothy as she closed the door again. But back somewhere before phones were ever invented, this formality was born of necessity until it became a right, a privilege of rank. And that was the great strength of the British, really; a tradition so strong that it sustained them even when the rest of it, the substance, went sour.

*   *   *

"You look beautiful, Dorothy."

She was leaning forward into the mirror, tracing the outlines of her mouth with lipstick, trying to enlarge her thin lips without looking tacky. It never worked very well. Joe grasped her shoulders from behind, kissing her on one cheek. He kept at it, day after day, year after year, until it was tempting to believe him. She examined her image, the maroon silk dress she had bought in London on a shopping trip with Samantha Fitch, her dark hair up in a bun, a necklace of pearls around her thin neck. *Not bad,* she thought. *But not beautiful.*

"Why, thank you. And you look like Charles Atlas." He raised thin arms and curled imaginary biceps. She had to smile, and kiss him back. "Do you like my dress?"

"It's perfect. And Wing Commander Calhoun will just love it. Oh, yeah. So I'm not alone."

"Wing Commander Calhoun is an ass. If he puts a paw on me tonight, I'll make him sorry, I truly will, Joe, I don't care if it makes them give you an unsatisfactory fitness report and they throw you out of the Air Force." She thought about it for a moment, picking up her gloves and small purse from the bed. "In fact, that would suit me fine."

"He's harmless."

"Harmless? A man asks your wife—no, a man *orders* your wife to be his mistress, and you say he's harmless?"

"That was six months ago, Dorothy. Nothing came of it. He was just feeling you out, and you couldn't have handled it better." Joe stood at their bedroom door, actually looking more like a concert pianist in his dress uniform than a military officer. Slim and smooth, she thought. Elegant.

"Feeling me *out?*" She placed her fox fur coat on her shoulders. "Feeling me *up* was more like it."

The RAF Henlow Officer's Club was Men's Country, a last retreat for the purest form of chauvinism, the camaraderie of warriors. Women could not enter the club, except for one small closet of a waiting room where they might announce their presence and await their husbands or friends, who were under a duty to immediately remove them from the building. The only female officer at RAF Henlow, who commanded the small Women's Air Force detachment, did not frequent the club. At the command's monthly dining-in dinners, she left immediately upon completion of the meal, avoiding the raucous, hard-drinking post-dinner festivities by unspoken, mutual agreement.

Twice a year, on Midsummer Night and at Christmas, the officers opened their guarded dominion for a formal ball. The women, who normally communicated through a network of teas, coffees, and bridge clubs sponsored by wives according to their husband's rank, appeared with their husbands, dressed in their finest regalia. They supped from a long table filled with food that was at once traditional and exotic; stuffed pig, an apple in its mouth, whole flounder and sole, mounds of turkey, and at Christmas, figgy pudding with an occasional shilling cooked into the custard. They danced to the music of the Royal Air Force's own small band.

It was the women's military task to bring harmony, to be pleasant. They spoke of the snow and of the new shops in Luton. Their husbands talked of Canberras and Hawker Hunters, of Whirlwinds and Javelins, of Britain's place in the world. The women deferred, at least in public: it was a mark on a military officer if he could not contain his wife's opinions. And Dorothy had done well, for eight whole months of it. But it was deprivation, starvation, as if she had gone without sex for that entire period.

"Well, hullo, the Yanks have arrived!"

She preceded Joe into the large dining room, smiling and waving to the gathered couples. A fire glowed from a huge hearth that dominated the room. The room itself was actually hot from it, a rarity in England. A large, ornate Persian rug covered part of the hardwood floor,

a lush and tasteful piece that had no doubt come directly from Iran
for a pittance in the halcyon days when Britain occupied that country.
The officers and their wives packed the room, surrounding the table,
which was overflowing with delicacies, the officers spit-polished and
bemedaled, their wives bejeweled and smiling. At the far end of the
room the Royal Air Force ensemble played, and a dozen couples
danced.

Air Commodore Fitch met them halfway across the room, shaking
Joe's hand and bowing to Dorothy as he grasped hers. She watched
the top of his balding head as he actually kissed her hand. His wife
sauntered over also, solid and rectangular in her sleeveless silk gown,
her gray hair recently done, and put an arm on Dorothy's shoulder.
Fitch was the senior officer at the Technical College. His wife had
grown up in the military and then married into it, and knew all the
nuances of military life. Samantha Fitch had looked after Dorothy as
if she were her mother. In fact, she had been responsible for their
being assigned a house that should have gone to a man with a much
higher rank than Dingenfelder. "Dorothy," she had said after their
first afternoon visiting over tea, "we simply must get you into The
Elms." In two days it had been accomplished, with the skill of a government negotiator.

"Well, Captain!" Fitch smiled brightly, two drinks ahead of them.
"We'll have to watch our jokes now that the representative from the
Colonies has arrived."

"That won't be necessary, sir." Joe grinned over to Mrs. Fitch. "You
can joke all you want, as long as you remember we beat you in the
war."

"The war?" It was Wing Commander Calhoun, his gray eyes dulled
from whiskey, the word "war" conjuring up visions of the Battle of
Britain in his dimmed brain. Dorothy watched him like a lioness,
ready to claw him. The moustachioed Scot, the only bachelor among
the senior officers, followed her like a lecher at every social gathering.
Joe thought it funny, almost a compliment to his own taste. Calhoun
called from a nearby group of officers, towering over them as he
peered at Joe. "Is Captain Dingenfelder saying that the States did
more in the war?"

"We're talking about America's War of Independence, Calhoun."
Fitch said it slowly, a mild rebuke.

"A bloody mess, that was. Well avenged in 1812 as I recall."

"Oh, for God's sake." Dorothy said it and Joe Dingenfelder immedi-

ately searched her eyes. She was looking down toward her small
purse, reaching for a cigarette. He had seen her do it too many times,
almost always prefaced with those words and with the nervous habit
of playing with a cigarette. In a moment, with one more small provocation, she would explode, covering Calhoun with acidic prose, vomiting an encyclopedia of evidence into his face. It was too early in the
evening for that, and he was still too sober.

"Dorothy, let's have some of this fish."

"We may as well. I've had enough 'boar' to last the evening." Noting the surprised looks of Air Commodore Fitch and his wife, Dorothy
smiled invitingly to them. "Would you care to join us?"

"Why, yes." Samantha had picked up the tension. "Come, dear."

Wing Commander Calhoun broke away from the group of men, his
eyes like slate behind the curving, red moustache. In a moment he
was at Dorothy's side, touching her as he reached for a piece of cau-
liflower. *What does he want of me?* Her shoulder was at his mid-
chest. He pressed against her with an insistence that ran down her
back. *I can make it miserable for your husband,* that was what he had
said six months before at the Midsummer Night's Ball as they danced,
he squeezing her with the grip of ownership, as if she were a chattel.
She edged closer to Joe but that only compressed the three of them together, like Siamese triplets. She felt watched, uneasy, angry.

Calhoun put a hand on her shoulder. "I would very much like to
dance."

"Good. Make us all happy and go do a jig."

"With you."

She turned toward him, staring up into his face as if she were a
child, her anger held back by one tiny gossamer of self-control. "Wing
Commander Calhoun, I do not want to dance with *you!*"

Air Commodore Fitch intervened, his watery blue eyes peering at
Calhoun as if he were an errant schoolboy. "See here, Calhoun, that's
no way to treat a guest of the crown. A bit into your cups, are
you?"

"Very sorry, sir." Calhoun's eyes stayed on her as if she were a pet
to be bought. His thin face remained above her, the chin just at the
top of her eyesight. "Just reliving fond memories of my Palestine tour,
I suppose."

So that was it. The mystery unveiled, thought Dorothy. Ah, the Jew
squats on the windowsill, patched and peeled in London, bedded in
Palestine. The fool, the simple fool. And where was Joe? Avoiding

again, talking quietly with Samantha Fitch, at the end of the table, as if it wasn't happening. That did it.

"Wing Commander Calhoun, I have never been to Israel." He began to answer, an apology, perhaps, although more likely an extenuation on his fond reminiscence. No matter. She cut him off with a crisp, knifing voice. "But I'm glad that you have fond memories of it, because few Israelis have fond memories of the British presence there."

The room began to go quiet, voice by voice ceasing as the officers and their wives turned toward Dorothy and Calhoun. The tall officer looked startled, as if he had been slapped. He grew formal, teetering on his heels and clasping his glass of whiskey to his chest, conscious of their larger audience. "My dear Mrs. Dingenfelder, I wish to remind you that less than two months ago, the British did Israel the greatest favor ever done for it, by intervening in the Egyptian War at the precise moment the Israeli Army's attack peaked. Our Air Force destroyed the Egyptian Air Force. Without us, you would have been demolished." He said it loudly, as if it were an official proclamation. The room was now dead quiet. She sneaked a look at Joe, who looked absolutely nauseated, as if he were trying to wish away what he knew was going to happen.

"Wing Commander Calhoun, I wish to remind *you* that I am not an Israeli, a delusion you apparently have been laboring under for the entire six months you have been bothering me." Calhoun looked as if he might faint, all straight and round-eyed, watched by his fellow officers and their wives. And it came out of her in a rush, an exuberant release, in a sense a payback to all of them for her months of smiling, deferential silence. She knew her politics and she had an audience and she might have been a diplomat, a government official, a news commentator.

"And as for the rest of it, I have great doubts about British altruism. As you know, Prime Minister Eden was desirous of once again controlling the Suez Canal, and in fact occupied it. He also wished to crush Nasser, who is loving up the Soviets, and to remove the continuing threats to Europe's oil supplies in the Middle East, not to mention cutting the flow of Egyptian arms through Libya to North African rebels, and generally restoring British prestige in an area where they are, quite frankly, on the run. I shall not go into the French motivations for joining your forces in this intervention. In fact, to be honest, I am happy that you both made what are being called pitiful efforts to reconquer old territories, since it did help the Israeli effort to keep Egypt from overrunning it. But for God's sake, don't talk to me about favors."

Even the band had stopped playing. Joe was walking toward her. She couldn't quit, not yet, anyway. "If you want to consider what you might have done as a *favor,* consider that the Soviets chose that moment to kill off Hungary. If what I read is correct, your Royal Air Force lost exactly four men in the Egyptian intervention. There should have been a few more left to go help the Hungarians."

"Mrs. Dingenfelder." It was Air Commodore Fitch. He appeared tired and hesitant. "I should tell you that the Royal Air Force did fly more than a hundred tons of emergency supplies to Hungarians who escaped to Austria. We *are* proud of that. And the United Kingdom accepted the bulk of the Hungarian refugees—more than twelve thousand, to be precise. I'm very sorry this has all happened."

"I am, too." Looking around the room at the solemn, appalled faces, she felt immediately ashamed. "You are a great country. I didn't mean to criticize." Her outburst had drained her, like the scrubbing of a wound. She wanted to be friends again. She looked back up at Calhoun, who wore a drunken, puzzled look, quite obviously never having been bested in a debate with a woman before. "Perhaps I should even dance with Wing Commander Calhoun, just to show how sorry I am."

The whole room laughed at that. That was the joy, yes, even the greatness of the British. They liked a fight, stilted as they were, and they were so deep into the ebbs and flows of their own historical luck that they had an ability to get on with it when the fighting was done. Dorothy curtsied to Calhoun, who now wore a beaten frown. "Wing Commander Calhoun, may I have this dance?"

They all applauded, and Dorothy dragged him stumbling onto the dance floor, where they danced alone for a full minute as the others gathered approvingly around. All the while she chattered at him with lively gossip about the snow, the new shops in Luton, and the wonderful constable who visited her house to drink bourbon and check her performance as an alien.

CHAPTER TEN

I

OCTOBER CRAWLED INTO ANNAPOLIS with a promise of early winter, and the cold wind pushed in those other wintry beasts, the gruff and hoary alumni, for their weekend of nostalgia known as Homecoming. Parade day was moved from Wednesday to Friday and the stands were packed with gray heads and leathery faces, the heavy overcoats of captains and admirals mixing with stooped retirees and erect, tight-faced ensigns. Later there would be receptions, a football game dedicated to the alumni, dinner in the mess hall, and a formal dance. But it was at the parade where the memories began.

Company by company the brigade moved out from Tecumseh Court on the crisp edge of drumbeats and bugles, past the chestnut trees that bordered winding roads, in front of the chapel and next to Sampson Hall and finally to Worden Field itself. Bayonets flashed in the cold sun. Thousands of heels clicked in unison on the pavement. Memories of youth permeated the stands, silent songs that played only to one man at a time.

Judd Smith wept inside himself, listening to his. He stood in the wooden bleachers and peered across the green fields of his youth at those younger visions of himself, measuring the distance he had traveled since he last marched on Worden Field. He was not measuring time, but rather events; successes, failures, marriages, births, deaths, and holding their surprises up against the mirror of the possible. He finally decided that it was a frail, doomed, uncomprehending innocence standing in formation in front of him. He knew. He had stood there and dreamed, and now he knew that dreams were no more than the young's unwitting shield against despair.

The parade began and he remembered classmates who had fallen in the icy trenches of Korea. They had died innocent; it was his duty never to forget them. He was now thirty and his own bones and insides ached in the morning and on cold days, little Korean promises of what would follow him into his old age. But he was still alive, anyway. Somewhat soiled by life, true. But better to be old and defiled, than to be forever twenty-three, dead in your innocence.

The sulfurous funk of a bygone chemistry lab for some reason tainted the edges of his nostrils. Perhaps it was having passed old Maury Hall on the way to the parade, and remembering his narrow escape from its fume-filled labs with a rock bottom "D"; had it been ten years since he took that course?

Julie was on his arm, his wife of two years, mother of his daughter. She hadn't wanted to come. She had believed that his classmates would talk behind his back about his being an FBI agent. Was this fragile, unfulfilled woman really the Forever After he had day-dreamed about during parades on Worden Field?

Sophie and Red Lesczynski stood next to him, already the parents of three children. They had brought little J.J. to the parade. Small patches of veins had gathered like road maps on the back of Sophie's slender legs. Her dark hair was flecked with gray, although she was not yet thirty. But for some reason she and Red still represented all the dreams to Judd Smith. They were both, simply, what they had planned to be, and that phenomenon was getting rarer and rarer.

Sophie clearly relished parades. Her brown eyes danced and her smooth viola voice called to her son, who had climbed to the top of the bleachers with three other boys. "Oh, here comes the flag. Stand at attention, J.J.!"

As the color guard marched past, the little boy appeared just next to Sophie and stood at a perfect attention, thumbs along the seams of his blue jeans, his feet at a forty-five-degree angle, his small jaw firm and his eyes unwavering, straight ahead. He had red hair and freckles and big teeth. His pale blue eyes were the same as Red's. He was five, going on thirty, a mature, thoughtful child who it was already clear would also someday have Red Lesczynski's physical strength. Judd Smith grinned at J.J.'s military pose. *Hey, J.J.,* he thought to himself. *You go be Real American too, eh?*

The brigade was passing in review. Smith nudged the little boy, who still held a serious attention. "Yeah, you stand tall, kid. That's my old company coming up." J.J. Seemed mildly surprised. He turned his head slightly, staring at Judd Smith's civilian overcoat. "You went here, Uncle Judd?"

"Of course I did. Your daddy and I were roommates, along with your uncle Dingie. See that company? I was company commander my first class year."

"I didn't know you were in the Navy."

"Now, nobody said anything about me being in any goddamn Navy, J.J. I was on loan from the Marine Corps for four years."

Julie tugged at his arm. "Judd, do *not* swear in front of that child. He's only five."

"I didn't swear. 'Goddamn Navy' is one word in the Marine Corps. You can't say Navy by itself."

"Is my daddy in the goddamn Navy?"

Red Lesczynski leaned over from the other side of Sophie, grinning wistfully at Judd and then at his son, the double gold stripes of a lieutenant looming on the wide shoulders of his overcoat. "J.J., only Marines can say that, okay? Don't mind your uncle Judd. He's only teasing."

"Are you still in the Marines, Uncle Judd?"

"No."

"You didn't like it anymore?" The boy seemed puzzled, his clear eyes now scrutinizing Judd Smith from behind a long red forelock.

"No, I liked it fine, J.J." Julie's arm had withdrawn from his elbow, as if dreading any detailed response. Actually, he didn't have anything left to say. "I just wanted to go catch bad guys, that's all."

"Your uncle Judd works for the FBI now, honey." Sophie saved him, stroking the boy's hair. "He catches bank robbers, and people who hurt other people. Sort of like 'Dragnet' on the television."

J.J. mulled it over, still inspecting Judd Smith's face and clothes, then nodded, giving his approval. "You must be pretty brave."

*   *   *

"They aren't getting along, Red. It's kind of sad, really." Sophie stood in front of the mirror in their small bedroom. "Oh, I just can't get my hair right."

"It looks fine, Sophie."

"You'd say that anyway. I feel absolutely *old* when I look at Julie! She's so beautiful I can't believe it." Sophie ran her hands along the outside of her waist and then down her hips. "I look like I'm forty years old."

"Sophie, you do not! I told you, you look fine, and I wouldn't just say that." Red Lesczynski leaned away from a second mirror, where he was affixing the bow tie of his Navy mess dress uniform. He smiled softly. "Well, maybe I would, but I meant it. You'll always be beautiful to me, Sophie, and I can't love you without loving every wrinkle."

"Am I getting *that* old?" She was suddenly only inches away from the mirror, studying her face closely.

"Oh, brother. *No!* I was just trying to be poetic, to tell you not to compare yourself with Julie. She may be pretty, but she's not happy. Anybody can see that. And old Judd scares me a little. I said something about wanting him to be happy, and he started talking like he was reading from a philosophy book or something, saying that happiness wasn't the natural state of man, that a baby is born crying and has to learn how to laugh, and that we do the world a disservice by saying that people should strive to be happy. He said it creates an artificial expectation, and when they fall into the natural state of not being happy they feel guilty about it and it makes them *unhappy* instead of just not being happy. Can you imagine Judd Smith coming out with a mouthful like that?"

She was putting on her earrings. "Well, he's miserable and he's trying to understand why." There were no mysteries in the world to Sophie, only answers that others did not yet see. "Did you see in the paper about that little boy out on West Street who chased a ball into the street and was hit by a car?"

"No." Red watched her fret over her lipstick, awaiting more.

She finished and shrugged, her soft little face awash with empathy for the dead boy's mother. "Well, that was terrible. Can you imagine anything worse happening in the whole world?"

Julie Clay Smith had no right not to love him. No, that wasn't it. She had no right merely to fall in love with love and make him the implementer, the object, the conduit through which that abstract principle flowed. Well, maybe that wasn't it, either. It it it. What *was* that magical "it," the element that was wrong and could be resolved? He didn't know, and the harder he pushed to find it, the further she withdrew. Everything in life was fixable if you pushed hard enough and long enough at it, that was what he had always believed, but pushing at her only made her disappear. He couldn't overpower her, because she did not react to power, except to go off in a sulky, confused silence, or to go home and stay for a while with Daddy.

And after he had passed all the tests and then taken the great unforgivable leap of faith, the leap away from a life of falsity and toward her (whether she knew it or not), she had made it mercilessly evident that he was now untrustworthy, a traitor. It took a year before he realized that he not only had not won, but had lost so dreadfully that her very marriage to him had been something of a punishment, a payment for having embarrassed her and her family. He would never understand it. No, that wasn't true, either. He would never allow himself consciously to understand it, because it would be a tragedy so deep, a failure so complete, that he would have to hate himself.

"I don't want to stay very long, Judd."

She said it without looking at him, through that Miss America smile, as they walked the center aisle of the cavernous mess hall toward the tables assigned to the Class of 1951, all the while waving to different people they knew. He would have felt sorry for her if he had not been so hopelessly in love with her, if she had not held the power to crush him like an eggshell simply by removing her presence from him. She had been in too many political campaigns. She had a fossilized public face, a compulsion to radiate that did not match her private moods. Yes, he thought again, I almost feel sorry for her.

The mess hall tables were on either side of them, two rows as long as a football field. The oldest alumni were seated just inside the door on the left, and the youngest classes had their tables just inside the door on the right, so that as they walked into the mess hall the continuum of men and their wives grew slowly younger on one side of them and slowly older on the other, until they met, at the same age, at the far end. It was as if they were watching two simultaneous time exposures of the aging process, the mode of dress varying slightly, a few aberrations here and there, but the clothes and the smiles and the loud exchanges almost a constant. Navy. Some of the old hunched bone bags just to Judd Smith's left had sailed and steamed with Dewey in the Spanish American War. The bulk of the mess hall's inhabitants had fought for the ocean in one or the other of the World Wars.

They reached the tables for the Class of 1951 and she came alive, actually performed. His classmates gravitated toward him and Julie. He was the decorated warrior, she was the flawless southern belle. As she shook their hands, asking just the right sort of probing, interested questions about each of them, their jobs, their families, he knew that even this was one of her little punishments. She was acting out the role he had denied her, demonstrating a very real and cultivated talent. She was a politician's wife with a humbug cop on her arm.

II

Professor Crane Howell was as ugly and yet as capable of conjuring up dignity as an old lunker bass. He had crooked, stained teeth, hollow cheeks scarred from acne, and a small chin that fell into a loose, long neck. He smoked a pipe and coughed a lot. He walked with a shambling, knock-kneed gait, cradling his pipe in one hand up around his neck, his head down and his shoulders sloped, as if he were much older than his nearly fifty years. Actually, he was. He had taught a mandatory course called "The History Of Sea Power" to Red Lesczynski in 1950, and it was now Lesczynski's greatest pleasure every morning to share a cup of coffee with Crane Howell not only as a colleague in the "Bull" department, but as a fellow professor of the same course.

Howell shared another distinction that had caused Lesczynski to gravitate toward him: he had spent more than three years as a Japanese prisoner of war in World War II. Howell had been captured on Corregidor in May 1942, after having commanded the supply detachment at the Cavite Naval Yard near Manila until December 1941, when the Japanese overran Luzon. He had endured the humiliating marches through occupied Manila, the nights in the old Bilibid prison, the imprisonment at various camps with their romantic poems of names: Cabanatuan, where more than two thousand Americans died, Cañacao, Cebu, and finally a year as a laborer in a Japanese coal mine. Following his repatriation, Howell was medically retired from the Navy with a list of war-connected ailments that filled a full page of typing paper. After obtaining a master's degree in history, Howell had returned to his alma mater to teach. And, although freely admitting he had reasons to be biased, Crane Howell did not apologize for his dislike of the Japanese.

"The Knights of *Bushido*," he drawled ironically, sucking on his pipe and taunting Red Leszynski from across the table in the faculty conference room. "That's what they would call themselves. 'We are the Knights of *Bushido*. We do not execute at sunset, but at sunrise.' Does this Japanese friend of yours mention the beheadings? How about rape and mass executions as a matter of policy in China? How about the use of prisoners as guinea pigs? Did your friend talk about that? I don't know why that hasn't been released yet. They used Americans as experimental animals. Is there a better indication of complete racism? They injected Americans with massive doses of plague and smallpox germs, just to see what would happen. They pumped Americans full of horse blood and radiation, and then cut the bodies up, killing the men if they were still alive, just to see if there was any damage. How can we forget that? Jesus, Lesczynski, almost 40 percent of our Japanese POWs—thirteen thousand of them—died in captivity. Compare that to the bloody Nazis: only 1 percent of our POWs died in German hands. And you're telling me I'm supposed to suddenly love those bastards?" Howell waved a hand casually into the air, his dark eyes honing in on Red Lesczynski as if he were still a student, which in a way he was. "Forget it."

"You were held longer than the German prisoners. And you were in worse physical shape when you were captured, after the siege of Bataan and Corregidor." Lesczynski knew it would irritate, even anger the older man, but it was a slow Monday and he felt like provoking his old professor a bit.

"Well, of *course* we were! And you don't take starving people and walk them sixty-five miles without giving them food or water, like they did after Bataan! You don't behead the slow ones and bury the weak ones while they're still alive, either. That wasn't the length of imprisonment, it was *Bushido*. They *hated* us for having given up. The only honorable conduct for a Japanese was to fight to the death, no matter what. Even if a Japanese was taken prisoner after being so seriously wounded that he couldn't move, he could never hold his head up in Japan again. He was thoroughly disgraced. So was his family! Even his *family* preferred him to die—can you understand how deeply that goes into the culture? They couldn't believe it when we told them that we wanted our families to know we were still alive!"

Howell tamped his pipe, spilling ashes on his plaid coat. He wore a striped tie that didn't match. Mismatched clothes were his trademark. Lesczynski had an affection for the aging professor that was almost palpable. Howell was reasoned, well read, and yet unyielding on principle. Being able to serve his tour at the academy in the history section was a blessing, and Lesczynski was spending every available free moment either studying the military classics or seizing a Socratic tutorial from Crane Howell. Lesczynski admired the Japanese, but still allowed himself a tickle of doubt, a gossamer of wonder, and Crane Howell was a repository of knowledge for him to probe.

"Look, Crane. We've got to work with them, I suppose you can agree with that premise, particularly after China has gone communist.

You say they're using us because we're defending their economy without their help and then you say they were such barbaric soldiers that they shouldn't be allowed in uniform again—"

"—I didn't say that."

"So, what are we supposed to do?" Red Lesczynski shrugged mildly, finishing his cup of coffee. "And they *have* renounced war. It's even in their constitution."

"Well, that's a pretty neat trick, isn't it? Do you know what *jujitsu* is?"

"Of course I do. It's a Japanese martial art, a form of self-defense where—"

"—where you use an opponent's strength to your advantage. He comes screaming after you and you step aside and toss him with his own momentum. Check?"

Lesczynski thought about it, his wide pink face grinning at Howell. "Well, yeah, I guess. Check."

"It's the Japanese philosophy. *Jujitsu*. Renounce war but continue aggression. Take America's strength and throw it at your enemies, without the cost in either blood or treasure. I admit I'm biased. But they used to tell us, right up to the end of the war, that the 'Japanese spirit' was going to prevail, that they were going to win, that it was just a matter of time. *Bushido*. And it may yet, Lesczynski. You don't toss off a way of life, a whole national perspective, the same way you change your clothes from a kimono to a three-piece suit. Scratch a Japanese businessman and you find a samurai."

"You really hate the Japanese, don't you, Crane?"

"Well, no, I don't hate them. Let's just say I've lived among the natives when they were running the jungle." Howell peacefully smoked his pipe, gazing at Lesczynski. "So now your friend Kosaka writes that his little business is getting ready to enter American markets. Is that what you said?"

"It's amazing what Toyota has done. Amazing. When I first went to Japan in 1952, they were making four thousand cars a year. This year they'll make twenty thousand. That's five times the cars, in five years! Come on, Crane, you've got to hand it to them."

"Yeah, I'll hand it to them. We're fielding a fleet of a thousand warships, draining money off our economy, so they can make Toyotas and send them here on the sea-lanes we're protecting. *Why do we stand around like proud parents, viewing them as our children?* I'll never understand that. They smile and bow and talk funny and everyone thinks they're damn children!" Howell shook his head, still sucking on his pipe, totally bemused. "What a ride they're taking us on. Americans are such suckers for a smile, so eager to be loved, especially if it's someone who used to hate us."

Lesczynski leaned back, large hands behind his head, the white shirt and black tie of his service dress blues giving him the look of a business executive surveying a profit chart on the far wall. "That's the other thing that makes me want to disagree with you, Crane. It's amazing to see them with their children. Until their kids reach school age, they have a completely free rein on life. The parents let them do anything. It isn't until they begin school that all of this, I don't know what you would call it—"

"Repression."

"All right, close enough. That this repression begins." Lesczynski smiled, a small victorious look on his wide, comfortable face. "Look at American families, whacking the kids around, always disciplining them. Then tell me which society is the more violent and abusive."

"You're confusing yourself. The principle still holds." Howell was consciously professorial in his response. He hobbled over to the coffeepot and poured himself a second cup, his back to Lesczynski. Finally he returned to the conference table, briefly checking his watch as he sat down. "Society, or family?"

"I don't understand what you're getting at."

"I see an inverse relationship." Howell relit his pipe. "The greater the structure imposed by the society, the less it is needed inside the family. Our children go out into a society that is going to demand nothing of them, unless they decide to do it. That's America in a nutshell. So, if an American kid doesn't get a sense of self-discipline from his family, he plays hell finding it later on. On the other hand, Japanese society is overwhelmingly repressive. If a kid doesn't get a few years of freedom before he enters school, he'll never know what the word meant. Actually, they all *are* children, in a way. At least the ones who take their culture seriously. The culture is the parent, whether it's the Emperor or the *zaibatsu* or their million little shrines. Did you ever hear about the first two Japanese students to study in the United States, at the end of the last century?"

Lesczynski grinned ironically. "Don't tell me. They were both valedictorians, and the Emperor purged them of their knowledge."

"No, worse. They both worked themselves to death. They couldn't bear the thought of going home without bringing straight A's on their report cards." Howell chuckled. "Of course, the Japanese were able to turn *that* into a victory, too. They gave everything for the honor of their culture, you see, and their graves up at Princeton are now something of a shrine for other Japanese students." He measured Lesczynski and drained his coffee cup. "Sort of the *banzai* approach to education."

"You make them sound like they're a mess, Crane."

"They're hardly a mess, Stanislaus." The shuffling, stooped former prisoner of war picked up his pile of history books and notes and roll books and headed slowly toward the door, on his way to teach class. He pointed the stem of his pipe at Red Lesczynski. "In fact, we're the ones to be pitied, I'm afraid. Because they're going to be taking us to the cleaners." Howell laughed aloud, shuffling out the door. "Or at least they'll die trying."

❉   ❉   ❉

Sophie loved being assigned to the academy. It was the first time in ten years, since Red had left Ford City to become a midshipman, that they had the sort of routine she had thought would be a part of married life.

Not that she complained about the rest of it. That was Navy life. It alternated, and she alternated with it. He had sea duty, and then he had shore duty. When he was at sea she kept the family together, paid the bills, worried about his flying on and off the floating runways of an aircraft carrier, and lived for the day he would come home. When he was ashore she went out of her way to allow him more time with the kids. She paid the bills because she wanted him to enjoy his precious days ashore. And she worried about the inevitable day he would have to go away and fly again. She didn't tell him that she worried, because it might affect his split-second timing, and then she would have to worry more because she had let it out of the bag. She didn't tell him how hard it was when he was at sea because it didn't make it any easier if he knew; he couldn't do anything about it and he had enough to worry about.

This whole business of flying jets was more than his job; it was the way he defined himself, and to interfere with that would be to destroy him. So she hung on, and he passed through those turmoils with a growing simplicity that actually seemed to believe that there was nothing difficult about the mundane part of life. Dinner was always on the table and his clothes were always clean. The car was always fixed and the bills were always paid. He didn't change diapers and he didn't vacuum floors. He flew and studied and kept himself in shape.

But he loved her, really loved her. And wasn't that the bottom line, anyway? Wasn't that what people moaned for, wrote songs about, went to psychiatrists and cried over? Well, here it really was. Nobody ever said that Monaco and the Riviera came with it.

On his first WESPAC cruise (the Navy abbreviation for Western Pacific, that area beyond Hawaii) he sent her a little Japanese fan made out of ivory, or at least it seemed like ivory and she told everyone it was, and he wrote her every day. He wrote her from Hong Kong and he wrote her from Manila and he wrote her from Japan. He spent a lot of time in Japan and he learned how to play a game called Go and he became friends with this man Kosaka, who had two brothers killed in the war, one by a naval aviator. He dropped bombs in Korea, along supply lines and into rail depots and power plants, but he felt vaguely unfulfilled about his contribution. It haunted him that he hadn't really done enough. Judd Smith had done enough. When he came home they made another baby. Katherine was born on his second WESPAC cruise.

On his second WESPAC cruise they were making more money and he bought several Japanese screens and paintings and dried flowers. He really seemed to admire the Japanese. The Kosakas became something of an adoptive family to him. He still wrote her every day and it was amazing how many boxes you could accumulate over the years, stuffed with neatly arranged envelopes that had been mailed from Annapolis and Tokyo and somewhere in the middle of the South China Sea. She would sit in their small Coronado home, nursing Katherine and keeping J.J. busy on the floor, and stare at the screens and paintings and wonder what it felt like to be in Tokyo. She knew he spent most of his time at sea, but there were days when she couldn't hold back that old green monster, envy. *Yeah, Red Lesczynski, write me cards from Hong Kong and Tokyo and tell me about how lonely you are, uh huh.*

But mostly she had to keep herself busy. The key was not to allow herself to become a WESPAC widow, haunting the bar at the officer's club or the lounging chairs beside its swimming pool. She learned to refinish furniture. She learned to play bridge. She learned about antiques and spent a great deal of time shopping at local flea markets and swap meets.

She spent a month with her parents in Ford City. The factory had laid off 10 percent of the work force and the union was threatening to strike. Ford City was not a happy place to be in these humdrum days of Eisenhower, and there was no indication that it would get better. The town chafed under the first Republican President in a generation. If you said the word "Republican" in Ford City, the automatic, unthinking response was "Herbert Hoover."

Red came back from his second WESPAC cruise and Johnny was born and finally there were orders for shore duty, three glorious years of normalcy at the Naval Academy. Red took it with mixed emotions, not fond of the thought of leaving the cockpit for three years in an era of quantum leaps in aeronautical performance. He compared it with taking a heart surgeon out of the operating room for that long, to go lecture somewhere. You ended up outdated, if you weren't careful, and unfamiliar with the hardware, and that could kill you.

But there were long talks with Professor Howell and the nights at his little desk under a reading light, devouring all of the histories he had avoided when in school. Book after book, and he filling a loose-leaf binder with notes to himself, comparing the decisions of commanders on various battlefields, of statesmen in different eras. How did the Japanese beat the Russians? How did the Russians beat the French? How did the French beat half the world, and then manage to lose it? Why did it take half the world to beat the Germans? What happened to the Poles? He talked about these things at dinner, and when they went to bed. She liked to hear him talk.

The midshipmen loved him. He helped coach the football team and he liked to have students over for dinner. His kids loved him. He was fond of taking little J.J. over to the workout rooms in MacDonough Hall, teaching him how to climb the ropes that the gymnasts used, and wrestling with him. J.J. was going to be a horse. He read stories to all three children every night, and put them to bed. She loved him. They went sight-seeing in Washington on the weekends and he even learned to play bridge for her. It was so incredibly *normal* that it scared her, even though she knew it would end in another year, with another deployment on another ship.

One night, watching him reading a story on the couch, Katherine on one side of him, J.J. on the other, little Johnny chattering away on his lap, she decided that the going away had become an essential part of it. If he were around all the time, she mused, they might all get too used to it.

CHAPTER ELEVEN

"*Hello!* ANYBODY HOME?"

Judd Smith had known before he called into the dark hall and the empty air that he was alone, but it was the way he always entered, as if his noise might stir up the ambience, create a current of energy. The apartment was dead of noise or motion, like ashes.

More often, it was their battleground, the nexus of their inability to comprehend each other. The hallway walls were stained brown with water marks from a leaky ceiling. She had hung exquisitely framed paintings on the walls; a Renoir print, and some originals, including two from a Washington artist named Peter Marvullo, a man she had once dated. She couldn't understand how Judd could live with stained walls. He couldn't understand how she liked the paintings, or her insistence in hanging Marvullo's works in his home, as if they were hunting trophies. It was like having another lover in the home, a reminder of his own inadequacy. The rosewood table inside the door with its porcelain figurines and dried flowers stood like a shrine to the unreachable mesas of pristine culture. It did not belong in his house. Or maybe he did not belong in hers.

He called again, just for measure. No answer. She had taken the baby and gone for another visit to her parents' house in Washington. He was not surprised that she was gone; in fact, he had come to expect it. But he had hoped. He had a story for her, a little love offering, a piece of pride that might somehow, finally, buy her love.

He needed a beer. He walked into the kitchen and flipped on the light. He stopped then, shaking his head with anger, yes, but also with a small release, as if he were finally going to be free, whether he wanted to or not. He stared at the cat lying sprawled and unmoving on the kitchen floor and thought, *Now it will end, if she wants it to. Because she is a woman and women need reasons. They are not like men, who leave for other women or because of things they can't articulate. They wait and then they come up with a reason.*

"You goddamn cat!" The cat had been nothing but trouble, from the beginning. But it had outdone itself this time.

It was the kind of a cat that any sane, self-respecting man had the right to just plain hate, and Judd Smith hated the hell out of it.

It was the kind of a cat that the Cat Lovers of America would pin a ribbon on and put on the cover of a cat food can, the kind that Montaigne would remind his readers found humans more of a playful pastime than humans found the cat to be. It was one of those foul-breathed, purring, hissing Chinchilla Persians with big, shocked eyes, which every now and then would appear with false regality and allow a human to stroke its long gray hairs and scratch behind its almost hidden ears, all the while rubbing against the legs of the person so honored, and then would abruptly hiss into its admirer's face and strut away to its daytime haven. It was the kind that would hiss and actually spit if you opened the closet where it was spending its day after having made a nest on the towel you needed to dry your face, the kind that assumed a sort of eunuch's power in the palace of your home. Its claws had been removed and its sexual capacity sliced away by a veterinarian's scalpel, so that its whole *catness* now depended on how badly it could ridicule the person who had caused it to become a changeling, a caricature of a real animal.

My owner loves me. She cut my box out, thought Smith again, this time without humor, thinking of his frequent taunt to Julie.

It was the kind of cat that would take a dump in a box inside the house and then come out from its hiding place just to sit, yawning in a way that was beyond doubt its version of a laugh, and watch you while you cleaned it up. Judd Smith hated that cat, almost as much as Julie loved it.

Godiva. The cat had become the greatest symbol of his and Julie's inability to understand each other, the unspoken summary of why their marriage had been a disaster since the very beginning. In Bear Mountain County you grew up around every variety of animal under God's creation. You raised them, you milked them, you fed them, and sometimes you shot them. But you didn't keep them inside your house and you for sure didn't let them *crap* in the house.

And you for stomp-down a hundred *percent* sure didn't let any animal climb into bed with you. Animals were to be trained and controlled, or hunted. If an animal didn't show you respect, you kicked it out of the way. All of which caused Julie to believe he was a form of barbarian. He had knocked Godiva silly the first time she had climbed onto their bed, on her way to curling up next to Julie, a nightly ritual until then. Without hardly thinking about it, he had thrown the cat off the bed, against the nearby wall. Julie had jumped from the bed screaming, and sat on the floor, stroking Godiva, who kept shaking a stunned head with quick snaps, as if trying to throw a dash of water off her nose.

From that moment forward it had been a battle. Julie would periodically quote something from St. Francis of Assisi about how a man's attitude toward animals was the key to his real attitude toward humans. Judd would ask her if she loved rats and roaches, too. Godiva would hiss if Judd merely walked into the same room, and Judd would immediately slap the righteous, disrespectful creature, sending it against the wall again with a solid thud. The cat would groan for a few minutes, its fat trunk undulating with hate, and then finally summon up another hiss, which would be met with another whack across the face by Judd. Now and then, to demonstrate its continued hostility and independence in the face of Judd's quick slaps, the cat would defecate right on the spot, and prance away to hide under a bed or in a closet as Judd screamed after it and Julie screamed at him. It was an unapologetic cat, an undisciplined cat, a senator's daughter's cat.

And there it was, lying sleek and dead on the kitchen floor, having managed to kill itself when Julie was not around, the sneaky, mischievous, grudging ball of fur and halitosis. Judd walked slowly toward it and gave it one hesitant little kick in its abdomen. Stiff, sure enough. One of its front legs was caught inside the new leather collar Julie had pridefully bought for it a week before, and the animal had apparently strangled itself while attempting to fling the collar off. Smith had seen it perform the feat before, a leap into the air as the paw pressed upward, the collar sailing across the room and the cat imperiously striding back under a bed. He kicked it again and sat down at the table, lighting a cigarette.

"Got you this time, you sad piece of ragshit. Can't say I'll shed any tears over you."

There was a note on the table. *Back Friday night. Casserole in the fridge. Don't forget to feed Godiva, and clean her cat box. J.* Great, he thought, smoking the cigarette and staring at the dead cat. A whole day, at least, before she's back. So what the hell am I supposed to do with the cat?

It had been his first, immediate thought, a vision clear and unerring as a look into the past, that she would blame him for Godiva's death, and in fact would believe that he had killed the animal. He had made fun of it, ridiculed it, declared his hate for it on every available occa-

sion. He had offered to take it down to the turnpike and let it play in
the traffic, to throw it over the nearest bridge with the fond farewell,
"If you don't know how to swim, cat, you better learn to fly." And that
was when he and the cat were getting along. Nope. Julie would never
believe that the cat had up and killed itself out of its own Chinchilla
Persian inbred stupidity, at one of those rare moments when she was
not around and Judd Smith was. Uh-uh. That cat lying dead on the
kitchen floor was the major crisis of a marriage that had fed on crisis
in the same addictive way that a nymphomaniac goes after sex.

And he had such good news, such a proud love offering. He had just
helped capture Franco "Pinky" Linz, one of the FBI's "Ten Most
Wanted Fugitives." Linz, while hardly a murderous monster, was one
of the cleverest and most imaginative fugitives in history. A bank robber who had been eluding the FBI for more than three years, he had
used forty different aliases and stolen thirty-three cars and five airplanes, while moving freely through Canada, all of the United States,
and Mexico. And Judd Smith had figured the angle that had caught
him.

Linz, a gregarious, prematurely balding fellow who usually posed as
either a college student recovering from a nervous breakdown or a
professional golfer taking a break from the PGA tour, had developed
four consistent patterns. First, he liked to leave stolen cars on old used
car lots or in large parking areas, where they would not be found for
several days. Second, he always wore a hat to cover his baldness, even
when swimming or dancing. Third, he liked to double back on his
trail, reversing his movement and returning to the place he was last
reported when any pursuit became intense. And fourth, he liked to
send postcards. He sent them to his son in Indianapolis. He sent them
to his numerous teenage girl friends. He sent them to the owners of
rooming houses where he had lived. It was his little way of remaining
famous, a "Lone Ranger" touch: the getaway, then people standing
around wondering, "Who was that masked man?" His son and others
had collections of postcards that included Akron, Ohio; Toronto, Canada; Kalamazoo, Michigan; Alderwood, Washington; Baltimore, Maryland; Washington, D.C. (a picture of the FBI building, no less), a
remote area of Idaho, Cypress Gardens in Florida, and just about
every place in between. The FBI started joking that Linz was robbing
banks just to pay for postage stamps.

A bank had been robbed in a little town called Millville, New Jersey, by a polite, well-spoken gentleman wearing a black derby. That

evening, a car stolen in Atlantic City was found in a grocery store parking lot in Millville, and another car was reported stolen. Two days later, Linz's son received a postcard from his father, postmarked in Philadelphia, the FBI having intercepted it and read it first. So Judd Smith had gone out with another agent and sat along State Route 47, where it passed through Millville on its way to the beaches of Wildwood and Cape May from Philadelphia, watching for drivers who resembled Linz. It was a long shot, a triumph of intuition over science. But at three in the afternoon a man wearing an Irish walking cap (and this in the heat of July) drove into Millville and parked a well-polished 1957 Chevrolet in a supermarket lot. When they approached him he seemed actually honored to meet them.

"You guys are really sharp," Pinkie Linz had said in admiration as they drove him away to certain jail. "I read *The FBI Story* and I liked it a lot."

See, he had wanted to tell her by not having to say it, *see what you got, how lucky you are? Can't you see that it doesn't matter about the rest of it, that you got more this way?* But he couldn't even be allowed the honor of not saying it because she was not there. All that was there was this stupid, stiff dead cat that she was going to refuse to believe he hadn't killed.

He stepped daintily over the carcass and took the casserole from the refrigerator, grabbing a pan from a cupboard and reheating it in the oven. He stared pensively at the dead animal as he ate, disliking it even more in its death than he had when it was alive. Somewhere up in that Nirvana where dead cats gather to hiss and preen, it was laughing at him, just as certainly as if he were scooping up poop from its cat box. The large, dead marble eyes, the left paw stuck motionless inside the new collar Julie had so proudly affixed to it a few days before, the lengthy stretching of its frame. It was so ridiculous to believe a dead cat might blow his marriage apart.

It was eighty degrees inside the apartment. The cat was going to start smelling before too long. He thought about burying it. She wouldn't believe his story. He thought about putting it on the back porch. The bugs would get to it if the rats did not, and the neighbors would not appreciate the clinging, rancid death odors that would soon float out of Godiva's pores. Finally he sighed, taking out a roll of plastic wrap, and began wrapping the animal's body, again and again, around and around, until it appeared to be a luminescent mummy, a funny gray butterfly inside a clear silk cocoon.

* * *

The door slammed on the little 1958 Mercedes Diesel that her father had bought and loaned to her because Judd Smith would not allow her father to buy it *for* her, a point of useless pride, one of many, but that was what it had come down to after three years of marriage—naked pride. He walked down the stairway from their small bedroom, turning on the hall light, passing the antiques, the porcelain jars, the intricate baskets, the paintings inside heavy wooden frames, all the things she had purchased before they married, things he could not fully appreciate and consequently had a tendency to ridicule. Things that appeared just as foreign along the halls of their Newark apartment as a tea set in a cow pasture.

"Hi, honey." He looked briefly at Julie, his eyes heavy with anticipation, and then smiled widely, reaching for his daughter, who was suddenly in his arms. "Hey, kiddo."

"*Da!* Uh-uh!" Big round smiling face, eyes rounder still, a mat of brown curls that dangled in every direction. She was all smiles and energy, hugging his neck and grunting, as he had taught her, to the chagrin of her mother. He grunted back.

"Uh uh uh! That's my baby."

She was babbling to him, pulling on his nose, pointing, telling him all about her trip and how she had missed him. It was hard for him to believe, but soon she would be two years old. He looked into her smooth innocent loving face, feeling a wholesome, almost sad form of purity. "Loretta, you stinker, you need new diapers. Hey, you wet?"

Her wide-eyed, serious little pout looked as if it held the whole world's angst. She was embarrassed. The word dribbled out over a jutting lower lip. "Potty."

"Yeah." He was laughing at her and she pouted more. "That's what I thought, you little smack."

"Where's my little darling?" Julie set down their small suitcase and began looking for the cat. "Go-DI-va! Kitty kitty!" She walked into the kitchen, and peered up the stairs. "Judd, where's Godiva?"

Loretta was playing with one of his ears, somberly inspecting it with both hands, as if it were a steering wheel. "She's in the freezer."

"Come on, Judd. That isn't very funny."

"I don't think it's very funny, either, but she's in the goddamn freezer, all right?" Smith looked at her for a quick second, then walked toward the stairway, thinking to change Loretta's diapers.

"What do you mean, she's in the freezer?" He began walking up the stairs. Behind him, Julie shrieked almost loud and clear enough to break crystal. Loretta started crying. He walked back down the stairs. Julie was still screaming. Loretta was holding her own ears now, screaming also.

"Mama! Mama! Uh-uh-uh."

"What have you *done*, Judd Smith, oh, my God!" Julie stood in front of the refrigerator, holding the freezer door open with one hand, the other one on her stomach. Clouds of frost mixed with the musky summer air. She reached into the freezer and then withdrew her hand as if she had almost put it into molten lava.

"*Da*. See? Uh-uh-uh."

"I didn't do anything. I knew you wouldn't believe me, so I saved the evidence."

"The *evidence?* Oh, my God." She slammed the freezer door closed and sat down at the small, circular kitchen table, a piece of rosewood given them by her mother. "The evidence. You had to make it sound like the FBI, didn't you? Special Agent Smith preserves the evidence."

"*Potty-y-y*." Large pearls of tears gathered at the edges of Loretta's eyes. She was pouting again, one hand between her tiny legs.

"It choked itself to death. I can show you what happened."

"*Choked* itself to death?" She watched him severely, her hair pulled back tight into a bun and her eyes like her mother's, always afraid and always reaching, part of the fear an intuition that she would never understand and a knowledge that if she admitted this permanent misunderstanding she would also have no buffer from the fear that would not go away. Or maybe it was just a fear of him. He recognized that, watching the reaching eyes. "A cat can't choke itself. I've never heard of such a thing, Judd Smith. And how could you put it in the *freezer*, for God's sake? You've probably contaminated every piece of food in there. This is just *crazy*, Judd!"

"*Potty-y-y-y!*"

Loretta was crying, her little legs jumping against him. He felt a warm, wet spot on his side, where she had just gone through her diaper. He set her onto the table. Julie shrieked again, taking the baby off the precious rosewood and immediately wiping up a urine stain. He opened the freezer door and dropped the dead cat onto the floor. It was a stiff cellophane package that bounced like a large, wrapped brick. Julie and the baby were both screaming. He began to unwrap

the cellophane, the cat's carcass clunking again and again as it
twirled. His voice was an angry, defensive growl.

"She tried to throw off that cute little collar you bought her. Her
paw got stuck in it. I don't know if she choked or had a heart attack.
Maybe you can get a goddamned coroner to tell you."

"Kitty," said Loretta, wiping away a tear with one tiny hand and
pointing to the dead cat with the other.

He had fifty feet of cellophane in his arms. He tossed it onto the
floor. "What the hell was I supposed to do with it? I knew you
wouldn't believe me. I figured you might if I saved the body. So, there
you are." He couldn't resist one last barb. "Stupid cat."

"Ohhh," said Julie.

"Kitty kitty," said Loretta, a smile creeping onto her face.

"You hated my cat." Julie seemed to be recovering from the shock.
It was an accusation.

"I hated the *shit* out of your cat, but I didn't kill it. Look, Julie.
Remember when the Marstons were going to take that hang dog to
the pound to have it killed? What was its name—"

"Sonny."

"Yeah, and the night before they were going to have it gassed or
whatever they do to old dogs it got out of the house and was running
down the street and they were out trying to catch it, and the old dog
ran right up to me, its tail wagging, wanting me to pet it, and Mr.
Marston yelled at me to catch his dog? Remember that? And I chased
the dog away, yelling at it, 'Run, Sonny, they're going to kill your fat
old ass! Get the hell out of here while you still can!' Remember that?"

"Yes." She was staring quietly at Godiva, as if peering into a casket.

"So, how could I kill an animal that was a pet if I wouldn't even
help them catch old Sonny? Answer me that."

"Sonny was a dog. You liked Sonny. You ruined all the food, too.
You're really stupid, Judd. I'm serious. You're stupid." She said it in a
quiet tone that bordered on pity.

"I didn't ruin any food. I wrapped that cat up tight."

"You ruined the food." She stood and began methodically emptying
the freezer, placing frozen hamburger and chicken, ice cubes and orange juice onto the counter next to the sink. Then she began on the refrigerator, taking milk and ketchup, leftovers and lettuce and stacking
them also near the sink. She seemed disoriented, bent on motion as a
respite from thought. The baby approached the dead cat, as if to pet
it, and Judd silently picked her up, holding her.

"Ki-i-tty kitty kitty." She pointed to the cat again, her other arm grabbing onto Judd's hair. Her diaper soaked through his shirt.

"I didn't ruin the food!"

"You did! You ruined the food and you killed my cat, Judd Smith, I won't have you deny it!" She had turned and was facing him, her delicate white hands in little fists, the smooth skin of her classic face tight with anger, suppressing the fear. "You have a violent streak in you! I can see it in everything you do! You are *filled* with violence and you are stupid and you killed my cat and you ruined the food."

"Oh, for Christ's sake."

"And swearing about it won't change it. Does it make you tougher to swear like a—like a roughneck? You're a crude man. I can't take any more of you."

"Then go away, Julie. That's what you've been after for at least a year, now. I can't give you what you want." They stood silently, staring at each other for a long moment. The baby played in his hair, cooing. He began walking toward the stairs again. "I'm going to change Loretta."

He could hear her in their bedroom as he changed the baby. By the time he had finished, she had packed another bag. He watched silently, holding Loretta, as Julie threw more of the baby's things into yet another suitcase. He wanted more than anything in the world to be able to say the right words that would make her understand and respect him, but he wasn't smart enough or maybe attuned enough to her to know what those words might be. He was exhausted from trying to find them, so he said nothing.

"Would you help me load the car?"

Silently, awash with a dead pain that denied this moment was finally happening, was really occurring after months of threats and rehearsals, he loaded her suitcases into the Mercedes. The baby played with his ears, still on one arm. Then Julie took Loretta from him, and it felt as though she had ripped something out of him from deep inside, stomach or lung or heart. Loretta saw the car seat and giggled, "Go go go," and he walked to the car and kissed her soft little cheek, knowing viscerally that now she would grow up without him, that he would be denied the daily opportunity to do all the little things, those osmosis chores of parenthood. It was the most painful, dreadful, meaningful kiss of his life. She grabbed his ears and tears sprang from his face like a burst of sweat.

He ran into the house, not even saying good-bye to Julie. The Mercedes started up with its smooth sewing machine precision, a smoothness he could not bring into Julie Clay Smith's existence, and then was gone.

❖   ❖   ❖

He spent the weekend inside his Indian self. On Saturday, he ran ten miles, beating himself against the pavement, the ankle that had caught a Chinese bullet screaming with pain and then numb to it, and later swollen from it. He spoke to no one, not even to himself. That night he took the cat's carcass, now soft and beginning to smell, and skinned it like a squirrel, cutting it under the tail and down its back legs and then pulling the skin off the meat. He buried the meat and nailed the skin to a piece of plywood, stretched out like the raccoon hides he once sold as a boy.

On Sunday he went to church. He neither sang nor prayed, but rather allowed a part of himself beyond his consciousness to search the perimeter of his spirit and communicate with God. He did not intellectualize as to whether the contact had been made. That night he got drunk, and bought a whore. It was the first time since he was eighteen that he had paid for sex. He did not speak to her after he negotiated the price, and he did not speak to himself after he left the musty stark hotel room.

On Monday he mailed Godiva's skin to Julie, care of her parents. He knew that it had already ended, but that she was a woman and needed a reason, something that would make concrete what she had been trying to explain to others about him, so he decided that he may as well get it over with. He attached a short note.

So what did you want me to do with it? You never said.

CHAPTER TWELVE

I

"MISTAH PRESIDENT. *Sah!*"

Flight Lieutenant Whiteside stood on top of the mess table at attention amid the dishes and the ashtrays, trim and bemedaled in his dress uniform. His thin, hollowed face was dominated by a dark moustache that curled up at the ends, like the villain's in the old silent films. His straight black hair was greased, and parted in the middle. He held a glass of wine in front of his chin.

Air Commodore Fitch nodded from the head table, recognizing Whiteside. "For what purpose does the gentleman rise?"

"*Sah.* I wish to propose a toast."

"Very well." Air Commodore Fitch banged his gavel. "There will be order in the mess. The gentleman has asked to propose a toast."

Flight Lieutenant Whiteside took a deep breath, summoning the depths of his vocal cords, and gave Joe Dingenfelder a glance as he began. "*Sah.* We have toasted the Queen, the President of the United States, the heads of state of the NATO countries, the King of Thailand, the various of our sister services"—he took three full seconds to say the word 'services'—"and quite frankly, *sah,* I am completely in my cups." The mess filled with laughter, and dozens of officers banged their hands on the table, a form of applause, a few of them joining in with the chant, "Here here!"

"However—" Whiteside cut their poundings short, throwing the word out like a dagger, swaying as he viewed his fellow officers around the room. "We are dining out a gentleman tonight who has given us a great deal of friendship over the past two years, a man who is as competent an engineer as any I've ever had the pleasure to serve with. With the bloody Russian buggers—"

Fitch quickly pounded his gavel, severely eyeing Whiteside. "There will be no swearing in the mess, Flight Lieutenant Whiteside. Proceed with your toast as an English gentleman, should that be possible." The mess table rippled with exuberant laughter, rattled with the further thumping of hands, and Air Commodore Fitch again banged his gavel, restoring order. "Proceed."

"Yes, *sah*." Whiteside looked wobbly on top of the table. "Where was I? Oh yes. With the—" Whiteside looked drunkenly lost for a moment, and then smiled brightly. "With the bleedin' Russian scum." He paused a moment, waiting for the air commodore's gavel, then proceeded, still smiling. "Very good, *sah*. I thought I had it." They were all laughing now. It was by far the longest toast of the evening, but the majority of the mess was intoxicated, after the predinner sherry, the succession of wines during the meal, and the string of toasts. Whiteside continued. "Anyway, with all of that, the putting of the Sputnik into orbit, the desire of the Bolsheviks to conquer space and then us, God forbid, I cannot help but feel good for the future of the free world knowing that our Captain Dingenfelder will be working on the American missile program." The entire mess joined in, pounding the several tables and shouting, "Here here." Joe Dingenfelder stared self-consciously into his plate, moved.

Whiteside continued. "So, I propose a toast. *Gentlemen!*" They all stood, raising their wineglasses into the air. "To Captain Dingenfelder! May he find a way to blow Russia off the bleedin' map!"

The mess chanted, "To Captain Dingenfelder!" and the glasses drained, then clunked back onto the tables.

"Speech! Speech!" They pounded on the tables again, calling for Dingenfelder.

Reluctantly Joe climbed on top of his chair, and then onto the table itself, feeling tipsy and exposed. He gave a small smile, peering at the lit faces of a hundred men he had worked with and lived among for two years, true professionals, more competent perhaps than even their own country could fully appreciate at this stage of its history. No, that wasn't true. Their country could appreciate them; it simply was falling over a cusp to a point where it might not be able to take full advantage of their professionalism. Rolls-Royce aircraft engines led the world, but Rolls-Royce was in trouble. The Hawker Hunter, the Vickers Valiant, the Canberras, the Gloster Javelin, the Avro Vulcan, were all world-class aircraft, but advancing technology was demanding newer versions every year, and it was not clear that Britain's lethargic economy could keep up. An image flashed in his mind as he sought words for his speech, a remembrance from World War II's shocking beginnings: the brave men of the Polish cavalry riding quixotically on horseback to their doom, in the face of modern German tanks. Would these plucky Brits someday end up that way, in the face of the competition signaled by Sputnik? He hoped not.

He looked down at his shoes, then at his friends. "As I suppose most of you have found out over the past two years, my wife is the one who likes to give the speeches." They laughed, pounding the tables; dozens of them had been exposed to Dorothy's biting, irreverent tongue by now. Joe Dingenfelder experimented with a grin, nodding his head slowly in agreement with their response, putting his hands inside his pockets and growing casual. "So, anyway, I was going to put in for an extension of duty here at Henlow, but Air Commodore Fitch wouldn't allow Dorothy to stay for another year. He said she'd organize a wives' union, and they'd take over the club." The tables were being pounded so hard that the dishes were vibrating and glasses were falling. Air Commodore Fitch was red-faced with laughter, leaning back in his chair and shaking his head.

Dingenfelder grew serious. His voice became shy, almost docile. "I'd like to thank all of you for your friendship. I'll always feel close to England, and it means a lot to me that my son has been born here. Every time I look at him I'll think of these years. You're true professionals, and it's been a privilege. Thank you."

"Here, here! Jolly good, Dingenfelder!"

He climbed down from the table and almost as soon as his feet found the ground, Air Commodore Fitch pounded the gavel one final time and the stewards cleared the last of the dishes as the men moved all the tables toward the walls, making the dining area a gymnasium floor. The sole female officer quietly disappeared, leaving the club without so much as a farewell. The games were about to begin, and there was no place in them for a woman.

"Tug of war, over here!" Air Commodore Fitch and the group captains acted as referees and judges, the British passion for intricate legality showing even in such informal sports as drunken frolic. Air Commodore Fitch carred a derringer starting gun. Dingenfelder lined up, as always, with the foreign team, little Thais, huge Norwegians, dark Greeks, pretentious, complaining Frenchmen, laughing Italians. The disjointed foreign teams never did very well against the tenacious bulldogs of Britain.

Air Commodore Fitch held a broom handle between the two groups, just above a "pull line" that had been drawn on the wooden floor. A tall Norwegian grabbed it for the foreigners, and a squat Ulster Irishman held it for the Brits, his eyes intense and his lips tight in a smile. The others fell in behind, grabbing the waist of the man in

front of them, a paradoxical sight in the grandeur of their dress uniforms.

"Ready, *pull!*"

The starter gun fired and they grunted and growled, Air Commodore Fitch leaning forward and peering at the space in between
them, his hands behind his back, measuring the inches from the pull
line. Dingenfelder held the slim waist of a Thai, the garishly ringed
fingers of a Greek around his own stomach. They strained and called
to each other, but it was no use. Soon the Brits had them over the pull
line, and Air Commodore Fitch straightened up, pointing to the British team. The others who had gathered around cheered. The reward
for the winners: free drinks, and a new group of challengers.

They played chug-a-lug, a drinking relay race, lined up again as the
"foreign team." Each man threw down a full pint of warm beer, turning the mug upside down on top of his head after draining it. Group
Captain Turner refereed (always there was a referee, an arbiter of
facts and emotions, a preserver of order, that was the British), pointing to the next man when he might begin. The Norwegians were great
beer drinkers; the poor Thais looked as if they were sipping sherry.
The foreigners lost again.

Across the room, two teams of a half-dozen men were playing catch
with a heavy leather sofa, tossing it back and forth across the room
with small running starts and loud cries of "ready, *heave!*" Another
dozen or so were playing "high cockalorum," one man standing
against a wall and others running across the room and piling on top,
piggyback style, to see how many could stay on before they all
crashed laughing to the floor. On the floor in the center of the room,
two men lay blindfolded, their wrists tied together, each free hand
holding a rolled magazine, as if it were a club. They squirmed silently
on the dusty floor in their elegant uniforms, trying to position themselves without giving the other man a clue through the movement of
their joined wrists. One man called tentatively, as required by the
game, "Moriarty, are you there?" and the other suddenly rolled, following the voice, and smashed him with the magazine again and
again. The first man fought back, creating a laughing, growling brawl.

At the edge of the room, one quiet officer, very drunk, was unfold-
ing the mess tables again, and stacking them on top of one another,
building a tower. The first two were easy. After that it took patience
and concentration. The round, bespectacled man would kneel on the
top table and drag another up the side, then actually unfold it above

him as he lay on the top table, and finally climb around the edge onto the newest top table. He spoke to no one. When Dingenfelder had first observed Flight Lieutenant Hughes perform this feat two years before, he had wondered what the shy, normally cautious man had done during the war. With such concentration, Dingenfelder had reasoned, he should have been a dam buster. Finally someone had told him that Hughes had been a Japanese prisoner in the China-Burma-India theater, at the famous camp on the River Kwai. The Japanese, the man explained dryly, had imbued in Hughes a lifelong passion for bridge-building.

The tower came crashing to the floor and Hughes fell with it, suddenly awash with bubbling laughter, rolling amid the wreckage of his little structure. A few officers stopped from their frolic and applauded him, but the others merely smiled knowingly. It was Hughes coming back from the war again. His antics were predictable, every month at dining-in.

Joe Dingenfelder stood watching the circus, glowing with good humor. He loved the very paradox of it; the stiff, formalistic public image and its riotous private counterpart. It was as if he had been let in on a special secret, kept from an undeserving, judgmental world.

"It's a disgrace, isn't it, Captain?" The American commanding officer from nearby Churchton Air Force Base, a joint American-British facility, had come to his first RAF dining-in as a farewell gesture to Dingenfelder. He had grown visibly disgusted during the toasting period following the dinner, watching the officers grow convivially drunk, and had declined several invitations to participate in the games.

"No, sir. It's their way of unwinding, that's all." Dingenfelder downed his beer and smiled as a tall, red-haired Irishman climbed onto the mantel above the glowing fire and began reciting poetry by William Butler Yeats, the poet laureate of the Irish republic. He was being rather politely jeered.

"Well, it's not *our* way." It was a judgment, not on the British, but on Dingenfelder. The colonel peered into Dingenfelder's drunken face. "Frankly, Captain, I'm ashamed of you."

"Eh, *wot?*"

Wing Commander Calhoun, the lecherous old Scot, Dorothy's former pursuer, had drifted behind the Americans, probably to eavesdrop on the conversation. He now stood in front of the surprised colonel, his curving moustache and gray eyes giving his face a warlike avidity. "Begging the colonel's pardon, sir, what has this"—he gestured almost contemptuously toward Dingenfelder—"this mild-mannered imitation of a *true* pub crawler done to make you ashamed?"

Calhoun's rich, echoing voice caused a half-dozen others to turn and watch. The colonel swallowed uneasily. He was an unmuscled man with flitting eyes and a sagging chin. He had small hands. He did not like controversy. He swallowed again, and cleared his throat. "I only meant—" He thought about it some more, probably wondering how this incident would be described on his fitness report when the embassy found out about his insult to the Brits. "I wasn't passing judgment on your games. Actually, I only meant that we are here more as observers than participants, that was all."

Several catcalls floated toward the embarrassed colonel. Wing Commander Calhoun towered over him, his eyebrows furled in mock seriousness, imperiously studying the colonel's averted eyes. "Perhaps it's because you haven't found your own game, Colonel. See here—" Calhoun walked over and stood next to one of Hughes's fallen tables. "I'm going to show you something, and I'll give you ten pounds if you can do it. Ten pounds, Colonel. That's about twenty-five Yankee dollars. Here. Watch this."

Calhoun lay flat on top of the table, hooking his large feet over one end, then signaled two other officers to raise that end. Up it went, until the table was perpendicular to the ground, and Calhoun was hanging by his toes, his head inches from the floor. He rested his elbows on the table, his hands comfortably underneath his chin, and stared at the American colonel. "See here? Nothing to it, Colonel." Finally they lowered him again. "All right. Your turn."

The colonel walked slowly toward the table. A dozen RAF officers now watched, holding back their smiles. He lay flat on the table, tentatively hooking his toes over one end, as Calhoun had done. They began to raise him and his unsteady eyes grew round with fear. Finally he was perpendicular to the ground, though, and his whole face brightened with accomplishment.

"I'm doing it! Hey, I'm doing it!"

Two officers jogged up, each carrying a seltzer bottle, and squirted soda water down his trouser legs as he screamed with surprise. He fell crashing to the floor and three others immediately grabbed him, laying him flat, and rolled him tight as tape inside a huge Persian rug, completely paralyzing his movement. Then they stood the rug in a corner. Only the colonel's head showed at its top, abandoned and forlorn, as if he were part of a war trophy from some expedition to the colonies.

Calhoun took a collection from the other officers, and finally presented Dingenfelder with ten pounds. Dingenfelder walked to the colonel and stuck the money inside the rolled carpet, underneath his chin. The colonel attempted, just for a moment, to appear officious.

"Captain, get me out of here! I don't want that money, stop it! *Get me out of here!*"

"Sorry, sir." Dingenfelder walked away, accepting another beer. "Like you said, we're just here as observers. I wouldn't want to meddle in the affairs of the Royal Air Force."

* * *

They were such fun, the Brits, such a mix of spunk and propriety. He would miss it all, the formal work environment, the curious, stratified economy that created such anomalies as having to shop at the stationery store for everything from newspapers to Dorothy's sanitary napkins because it all came under "paper," the open-air markets on Saturdays at Hitchin, the blackout curtains and wooden shutters that still dressed the windows of his home in case of air attack, the wonderful ambassadorial feeling from being the only American at the base.

But on October 4, 1957, while he had peacefully driven to work through the bicycles and dogwoods of the English countryside, the plodding peasants of the Soviet Union, the people who had marched 7 million soldiers to their deaths in World War II, sometimes preferring to expend a legion of men before losing a truck or a tank, the trucks and tanks themselves quite often donated to their cause by the United States, had launched Sputnik I into orbit, sending waves of fear and humiliation through the free world. And less than a month later, Sputnik II had thrown a payload of more than a thousand pounds circling the earth, replete with a space dog named Laika.

The United States had been caught dallying, and was faced with the prospect of losing a technological war that might leave the free nations of the world at the mercy of missile delivery systems that could not be countered. In December of that year, only five months before Dingenfelder's last dining-in at Henlow, the United States Navy had failed miserably in its attempt to put a four-pound payload into orbit on the nose of a Vanguard missile, the missile blowing up on the launching pad. The headlines, appearing ironically on December 7, had proclaimed a new Pearl Harbor for the country, this time in the area of technology. In January 1958, an Army team from Huntsville, Alabama, led by German expatriot Wernher von Braun, successfully launched Explorer I, a thirty-pound payload that achieved orbit. It was good news, but for the first time since World War II the country was truly afraid. America was gearing up for the space war, no holds barred, no cost spared, and Joe Dingenfelder was going to be a part of it. In a perverted way, it was a dream come true.

When it came time to leave England, Air Commodore Fitch threw a large dinner party for Joe and Dorothy at a restaurant in Letchworth called the Georgia Dragon, and after dinner the doting old officer insisted that they come by his house for nightcaps. When they finally returned to their own home they found the whole crew, several dozen officer friends and their wives, waiting inside. The friends had parked their cars at a pub down the road, and turned every piece of furniture in the house upside down. Dorothy's shrieks upon entering the house were greeted by a raucous *"Surprise!"*, people appearing from behind upturned couches and from inside closets and even from the dank cold of the haunted basement. In a few minutes a cherubically grinning Air Commodore Fitch arrived, and they partied again, drinking and singing until the heavy fog outside took on a scintillating gray, the English version of a sunrise.

II

Los Angeles was like a melody, alluring and exciting, one that she had never before heard. The city sang to her of home, of contentment. She immediately loved it, all of it, the palm trees and freeways and even the smog that she could taste on her tongue and feel like salt in her eyes. She embraced the smog. It became a symbol of her yearning. It was a new phenomenon, just as Los Angeles itself was, a peculiarly American substance making a lid over a new, dynamic culture. It hung like an amber mist on the skyline, a hazy umbrella over millions of people. The thought of so many people, most of them new to California, gathered in one place, creating a totally fresh style and value system, hit her like the first shot of water given one who had survived the desert. *Finally, finally! This is me, this is where I belong!* She watched sprawling houses from the freeway, and the parched mountains to the east, and the people inside their cars, and thought she saw it, everywhere: Los Angeles had delivered them from the drudgery and the rigid culture of Peoria and Queens. They dressed casually. They drove convertibles. They had suntans and they all looked as if they lived on the beach.

North of Los Angeles they drove into the mountains and then along the sea. Her feeling of deliverance disappeared, abandoned her, and Joe started talking again about this place called Burton Mesa. It had sounded exotic a few days before, but it was becoming more and more threatening as the smog and the self-satisfied city dwellers fell behind the horizon. Joe had researched it, of course, and had become an expert on its history. So the miles clicked off and he unfolded his arsenal of tidbits, and she felt as if she were heading off in a covered wagon toward a frontier outpost.

They passed through Santa Barbara, a palm-lined oasis, and then broke into rough, winding mountain roads, seventy-five miles of wilderness. Little Joe grew woozy on her lap and repeatedly threw up. Natasha howled in the back seat. And Joe calmly recited his facts, his trivia about Burton Mesa—the Japanese current along the beach that kept the water icy and the rip tides treacherous, the fog so thick that an entire squadron of Navy destroyers once had steamed into the rocks at Point Arguello and unanimously sank, the surrounding hills that boxed Burton Mesa in from three sides, against the sea. He went on about deer and lynx and bobcat, rattlesnakes and seals and cormorants. He sounded professorial as he mentioned the eighty-six thousand acres claimed by the Army for a training base during World War II, Burton Mesa becoming Camp Cooke, where three armored divisions and two infantry divisions had trained, and how the Air Force had recently chosen the abandoned base for its operational missile squadrons. The rugged isolation allowed missile launching pads to be dispersed. The shots would go over the Pacific, eliminating overflight dangers from unpredictable launches. Its relative nearness to defense contractors operating out of Los Angeles made it ideal.

Ideal for the Air Force, anyway. They drove up and down brown mountains, past scrub oak and mesquite and manzanita, and finally at the top of one brushy hill she saw the chain-link fence topped with barbed wire that marked the base perimeter. On the other side were hundreds of abandoned yellow buildings left from World War II, and then new, red roads scratched into the mud, and bulldozers working, and a mass of skeletal structures that would be new homes. They sat on treeless, grassless plots, half-built and forlorn.

It was August 1958. Soon Camp Cooke would be renamed Vandenberg Air Force Base. Thousands of personnel would come pouring in from Air Force installations around the world, making a Gold Rush town on the mesa. But it would always be isolated, and at that moment it was stark and raw, abounding with ugliness.

The HELL with this! I'm going back to Los Angeles! "Let me out of this car! I demand that you let me out!"

"What do you mean, 'Let you out of this car'? Dorothy, we're in the middle of nowhere. Calm down!"

She stared out at the edges of the base as the car made yet another slow turn on the narrow, winding road, the car swaying, the road dropping off on the left or the right, little Joseph crying and throwing up from motion sickness, Natasha yelling now and then merely for effect, searching Dorothy's reactions with dark wondering eyes. Dorothy had expected *something* at the end of the ride, a reward of sorts, if not an oasis then at least a community. But here they were and the reward for a journey through wilderness was wilderness; no, an unhappy bracketing, decay on one side and raw beginnings on the other, with nothing in the middle. *Nothing.*

"*I'm not going in there!* This is it, Joe Dingenfelder. This is the end. I'm *not* going to live in this place! Oh, my God, I think I'm going to throw up."

"Dorothy, you haven't even seen it yet."

Little Joe began howling again. His chest was streaked with vomit. He needed to be changed. She picked him up from his car bed in the back seat. "If you don't let me out of this car, I'm going to throw this baby out of the window."

Joe pulled the car over to the side of the road. The main gate was less than a quarter mile away, a little white sentry post left over from the World War II Army days. He turned to her, the strain of the drive having deepened the wrinkles at the corners of his eyes. He spoke softly, as he always did, gesturing toward the empty road, the rolling hills of scrub and thistle, the sentry post where the lone air policeman now watched them with what might have been anxious curiosity, a reprieve from boredom.

"Shall I call you a cab?"

She dumped little Joe onto the seat. He whined softly, exhausted. She slammed the car door and began walking along the narrow road. The summer wind was brisk, coming from the sea. Her hands touched her thighs as she walked, an unconscious gesture that allowed him to peer secretly into her uncertainty, her unannounced awareness of their heaviness, then she clasped her arms around her chest, fending off the chill. She strode almost purposefully away from him, her shoes kicking up loose curtains of dust and mashing down spikes of dark green ice plant. A car came from the other direction and slowed down. Two men stared at her, covetous looks. They were airmen from the base. Their unsmiling faces petrified her.

She stopped walking and stood halfway between the car and the gate, her arms still around her chest as if she were embracing herself, looking inside the fence. In the distance she could see the mounds and ditches of raw, red earth and the bulldozers flattening out new housing plots. Dear old Senator Capehart. He had indeed gotten his name into a housing development. Soon hundreds of Capehart homes would scar the hillside, and if she stayed she would be one of his blessed tenants.

"Want a ride?" Joe had followed her in the car, and now leaned over, calling from the open window on her side. "I could at least take you to the bus stop. I would imagine they have a bus stop. Either that or they will have one when—"

"Joe, you can't laugh this away. Not anymore." She still faced away from the car, staring out at the base. Far away, off to her left, old yellow mobilization buildings from World War II stood amid a stand of eucalyptus trees. And just in front of her were the acres and acres of those God-awful Capehart homes. "I've picked sand out of my teeth in Texas, swatted mosquitoes in Florida, lived next to a cornfield in Illinois, and sipped tea with the ladies in England. I'm not doing it anymore. It's got to stop, Joe. You've got to think about *me* for a change. Is there something wrong with doing that?"

"Dorothy. Come on." His voice was soft, persuasive. "At least get back inside the car. Huh?"

She turned around toward the car. Natasha was looking at her from the back window with eyes that had always known too much, reading her, her small dark head tilted in an unspoken question. It always made her uneasy to look at Natasha when she and Joe were arguing. Perhaps it was simply Natasha's reaction to her. Perhaps it was simply Natasha.

"Come on." Joe gestured to her seat in the car. "Get in, please?"

She opened the door and picked up little Joe. He was sleeping. His eyes rolled for one quick second as she put his head on her shoulder, then he fell back into his exhausted slumber. "All right. Now what?"

"I love you."

"Well, I don't love you. Not enough to go through this again." She peered out of the window. "I'm *leaving*, Joe. I'm getting out of this. I feel like my life is getting away from me. Oh, for God's sake. You talk about putting a man on the moon? Who needs the moon when you can come live at Cooke Air Force Base? Well, I've had it."

Joe watched her almost involuntarily stroke the baby's small back, and then he looked west, searching for the horizon, feeling a surging elation that was so fundamental and deep that it was as clear in his brain as a shout. Six miles away the crags and rocks fell into the rough sea and somewhere along that wilderness men were pouring concrete, erecting blockhouses, preparing to penetrate the outer edges of man's knowledge. He was going to be a part of it. He would be a pioneer. "Do you realize what we're going to be doing, Dorothy? Can you appreciate that?"

"We? Oh, I like that. Who is 'we'? You and your buddies. Do you realize what *I'm* going to be doing?" She watched him closely. He must have studied Chiang Kai-shek, she thought almost humorously, remembering her own readings at Radcliffe. *When in doubt, do nothing*. Joe was becoming a master at offsetting her moods with mere delay. But this was it. "You're just going to have to make a decision, Joe. Which is more important, your missiles or your marriage? Because I've already made mine. Either we leave, or I leave. I am definitely getting out of the Air Force."

"You should at least give it a chance."

She had managed to light a cigarette without disturbing little Joe. She laughed. "Give it a chance? I've given it five *years* of chances. I'll tell you what, Joe. You give *me* five years of chances. How's that? Because I'm going back to work, Joe. Don't ask me what I'll be doing, because I don't know. And don't ask me to feel guilty. I'm just done staying at home. *You* stay at home for a while."

That somehow seemed to satisfy Joe, perhaps because of its absurdity. *Ah, yes. The little woman's high strung, with all this moving.* He put the car back into gear and slowly drove toward the main gate of the base. A sign had been erected above the sentry post: "U.S. AIR FORCE. PEACE IS OUR PROFESSION." The air policeman noticed the officer sticker on the car's front bumper and waved them through, saluting Joe. It appeared as though he were suppressing a voyeur's sardonic grin. Dorothy scowled at him. Following the airman's gaze toward the back seat, she noticed Natasha looking at the man with an identical scowl.

Joe turned at a sign marked Ocean View Boulevard, and drove along a dirt road edged with freshly poured concrete, which in time would become the boulevard. Half-built homes sat on red, bulldozed yards as if adrift on a scummy sea, hundreds upon hundreds of them. He turned again at a sign marked Korina Avenue and followed it down a steep hill past other frames. Finally he stopped, turning off the car's engine and gesturing grandly to a boxy unit with a flat roof, undistinguishable from every other Capehart dwelling. "Home sweet home. They'll be ready in about a month. They're really pretty nice. We'll have three bedrooms, a dishwasher, our own yard, and even a garage!" She had not so much as glanced at him. "And look, you can see the ocean." It was true. Six miles away a tiny triangle of the Pacific showed itself, from between two sloping hills.

Finally she spoke, the knives out of her words, replaced with a flat calm. "You told me six years, Joe. Remember? You've got one year left on your obligation to the Air Force. All right, I'll give you a year, Joe. One year."

✻ ✻ ✻

The dank smell of a relit cigar. A roaring laugh, just before he turned the corner into the office. A ragged, pink finger, gray along its edges, sitting inside a jar of formaldehyde at the center of the desk. On the wall, the mournful fat man with elephantiasis of the gonads, staring down at a sack that stretched from his chair to the floor. *THIS MAN HAS BALLS.*

Colonel Henry Pattakos. His very self.

"Get in here, Dingenfelder!"

"Yes, sir. Captain Dingenfelder, reporting as ordered, sir."

"Ha *haaa,* well, goddamn." The colonel returned Joe's salute with one of those perfunctory eyebrow grabs and jumped up from his chair, pumping his hand with glee. "I thought you might have defected to the Royal Air Force by now."

"No, sir. They told me that, with my background, they'd put me into their Thor training program and send me to Vandenberg."

"Pretty good comeback, Dingenfelder. You always did have a sense of humor." Pattakos slapped his thigh and lit his cigar again, the thick column of tobacco jutting out of his black moustache like a cannon from a bushy camouflage. "Well, let me tell you something, Captain Joe, you are one lucky Jew!" Pattakos laughed at Dingenfelder's quick surprise. "Oh, yeah! And you know why you're so lucky? Think about it."

Dingenfelder retained his casual position of attention in front of his old boss from Scott Air Force Base. "Well, I can think of a lot of reasons." He studied Pattakos, grinning shrewdly. "The first of which is that I get to watch you raise holy hell, without getting fried in the process. Sir."

"Well, that's part of it." Pattakos gave off one of those deep, melodic laughs again, as if the whole thing were at once important and also wonderfully absurd. "The other part of it is that I don't know a goddamn thing about missiles! And for that matter, neither does anybody else!"

Pattakos rose from his chair and looked out from the rundown World War II building that contained his office, across a small field of scraggly thatched grass, toward the scrub-filled mesa that led down to the sea. The land was lost in a morning fog that rivaled London's. The fog poured in from the sea every morning, rolling down hillsides with the heavy motion of water itself, splashing and curling at the bottoms. But by noon on Burton Mesa, the dry wind and the sun melted the fog away.

"Just think of it, Dingenfelder! I've been in this business for twenty years. Twenty years—that's nothing more than a blip on God's radar screen, *blip*, and yet I've gone from flying *biplanes* in my primary training, all the way through jets. I'll tell you, I was beginning to feel old. I thought I'd done it all, fighters, cargo planes, bombers, jets. No fooling, I was starting to get bored. Then SAC pulled me off for this program. They just took over the First Missile Division." Pattakos shrugged, as if apologizing. "It makes sense. Strategic Air Command—missiles are strategic, and they go into the air. So, now we're going to be shooting missiles! I'm so excited I can hardly shut up about it." Pattakos turned back to Dingenfelder, his dark face beaming. "And you're so lucky you should be puking with joy. In a few months, Dingenfelder, you're going to know more about the Atlas missile than anyone in the entire United States Air Force."

"The Atlas, sir?" He had read about it. The first truly intercontinental ballistic missile system, a weapon that the United States could actually aim at Russia from a California launching pad, a thin-skinned, fragile steel structure eight stories high that you blew up like a balloon, filling it with liquid fuel. It had a range of more than six thousand miles, and a loaded weight of a quarter of a million pounds. The Air Force had never shot one before.

"We're taking them over, like ASAP. Convair has had them for a couple years, dinking around down at Cape Canaveral, blowing them up on the pad. We've got to make them work. We're playing catch-up ball, and everybody's nervous. SAC wants operational, manned sites with nukes pointing at the Russians. Convair's moving out here, they've got the prime contract. General Electric is doing the guidance systems. Rocketdyne's got the engines. SAC just activated the 675th Strategic Missile Squadron to sit side by side with the contractors. They've got people down in the plants undergoing training right now. We've got people out there building the launch pads, too. We're going to figure it all out, and then we're going to run the show, just like we fly our own planes." Pattakos' enthusiasm was unbounded, and infectious. Joe Dingenfelder found himself wanting to do something, anything, right then, just to demonstrate he was a part of it.

"So, what are we doing, Colonel? I mean, you and I? You're Director of Materiel, sir?"

Pattakos threw both arms into the air, embracing the entire base and everything in it. "We represent SAC out here. We're the direct liaison. If we don't sign off on a site or a piece of equipment, SAC doesn't accept it from the contractor. We make sure that SAC gets everything it's supposed to get when it buys off on the combat-ready missiles. We make sure that it all works, that the Air Force can operate and maintain it." He waved toward the window. Outside, beyond the morning fog, missile crews and support mechanisms were erecting their facilities all over Burton Mesa. "We have to follow everything; supply mechanisms, maintenance, transportation, technical data on the missile, training programs. We're going to be the brains of SAC on this one, Dingenfelder, and you're a lucky son of a bitch, I'll tell you." Pattakos walked across the room and exuberantly beat Dingenfelder on the back. "You're the Atlas Technical Evaluation Officer for the whole goddamn Strategic Air Command, what do you think about that?"

"Good, sir." Dingenfelder smiled wanly, his insides churning with mission and excitement, trying to look somewhat dignified as Pattakos beat his back again and again. "So where would you like me to start?"

Pattakos waved absently into the air. "I got you for this job because you're the smartest guy I know. Don't ruin it by asking stupid questions." He almost shouted, so great was his enchantment with a task so large and necessary and unknown that a man with the talent of Joe Dingenfelder could start anywhere he wanted and not be wrong. "You're my bird dog. Just go on out and make yourself an expert on the missile! Wherever the contractors go, follow them like a shadow. When they meet, go to their meetings. When they read, ask for a copy of their book. Talk to the engineers, the scientists, the goddamn guy who's driving the tractor that carries materials to build the block houses!" He patted Dingenfelder on the back again, sending him out the door. "Go buy us a missile that'll blow up Russia. In a month, I'll be expecting you to tell *me* what needs to be done."

* * *

He drove along an old tank trail, its dirt bed made into a brittle washboard by years of winter rain that came in quick torrents, creating gullies that led toward the sea. A jungle of weeds and scrub grew like thatch along its edges, dry and matted, making him wonder for a mile or so whether he was lost. The sun was high, and a sparrow hawk flitted across it several times, gliding, looking for small game. He rounded a bend and a mountain lion moved away from him with a slow dignity, staying twenty feet in front of the car, wheat-colored and heavy pawed, its large muscles swaying and casually rippling at that slow pace as if it were burdened by a lack of challenge. Finally it broke off into the brush. Jackrabbits flitted and scurried across the road. A deer broke cover underneath a scrub oak where it had lain at rest, bounding across the field with little jumps, as if it were a gazelle. He was city-born and raised, and the wildlife made him uneasy. If he were indeed lost, he might have to spend a night in his car. Would they ever find him?

Bivouacs from World War II training encampments appeared and fell behind him as he drove, old fighting holes mixing inside long stands of eucalyptus trees, their high pale branches holding dry leaves covered with dust. Finally in the quiet he could hear the sea, roaring and pounding on a craggy shore. His heart quickened. As he approached the sea, he could discern the motorous digs and surges of heavy equipment. The car crawled down into a dry arroyo and when it came over the other side he saw the sea. Clumps of ice plant grew down steep bluffs and mounds of reddish sand dunes. Over to his right, toward him from the bluffs, was the Atlas site. Earth movers were everywhere, churning up dust.

In the middle of it all was a mass of concrete two football fields long and fifty yards wide and several stories high. It was as curious and out of place in this wilderness as a Sphinx uncovered in the desert.

He parked the car next to it and walked around it. Underneath the foundation were the beginnings of a huge basement that would soon house several fuel tanks, each one larger than a railroad car. They would hold liquid oxygen and kerosene and liquid nitrogen, the stuff that made the Atlas go. Other gaping holes would later be filled with plumbing and launch-pad support equipment. A disked, steel flame bucket, several stories high, curved down toward the sea. When the Atlas was launched, the flame bucket would absorb and redirect the heat from engines giving off three hundred thousand pounds of thrust, and would be washed by thirty thousand gallons of water a minute, from cooling pumps that would preserve the bucket's steel. The foundation would also provide a launch stand, with a gantry tower to support the missile until ready for launch, and tracks where the tower could be wheeled in and out.

Staring at the raw concrete with its mass of metal tubes protruding as if they were veins from an organ that had been ripped out of a living body, Joe Dingenfelder could visualize the finished site, the launch, the huge missile soaring up with a bright flame three times as long as the missile itself, the beauty, the perfection, the triumph of the scientific mind. He no longer saw the wilderness. He did not see the awesome difficulties of the coming months. He saw himself, watching the missile go, feeling that he was its creator and its master.

This sort of chance only happened once in your life. Dorothy would have to understand that.

CHAPTER THIRTEEN

I

SHE TWISTED, OH, SHE ROLLED, her head turning one way and then the other, her bare arms out on the rumpled sheets as if she were a martyr, suddenly along his sides, scratching, and then digging into his buttocks. She called to him, her hair like clouds on the bed, the very bed where Julie Clay Smith had once primly offered him her passion wrapped up in a perfunctory ball of duty. She bit him, she kissed him, she moaned. She drew it out of him and he shuddered over her, pounding her with the pulsing of his body.

And then it was over and he rolled away from her, not quite disliking her but simply wishing she would leave. Julie Clay had fallen in love with love and used him as the object, the conduit, until his harsh reality had driven her away, back into her bookish view of it; the dry, safe, unchallenging demonstrations of pure affection. Someday, he mused again, now stroking this latest replacement's dark hair, Julie will find a dry, safe, unchallenging man, and she will marry him. He will defer to her, take her only on her own terms, maybe even run for the goddamn Senate. A storybook prince come alive. A piece of cardboard.

But he had been the object, the conduit in an abstract sense, and now he used objects. It was different from what had happened to him, almost the flip side, but it was the same, really, because at the bottom of it was the same refusal to love, Julie's because she loved the idea and didn't know how to love the man, his because he had tried love and come away scorched and twisted inside, hating himself, and had decided to try and love the idea.

"Oh, Ju-u-udd, that was terrific."

"Yeah, it was. It was really good." He almost didn't remember her name. He was pretty sure it was Sharon, but it could have been Sherry. He decided it was Sharon, but he avoided any mention of it, in case he was wrong.

She kissed his chest, rubbing his stomach with her hand. She wanted more. That was always the problem, wanting more. It was never enough because it didn't mean anything. "I never thought it could be this good." She had small breasts and a tight stomach and slim hips. "Judd, does it bother you that I'm married?"

"No." He reached to the end table and found a cigarette, lighting it, for a moment viewing the starkness of a room that had once been filled with antiques, impressionistic paintings, and heavy wood furniture. All gone, like the days of Julie's discontent. "I believe I've probably been involved in more triangles than Pythagoras himself."

"Pythagoras? I don't get it."

His eyes began to roll and he stopped them because she was watching his face. "I didn't think you would."

She stared at the ceiling with dark eyes, one finger pressed into a cheek. "I've heard of Casanova. Is that what you mean?"

He chuckled sardonically, shaking his head. He wished again that she would leave. "No, that wasn't what I meant. Forget it, all right?" He wanted to call her Sharon but he wasn't sure. Maybe if I call her Sherry she'll leave, he thought.

"You probably think I'm dumb. Do you think I'm dumb?"

"I don't think you're dumb, Sherry, it's just—"

"—Sharon." It hadn't even fazed her.

"It's from geometry."

"It is?" She still rubbed his stomach. She watched him with delighted eyes. "What is?"

"*Pythagoras.* Forget it."

The way he said it stiffened her, caused her to withdraw from him and contemplate him from a foot away with puzzled eyes. "You can be so cold, Judd. You just turn it on and turn it off. Sometimes it really hurts."

"Well, nobody told you to keep putting up with it."

"Do you want me to leave? That's it, isn't it? You've got what you wanted, and it's time for me to leave. Throw me away like you flush a rubber down the toilet. Is that it, Judd?"

"Sort of." She jumped from the bed, her small breasts bouncing, their purple nipples gathered like prunes. She began dressing. He felt immediately sorry, that dark nimbus of anger now turning into himself. "Hey, I was only kidding, Sharon. I'm sorry."

"No, you're not." She watched him in the weak, pale light that came from the hallway. Just around the corner, little Loretta used to laugh and call to him. He missed her and the echoing ghosts of her giggles bounced along the empty walls. He *was* sorry, that was the truth, but he did want Sharon to leave. How could he explain that she was an interloper, trouncing on the gardens of his past?

"I am. I really am sorry." He tapped the ash from his cigarette into an overflowing ashtray, his sheets now gathered around his chest. "You've been really sweet, and my mind just got onto other things, that's all."

"What do you want out of life, Judd Smith?" She had snapped her bra back on, and was looking at him from inside a wreath of gorgeous black hair, tangled from her passion, her sweater clutched against her. It was she who was waxing philosophic now. "Have you ever thought about that?"

He grinned, tapping his cigarette and staring back at her. "My secret wish?"

"All right. Yeah. Your secret wish."

"My secret wish is that when I die, all of the women I've ever loved will come to the funeral and gather at my graveside and say wonderful things about me. They'd all meet each other for the first time and congratulate each other on their taste. Maybe they'd even compare notes." He was smiling widely now, his eyes on the ceiling. "Ah, what a beautiful sight that would be!"

Her sweater was on, as was her skirt. She held her nylons in one hand, preparing to stuff them into her purse. She stopped at his bedroom door, shaking her head with a mote of pity. "Well, I'll keep my eyes on the obituary page, then. So long, Judd."

"Wear red."

"Huh?"

"Red. Wear red. Black is such a depressing color."

She sighed, as if helpless from his commands. "All right, Judd. I'll wear red."

He put out his cigarette, giving her an inviting look that made her smile. "But if I'm not dead by next week, call me."

She lowered her chin, grinning back with a sultry promise. "All right, Judd. I'll call you."

*　*　*

You don't have to run your truck into a wall or stuff yourself with sleeping pills to be committing suicide.

In fact, you don't even have to be wanting to die. All it takes is for the moment to be so unbearable that you'll purchase any ticket, take any voyage, to escape, never mind where. Never even mind how long. *Just get me past this moment.*

Sometimes he found it in the brown burn of straight whiskey, taking it right out of the bottle, warm and mean like scalding water as it coursed his esophagus and splashed, firelike, in his abdomen. If he drank it fast enough and had enough of it, the floating falsity, the hypocrisy of its good will, carried him away from his dark moods and put him in his very own padded cell, a sterile world without joy, yes, but without pain, either. Then in the morning his head ached so badly and his body was so nauseated and weak, disgusted with him, that the other pains were still defeated, successfully avoided by his very misery.

Sometimes he found it by running, the pain of the pavement pushing on his old wounds and overriding all the other hurt until he could not focus on his spirit anymore, only on what the exertion was doing to his body. He ran and ran. He was in great shape, everyone agreed.

Often he found it in women; bar girls, secretaries, schoolteachers, stewardesses, other people's wives, *they love me, they all love me, and if they all love me you made a mistake, Julie Clay, it was you.* His life had become a litany of dark nights in other people's beds, waking up wordless, disappointed that it came so easy, afraid of what it would do to him if he exposed himself again to something beyond what he perceived as body worship. It was nihilistic, it was sad. He was a turtle with its head and legs inside its shell, skidding and bouncing down a rocky slope, the slope that Julie Clay had kicked him over. No, that was too harsh; the slope over which he had by his very nature teetered, and she had by hers allowed him to fall. But he was bouncing and rolling, touching no one, and no one was allowed to reach inside that shell and touch him.

He found it, easily and at will, in his job. He was a hunter, a stalker, from his earliest mountain days. It was a trait that had helped him in his relentless pursuit of women, one that had made him among the best of his lot in war. He had no fear of death, none whatsoever anymore. Not that he ever consciously considered dying; it just didn't come up. Happily Ever After was gone. His wife, the only woman he had ever loved, the source of his aspirations to normality, had abandoned him, was even afraid of him. His daughter would grow up as a stranger. Sometimes he would sit and wish that he had tasted this irresolvable disappointment before he had gone to war, because it would have kept him from believing in either the bad part of war or the good part of what awaited him when he returned. War would have just been life. Accelerated, impacted, but simply life. And that was what working for the FBI had become; a simple intense version of life. The good guys were here, the bad guys were over there, sometimes you got them and less often they got you. And whichever way it went, at night unless you were lucky you ended up alone.

II

"All right, Smith, what the hell are you up to now?"

Vernon Drought stood in the doorway of their little office in the sultry afternoon heat, looking gray and somewhat worn under the fluorescent lights. He perpetually smoked a fat cigar from the center of his mouth, as if it were a fixture. Judd Smith had never seen Drought without a cigar. It was his partner's trademark. Drought smiled with an ironic expectation, his large eyes the color of a rain cloud under a bald, wrinkled forehead, gray hair cut short above the temples. He carried a gray felt hat. He wore a rumpled gray suit. He looked old enough to be Judd Smith's father, and he sometimes treated Smith as a recalcitrant son.

"What am I doing? Exterminating flies." Smith chuckled, leaning away from his small metal government desk and pointing to the floor fan. "Actually I'm conducting an experiment." Flies buzzed slowly around the room in the lazy summer heat of 1960. The world was secure. Red Lesczynski would soon return from sea duty in the Mediterranean, for assignment with the prestigious Blue Angels. Joe Dingenfelder was shooting missiles into the sky, on the cutting edge of modern science. And Judd Smith was still in Newark, New Jersey, catching crooks and killing flies. "Look at all these goddamn flies, Vern."

Drought sat heavily into his desk chair. "So? It's July. What did you expect, a room full of penguins?" He pulled out a sheaf of folders from his gray briefcase. "Look at this. Did you ever go to Miami, Smith?" He held up a brochure from some company called Florida Development.

"Yeah, I went to Miami once. With you, don't you remember? The Enrico case. I hate Miami. All you've got in Miami are Cubans getting away from Castro and old folks getting away from the fact they're going to die. Christ, I felt like I needed a spatula walking along Miami Beach, so I could turn over all the old bone bags that were frying themselves on the lawn chairs. So, don't tell me. You and the wife are going to retire in Miami."

Drought hesitated, staring at the waterfront home on the front of the brochure like an alcoholic trying to turn down a free drink. "Well, we been thinking about it. What's the alternative, staying in Newark? Moving to New York City? Hey. New York City is the only place in the world where the pigeons mug the other pigeons, and the way you figure out winter is the dog shit just froze on the sidewalks. I can go to Miami, not have to worry about heating bills or winter clothes. And what's the big deal about Cubans? There's more Puerto Ricans in New York City than they got in whatever that town is down there, Rio—"

"—San Juan."

"Yeah. And the niggers are everywhere, you're not going to get away from them." Drought rubbed his fleshy face and shook his head slowly. "Six more months, that's all." He was a tough, methodical man, but the cigar gave him an almost childish look, as if he were sucking on a pacifier.

Judd Smith nodded, commiserating. "If anybody ever earned a government pension in his life, you have, Vern. You've been in more cesspools than a whole army of roaches."

Drought's eyebrows raised in agreement, his lips tight around his cigar, giving him a startled appearance. "I've seen my share of the sick side of life. Yeah, I'll go down to Miami, Smith, and you come down every now and then and flip me over with your spatula."

Judd slowly rose from his chair, his eyes intent on a moving speck in the air. He lifted his hand slowly, almost imperceptible in its movement, until it was in front of his face. Then, as if he were a boxer shooting out a jab, Smith caught a fly, and cupped it gleefully in his hand as he moved behind the floor fan. Drought watched him all the while, his nose squinched as if a sudden stink had permeated the room. "What the hell you doing?"

"I told you. I'm running an experiment." Smith tossed the fly into the back end of the fan, and watched on the other side of the blades to see if it emerged. It didn't. "Eight to two."

"What do you mean, 'eight to two'?"

"I've tossed ten flies into the ass end of that fan this afternoon, and two have actually made it through the blades and flown out the other side." Smith stared at the fan with a philosophic profundity. "Those were two tough flies, Vernon. Either that, or they've got Somebody up there liking them."

"So what are you trying to do, breed Superfly? Those studs that made it through the fan are going to go out and perpetuate a bunch of armor-plated fan killers." Drought grunted. "We got enough trouble with flies. I'll tell you Smith, for an Annapolis man sometimes I don't think you're very smart."

The phone rang and Drought took the call, holding the black receiver into his ear with a heavy shoulder, the mouthpiece settling into his jowl as if it were pushed into mashed potatoes, partially submerged. He was like a doctor as he asked questions and took notes, his gravelly voice a patient monotone, each question as relevant as a trial lawyer's, narrowing down the parameters of his mission.

Judd Smith watched Drought query and scrawl, and automatically inspected the chamber of his .38 Smith and Wesson revolver, counting the bullets, ensuring that the primer on each one was smooth rather than having been dented by a firing pin, indicating a spent round. It was a perfunctory habit, almost a superstition. He had never left a spent round in his weapon, but checking it gave him a necessary mood, in the same way that putting a working collar on a sentry dog makes it intent on the dreadful aspects of its training. Much of his work was interrogations, the gathering of evidence, the mundane paperwork of any profession. But Drought was talking arrest, the buzzwords of violence being repeated and jotted down; murder, unlawful flight, escaping federal custody, robbery. The older man's conversation indicated that a warrant had already been issued. Judd Smith was suddenly high on fear; not death fear, but the fear that he might fail in his job and allow this slimy bastard to get away.

Drought hung up the phone. He spoke with clipped authority as he stood up. "Okay, Navy Cross. Okay, hotshot." He grabbed his hat. "Looks like we got that prick Wayne McCoy taking a little nap at the Turnpike Inn."

The Newark summer beckoned all the odious parts of life. It emanated a gaseous heat, the air heavy with the discharge of a hundred refinery smokestacks until it mixed streaks of gray and amber, hovering over a brown and churlish landscape. They drove past decaying houses that seemed to have imploded from anger and loss of hope, past groups of people on broken porches, peering through faces scarred and wrinkled from years of amorphous hate. Newark always reminded Judd Smith of a pile of dry, useless sawdust, waiting for a match, or maybe even a small, stray spark, to set off an explosion.

Night crawled along the eastern sky, chasing sundown into the stink of the smokestacks. They exited their car and headed toward the manager's office at the Turnpike Inn, the cars and trucks on the nearby turnpike causing a roar that resembled the ocean. Not many people slowed down at Newark, much less stopped for the night.

The manager was a small Italian with a big neck and a fat, hairy trunk that seemed to ooze out of the edges of his golf shirt. A bald spot shone through a long tuft of hair that he combed from one side, over it. He watched them with worried eyes and sighed with relief when Drought displayed his FBI badge. Small hands waved in front of him as he spoke, his eyes never leaving the door.

"I don't know who he is, and I don't want to get involved. I don't want him to know I called anybody, do you know what I mean? I don't mind helping you guys but I don't want anybody to know. I don't even know *why* I called, except this guy is scary, really scary. I don't normally call. We get all kinds in here. But I get the feeling he could kill me just to keep from paying his goddamn bill. He cased this office in about two seconds. I've seen those kind of eyes before. I just called up and ran his name by the cops, that was all I did. He signed it Wayne Miller. I guess it's an alias. They picked it right up."

Drought placed a "Most Wanted Fugitive" photograph in front of the manager. The small man's eyes rolled with dread. "Oh, my God, it's him. That's the man."

"Where is he?"

"Room 121. Along the side. He came in a '57 Pontiac. Don't tell him I said anything."

"Is he in there?"

"As far as I know. He was in there a half-hour ago. *Please* don't tell him I called. You don't know what it's like to have to live with these people."

Drought snickered at that, staring almost contemptuously at the frightened man, his cigar now unlit, like a button at the center of his lips. He turned back to Judd Smith. "We should probably call for more firepower if he's in there. He's killed three people already, including a guard at Lewisburg when he broke out. He won't go easy."

"I don't know if we have time to get anyone else here. If he smells anything at all, he'll be gone."

"Oh, Jesus Christ, maybe you should just let him go." The manager was on the verge of whimpering. He actually crossed himself, staring down at the floor, wearing a sad clown's face.

Drought ignored the manager now, his air that of a surgeon in an emergency room. He and Smith walked quickly from the office, back to the car. He grabbed the handset on the radio, his eyes peering down the side of the motel as he talked. "Roger, we got an armed and dangerous fugitive at the Turnpike Inn, Newark. Wayne McCoy. He's on the List. Murder, robbery, escape from custody. He's in a room. Get us some more firepower out here, ASAP. We'll go surveil." He slammed the handset down and nodded to Judd Smith.

They moved around the office toward the side of the building, drawing their weapons from shoulder holsters and instinctively spreading out, one on each side of the road. In the parking lot they shifted to a slow, hunter's gait, the roar from the turnpike drowning out nearby noises, lights now flashing from the roadway on the other side of a fence as a stream of cars followed a curve. The air was rancid with exhaust fumes, heavy in Judd Smith's lungs, like smoke. He followed a small sidewalk just next to the rooms, momentarily underneath a spotlight as he passed a lit doorway, then in the musky dark again. Drought was on the asphalt, on the other side of the few parked cars. Smith saw the Pontiac and shortened his stride, gripping his revolver tightly and squinting through the flashes of headlights that blinded him every few seconds. They lit Drought, too, every few seconds, like a strobe light.

Drought suddenly crouched, screaming. "Drop it! FBI!" Somebody shot and Drought fell forward, limp, caught in headlights for a moment as if snapped by a flash camera. Smith watched him fall and searched forward through the blinding glare. A muzzle flash erupted in front of him and at the same time his head twitched, his left ear going deaf and he bounced against the building, screaming, and he saw another muzzle flash and he shot at it, now running madly toward it, still screaming, completely mindless, overwhelmed by the fear and fury of it, in a gory Korean trench again, exposed, his whole life nothing but a blur of screams and muzzle flashes, the only answer to race from his nakedness toward death. A tall shadow had sprinted to the Pontiac and opened the front door and was firing from behind it now and Judd charged it like someone insane and possessed and finally from four feet away he shot the murdering bastard in the face. The man slumped to the ground and Judd Smith fell on top of him, for the first time hearing his own ravening voice as it gurgled and chanted with his furious hate, and he had to consciously order himself to stop bludgeoning this melanoma, this blight that too many courts were sorrowing over and excusing as it killed its way across a forgiving country, this carcass who had just put an end to Vernon Drought's sad dream of retiring to the innocence of a sunbath in Miami.

Judd's face and neck were soaked with blood. It was pouring out of him with the rapid pulsing of his own heart. He knew the feeling and the odor and he knew that with a head wound he would soon pass out if he were not treated. He had also seen too many men die even to pretend that there was any use in checking Drought's body. Drought had fallen to the ground like a dead man, and nerveless muscles never lied.

*　*　*

"Well, good evening, all you wunnerful God-fearin' Christian folk here in Charleston and out there in TV land. Yessir, this is the Reverend Gabriel of the Lord and His Angels, that's right, the Reverend Gabriel of the Lord and His Christian Angels, and the Lord has given me the power to cure the sick, to heal the lame, and if you got the faith in the Lord it can happen to you."

Smith summoned up a gob of saliva, wanting to spit it at the television screen, but thought better of it and swallowed. "Turn it off!" His head ached so badly when he screamed that he at first feared he had reopened his wound.

". . . All you got to do is say, 'Come in, Jesus,' and let the Spirit in, and . . ." On and on the fat, pompadoured man babbled, dressed up in a white suit as if he were a used car salesman. Smith absently checked to see if he were carrying snakes, like some of the faith healers from the mountain country. No snakes. Reverend Gabriel of the Lord and His Angels was a smoothy, right down to his patent leather shoes.

Smith pressed the nurse buzzer. The Reverend Gabriel was curing a little deaf boy on the screen, the boy's awed, frightened textile worker father standing lean and toothless behind him, peering at the Reverend Gabriel as if he were indeed an emissary of the Lord, a true demi-savior. Reverend Gabriel had his fingers deep into the little boy's ears. He stared up into the heavens, his face visibly sweating from the glare of studio lights.

"In the name of the Spirit, in the name of Jesus, create the eardrums! Those deaf old spirits come *out!*"

Reverend Gabriel pulled his fingers out of the boy's ears, the sudden popping causing the boy's eyes to go fully round, the pain of it startling him. Triumphantly, the Reverend Gabriel turned the boy to face the crowd. They applauded upon seeing the boy's stunned expression.

But Reverend Gabriel of the Lord and His Angels wasn't done yet. He leaned forward, his face close to the boy's, his eyes gleaming with authority. "Now, say 'baby.' 'Baby.'"

The boy watched his lips, and imitated them. Finally he managed to utter, "Ba—ba," in a throaty, deaf boy's scream.

The crowd of thousands applauded yet again, their worshipful eyes captured by television cameras. The Reverend Gabriel put his hands on the boy's small shoulders, his face again up to the heavens, with a look that approximated pain. "The deaf old spirits are gone, the dumb spirits are gone, and I command them never to come back again."

"For God's sake!" Smith screamed again, pushing the nurse's buzzer in Morse Code, spelling out S.O.S. Finally she appeared, just at the end of the commercial, saving him from another episode of the Reverend Gabriel.

She leaned in the doorway, very young and very tired. "What is it now, Mr. Smith?"

"Turn that goddamn TV off, okay?"

She reached over and clicked it off. "Is that it?"

"No. Talk to me."

"That isn't in my contract." She checked her watch. "Aren't you tired? It's one o'clock." She folded her arms, her breasts resting comfortably above them, pointing at him like silent invitations. He wanted to make love to her. He briefly wondered if she thought him ugly, with the left side of his head shaved, and half of his ear shot off. He had never felt ugly before.

"I just don't want to be alone tonight."

She smiled sympathetically, as if consciously forcing her weariness away. "I think I can understand that." She had a kind face, with the perpetual look of a child who had just picked up a kitten. Nurses were always such suckers for vulnerability, thought Judd Smith again. It was almost a prerequisite for entering a profession designed to pick up the broken pieces of life. "You've been through an awful lot today. I heard the whole story. The FBI is even writing you up for an award."

An award? Smith was almost paralyzed by the very *déjà vu* of it; the death walk into the unknown, the mad, screaming slaughter, the loss of control, the choking, crying emptiness, the purchase of blood, the hospital. "I really don't think I can handle an award. I don't even think I can handle the hospital. I need to get out of here."

"You can go in a couple days, probably. They can reconstruct your ear. Did you know they can do that? You shouldn't worry about that."

"I don't want them to."

"You're really a funny guy, Mr. Smith. I think you need to calm down a little, actually. You don't want an award, you don't want your ear reconstructed, you want to leave the hospital in the middle of the night but you don't want to be alone. You might still be in shock. You did lose quite a bit of blood from where that bullet grazed your head after it hit your ear. You're quite a lucky man to be alive."

"I've heard that before." He pushed down the sheets and raised his pajama top, showing her the burn-slick scar in his lower abdomen from eight years earlier, subconsciously hoping to entice her interest in him by a display of flesh. "You want to see a wound? Now, *that's* a wound." She examined the scar with removed professionalism, nodding in agreement. He covered the scar with his pajamas again. "I've played this whole silly game before. That's twice I should have been dead, beyond all rights to complain. That does something to you."

"What?" She stood just over his bed, a shapely shadow in the dim light, the brows on her pretty face furled. "What does it do to you, Mr. Smith?"

"I don't really know. It changes you." She looked at him, obviously expecting more. He shrugged, the bandage on his head making him feel slightly claustrophobic. "It just changes you."

"Would you like a sleeping pill?"

"No. I hate pills."

"Well, try to get some sleep." She walked slowly out of the room, stopping for one quick moment at the door. "You're all right, now?"

He lay back, closing his eyes. "No, but you'd better get out of here before I fall in love with you."

He slept fitfully, no more than a few minutes at a time. His mind was a colorless mush, unable to really distinguish its multiplicity of angers, dejections, and pains. Reverend Gabriel of the Lord and His Christian Angels mocked what was left of his beliefs from the empty television tube—just say come on in, Lord, just say it. Judd directed his anger for a few minutes at the Reverend Gabriel. Who was that fat, greasy-haired phony to be bringing God to the world? After a while it frittered away, though, falling into the rest of his cerebral muddle. Who was he to go after the Reverend Gabriel?

Do you see yonder shining light? It popped into his consciousness as he dozed, from a reading of *Pilgrim's Progress* during his last year at the Naval Academy. The book had appealed to his failed fundamentalism, and he had secretly liked knowing that they had said "yonder" back in the old days, just as they still did in the mountains. In the book they'd asked the pilgrim, *Do you see yonder shining light,* and the man said no, and Judd Smith had said no, too. Then they'd asked him if he saw the low wicket gate and he said, *I think I do.*

Judd Smith grimaced in the dark, alone and beaten. *Yeah, I think I do, too, Lord. I've been breaking my knees on low wicket gates since I've been big enough to walk. What I need is some of that yonder shining light.*

Low lights, blue lights, moon lights, yonder shining lights. His mind went spooked and amazed as he let it drift inside its back edges, its forgotten corners of past emotions, all the way inside the helpless terror of a long-ago Korean night when he had teetered on the razor edge of death, that Voice growling calmly, luring him,

> *Just say yes, Judd, come on and say it*
> *Yes to what, Lord, I don't need to die*
> *Just yes. Just say it*
> *Yes yes yes yes yes*

He was crying. He was on his back in the bed and his tears went down the sides of his cheeks, trailing the lower edge of his bandages, and dripped off his neck into the crisp fabric of his hospital pillow. Without consciously willing it he found his hands moving from his sides in the dark room, clasping together at his waist, shivering with a bouncing motion on his stomach.

His first reaction at this warp of despair was disgust, and then a fear that he might somehow lose out in his nonexistent chance of bedding the pretty little nurse whose name he no longer even remembered, anyway. Then he prayed a little, an apology to God for everything. It made him feel better. He stopped crying. He began hoping for a vision, perhaps the kind his aunt had always related, Christ appearing at the foot of her bed surrounded by a golden light, soaked from the blood of the Cross, His arms out to her, commanding in a warm embracing voice, *confess Me before the world,* after which she had burst into the middle of a church service and stood in the back of the room and cried, "I'm a sinner before God!"

No vision. Only a memory engulfed by lament, and Judd Smith feeling calmer about things. He prayed some more. He remembered a verse from the Book of John that came to him from his childhood Sundays, sitting in the front pew and making the preacher mad; *I am the resurrection, and the life: he that believeth in me, though he were dead, yet shall he live: and whosoever liveth and believeth in me shall never die. Believest thou this?*

Yes.

That which is born of the flesh is flesh. And that which is born of the spirit is spirit. Marvel not that I said unto thee, ye must be born again.

Yes. Yes, I can handle that.

He prayed some more. He found himself wanting to live in repentance, to deny himself, to wear a wool undershirt filled with lice like Martin Luther, to whip himself like an order of monks he had read about somewhere, to remain ugly, scarred, and earless. He heard himself promising things to God that might right the order of his life. He was feeling pretty good.

"How are you doing?" It was the cute little nurse. "Are you sure you don't want a pill?"

"No. I told you about the pills." He smiled to her from a sudden inner warmth. "I'm fine." Then he said it, as if he might have announced that he had discussed it all with J. Edgar Hoover himself: "I've been praying."

Part Three

THE PETALS OFF THE ROSE

CHAPTER FOURTEEN

I

SHE HAD GIVEN HIM A YEAR and already he had taken two and there was nothing left to do but leave.

It wasn't that she wanted to leave him and it wasn't even a matter of pride anymore, either. It was just something she had to do, in the same way that tradition or time of life or perhaps foolishness had caused her to marry him in the first place. And it wasn't an absolute decision, anyway. Maybe he would come with her, once he realized that she was serious and not simply going through a remonstration, a memory of what might have been had she kept her wits and refused marriage seven years before. He could still work on missiles as a civilian in Los Angeles, and make a lot more money doing it, too. But there was no way she could go to law school in Vandenberg.

Actually, it wasn't even a decision at all. In October 1960 it was somewhere between a thought and a fantasy.

There was no way to reason with him about it, though, and that alone was making a decision inevitable. It was hard enough even to have a conversation with him anymore, much less a good, old-fashioned argument. He had blissfully passed off her frustrations for seven years, believing they would wither up and blow away as she aged, tolerating them as more of a proud display of her intellect and passion than as a verity, a rock at the center of her married soul.

Joe Dingenfelder was in heaven at Vandenberg. He did not see the chaos of a community that had grown from nothing to fifteen thousand people in two years on the isolated mesa. He did not see his own wife gnashing her teeth, feeling she was on the verge of growing old in the shadows of his exuberance. He saw instead the future, the edge of eternity, sitting tall and silver and pencil-thin on the launch pads near the sea.

He was gone every morning by dawn, and did not return before nightfall. He worked weekends. He was good; no, he was brilliant, a man who had achieved by luck and coincidence the perfect union of his mind to a new idea. Colonel Pattakos had turned Joe loose, and he

had his nose into everything. He was now probably the most knowledgeable man in the Air Force about missiles.

In the past two years, Joe Dingenfelder had written the book for
the Air Force on procedures for accepting missile sites from civilian
contractors, another one on technical requirements for handling cryo-
genic fuels—liquid oxygen, nitrogen, and hydrogen, which were highly
explosive and were dealt with at temperatures down to 325 degrees
below zero. He had done a manual for the Strategic Air Command on
the intricate Atlas guidance system, which could measure time in mil-
lionths of a second and velocities with distinctions of one foot per second at a speed of twenty thousand feet per second. He had done another book on the huge Atlas turbines, which could go from zero to
thirty thousand revolutions per minute in half a second. He had mastered, as a technical adviser on the Atlas sites, the problems of mesh-
ing one contracting company's computer equipment to another's—
something Colonel Pattakos had proudly described as similar to plug-
ging in a hundred different plugs at the same time.

He was good in the field, too. He had conducted demonstrations on
every tool needed to work on an Atlas missile, alternately changing
engines, putting on a nuclear warhead, using guidance equipment,
simulators, and calibrators. And he had supervised the first rebuilding
of a launching pad after the destructive heat and debris of an actual
launch.

He wanted to help beat the Russians. He actually had come to see
the world in those terms—who could blow up the other more completely. He dreamed about it, brooded over it. He was turning into a
warmonger, a *warmonger,* she thought again and again, thinking of
how he might use his brilliance to help move the world in other ways.
Part of her frequent complaining before had simply been her demand
for reassurance. Now even that was gone. In its place was the reality
that she had lost seven years and her equal footing with him as well,
only to be stuck in a California wilderness and to hear him speak in
hurried sentences about blowing up Moscow on fifteen minutes' notice.

She was starting to look like a man. Not really, but her features
were hardening and becoming angular, just the very slightest changes,
and the quicksand of her life at Vandenberg made the wrinkles and
the fadings luminesce before her as she studied them. *Then it will be
all over, he'll leave me and I'll be angular and old, the petals off the
rose, shrill in the possibilities of what might have been.*

Enough of this.

Vandenberg itself had arrived, and the Air Force was outperforming all expectations. Throughout 1959 and into 1960, missiles soared from Vandenberg like Roman candles, alternately bursting, flying sideways instead of upward, forgetting to roll into a turn, and blowing up on the launching pads. Many were also successful. Ten launch efforts were made on the Discoverer series, the first polar orbiting missiles, a modified Thor with a second-stage system and a 1,300-pound satellite. Six made it into orbit, and the Air Force began talking about a plan to eject space capsules from orbiting satellites and then recover them either in the air or from the sea, a precursor to manned space flights. The Royal Air Force launched twelve Thor missiles, including several simulated combat launches. They had given the inhabitants of Burton Mesa the most spectacular firecracker in history, a glowing starburst huge as the western sky when one missile blew up over the ocean during a night shot just before Christmas.

And in September 1959 the officers and men of the 675th Strategic Missile Squadron had launched the first Atlas from Vandenberg Air Force Base, a successful shot toward a target more than four thousand miles distant, in the Marshall Island group of Micronesia. Earlier attempts from Cape Canaveral, Florida, by civilian contractors had met with repeated failures, and the ability of Air Force personnel to so precisely put an Atlas onto the target on their first attempt was surprising to many. But not, of course, to Colonel Three Fingers Pattakos and his cerebral assistant, Captain Joe Dingenfelder, who had cheered like schoolboys from their observation post across a valley from the huge launching pad, then beaten each other on the back and stared dreamily into the sky as a flame torch drove the silver bullet out of sight.

In November 1959 the 675th had become an operational combat squadron. A message went out to the world from the Pentagon: "The Atlas squadron at Vandenberg Air Force Base, California, is now integrated into the Strategic Air Command's emergency war plan and is ready to launch on fifteen minutes' notice." Thus, with a terse sentence uttered from three thousand miles away, Vandenberg Air Force Base became at once a nuclear platform and a nuclear target.

So here we are, Dorothy had thought, the Doom Brigade, marching along toward mutual destruction with Joe Dingenfelder carrying the baton.

The world had begun to notice that Burton Mesa existed. In September Nikita Khrushchev had taken the train from Los Angeles to San Francisco, part of an American visit that had included Disneyland. As the locomotive broke through the Santa Ynez Mountains and chugged slowly along the seacoast at Surf, actually entering the base itself, Khrushchev refused even to look at Vandenberg, ceremoniously turning his back to it and standing with folded arms and a mischievous smile on his warted face, staring out at the angry surges of the sea. Joe talked about Khrushchev for days after that, as if he himself had slapped the old bastard in the face.

* * *

Then shortly after the turn of the year the beatniks came, and she knew that she must leave Vandenberg and the Air Force and maybe even Joe as soon as she could garner up the courage to decide. At least that was what everyone had said they were, beatniks, the word new, full-tongued, and entrancing at the same time, like that first taste of spicy foreign food. The beatniks provided Dorothy Dingenfelder with one of those pure, narcissistic moments, an unexpected look into a sudden mirror where she for the first time saw herself.

They didn't do much and they didn't stay long and it wasn't even clear what they had been after once they left. They simply appeared one Saturday morning, outside the fence that adjoined the housing area, and walked slowly in their mottled group, the poorest excuse for a crowd ever presented, toward the main gate. But it was impossible for someone to simply *appear* outside the fence at Vandenberg, particularly from around the hills that led north. The nearest community of any size was Santa Maria, twenty-five miles away, and there weren't forty bearded and unkempt people in the entire town, much less that many who would elect to spend a precious Saturday painting posterboard signs that said "BAN THE BOMB" and "STOP NUCLEAR WAR" and "DEATH MISSILES OUT OF CALIFORNIA," and then walk God knew how many miles to parade in front of some lonely gate guard who had probably never seen a missile up close in his life.

No, they had to be from somewhere else, and the mystery of their origins, as well as their dramatic appearance, this bedraggled group shambling along a road that came from nowhere, caused fear and rumors to ripple through the housing area as they passed. *They were from San Francisco. They were beatniks. They were going to enter the base and sit in at the missile sites. No, they were going to parade through the housing area. No, no, they were going to beat up the children.*

So the beatniks walked, unshaven, unwashed, unsmiling, unspeaking, along the outer fence in the powdery dust and patches of ice plants, past the rows of Capehart houses, past the baseball diamond, stark colorful figures in the clear winter sun, their silly signs on their shoulders, making for the main gate. And inside the chain-link fence with its strands of barbed wire at the top, dozens of children followed them, speaking among themselves with bright eyes and hushed voices, their mothers now and then calling them away. *Are they really going to try and beat us up?*

The provost marshal dispatched a fire truck to the main gate and it parked sideways in the road, blocking all traffic. Kids and mothers and dogs and even an occasional father, stiff with military machismo, gathered behind the fire truck. The group of beatniks or whatever they were mulled around on the other side of the highway, forty heads together in something of a command conference, then solemnly walked toward the main gate, waving their signs with what shrieking kids and barking dogs perceived as a threat, still unspeaking and unsmiling, and in a short minute, as soon as the first bald, bearded man put a tennis shoe onto base property, the firemen cut loose with a fat canvas hose and blew the whole lot of them all the way back across the road on a heavy stream of water, as if they were pieces of flotsam to be cleared off the road after a flood. The kids and mothers cheered and the dogs yapped excitedly and the fathers nodded, agreeing with each other that the beatniks had needed a bath anyway. And then the motley crowd retreated back down the road again, wet and dirty and walking slowly, presumably to trudge on home to San Francisco or wherever, their mission either impossible or accomplished, it wasn't clear.

A story appeared the next morning in the Los Angeles *Sunday News* about an antinuclear rally held at the main gate of Vandenberg, and above it was a picture of the beatniks or whoever nobly standing their ground in the face of a military firehose that was snuffing out their right to dissent. The picture did not show the fire truck or the kids and dogs behind it, screaming and yelping. It showed the provost marshal and his minions excitedly blasting away at the sign carriers, who were out in the street, off base property. In the picture there appeared to be a lot of sign carriers.

The whole incident, watching it and then reading about it, touched off an irreversible compulsion in Dorothy Dingenfelder. She understood the demonstrators, both philosophically and tactically. They had gathered around an issue and had taken action; they had *made news*. Watching them walk along the outside of the housing area's fence, she had felt an urge as deep as pain to walk with them, to let her hair grow long and to carry a sign, to proclaim that what her husband was so proudly and competently doing was the first step toward the end of the world.

They made her feel ashamed, not merely of her husband but of herself. This was more than Joe; it was all the fear and anger she had felt from her childhood, the fight against embryonic fascism to which she had once proclaimed she would dedicate her life, before Joe Dingenfelder lured her away, not only from the issues, but unwittingly to the other side. At that moment, staring at the picture of the beatniks that she had been unable to join because of her hair and clothes and the high chain-link fence with its barbed-wire top, she hated Joe Dingenfelder. He became a robber in her mind, and he had stolen more than years.

II

Natasha was beating up little Joe, but that was all right. It was happening in another room. Big Joe had gone to the blockhouse at five-thirty; it was launch day for another Atlas. And Dorothy sat at the kitchen table, sipping a second cup of coffee, lost inside the *Style* section of the Los Angeles *News*.

She read the Los Angeles *News* every morning, every sentence of all but the most mundane articles, a ritual that had itself become a religion. It had to be the Los Angeles *News*. Not the Santa Barbara *News Press*, not the Lompoc *Record*, not the Santa Maria *Times*. The Los Angeles *News*, because Los Angeles was going to be her deliverance and if she read about it long enough and reminded herself of what was awaiting her often enough, she would get mad enough not to feel guilty when she told Joe that his year had been up for a long, long time. The city itself was like a swooning lover, luring her away to a second chance at life. And it had to be Los Angeles. There was nothing to go back to in New York; her father had recently died, so there was no more family. And she had fallen in love with the freedom of Los Angeles; it grew with every visit. And Joe could still work on missiles in Los Angeles. The city was the aerospace contractors' capital of the world. If he didn't come with her to Los Angeles it would be his own goddamned fault.

And look at this. A final party for Kennedy supporters, its pictures filling up the *Style* section. Kennedy wouldn't carry California. She didn't really know that from her viewing post in the outback, but her political sense was almost uncanny. No one loved Richard Nixon, but no one really knew him, either, so a lot of people voted for him because he was so shrewd with his disguises: the tough man on communism, Eisenhower's protegé and pseudo-son, the family man replete with puppy dog and wife in cloth coat, the poor Whittier boy who made his own way to the top. He'd carry California. He might even win the whole thing. She felt a sudden admiration for his cleverness, even though she despised him for the way he had used the fearful days of McCarthyism to catapult himself into national power.

But enough of that. She mocked herself: *One mustn't dally in politics when the geniuses of tomorrow are awaiting their intellectual gruel.*

"Come on, you two! Stop it!"

She separated Natasha and little Joe, and urged them both out of the door, into the old Plymouth. They drove up Korina Avenue to Ocean View, the main road of the housing development. The streets and sidewalks were almost empty, something she had never gotten used to after growing up in New York. A Chevrolet chugged along in front of her, going the regulation fifteen miles per hour. The blue Air Force shuttle bus lurched through the housing area on the other side of the road, making its morning run. A sergeant whisked by on a little Lambretta motor scooter, on his way home from a night shift on the missile pads. So quiet; not city, not country, just there, in the middle of nowhere, artificially spawned, unnatural, new, and *quiet.*

At the edge of the housing area the fields extended forever, broken only by neat rows of eucalyptus trees every half-mile or so. The morning fog made the whole outdoors resemble a black-and-white movie. On the far side of the eucalyptus trees, all the way to the edges of the sea, Joe was puttering around with his goddamned three-fingered Greek friend, getting ready to shoot off an Atlas missile.

She turned onto a road, in the middle of a complex of old World War II buildings. They were square and worn, a few recently converted into recreational facilities, the rest forlorn from abandonment, roofs hanging, windows broken, a ghost town from another era. She stopped the car in front of one building marked with a brand-new sign, BASE NURSERY, and left her children in a room filled with wailing infants and screaming kids. It was primitive, but there was no alternative within at least fifty miles.

For what, Joe Dingenfelder, for what? You tell me.

The Air Force had remodeled an old hospital complex and made it into the base school, from kindergarten through the ninth grade. She halted her car in a space of dirt marked for faculty parking and slammed the door, walking toward the wing that housed the school's main office. The old hospital had twelve wings, connected by long, dark hallways. Each wing had another hallway marked with small rooms that once had housed doctors' offices and intensive care patients, then opened up into a large, low-ceilinged ward. They had put blackboards on the walls nearest the corridors, then filled each ward area with desks, and had declared the hospital to be a school. It reminded her of the famous legal case where someone had stuck feathers into a horse's saddle and then proved, statutorily, that it was a bird.

The classrooms were dark and musty. Skunks nested underneath some of the buildings. Occasionally they unleashed their unbearable odors when the floors above creaked and rumbled. The buildings remained a sickly, World War II hospital white. The grounds were grassless, brown with a powdery dust. Jackrabbits flitted about in the field across the street. Snakes and toads were common, still unused to having been uprooted from their havens. And there was too much empty space in the complex, too many places for the mischief of boys and girls who had been suddenly thrown together in this isolated morass of confusion so that their fathers could shoot missiles up at the moon or maybe at the Russians.

As she walked along the seemingly endless main corridor toward the ward that held her classroom, Dorothy watched three boys in the parched dust of the schoolyard. The boys were throwing rocks at the windowpanes of another hallway. They had drawn a line in the dirt and were trying to see who could break the most windowpanes before class started. She thought to call to them but was weary from the continuous battles. Being disciplined was a badge of honor to many of them. It didn't do any good. Who needed it? Base Maintenance would fix the windows.

She feared many of them, detested others, yet at the bottom of it she felt sorry for them. Before World War II the military had its posts, its traditions, its tight small community. But chaos had come with

America's larger commitments; new bases, more people, more moves. The children were like perpetual immigrants, especially those whose fathers were in the more dynamic military areas. The missile program had brought the turmoil to an almost unbearable extreme. It was like having a father in the California Gold Rush of 1849. The children had come to expect the chaos and eventually became hooked on it, like a bewildering drug.

She turned down the long dark hallway toward her own classroom and immediately became wary, like a cat entering a strange house, wondering if one of her students had decided to surprise her or confront her from one of the side rooms. A firecracker exploded inside the classroom at the end of the hall, and she heard loud shouts, then another firecracker. Her steps shortened as she approached the room. She clasped her thermos jug of coffee against one side, and her purse against the other, building an unconscious shell with her arms, lowering her head and shrinking inside herself. *I'm getting out of this,* she litanized for the thousandth time that week. *I hate it I hate it I hate it* . . .

Outside the door Paul Wilhelm leaned against a wall, a cigarette tucked behind one ear, absently fondling the breasts of a girl through her sweater. Paul Wilhelm was a member of the Blue Jackets. The Blue Jackets were kings among the children, reigning through fear and disruption. A group of them had filed into one of their errant member's own home and beaten him up in his bedroom a few months before. Nothing had happened to them; the beaten boy threatened his own sort of violence if his parents prosecuted.

Paul Wilhelm smiled slowly as Dorothy approached. It was a James Dean smile, from behind a lightly pimpled face framed in a ducktail haircut. He raised his eyebrows, nodding to her, and slowly dropped his hands from the girl's chest. The girl stood like a small child in the shadowed hallway, her feet together and her small hands folded below her waist, a baby's innocent eyes meekly apologizing to Dorothy as she glared at both of them. It was Tina Morrel. The boys had nicknamed her Pro, and it wasn't for her tennis, either.

"Good morning, Mrs. Dingenfelder."

"Get into the classroom." They're only *fourteen.*

They had hung her pet skunk. It was not a real one, only a stuffed skunk that Dorothy had seen at a garage sale when a family down the street had transferred out. She had bought it in her early, more optimistic days to share a joke with the class after her classroom had been victimized by a scared skunk from underneath the floor. But there it hung on the cord that dangled from the fluorescent light switch, just above her desk, its neck twisted and stretched.

The class tittered expectantly. A few boys, probably the perpetrators, howled with delight, calling attention to themselves. She tried to untie it but the knot was too tight, so finally she jerked the entire light cord from the fixture. It was too embarrassing to stand before thirty mocking faces, playing with the knot. And anyway, Base Maintenance would fix the cord.

She tossed the skunk onto her desk and sat down abruptly. "Take your seats, please!"

They slowly moved from along the walls toward their desks. The joke of the day was over. The week before, someone had killed off the fish in her small aquarium with tincture of merthiolate. Before that, she had opened her thermos during one third-period class and found it stuffed with snails, all gathered at the top around the lid, trying to escape the heat of the coffee. There was always something. And at almost any moment a fistfight was possible, small whispered arguments suddenly erupting into a brawl that would send desks careening and the other students heading for the safety of the outer walls as she worked her way through the wreckage and tore the fighting boys apart.

And you didn't expect cooperation. One boy had done something, been overly nice to her in some forgotten way, and during a recess had lost his blue jeans to a sudden crowd of other boys, who had stripped him down in the dust yard and left him naked and crying. His trousers were found soaking in a toilet. It wasn't just the boys, either, although they were the worst. She had broken up a fight between two girls after school one day, apparently over the honor of wearing a boy's jacket during school, a symbol of his "love." They were using razor blades. Luckily, they were cutting each other's clothes rather than their bodies, but both came away in rags and bleeding in several places.

Sort of like the squabbles of prep school, Dorothy thought sardonically, beginning to call the roll. Only these kids play for real.

A match flashed at the back of the row immediately in front of her desk, and as she called the names from her roll book she heard the quick hiss of a fuse. The boy in the rear seat then calmly handed a large red firecracker to the girl in front of him, who quickly passed it up the row. Dorothy raised from her chair, speechless, unable to decide whether to run from the room or to rush the firecracker.

The boy in the desk nearest her stood, grinning, and placed the firecracker on her desk. It was three inches long, as big around as a nickel. Dorothy had inched backward until she was flush against the blackboard. She stood frozen, her hands in front of her face to protect it, her large eyes now round with fear and anger.

Finally the fuse burned down, and went out. It was a dud, one of those fake firecrackers that novelty stores sold. The students mocked her with their laughs and screams and she stood for one moment more, frozen now more by anger than fear, feeling it well up in her like hot vomit, tightening her stomach, drawing her face into a grimace of pure rage. There was no more backing down, no more room for compromise with these twisted little aliens, these children of the doom brigade that now was building dozens of ugly carriers of death all over this remote, unwanted prairie. She rushed her desk, tossing the firecracker into the trash can, and picked up the wooden pointer she had used in so many futile attempts to press knowledge into their unwilling brains. They grew silent as she held it overhead and several cringed when she smashed it across her desk, emitting something resembling a scream. The pointer flew in three pieces across the room. She held a small, remaining piece in her hand, and finally threw it at the student who had lit the firecracker. He sat, suddenly small and scared, watching her with wide brown eyes.

"That will cost you, Jimmy Brandt, that will *cost you!* I'm calling your father tonight—"

"—he won't be home."

"—and if he doesn't get the word about conduct in this class, I'm calling his *commanding officer* the first thing tomorrow."

The whole class was suddenly quiet. It was a new tactic, a military threat that they all seemed to understand. They may not be afraid of me, thought Dorothy, but at least they've got to wonder what their dads will do to them if they get chewed out by the colonel. Anyway, it would slow them down for a few hours while they thought about it.

"All right." She tightened her lips, picking up a biology book. "Open your books to page fifty-seven."

* * *

Oh, beautiful, beautiful, all tall and slim and statuesque, so power-
ful and new, pointing to the sky like a phallus, like the Washington
Monument, like a tower, yes, like the Tower of Babel . . .

Joe Dingenfelder nudged Colonel Pattakos, leaning against a small
white blockhouse wall and staring across a half-mile of manzanita and
tumbleweed toward the launch pad, where the Atlas sat ready to
erupt. Wisps of liquid nitrogen and oxygen gathered along its base, as
if the missile deserved its own personal, scarifying fog.

"She sure is pretty, isn't she?"

"Just like my last wife: pointy head and straight down the sides."

"ATTENTION ALL PERSONNEL." The launch control officer's
voice broke over the loudspeaker, its flat, Victrola tones carrying
across the small valley to their observation post. "TASK EIGHT,
COUNTDOWN EVALUATION IS COMPLETE. ON MY MARK
WE WILL PICK UP THE COUNT AT T MINUS TWELVE MIN-
UTES. THIS IS PHASE ONE OF THE TERMINAL COUNT-
DOWN. PHASE ONE WILL BEGIN ON MY MARK. FIVE, FOUR,
THREE, TWO, ONE, MARK. T MINUS ELEVEN MINUTES AND
FITY-FIVE SECONDS."

A reporter called to Pattakos. "Where's this one going, Colonel?"

Pattakos pulled from his cigar and blew a smoke ring into the quiet
morning air. Then he grinned, obviously enjoying the attention.
"Come on, Wilbur, you know I'm not allowed to say. Just somewhere
in the Pacific. Near Kwajalein."

"And what is the Air Force shooting at down there?"

"Natives. Dolphins. Little grass shacks." Pattakos laughed loudly,
staring at the wondering looks from the other reporters, who were not
used to his inanities. "Nah. Just trying to hit the center of a lagoon,
Wilbur." Pattakos grinned again, turning to face the man. "I'll give
you a hint, son, just because you're my friend. Take a map and draw a
radius from around Kwajalein, and keep going. Not a flat map, do you
get what I'm saying? Keep drawing the radius north, you get what I
mean?"

"Are you saying that this target is a substitute for Moscow?"

It was another reporter, a man from the New York *Century*, new to
the missile beat. Neither Pattakos nor Dingenfelder had seen him before. He stood with a small group of reporters and Pattakos walked toward them now, considering them. They had gathered at this closest
permissible point to the launch pad in order to report the third Atlas
"simulated combat" launch by Air Force crews. Pattakos deliberately

played with his cigar, inviting them to stare at his fingerless hand, then spoke with slow humor. "Now, come on, guys, have a little sympathy for a workingman, will you? One of you quotes me on something like that and I'll have to go plant potatoes in Idaho. I didn't say anything. I just told my friend Wilbur here, who's been with us a long time and covered all of the shots for the Santa Barbara *News Press* and is a good guy who drinks beer and chases tail, that we're trying to hit a *lagoon* in the goddamned Pacific Ocean! Now if Moscow's in the middle of a fucking *lagoon* in the goddamned ocean, then we're trying to hit Moscow. Jesus, you all should be playwrights or something."

The *Century* reporter persisted, staring at his notes. "Look, Colonel, you just said—"

"So use your imagination. That's all I did. Just don't substitute mine for yours."

"Colonel, you're a direct representative of the Strategic Air Command. When you use your imagination in front of the press, it carries a little more weight than my own speculation."

"I didn't use my imagination in front of you. I used it in front of Wilbur." Pattakos was heating up. Dingenfelder could see the blood creeping up the back of the big Greek's neck. Poor Pattakos. He would never make general. He simply didn't know how to stroke the Big Boys. Pattakos deliberately bit off a half inch from his cigar and spat it onto the ground, staring at the reporter as if he were dumb. "Wilbur isn't the press, he's my goddamn friend. You, you're the press. Did I say anything to you?"

"You said it publicly, in front of all of us."

Pattakos paused, sucking in air through tight lips, then threw both hands into the air, an act of adamant energy. "Oh hell. What the fuck do I care, anyway."

The launch control officer's flat monotone floated over to them. "ENGINE EXTERNAL SLEW COMPLETE. PHASE TWO COMPLETE. PHASE THREE PROCEEDING NORMAL."

Pattakos pointed toward the Atlas. He stood in his khaki uniform with its rows of ribbons won in a simpler war, in another age, looking every bit a warrior of the old way with his thick gash of a moustache and his cigar and his burning brown eyes. "*If we can drop that missile into a lagoon in the Pacific, we can damn well put it right on top of Lenin's fucking grave, you creep, and you can write that in your book!*"

Oh, God. Dingenfelder visibly shuddered, imagining the headlines as Pattakos launched into a tirade against everything Russian, and a half-dozen reporters busily filled their notebooks with the wit and wisdom of Colonel Three Fingers Pattakos. He and Pattakos would hear all about it when SAC found out. It might even cost Pattakos his job, although he had been invaluable in the early, creative stages of the program. It was now clear that the Atlas program, for all its continuing ups and downs, was going to work, and it was time, mused Dingenfelder, for the bureaucrats to start easing out the pioneers. Pattakos was too eccentric and too honest for the sophisticates.

"PHASE THREE COMPLETE. FUEL RAPID LOAD VALVE OPEN."

"Colonel! Hey, Colonel, come on over here. It's about ready to go." He grabbed Pattakos by an arm and pulled him back toward the side of the blockhouse, and they sat by themselves against its wall as if sunbathing, under the warm October Santa Ana sun.

"VERIFY BTL ON INTERNAL. VERIFY MISSILE ON INTERNAL."

"Oh, God, I love this." Pattakos was the happy warrior again, free from the demands of the reporters. He watched across the dry little valley as the missile steamed heavily, loaded with its liquid fuel, as much a mass of energy and tension as a bomb one second away from exploding.

"LAUNCHER CLEAR TO FIRE."

The last two years had moved so fast. Dingenfelder pondered it, staring at the Atlas and trembling slightly from his own excitement. By the time the gantry cranes were perfected they had been obsolete. By the time their replacement cranes, the elevators which raised a missile up from the horizontal, were perfected, they were outmoded, surpassed by a silo concept, where the missile would be fired from underground. It took fifteen minutes to fuel an Atlas. Inside a silo such a system would not only be obsolete, but dangerous. The Titan would soon become the Air Force's principal combat missile, using a preloaded, self-igniting fuel system. The Minuteman missile, which was on the way, would use solid fuel that would burn from one end to the other, like the gunpowder in a Fourth of July skyrocket. Joe Dingenfelder was watching his love, indeed in many ways his creation, on the concrete platform across the dry field, with an enormous pride but also with the sad knowledge that it was already on its way out as a combat system. All that energy, all that thought, poured into the creation of a century plant, a flower that would bloom for only a day or so.

"FIRST STAGE READY TO LAUNCH. ALL SYSTEMS CLEAR FOR LAUNCH."

Pattakos raised a fist, screaming into the hollow empty air. "Go, you son of a bitch!"

"TEN, NINE, EIGHT, SEVEN, SIX, FIVE, FOUR, THREE, TWO, ONE, ENGINE START."

A white bowl of flame erupted underneath the missile, mixed with the heavy steam of the fuel, and then a roar beyond belief hit them from across the field, pressing them against the building with its force, warbling on their faces and arms like pellets. They held their ears, screaming mad indecipherable joys to each other, and watched the missile slowly, after several anxious seconds, begin to rise from the pad. They did not hear launch control's faint Victrola announcement.

"NOW, LIFTOFF."

From seven miles away the same roar shook the raised timber foundations of the abandoned hospital pretending to be a school, and the rooms full of children pretending to be students poured onto the weeds and dust of their outer yard, staring up into the sky. Launches were the only times that Dorothy saw them proud, enthusiastic, cheering, speaking of their fathers. She followed them outside and caught the pencil of white and yellow flame as it rose above the far trees and bent gently toward the sea. The children were chanting, "Go, go, go," their enthusiasm unbounded for this pure, loud, and entrancing half-minute, their fathers having worked to offer them up a personal firecracker, a special skyrocket, an instrument of death that might somehow compensate for the long days and nights away from home, for the misery of an isolated life in the middle of a manzanita prairie, for the personal damage that they might never perceive because they might never recover sufficiently from it even to be conscious that it was damage. She watched them and felt again relieved that they were capable of constructive pride, and then felt sorry for them again.

The white and yellow flame arched sideways as it always did, into its pitch and roll, curving gently toward Kwajalein or wherever, becoming tiny, a hot dot of sunlight. And then suddenly, incredibly, it turned all the way around, heading back toward the launching pad, leaving a snaking trail of smoke in the sky and becoming larger again. Below her in the yard they screamed. She could not decide whether it was terror or fascination. It was going to go back and take vengeance on its creators, their fathers, her husband. For a small moment, she had to suppress a secret warmth, a small congratulation: Take *that*, Joe Dingenfelder. And then she was afraid.

"My God, it's turned! They've got to blow it up!"

Here it came, the equivalent of 130 large Cadillacs packed into a ball of steel eight stories high, hurtling through the air at a thousand miles an hour, right back at them. It had happened so fast that when the range safety officer finally was able to push the button and destroy the missile, it was above them, a flaming dark pencil that suddenly exploded, making a large, brilliant ball of yellow and black on the canvas of the bright blue noonday sky. That slinky metal mistress, that inheritor of Einstein's brooding theories, had become a quarter-of-a-million-pound bomb that had air-burst over California. The United States Air Force had attacked itself.

Chicken Little had not been wrong; the sky was raining metal. On the observation post, reporters were scrambling, screaming, lying down, and getting back up. There was nowhere to run, nowhere to hide. The New York *Century* reporter was running, though, his eyes skyward, as if he would be able to avoid a hundred-pound jag of metal falling at hundreds of feet per second if he could only see it coming. He ran smack into a chain-link fence, bounced off, got back up, and ran into it again, never taking his eyes off the wisps of black smoke up against the edges of the sun. The driver of the truck that had brought them all to the outpost panicked and raced his truck out of the gate, careening down the pocked road toward small rolls of hills, perhaps thinking a moving target would be harder to destroy. As he roared away, five stunned reporters looked up from where they were lying and followed his progress, holding unbelieving arms over the back of their heads. They had been hiding underneath his truck.

Twenty-five miles away, in a Santa Maria strawberry field, a somnolent farmer heard a thud from where he had been working on irrigation lines. He walked fifty feet, and found a piece of twisted metal as large as a car. In the base housing area, an off-duty sergeant watched the explosion and ran through a sliding glass window in his haste to get back indoors.

And up against the blockhouse wall, watching with an almost casual interest, Colonel Henry Pattakos blew a smoke ring after pulling on his half-smoked cigar. He was watching reporters scramble in the

dust, his face holding the delight of a man who has seen his antago-
nists stripped naked. "Goddamned civilians." He banged Joe Dingenfelder's shoulder and then his head as he lay flat against the edge of
the building, and laughed uproariously. "Ha *haaaa!* What's the matter, Dingenfelder? Do you want to live forever?"

Dingenfelder looked up, feeling sheepish, and then joined the colonel sitting against the wall and surveying the launching pad across the
little valley. It still smoked from the flames of the dead missile. Dust
swirled in small tornadoes from the hot currents. Pattakos suddenly
laughed again, and slapped Dingenfelder's back, declaring the day to
be a success. "Jesus Christ. You're not going to let your old lady take
you away from this, Dingenfelder. You love it too much."

"She's got her mind set on it, sir. I don't know what to do."

"She doesn't like it, fuck her. Get yourself another wife." Pattakos
laughed again. Vandenberg was his heaven. "There are a million
women in the world to screw, Dingenfelder, but there's only one Vandenberg. Ha *haaa!*"

*   *   *

*All the years, the warnings, the secret thoughts, and the unan-
nounced frustrations boiled down to one cliché.*

"I'm sorry, Joe, there isn't anything left to talk about."

She examined an expression that seemed genuinely hurt and surprised. That in itself amazed her. She shrugged, though, sitting up in
bed as he stood half-dressed in front of her, just home from another
glorious exciting day. Kennedy had become President, Three Fingers
Pattakos was being transferred to the Strategic Air Command headquarters at Offutt Air Force Base, Nebraska, Joe Dingenfelder had
been selected for an operations billet with the 675th, and she was putting an end to her part in it. "I've made up my mind and that's it. I've
been accepted at UCLA and I'm going. If you want to come, come. If
you want to stay here and then end up in Nebraska, go ahead. I'm not
going to feel guilty about this. I said a year and it's been two and
I'm not going to suddenly realize that it's been twenty."

"Aw, Dorothy—"

"Aw, Dorothy, *nothing*. For God's sake, I don't have to go through
the list again." She scrutinized him, her face puzzled. "What I don't
understand is why you would even *want* to stay in the Air Force! I
just don't understand it, Joe! You've got a degree from MIT. You've
got the hardware experience out on the sites. You can make a *mint*

with Lockheed or Douglas or General Dynamics, doing almost the same thing you're doing now. You could work for a contractor and buy Air Force majors for lunch. And look at your hero Pattakos. He's going to *Nebraska!* That isn't even missiles, not in the same way. How can you trust your career to that sort of instability? Living out in the middle of nowhere . . ." Her voice trailed off and she watched a bedroom wall, then she snapped her face quickly so that her eyes locked into his and would not let go. "*Nebraska!* For God's sake, what would I do in *Nebraska?*"

"He's going to be working in the Hole, Dorothy. In the most sensitive command center in the world. Can you imagine how important that is? It's more than money. It's—" He sighed, knowing he was not getting through to her. "It's bigger than missiles. It's keeping this country free, watching after the Soviets. It's being involved with history."

"Good. Then go get involved with history, Joe. I'm going to get involved with the law. In five months, I'm starting at UCLA, and if you don't like it you can go to hell." She turned out the light, facing away from him, then added whimsically, "Or to Nebraska."

As he finished undressing, he heard a small giggle in the dark, and then she spoke, newly calm and completely independent, apart from him, a severance. "Or maybe they're the same goddamned thing. Whatever happened to the music, Joe? You told me there would always be music."

CHAPTER FIFTEEN

One hundred miles out.

"Okay, gang, get ready for maneuvers on arrival."

"Skip."

"Hank."

"Red."

"Don."

"Dave."

Red Lesczynski peered out of his pristine canopy toward the far edge of the green earth. From the ground, looking up, it would have seemed like freedom, the six planes piercing through clean summer air alone and powerful, blue metal birds migrating west. Inside the cockpit it was closer to prison. Lesczynski was flying at nearly the speed of sound, surrounded by five aircraft, each of them almost touching his jet in different places, nose and tail and wings, as if he were all the points of a flying star on which they guided.

He looked like Superfly. A round, golden flight helmet made his head appear overlarge and bald. Bulbous green goggles went from the top of his forehead, where the helmet ended, down to his cheeks, and around from ear to ear, giving him fly's eyes, dark and protruding. A voice microphone hung just in front of his mouth, affixed to the helmet. He wore a blue one-piece flight suit that hugged his body like a leotard.

Superfly, superpilot, superman.

His gloved hand gripped a custom-fitted stick that rose in front of his seat, between his knees and crotch, surrounded by dozens of dials and gauges. A lot of pilots gave a lot of reasons about why they wore the gloves. Lesczynski wore them to keep the sweat off the stick. It wasn't simple fear that made him sweat, and it wasn't exertion, either. It was the hours of tiny, microscopic adjustments, the almost indecipherable nudges and caresses that went from his hand into the stick and kept him alive. Whenever Red Lesczynski finished a Blue Angels show his flight suit was soaked, and his right hand trembled for hours.

From the canopy of his F-11F fighter, Lesczynski could peer down on either side and see another jet. The gold wing tips and long blue wings of the other planes were so close that they seemed to grow out of his own fuselage. Sometimes they did push into his aircraft, as if they were trying to meld together into one clot of metal. The winter before, when the new team was training off Key West, the formation had come too close together during an echelon roll and when they had landed, Lesczynski had found a scar in the metal of his fuselage, where his aircraft and Hank Sowell's had gently embraced at five hundred miles an hour. That could make a man's hand shake.

Most of the time they didn't touch, though. Most of the time the aircraft flew together as if they had been glued onto four or six little slots on the same flat hidden surface, a pane of Plexiglas up in the air, an engineering marvel. In front of Lesczynski, the exhaust from Boss Heckler's jet glowed hot and red. Behind him the two solo aircraft had closed in for the arrival show. His slot position in the formation was vulnerable to the judgments of five other men possessed with the same human frailties as he, any one of whom could kill both himself and Lesczynski with one small moment of distraction. That made a man sweat into his glove as he held tight onto his stick.

Fifty miles out. Boss Heckler was talking to the tower, getting clearance for maneuvers on arrival. If Lesczynski had been able to see beyond the wing tips and Boss Heckler's tail, he would have noticed the amber mist of Pittsburgh growing on the edge of the horizon. Pittsburgh, factory town, and down along the Allegheny, stuck inside one of the endless corduroy ridges, Ford City.

Hey, you glassmaker's town, you Hunkytown, you layer cake of dreams, Red Lesczynski's brought home his toys. Can you see me screaming by? I'm a bullet in the sky, I was born to fly, the Polish Falcon, eh?

"Okay, boys, let's give 'em a good diamond roll."

On the ground the people of Pittsburgh were treated to an unexpected display of beauty that swept the early summer foulness from their lungs, and erased the laziness of a Friday morning just before the July 4 holiday. The two solo aircraft peeled away from the tight formation and the other four blue jets surged straight up into the air with a piercing roar that spoke of power and exactness, twisting as they climbed, then floated weightless, upside down, spewing red and blue smoke like streamers from their wing tips. The diamond of overlapping wings continued to twist as it fell, smoke twirling like a clutch of ribbons, until it righted itself in its original formation, roaring at almost five hundred miles an hour in a vertical power dive that ended a hundred feet off the ground.

"Real nice," said Boss Heckler. "Reversing, to tuck under break. Right echelon landing."

The two solo jets barked over the runway then from opposite directions, thirty feet off the ground, spinning like bullets, screwing their way through the air as they shot a series of horizontal rolls.

"Don off."

"Dave off." The solos disappeared.

The diamond even landed in formation. They were not four aircraft, not while they were flying. They were not even four people. They were simply the Blue Angels. They had managed to straddle the most difficult demarkation of the human spirit, first to perfect an individuality that made them among the best in a trade that killed a man quick if he could not, and then to sublimate that individuality even as they used it. You had to be both to be a Blue. You had to be able to fly the jet, fast and subtle. But you had to be able to follow the Boss, too, to make yourself a part of his mind and reflexes, to go up when he went up, to twitch when he twitched, to ride on the same sudden puffs of air currents. It was piloting with a surgeon's precision, rather than with the abandonment of the Red Baron's mythical soarings.

On the ground a hundred people waited to greet them, even though the air show was a day away. Boss Heckler left with a representative of the Federal Aviation Administration to negotiate and sign a clearance for the next day's show. Skip and Hank and Dave and Don were off on their weekly goodwill stops. They would spend the day visiting hospitals and schools, signing autographs and giving speeches. The maintenance crew would soon arrive on Navy Eight, a Douglas R-5D transport filled with spare parts and special tools, and would likely work into the night to ensure that the aircraft were up for the next day's show.

And Red Lesczynski was going home. He grinned widely as he walked down the flight line, lithe and powerful in his body-hugger of a flight suit, searching for Sophie and his mother. They were driving out from Ford City to meet him. He was remembering the day, fifteen years before, when the Naval Academy recruiter had left his home after signing him to a letter of intent to play football. He was hoping that the recruiter was still alive, and had seen in the newspapers that the shy, bulky Hunky boy had not let him down.

He saw them inside the operations terminal, his mother trying to look as if she met the Blue Angels every day, but her tightly clenched fists pressed into her chest a giveaway. From twenty feet away he could see her tears. She was so overwhelmed with pride that she was in awe of her own son. *Aw, Mum,* he thought. *It's only flying airplanes.*

Watching Sophie and his mother he felt a sudden surge that made his nostrils burn and dared tears at the edges of his eyes. Baba had died, two years before. He imagined her, bundled in her ever-present shawl, dressed in the black shoes and babushka of the old country and caressing the large cross she would have worn around her neck for the occasion. She would have been nodding with the certainty of the endless Slavic ages, as if only she had known because she had seen it in a dream while calling hogs in another century on the flat plains of Poland.

*   *   *

"I tell you, Sophie, and you don't got to believe me, but that Mattie Gwalcek is a witch." Mama Lesczynski nodded mournfully, resting against her own fat bulk, spilling over the sides of the rocker as she peered out from her back porch toward the small infinity of her Ford City neighborhood. "She's been trying to put a spell on me."

"Now, Mama."

"Now, Mama, nothing. She's a witch. What you know, baby? You been away."

Mama Lesczynski was watching Mattie Gwalcek's house. The Gwalceks' backyard adjoined the Lesczynskis'. The lots were hooked up end to end, with the homes on different streets. On either side of them, hundreds of same-sized houses sat on same-sized narrow plots of land, each with their back porches and small summer gardens and rusting clothesline poles. The day's wash was on the line, all across Ford City. In the humid summer heat the porches filled with little coveys of clucking, laughing women. The houses were not air conditioned. The men were at the union hall, or on the picket line.

Mama Lesczynski rocked, her eyes fixed on Mattie's house, comfortable in her delusion. "A damn witch."

J.J. and a cousin wrestled in the backyard, next to Mama's garden, their laughs and calls floating up to the porch. Off on the road a few lots down, Katherine and Johnny were playing with neighborhood children, riding bicycles and throwing rocks up the hill that caused Ford City to sit so compactly against the factory walls and the Allegheny River. Sophie glowed from the normality of it. It was the way she had always dreamed of growing old, and here she had a full three weeks of it, up from Pensacola while Red was on one of his longer Blue Angel deployments. She settled back into her metal lawn chair and winked at her mother, who sat near Mama Lesczynski.

Mama Lesczynski caught the wink, and took it for disbelief. "Oh, now, would I lie to you, Sophie? You just been away, that's it. You should see this woman. Always over here to try and get me to hand her something! You know if you hand something to a witch, she can put a spell on you! So, I never handed her a damn thing."

"No, I believe you, Mama." Sophie's years away had not dimmed her belief in such realities as witches, although she strained hard to apply that fear to Mattie Gwalcek. "So, what does she ask for?"

Mama Lesczynski rocked gently, watching J.J., who had pinned down his older cousin and was sitting on top of him, pulling his nose. "Ohhh, anything she can get, that woman. She comes over when I'm in my garden and tries to get me to hand her one of my tomatoes. 'Could I just have one,' she says. So I let her take as many as she likes. I don't hand her a damn thing. Same thing with my flowers. She takes clothespins." Mama Lesczynski raised her hands, palms up, resting her case. "Anything."

"Maybe she's just turned into a beggar." Sophie's mother, small and wizened in contrast to Mama Lesczynski, leaned back and offered a tentative rationale, and then hastened to add her support. "It's just a thought, because you know I believe you, too, honey."

Mama Lesczynski continued to rock, her face momentarily sagging with her burden, secretly enjoying the distinction of being pursued by the agents of the supernatural. "I know you might not believe me, Sophie, but you tell me after a couple days. You and Red peek out into the backyard tonight. There she is, Mattie Gwalcek, sweeping off the sidewalk and then the *road,* at two in the morning! Now, who else would do that but a witch?"

"Somebody who's drunk or crazy." Sophie's mother caught herself, not wanting to destroy the harmony that Mama's special predicament had created. "I'm not saying she's either of those, now. I just heard about other cases, that's all." She wiped sweat off her forehead, onto her cotton print dress. "Just look at little J.J., will you? He's going to be the picture of his papa. I never seen a kid so strong, and here he is only nine."

"Besides, her sister told me." Mama Lesczynski reached out and picked a bunch of honeysuckle from the trellis next to her porch. She buried her face in the leaves and blossoms, then turned toward the backyard and called to the two boys, not wanting to appear self-centered in her obsession with Mattie Gwalcek. "J.J., you stop putting dirt in Peter's hair, son. That ain't nice." She looked back to Sophie. "You know Henna Zercoe? Mattie's little sister. She told me one day, she said, watch out, because Mattie's trying to put a spell on you. Don't you hand her a damn thing."

"Henna's a drunk, for sure." Sophie's mother hedged again. It wasn't worth offending Mama Lesczynski's little fantasy. "It's a wonder she's keeping up with everything Mattie does, these days." She yawned then, tiring of Mattie Gwalcek. "Anyway, I just wish she'd put a spell on Pittsburgh Plate Glass, so the men can get back to work. I run out of ways to cook Spam."

Mama Lesczynski nodded solemnly, agreeing. "*Jesus Maria,* I wish they'd get this strike over with. It ain't gone anywhere." She patted Sophie on a shoulder. "Sophie, girl, we miss you'ns but I think you'ns are lucky you and Red moved away. Red's papa and the boys who stayed, they been in bad shape."

"I know, Mama." Sophie wiped her forehead and then her hands in the sweltering heat. She felt both cursed and blessed, missing the daily contact with her family and yet thankful that she and Red had managed to avoid the numbing, hateful dependence of factory work. She had seen the strike's toll in the faces of a hundred families, just in the past two days. It had gone on too long. It was a bad strike, for the wrong reasons, and they were going to lose. It had been more of a political strike than an economic one, a strike aimed at national issues rather than worker needs. Many of the men had resisted it from the outset, but once the vote had come in, they had all walked out. That was the essence, the nub of everything in the mill country. No one was more hated than a man who would cross a picket line. *Scab laborer.*

She worked to find a piece of thanks, and sought to brighten them to Red's proud homecoming. "And Red works so hard. He's done so *well,* oh, I just feel like God's blessed us."

"It ain't been easy for you'ns, either, honey."

"I know, but look at what he's done. He's just been such a part of the world. Over there in the Mediterranean a few years back, flying cover when the Marines landed in Lebanon. That was the edge of World War III! Then his squadron won the air-to-ground weapons competition at the Naval Air Weapons Meet in California—and he gets the award for the outstanding fighter pilot in the whole Navy! And now he's on the Blue Angels. I just don't know how it could have turned out better, Mama."

Mama Lesczynski rocked, clucking her tongue, her full face reeking with pride yet suppressing it, in order to give Sophie her due. "And that boy is gone all the time. Here he's home from working on the boats, always out on the ocean, and they've got him flying all over the *world* with these Blue Angels. He told me he's flying in something like seventy shows, just this year. The way them boys fly, that's plenty to be worried about. I tell you, Sophie, that's a hard life."

Sophie's brown eyes sparkled and her face was a child's again, watching her two mothers and staring out at her own children as they played on the streets of her childhood, the very streets where she and Red had cavorted from the time they both were nine. "Oh, I can't tell you what it makes me feel to watch him fly. Sure, I get scared sometimes, but I think of all the nights he used to sit up when we were in high school, talking about how he wanted to be a pilot. It's so much a part of him that he'd just wither up and die if they took it away from him. And it makes him so, so *full*. I can't explain it. It's just something you can't separate out from the rest of him. Like God from a priest. So it isn't a hard life, Mama. Not really. The Navy's good to us and he's doing what he wants. He's living out his dream. How many other people can say that?"

Mama Lesczynski had satisfied her pride in her youngest son, and was peering out over her domain again, those dozens of backyards whose movements she had mastered. "Did you see that girl walk by on the other side of that house over there?" She pointed expertly, demonstrating her mastery of the terrain.

"No, Mama, where?"

"Just over there. You remember that funny man, Lazeretti? Fat, greasy man with kidney trouble? He drives a De Soto."

"Kidney trouble?"

Mama had a detective's certainty on her heavy wrinkled face. "Well, his bathroom light goes on every fifteen minutes all night long, every damn night. I'm laying there in bed trying to get some sleep and here comes the light, I can see it even when my shade is down. He must have kidney trouble. If it was the runs every night he'd be skinny. So, anyway, his little girl, you probably don't remember her, Sophie, she's maybe ten years younger than you are, honey. Well, she's about half retarded, I think. Always going around wetting her pants when she was little, smelled like pee all the time. And now she marries this boy who drives a Good Humor truck over in Kittanning, he's pretty slow himself. *Jesus Maria* he was even too dumb to get into the Army, that's what Red's brother Steve said. But that's how slow he is. And anyway they just had a kid. I wonder if that kid's going to be dumb, too. What you think, Mary?"

Sophie's mother leaned back in her chair, considering not the question but how she could safely answer it. "Did the priest bless the baby?"

"Oh, yeah. Down at the Dago Catholic church, not two months ago."

"Then it's in the Lord's hands."

Mama Lesczynski nodded her agreement, stunned at the simplicity of the other woman's approach. "Well, so it is." She turned, touching Sophie on the arm. "Where's your Red, honey?"

Sophie swallowed, not wanting to talk about it, her eyes going round and sad. "He took Pete's little Carol down for a visit. She misses her daddy so, and Red wanted to see Pete, too."

Mama stopped rocking and rubbed her fleshy face, fighting the tears that had come so often over the past nine months, the reality she avoided with her witches and her spying, the pain from having wed and mothered foundry folk.

"Oh, that's so sad, so sad. My poor darling Pete."

❊   ❊   ❊

Little Carol Lesczynski was sniffling, tears traveling the round terrain of her fat cheeks. She absently wiped at them with the back of a hand, staring over at her father. She was wearing her prettiest pink dress. It flared out above her dimpled knees, on the outside of three full slips. Her straight blond hair was bowl-cut in the Polish tradition, making a line from just above her eyebrows, past the tops of her ears, around her head to her neckline.

The Salvation Army Band was playing "God Bless America," slowly and off-key, until it resembled a dirge. Salvation Army members were passing from cell to cell in the Armstrong County Jail, handing out religious materials. A fat, mournful woman in the dark Salvation Army uniform stood in front of Pete Lesczynski's cell and handed him a packet, avoiding his eyes. He took the materials with Catholic ca-

sualness, awaiting the moment during the July 4 combined concert
and religious service when he would have a few minutes to visit with
his daughter and his brother.

The drum boomed methodically. The trumpets sang with hollow
metal screams. Pete watched his little girl through bagged, red pools
of eyes, matching her tears. Her uncle Red was kissing the top of her
head, whispering soft consoling words that became lost in the trumpet's noise. He was wearing a khaki Navy uniform, carrying a hat in
one hand. He had three gold stripes on each black shoulderboard, and
golden oak leafs on his shirt collar. He had ribbons and golden wings
above his left chest pocket. He looked entirely too good, too powerful,
too free to be a Lesczynski.

"Hey, Red!" Pete's head bobbed from side to side, his chin lost in
the heavy flesh of his neck. "God, you look good, boy!" Pete went
down onto his knees as little Carol, the youngest of his five girls, raced
toward him and reached through the bars of his cell. She was wailing.
"Here, honey, it ain't that bad, now. Hey, you going to watch your
uncle Red fly his jet tomorrow, huh? Won't that be a treat, now?"

"Why won't they let you come with us, Daddy? When can you
come home?"

"Not for a while, hon." Pete reached out and grabbed his brother's
hand, shaking it furiously through the bars. "*Damn* it's good to see
you, Red! You don't get home that much anymore." Peering at his
brother's crisp uniform, Pete thought of other days, now more than
ten years gone. "How's your buddies? You know, the ones who came
to Ford City from Annapolis? The Marine got all blown up, and that
Jew fellow?"

"Dingenfelder just got out of the Air Force. He's working for Aero
Dynamics down in Los Angeles. I think he hates it. Smith is back
home in Virginia. I don't know what he's doing for sure. I know he's
going to school. I think he's gotten pretty religious, at least from his
letters."

"Well, that would be a switch. Remember Christmas before you
graduated, him and that—" Pete grinned and then caught himself,
staring uneasily from the mournful, attentive Salvation Army dowager
down to his daughter, who had been clutching one of his legs and
now was playing with the fabric of his trousers. "Anyway, sounds like
you made a pretty smart move, staying in the Navy."

"So"—Red Lesczynski shook his head, half with bemusement and half with his melancholy joy at seeing his older brother again—"you went and punched out a scab. Pete, I never thought you'd do something like that."

"Daddy hit a man who tried to take his job." Little Carol was reciting her understanding of the situation as she clutched Pete's leg. It was a lesson that had been taught to her by rote.

The Salvation Army Band was playing "This Land is Your Land." The mournful fat lady handed Red an extra leaflet and moved on. In the next cell, a young man reached through the bars and embraced his wife with unmuted passion. A guard walked over and glared into his face until he stopped.

"So what the hell is a man supposed to do, you tell me that, Red. Nine months watching my wife and kids line up at the union hall for food like they gave me in the field when I was in the Army. Nine months hanging around the union hall all day, talking and waiting. Nine months staring at that plant, hating it but wanting to go to work in it. You know what that does to a man? When those scabs started walking through the picket line it was like somebody breaking into your home in broad daylight." Pete reconsidered. "No, it was like watching somebody rape your wife." He shrugged, searching his younger brother's face for understanding. "I guess I could have moved to California. That's what management wants, anyway—to bust up the union. But you try that with five kids and no savings. Red, you never worked the foundry, or in the tank. What do you know about the grinders and the rollers? That's the luckiest thing that ever happened to you."

Red Lesczynski massaged the small back of his brother's child. He shook his head helplessly, his dialect taking on all the old idiom of Hunkytown just as easily as his emotions blended with his family's upon his return. "They been picking away at you'ns for a long time, now."

"A hundred men a year they been laying off, ever since you left. Four thousand men working at PPG in 1951, three thousand today. And they'll kill us off over this strike, Red. I can smell it coming. They think they been too good to us. It'll be a runaway factory. The union pushed too hard."

"On the wrong things." Red Lesczynski took a secret breath and said it anyway, knowing it would offend his brother. "Thought you'd tie the strike in with the election, did you now?"

"Kennedy carried Pennsylvania, didn't he? And that made him President."

"Lucky you, Pete. Lucky you."

This land is your land, this land is my land—
This land is made for you and me.

"He's a Democrat. And he's a Catholic. You know what that means?"

"Yeah. It means you're out of a job, and you're in jail. What do you want me to do, congratulate you?"

Pete looked as if he might either rage or cry, his fists white as they grabbed the bars of his cell. "So, don't tell me. You moved away and got a little money and now you're a goddamned Republican."

Carol tugged at her father's shirt. "Don't get mad, Daddy. Uncle Red loves you."

Red Lesczynski reached inside the bars and grasped his brother's heavy rounded shoulder. "No, Pete. I ain't any Republican. I ain't a Democrat, either. I'm a Navy man, that's all. I go anywhere in the world they tell me to go, any time they tell me to, to fight anybody they want me to fight. I move my family anywhere they tell me to move, on a day's notice, and live in whatever quarters they assign me. I work whenever they tell me to work. Hell, I work twenty-four hours a day if they need me to. I don't belong to a union and I don't strike if I don't like what they're doing to me. And I like it. Maybe that's the difference." He shrugged, grinning gamely. "But I'm a peon, just like you."

"That ain't true, Red. Don't even say that. You got any idea what a hero you are? Jesus God, Red, half the people in Ford City live through you! Go on down to the Falcon Club and see the Red Lesczynski wall, eh? Navy football, Fighter Pilot of the Year, Blue Angel. All-American Boy." Pete had an ability to make "All-American" sound as if his brother were faintly foreign, deserving of awe.

"Aw, Pete."

The band had stopped playing. It was almost time to go. Little Carol sensed it, and had started sniffling again, clutching Pete's legs through the bars. Red Lesczynski bit his lips, studying his brother. "Is there anything I can do while I'm home?"

"Make sure you spend some time with Dad, Red. He's taking all of this pretty hard. He's been through the strikes before, but it ain't easy to be his age, with forty years thrown into that hole and your pension on the line." Pete shook his head slowly, as if he were staring at an inalterable sadness, his eyes wet from the ache of his own predicament and from the memories that rolled clear and saline down his cheeks. "He misses you so much. Six sons he's got, and all of us he loves. But he never gets over you being gone, Red. He talks about you all the time. I guess that's the price you got to pay for doing more than the rest of us, eh, Red? You can't know your family anymore."

* * *

Along the railroad tracks the grass grew knee-high where the two men walked in the hot bake of an afternoon sun, in places where the trains once kept it oiled and dead. They seemed a mimic age mirror of each other as they walked, the reflection showing one man his former athletic grace, the other his future frailty. They seemed to hobble, taking awkward steps that avoided protruding railroad ties. A film of rust grew on the rails themselves. Before the strike, two trains a day had kept the rust away.

They were surrounded by common, usually calming things: the town, the factory that was a constant in their lives, each other. Far in front of them the Allegheny River bent underneath a small metal bridge. Children jumped off the bridge into the river, enjoying a merry summer swim day. Red Lesczynski could see them leap and splash. What did they yet know, he wondered, of humiliation, of indignity, of the all-consuming uncertainty of being cut off from a life's work? For that moment he hated the factory and the union both, just as deeply as he loved his father.

"It's so quiet, Dad."

The old man snorted. "Quiet, hell. It's dead."

On their right the factory stretched behind them and before them, a mile-long, empty building that paralleled the river on one side and the railroad tracks on the other. Inside its bleak walls was a foundry that cooked steel and coke, as well as the tank, which boiled up sand and chemicals and made them glass, a grinder and a polisher, transfer cars and turnover cranes, a stripping yard and a washer, racks and ware rooms and examination rooms, cutting tables and more examining rooms, and finally heavy cars that took the merchandise out for the railroads to haul for shipment all over the world. Nothing moved inside the building. It was quiet, abandoned, as fallow as a burned-out cornfield.

Down the railroad berm to their left, Ford City clung to the factory gates, an appendage, a life sack. They could see the small town square and the elevated statue of old John Ford, peering across the tracks toward his plant like some Ozymandias staring out into the empty desert; *look on my works, ye mighty, and despair.*

Reaching down amid the growing weeds, Red Lesczynski picked up a fist-sized chunk of processed glass, and then another. Those vestiges were antiques, chunks of slag from the pots that made up the casting hall of ancient days. The tank, though obsolescent, had been a modernization. The slag rocks were at least thirty years old, and were scattered on the railroad tracks like bullet casings on an old invasion beach, having been scraped out of the pots and dumped outside the factory in those early days.

The glass was soft-edged, like volcanic lava, its translucent green interior shot with little air bubbles. For that moment it was precious, a symbol of the toil that had been expended inside the once vibrant building. His father had walked sand up the pot house ramp in heavy wheelbarrows for forty years to make such jewels. His brothers had done it for twenty. They were factory people, born and reared, with forearms that could snap a broomstick like a pencil, backs that looked as if they belonged on wrestlers, bellies that grew large and heavy from beer. Now the factory was old, outmoded, riven by labor battles. The factory was running away, to be reborn, perhaps, in newer, fresher surroundings. *They can't do that to my dad.*

He was remembering Pete's comment about the past ten years, a hundred men laid off every year during that period, the factory at only 75 percent of its 1951 level even when the strike began. It had made him think of a recent letter from his friend Yukichi Kosaka. Toyota had sold a quarter of a million cars and trucks in 1960, and made a profit of 7 billion yen. They employed eight thousand people now. Those sales and profits were more than ten times the levels Kosaka had mentioned in 1952, when they had first met. Toyota was booming. Pittsburgh Plate was dying. He didn't know if there was a connection, and if there was he didn't know what it was. The contrast simply made him more restless, more upset for his family. *This isn't happening everywhere, I'll tell you that.*

He felt like throwing the chunks of glass back through the window of the factory that had boiled them out of sand those years before, an act of emotion more than defiance, a returning of the seed back to the soil around the roots of its mother plant. Instead, he casually tossed the two pieces in front of him as they walked. It wouldn't do any good to upset the old man any further.

"That's going to be some show tomorrow, son. I bet half of Ford City's driving in to Pittsburgh." The old man chuckled. "There'll be a traffic jam over in Kittanning like they've never seen."

He had found his father at the union hall and had been besieged by a hundred exuberant men, all thankful to be gathering around someone bright and powerful, someone with romance and a future. It was as if he were Theseus, with ichor in his veins, come back to slay the Cretan bull and save his people from their sacrificial slaughter. Pittsburgh Plate was the bull, or perhaps the union was. He didn't know anymore. Either way he was helpless, a figurehead. He was not Theseus, and he knew it. Rather, he was simply a fortunate escapee to a foreign land.

Down the berm the churches raised above the simple tawdriness of the little town, their steeples pointing toward the only hope for eventual equity from life's little twists. Watching them, he remembered other days, and their fond place in his childhood. The church, the Falcon Club, the union hall. On holidays the children of Ford City would line up by family and receive sweets and presents at the union hall, a Big Brother reward for their fathers' long hours in the plant. They loved the union, that dispenser of treats, with the innocent completeness that could only be conjured in a child. Afterward they would stand outside the Chrysler dealership next door, sucking their candy and admiring the latest models. His father had always owned a Chrysler. It was an act of loyalty to the dealer. Red Lesczynski had just bought a Cadillac. The very opulence of it, when his father and brothers were bringing home Spam and beans, bothered him at that moment. No, sir. The Navy wasn't half bad.

"So what's going to happen, Pop?"

The older man, that thicker, slower version of himself, spat with resignation. His spittle melted into the rust of a railroad track, spreading and then quickly disappearing under the hot summer sun. At the end of the tracks sat a lone railroad car. It looked battered and rainwashed. Its wheels were almost locked from rust. The car contained the last load of industrial glass the factory had produced before the strike. The company had hired a "dinky" railroad engine to pull it out after the strike had begun, as if it wanted to extract the last measure of energy from the aging plant before it died. Two thousand somber workers had gathered on the railroad tracks and placed their bodies between the dinky and the railroad car. The dinky had left without the car. The car had begun as the symbol of their resistance. Now it was the rotting summation of their defeat.

"We already lost." His father stared from the railroad car toward the black windows of the silent plant, as if he were watching a monument, or perhaps a tomb. "They'll keep enough men on the line to say they ain't a runaway factory, and they'll disappear. What the hell is a man supposed to do, move to Altoona? Who'd buy a home in Ford City, even if I wanted to sell it?"

The old man worked heavy, fleshy jaws, consciously changing his mood. "Come on with me over to the Falcon Club, son. I want to show you your wall. God *damn* I can't wait to see you fly tomorrow! I seen all them pictures but I never seen the real thing. Come on! I bet they got thirty men in the Falcon Club, just waiting to talk with you."

Walking down the berm and through the little park where old John Ford stared complacently toward the full car and his empty buildings, neither man looked up or back.

* * *

"Good afternoon, ladies and gentlemen. I'm Lieutenant Bruce Watkins, narrator for the United States Navy flight demonstration team, the Blue Angels."

They packed the sides of the National Guard air strip near the Pittsburgh airport, gaudy in their summer shorts and T-shirts, small children on their shoulders and cameras dangling everywhere as if they had been mandatory for admission to the show. They cheered the trim officer who stood before a microphone at the edge of the runway. Rich and poor, boilermen and lawyers, Navy men from World War II come back to view their legacy, high school boys making a pilgrimage to their dreams, wives and girl friends, bored dowagers and secretaries on the make, cramped together with one overriding excitement: to watch man and machine approach perfection, to secretly share the horror that these demigods might tempt the whims of fate one time too often and cash it in, buy the store, *break an airplane.*

Watkins continued over the subsiding applause. "For fifteen years, since the end of World War II, the Blue Angels have been demonstrating the precision techniques of naval aviation to the American public, thrilling an estimated 35 million people with the most exact low-level formation flying ever performed. The maneuvers you will watch today are not stunts, but represent the stock-in-trade maneuvers taught to every Navy and Marine Corps fighter and attack pilot. Ordinarily, these maneuvers are performed by single aircraft, at an altitude of thirty to fifty thousand feet. Today, of course, the Blue Angels will perform in close formation and in a low-altitude environment, so that you may view the skill and precision possessed by these Navy and Marine Corps aviators.

"The Blue Angels are flying the supersonic, after-burner equipped F-11F Tiger. You are about to see maneuvers that will vary from six hundred miles an hour to just above stalling speed, all in the space of less than a minute. We hope you will enjoy it."

They applauded again, tentatively this time, with anticipation. Lieutenant Watkins nodded from his microphone and then peered out at the runway, where the six F-11Fs sat sleek and blue.

"Now, if you will direct your attention to the ramp area off to our right, you will see the six demonstration pilots who will fly this afternoon's aerial demonstration. I ask that you note the military manner in which each pilot approaches his aircraft, is saluted by his crew chief, and then performs a rapid walk-around inspection of this already thoroughly preflighted machine.

"Flying Blue Angel One, the officer in charge and flight leader, from Catawba, North Carolina, in his second year with the team, is Commander Tom Heckler.

"On the right wing, flying Blue Angel Two, our Marine Corps representative from Little Rock, Arkansas, Captain Skip Bankester.

"On the left wing of the diamond formation, flying Blue Angel Three, is Lieutenant Hank Sowell, from Garden City, New York.

"Flying Blue Angel Four, in the difficult and hazardous slot position, in his second year with the team, from nearby Ford City, Pennsylvania, is Lieutenant Commander Red Lesczynski."

The crowd burst like a balloon with applause and screams, several hundred people in one cluster yelling at Lesczynski as he walked toward his aircraft. They were only a few hundred feet away from him. He peered at bright, beery faces with their thick chests and raised fists, and saluted them, grinning shyly. The last two pilots were being announced over the noise. Reaching the aircraft, he laughed aloud, a private exultation of his people and his blood. Crazy hunkies, he thought, climbing into the cockpit. Don't they know that sort of stuff is supposed to make a pilot nervous? But what the hell. This one is for you, Ford City.

He strapped in. Bruce Watkins was explaining that the huge Wright

J-65 turbojets which powered the Tigers would soon make the noise level too high for him to be heard, an ironic announcement since Hunkytown had already drowned out his microphone once.

Zzzip. The canopy closed over him and he was sealed inside a silent world, down in the belly of Judd Smith's whale.

Sophie loved it, that was all. Sometimes people asked her if she wasn't continually afraid, and she would answer that there wasn't any need to be afraid. Red was too good to worry over, and the only other possibility was that Boss Heckler would somehow make a miscalculation, one tiny twitch of his stick in a power dive, perhaps, and lead them all to death since they all keyed on him rather than each other or the ground. But Boss Heckler had more than seven thousand hours inside Navy fighters. You didn't last that long, and you didn't make hundreds of landings on aircraft carriers, those little specks in the ocean that pilots hit at hundreds of miles an hour, unless you were good.

Besides, fear was a useless emotion. It was all or nothing when your husband was flying at five hundred miles an hour with his wing tips actually overlapping two other aircraft. You felt fear when you wanted someone to be careful, to avoid hurting himself out of carelessness or accidents. Accidents were unpreventable, and unworthy of fear. Carelessness was inappropriate when Red Lesczynski himself knew what a moment of inattention would do. That was why his hand trembled at the end of a show, all the way into the night, so that when she was able to be with him afterward she would clasp it inside hers as they slept, to absorb its vibrations. He knew those things so well that Sophie even felt secure watching a show, and indeed sometimes felt guilty because she was unable to conjure up this dread that everyone believed was her duty.

"Oh, there he goes, just look at him!" Mama Lesczynski's eyebrows were arched in fear and adoration, her heavy hands clasped at her chest, for that moment a celebrity herself as other people watched her glow. "My baby my baby my baby . . ."

"Who's your baby, Grandma?" J.J. squinched up a freckled face as if he thought the proposition were absurd. "Dad?"

"Hush, J.J." Sophie put her hands onto a back that already rippled with muscles, and smoothed down her eldest boy's red topknot. "Someday you'll be bigger than your daddy and you'll still be my baby."

"Aw, Mom, come on."

The air filled with the roar of six jet fighters at full throttle, taking off in formation. The noise was in front of them, behind them, inside them. It vibrated their skin. The jets lifted off on the other side of a warpy mirage of heat from their exhaust. It was awesome, it was beautiful. She had seen it dozens of times but it never lost its freshness. It was raw and primeval, and at the same time so advanced that it was beyond her, like spaceships.

From all around her the fists of Ford City raised as the engine roar went louder, and she could see that the men were screaming from some mad elemental energy that sought to match the jets, and also from their collective pride. Red Lesczynski had put them on the map, lifted them from the doldrums of their dying trade, made a figure of himself without guile or treachery, without feeding off their misery. Was it any wonder that their hearts filled up his cockpit, just as surely as if it had been stuffed with joy?

You, Red Lesczynski, she sang, her own spirit lifting with his plane, her high little chin and gleaming eyes no longer able to conceal her pride. *You . . . you, Falcon.*

"Solos clear."

"Don off."

"Dave off."

Only Boss Heckler spoke at any length on the radio. The other pilots simply acknowledged his commands. There was no need to chatter; it had all been done so many times that all they needed to do was listen to the Boss, to follow his tail, to concentrate . . .

"Okay. Ready. Reversal." Up they went, into a steep climb.

"Ready, burner. On. Now." Straight up now, like four missiles, leaving white smoke in the blue summer sky.

"Burner. Off. Now." They floated together over the top of the climb, upside down, almost halting up there next to heaven. Lesczynski watched his air-speed indicator drop lower and lower. He couldn't hold it back, it just floated out of his throat like a wispy pant.

"*Fifty knots,* Boss."

"Ten to spare, Red." A moment of silence. "Hold on. Okay, diamond roll."

"Skip."

"Hank."

"Red."

Straight down they went, like falling from a cliff. The air-speed indicator hit four hundred and kept moving. Lesczynski concentrated on the Boss's tail: *Pull it up, Boss, pull out of it I'll never do this again I'm going to quit this goddamn foolishness tomorrow . . .*

Boss Heckler said it again, just to be sure: "Diamond roll."

"Skip."

"Hank."

"Red."

Get me *out* of it *out* of it . . .

Boss Heckler pulled hard and they leveled off at two hundred feet, roaring past the awed and frightened crowd. "Water. On. *Now.*" Colored vapor streamed from their wing tips, blue from each left wing and red from the right. It was beautiful and eerie, like Christmas and death.

"Up we go." Boss Heckler pulled hard, and they matched him. It was working today, everything was going like it should in Pittsburgh on July 4, America and freedom and Big Red coming home. They went straight up, so hard and fast that each of them suddenly weighed four times their normal poundage as they climbed. Red Lesczynski's face was stretched somewhere behind his ears from the G pull and he focused hard on Boss Heckler's tail, his hand tight on the stick.

"Okay." They rolled as they climbed, their colorful vapor trails twisting together.

"Reversing." They were upside down.

"Twist." They turned out of it, slowly regaining position and righting themselves.

"Down we go." Here it came again, the worst part, following Boss Heckler into that power dive, wings from the other two jets overlapping his. Red Lesczynski was alone with his stick as they dropped from the sky, alone in the knowledge that he was so afraid that he would do anything in the world to get out of doing it again, except suffer the loss of his self-esteem, alone because if he ever told anyone he was afraid they would all be afraid, and that might make him die, alone because he knew that he would do it again and again and again and each time swear to himself as he fell down this voluntary cliff that this plunge toward the hard ground was the last one he would allow himself to take. *No more, Boss. No more. Pull it up, take us out of it . . .*

On the ground the four fighters finished their dive and shot past once again, roaring and spewing colors, only a hundred feet off the ground this time. Mama Lesczynski and several Ford City friends were actually crying from the tension. The diamond flew off to ready another maneuver and shortly the two solo jets screamed past each other at the center of the runway, having closed at a rate higher than a thousand miles an hour and passing within a hundred feet of each other in what was called the knife edge, turning at the same time so that the wings were vertical, only fifty feet off the ground, as if they wanted to peer inside each other's cockpit as they passed.

Mama Lesczynski was exhausted, as if she were absorbing her youngest son's secret fears. She wept and clutched at herself, wanting it to end. Sophie knew that once it was over, Mama would beam more broadly than anyone, with a small claim to having created the day's show.

"My baby my baby . . ."

It was more interesting to watch Red's father, and her oldest son. Sophie smiled with her own fond feeling of creativity. The old man and J.J. were standing somberly side by side. Their faces were tight-lipped and serious, staring into the sky. Their bodies were at identical positions of attention, chests out and hands made into large fists at their sides.

They were watching their blood up in the air as if he were the Flag.

CHAPTER SIXTEEN

Comb your hair and paint and powder,
You act proud, and I'll act prouder
You sing loud and I'll sing louder—
Tonight we'll set the woods on fire!

I

JUDD SMITH WAS DEEP into a sermon. Sort of. He smiled across the table at those warm adoring female eyes and wanted them to know everything about music, about life, yes, about the whole world, especially *his* part of it. It was love, love . . .

"Now, Hank Williams. There was a good old boy. Hear that music, hon? He died an honorable death, I guess. Car wreck, sort of. Right when I was getting shot over in Korea. Seems like half of hillbilly heaven is made up of men who died in either car wrecks or wars."

"Well, I know why they shooted you, Dad." She looked at him with such certainty and finality that for a moment he actually believed that this tawny little six-year-old, the only repository of his blood and anguish, had seen more deeply into it all than he. She sipped her 7-Up, still staring at him with that serious, embracing adoration.

He chuckled softly, lighting a cigarette and peering into owl's eyes. "You're not up for just listening to the jukebox and eating hamburgers, huh? You got to talk philosophy."

"What's that?" She squinched her little nose.

"Never mind, honey. If I started to tell you, you'd end up explaining it to me."

"Anyway, I know." She sipped her 7-Up one more time and delivered the disastrous news, the most unpardonable judgment of the first-grade social order. She almost whispered it. "They didn't like you."

He leaned back against the torn vinyl seat of this rundown diner just off the Robert E. Lee Highway outside of Richmond and laughed, clear and full-toned, his head up to the ceiling. It was so wonderful to be loved, to be puzzled over.

"*Daddy!* It isn't funny!" She was somewhere between hurt and indignation. Clearly, she had been trying to figure out why anyone would want to shoot her father, this fleeting, good-natured figure who swooped up from the far hills on weekends and kept her so enraptured. "Daddy, *why?*"

This was going to be rough. He didn't want to make it simple, because it hadn't been simple. But he hated people who told war stories to children. Someday he'd tell her. "Because somebody told them to."

Her eyes grew round, astonished, and she sat tall in the booth. "*Why?*"

"Because I was trying to shoot them."

"Because you didn't like them?"

Damn it, why does she have to be so smart? Why can't we just talk about Hank Williams? "No. Because somebody told me to."

She drained her 7-Up, a small frown on her round face, peering into the bottom of the glass, contemplating those complexities as if she were a judge. The jukebox was hot with Johnny Cash now, burning up from that ring of fire, blistered from those pills, gravelly and mean as hell. Finally she stared up at him again, her lips in a grimace.

"Anyway, you missed."

He started to laugh again, and then noted her seriousness. He dragged on his cigarette. "No, I didn't miss all of them. I only missed some of them."

"And some of them didn't miss you?"

"That's right!" He felt almost exultant. He thought he had finally satisfied her.

"Daddy, *why?*" She stared up at him from that little round face, looking so much like her mother that sometimes it pained him just to watch her. He shrugged helplessly, beaten by her persistent search for logic. She focused in on his half an ear. "What about the man who shooted you in the head?"

That one was easy. "He was just a bad man."

"Oh. Did you shoot him back?"

"Yeah." Again, someday he would tell her the story, but he did not want her to mix and confuse the gore of the event with her love for him. They were two separate things, that was all, and he did not want them to connect in her mind when she thought of him. He had a secret, unspoken fear that her child's mind might cause her either to love gore because she loved him, or hate him because she detested the violence that his body proclaimed. "Did I ever tell you about Johnny

Cash? Johnny Cash is from over in Arkansas. His daddy was a dirt farmer, just like my daddy. Now he's on every jukebox in the country—"

"*You cocksucker, give me that fuckin' pitcher!*" It came from the next booth, just behind Judd Smith.

"I'll give you a kick in the ass, if you don't shut your face, turdball."

There they went again. They were two men of about his age, crew-cutted and knobby-faced, letting the world know they were drunk and disastrous. Loretta was staring expectantly at him, just the way her mother might have five years before, a natural (was it inbred?) antici-pation that he would resolve the embarrassment, eliminate the foulness from her surroundings. Outside, a stream of cars raced by, their lights flashing against the large window of the diner. Judd Smith said a small prayer for patience, wishing he had brought his daughter to a real restaurant, the kind her mother would have liked.

"Tell the waitress to bring us another pitcher."

"Tell the waitress to lick my dick."

She squinched her face. "Daddy, what does it mean to lick a dick?"

That did it. Judd Smith rose and walked slowly to the next booth, standing over the two thick, slouching men. They peered up at him for a quick moment, taking in his thin frame, the bottom of his eagle tattoo that showed below the sleeve of his T-shirt, his half an ear. Then they smirked to each other, dismissing him.

"Excuse me." They continued to ignore him. The small waitress edged by him, setting another pitcher of beer between them. "Hey!" He leaned forward, making himself a part of their presence. Finally, they looked at each other, and then up at him. "Listen, I've got a six-year-old over there. I'd appreciate it if you'd hold it down a little, all right? She's not used to that kind of talk."

They looked at each other again, grinning balmily from their beer and their self-adjudged badness. The man on the right started it. "Fuck off, buddy."

The man on the left nodded, still looking at his partner. "If you don't like it, leave."

"What did you say?"

The man on the right sat straighter in his seat. "He said leave, hoss! Nobody asked you to bring that girl into a place like this. Just buzz the hell off."

There were a dozen other people in the restaurant. All of them were staring at Smith as if he were an intruder. Loretta was indeed the only child inside. Suddenly she appeared next to him, in a way taking charge of the situation, handing him his cigarettes and grabbing his arm, dragging him toward the door.

"Come on, Daddy."

Judd Smith allowed the child to pull him slowly toward the door, his eyes never leaving the two men's gloating faces, staring them down to show them he was not afraid. At the cash register, he dropped a five-dollar bill.

Outside, the air was hot and wet, swamp air that clung to them, Virginia summer air, like someone else's breath. He approached his car and looked back inside the large window and saw that they were all laughing at him. He said another small prayer, begging God for patience and humility.

"Come *on*, Dad." She pulled hard on his arm as he slowed, facing the two men through the window. "*Daddy!*"

The two men flipped him the bird, then leaned back into their booth, laughing at him and pointing at him as if he were a humiliated fool. He tried to say another prayer but found himself walking back toward the restaurant door.

"Assholes."

"Daddy!" He could hear her cry, but he could not bear to have her remember him in defeat. "Oh, no-o-o-o! Daddy!"

He walked slowly toward them, staying cool. He wanted them to be sitting down when he got there. He wanted them to think he was going to talk to them. Other eyes watched him and he nodded gently, in control, and then as soon as he reached their table he grabbed their beer pitcher and tossed it into the face of the man on the right, then dropped it, and hit the man on the left with a ferocious right cross just under the ear. The man on the right started to get up and Judd hit him, too, just under the solar plexus, his hard ball of a fist sinking three inches into the man's soft stomach. The man leaned over and threw up across the table, his vomit reaching the sagging, unconscious frame of his partner.

That was all. No one in the grimy little restaurant had screamed or even moved from his seat. No one reached out to grab him. They were either terrified or used to it, it wasn't clear which. Loretta's face was pressed against the window, her tears wetting the glass. He dropped another two dollars on the counter on his way out the door. He was breathing hard, from release. He tried to smile at the waitress, but he wasn't a very good John Wayne. His lips shivered from tension. He rubbed his knuckles. They hurt from where he had hit the man's head.

"I think I broke the pitcher."

*　*　*

He was all right as long as he didn't see her. But to walk their daughter up the high steps of her Richmond home and deliver her to the opulent, careful taste that he had once aspired to, if not owned, created a fresh wound every visit. His former wife lived in one of those Xeroxes of an antebellum mansion, a large, columned, three-story home set on too small an acreage, grandiose to be sure, but at the same time pretentious. Julie Clay had married her lawyer after all. The senator had retired. Her mother was dead. Her new husband was related to the Williams family, which owned T. R. Williams Tobacco. Judd Smith had read in the newspaper that Anthony David Williams was declaring for the state legislature. But he couldn't help but wonder, every time he secretly searched the parameters of his former wife's milky translucent face, if she had really gotten what she wanted after all. *Was I that bad, Julie Clay?*

"Daddy got in a fight."

"Oh, Judd."

She had that look in her face as she stood in the lit doorway, dressed in a yellow lounging suit that reminded him of the movies, the look that told him she had never really understood him and because of that she had always feared him a little, held him out at a distance, measured him rather than embraced him. Not that it was supposed to matter anymore. But it did.

"We were in a restaurant and these men said some bad words. Daddy beat them up."

"Judd Smith." She shook her head from side to side, smiling slightly as if she were now remembering, watching him from a safe place, and could thus afford to appreciate and even enjoy his eccentricity. "Are you all right?"

"Yeah. My hand hurts a little, but I wouldn't want to be inside the other guy's head right about now." He grinned sheepishly, watching her giggle. "I'm sorry, Julie. I really didn't want to get involved in something like this in front of Loretta. These things just have a way of happening to me, I guess."

"Let me see your hand." He held it out and she took it, examining it as if he were a puppy with a thorn in its paw. "Oh, it's swollen." It was torture to him that she would hold him so gently.

"Can Daddy come in, Mom?"

"Of course." She smiled sweetly, a reassurance. "Tony's off at a meeting. Would you like some coffee, Judd? It's a long way back to Bear Mountain."

I won't go inside that house, like some sharecropper up to pay the rent, Bear Mountain roughneck hat in hand to be catered to and drink from a china cup and have her worry whether I'd drop it or spill an ash on the rug, to watch my little girl sit on furniture I can't afford and measure me from a referent I could never share, violate my sense of self just for five minutes with a woman I could never stop loving no matter what she did to me or said about me, five minutes of studying the face I can never touch again and the body that another man violates with the false notion that he is her husband before God, my God, my partner, where are you, Lord?

"Well, all right. But I have to get going pretty quick."

"Oh, goody! Daddy, let me show you my bedroom!"

"So, tell me, Judd." Her back was to him as she made coffee and he studied the lanky curves underneath her lounging clothes, through eyes that reached back to a moment almost eight years removed, when he had grabbed the throat of a long-forgotten military rival and escorted her down a White House corridor toward Happily Ever After. "Does Bear Mountain like fighting preachers, or are you going to have to keep all of this a secret?"

*   *   *

She still loves me. Or maybe she loves me for the first time. I can see it in the way she watches me in the chest and neck. I can feel it in the way her small hand lingers on my arm. I can hear it in the way she says good-bye. Not that it's supposed to matter. But it does.

The windshield wipers beat a rhythm as he drove down slow lonesome roads toward southwest Virginia, a four-hour night journey in an ugly summer rain. Soon the mountains would rise to meet him and he would fall deep inside their hollows, further and further away, an isolation, a cloister from his pain, a ready, warm embrace. The drive from Richmond wasn't bad. He kept the radio off, and used the time to think.

Tell me, Lord, answer this for me. They say you gave Man the ability to reason and that made him closer to You, different from the beasts. But isn't it his ability to feel pain that makes him more unique? Isn't there a consciousness in pain that is spiritual? Isn't that why You

felt pain on the cross for all of us? What other animal can be emo-
tionally wounded? What other animal is capable of self-destruction
due to emotional pain? You gave us a brain and this ability to reason
and the greater our ability to reason the more we are able to perceive
inequities, to realize when life is not going to work out. Isn't that why
retarded people are usually happy, because they lack the intelligence
to discern? We have to contemplate complexity in order to understand
that life isn't going right. What other animal commits suicide? I won-
der if the suicide rate goes up as a function of intelligence? Perhaps
it's the ultimate elitism.

And tell me, Lord, when you only get one shot at life, and you
screw it up, so that no matter how good you are or how repentant you
are it doesn't fit all the way back together, should that make me be-
lieve more in You or less?

The black sky wrapped him up inside its blanket as the road cut
into mountain forests. The windshield wipers beat like a drum against
his silence. The warm rain whispered to him that he'd always be
Christ's lover.

* * *

He had recently come home, having finished divinity school at
nearby Lynchburg, and moved into the small cabin that his grandfa-
ther had built sixty years before. He lived alone. He had no indoor
plumbing or electricity. The cabin sat next to a swift stream, just up
the edge of a slope, and he used the old spring house for his refrigerator. He had to ease his car over a shaky, handmade wooden bridge
in order to park in his yard.

The cabin was dark. His three dogs met him at the car, barking and
prancing, their tails wagging wildly. They were dirty and odorous
from a day in the water and the woods. He hit one of them in the
muzzle.

"Get *down*, dog!"

Inside, he lit a kerosene lamp and sat at a small desk he had made
from an old military footlocker. He pulled a thick notebook from an
alcove in the desk. It was a binder, the kind students carry to class.
He opened it up and flipped quickly through hundreds of pages that
were filled, margin to margin, with his tight, controlled scrawl.

He picked up a pen and put it thoughtfully to his mouth, then
began to write.

August 1, 1962. I saw you again today and it all came back so hard.

I long for innocence, yearn for simplicity with a pain that rides my days like an ugly bloodsucker. I can see it in the faces of small children and in the trees that go bright with summer leaves. I can grasp how it left me, just as swiftly as a frost can strip those trees of their gaiety; no, just as slowly as the small child's face takes on life's scars. I watch young lovers clasp each other in that first sure embrace that says forever and I wonder, I wonder, how long is forever this time? It was not long for me. I am foul, I have floundered in the Pit, I have fornicated freely and I have killed my fellow man. I do not deserve you, much as I wish for you, much as I once claimed you were too soft and spoiled to deserve me.

Good night, Julie Clay. Good night, my love. Take care of our child. We are all the joint heirs of God's grace, and on the other side of earthly life, He will marry us again.

II

The newly Reverend Judsonia Smith stood tall at the pulpit, surveying the dark interior of his very own church. He cleared his throat and tenderly massaged the onionskin pages of his Bible.

"The Scripture reading for today is from The First Book of Peter, Chapter Two, verses one through six."

He peeked up from the Bible and surveyed his parishioners, all five of them. They seemed attentive enough. He felt encouraged. He was surprised at his own nervousness. He had been less nervous when he knew he was going to get his guts blown out in Korea. He thought about that, and decided it was appropriate. In Korea, he had been in the Lord's hands. Today, and for as long as he kept preaching, the Lord's message was in his. It had been less demanding the other way around.

"So put away all malice and all guile and insecurity and envy and all slander. Like newborn babes, long for the pure spiritual milk, that by it you may grow up to salvation; for you have tasted the kindness of the Lord. Come to Him, that living stone, rejected by men but in God's sight chosen and precious; and like living stones be yourselves built into a spiritual house to be a holy priesthood, to offer spiritual sacrifices acceptable to God through Jesus Christ. For it stands in the Scripture, 'Behold, I am laying in Zion a stone, a cornerstone chosen and precious, and he who believes in Him will not be put to shame.'"

He looked up at them, staring into each suddenly self-conscious pair of eyes. He worked hard to keep the edges of his voice gentle, devoid of pride. "My friends, St. Peter was the rock, his church was the rock, this church that we dedicate today will be the rock, and I will be the rock, so long as God wills it."

They gathered at the door when he was done, shaking his hand and smiling politely, seemingly happy with the content of his message. Inside, he glowed. It was a start, anyway—five parishioners, two of them his parents, two the Baxters, because he had fixed their well pump the week before and had cornered them into coming to the service in lieu of money or milk or even thanks, and a cousin who was probably more curious than religious.

His father slapped him on the shoulder as he left the church. "Buddy, you always had a magic with them words."

His mother nodded in agreement, no doubt congratulating herself on having kept the evil away from her midnight baby thirty-six years before, knives in the cradle and the name given on a piece of paper to the preacher when Judd Smith himself was baptized. Wild and brilliant, that was her bad boy, now come home to settle down.

After everyone had left he paced the inside of the small frame building for a few minutes, savoring his first service, and then walked outside, into the dirt parking lot. He had rebuilt the old abandoned church by himself, plank by plank, pew by pew, shingle by shingle. It had taken him six months, but it had been a labor he had enjoyed like no other. The church sat on a small knoll, among a stand of white oaks, flanked by two outhouses on one side, and a picnic area on the other. It was his church, now, up from abandonment, just like its pastor.

It was March 1963. The mountain nights were still icy, their winds brick hard when they came across the Alleghenies from the north, but along the rolling, cascading peaks he could already see the earth aborning, juicy with fresh green fields and budding trees. *My people have been lost sheep; their shepherds have led them astray, turning them away on the mountains.* It was from the Book of Jeremiah and he was immediately sorry he had thought it because it sounded bitter and at that moment he felt only contentment. He had been the lost sheep, not his people, and he had come back to the mountains to be reborn.

*   *   *

Mrs. Floyd started coming because he stopped by her little country store every day to ask how she was doing and to buy a cola. She got to telling people about how he was just the nicest man, and when her boy Henry fell off the barn and hurt his back it was Preacher Smith who came by the house every morning to let the cattle into the back pasture and spread hay. One night they had to pull a calf that was breeching, its mother lowing and dying on the barn's straw-covered floor, and the reverend put poor aching Henry at ease and pulled it himself. He even helped Henry cut the oysters off the bull calves that were going to go for beef, a sad and bloody job if you let yourself think about it. Henry and his wife and three children started coming just after that.

Ward Andrews started showing up with his family because the reverend had spent the good part of one week helping him take his tobacco plants one by one from the seedbed and plant them into the scrabbled earth on the side of the steep hill that he sharecropped in order to keep living in his small tin-roofed house. It was back-breaking work, like pulling onions and then replanting them again. Ward Andrews didn't even own a tractor, but Henry Floyd loaned his to the reverend to use.

The Callahans trickled in, a large group each Sunday until pretty soon close to a dozen of them were coming regularly, because the reverend had brought them twenty pounds of dressed venison he had killed and cleaned, knowing they could always use meat. They'd asked him with their shy mountain indirectness if it wasn't a bad idea for a preacher to be out hunting, and he'd answered that God wouldn't judge him if the meat was eaten, any more than He would judge a man who slaughtered a hog for Thanksgiving. They'd never heard of a preacher man who could justify living like the rest of them.

The rest of them began pouring in from the ridges and the hollows, and even from the small town itself five miles away, because they heard that a man had built a church with his own two hands and was talking inside it each Sunday with the rare power of someone who was not hiding behind a preacher's collar, of someone who had been out and seen the world and been cut up and shot and hurt by life, until he could look inside all of their souls and truly forgive, absolutely understand, because he had overcome it all himself, and found a sense of Grace.

The dirt road up to Judd Smith's little church looked like rush hour on Sunday mornings, and the hills filled with the echoes of unfettered, joyous hymns.

CHAPTER SEVENTEEN

I

IT WAS OCTOBER 1963, and Japan was back. The cityscape between Yokosuka and downtown Tokyo almost jumped with energy. Red Lesczynski peered out from the train and remembered a trip eleven years before on the creaking *densha*, people climbing into windows and hanging out from compartments, the towns still quaint or recently up from rubble.

Now there was power out alongside the rails. Professor Crane Howell's thoughtful analogy of years before stuck in Red's mind as he watched: *jujitsu.* You take the strength of your adversary and throw him with it. Here it was, the best of Western culture picked up like unbruised apples at a supermarket, assimilated by the Japanese, and the rest thrown away. The essence would always be Japanese, and that was the point. They wore Western clothes, most of them. They made cars and refrigerators and stereo systems, instead of silk and trinkets. But that was all window dressing; they could make anything and market it. The product wasn't important, and he felt it as he moved among their people. The making of it was. It was not the product, but the process itself, and what it did to their people. And the process would always be Japanese.

He reached the Sanno Hotel, and stared across the car-choked Sotobori Dori to a raw construction site, where a new office building was going up. A gritty Japanese worker sat on a stack of steel girders that a crane was lifting hundreds of feet into the air, to the top of the structure. The young man wore a hard hat, green work clothes, and gray Japanese workshoes that resembled mittens, with a separate pocket for his big toe. His left hand grasped a steel line. His right hand held a book six inches from his face, as if he would be wasting precious minutes if he were not studying as he dangled in the Tokyo sky.

Nope, thought Lesczynski as he picked up his suitcase and walked toward the Sanno's horseshoe entranceway, *nobody's going to hold these people back.*

The old hotel stood in the Akasaka section of downtown Tokyo, just a few blocks from the National Diet Building and the Japanese Supreme Court, and halfway between the Imperial Palace and the hallowed Meiji Shrine. Since 1945 it had served as an American military hotel, but the Sanno was something of a memorial itself. During the two decades before the beginning of World War II, the Sanno was the headquarters for Japan's intelligence network. Government operatives returning from secret missions, as well as businessmen who traveled abroad, always stopped at the Sanno, reporting any tidbit of information that might relate to national security. During the war, several radio programs every day emanated out of Room 426 of the Sanno. "Zero Hour," "Humanity Calls," and numerous propaganda messages designed by Japanese Army Intelligence had been created and scripted in the so-called "Quiet Room" on the fourth floor.

Before that, the Sanno had been the launching pad for Japan's militaristic era. On February 26, 1936, a small group of young Army officers headquartered at the hotel had committed *gekokujo*, a series of assassinations intended to help redress Japan's social ills. The infamous "2-26" uprising ended in death for the officers who had dared to murder Japan's leaders. At the same time the incident brought about martial law and military control of the government, and eventually provoked the instability that caused Japan to fall berserkly into war.

And in a way, thought Lesczynski, walking into the building and returning the smiles and bows of the Japanese doorman and the bellhop, the Sanno represented what had happened to Japan's view of militarism ever since. Under the old Samurai Code, warriors were at the top of the social order, and merchants at the bottom. The United States military moved into the Sanno Hotel at the same time it occupied the country and took over Japan's defense responsibilities. This rundown four-story hotel, once among the best in Tokyo, was becoming dwarfed by huge luxurious monstrosities that were monuments to the inversion of the old code. Business conquests had captured the national imagination, and warriors were no longer held in awe and esteem.

He handed the eager, deferential bellhop his bag. Unless they're American warriors, that is.

*　*　*

"Renshki-san!"

"*Kamban wah*, Yukichi! It's so good to see you again."

They bowed deeply to each other, from the waist, smiling like schoolboys. Lesczynski then put an arm around Yukichi Kosaka, and led him into the Sanno's dimly lit bar.

Kosaka had changed, while the Sanno had not. The bar seemed a holdover from the occupation days. A Japanese woman played American songs from behind a grand piano. Young, plain girls from the countryside walked from table to table dressed in shorts and black stockings, revealing plump shapeless legs. An old Japanese man tended bar in front of a large, gaudy mirror. Across the red carpet, in the back room, someone had scored a jackpot on one of the slot machines. The bell buzzed interminably and a Japanese woman was giggling and shouting, drowning out the plaintive piano notes.

Kosaka stared with disapproval as he examined the bar girl who took their order. When the woman in the next room shouted, he frowned. The Sanno was not Japan, not anymore, and it was clear he wanted no part of it.

"You are my guest tonight, at Japanese night club."

"*Geisha,* huh?"

"Oh yes. Very nice." American military men called loudly to each other, seemingly anxious to show off their Japanese women. Kosaka consciously ignored them, smiling politely to Red Lesczynski. "Ah, Renshki-san. Six years is too long. I am happy you survived Blue Angels and are back in Japan. You are here maybe for a month?"

"No, only a week."

"Only one week? No-o-o, that is too sad to come all the way to Japan and be here one week. Where you go from here?"

"Vietnam." Lesczynski watched Kosaka's thick eyebrows arch with surprise and interest. "I work for the Secretary of the Navy now. He sent me as an escort for a congressional fact-finding mission. I'm traveling with a dozen congressmen and senators. They've been getting briefed at Hawaii, then here at Yokosuka and Yokota Air Base about our defense capabilities in the Pacific. Then we're going into Saigon." Lesczynski drained the last part of his beer and banged the glass onto the table, calling for another. It was a measure of camaraderie among the Japanese to drink hard. Hard drinking opened up your heart. "It's pretty bad over there, now. We're trying to figure out what to do about it."

"Indochina will always be at war." Kosaka smiled, gulping scotch whiskey, then consciously softened his unusually direct statement. "For maybe another thousand years, anyway. Then they will be one people, like Japan." Lesczynski watched Kosaka carefully, a bit uncertain after six years, and the Japanese businessman picked up his tension. "All great Asian countries have come together after many civil wars, when one strong leader can unite them. Like the Emperor Meiji in Japan, a hundred years ago."

"Like Ho Chi Minh?"

Kosaka shrugged casually, his face unreadable, parrying the analogy. "The mistake of Japan in the war was to believe that our country could unite other countries under feudal rule."

"Maybe that's what China wants to do today, Yukichi." The small Japanese man shrugged, smiling again, as if he did not wish to pursue it any further. Lesczynski absorbed Kosaka's sleek, prosperous look, and the manner that indicated he was used to making hard decisions. The past eleven years, since Kosaka had first bowed and smiled and deferred so gratuitously to Red Leszynski, had toughened him. "I didn't drop bombs on Koreans in that war, Yukichi. I dropped them on Chinese. And they'll have their own nuclear capability within the next year. We don't know what they're up to. It's the communists who believe they can unite other countries under feudal rule, not the Americans. That's what we're trying to stop."

"Renshki-san," Kosaka was smiling patiently, unyielding in the point he had not directly made. "You have many soldiers in Vietnam."

"About sixteen thousand, now. Fifteen thousand more than we had when Kennedy took office."

"How many soldiers do the Chinese have in Vietnam?"

"Who knows? The Chinese were the main supporters of the North Koreans, and of the Viet Minh when they fought the French. They supported the Malaysian communists. They're active right now with the Indonesian communists. And they can come into Vietnam in a day. That's what they did in Korea." He stared into his beer, then up to Kosaka. "Do you want to see all of Asia go communist, Yukichi? Answer me that. How many Toyotas do you think you'd sell if Asia went communist?"

"We will always be thankful to America for helping Japan again become a strong country, and for America protecting Asia from the communists. I must speak from the heart, and tell you I am not worried for Japan, or for America. I worry for my friend." Kosaka drained his scotch and stood, bowing slightly as he indicated to Lesczynski that they should depart.

The Marunouchi subway line's entrance was inside a new shopping plaza, just across from the expansive Akasaka Tokyu Hotel. Lesczynski

followed Kosaka across a busy street, losing him for a moment
in the packed crowd. The people took off like cross-country racers
once the little green light indicated that they should walk, driven by
deadlines, and the husky Kosaka in his gray wool suit blended in with
all the others. An occasional kimono-clad woman broke the Western
monotony, but it was as if the bulk of them had learned to dress in
London. One could not have guessed from Kosaka's understated
clothes or the way he moved that he was among the most talented
young executives at one of the fastest growing corporations in the
world. And how Japanese, thought Lesczynski. He works for Toyota,
but he rides the subway. I wonder if he even owns a car?

Blue-uniformed ticket-takers waited at their stalls, faces impassive,
clicking their punchers endlessly like barbers working scissors over a
man's hair, click click click, sometimes onto tickets and some into the
air, a mark of their profession, a matter of style. Downstairs, on the
platform, people lined up in urgent little rows along marked lines.
Soon the train came and the doors opened and immediately everyone
pushed, unspeaking, as if in a rugby scrum or attempting to flee a fire,
jamming into the subway cars. Lesczynski felt himself carried along
into the car by their force. Next to the cars, a conductor looked up
from his stopwatch and blew a whistle, and the train doors slammed
shut, excluding anyone who had not jammed himself inside. The train
lurched forward immediately, into its underground tunnel—*exactly* on
time.

They were so incredibly industrious, so driven, the Japanese. Even
on the trains, after a day of work or school, their moments were carefully spent, most people either reading or sleeping, making use of this
little block of time. Kosaka did not converse with him on the subway.
It seemed almost a matter of protocol to be within one's self, chatter
being a sign of something weak, perhaps idleness or a lack of concentration.

They offloaded at Shinjuku, Tokyo's Sin City, colored signs and
bright lights, pimps and hard-driving American music assaulting them
as they walked quickly down streets that were never empty. Some of
the clubs and restaurants were as small as an American living room.
American clothes were as dominant in Shinjuku as the heavy gray
wool had been in Akasaka, jeans and bright sweaters and even bobby
socks, although Lesczynski strained to see another American face.
Eleven years before, on his first trip to Tokyo, Americans had been almost as commonplace as the Japanese themselves.

Kosaka walked quickly, his head down, ignoring the catcalls from the pimps. Lesczynski followed alongside, drawing frequent stares, unable to stop gawking at everything, little restaurants and masses of people and night clubs that reminded him of New York. Japan had grown up. He thought he liked it, but he wasn't sure. He felt vaguely like he had contributed to it, but he didn't know how.

Finally Kosaka turned down a concrete stairway and knocked at an unmarked door. It opened slightly, and he showed the doorman a card. The door opened all the way and Lesczynski followed him into a luxurious entranceway. Beyond was a large, thickly carpeted room, ornately decorated with chandeliers and mirrors, dining tables, and a dance floor.

The patron of the club, dressed in a Western tuxedo, was delighted to see Kosaka. He bowed deeply, and conversed excitedly with the stocky Toyota executive for several minutes. Lesczynski stood awkwardly at Kosaka's side. He was the only non-Japanese in the club.

Kosaka grabbed his arm. "Tanaka-san, this is my friend Renshki-san. He is a Navy pilot, the best pilot in the American Navy."

"Ahhh, so!" Mr. Tanaka bowed deeply. "Kosaka-san says you were Blue Angel pilot. Very good! We hope you enjoy your stay with us tonight!" The man was old enough to have fought in World War II, and no doubt had. His little smile told Lesczynski again that such men would always feel a certain loss of face. *Or did they secretly wish they had it to do over again, so they could make it come out right? Or had it come out right in the long run, anyway, if you could forget the cost?*

Lesczynski bowed back. "It is an honor to visit you."

Inside the room, four kimono-clad young *geisha* girls folded their hands below their chins and trotted toward them like nymphs, as if two idolized movie stars had just arrived. The girls fawned over them, drawing them to a small table and seating them, then kneeling next to them on cushions. Kosaka glanced absently at a pack of cigarettes and almost before he raised his eyes one winsome, oval-faced beauty had placed a cigarette between his lips and was lighting it for him. Kosaka must have ordered drinks from the patron because Lesczynski no sooner thought about having a beer than another giggling, lightly chattering young lovely was pouring him one and raising the glass to his lips.

No woman, however rich or powerful, was allowed to visit such a club. It was the *geisha* girls' domain. They didn't speak English; at least, not well enough to converse. They were all in their twenties.

They were not prostitutes. They were trained to worship men for a living, to provide a fantasy of gaiety and coquettishness, to take the hard-driving Japanese businessman back to the romance of another era, to help him forget for a night every month or so that his employer demanded total effort and allegiance, while his wife controlled all the family decisions. They sang, ancient Japanese songs and more modern ones if a man requested it. They danced, alone in the old way or with a man if he desired. Their presence required a small fortune from the beneficiaries of their sweet little lies, but that was all right, and Lesczynski knew it. Japanese men's clubs were a business perquisite, a reward. Toyota sent Kosaka out like this as a small payback for his competence.

Lesczynski drank from the glasses they held to his lips. He ate food out of their tiny fingers. He watched Japanese executives move crudely with them on the dance floor, jutting aging pelvises into their nubile warmth as they giggled and endured. He was entirely content, and talked for hours with Kosaka about Japan, about Vietnam, about Toyota. Toyota had made 230,000 cars and trucks in 1962, and would produce 310,000 in 1963. In 1952, they had made 10,000. Yukichi Kosaka wanted to see them produce a half million by 1964, and thought they would reach that goal. He saw Asia as a gigantic Go board, with Toyota filling up the corners, area by area, surrounding marketplaces and capturing the locales until, just as in a game of Go, Toyota would own the board and totally dominate the markets.

Kosaka became very drunk. He described his Go analogy in detail, waving his small hands in the air, with the *geisha* girls smiling and nodding at his English descriptions, speaking of "killing off" competitors and leaving their products "dead," just as an opponent's stones were killed off and left dead on a Go board. Finally his eyelids narrowed and his high voice took on a teasing intonation. "Maybe America is a Go board, too."

"Maybe. I don't know, Yukichi. I'm a warrior, not a businessman."

"That should change, Renshki-san." A cute *geisha* giggled as Kosaka nibbled her fingers while she fed him *yakitori*. "Businessmen are warriors, now. It is a new world since the war. The old rules don't apply anymore. You don't control a country with guns now. You only make its people angry. You control a country by making it need what you can bring to it."

"Maybe for you, Yukichi. Japan hasn't had to worry about defending itself since the war. Isn't that ironic? Your merchant fleet has gone from 2 million tons to almost 9 million tons, just in the last ten years. You've got more than four thousand merchant ships, and what does your Navy look like? A hundred tiny auxiliary craft. Twenty destroyers. Twenty-eight small frigates. Eight submarines, none of which leave your coast. What do you think would happen to your businesses if they couldn't ship on sea-lanes that the American Navy's nine hundred ships protect? Why do you think we have 860,000 sailors and Marines on active duty around the world?" Lesczynski consciously softened his tone, not wanting to further offend Kosaka, who appeared chagrined. "The old rules still apply, Yukichi. Japan just doesn't have to deal with them anymore. You're not going to stop communist aggression in Vietnam with transistor radios, I'll tell you that."

"Ah, Renshki-san." Kosaka seemed weary, sad for his naïve American friend. "I have a gift for you. But first you must come with me to another place. A different, very important place."

"Tonight?"

Kosaka checked his watch. It was eleven o'clock. "It's not far. We can take the Shinjuku line to Ichigaya, and walk."

*　*　*

They passed two concrete lion-dogs at the entrance gate as they walked underneath a huge stone *torii* in the black October night.

Lesczynski immediately remembered where they were, although he had not visited the shrine since 1952. Yasukuni, the hallowed resting place of the spirits who had fallen in all of Japan's wars, more than two and a half million of them. The shrine was as large as several football fields, and they had it all to themselves at midnight. Side by side they strode along a gravel path lined with trees and bordered on each side by rows of tall stone lanterns. The lanterns were unlit, cold and haunting. Leaves sailed in front of them and around them on crisp, puffy autumn breezes as they walked. Halfway to the main hall they stopped for a moment, not speaking, and peered through the darkness at a large bronze *samurai* soldier standing proud and fierce in the old warrior garb, on top of a ten-foot pedestal.

Kosaka did not seem drunk. He trudged steadily, his body gathered and his hands in tight fists, almost aglow with the quiet conviction that he was in the presence of the gods. Lesczynski walked alongside him. The sounds of heavy traffic on the nearby Yasukuni Dori wafted up to them on gentle bursts of wind, punctuated by an occasional horn, but the dominant sound was the crunching of their own feet as

they strode through gravel and dry leaves, past further rows of concrete lanterns, and the sibilant whispering of other leaves overhead in
the trees.

They passed underneath the tall bronze *torii* that marked the entrance to the courtyard. Inside, white doves flitted about in the dark,
pecking at isolated kernels of grain left over from the day's visitors,
who bought food for the birds at a nearby stand. The main hall's front
facade was immediately before them, draped by a white curtain that
was marked with black chrysanthemums, the symbol of the Emperor
Meiji, who first created the shrine.

Kosaka hesitated, moving slowly inside the courtyard. He looked at
Lesczynski and then left him at the courtyard entrance, climbing the
outer steps of the main hall. Inside, in a place no mere citizen could
visit, were scrolls that contained the names of every Japanese soldier
who had perished on the battlefield since the unification of the country in 1868, along with his home town, the date he died, and the location of his death. Lesczynski knew that two of Kosaka's brothers were
on the scrolls. He watched in respectful silence as the squat little businessman clapped twice, awakening the spirits, bowed deeply to them,
and then tossed a handful of coins into a long, thin box. Kosaka
remained at the altar for a full minute, his head bowed in prayer, and
then finally rejoined Lesczynski near the *torii*.

"You know what this is?" His breath made frosty clouds in the
night.

"Yeah. I've been here before, Yukichi. A long time ago."

"I come here every week." Kosaka took a small, square piece of
leather from his pocket. He held it up in front of Lesczynski. On one
side was a gold-embossed *torii*, on the other was a chrysanthemum.
He opened it up. Inside was a square of white paper.

"You know what this is?"

"No."

"This is cut from the Yasukuni scroll! Oh yes! If you carry this with
you, the gods of Yasukuni will protect you. No bullets will hit you!
You cannot die in accident, only of old age. Very special! No give foreigners, Renshki-san."

Lesczynski nodded slowly, appreciating the magnitude of that
black, chilly moment.

Kosaka pressed it into his hand. It was not much larger than a
matchbook. "I will pray to the Yasukuni spirits for you, every week
when I come here to remember my brothers and my friends." He

closed Lesczynski's hand over it, holding the meaty hand that so intricately guided jet aircraft in his own two small but muscled paws. "It makes me very sad, Renshki-san, *very sad!* But you are going to war in Vietnam. Soon."

II

They landed at Tan Son Nhut and the dank perfumed air welcomed them as foreigners, warned them of its equatorial powers, surrounded their nervous excitement with its biting odors and kissed the insides of their lungs with promises of asphyxiation. It crawled along their skin, coaxing sweat out of their pores as if it were a special kind of magnet. It hung over nearby Saigon like a pretty little orange umbrella, rancid and cute at the same time. Breathing it was like sticking your head inside the exhaust pipe of an idling truck. Red Lesczynski took from it cautiously, shallow breaths, slow and spare, not trusting its deceptive sweetness and not liking his first hot green look at Vietnam.

The road toward downtown Saigon was cluttered with bicycles and *sigolo* motorbikes and little cars and people afoot, many half naked and pushing cattle, children staring at the American bus with idle curiosity. Along the road, masses of tin houses piled on top of each other in cluttered, dense green weeds and trees, heavy with people who seemed to ooze out of the surroundings, frail and long-limbed and blank in the face, like spider monkeys. Southern Asian towns had a sameness at their outer edges, before one reached the places more affected by now-departed European sponsors. They were dense with voyagers, families in from the hinterlands to try and savor a piece of their city cousins' pie.

Near the center of the city the air filled with a heavy sweet citrus aroma, and they drove past block after block of lime trees. After that, Saigon became an oriental improvement of Paris, heavy with French architecture, drowning with noise and people. The driver dropped the delegation at the Continental Palace Hotel just off Tu Do Street, a famous French vestige from Saigon's supposedly happier days. The hotel had a huge walk-around portico, and the most elegant whores in the world lounged at tables covered with stiff damask tablecloths, dressed in silk *ao dais*, drinking gin and tonics served by white-coated waiters. Many of them were obviously half French with their pale skin and full physiques. They moved slowly, as if in a trance, sipping their drinks and openly studying the dozen members of Congress who had just entered the hotel.

Inside the hotel's entranceway, huge, stately trees burst forth among bright flowers in the center garden. It was the most beautiful hotel Lesczynski had ever been in. He followed the delegation to the large front desk, checked quickly into his room, and immediately escaped, wandering through the heavy air and bustle of Tu Do Street.

He wanted to see a soldier, any soldier. He was trying to believe that Vietnam was at war.

*   *   *

"Well, General, I've got myself a real problem, and maybe you can help me get to the bottom of it." Senator Clem Handley, the second-ranking Democrat on the Senate Foreign Affairs Committee, pulled his pipe out of his mouth and rubbed his large beak of a nose, his blue eyes hollow and bright, emanating perplexity. Handley was either in a dilemma or feigning one, it wasn't clear which. The old Oregon lawmaker was a master at playing possum, giving off weakness and confusion as a negotiating technique so that he might flush out an opponent and go for his jugular. "I've been around Asia off and on for pretty near all my life. Served in China as a young Marine just off the farm, way before the war. Came back to Japan just before the war as a businessman. Traveled all around. Came here in 1955, just after the partition, and again in 1961. I care a lot about our interests in Asia. You know what I'm getting at."

"Yes, sir." Brigadier General Mark Crawford stood before a large map in the briefing room at the Military Assistance Command, Vietnam (MACV) headquarters. In front of him were nearly thirty men: four senators and eight members of the House of Representatives, the others congressional staffers, State Department and Defense Department civilians, and military aides such as Red Lesczynski. Crawford held himself erect as he peered at Senator Handley. He was starched and shined. He held a pointer in his hand. He was obviously straining his mind furiously to keep up with the senator's slow western drawl, to figure out what he was indeed getting at. The data was on the map and in the brief itself. Most of the congressional delegation in the seats in front of Crawford had both comprehended and approved of it.

And Crawford himself was no slouch. Lesczynski was sure of that, having breakfasted with the trim athletic infantry officer that morning, along with the other military and State Department escorts. A Vietnam assignment in 1963 was a true plum, and particularly a billet as the G-3 on the MACV staff. Germany was potentially hot, after the erection of the Berlin Wall and the Soviet threat to blockade the city again. The Caribbean was a mess, after the near war of October 1962, and the American blockade of Cuba. But Vietnam was a true shooting war, as the military termed it. To serve as G-3 for sixteen thousand men, overseeing their multitude of activities across the country, was as important a post as any brigadier general might have in the entire U. S. Army. The Army wasn't wasting it on dummies or cowards.

Handley tamped his pipe, leaning back in his front row seat and crossing long, spindly legs. His thin mouth worked slowly, pursing and grimacing as he examined the pipe, keeping Crawford on a nervous hold. The air conditioner at one side of the room whirred, sucking smoke out of the room. A fluorescent light above them blinked and buzzed. Handley looked up again, uncrossing his legs and leaning forward, his pipe stem a pointer directed at the briefing map.

"Now, you're telling me that since you developed this 'Strategic Hamlet Program' last year, the Diem government has moved 10 million people from their homes into fortified villages—"

"Yes, sir. Since February a year ago, the government has established 11,864 strategic hamlets, holding close to 10 million people." Crawford glanced at the map again, as if for reassurance, his trim features consciously erect.

"And that the other areas, the—" Handley seemed to falter.

"'Open areas,' sir."

"Yes, yes. Of course. The 'open areas.' The 'open areas'"—Handley played with the words, drawing them out, letting them roll off his tongue as if he were tasting something foul—"are subjected to intermittent bombing and artillery fire, in order to—*encourage*—the villagers to move into the strategic hamlets."

Crawford was indeed no dummy. He could see the rest coming. He exhaled heavily, rubbing the back of his shaved head with one hand and holding his pointer toward the ground with the other, as if mildly perplexed himself. "Yes, sir. It is considered necessary at this point to evacuate the villagers and place them in the strategic hamlets in order to provide physical security from Viet Cong terrorism, and to sever the social ties the VC have established. It's a temporary measure, in order to gain control over the countryside and minimize civilian casualties while the war is being fought. I know it sounds somewhat distasteful, sir, but—"

"Distasteful?" Senator Handley's owl eyes cut a hole through General Crawford's face. "Di*stasteful?* For Christ's sake, it's the most unworkable goddamn thing I've ever heard of! We're interested in keeping communism out of South Vietnam, General, not creating the ideal laboratory conditions for it to grow!"

Handley drew back a bit, pressing his assertion by his very silence. He packed his pipe, his voice calm again. "I assume you've spent a good deal of time in Asia, General?"

"Korea, sir. Two tours."

"Then I may also assume you are familiar with the special place the village has in an Asian's heart?" Handley lit his pipe. "You can ask a Japanese living in Tokyo where he's from, and he'll tell you the village that his family moved from two generations ago. Do you understand what we like to call 'the village mentality,' General?"

"Well, yes, sir." Crawford searched among the other members of the delegation for support. They were silent, either lost, uninterested, or curious. "That's why we depend so heavily on the advice of our Vietnamese counterparts, Senator. It's their country, and their war to lose."

"Well, they're doing a damn good job of it, aren't they? Look, I'm not trying to be an obstructionist. I want to keep the communists out as badly as anyone. But examine this program of yours, General. In the first place, you don't have 10 million people in these, whatever you call them, refugee centers. Your Vietnamese counterparts are lying to you. It's obvious. They're mandarin. They don't want to have to lose face by admitting the program is a failure, and I can guarantee you that it is. Most of these Vietnamese families have been in the same village for five hundred years. Their ancestors built those little rice paddy dikes with their bare hands. You're not going to move 10 million of them away and into goddamn *stockades* in one year! And that's what they'll think they are, too. Stockades. And that's the second point, General. The villagers don't see the big picture. They see the government troops coming in and disrupting their lives and bombing the ones who won't cooperate. I don't doubt that many of them come into the hamlets from these 'open areas' to keep from getting killed by the government! That's a hell of a motivation!"

Senator Handley was almost shouting now, totally intimidating General Crawford. Lesczynski had no doubt that even that outburst was carefully considered, tactical. Handley was a master. "So the communists come to the villager and tell him they're trying to help him keep his land, that they'll drive this Diem bastard away just like they did the French, and that the Americans are coming to persecute them, to make them a colony again! And what the hell is the villager going to think, General? You've scared the death out of him! You've taken his farm away from him, or at least you're claiming to the world that you have! It's *disgusting!*"

Handley calmed down again. He had an almost musical ebb and flow in his moods, a symphonic way of manipulating an antagonist. "So, my little problem, General, is how I can continue to support what we are doing here, knowing that we are going about it wrong? You tell me."

"Come on, Clem, hold your fire. Let's not throw the baby out with the bath water."

Roscoe Mantle was a Democrat on the House Armed Services Committee, and the second-ranking member of its Veterans Affairs Committee. He was a tough bulldog, an infantry veteran of World War II, who still limped from his wounds in that war. The Nashville congressman had developed a respected strategic expertise during his seventeen years in Congress, even though he couched his thoughts in down-home rhetoric. "We've got sixteen thousand troops in here to stop communism. That's our job: *stop communism.* And that's a military job, because we're seeing a thousand North Vietnamese soldiers a month coming across that border to fight. A thousand a month. They and the VC have been killing off village chiefs and police officers and schoolteachers, anybody who looks like they're capable of bringing order and decency to the people of the South. Ten government officials a day they're killing! A dad-blamed *day!* Anybody who wants to read their book knows what they're up to: phase one, secret propaganda. Phase two, terrorism, assassination, and sabotage—that's where we are in this mess. Phase three, attacks on isolated outposts, progressing to open, mobile warfare. Phase four, a general offensive to overthrow the government. These strategic hamlets are designed to protect government officials, as much as anything."

Mantle raised his chin stubbornly. "I can't help but think of what the President, God bless him, said about Vietnam in his State of the Union message last year. Remember? He said Vietnam isn't any 'war of liberation,' like the North Vietnamese say, because South Vietnam is already free! It's a war of subjugation, that's what it is, and we're just going to have to take whatever means necessary to kick the communist bastards back across the border. Vietnam is a test case. If Vietnam falls, the United States is going to be held responsible in the world community. A country that won't come to the aid of its friends pretty soon won't have any friends, that's what I think."

Handley stared coolly at Mantle. "Roscoe, if we keep up what we're doing here, we won't have any friends inside *Vietnam!*"

Mantle waved a hand at the lanky senator, brushing a particle of lint off his white trousers. "Ah, the hell you say. The general has the data, and you're going on speculation. We should at least trust his figures unless we see something different. We're going out with President Diem tomorrow to see a strategic hamlet ourselves. There'll be plenty of time to look and talk. Clem, you can't just go back to the American people and tell them we're going to abandon Vietnam to the communists because the South Vietnamese government isn't being very nice to its people! The South Vietnamese are working under some terrible constraints! They're under attack, goddamn it! And it's an *external* attack, don't fool around with this talk of civil war I keep hearing. Do you think the South Vietnamese would have any say in a communist government? Get serious!" Mantle sat back, ignoring Handley and lighting a cigar.

"General, can you tell us about Diem? I hear bad things." Domenick Santoli, who represented a portion of Queens, in New York City, was a small, bland man with a quiet voice, who had specialized in negotiating compromises during his ten years in Congress.

"Sir, it would be inappropriate for me to comment on the political leader of an allied country. My position here is strictly the operational military."

Santoli persisted, speaking quietly, as if he were a gentle defense attorney adducing facts from a victim. "He's a Catholic in a nation that is 80 percent Buddhist, right?"

"That is correct, sir."

"He's terrified the Buddhist elements of his country, right?"

"Sir, that goes into opinion, and I'm—"

Santoli looked toward the back of the briefing room, suddenly ignoring Crawford. "Who the hell is allowed to answer questions like these? Anybody from the State Department here?"

"Yes, Congressman." A slight man with a thin moustache stood from a chair in the rear of the room. "Nick Karoulakis, from the embassy."

"Well, what about it?"

"This is all off the record—"

"Of course it's off the record! This whole meeting is off the record, Mr. Karoulakis! Why do you think we're being so goddamned honest?" The briefing room filled with laughter, Handley and Mantle grinning toward each other like conspirators, and Santoli himself smiling comfortably, pleased with his little joke. "Now, what's the story with our man Diem? Does he hate Buddhists, or what?"

"Well, Diem started out pretty well, as you know." Karoulakis clearly enjoyed the spotlight. It was going to be a long and academic answer, Lesczynski could see it coming. "He was considered ideal for the job. Born in Hue of an old and revered family, educated under Confucian principles, a mandarin, an ardent patriot, and a believer in national independence. He wasn't identified with the French or the Americans, either one. Bachelor, extremely hard worker, and he hasn't changed his lifestyle that much since he took power. He's enjoyed a lot of respect among world leaders. When he came to Washington, Eisenhower even met him at the airport." It was a little bit of trivia, delivered with the smile of the fully researched assistant. "He fashions himself to be a father figure for the country, a sort of flip side to Uncle Ho. He's tried to develop the same kind of personality cult— it's a requirement at all public gatherings that citizens sing a song called 'Adoration of President Ngo.' But it doesn't work here. The Vietnamese prize modesty."

Santoli was unimpressed. "So does he hate Buddhists, or not? That's what I asked you. Why has the man been kicking all the Buddhists around? It's been making the papers all over the world, these goddamned monks setting themselves on fire in the street."

"I don't think he hates Buddhists, Congressman." Karoulakis spoke slowly, as if he were not certain he should bare his soul. He stroked his thin moustache with a delicate hand. "This *is* definitely off the record?"

"We could always put you under oath." The room again filled with laughter.

"That won't be necessary, believe me." Karoulakis grew suddenly serious, seemingly as afraid for himself for what he was about to say as he was for Diem. "Diem's in big trouble. I think he's gotten a little paranoid, to tell you the truth. He's survived an assassination attempt a few years back, and two *coup* attempts, one of them just last year. He's gotten so mistrustful that he's putting his family and his childhood friends into every key position in the government. His brother Thuc is the main Catholic archbishop for the country. Another brother, Nhu, is his main political confidant. Nhu's wife leads the Women's Solidarity Movement. She has probably a million members. Go downtown and look at the statue she had erected in memory of the Trung sisters, who led the repulsion of the Chinese invaders two thousand years ago. The sculptor put Madame Nhu's face on both of the figures!"

Karoulakis gathered himself. He wasn't enjoying the spotlight anymore. "She and Nhu hate the Buddhists. They've made sure that Catholics get preferential treatment in the military and in government positions. In June, an old bonze named Thich Quang Duc immolated himself on a street in Saigon. The old guy died without making a sound or a move. The public think he's a martyr. Madame Nhu called it a 'happy barbecue.' Nhu's the man who used the Army to raid the Buddhist pagodas two months ago, and send fourteen hundred people to concentration camps, a lot of them Buddhist priests. They're poison, and they're bringing Diem down with them, but he can't be reached on it."

Santoli measured Karoulakis. "Is Diem on the way out?"

"He may be."

"What happens to the war if he goes?"

"No." It was Handley. "What happens to Vietnam if he stays?"

"No, no no." Mantle puffed absently on a long cigar, staring at the large map and at General Crawford, who stood forlorn and forgotten in front of it, his pointer still aimed at the floor. "What happens when them damn North Vietnamese communist bastards start pouring across the border with their mortars and machine guns?"

An anonymous voice filled the silence, floating from the back of the room, just above the whir of the air conditioner. Red Lesczynski had not actually known he was speaking that loudly until he perceived the acknowledgment that accompanied two dozen sets of eyes on his own querulous face.

"Well, whichever way you slice it, we're getting screwed without getting kissed, aren't we?"

*　*　*

"Mind if I join you?"

"No, help yourself." The senators and congressmen were having lunch with the ambassador at the embassy. Red Lesczynski was eating a hamburger and a milk shake in the MACV cafeteria.

"I'm glad you said what you did at the end of that meeting. That took balls."

"Not really. Actually, it just slipped out."

The man was about forty, fit and very tanned, with the bulky arms of a construction worker. He had shocked brown eyes, framed by peppery, close-cropped hair. A wild gray moustache grew underneath his bent nose. He was not a bureaucrat. He looked as if he lived outdoors. He held out his hand. "Jerry Schmidt."

"Red Lesczynski."

Schmidt put his tray on the formica table and sat down. "How'd you get hooked into baby-sitting these turkeys?"

Lesczynski chuckled. "To tell the truth, I volunteered. I'm on the Secretary of the Navy's staff. He wanted someone to go as a liaison. I had a friend in Japan I wanted to see, and I've been curious about what's really happening over here."

"Well, you're not going to find out if you go on the dog and pony show tomorrow."

"What's that?"

Schmidt smiled ironically, chewing his sandwich. He washed it down with a swig of cola. "They'll probably take you guys up to Bong Son or something, and let you stare at a Self-Defense Corps Unit. The district chief will have little portable trees along the roadway that he'll remove as soon as you leave, to save for the next village that's going to be inspected. Diem will wear his white fedora and a silk suit and everyone will smile and the senators and congressmen will return to the United States and proclaim that it's all working."

"You sound pretty cynical."

Schmidt shrugged good-naturedly. "Hell, when I first got over here I was the action officer on a half dozen of the goddamn things."

Lesczynski eyed him closely; the tan, the athletic body, the quick eyes. "So what do you do now?"

"State Department." That covered everything; it meant only one thing. Schmidt smiled again. "I can get you out to a Vietnamese combat unit if you want to do it. I think you'd get a lot of meaning out of it. I think your boss would, too." He shrugged. "I'm not pushing it, don't get me wrong."

"No, I'd like to. Maybe I even *need* to." Lesczynski smiled back. He threw down his milk shake and checked his watch. He felt the exhilaration of the utterly irresponsible, as if he had just accepted a dare to jump from a hundred-foot tower into three feet of water. "They won't miss me on the trip tomorrow. When do you want to go?"

"You really want to do this?"

"I wouldn't be much of a military man if I turned you down, would I?"

"You'd be surprised." Schmidt was eyeing him with a sardonic look. "It's pretty hard to get visitors out to the war, you know." He checked his own watch, his voice suddenly enthused. "We should go up to Quang Nam Province. There's a lot going on up there. I can get us a flight into Da Nang tonight, and we'll head out for one of the outposts tomorrow morning."

*   *   *

Jerry Schmidt had enlisted in the Army in 1943 at the age of eighteen, and had served in the Pacific as a member of the OSS, the precursor to the CIA. After the war he had gone to Yale, and like so many of his contemporaries, had chosen government service as the noblest imaginable undertaking. In his thirteen years with the Agency he had spent six overseas, including three in Vietnam. He had explained to Red Lesczynski as they drank beer in Da Nang's old Grant Hotel that Vietnam was the litmus test for the viability of democracy in former colonial structures It had not been a passionate speech, nor had it been a terribly optimistic one. In contrast to his earthy appearance, Schmidt was analytical about it, almost to the point of dryness. It was simply true, on the facts, and it was so true that Schmidt was foregoing more exotic places and more important positions in order to see it through to the end.

They awoke before dawn the next morning. Schmidt had given Lesczynski a set of camouflage fatigues. He dressed in them, feeling somewhat like an impostor as he stared dully at his image in the mirror, then joined Schmidt for breakfast. An American soldier in an Army jeep waited for them in front of the hotel. Schmidt climbed into the back, tossing several C-ration meals onto the seat before he entered the jeep.

"You've got shotgun, Red."

"Literally." The driver chuckled, handing him an M-14 rifle. "There's bad guys out there. Keep your eyes open, Commander."

Where? They began on the narrow asphalt roads of Da Nang city, winding through children pushing cattle on the streets, passing the same clusters of tin and thatch that formed a perimeter around Saigon. The smells were heavy and warm; dung and incense, strange cook-fire odors, the musk of tropical vegetation that rotted just underneath mad new growth. Every now and then other military vehicles passed them, but beyond that they might have been in southern Thailand.

Outside Da Nang the road turned quickly to sand and then clay dust, and within an hour they were alone, one jeep in the countryside cutting through flat valleys and over tree-packed ridgelines, along the edges of mountains that were so green they appeared blue, then following a wide, clear river. Villages sat on the ridges and among long tree lines in the fields. The valleys were filled with rice paddies, squares of varying sizes that extended for miles in many places. Water filled the paddies from the recent monsoon rains, and children rode like rajahs on the water bulls that waded in the muck. The circular mounds of Buddhist cemeteries pimpled the fields. It was tranquil and yet primeval, like the beauty of a panther just before it pounced.

They crossed a one-lane bridge. On the other side, Lesczynski could see a military compound that scarred a low foothill. Beyond that, now interminable, were more wide fields and then steep, craggy mountains that went all the way to Laos, fifteen miles distant, the green canopy so thick on them that it looked like heavy fur. Two towers rose up from the compound. Barbed wire was thick around it. At its edges, in a rough circle, green sandbag bunkers proclaimed its perimeter. South Vietnamese soldiers stood in the towers and sat on top of many of the bunkers, weapons beside them or on their laps, even in the noonday heat.

A soldier opened the concertina gate for them, and they drove inside, becoming the objects of mild, smiling attention. Schmidt halted the driver.

"Okay. Wait here for us. We'll probably be a few hours." He smiled to Lesczynski and gestured toward the mountains and the river and the foothills that surrounded them. "Welcome to the war."

An American officer appeared outside one square bunker, and walked toward them. He was tall and tanned, and wore the tiger suit fatigues of an adviser. His head was shaved down to the scalp, with only a small tuft of hair in front. He had the slim muscularity of a decathalon man. He waved fondly to Schmidt.

"Hey, Jerry." He examined Lesczynski from ten feet away, with the fierce, natural arrogance of a man continually exposed to danger.

"You're from the Pentagon, huh?" He said the word as if he might
have spoken a curse.

"Not normally. Normally, I'm a fighter pilot."

"He's all right, Mike." Schmidt was smiling knowingly at the adviser, one hand on Lesczynski's shoulder. "McCormack doesn't like
McNamara's whiz kids very much, Red. He thinks they're trying to
make Vietnam like a movie. You know, fancy machines and a happy
ending."

"He's right." Lesczynski surveyed the countryside, noting that
McCormack had smiled slightly at his comment. "Why are you here,
Major? I mean, why is the outpost right here, on this foothill? You just
seem sort of—stuck here, for nontactical reasons."

McCormack tilted his shaved head toward Lesczynski and raised
bushy eyebrows, staring at Schmidt. "I thought you said he was a
Navy fart." He turned back to Lesczynski, his mouth scrunched into a
grimace. "We're here to control the road, which comes in from the
Nong Son coal mine over at the edge of the mountains, and the river,
which goes from the mountains, all the way to Hoi An, by the sea.
Nong Son's a special government project. The VC try to disrupt the
mining, and they do a pretty good job. If the bridge is blown, the VC
will have cut off the whole valley over here from the government. We
patrol during the day, defend inside the compound at night. I've got
maybe eighty men to cover this whole basin. If they attack us, we do
all right, but you can't be everywhere at once. We don't do that much
good as a show of force. So, to answer your question, there's a reason
why we're right here, but it isn't a very good one."

He saw that Lesczynski was wearing a curious frown. "Look, the
thing you've got to understand is that the VC don't give a shit about
fighting us, except to try and embarrass us once in a while. They don't
need to fight us, at least right now, because it doesn't matter if they
beat us or not. If they can shut down the coal mine and blow up the
bridge and keep killing anyone who says anything good about the
Diem regime, they're winning. They want to shut this country down
and make the whole population hurt, and convince them it's the Saigon government's fault because its leaders are corrupt—you know the
line, Lesczynski—American puppets, keeping Vietnam colonized."

"Are your troops from around here?" Lesczynski watched them
sauntering slowly around the compound, squatting before small cook
fires. They had the bored look of occupation forces.

"No, and that's a problem." McCormack watched the hard little men with their soft, smiling faces, as if he were their collective father. "They're not bad troops. That's a message you should take back to the fucking Pentagon. But they're sent out into areas they don't know, and ordered to operate militarily, when the real problem has been a political one. It makes it easy for the VC to use our presence as a straw man—you know, to say that Diem has sent them in to make war against the villagers. The real problem is that the VC are killing off local governments as fast as Saigon can appoint them. Hell, man, it's gotten so bad that the last guy who was appointed district chief out here moved to Da Nang as soon as they appointed him! That's a hell of a message, Lesczynski. Americans don't understand it, but they do out here. That's fucking power, man, when you can kill anyone who cooperates with the government. The VC are in *charge* out here. And they couple it with kindness—kind of the carrot and the stick. They separate out the people from the government. As long as you don't have anything to do with the government, they love you. They help you fortify your village. They help you harvest your rice. A lot of them are from this area, and they're recruiting most of the men. Who you gonna fight for? The invaders up there in the compound, who spend each night behind barbed wire because they're so outnumbered and isolated, or the home boys?"

McCormack raised both hands into the air, an act of complete frustration. "Sometimes they catch us wrong and claw us up, but for the most part our little guys do damn well. But it hurts them to be hated like this by their own country people. It confuses them. They're just farm kids, mostly like these people out here. We should let them go back home and protect their own villages."

"What about the North Vietnamese, and the VC out here?"

"Look, I don't have all the answers. I'm just a goddamn soldier." Behind them, a 60-millimeter mortar crew was holding gun practice, shooting high explosive rounds onto a nearby hillside. They held their ears for a short moment. McCormack lit a cigarette. "I guess people should have thought of that a few years ago. We're playing catch-up ball. Maybe American troops should come out here and fight and let these guys do the villager stuff back home. It's getting to be a real shooting war, let me tell you."

"You think Americans should fight here?"

McCormack grinned sardonically to Schmidt. "What the hell have they been telling this guy in Saigon, Jerry?" He shook his head slowly, as if Lesczynski were hopelessly naïve. "We've already lost seventy men killed here this year. The Air Force has flown six thousand missions. We're in this one, and I think the only way out is to fight like hell. They've beat us bad where it counts, and it'll take years to straighten that out. If we've got the guts to hang on that long." McCormack dragged on his cigarette. The mortar tubes fired again. "I'll tell you something. I've got a ten-year-old boy at home, and it wouldn't surprise me a bit to see him fight in Vietnam. That's what we're up against here. You tell that to McNamara."

The sky had just begun to gray as they again reached the outskirts of Da Nang, the little jeep having raced against dusk all the way down lonely, dusty roads. Red Lesczynski loosened the grip on his M-14 as they were once more surrounded by the mass and confusion of the city. Schmidt leaned over from the back seat.

"So, what do you think?"

"What do I think? We're trapped, aren't we? We want to save this country from the communists, but it's like we're propping up a shell, at this point. I hate to say that, you know." The jeep turned along the riverbank, heading back to the Grant Hotel. Lesczynski pondered the small boats on the water. "Even Diem's got us by the balls. He knows we need to keep the communists out even worse than he needs to." Lesczynski shrugged. The M-14 now seemed ugly and out of place in his hands. "I'll stick to my original assessment. We're getting screwed without getting kissed."

Schmidt chuckled appreciatively. "Not bad. You ought to come work for the Agency, Red."

"No, thanks. I like to fly them jets. So tell me"—they exited the jeep, going into the hotel to claim their bags—"you must believe it can come out all right, or you wouldn't be staying in Vietnam."

"Ah, it's a living." Schmidt was being facetious and Lesczynski knew it. The CIA agent grabbed his bag from behind a counter and stood for a long moment, contemplating Lesczynski's question as he peered out toward the river. "First, if Kennedy will just lay it out to the American people about how bad we've screwed it up and how long it's going to take to fix it, we've got a chance. Second, the South Vietnamese need a leader. I'll tell you, Red, Diem's on the way out. You can smell *coup* all over Saigon. It's going to take a hell of a lot to stabilize this country after he's gone. We've got to hold on until that can happen. It'll be an American war for a while. And that's point three." He looked almost apologetically at Red Lesczynski. "The

North Vietnamese are going to hit this place hard once Diem goes. There'll be an invasion. They've got sixteen divisions of well-trained troops. It'll be rough, but it's our chance to make what they've been doing for the past few years visible to the world. We can beat them on the battlefield."

He pointed a finger into Lesczynski's chest, tapping it there. His eyes searched Lesczynski's face. "That is, *you* guys are going to beat them on the battlefield, if our government will turn you loose without a million restrictions. I think Kennedy understands that. And when we beat them on the battlefield, they'll stay the hell out of South Vietnam, just like they've stayed out of South Korea."

*   *   *

By the time the delegation reached Hawaii on November 1, 1963, it learned that Diem had been overthrown and assassinated by a military coup. Within three weeks, Kennedy himself was dead. And in December, the Department of Defense received intelligence reports of the highest reliability that the Vietnamese Workers' Party of Hanoi, Ho Chi Minh's political organ, had ordered an offensive military strategy in the South.

Reading the intelligence report at his desk in the Pentagon, immersed in the sudden chaos of a world that had begun to turn on its ear, Red Lesczynski found himself absently toying with the little square of leather that his friend Yukichi Kosaka had given him at midnight at the Yasukuni Shrine. He massaged it, studying the chrysanthemum and daring to touch the hallowed fabric of the Yasukuni scroll itself, and felt a strange, almost frightening certainty.

Part Four

WE
ARE
NOT
OURSELVES
ANYMORE

CHAPTER EIGHTEEN

I

SHE HAD SIMPLY APPEARED on their doorstep the summer before, this short, diminutive, obsessed woman with her tiny hands held in front of her chest like kangaroo paws, clutching a wide and heavy purse, her small, pinched face demanding and yet inquiring, as if she were selling trinkets house to house. She had been wearing a jean skirt, a western blouse, and turquoise Indian jewelry. She had looked as incongruous in such sporting clothes as if she had dressed for a costume ball, a thirty-four-year-old Austrian-born, New York-raised, Jewish law student dressed up like a cowgirl.

She hadn't even apologized for not calling beforehand. Her expression was almost that of a child getting ready to swallow castor oil. She had stood for a moment after Sophie answered the door, first measuring Sophie's athletic figure, the slim brown legs that still could stop a man on the street when she wore shorts, as she was doing that day, the bulbous breasts, the slightly thickened waist, still trim enough to show fetchingly beneath a shirt tied in a knot at the front, above her shorts, and then inspecting the almost unnerving placidity of Sophie's smooth Slavic face, as if there were something she was desperately seeking so that she could properly register a preconceived disapproval.

"I'm Dorothy Dingenfelder. I'm here in town for a few days, and I promised Joe I'd stop in and say hello. I just realized I was only about a half mile away, so . . ."

"Oh, my! Well, this is *wonderful!* Dorothy, you don't know how much we've wanted to meet you! Red was just saying the other day, 'Sophie, can you believe that Joe's been married ten years and we've never met his wife?'" Sophie had grabbed the hesitant woman's elbow and almost dragged her into the house. "Red's at work but he'll be home any minute now. He doesn't work *every* weekend but you know the Pentagon. Oh, is he going to be surprised!"

"Actually, I only have a few minutes. I—"

"Oh, nonsense, Dorothy Dingenfelder, I didn't wait for ten years just to have you stay a few minutes! You're just going to have to stay the afternoon, and maybe we can go sight-seeing later on, and tonight Red can cook up a barbecue out back."

"Well, that would be nice some other time." She had physically resisted Sophie's hand on her arm. It gave her a small, secret pleasure to make the statement that had been denied to her for so long. "But I'm here on *business,* and I'll have to get to a meeting in about a half-hour."

"Business?"

It delighted her to see Sophie's stunned face, to experience her quick silence. *Yes, yes. Women can go out of town on business too. We don't all have to sit at home and think of sight-seeing trips, you know.*

"Yes. I'm here for the march."

"The march?" Sophie seemed disoriented, in contrast to her earlier control. "On the Lincoln Memorial?" Dorothy had nodded. "Oh. I thought that was for the Negroes."

It was almost as if Dorothy had been waiting to expose a particular flaw, to be able to seize an excuse and explode. She faced Sophie in the hallway, not even waiting to reach the living room of the little Arlington home, and struck a righteous pose, one hand on her hip, holding the purse, the other in the air. "What kind of society do we live in when it becomes a natural reaction that something is 'for the Negroes'? Are we so segregated in our own minds that a march led by a black man, for the benefit primarily of black people, is simply 'for the Negroes'?"

Sophie had cocked her head, peering uncertainly at Dorothy Dingenfelder, wondering how she had so quickly provoked her guest. "Oh, gosh, I didn't *mean* anything, Dorothy! I'm sorry. I was just reading in the *Post* this morning that two hundred thousand Negroes were expected to walk to the Lincoln Memorial to hear this Martin Luther King and some others give speeches about the hundredth anniversary of freeing the slaves." She shrugged, her face pixie-like. "That's all." She brightened hopefully. "Now, let me get you a cup of coffee, and you can tell me all about the march! How did you ever get involved in it? It sounds exciting."

Sophie could melt dry ice with her infectiously warm and upbeat interest. Children poured in and out of the house, dropping baseball gloves and stealing food from the refrigerator as Dorothy sipped iced coffee in the August heat, telling Sophie of the civil rights movement,

of Martin Luther King's freedom rides and sit-ins, of the recent victory in Birmingham, Alabama, where they had changed law because
thousands of blacks and whites together had allowed themselves to be
arrested and jailed in the cause of destroying bigotry. The little
woman in the cowgirl costume spoke passionately and hard. She described her own volunteer work during law school with the American
Civil Liberties Union in Los Angeles. She mentioned that she had
helped edit Dr. King's speech for the march. She parroted it, her small
hands clasped in front of her and her bright, adulatory eyes on Sophie's ceiling.

"'I have a dream today, a dream that my four little children will
one day live in a nation where they will not be judged by the color of
their skin, but by the content of their character. I have a dream, that
all God's children, black men and white men, Jews and Gentiles,
Protestants and Catholics, will be able to join hands—'"

"Why, Dorothy, that's *wonderful!* I think that's just beautiful." Sophie had taken the unbelieving Dorothy's hand across the kitchen
table and congratulated her.

And by the time Dorothy Dingenfelder had left for her organi-
zational meeting, she was effusively promising Sophie that she would
return for a longer visit, at her very next opportunity.

* * *

And here she was again, finally, almost a year later, on July 1, 1964,
husband in tow, knocking again on Sophie Lesczynski's door.

Sophie opened the door and threw both hands wide, an embracing
gesture. "Oh, my word, Dorothy, come on in! And, *Joe,* oh, it's just so
good to see you!" Sophie almost lunged into Joe Dingenfelder's surprised arms. He had lingered behind Dorothy, his face dark with
uneasiness as they waited for the doorbell to be answered. Sophie
peered up into his face, her chin on his chest, and touched his temples
affectionately as Dorothy watched, her own eyes squinting. "Getting a
little gray, huh, Joe?"

She almost danced in her hallway, a child's delight moving her feet
in stutter steps. "Oh, you'll never believe this! We called Judd after
you told us you were coming, and he's driving up from Bear Mountain
today. He should be here any minute!"

Red Lesczynski walked down the stairs near the front doorway. He
was shirtless. His round shoulders and deep chest muscles shimmered
in the shadowed light of the stairway as he hauled his youngest son

over his shoulder, upside down. The boy was laughing, filled with excitement, beating his father on the back. Lesczynski saw them and beamed, setting Johnny down on the floor and slapping his backside as the young boy ran toward the back door.

"Get out of here, kid. Go beat somebody else up." He trotted up to the entranceway. "Dingie, you fink! I can't believe how long it's been." He hugged Joe Dingenfelder, and began to reach for Dorothy.

She saw a hairy sweating red armpit coming her way, and took a quick step back, her nose involuntarily squinching. She gamely stuck out her arm, offering a handshake. "I'm Dorothy."

"Well, I certainly hope so." Lesczynski chuckled and hugged her anyway, leaving her cotton shirt damp where his armpit had pressed into her shoulder.

Sophie grabbed Joe by the arm and began pulling him along the corridor toward the back door. "Joe Dingenfelder, you come back here and build me a charcoal fire. I want to hear everything you've been up to." She called to Lesczynski over her shoulder. "Fix everyone a drink. Dorothy can help you. Then *you* put a shirt on!"

Lesczynski's wide smile seemed to cut his face in two. He unabashedly scratched at a mosquito bite on his stomach, taking in his first look at Dorothy. He could feel her uneasiness as she watched him in the hallway, just as deeply as if she were screaming for help. She seemed alone and vulnerable, almost abandoned. Her arms were crossed in front of her and her feet were together. Her small chin was tucked down, almost touching her neck. He wanted to reach out to her, to coax her into some form of comfort.

"Sophie says you're here for the signing of the Civil Rights Act. That's pretty good."

"I'd say it was, pretty good, yes. I'd say it was about time, too."

"Huh? Oh. Yeah, you're right. Can I get you a beer?"

She followed him into the kitchen, waving a hand into the air, suddenly out of her cocoon, speaking with an intensity that washed over him, as if he had opened a floodgate and then attempted to stand in the way. "Tea. Iced. It will desegregate all public places, and make it illegal to refuse someone a job because of his or her color."

"Sugar?"

"Lemon. It was Kennedy's top priority for this year. Johnson had no choice but to push it. He's going to try and take all the credit, but what can you expect in an election year? And Goldwater's going to carry the South, so Johnson had better take up all the liberal slack he can get."

"Does Dingie still like beer?"

"*Dingie?* Why do you still call him *Dingie?* How silly."

The doorbell rang and Lesczynski jogged quickly to it, thankful for a respite from her, leaving her in the kitchen. He opened it and Judd Smith burst into his house, half eared and tattooed, throwing an elbow into Red's heavily muscled stomach and then attempting to slam him against a wall. The two men wrestled for a moment in the hallway, laughing and growling. Smith finally broke away and grabbed his hand, shaking it.

"Yeah, yeah. Still think you're a tough guy, huh, Lesczynski? Try me again in a couple years. I may have slowed down a little by then. *But I doubt it.*"

Red Lesczynski laughed softly, still leaning against the wall. Little welts were raising on his chest and stomach where Judd Smith had manhandled him. "The Reverend Mr. Smith. In person."

"So where's Dingie? Did he wear his cashmere coat?"

"Do you know Dorothy?"

Judd and Dorothy stood at opposite ends of the small kitchen like statues, measuring each other. It was an immediate tension, as natural as cat against dog. "We argued over a drink once. It must have been nine or ten years ago, I guess. Right here in Washington. And we've written a few cute letters to each other, particularly when she made Joe leave the Air Force. Hello, Dorothy. Castrate your husband yet?"

"Well, for the record I should point out that it didn't take very long for your pretty little politician's wife to have had enough of you, did it?"

Judd Smith laughed comfortably, staring up at Lesczynski's stunned face and then patting him on a shoulder. "Take it easy, Red. I think Dorothy and I just understand each other, that's all. Don't take it to heart."

"I was just going to put on a shirt." Lesczynski struggled for the foundations of a decent conversation. "Dorothy was just telling me about the Civil Rights Act. She helped get it through, Judd. She was telling me what it's going to do."

"We've all got a pretty good idea what it's going to do."

Dorothy examined Judd Smith. His scarred face and tattoo were repulsive, and she could not believe that a man of his age and profession would wear a T-shirt to someone else's house. But at the same time she found his energy fierce and attractive in some fundamental, unexplainable way. She felt provocative, hateful, faintly aroused. She knew she would anger him and she even liked that. "Yes, I was just saying that it's hard to imagine that a country that bills itself as the hope for freedom in the world has kept black people in a state of quasi-slavery for a hundred years after they were supposedly free."

"Did you arrange this, Lesczynski? You know I'm not going to stand here and listen to that." He faced her, shaking his head as if she were a stupid child. "What is this 'quasi-slavery'? That's a bunch of lawyer's gobbledygook."

"Oh, come on! How can you deny the truth of it?" She paced a bit in the narrow confines of the Lesczynski kitchen. "For God's sake, *Reverend* Smith, you call yourself a man of God? Separate bathrooms, separate water fountains, separate places to eat and to sit on public transportation? No voting rights? Job and housing discrimination?"

"You were from New York, and now you're from California. Are they any more successful in New York and California? You tell me that. Are they, Miss Righteous? Why do the colored folk live in Harlem and Watts, if the problem is in the South? Why aren't they living in Scarsdale and Beverly Hills?"

"Maybe New York and California inherited the problems the South created."

"Like what?"

"What do you mean, like what? I just listed them for you. The Constitution calls them the badges of slavery."

"Did you know there were sixty thousand free Negroes living in Philadelphia *before* the Civil War?" Judd Smith smiled blandly, knowing she had not. "So, if those things were just 'the badges of slavery,' if the South has been so perverse, and the North has been so blessedly pure, *why are the Negroes in Philadelphia still living in the slums?*"

She stared quietly at him for several seconds, trying to regain her composure. Her lips were tight and her hands rested on her hips. "The Civil Rights Act isn't aimed just at the South. If its impact is going to be greater there, it's because the problems are greater there."

"The Civil Wrongs Act, you mean." Smith could see she was ready to explode. He wondered how violent she might get. She was certainly capable of extreme emotion. He rather liked seeing her at the edge. The whole argument was ironic, in a way, since Judd Smith had once taunted old Senator Clay from the other perspective, trying to convince his former father-in-law that segregation was not ordained in the Bible. "You know, I'm not unsympathetic to colored folk—"

"I can tell you're their greatest friend."

"—I just have a hard time with all of these supposed white protectors, who romanticize the whole thing without understanding white Southerners, or even trying to. Don't get me wrong. I'm not saying you haven't done any good at *all,* I mean, even a blind hog snoots up an acorn every now and then. But I guess you can't view yourselves as heroes unless you can see other people as villains. Look, why don't you and your friends go solve the problem in Los Angeles before you come riding through the South and creating stereotypes, as if everyone who disagrees with your methods is a Ku Klux Klanner? The South will take care of itself; it always has. Go look at Watts. And then look at Detroit and Harlem and Cleveland and Chicago. You know the worst race riot of this century was in Detroit? That's right, in 1943. Thirty-four people were killed. Or go look at Newark, for Pete's sake. I worked up there for the FBI for four years. It's a time bomb. Only you won't get the same kind of media coverage if you go up North. No pot-bellied, tobacco-spitting sheriff to excite the minds of the producers."

"The Negroes all live in one end of the town in Ford City. I guess they like it like that. I never thought about it." Lesczynski sipped on his beer, sweat dripping from his chest down his muscled stomach. He wasn't even sure on which side of the argument his comment had fallen. He was trying to find a way to end it.

Dorothy had caught her breath. She sucked on a cigarette. "If we'd waited for the South to solve its little problem by itself, we'd still be waiting long after you and I were dead, *Reverend,* and you know it."

"Well, I'm not sure how much you've helped to solve it." Smith's eyes were bright, and he had not lost his smile. He drank his beer, gulps from a can. "Look, separate bathrooms and seats on the bus are easy. Most people in the South would agree with that. But when you start talking all these 'equal opportunity' measures in the Civil Rights Act, you're talking about something else. You're talking about eventually setting up quotas for hiring and schools, and *you* know it. There's no other way the law can be enforced, except looking at the bottom line—how many whites, how many blacks. That's not equal opportunity, that's social engineering."

"All right, I'll admit it." Dorothy gave off a small smile of her own. "So what's wrong with that?"

"You're talking about eliminating discrimination, and yet you're building it right into your law. Discrimination *against* whites."

"One form of discrimination—against blacks—was invidious. It was a badge of slavery. The other—against whites—is benign. It's designed to eliminate the impact of the other." She smiled widely now, a deliberately false sweetness meant to anger him. "That's the Supreme Court's interpretation, you know. It's been applied to charitable trusts, under the doctrine of *cy pres*, and we hope to apply it to the Civil Rights Act."

"Well, that's why the whole world hates lawyers! I never heard a bigger pile of owl dung in my whole life. They don't even *need* to teach you how to lie in law school if they can teach you to beat up on the truth like that! Discrimination is discrimination." Smith considered her. "Have you got any idea of how hard the average white Southerner has had it? You probably don't even care."

"However bad it was, it was better than the average colored Southerner, I'll guarantee you that."

"Maybe we should go out back." Lesczynski looked at both of their faces hopefully. "Hey, Judd, Sophie doesn't even know you're here. Let's go say hello, huh?"

"In a minute, Red. I just haven't had a chance to talk things over with a real Freedom Rider before." Smith's eyes had not left Dorothy's. She was meeting his stare, a grim smile still on her lips. "So tell me how much you know about white Southerners. Other than they're bigoted and they have red necks and they all used to own slaves and they've had it so good while the Negroes have suffered mightily."

"That about covers it."

"Less than 5 percent of the whites in the South ever owned slaves." He noted the unbelieving lift of her eyebrows. "Oh, yeah! And only about 20 percent had anything at all to do with the slave system, even as overseers. John Hope Franklin wrote that. Look it up, you're the lawyer. And I suppose you've read President Roosevelt's 'Report on the Economic Condition of the South,' of 1938? No? It was the basic document of the Roosevelt Administration's economic recovery program. Did you know that there were almost 2 million sharecroppers in the South in 1936, and that two thirds of them were *white*? Did you know that in that same year, the average southern child had twenty-five dollars spent on its education, when the average New York school kid had a hundred seventy-four dollars spent? Did you know that the

average white in a whole bunch of the southern states has less education than the average Negro, nationwide?"

"What about the average Negro in the South?"

"They've had it worse, on the whole. I told you, I don't have anything against helping them. But your quotas aren't going to hurt *your*
kids. They're already plugged into the system. The quotas are going to
take it away from the poor whites, and give it to the poor coloreds.
The poor whites have never had anything, either, but all you care to
see is that they're mean. You're stomp down *right* they're mean.
Wouldn't you be, seeing spoiled, rich whites from the North coming
into your towns as if they held all the world's truths in the cup of their
hands, talking about you as if you were some kind of rabid dog?"

"Are you done?" Her head was tilted, her eyebrows raised. She
sipped tea coquettishly, still meeting his gaze.

"For now."

"Good. You've made your point, and it hasn't altered mine. *My* point
is that southern whites have kept Negroes from voting, from holding
office, from working, and from gathering as equals in public places,
and all the crying in the world isn't going to keep that from being
viewed as an historic disgrace. You had your chance to do something
about it, and you didn't. Don't complain when others did." She
searched for a point, her eyes averted for a moment. "Why, did you
know that right here in Virginia, it's against the law for a white and a
Negro to marry, even if they're really in love? It's *miscegenation!*"

"That's something I've struggled with, as a minister."

"The Reverend Smith has struggled with it?" She carried a small,
almost mocking smile on her little heart-shaped face.

"He has struggled with it. He, like a lot of other mountain people, is
the product of an earlier miscegenation, when it was illegal in Virginia
for whites to marry Indians." She seemed surprised, almost touched.
Her mocking smile melted in a pool of warmth. Judd Smith smiled
back. But white and *Negro?* It was an inner battle, his faith against
his cultural upbringing. "He has not yet resolved it."

"Let the record show that the Reverend Smith has the capacity to
ask hard questions, even if he does not have the sensibility to come up
with the answers. Now"—she gave a small, androgynous bow, silently
declaring herself to be the winner of the debate, and pointed toward
the backyard—"shall we? I've had enough bigotry for one afternoon."

Lesczynski looked relieved. "Let's get you two out back, then I've
got to put a shirt on before Sophie strings me up."

"Oh, Judd! You get over here and let me give you a hug!"

She looked so innocent, so naïve, running across the green grass past her flower beds and her garden, underneath the tall old trees, clasping her arms around him and unthinkingly pressing her breasts and thighs into him, as if she were ten years old and he were her father. She had fallen in love so completely and so early with Red Lesczynski that she had no idea of the power of her body, the explosive magnetism of her very lack of awareness. He hugged her back and as she chided him and played with his torn ear she became the nurturer, the earth mother. She had that power over all three of them. It had been that way since 1947. As Joe Dingenfelder watched Sophie coo playfully with Judd Smith, he emanated his own measure of contentment, a relaxation that Dorothy had not viewed on his face since their dating days eleven years before.

Sophie held onto Smith's head with both hands, scrutinizing him from three inches away. "Judd, you should go ahead and have this ear fixed. It makes you look like a pirate."

"Ah, Sophie. It was only in the way, big floppy thing. That's why it got shot off in the first place."

"Poor Judd." She let his head go. "What's going to happen to you next?"

"Well, if I'm not careful, Dorothy Dingenfelder's going to claw my eyes out before the afternoon's over."

"No, I'm more subtle than that." Dorothy stood at the edge of their gathering, holding her glass of tea. Smith noticed that Joe Dingenfelder's eyes grew immediately narrow as he watched his wife.

"You probably are." Judd Smith turned to his former roommate. "So how do you like being a Californian by now, Dingie?"

"It doesn't take much to be a Californian. You just put on funny clothes and throw away your values." Dingenfelder still stared quietly at Dorothy. Finally, he shrugged, giving Judd Smith a small smile. "It meant a lot to me to help put John Glenn into orbit. He went on top of an Atlas, you know."

"No fooling?"

"Judd, Joe built the fire. You have to cook the steaks." Sophie appeared, handing him a tray of marinated meat.

"Doesn't Red do any work around here? What is this?" He grinned playfully, taking the tray.

"I heard that." Red Lesczynski grabbed Smith by the nape of his neck from behind, having put on a blue T-shirt.

Smith froze before the barbecue grill, the tray hard against his stomach. "Well, what are you going to do about it, Polack?"

Lesczynski grinned, taking the tray. "I'm going to cook the steaks."

"We'll ask Judd to take the grace."

They all bowed their heads, sitting at the picnic table in the back-yard, flies buzzing near their food and the shouts of children at play drifting across from other yards. "Lord, we ask Your blessings on this food, and we thank You for bringing us all together today, to renew the bonds of friendship and love. We ask that You look after each of us as we carry out Your work. Bless Red and keep him safe should he be called to duty in Southeast Asia, watch after him and hear our prayers for him"—Smith looked up out of the corner of his eye, and saw Dorothy's sardonic grimace—"and bless Dorothy as she labors to make the world free of prejudice and hate. Amen."

"Amen."

He couldn't resist it. They were all reaching for food. He smiled across the picnic table to her. She seemed pleased, vindicated by his prayer. He couldn't let it go at that. "Even if she's going about it wrong."

"Are we going to start in again?"

"No, no." He smiled contentedly, cutting into a steak. "I'm done talking about Negroes for a while. I want to drink some beer, and talk about the flowers and the trees, and summer in Washington. I want to hear how everybody's kids are doing, and brag a little about Loretta. And I want to hear what Red has to say about Vietnam."

"Well, if you want to talk about Vietnam, we *are* going to start in again."

"Dorothy, why don't you just *stop it?*" Joe Dingenfelder stared across the table at his wife, unable to repress his anger any longer. He had deliberately chosen a seat as far away from her as possible, but now he leaned forward amid the potato salad and the beer, a beam that resembled hate riding from his eyes to hers, his voice low, but holding the intensity of a scream. "We didn't come here so you could show off about how *up* you are on all of the political issues. We came here to see friends, people I haven't been around for ten years. I've hardly said a sentence to Red or Judd either one, and you've been so busy making sure everyone knows you're smart and in tune that you haven't taken the time to even try and get to *know* anyone!"

It was apparent that it was a debate that had begun long before they arrived, perhaps one that had been ongoing for years. Dorothy coolly measured her husband, as if he were a dog that had just fouled her carpet. The others sat quietly, hiding their embarrassment with bites of food.

"Well, it's pretty clear I'm out of place at this little gathering." She stood abruptly, and began walking toward the back door of the brick home.

"Oh, Dorothy, that's not true!" Sophie rose also, and began to follow her.

"No, that's all right, Sophie. I can find my way out."

"But, Dorothy, won't you—"

"No, really, I'll be on my way." She slammed the door in Sophie's face.

Within thirty seconds, a car started in front of the house, and drove quickly away. They sat quietly at the table, Judd Smith and Red Lesczynski still chewing food, Joe Dingenfelder and Sophie simply staring at each other, reading looks. She noticed that Dingenfelder was beginning to get heavy-circled, drinker's eyes. It made her worry. Finally, Dingenfelder drained his beer and clanked the can onto the table top.

"I'm really sorry all of that had to happen. It didn't have anything to do with you guys, I promise."

Judd eyed Dingenfelder as he piled more potato salad on his plate. "That's a high-strung mare you got there, Dingie." He shrugged, smiling abashedly. "But who am I to talk."

"It's gotten so bad, I can hardly stand it." Dingenfelder rubbed his graying temples, shaking his head. He wanted to tell them about it. He wanted Sophie to help him with it. He wanted Judd Smith to make fun of his wife. He wanted them all to embrace him and console him, just as they had done so many years before, as they grew together as roommates in the womb of their adulthood. "Maybe I could have done something earlier, I don't know. I'll admit I wasn't being very sensitive to her frustrations. And she did follow me all over the world. If you can imagine someone like Dorothy enduring all the officers' wives protocol, living in Texas and Illinois and England and the California prairie. So, anyway, once I realized she was serious, I thought if I left the Air Force and allowed her some growing room it would end, but it only fed it. It's like it became a battle, and when I left she'd won. Like my leaving the Air Force was a sign of weakness."

He shook his head. He had the saddest voice Judd Smith had ever

heard, down past loss into self-pity, as if there were no hope for re-
solving it. "I should have stayed the hell in the Air Force, and let her
dump me. She's trying to make up seven 'lost' years and she doesn't
have a minute for anything else. She won't do anything, hardly, but
work, and she won't talk about anything but issues. She's dumped responsibility for the kids on me. If I can't arrange for a baby-sitter, I'm
supposed to stay home from work. She says it's my turn. It's getting to
be a joke at Aero Dynamics, can you imagine? Here I am working on
missile programs while my wife is doing radio shows for 'ban the
bomb.' And she's getting into this Vietnam thing, too. I just couldn't
stand to hear her go through her speech again. That's why I had to
shut her up a minute ago."

Judd Smith scrutinized him, a frown on his face. "Can't you talk to
her? You know, lay down the law?"

"She just doesn't *care* anymore, Judd. She says there's no such thing
as a good marriage, and then at the same time she clings to the *illusion* of a marriage, because it helps her in her work. You know, the
happily married little housewife who can also handle a career. And if
I leave, I don't know what would happen to the kids. There's the real
catch! I just don't know what to do." Dingenfelder attempted a grin.
It didn't work. "Did you ever think life would get so goddamned complicated?"

Sophie had put an arm on his shoulder. She gave him a small, moth-
erly hug and patted his back. "I'm so sorry you're not happy, Joe."

He stared into his beer, cupping pianist's fingers around the can. "I
really didn't mean to unload all of this on you. Forget Dorothy, all
right? She's already forgotten us."

"Yes, this is Dorothy Dingenfelder. Is the congressman in?"

She stood straight up in the rancid telephone booth. Someone had
urinated inside it, and the hot summer sun caused the odors to en-
velop her, leaving every part of its interior suspect. Someone else had
scratched on the metal next to the telephone, amid dozens of hastily
scrawled numbers, 'SUPERMAN (sex) CHANGED HERE.' She
pondered it, trying to understand the joke. She liked to stay on top of
all the latest trends. Finally she dismissed it, concentrating on what
she would say on the telephone. It didn't make a lot of sense to her,
but maybe it did to Washington's populous gay community. She
would ask someone about it when the right moment presented itself.

"Hello, Lou?" She smiled, pleased that he had so quickly answered the phone. Outside the phone booth, a steady stream of cars made it difficult to hear. "How are you? No, I'm only in town for a few days. I'm in for the signing of the Civil Rights Act. You're still coming, aren't you? Oh, what a moment that will be!" She took a little breath. "Listen, would you like to have a drink? My husband's over with some old friends, and I've got the evening to myself." Her smile widened, and her eyes took on an anticipatory delight. "The Rotunda? That's just off the Longworth Building, isn't it? Ivy Street, yeah. I had dinner there with Everett Prawn last year. You know, he has the Twenty-second District, just north of San Diego? All right. I'll meet you there. Twenty minutes? Good. Oh, it's good to hear your voice again, too, Lou." She had tried to make her enunciation of his name meaningful and promising. He was, after all, a lover, and lovers were supposed to occupy meaningful spots in one's heart. "Well, hurry. Bye."

II

Ron Levine had long black hair and wire-rimmed glasses that framed heavy-lidded blue eyes. Large, crooked squirrel's teeth could just be seen underneath a moustache that drooped down below his top lip, an apparent attempt to hide them. He wore blue jeans and a flowered shirt. He was tall and narrow-shouldered, and a growing pot belly hung over the top of his jeans. He smoked incessantly.

But his voice was deep and modulated, professionally trained. Half of Los Angeles could recognize it in a heartbeat: Ron Levine, king of the airwaves, master of controversy, the Rush Hour Maniac, capable of driving listeners into frenzies. *If I've made you mad, honk your hot little horns, you pigs!* And from the packed Harbor Freeway, down to the crowded parking lot called the Santa Monica Freeway, all the way out to Riverside, you could hear them pressing angrily into their steering wheels, a chorus of agreement that moved his show's ratings up, up, up, the greatest pratfall of democratic capitalism: dissent sells soap.

"You ready to roll, Mrs. Dingenfelder?"

"Sure, Ron." She gave him her sweetest smile, following him from the brightly wallpapered outer room of KISS Radio's studio, through a series of doors into the broadcasting room. "How are you doing today?"

"I'm hot, I'm hot." He waved his hands into the air, doing a dance as he walked into the room. "We're going to *piss 'em the hell off* today! *All right!* What do you say, lawyer lady?"

"Well, let's do it."

"That's what I like to hear."

She sat across from him at a circular table that held four microphones. The room was stark, green-walled, like the interior of a hospital room. On the other side of a glass partition, several engineers played with their consoles, readying sound levels and monitoring network broadcasts, in order to catch the news on the hour. The news began. A little man dressed in a suit came into the room and sat at one microphone, watching the producer behind the glass. The man behind the glass counted down for him, five, four, three, two, one, then pointed at him.

"And here's the weather for Los Angeles and vicinity . . ."

When the little man finished, they broke for a commercial. Levine pointed casually at her microphone. "Give them a voice level, Dorothy."

"This is Dorothy Dingenfelder, coming to you live from—"

"That's fine. You know where the 'cough button' is?" She nodded, touching it.

"Good, good." Levine checked a page of notes. "I'm going to do a short lead in about the riots, and then we'll get right into it." He smiled to her. She had done several shows with him before. He knew she could be both clever and caustic, a combination that was unbeatable. "Let's blow their asses away."

She was casually lighting a cigarette. "You take me there, Mad Ron, and you've got it."

"Well you know I'll get you there." The producer was showing him fingers now, four, three, two, one, go . . .

Levine cut into the airwaves, his eyes half closed, making love to his round foam-covered microphone, getting off on his own modulated voice and his ire-inducing words. "Good afternoon again, Los Angeles, you city of dirt, you sun and smog and smut capital of America, this is Mad Ron Levine, the Rush Hour Maniac, coming to you live *again* on radio K – I – S – S, and if you hate me, beep your horns, you creeps. Ah, I can hear you all over the roads and highways, a tribute, a love song. *Thank you*, Los Angeles, thank you."

He winked at Dorothy, and she winked back. "I've got a good one for your consciences today. You're a people with short memories, who love to avoid responsibility for the sufferings of others. You slobs!

That's why you left your wives back in Mason City, Iowa, and fled west in the first place. You *perverts!* But let's take a sober look back for a moment. It's been a little more than three months since those hot August days of Watts. You remember it, don't you? August 1965. A time of pride for America, with the *Gemini 5* space capsule going up into orbit, the farms of America registering record harvests, even the up and down waging of the Vietnam War registering some impressive gains. But here in Los Angeles, a city with the most affluent Negro population in the country, a city that has prided itself on good race relations with its three hundred seventy thousand blacks, we saw six dreadful days of hatred and violence, of raging fires and machine gun bullets and stores emptied by looters. Here in God's country, the land of sun and make-believe, we saw the very real grimness of our fellow citizens—black citizens who had come west to share the same California dreams as you and me—mired in poverty and despair."

Levine was aglow, his eyes toward the ceiling, immersed in the beauty of his voice and words. "You remember. How can you forget? Thirty-six dead, thirty of them black. Almost a thousand injured, more than four thousand arrested. Forty-six million dollars' worth of damage, fifty thousand thefts, almost eight hundred buildings destroyed. And more than twenty thousand police and National Guardsmen on the streets, occupying their own soil, guns pointing at their own countrymen. What went wrong? Who is to blame? Was it just the final burst of frustration from Negroes who were crying, 'enough,' a 'temper tantrum,' as Nobel laureate Martin Luther King claimed? Or was it something deeper, more sinister, more indicative of the lingering guilt white America must come to grips with?

"Dorothy Dingenfelder, my guest here today, is an attorney for the American Civil Liberties Union, and has represented many of those arrested during the Watts riots. Active in the civil rights movement for many years, she is a well-known figure in Los Angeles. She has marched alongside Negroes in Selma. She has testified before the Congress in Washington, D.C., on difficulties related to integration and other racial matters. She is also a former schoolteacher, and served a term on the Los Angeles county schoolboard when she was still in law school at UCLA. Dorothy, it's a pleasure to have you on the show again, and my first question is, when are you going to run for Congress?"

He winked at her again, and she winked back, her mellow little surprised laugh floating onto the airwaves. She grew properly coy, her blue eyes twinkling. "Well, Ron, whether I ever decide to run for Congress or not is a little off the subject. I think I'll let that one pass. And speaking of being off the subject, I'd like to clarify my position on something else you said during your lead in. Last August may indeed have been a time of triumph and pride for our country, but I would not include the barbarism that is going on in Vietnam as a point of pride or triumph, either one. Whether we are doing well or poorly in a war that is illegal, undeclared, and an unwarranted intervention into the internal affairs of another country is beside the point. The point is, we should not be in Vietnam, and our involvement there reflects our lingering shame, not pride. I want to completely disassociate myself from that portion of your remarks."

"Fair enough, Dorothy, fair enough. So let's get down to the issues of today's show. What were the primary causes of the Watts riots? President Johnson, the creator of the so-called Great Society programs, said the rioting Negroes were 'lawbreakers, destroyers of Constitutional rights and liberties, and ultimately destroyers of a free America.' Martin Luther King, last year's winner of the Nobel Peace Prize for his work in civil rights, called it a 'blind, misguided lashing out for attention, a temper tantrum by those at the brink of hopelessness.' What does Dorothy Dingenfelder say?"

"I think if President Johnson wants to look at the law and who is breaking it, he should examine the way it has been enforced by the Los Angeles Police Department and the state of California. As Senator Bobby Kennedy recently said, 'There is no point in telling Negroes to obey the law. To many Negroes the law is the enemy.' And Martin Luther King, I'm proud to say, is a friend of mine. Although he was given a bit of a hard time when he came to Watts for trying to urge nonviolent methods on its citizens, he did say something very important, which ties into the real issues of being black in Los Angeles. He said, and I quote, 'There is a unanimous feeling that there has been police brutality.' And I think that is the key. The incident which touched off the riot involved two white state troopers who needlessly kicked a black man after handcuffing him. They do that sort of thing all the time. Only this time, they did it in Watts, and the people began to fight back."

"So you endorse what the rioters did?" Levine was grinning merrily, leaning back and smoking a cigarette.

"No, no, of course not." Dorothy grinned back at him. It was going well, like slow pitch softball. "Although I certainly do understand *why* it happened. We have almost two thousand Negroes moving into southern California every month, most of them fleeing the racial oppression of the southern states. Sixty percent of them end up on welfare. Two thirds of the kids drop out of school before graduating from high school. The median age is young—sixteen years old. This group collects in areas like Watts. They've fled from oppression, and the first thing they see is a white cop who will beat their brains in if they look at him wrong. There just came a time to fight back, that's all."

"So what's the answer? Pin a medal on the Negroes who rioted, and call them heroes?"

"No, the Army's trying to do enough of that with their brothers in Vietnam. We *must* put limits on how the police are allowed to use their authority in this country, Ron. I've represented dozens of victims of false arrest from the riots. The police were arresting anybody on the street during the riots. They left a thousand people in jail for *days* without seeing a judge!"

"As I said at the outset, Dorothy, there *were* fifty thousand thefts. Televisions, clothes, you name it. What are the police supposed to do?"

"The law is very clear. You don't arrest someone unless you have probable cause to believe he has committed a crime. Being present on the street where you live is not probable cause. It reminds me of the policies that are being used on the civilians in the war zone of Vietnam."

"Dorothy, there are those who will accuse someone of your sensitivities of being blind to the reality of law enforcement. What do you say to them?"

"We cannot allow any crisis, *any* crisis, to turn us into a police state subject to mass enforcement policies. In a free society, it is essential that individual rights take precedence over efficiency. If we ever lose that foundation, we—"

Click. Joe Dingenfelder turned off his radio as he drove along the packed San Diego Freeway toward home. He couldn't stand to hear another minute of it; the high-pitched voice, the hard words thrown like righteous darts at the microphone, with the passion of a wholly convinced extremist. *What happened?* It was as if she were a satellite that had thrown its orbit and was careening madly, without direction, through space, at the speed of light. He mocked himself with a snide grin. She would have had a field day with his scientific metaphor, the

comparison of his wife with a missile. It would have been an indication to her of his narrow little world.

*To hell with her and her goddamn "advocacy law," or whatever she
calls it.*

Joe Dingenfelder was getting rich. Mercedes driving rich. Cocaine
snorting, country clubbing, vacation-in-Maui rich. In five years at Aero
Dynamics, he had risen to Executive Vice-president for Government
Affairs. He was smooth, low-key, and knowledgeable. He could talk
military with the military, and science with the scientists. He could go
out on the sites and pull off a part from a missile and examine it and
even fix it. He could sit in a board room and talk contracts, profit and
loss.

But doing things for money was boring, even oppressive, a poor
substitute for a sense of mission. And Dorothy was cutting into every
portion of his life, until there was no room for maneuver. They were
beginning to mock him behind his back at work. Pussy-whipped.
Capon. Mr. Dorothy Dingenfelder. It was unbearable, and it was going to get worse. *What kind of man says he's a defense-oriented con-
servative, and remains married to a radical who wants to disarm
America?* And if she ran for office, it would hurt him in the defense
business. Dorothy was a conflict of interest.

At home, there was neither love nor duties, really. There was only
presence, as if he were an ornament, essential to remind Natasha and
little Joe that there was indeed such a thing as a parent. Dorothy
seemed to go out of her way to find reasons to work late, anything
that could keep her from confronting him and the children. She was
rarely home, except to sleep. She traveled frequently. At home, she retreated to a study desk and read. They had a Mexican maid who was
good to the children, but this was no way to raise a family.

He wanted to be in love again. He wanted to have a wife who could
take care of the home and manage the children's lives, and free him to
grow professionally. He didn't think that was too much to ask, or even
selfish. It was the way it had always been, and it had no right to turn
around on him. If it was going to happen, it could have at least waited
for one more generation and happened to someone who had been
prepared for it. It wasn't fair. The deal had already been struck.
Dorothy was an Indian-giver.

They had a wonderful home, an old Spanish-style house with stucco
walls and a curvy red-tile roof and a high wall around it, so that it
looked like a villa. It sat on a high bluff near Pacific Palisades, in an

area with dozens of elaborate houses. In the morning when the smog
was down and the fog had lifted you could see the ocean. It was a
beautiful view, but it reminded him of Vandenberg, and he could not
watch the small triangle of sea without becoming overwhelmed by a
smoldering anger. *I gave up my Air Force career for her, the only
thing I've ever done where I've felt completely happy and immersed.
You'd think she would at least appreciate it, instead of treating it like
a liberation she's forced on me, the bitch.*

"*Cómo está,* Carmella."

"Oh, hello, Mr. Dingenfelder." She was putting away the dishes.
The house was spotless. He wondered briefly who was raising her
children, and cleaning her home, as she puttered about his house all
day. She was fat and sweet. She pointed toward the rear of the house.
"The kids are watching television."

He walked to the television room, and stood briefly in the doorway.
"What are you watching?"

Natasha replied, "Oh, junk."

They sat languorously on imported rattan easy chairs, watching a
family sit-com. Little Joe waved briefly. Natasha didn't even look at
him. They had a heavy, knowing manner about them that was as visible as a burden when they spoke with adults. He didn't remember
being so emotionally intense as a child. It upset him to see the nine-
year-old Natasha speak of depression, to fantasize about running away
to live with his parents in New York. They spent their summers there.
It was the only normality they had viewed in family life since Joe
Dingenfelder had left the Air Force five years before. Watching them,
he felt like a complete failure. Dorothy was able to rationalize it, to
say that family values and parental techniques were being modern-
ized, that it was not the amount of time spent with the children that
counted, but rather the quality of the time spent. But that was a cop-
out, and he knew it. It wasn't going well for Natasha and little Joe,
and it wouldn't be over when they left home, either. It was a permanent deprivation. They would suffer from it for the rest of their lives.

He changed clothes and walked into the large living room, feeling
the thick carpet grab at his shoes like lush grass. One entire wall was
glassed in, covered with sheer drapes. In front of the drapes was his
Steinway. He approached the old grand piano and let his fingers
lightly caress the dark wood. It was his favorite moment of the day,
the moment he lived for. All options opened up for him as he sat on
the piano stool and contemplated the soulful interior of his mind. He

could create, perform, make life beautiful, and bring joy into one small corner of the world, simply by moving his long fingers over the keyboard and freeing up his spirit.

He chose Chopin. His delicate touch gave the notes the consistency of rose petals falling from a clear blue sky. Little drops of music, soft notes played with the crispness of an artist. For those few minutes he was free, lost in the beauty of the ages.

"Hey, Dad!" It was Natasha, staring at him from the doorway.

"Yeah, hon." His fingers didn't miss a note.

"Can you hold it down? We can't hear the TV."

He needed to get away. Yes. That was the answer. To get away.

CHAPTER NINETEEN

I

HE WAS NOT A BIG MAN but he had a sort of power in him; not the affirmative directness of the achiever who must win, but the simple tenacity of a man who has never won and thus does not really even think about winning, but rather sees life as a daily refusal to be beaten. His body carried the stringy, acquiescent toughness of the mountains. With his gnarled look and his mousy, gray-tinged hair, he could have been anywhere from thirty to sixty years old. He had clear blue eyes and a certain set in his square, creased face, a posture to it, the thin mouth wide and firm, unyielding, the hollows of his cheeks and the slight tilt of his head a promise that he meant exactly what he said, and the world be damned all to hell. They could lock Havens Cox away forever afterward, but that would be afterward, and either way it was going to happen, so rich big city Dr. J. Compton Frank had better be getting used to it.

Cox grasped Judd Smith's hand with a palm that had the abrasiveness of tree bark. "Reverend, I don't mean to call you away from your dinner, now, but I truly do appreciate."

"That's fine, Havens. Don't you worry now. Where's Dr. Frank? I'll just go have a talk with him."

"He's over yonder to his office, there." Havens Cox pointed down a brightly lit hallway. "I don't mean to be hateful or to muscle you, Reverend, but the baby's plumb on the down-go and I ain't waiting but a few minutes. Hit's a small, bitty thing we're asking, and we just point blank got it to do."

Smith nodded to Cox, and then smiled in what he hoped was a comforting gesture to his worn-looking wife in her print dress and thin coat, and to the six children lined up like rag dolls behind her. They were all rough, quiet, and slightly unkempt, down from the ridges to say good-bye to Baby, and good-bye to Baby they were going to say.

You don't mess with a man's pride and culture like this.

Dr. Frank was on the telephone. From the sound of his voice, he was talking to the police. Judd Smith leaned over the doctor's desk and pointed to the phone, shaking his head negatively. He whispered. "Hang it up, Doc. You ain't got time. Tell them to *forget* it."

The way he said it gave such an unpardonable suggestion logic. Dr. Frank stared into Smith's face for one second, and then spoke to the other party. "Uh, listen. I think we're working this out after all. If I have a problem, I'll call you back. Okay? No, it's all right, at least for now. Don't trouble yourself. I'll get back to you if I need you. Thank you. Good-bye."

Dr. Frank hung up the phone and stood, shaking Smith's hand also, his damp, soft grip defining the paradox, the tottering seesaw on which Judd Smith had quickly become the fulcrum. "I'm glad you came, Reverend Smith. Maybe you can talk some sense into the man. He can't bring all those children into that room, and he for *damn* sure can't let them touch her. That baby is dying. She won't last the night. She's got a highly developed and contagious streptococcus that's gone into scarlet fever. She also has a secondary infection that's carried over into pneumonia and glomerulonephritis. Poor child."

"They won't be but a minute, Doctor. I think you'd better let them go in there, because one way or the other, Havens Cox is going to kiss that baby good-bye."

The doctor glanced again at his telephone. "I thought you came here to help!"

"Doctor, listen to me. A lot of people around here aren't used to hospitals. They only know their duty to their blood."

"If he'd brought that baby in earlier, we might have saved her."

"If these hospitals didn't cost so much, and if he trusted you, he might have done that." Smith and the doctor stared at each other from across the desk. "If you try and stop that family from giving their child her little kiss of death, you'll not get any of them back at all. And I won't be responsible for Mr. Cox's acts of grief."

"Is it really that serious?"

"Doctor, I'm telling you, Havens Cox is a simple man. But he's got his pride and his obligations. Don't stand in the way of his blood, now. He's in charge of that family, and he knows what he has to do. People around here take their own responsibility for their kinpeople. He won't be but a minute. Trust me. I'll go with him."

"All right, Reverend. I'll trust you."

The small baby was in isolation, strange tubes running into her and an ominous machine whirring next to the crib. Havens Cox entered

the room, his chin high, fighting tears with the dignity of a clan chief-
tain. He was, indeed, the inheritor of the old Scotch-Irish ways, even
though he was passing down a ritual from centuries before without
that historical knowledge. There was only one way to go about family
duty, that was as far as he had thought it through.

"Okay, now. We'll just kiss Baby good-bye."

The mother went first, and then each of the children passed the unmoving, comatose child. Tears dripped from leaning faces, soaking her
cotton blanket. Havens Cox held the youngest child over the edge of
the crib, and then kissed the baby himself.

"She's such a tiny little set along, sweet thing. Bye, sweetheart. We
love you."

Judd Smith went last. Her small forehead burned against his lips.
But it would have been an insult to fear disease more than he loved
his parishioners.

"Let's say a little prayer, then we need to let the doctor try and
work on her some more." They stood silently together, their heads
bowed. "Dear Lord, we pray that we can always be thankful for the
days this child was with us on this earth, and if it is Your will, we
must bless her to Your keeping. For as Paul wrote to the Thessalonians, concerning those who are asleep, we must not grieve as others
do who have no hope. 'For since we believe that Jesus died and rose
again, even so, through Jesus, God will bring with Him all those who
have fallen asleep.' Amen."

"Amen." Havens Cox nodded to his brood, pointing toward the
door. He was suddenly slouched, undone, like an unstrung bow. He
made some Bible talk with Judd, an attempt to show his courage
under duress. "You know, I bet them Thessalonians never even wrote
Paul back."

Outside the door he grasped Judd Smith's hand again. "We'll get
on, now. Reverend, this means more to me than I could ever rightly
say. I didn't want no hardness between me and the doctor."

"Don't you think about it another minute, Havens. You just call me
when you need me, hear?"

Outside the door, Judd Smith nodded slowly to Dr. Frank, who
waited like a guard. The Cox family had passed him without so much
as a moment of recognition. "Thanks, Doctor. Sorry to have troubled
you."

"Well, I hope I don't see eight more cases of scarlet fever next
week." The paunchy doctor considered Smith. "Nine, that is." He soft-

ened, a small, puzzled frown on his face. "I appreciate your wisdom, Reverend. I think that was the right thing to do."

"The man's got enough grief without having to believe for the rest of his life that he didn't show strength when it came time for him to do his duty, Doctor. Good night, now."

* * *

He slowly dialed the numbers, a ritual that never failed to summon the same mix of heady excitement and gut-wrenching nostalgia.

"Julie? Judd. Listen, I can't come see Loretta today. I just can't make it up there. I've got to do a funeral for a family that's really close to me. Their little baby died last night, and the father doesn't want to wait. He wants the funeral to go this afternoon."

"Oh, Judd. She's *so* looking forward to seeing you." There was a disappointment in Julie Clay Williams' voice that was palpable, and clearly not totally related to her daughter's needs.

Do I dare? Judd Smith's ears hummed from sudden tension. He held his breath, more afraid of rejection should he make the suggestion than of the pain of leaving it unvoiced.

"Tony's out of town, you know. He's in Miami Beach, for a conference." Tony was gone more and more. Judd sensed that there was indeed a nexus between that fact and the way she now dangled it out in front of him, like a worm wiggling in front of a hungry lunker bass.

"Well, why don't you drive her on down to Bear Mountain? You've never seen my church. I could bring her back up in a couple days. She doesn't go back to school from Easter break until next Monday, does she?"

She had already thought it through, he could tell. "I can probably find Bear Mountain, but I don't think I could *ever* make my way back through those roads to where you live, Judd."

"Give me a time, and I'll meet you in Bear Mountain. Just drive up to the courthouse. You'll recognize it." He chuckled whimsically. "It's one that still refuses to fly the Yankee flag."

"Is it *really?*"

"I'm afraid so. I'll be sitting in front of the Confederate Memorial."

She giggled. "Somehow, that seems appropriate. Daddy would love it, that's for sure. All right, Judd. What time is the funeral?"

"Two o'clock."

"We'll be there around five. Is the soldier facing south?"

"What do you think?"

"I think this might be fun."

She drove up in her brand-new 1966 Mercedes 230S, black with red interior, the dashboard wood-paneled, the engine running smooth and unhurried, like a lawyer's courtroom drone. Judd Smith winced as he saw the car, knowing the attention it would provoke in the All-American land of Dodges and Chevrolets. But what did Julie Clay know about mountain people? She had been unable to deal with him; that was a clue.

"Daddy! Dad!" Loretta waved to him, hanging out of a side window in the knifing April air. He waved back. Julie parked the car in a diagonal space, just in front of where Judd Smith sat huddled against the concrete base of the Confederate Memorial. Above him, a fully rigged Rebel soldier peered eternally south, long rifle in one hand.

Julie stared up at the Commonwealth of Virginia flag as it flapped in the breeze where the American flag normally would have flown. "Oh, my! You weren't kidding, were you?"

He rose to greet them, forcing back his exuberance at seeing both of them in Bear Mountain. "They haven't flown the American flag here since the Civil War. Hi, Julie. Come here, kiddo!"

Loretta raced into his arms, a ball of curly hair and lengthening, muscular limbs. It almost frightened him every time he was with her to see how quickly she was growing. Here she was nearly ten years old. What had happened to that decade? It had flown bright and ephemeral, like the falling stars he sometimes secretly wished upon, a hot, painful flash that in the end had left him alone at his origins, repenting for his loss by praying over other people's dreams and misfortunes.

"Why, that's terrible, Judd! This is 1966. Bear Mountain boys have died for the Yankee flag in the Spanish-American War, World War I, World War II, and Korea, and they're dying for it in Vietnam right now. You should do something about it!"

Here she was, already making new demands on him, having been in his community for perhaps five minutes. "Old ways die hard down here, Julie." He watched the Virginia flag for a moment. "It doesn't make a whole lot of sense, though, does it?"

"I'm famished! We've just got to get something to eat! We had a Coke on the way down, but that was it. I didn't want to be late. I

know how you hate for people to be late. Where can we get something to eat?"

He had Loretta's hand, and they were walking toward the Mercedes. "Well, I was figuring to fix you all some dinner at my place."

"Oh, Judd! Can't we eat now? Isn't there a restaurant in town?
Surely there must be *one*."

"Yeah, there's one, but—"

"Well, come on!" She misread his hesitation, watching his face with
those beautiful entrancing unknowing pools of rich-girl eyes. "Don't
worry, Judd, I'll pay for it."

It was still the Come On Inn, even after everything else in the
world had seemed to change. Her name was still Alma Coulter, although mad Buford, the man who had crushed a metal beer can with
one hand fourteen years before and tossed it casually onto the floor to
show his hatred for Judd Smith, had lost a coal truck down the side of
an icy mountain road five years back, dying in the second most honorable way for a mountaineer to go, a truck race from the Kentucky border on a fifty-dollar wager. And she still worked there, only now she
owned it, having bought the original owner out (rumor had it) with
Buford's insurance money. Judd Smith walked into the small, brightly
lit restaurant with Julie Clay and Loretta, dreading with all his heart
the meeting of his two former wives, the one he had married but still
refused to admit was ever his wife, the other who had divorced him in
the law and married another man, but who in Judd Smith's private
mind remained his spouse.

"Well, well. The Reverend Mr. Smith."

"Alma, how are you? We'll just take a booth over here."

There were perhaps a dozen others in the restaurant. Two wizened
old men and another man about Judd Smith's age noticed them, and
shyly rose from their booth, approaching Smith. They wore coveralls
and heavy cloth coats. They had bad teeth and thick, callused hands.
They stopped next to Smith and peered at Julie and then Loretta, as if
they would soon sing with joy.

One of the older men nodded to Judd Smith. "Howdy, Reverend.
Come in to have you a bait, is you?"

The other older man smiled encouragingly. "I'm fool about them
shuck beans Miz Coulter puts out. She cooked up rimptions of them
today."

Judd gestured toward them, smiling at Julie. "These here are the

Hardy brothers, Julie, Moe on the right and Jasper next to me. Behind them, that's Moe's boy Herbert. They live down the road a piece." He put an arm comfortably on Jasper's shoulder. "In town to buy some feed, are you, Grandsir?"

"Well, I had in head to plow today, but I couldn't work me up to it. Shame about the little Cox girl, ain't it?"

"It surely is, Jasper. We buried her this afternoon."

"My name's Loretta." She was so sure of herself, so in control, as if her mind and person were years ahead of the child's body in which they were trapped. She elbowed Judd Smith fondly from where she sat next to him. "That's my Dad."

"Well, now, ain't that the fetchinest little gal I ever laid eyes on! How you, honey?"

"Fine. This is my mom."

They watched Julie Clay Smith Williams with uncertain smiles, taken by her beauty and her style, yet naturally protective of Judd Smith, their friend, their working buddy, their reverend. Old Moe chanced it, making a careful inside joke, causing the other two to chuckle knowingly. "Well, that's our preacher for you. Was the frayinest man, before he got into this setting-down work! Went off awar and come back a hero, then feathered into that old criminal up New Jersey, got his ear put full of lead. And now the two prettiest old doney gals I ever seen right here face to face, and neither one of them owning a piece of him no more."

Jasper nudged his brother. "Moe, that's a sorry tale. Well, reckon we better get on, Reverend. Nice to see you all, now." They waved, and walked slowly out of the restaurant.

Julie had a quizzical look on her face, as if she did not understand anything the men had just said. A multitude of stares flitted her way from the other patrons. Judd Smith was wishing she had not worn a skirt quite so expensive or so short. The miniskirt was beginning to threaten Richmond, but it was a long way away from Bear Mountain, and her slim thighs were either exciting or offending almost everyone in the restaurant.

She watched the men leave. "The younger man—the son? He doesn't say much."

"Herbert? He's a little slow. They keep him pretty close, that's all."

"Daddy, what's a 'doney gal'?"

Smith watched Alma Coulter's hips and waist as she worked behind the counter, preparing a meal for a customer, and absently complimented himself for his taste, even as a youth. "A doney gal is a sweetheart, honey."

"They think Mommy and I were both your girl friends?"

"No. No, they were talking about something else."

"What, Daddy?"

Alma Coulter sauntered over like a coy, careful cat, her full breasts jiggling underneath the white uniform, her muscled hips and thighs pressing against its fabric also. She had listened in on Smith's whole conversation with the Hardy brothers, as well as Loretta's question, and her claws were out.

She plopped three menus onto the tabletop, her eyes glued on Judd Smith, as if she would turn to salt if she faced Julie or Loretta. At thirty-five, Alma had ripened into pure sensuality, like a juicy peach. She folded her arms underneath her breasts, accentuating them, pursing full lips with a mix of mild disgust and expectation. *The nicest teats in all Virginia,* that's what Judd Smith had proclaimed two decades before, lapping up their luxuries.

"You can have the dinner, or I can make you a hamburger."

He felt the weight of a dozen pairs of eyes as he answered her. "We'll take the dinners, thank you."

"Daddy, I want a hamburger."

"She'll take a hamburger."

Julie waved a delicate finger in the air, a command, as she studied the menu. "Do you have a choice of dressings with your salad, miss?"

For the first time, Alma Coulter stared fully into Julie's face. She had the look of the mortally wronged in her narrowed blue eyes. "Thousand Island or Italian. And I ain't a 'miss,' thank you. I been married twice. Judd Smith left me for the Marines, and Buford Coulter left me for the ever after when he piled up a truck."

"Daddy, *she's* the other doney gal!" Loretta exclaimed it as if she were now a master of the mountain dialect, the words rolling out of her little mouth with just the proper accent. Several muffled laughs floated to them from other seats.

Julie peered at Alma, her small mouth slack, open, and unbelieving. Alma stared back, a righteous smile sitting comfortably on her full face. "Thousand Island, ma'am?"

"No, I'd like to leave." She rose suddenly, and walked out of the restaurant.

"You never told me you'd been married before, Judd."

"Well, I wasn't, not really. Turn here." He watched her face in the late afternoon light. It was taut, offended. But sundown glowed on her cheeks and in her eyes, like a Cleopatra cream bath. It wasn't that he wanted to still love her; he just couldn't stop. "It was a marriage of false pretenses. I was eighteen, she was fifteen." He was conscious of Loretta in the back seat, her eyes carefully watching steep hills and woods and rushing streams, but her ears no doubt straining for every word. "She thought she was pregnant and it turned out she wasn't. That was the basis for the marriage, and when it turned out to be false, there wasn't a real marriage." He continued to watch Julie, searching for a reaction. "I'm comfortable with that notion, even now."

"But you never said a word to me about it, for all those years!"

"I don't know that it really matters anymore, does it, Julie?"

She glanced quickly at him, then again concentrated on the narrow, winding road. The pavement ended, her tires suddenly roaring and grinding on gravelly dirt. "I don't know. I guess not."

"It's right up here. The next place on your right."

"*That?* You live there, Judd?"

She braked the Mercedes, and then turned onto the wooden bridge. It creaked dangerously underneath the weight of the car. His dogs, four of them now, surrounded the car, yapping and jumping, their muddy paws leaving brown prints on the fenders and doors.

Judd jumped from his door. "*Git* now! Go on, dogs, *git!*" He chased them, and threw a few rocks. They retreated across a small pasture behind the cabin, still yapping, playfully nipping at each other as they ran.

"Oh, Dad, it's neat!" Loretta threw her little arms apart, embracing it all; the small cabin, the stream before it, the pasture and woods behind, and all around, the steep rolling mountains now bursting with the green of spring. "Let's move here, Mom."

"You don't even have electricity, Judd!" She carefully took it all in, obviously trying to place herself living in such primitive isolation. Inside, she conducted a thorough inspection. She touched the hand pump at the small sink and the kerosene lamp as if they were antiques. She studied the tiny cookstove, tracing its fuel line to the gas bottle, and then the wood stove, following its pipe up through the ceiling with her eyes. She pushed her hand once into the cushion of his couch, and then finally stood next to his military footlocker of a desk, motionless and moved, and contemplated his double bed against the back wall, with its massive pile of brightly colored quilts.

"Are you happy here?" She sounded as if it were somehow possible.

He cooked them a quick batch of scrambled eggs. The country ham was too salty for Julie's taste. Loretta ate five pieces of bread. Afterward they walked the rocky back pasture, up the hill to a barbed-wire fence. Beyond it, dark woods rose up the side of the mountain. The pasture smelled of sweet grass and cow dung. Loretta threw sticks and rocks for the dogs, who followed them, making circles around them and occasionally disappearing into the woods. The only sounds were animals and birds; the dogs yapping and pounding their paws, mocking birds and bluejays and his old friend of a screech owl in the woods, the mournful lowing of Fred Pennypacker's cattle as they trundled down a far ridge, heading for their night visit to his barn.

"It's so peaceful, Judd."

Back inside he stoked up the wood stove until soon the whole cabin was warm as an oven. He lit the kerosene lamp and they told stories in its shadows. Soon, Loretta grew sleepy, and he put her in his bed, covering her with three quilts.

He did not ask Julie to stay, nor did she mention it. They sat next to each other on his couch and drank warm coffee and talked in soft whispers with a relaxation that had been absent during all those other months of Washington and Newark, as if the remote peacefulness of his hollow had permeated their view of each other. He spoke of his church. They talked about Loretta. She told him for the first time of her mother's death, all the sad quiet alcoholic details, and of her father's loneliness, his refusal to allow himself to be coddled or kept. In a moment, the unquantifiable heartbeat or lifetime it takes to peer deeply into the soul of one you love, it was midnight.

She looked at her watch, feigning surprise. "Oh, Judd, I could never find my way out of here in the dark."

"You can stay. There's plenty of room in bed with Loretta." He eyed her steadily. "You know you were going to, anyway."

She leaned back on the couch in the low wick light, emanating delicacy, her miniskirt halfway up her thighs and her pullover blouse gathered in front, accentuating her small breasts. The shadows of the lamp danced on her face and chest, making her alternately light and dark, as if small clouds were passing between them. She slowly licked her lips, watching him.

"How long has it been since you've made love, Judd?"

"Five, six years, I guess. Since I got shot."

"Judd! *You?*" She crossed her legs, turning toward him. She was only two feet away. He could see the deepening lines on her forehead and around her eyes. He could smell her perfume and he could feel the way she wanted him, as if she were massaging him with her words. "I'd like you to make love to me, Judd. How sinful is that?"

"It isn't, as long as you accept basic principles." He still watched her with an almost expressionless face. "As far as my relationship with God is concerned, you and I are still married."

"We are?" She seemed curious, almost amused. She was only a foot away.

"I made a vow that said 'forever' and I meant it."

She stood slowly, and blew out the lantern light. He could hear her sibilant movements in the dark, and in a moment she joined him on the couch. She caressed his ear with soft fingers, and unbuttoned his shirt, a hand finding his brittle moon of a scar just above his pelvis.

"Poor Judd. Why do they always hurt you?"

She was all over him, touching and kissing, like feathers. Before, it was she who had demanded to be loved and fondled, but now Judd Smith might have been Kaw-Liga, the cigar-store Indian Hank Williams had sung about those years before. He was indeed hard as wood, and she mounted him, her soft lips and breasts and thighs pulling him under like a drug.

"What I wouldn't give to have the last ten years back, Judd. It's so scary to be old and wrong, too. Love me, Judd. Love me love me love me . . ."

She fell asleep in his arms. *You're such a wonder, Judd Smith.* She had whispered it just before she dropped off to sleep. *A wife you married and swear you didn't, a wife married to another man and you swear isn't. A preacher who gets in fights and shows up at all the wrong places. And cockfights. Do you really go to cockfights?*

He didn't actually perceive it as crying, but he could feel the tears run from his eyes and catch inside his ears as he held her to him. A quilt covered them. He had so many quilts; they were gifts from doting ladies in his congregation. Loretta slept peacefully at the other end of the cabin, not twenty feet away. It was the way it was supposed to have been, the way he had imagined twelve years before that it might be, but it was also wrong. Was it theologically wrong or was it just a cultural trespass, an antisocial act? He didn't know. He did not feel soiled by it. More than anything else, he was simply afraid. And his greatest fear was that, when the sun rose, and it all went away again, it would have hurt him beyond what he could bear. It had been more of a fantasy in this dark mountain cabin than anything else. What had it been for her? A respite from boredom? How could life get so complicated that making love to your wife created such anguish?

Firelight peeked around the edges of the wood stove door, silhouetting her profile. Her high forehead and her little nose and the small rise of her mouth were devoid of any emotion, completely relaxed. Examining their calmness, he could not help but think that he was staring at the way she would look when she was lying embalmed, peaceful in her casket. How would he feel, peering into it, about her, about the way they had hurt each other, about this? Those were the questions, and in the dark night, under the narrow, teasing flickers of stove light, he had no answers.

II

Clifton Marberry had the finest collection of nigger roundheads in all of southwest Virginia and maybe even in the whole world. He liked to wave a hand and shake his head modestly when people complimented him, saying that after all it was in the breeding more than anything else, but Marberry spent almost his entire workday training them up, running them and sparring them, and even keeping them on a secret vitamin formula in addition to their rather regal menus of chuck steak and eggs. People liked to tease Marberry that his nigger roundheads ate better than his family. Marberry would tease back that they worked harder, too, and made him more money. A few years before, he had even fought a truckload of them in northern California, and they'd done right well, even though they'd had to fight with knives instead of spikes.

When the gamecocks were hardly hatched, Marberry would hold a pair of them, one in each hand, and push their faces into each other, seeing which birds had more of the natural, inbred fighting spirit that would make them winners. By the time they were a few months old he would be training them, holding them into the air upside down and dropping them hundreds of times a day to strengthen their wings, running them along tracks near his barn to toughen their legs and their endurance. Later, he would fix boxing gloves to their spurs and match them up in a sample ring, closely evaluating each bird as it screeched and pecked and kicked. And by the time one of his brightly colored, heavy-feathered cocks was thrown into a pit inside someone's country barn, to battle for a minute or so and then probably die, Clifton Marberry had a full year of work into him.

Some people called them killer roosters, but Clifton Marberry didn't mind. They only killed each other. And some claimed that it was a cruel and violent sport, but that didn't bother Marberry, either; nor did it offend the hundreds of mountaineers who gathered in various barns each Saturday night from November through June to watch them fight. It was an ancient, even an honored sport, except for the past few squeamish decades. George Washington had liked cockfighting, and so had Thomas Jefferson. And besides, anyone who had ever chopped off a chicken's head so he could cook the bird, and then watched it run around in its mad, mindless jerky little circles, knew that dying dramatically was the primary contribution chickens made to the whole world, anyway, unless you were a person who preferred to gobble them up as omelets before they were even born.

And those nigger roundheads just *loved* to fight. Marberry was holding a pretty red and brown and green rooster in his arms, just outside the round dirt pit as the bets came in, and it seemed to be all he could do to restrain his cock from getting down to business. His rooster had caught sight of the other bird and was attempting to struggle free. Two hundred years of breeding had taught him to want to kill. Marberry stroked his rooster with a fat, doting hand to calm him down a little, as if he were a newborn infant screaming for his mother's teat.

An old, rail-thin farmer with a shaved head and bib overalls that hung on him like a barrel was walking along the edge of the pit, pointing toward Marberry's opponent. Earlier, he had served as usher and director of admissions. Now he was keeping book. Thousands of dollars had already changed hands in the first eight fights, and the final four, which pitted the best roosters of the bunch against each other, would see even heavier betting. "Still need a hundred dollar this side." No fights began until the betting was even.

"Think I ought to take a chance on that Gray, Judd?" Senator Jackson Clay sat with Judd Smith in the front row, comfortably disguised in a pair of overalls himself. "He looks a bit bigger than the other bird. I'd say size gets the money."

"Well, Senator—"

Clay nudged him. "Hold down on that, I told you! Just say 'Amos.'" Clay was clearly enjoying both his anonymity and his surroundings.

"*Amos?*" Smith chuckled, shaking his head. "Okay. Anyway, 'Amos,' I'm not a betting man, but I wouldn't put money against Marberry's birds."

"Ten dollars on the Gray!" Clay held up the money. The bookmaker nodded, writing down the bet.

"Name?"

"Amos . . . Jackson." Clay smiled with satisfaction as the bookmaker wrote the name next to the bet.

Judd Smith watched the enjoyment on the old man's creased, baggy face. Senator Clay was in his late seventies. He had developed large jowls and a heavy paunch. Sometimes his lower jaw shuddered when he concentrated, the lip falling away, revealing stained brown teeth. But his mind was still as active and combative as ever, and Judd Smith was still the only man who had ever stood up to him and prevailed, no matter how pyrrhic the victory had been. It had been the first thing Clay had mentioned following the "howdy do's," as he called their fifteen minutes of feeling each other out after eight years apart.

"Amos, listen." It was fun, almost comical to call a man who had been the greatest authority figure in Virginia politics for a generation "Amos." "You ever watch a rooster in a barnyard? You know it ain't the biggest rooster that's always the dominant one. It's the fightingest one. And once that little fellow fights his way to the top, he bites himself off the biggest flock of hens he can handle, and he handles them with a passion, if you know what I mean."

"Well, that might be true, but—"

"But what, Amos? You bet on the size of the fight, not the size of the rooster."

"*But you've got two of the fightingest goddamn roosters in Virginia out in front of you right now, Judd Smith, so I say bet on the size!*"

"*Bet on whatever you want, Amos. You've got a right to be a fool. But if it was me, I'd sure enough bet on that nigger roundhead, because Clifton Marberry knows how to breed fighters!*"

Clay and Smith both had fairly shouted their exchange, acting like ferocious, age-separated siblings, weaned on the same pugnacity. Owen Ford, who owned the A&P Store in Bear Mountain, leaned over from the other side of him, chiding Smith. "Reverend, I hate to go against you, but the man's probably right, you know. The best middle-weight in the world is like to get stomped by the best light heavy. Look at Ray Robinson and Joey Maxim." He smiled warmly to Clay, taking in his age and manner of dress. "You from around here, Amos? You durn sure look familiar to me."

"No, I'm down visiting the reverend for a couple days."

"He's a city fellow, mostly. Up near Richmond." Judd Smith let it hang, and Clay appeared relieved.

The bets were even. Side bets were being arranged throughout the large barn, men calling out numbers. Judd Smith heard a two-hundred dollar shout and counter-shout. Cockfights themselves weren't illegal but the gambling was, and of course there wouldn't be cockfights without the gambling. Every now and then the sheriff's department made an obligatory raid, but it was a matter of form, a way to stifle criticism of "unbounded lawlessness." Smith had freely given his own opinion to the sheriff and anyone else who would listen to him that betting on a cockfight was no more immoral than throwing a bundle of money into the stock market. Both were gambles, the only palpable difference being that the average mountain man had neither the funds nor the insight to win on Wall Street, while he might well possess a few dollars and some rooster sense. So it was just another foolish law, and mountaineers had a long history of ignoring foolish laws.

Marberry and the other handler slowly carried their roosters toward the center of the pit, cradling them in their arms like children, the birds peeking out from just above the handler's elbow as if both were lying in ambush. The cocks became immediately jittery at the sight of each other, their heads jerking this way and that, their feet working to get free. In the pit the trainers held them out to each other and the two birds screeched and strained some more, pecking and trying to move their wings, getting a taste for the fight. The crowd murmured approvingly. A few more side bets were shouted out and accepted.

Slowly, the handlers pulled the birds apart, first sideways, their arms making an arc, and then back, retreating to the edge of the pit. Each cock had been fitted with a sharp spike where his spur once grew. The handlers removed a sheath that covered the spike, watching each other from across the pit. They nodded, and then simultaneously they tossed the birds toward each other from the edge of the pit, giving them a small push upward, a prayer that their own cock might get high enough to land on top of the other bird and immediately spike him.

"Come on, gray bird!"

"Don't broadcast your foolery, Amos."

They closed with high hops, their wings flapping hard, whap whap, like the sudden sound a covey of quail makes when it breaks cover, their legs kicking out, stabbing forward with the spikes. They crashed into each other with wings and beaks and legs, mingling their feathers and screeching. The crowd screamed. They struggled, the metal spikes submerged under the mass of feathers and then suddenly gleaming.

In twenty seconds they both were still, lying in a heap together. Jackson Clay raised a fist.

"Get up, gray bird!" He turned to Judd Smith. "What happens if they're both dead?"

"Ah, they ain't either of them dead, yet."

"So what happens if they are?"

"You take them over to the drag line, over there, and lay them head to head. The last one that makes a move of any kind wins. He's got to peck the other one. They'll peck even if they're dead. That's the breeding."

The handlers had picked up the birds, now wet with saliva and blood, their feathers matted, making them look thin and wasted. Clifton Marberry lifted his cock and examined him carefully. Then he put the bird's head inside his mouth and blew gently, steady puffs, his cheeks going round each time as if he were playing tuba. The cock's eyes were open when Marberry took his head back out. The old handler then lifted up the rooster's tail, and blew a few toots toward his anus. The bird crowed, and many in the crowd cheered.

The other handler had partially revived his bird also. They nodded again to each other, and tossed the cocks together. Marberry's nigger roundhead took a high leap and came down onto the gray bird's neck with his spike. Purple blood shot out in a quick, thin gush for several feet, like a man urinating. It pattered on the dust of the pit and Marberry's supporters screamed with delight, calling for their money. The gray bird was dead. It didn't matter that Marberry's cock would also die within minutes. The fight was over.

"Hot damn, got him right in the huckleberry vein!"

Smith smirked a little bit, teasing old Senator Clay. "I told you, Amos. Ain't nobody can blow up a rooster's tail like Clifton Marberry."

*   *   *

Jackson Clay was quiet as the car sighed and swayed along dirt mountain roads, making its way back from the farm that had hosted the cockfights. Judd Smith could tell that the old man was gathering himself. He had not driven down from Richmond merely to watch the roosters. It was a measure of his honor, and of Judd Smith's admiration for him, that Clay would do anything—badger, complain, fight, kill— to see his daughter happy.

"You know you really set me off when you turned down law school and went working for the FBI, Judd."

Smith watched the road, his face an Indian's mask. "I know that. But I had to be my own man, Senator." He glanced over at Clay, catching an intent, almost apologetic stare in the dark. "I think you might have even done the same thing yourself."

"I probably would have. I can see that now. I was so bent on making sure everything was going to work out for you all that I guess I caused all the rest of it to happen. Julie picked up on a lot of the way I felt. You get used to having your way in politics, to having everyone kiss your ass. I guess I'm glad you didn't." He grew silent. The only sound was the tires growling on the hard dirt road. "I'm an old man, Judd. I'd like to go to the grave knowing Julie's going to spend the rest of her days without all this torment."

"I love Julie. I always have and I always will."

"So what are you going to do, Judd? By God—" From the corner of his eye, Judd Smith watched the old man slip a nitroglycerin tablet underneath his tongue. Clay sat quietly again, and then spoke with a new calm, as if beginning over. "You know, people say I'm a success, and I guess I was. But the only really important measure of success is here, in your personal life. You know about Julie's mother." He did not wait for an acknowledgment. "Julie loves you, too, Judd. But she's married to another man, now. And Tony Williams is running for lieutenant governor next go around. Do you know what kind of scandal it would cause if she left him in the middle of all that? I don't know if either of you would ever get over it. It would be in the papers. They'd follow you around. The Williams family has a lot of money and a lot of connections. They'd try to destroy you. And her." He was shaking his head, in a knot again. "I just don't know which way to go on it, I swear to God."

"Senator," Judd Smith spoke evenly, his eyes still on the road, his voice filled with a peace that washed over the older man and made him smile. "It's not like you've got to vote it up or down, you know!

The last time you tried to control things, they couldn't have ended up worse. That wasn't all your fault, don't get me wrong. But you can't push people's lives to where you want them like you can a piece of legislation." He glanced over and caught Clay's smile. He smiled back. "I won't hurt her, Senator. I'd do anything to keep from hurting her, I think."

Clay seemed content. "These people down here love you, Judd. That's a real trick, to keep their respect as a man of God and to show up at places like cockfights."

"I don't feed them anything phony."

"Did you ever think about politics? You'd be good."

Smith chuckled softly, turning onto a two-laned asphalt road. In ten minutes they would be back at his cabin, and Senator Clay would spend the night in his bed while he took the couch again. "Oh, I don't know. I just don't plan anymore. Life happens to you soon enough without planning it and getting disappointed, either because you planned too low or too high." He thought about it some more, taking a tight turn past ridges with their little cottages aglow in the dark. "But this war bothers me, it really bothers me. I fought in a stalemate in Korea, remember, just sitting there spending people and waiting for the politicians to end it, and it cuts you up from the inside. You know what I was thinking the whole time we were watching those cockfights? I was thinking of Red Lesczynski, my big old blood brother, out there on the carrier right now, running missions into North Vietnam. It's just like a cockfight. He's thrown in there again and again, on such controlled terms, with the option being to fight and get back out, or to die. No wonder they call the pilot's seat in a fighter the cockpit."

CHAPTER TWENTY

A GARBAGE DETAIL WAS THROWING trash off the fantail of the U.S.S. *Shiloh*. Leftover food, bags upon bags of paper and cans, large wall lockers, unidentifiable boxes, all bounced and rolled in the white wake of the steaming ship, mixing with the foam. Red Lesczynski could see pieces of garbage for miles behind the ship, all the way to the horizon in the late afternoon sun, as if the *Shiloh* were marking off a trail on the otherwise amorphous reaches of the blue, unending South China Sea.

He and a dozen other pilots were shooting their .38-caliber survival pistols, using the trash as targets. Lesczynski practiced often off the fantail, although he did not know many downed pilots who had either dared or had a useful opportunity to fire the .38 at the North Vietnamese. When you were hoping for rescue, you evaded, as silently as possible. When rescue was hopeless, you didn't commit suicide by firing your weapon at a people who outnumbered you 17 million to 1.

But it was a way to let off steam, to relieve the boredom of shipboard life. Except for the combat missions, he might have been a monk at a retreat, alone in a midocean cloister with the other members of his sect. It was flat, tedious, with a day's highlight being dinner in the wardroom and the movie afterward, or perhaps a game of chess or Go. That in itself heightened the tension of the missions, rather than allowing one to gear up for them. There was so little movement or variation on the ship, and yet three of every four days the *Shiloh* was "on the line" he was flung off the carrier deck two and sometimes three times a day by a steam catapult, as if his F-4 Phantom were a pebble in a slingshot, to form an attack group over the sea and then race through ground fire and missiles toward a bombing target where for ninety seconds every fear in the world was real, exploding all around him, calling for the most minute recesses of his concentration. Then it would be over and he would find the boat again, that square little speck in the sea, and set the tail hook of his aircraft on top of a cable on its angled deck, jerking to a violent stop. The whole thing took little more than an hour, and he would again be surrounded by the tedious calm. It was the paradox that taunted him, as if he were a lobster being dangled over a boiling cookpot for a few seconds every hour, only to be returned to the tank. What would the lobster think, if it could think, when it was again safe in the tank but knew it would soon be once more dangled over the pot?

Salt air covered him like a scab; he loved the smell and the taste. The snub-nosed pistol jerked in his hand as he fired again and again at a five-gallon can that had once held cooking oil. He couldn't tell whether he had hit the can. It bounced in the churning wake like a Ping-Pong ball, and was soon out of range.

"Ah, the hell with it." He returned his weapon to the chief petty officer in charge of the "famfire detail," and left the open platform of the fantail, entering the bowels of the aircraft carrier.

More men lived on the U.S.S. *Shiloh* than in Ford City. And all of them had jobs. The huge *Forrestal*-class supercarrier was home to 4,100 men, and 80 aircraft. It weighed 76,000 tons, fully loaded. It was longer than three football fields, and had four acres of flight deck. Its power plant could summon 280,000 horsepower from four geared steam turbines, enough to push the *Shiloh* through any sea at 35 miles an hour. It carried more than 26 million pounds of fuel in its hull. The *Shiloh* had deployed from Alameda, California, just after Christmas 1965, and had been operating as the center of a twelve-ship task force on Yankee Station off the coast of Vietnam since mid-January 1966. In its five months of Yankee Station duty, the *Shiloh* had been to Subic Bay, Philippines, twice, for four days each time, and to Yokosuka once, for three days. Other than that, the *Shiloh* had been constantly "on the line." Its pilots had flown 17,000 missions, and dropped 22 million pounds of ordnance onto North Vietnamese targets.

Lousy targets, mostly. The wrong targets. Lesczynski exited a narrow, honeycombed passageway and began crossing the hangar deck. It was filled with aircraft undergoing maintenance or being rearmed and refueled. A-4 Skyhawk and A-6 Intruder attack craft, EA-6 Prowler electronic warfare planes, RA-5 Vigilante reconnaissance jets, S-2F antisubmarine planes, and SH-3 Sea King helicopters variously mixed with his own F-4 Phantom fighters across its reaches. The hangar deck was long and wide and dark, its bulkheads and deck a musty gray, like a basement. The flight deck was two levels higher; planes moved up and down on four huge elevators.

He was the executive officer of his squadron, and was slated to take command of it within six months. He stopped for a few minutes, chat-

ting with crewmen who were working on the F-4s, checking their
efforts and assuring them, with simple words, of the importance of
their jobs. Then he set out again, heading for the flight wardroom, for
dinner.

In one corner of the hangar deck a group of sailors was playing a
fast game of basketball, shouting and running, shirtless in the tropical
heat. Across its middle, a line of men extended from a ladder that
went to the deck below, waiting to enter the main galley and eat dinner. A few of them wore the tight, multicolored shirts of flight deck
personnel, but most of them were dressed in blue dungarees and baseball caps. Many were reading from ever-present paperback books that
fit perfectly inside rear dungaree pockets. Others conversed, clowning
around and raucously taunting each other. Many wore tattoos on their
forearms.

Lesczynski grinned blandly as he passed the different groups of
sailors, waving to a few of the men he recognized. They were young
and they all worked hard, twelve hours a day for months on end, enduring cramped quarters, long lines, and the lonely isolation of shipboard life. They worked because they believed, or because it was a
job, or because it bought them liberty in arguably exotic ports. Some
worked because they didn't want to go to the brig. It didn't matter.
They kept the ship going twenty-four hours a day, no matter what,
and for that you had to hand it to them.

The 1-MC blared into every compartment, preceded by a boat-
swain's eerie whistle. It was Big Brother. *"Now hear this. Now hear
this. The smoking lamp is out, throughout the ship, while handling
ammunition. I say again, the smoking lamp is out, throughout the
ship, while handling ammunition."*

Lesczynski walked out the forward end of the hangar deck, and
climbed a ladder up to the "o2" level, between the hangar deck and
the flight deck. The flight wardroom was on the "o2" level. It was less
formal than the ship's wardroom below, designed cafeteria-style to ac-
commodate the more fluid schedules of the pilots. In contrast to the
main wardroom, there were no Filipino stewards to hold a tray of
food in front of an officer, as if he were an aristocrat dining downtown. No seating by rank. No careful conversation, designed to teach
one the art of gentle avoidance. Lesczynski liked the flight wardroom.

Commander Jimmy Maxwell was holding court with two junior
officers. Lesczynski's friend since his first days of flight training was
now the executive officer of the A-6 attack squadron, and like Le-

sczynski was on the "fleet up" program, which would give both of
them command within a few months. Maxwell had gone spry and gray
after fifteen years in the cockpit. Crow's-feet were etched deeply into
the corners of his eyes. His tight hawk's face was self-assured, and animated. Maxwell waved to Lesczynski, who joined them. Then he
smiled sardonically, without joy, his leathered face emanating a resignation that might have been anger, had he the luxury to question
policy.

"They bagged another A-4 today."

"Over that Dong Khe site?"

"Yes, sir, old LBJ sure knows how to treat his boys. You know why
he calls us his boys, don't you? Son, I'm from Mississippi, and I know
what that means. It means he thinks he owns us. What was it he said?
The military can't bomb a shithouse without his approval."

Lieutenant Nick Damsgard, new to the squadron and on his first
Western Pacific deployment, leaned forward, his heavy brows furrowed earnestly. "If he'd let us go after Dong Khe a month ago, we
could have flattened it."

Maxwell feigned alarm. "You don't shoot up missile sites before
they're ready for you! They're not part of the war until then. What do
you want to do, win this goddamn thing?"

They all laughed, staring into their food, dry chortles that indicated
none of them really thought it was funny, not when they were dangling their very lives over the North every day in pursuit of a goal
that Lyndon Johnson had never made clear to himself, much less
them. Maxwell snorted again. "If Goldwater had won in '64, this war
would have been done within a week, and there wouldn't have been
enough of North Vietnam left over to plant rice on."

Frank Salpas, also a new lieutenant, stroked his moustache, staring
down into his food. "I'm not so sure, Commander. This is a different
kind of war. Johnson seems pretty serious about doing the right thing.
I mean, he's trying. He's putting at least a half-million ground troops
in the South."

Maxwell snorted again. The constant attrition of the air war was
getting to him, Lesczynski could tell. "It's not how many troops he's
got on the ground, any more than it's how many goddamn bombs
we're dropping. It's what you're *doing* with them! You tell me what
the hell it means to fight a 'limited war,' all right? Do you think North
Vietnam is fighting a limited war? Shee-it. Do you feel like you're a
little bit at war when you're jinking up there, dodging SAM missiles?

Johnson won't let us knock out SAM sites while they're being built. He won't let us take out ships in Haiphong harbor that have SAMs visible on their goddamn decks! He won't mine the harbor. He won't let us go after operational MiG airfields. But we're 'his boys' when we get our asses shot off! He must think this is a goddamn *golf* game or something, and he needs to give the North Vietnamese some kind of *handicap!*"

Damsgard looked up from his tray, smiling ironically. "He's stuck with a war that he doesn't know how to fight. He just wishes it would all go away. This whole 'Rolling Thunder' operation is a joke. Tell me how much we've disrupted the average North Vietnamese person's life."

Maxwell nodded earnestly, agreeing. "Here we've got a whole fleet of B-52 bombers that could put Hanoi back into the Stone Age, and old LBJ sends them off to make toothpicks out of trees on the Ho Chi Minh trail. And here we've got light attack planes and precision fighters, and the man sends us against the North day in and day out. Not against targets that will hurt the North Vietnamese, but against 'interdiction targets.' I don't know how many pieces of railroad track I've blown away in the last five months. But I can guarantee you that Russia and China and the other communist countries have been replacing them as fast as we've been blowing them away. The North Vietnamese probably *love* what we're doing. It keeps their people united. It doesn't really hurt them. And it keeps the aid rolling in from the communist bloc."

"Can you imagine these sorts of restrictions during World War II?" Lesczynski had listened quietly, eating his food, but could no longer restrain his own frustration. "We couldn't have hurt the Japanese by simply shooting down the aircraft that attacked us. Hell, they'd *still* be regrouping, putting together fleets and forays! We went to their hearts. We took the war to them. We blew away their planes on the ground, we knocked out their industry. We took out Tokyo." He pointed a fork, growing animated. "Last week. Remember? Knock out the Sai Thon rail yard, they say, but if one bomb hits the steel mill next door you're in deep shit!"

They all three watched him attentively. He did not often philosophize aloud about the conduct of the war. For the most part, he viewed it as unproductive, a negative morale factor for the men who served under him. But tonight he felt unsettled, provoked. "This isn't going very well at all. Are we going to say that the Japanese were more evil than the North Vietnamese, and that they deserved more of our wrath? Why? The North Vietnamese are clearly trying to take over the South by military force. It's the North Vietnamese who have almost their entire army in the South right now. We have stated to the world that the South should not be subjugated against its will. If that's worth fighting over, then it should be worth a serious, total effort. How long is it going to take Johnson to understand that the North Vietnamese believe they're winning, and that this sort of bombing reinforces that belief?"

He had grown his moustache back. His lips curled into a whimsical smile underneath its thick red gash. "I'll tell you the truth. I don't think McNamara has the guts, and I don't think LBJ has the clarity of thought, to fight this war. It's that simple."

Lieutenant Salpas grunted once, then nodded, a slow cynical grin growing underneath his moustache. "Did you hear about LBJ's big Silver Star for gallantry in action in World War II? Went out on a reconnaissance flight as an observer from Congress, and the plane got shot at. He sat there in his seat and watched, and then decided that since he didn't shit his pants, he deserved a medal. Take a look at his pictures. He loves to wear the lapel pin."

Maxwell grunted back, a combative grin streaking his narrow face. "Uh-huh. Well, if that's what it takes, he can come out here and go on that Alpha Strike with us 'boys' tomorrow, I can make sure he gets the goddamn Medal of Honor."

* * *

The real question was why they kept doing it, so well and with such precision, day after day, week after week, in the face of a steady trickle of losses that had been deceptive at first, but eventually overwhelming. So many shipmates, so many planes, downed for the honor of interdicting a system that by the very nature of their bombing would grow stronger with greater outside support.

Sitting in his stateroom after dinner, Red Lesczynski scanned the classified briefsheets from the past few weeks' activities, one of his perquisites as squadron executive officer.

June 12–19: Interdiction. 100 railroad cars damaged or destroyed, Qui Vinh, Pho Can, and Nam Dinh rail yards damaged extensively. 5 major highway bridges dropped. Junks and barges "lucrative."

June 20–26: Interdiction. 40 trucks, 100 junks and barges damaged or destroyed. Me Ka highway bridge, Mai Duong railroad and highway bridge dropped, considered essential to the Hanoi/Haiphong transportation system. Russian SA-2 missile site damaged in conjunction with attack on Mai Duong. Extensive damage to yards and facilities at Qui Vinh, Sai Thon, and Van Coi.

June 27–July 2: Interdiction. 200 railroad cars, numerous trucks and bridges damaged or destroyed. Major strikes against Dong Khe SAM missile site, the Dong Can military area, and Bien Son barracks.

He tried to measure those frail statistics against the terror that produced them, and the loss:

June 14: A-3 lost over North Vietnam. Orange ball seen by observers. Crew MIA.

June 15: F-4B hit during attack on PT boat. Pilot, RIO eject over water, rescued by SH-3 helo.

June 15: A-4E downed by ground fire, North Vietnam. Pilot ejects, is seen on ground. POW or MIA.

June 17: A-4C hit by ground fire during pullout from dive on Vinh railroad. Pilot ejects, radios from ground that he is about to be captured. POW or MIA.

June 19: A-1F crashes ahead of ship after night catapult launch. Pilot missing.

June 20: A-1H crashes ahead of ship after night catapult launch. Pilot not recovered.

June 21: RF-8A downed by antiaircraft fire. Good ejection. Enemy defenses prevent helicopter approach. MIA.

June 21: F-8 damaged by MiG-17, 4 F-8s respond. 1 F-8 downed. Good ejection observed. Another F-8 downs MiG with Sidewinder missile. 1 MiG destroyed. 1 pilot MIA.

June 25: A-4E hit by antiaircraft fire. Pilot ejects over water, rescued by SH-3 helo.

June 25: A-6A lost directional control on bombing run. Pilot and RIO eject. Pilot rescued by SH-3 helo. Chute of RIO seen, but not located. RIO MIA.

June 27: A-4E crashed during bomb run on barges. No ejection sighted. Pilot MIA.

June 27: A-4E caught fire en route to strike. Pilot ejected, rescued by Air Force HH-43 helo.

July 1: A-4E hit by ground fire during withdrawal from strike. Good chute sighted. Pilot not recovered. MIA.

Well, let's see. Two years of time and salary, minimum, to get an adequate jet pilot to the fleet. A half a billion dollars, I'd say, to build this carrier, equip it, and put it on the line. Millions of dollars for every plane, and the load it carried. The reputation of our country riding in every cockpit—its military reputation, its sense of political wisdom. And people, count two weeks of them, lost blowing away railroad tracks. Railroad tracks! Pissed down the tube, Lyndon Johnson, pissed down the tube.

The feeling had grown over the previous six months until, every time he read such statistics, Red Lesczynski felt as if he were somewhere between a gladiator and a whore, although he would never publicly relate this to his men. There was something almost malevolent in the way Navy and Air Force pilots were being wasted, in the restrictions forced on them. God forbid that they should go after the enemy's political centers, even though the communists had been killing government officials in the South for a decade. There was something supposedly inhumane about attacking any area where there might be civilians, although no such inhumanity had been seen in any other war, or even in the South in this one. They flew against railroad yards and were not allowed to attack MiG training bases. They could not attack Soviet missile sites until they were operational, and then, of course, it was like walking down the tube of a cannon. They had indeed, as Jimmy Maxwell had lamented over dinner, produced photographs of ships unloading missiles at Haiphong harbor, and were ordered to stay away. In fact, the North Vietnamese had protested before the International Control Commission a few weeks before that U.S. planes had made "provocations" against foreign ships at Haiphong, causing further admonitions from Johnson and McNamara to his "boys," rather than warnings to those supplying the communists.

When did a missile become a missile? When did a war become a war? When did a military professional finally cry "foul" to his commander in chief? At times Lesczynski tried to empathize with Admiral Kuribayashi, who had commanded the Japanese defenses at Iwo Jima during the Second World War, fully knowing that he would lose the battle. Like the Japanese commander, who died in the battle, Red Lesczynski believed not in the specifics of what he was doing, but in what his effort represented.

He thought a lot about Jerry Schmidt as he whiled away his hours on the *Shiloh*, wondering how the muscled, intense CIA agent was dealing with the similar botching of the war down South. Johnson and Westmoreland were obsessed with world opinion, on the one hand knowing that it would take a half-million American soldiers to establish a combat presence and the support functions it would need in order to operate halfway around the world, and on the other not wanting to appear to be the "aggressor" in the war. The result was piecemeal escalation, with the North Vietnamese controlling the pace and thus the entire initiative in the war. The units in the field were performing admirably, but the United States was continually reacting, continually behind. It was not a happy time if you were a believer.

Sophie wrote him every day. The letters came in bunches, with the resupply. When he had been young, he had believed that a man could get used to being away, could program it into the other cycles in his life. But it had gotten harder each time, so that now, at thirty-seven, it was as if he had split himself in two. So much of him was left with her, and with the children. J.J. was starting high school. How he longed to watch his son on the football field. Katherine was going through puberty without his manly advice. There were so many questions about dating that she would now throw at J.J. Little John liked to fix things; bicycles, even cars. At home, Lesczynski's Saturday afternoons belonged to John and his tools. There would be other times, and he dwelled on that, but he would never be able to see his children through the same lens as before.

He read several hours a day. That was the one salvation of shipboard life. He had brought more than thirty books, and would soon be finished with them all. He had made meticulous notes. They were a mixed bag of classics and military oddments. He was trying to understand this war, the Pacific, Japan. Japan was the key, and always had been.

He pulled out an old, faded volume written in 1920 by a Russian general, Nikolai N. Golovin, in collaboration with Admiral A. D. Bubnov. *The Problem of the Pacific in the Twentieth Century.* He had found it in a secondhand bookstore in Washington. Among other things, the book had accurately predicted both the timing and the course of World War II.

He checked his notes:

p. 43: "Japanese imperialism is not an invention of a handful of politicians. It is the expression of the spirit of modern Japan."

p. 81: "The motives that will prompt Japan to engage in the struggle are so deep and so vast that not one but several wars will have to be waged before a solution is reached."

p. 38: "When Europeans fight they always endeavor to set their own strength against that of their opponent. The Japanese endeavor to use the opponent's strength against him. By this method you add your opponent's strength to your own and may therefore win in spite of being weaker."

He pondered the last paragraph for several minutes before opening up the book. It made him want to show it to Kosaka. It represented a combination of those two favorite Japanese games, *jujitsu* and Go. It also made him wonder, in an oriental triple-thinking way, whether there was indeed some connection between what he was doing and Japan's growing strength. He didn't feel smart enough to figure that out, at least not yet.

He read carefully for an hour, marking the book and taking notes. The last paragraph of Russian wisdom that he added to his thick three-hole binder stayed with him as he left his small desk and climbed into his bed.

p. 153: "The realities of the Pacific include the necessity of all international agreements being backed by actual force. We may deplore this fact the more bitterly that mankind has but recently suffered such heavy losses in blood and treasure, but such is the present condition of the world, and the primary principal of positive science in search of the truth."

* * *

"Now, pilots, man your planes. I say again, pilots, man your planes."

In the gray sea dawn a stiff wind pushed into the *Shiloh's* prow, beating insistently against the faces and chests of pilots and sailors who busied across the long, plane-cluttered flight deck. The aircraft carrier had turned north, into the wind, and geared up to thirty-three knots for launching. The steady wind across the deck would help lift the aircraft by increasing their relative ground speed. In minutes, thirty-two of them would scream off from three different catapults of the *Shiloh*, each plane taking a small dip in front of the bow as it shifted from the pull of the catapult to its own power, and then disappear.

Red Lesczynski left the F-4 ready room with seven other pilots and reached his aircraft. He did a quick but thorough preflight, walking around the sleek, long-nosed jet alongside its blue-shirted plane captain, an act that had his life in its hands, but one that had been done so many thousands of times that it was down to a series of quick looks and jokes with the plane captain.

"All set, Christianson?"

The plane captain grinned through snaggled teeth. Underneath the tight cap and the Mickey Mouse sound attenuators was a boy hardly older than his son. "It'll get you there, Commander. Big one today, huh, sir?"

It was indeed, one of the largest raids of the air war, and one of the closest ever to downtown Hanoi. He checked his payload. A cluster of Mark 82 five-hundred-pound bombs hung close to each wing, above cylindrical pods that would fire Zuni five-inch rockets. Four F-4s, including his own, would go in first, taking out as many of the radar-controlled antiaircraft guns and missile sites as possible. Twelve A-6 and six A-4 attack planes would follow with heavy bombloads, going after the Bac Giang petroleum storage area outside of Hanoi. Four of his F-4s would hold back as a RESCAP, to come to the aid of aircraft under attack by MiGs or damaged by ground fire. Two A-3 tankers would accompany the flight for emergency refueling. Two "shrikes," especially configured A-4s, would provide immediate counter-battery fire to missile sites that locked onto the group as they went toward the target. An EA-6 "Q" aircraft would fly at the head of the group with the F-4s, in order to provide electronic jamming and surveillance. And finally, an RA-5 would follow up the strike, making a photograph for damage assessment. Once Lesczynski's F-4 flight rolled in, it would only take ninety seconds for the whole strike to be done with.

"Now, pilots start your engines. I say again, pilots start your engines."

He checked his survival gear inside the cockpit. The kid in the blue shirt gave him the signal and he fired it up. The A-4s went off the forward catapults, followed by the A-6s. The sun was burning a narrow streak across the sea to their right, the east, where eight thousand miles away his family was then finishing dinner and speaking sorrowfully of his absence. It was the July 4 weekend and they were in Ford City. The flight deck was filled with aircraft roaring down catapults and others taxiing toward them, with thin sailors dressed in colored jerseys, red and blue and white, yellow and purple and green, each jersey indicating without words their jobs. He followed a series of yellow-shirted men who looked like funny insects with their goggles and bulbous sound attenuators, the men pointing forcefully at him, ensuring they had eye contact with him, and then pointing again to the next yellow shirt, who guided him through an intricate maze of equipment and aircraft toward his launching catapult.

On the forward left catapult they hooked his Phantom into its bridle. He spoke briefly with Ted Cunningham, his back-seater, a young lieutenant (jg) on his first combat cruise, ensuring all their gear was a "go." His thumb went up and then he saluted, a signal to the NCO outside, and suddenly he was being slung along a ramp toward the ravening, empty sea, all the while gunning his Phantom with everything it had, going from a full stop to 240 miles an hour in the time it took him to whisper "Please, God," and then the jet gave a sighing dip just in front of the bow, down toward the waiting water, and after that he was free, airborne, making a slow turn to the left, picking up the rendezvous TacAn: 335 degrees, 15 miles, 10,000 feet, circle to your left.

They gathered quickly, the A-6s below him at 9,000 feet, the A-4s below that at 8,000, the "dogs and cats" below that, all circling with undeniable beauty in the clear blue sky. Each of the flight leaders checked in and he then heard Maxwell, the strike commander, give the word back to the ship.

"Combat this is Mad Dog One. All aboard. Departing with thirty-two."

They flew in loose formation, the F-4s and the "Q" up front, the others spread laterally behind them in four plane flights. As they approached the coastline Maxwell checked in with the airborne coordinator, a C-130 orbiting in a safe area over Laos, giving him the on and off target times.

"Combat Nail this is Mad Dog One with thirty-two, estimated eight oh five with estimated eight oh seven, over."

"Roger, Mad Dog One, you're clear. New time on target zero eight ten."

Lesczynski grinned nervously, imagining Maxwell's curses as they pulled into a wide, five-minute circle. The Air Force was hitting the southern outskirts of Hanoi from bases in Thailand. They'd either been late or had a pilot down.

Then it was their turn and they powered in hard and low, just above the green as it slipped suddenly under them. They were "feet dry" now, over hostile ground. They jinked as they flew, moving suddenly left and right to throw off SAM missile radar intercepts.

"Okay, let's go."

Lesczynski pitched up suddenly, moving almost vertically, as if rising from the green earth itself. The other three F-4s followed close behind. He came down in a straight line, directly toward the target. The attack aircraft would come in afterward at various angles, avoiding a pattern that might be picked up by North Vietnamese radar.

"Red One, in!"

He had seen the gun sites on the photos during the preflight briefing and they were clear now as he roared toward them, their little puffs going off around him. His aircraft unleashed a string of Zunis, their smoky trails impacting again and again, and then he pulled out of the dive, away as the bombs fell behind him. It all happened in a few seconds, and the Phantoms made their turn, heading back toward the new rendezvous over the sea.

"Red One, off."

The A-4s were next. "Blue One, in."

He could hear the chatter as they talked to one another, quick instructions.

"Heads up!"

"Look out, John!"

"Go left, now."

"Blue One, off."

Here came the first flight of A-6s. "Hawk One, in."

It was all so sterile once you'd made it through.

"Hawk One, off."

It was almost over. "Mad Dog, in."

"Break break break, be advised Mad Dog One is down."

The mission, his obligations, the world, all changed in five seconds. Jimmy Maxwell had been bagged. Lesczynski immediately began to turn his fighter around and return to the site. He had no munitions left, but he could not bear the thought of having to stand before Louise Maxwell and not assure her that he had done everything in his power to help her husband.

He heard Maxwell's wingman, speaking with a forced calm. "Okay, we got two good chutes. I've got them in sight." The wingman contacted the airborne coordinator. "Combat Nail, this is Mad Dog, got a bird down just off the target. I see him on the ground. I'm over him. We got two other birds out to tank, and they'll be back directly to you."

"Roger, Mad Dog, we'll direct."

The fire from the petroleum tanks rose twenty thousand feet, red and orange with oily curls of smoke. Lesczynski jinked and zigged and zagged, changing altitude, shaking radar scopes, moving back toward the target. They were too far inland for the Search and Rescue helicopters that operated off forward destroyers. The only hope was for a Jolly Green Giant to come overland from Thailand. That would take twenty minutes or so.

"They're locked onto us, Commander!" Lieutenant (jg) Cunningham was a seatful of terror in back of him. Red lights flashed on the instrument panel, indicating that a SAM radar had indeed locked them into its sights. He jinked several times. A missile flew past them. It looked like a telephone pole as it raced toward the heavens.

"That was too close!"

Maxwell was talking on his "beeper" survival radio. He was about a mile west of the target. The Jolly Green was on its way. Lesczynski could hear Combat Nail instructing it. A group of enemy soldiers was moving across a wide field, sweeping, looking for Maxwell and his bombardier. If the soldiers got too close it was all over. Lesczynski dove at them from the sky, thinking to pin them down, to distract them. They wouldn't know he was out of ammunition.

The 85-millimeter battery was in a hidden emplacement, off to his left. It puffed once and he saw it for the first time, all six guns firing until his field of vision on that side was loaded with its flashes. A dozen orange balls were coming at him, drifting up into space with a filmic slowness, an unreality, and he knew he was bagged. A shell ripped through his lower canopy as he tried to pull out of the dive and the stick became uncontrollable, the aircraft unresponding, a dead horse on which he was saddled, rolling slowly to the left. In the space of a half second, the time it took to let go of the stick and reach for the ejection lever, he realized that both his legs were wounded, his oxygen mask had been torn off by shrapnel, the oxygen bottle near his feet had exploded and set the cockpit aflame, and he was peering at the ground through a hole in the underside of his Phantom, a mere thousand feet below. The ground, Victnam, death, was coming up to meet him. His Phantom was still going five hundred miles an hour.

He pulled the ejection lever and nothing happened. He pulled it again and he was propelled through the closed canopy, the jet now at five hundred feet. His chute opened just enough to break his impact. He hit the ground at a forty-five-degree angle and bounced into the air again, doing a full, almost graceful loop and then landing on his knees and forehead, a three-point thud.

It was all so *loud*. That was his first, woozy thought as he staggered to his knees and then tried to stand. In the cockpit it had been sterile, except for the radio chatter. Suddenly the world was swimming with roars and explosions; missiles going off, the 85-millimeter battery pumping out three shells a second at other aircraft overhead, bombs and missiles coming back down from the covering jets, rifles and pistols shooting into the air with futile pops. The petroleum storage area was a towering, crackling backdrop a mile away, whose flames reached forever into the sky, as high as Mount Everest.

The soldiers who had been searching for Maxwell were now sweeping toward him instead, spread laterally across the dry rice paddy, their AK-47s pointing at him. They filled his vision as he tried to stand, thirty of them moving in a half jog. He reached back to disconnect his parachute, an automatic, unthinking move, but it wasn't coming off. Then he looked down and noticed that his left arm was hanging useless, unresponding but for little twitches, like a chick trying helplessly to fly. The bone in his upper arm had snapped completely in two, and the part still attached to his shoulder was jiggling, causing the rest of the arm to flail around.

He couldn't even surrender. He raised his right arm into the air and they took it for a threat, half of them dropping into firing positions and the other half rushing him. A soldier grabbed the dangling arm and twisted it behind him, in a tight hammerlock that kept on going until his detached wrist was up behind his head. He hit the man unthinkingly, trying to stop the pain. The others charged him, then noticed the arm was loose and merely beat him up instead of shooting him.

They acted as if they had never seen zippers before. They cut his flight suit off him, stripping him down to his undershorts, and tied a rope around his neck. In the distance, he saw a Jolly Green Giant helicopter pop in just over the trees where Maxwell had been and then disappear, under heavy air cover. He had seen nothing of Cunningham, his back-seater. They walked him across the dry field. Loudspeakers were everywhere, blaring terse urgencies he did not understand. An old man tried to come at him with a scythe, and the soldiers pushed him away. The soldiers took a delight in suddenly yanking the rope and making him fall. Both his legs were bleeding, the blood gathering in the nonregulation, powder-blue socks Sophie had sent him. He felt silly, as much as anything else, in his white boxer undershorts and the funny socks.

Under a clump of trees a nurse dressed the cuts on his head, ignoring his arm and legs. It grew quiet. Finally the all-clear siren sounded over the ubiquitous loudspeakers and they walked him to a dirt road, where he was loaded into a green munitions truck. A blue uniformed commissar met the truck in front of a small cluster of buildings. He had a terse, bulbous face. He seemed amazed at Lesczynski's size. The commissar was the first person to speak directly to him. He closely examined Lesczynski's features, then made a judgment.

"Russki?"

"Polski." He didn't know what else the man might have meant. "American."

They took him into a large, bare room and made him sit on the floor. People gathered at its open windows and stared at him. Shortly, an officer in green clothes, wearing a pith helmet, entered the room with three armed soldiers. The officer's face was expressionless, but his eyes had the frozen intensity of a professional killer. He stood in front of Lesczynski and spoke in fluent English.

"I am going to ask you some questions. If you do not answer you will be severely punished."

"I need a doctor."

"Later, if you demonstrate a proper understanding. What is your name?"

"Stanislaus Lesczynski."

"What is your rank?"

"Commander, United States Navy."

"What ship did you take off from?"

"I can't answer that, according to the Geneva Agreements."

The officer issued a command in Vietnamese. Someone behind Lesczynski kicked him hard in the head, knocking him over. Two men grabbed him by the arms, dragging him to the center of the room. His bad arm was up around his head again and he screamed in agony. The crowd outside the room responded with a chant, louder and louder. He felt alone, so alone. *I'm going to die in the midst of strangers who hate me.*

They tied his ankles together, and then his wrists and his elbows so that they touched, the ropes so tight that they cut the blood off like tourniquets. It was done with one rope, so that his back was arched and his frame was immobile.

They kicked him and beat him and pinched his hands and arms with pliers until the skin was completely numb and the limbs were paralyzed, as if they did not exist. Each time they asked the same question. Finally, awash with guilt at such a small surrender, he relented.

"U.S.S. *Shiloh.*"

"What squadron?"

The same routine. The three guards took turns to see who could hit his face the hardest. He began to realize that he was in a small sense winning, because he was making them pay for information they already had. Finally, he could stand it no longer.

"VF-907."

"What kind of plane were you flying?"

"You ought to know. You shot it down."

"What was your target?"

Out of one window, past the hateful enjoying faces, tongues of red flame still licked the noonday sky. "Where all that fire is coming from."

The interrogator left the room for a few minutes. He returned with four photographers, who immediately began taking pictures. He walked directly to Lesczynski and shoved his head down to the floor. A soldier pointed an SKS rifle into the back of Lesczynski's head, and pulled the trigger.

In the millisecond it took for the trigger to squeeze and click, Lesczynski came to a sort of unrelenting peace with his captivity. He was in such pain at that moment that he welcomed any relief, even death. His mind went to other things as he stared into the dirt floor. *I wonder where they'll bury me. I wonder how long it will take for Sophie to find out. What is it like for a bullet to hit your head?*

The trigger clicked. The firing pin hit an empty chamber. The crowd outside taunted him. And he knew that, for some perverse reason, they needed to use him more than they needed to kill him.

They blindfolded him and loaded him into the bed of a truck, and in twenty minutes he was in Hanoi.

* * *

"Put these on. You are going to a press conference."

The interrogator threw him a pair of oversized flight boots and an Air Force flight suit, freshly washed. They untied his hands. He had been sitting on a small stool in the Hoa Lo prison's interrogation room for five hours, going through the same string of questions and beatings

as before. They had to help him into the clothes. One of the guards
fashioned a sling for his arm out of thin gauze.

They loaded him onto the back of a military truck and made him
stand at the front of the truck bed, holding onto a bamboo pole. The
truck lumbered through endless Hanoi streets, another truck in front
of it with a spotlight on him, another one following, filled with jour-
nalists. Crowds gathered on every street at the urgings of the Big
Brother loudspeakers, chanting at him and throwing things. Warm
urine covered one side of his face. Feces impacted on the bamboo rail
near his hand. The crowd periodically surged against the truck, forced
back by troops with bayonets. But even Red Lesczynski could tell the
whole thing was staged. The demonstrators were somehow flat, me-
chanistic. They looked sideways, for their controllers, as often as they
did at him. *Wonderful stuff for pictures. Red Lesczynski on display.*

Hanoi was actually a beautiful city. He preoccupied himself with
that thought. And far away, in the corner of one eye, he could see the
petroleum plant still burning.

At the International House they kept him outside, in a flower garden, for ten minutes. When the guard came to guide him inside, he refused to move unless they gave him water. He had asked before, and
been denied. He had not drunk anything since breakfast, a lifetime
ago on the South China Sea. Finally the guard relented, and gave him
two glasses of ice water. He knew he would pay for his obstinance,
but it didn't matter. There would be so many things to pay for that
they would all blend in, anyway.

There were Caucasian reporters in the press room, as well as Asians.
He did his best to march up to the podium, and saluted when he
reached it. *In the Orient, the man who shows no fear is king*, that's
what MacArthur had said, but he was not really thinking about Mac-
Arthur at that moment. He was remembering Crane Howell, the hobbled, irascible professor at the academy who had grown old before his
time, who had survived the work camps and the beatings of the Japanese. If he was lucky, he would live to be old and beaten also. There
was no use hoping for more. It was now his fate.

The reporters asked him no questions. He was merely meant to be
an object on display, like elephant tusks after a safari. Afterward, the
trucks drove him back to Hoa Lo prison, better known among American fliers as the Hanoi Hilton, through a different section of town,
through the same groups of chanting people. And then the fun began.

For ten days they beat him. For ten days they did not let him sleep.

For ten days they asked him the same questions, over and over, slapping and punching, keeping him in leg irons, laughing as he urinated and shit on himself. For ten days they allowed his wounds to fester, until his legs were swollen and the gashes had turned black, the blisters splitting and draining onto the floor, as if he were a frankfurter on a spittle over a hot fire. For ten days they worked the ropes, tightening them and loosening them to regulate his pain, until he developed infected blisters that would make permanent scars, his "varsity stripes" along his wrists and upper arms. For ten days he saw no one but the guards, heard no voices but Vietnamese, found himself locked inside a seven-foot-square repository of darkness and filth that made him wish over and over that he could merely die and see the end of it.

And after ten days, he found himself writing with numbed fingers the words that they dictated into his delirious, semideadness:

1. *I condemn the United States Government for its aggressive war against the Democratic Republic of Vietnam.*

2. *I have encroached upon the air space of the Democratic Republic of Vietnam.*

3. *I am a war criminal.*

4. *I have received humane and lenient treatment from the people and the government of the Democratic Republic of Vietnam.*

CHAPTER TWENTY-ONE

SHE HAD KNOWN AS SOON as it happened.

It wasn't witchcraft. It wasn't hindsight or melodrama. It wasn't an attempt to involve herself with the experience beyond the truth. It was an inescapable entanglement with his emotions, the result of twenty-three years of loving the same man, of communicating with him for almost half of that time while he was away, so that this unexplainable visceral bonding grew stronger, as if it were a muscle, from all of the exercise. When he was home, she knew without a look or a word when he wanted to make love to her, and she knew when he wanted to be alone. And when he was at sea, she could frequently feel his moods. Then she would get his letter five days or a week afterward and he would mention an especially good flight, or the loss of a comrade, or a period of gloom where he missed her and the family, and she would have been right. She sometimes made a game of it, mentioning to a relative or friend as if she had just spoken with him on the telephone that Red was in a good mood that day, and then later producing his letter as proof.

The Fourth of July fireworks display on the ridge behind the VFW hall had bothered her. She had stood in the grass, watching the rockets and the explosions on one side, and looked down the steep hill on the other to Ford City, somnolent and dying on the edges of a factory that had run away, and felt bracketed by despair. No, despair was too strong a word. Gloom, perhaps. Anxiety. Uprootedness. She couldn't decide. The crowd, a mix of older people and children, oohed and clapped at the bursts of pyrotechnic color. The town lay motionless under its dim moons of streetlights. Why was he gone, why was he facing real rockets and explosions? And after he was finished with the Navy, could he ever come back to this? No, they had outgrown their roots, or maybe their roots had burrowed into unfertile soil. Either way, life had pushed them along until they couldn't be themselves anymore.

Or maybe it was just her mood, the mix of memories and her loneliness. A heavy, aching weight inside her stomach kept pulling at her.

Something was wrong, *really* wrong. On the walk down the ridge after the fireworks had finished she took Mama Lesczynski to one side and put a hand on the old woman's bulky back.

"Something's happened to Red, Mama."

"Now, honey, don't you worry about a thing. It's only another month or two, and they'll be back. Why, you got a letter from him just yesterday. He even told me in one of his letters it was just like flying when there wasn't any war, except they been dropping real bombs."

"Mama, I don't want to scare you, but I *know*."

Then at three in the morning the man had come with the telegram and her foreboding turned into an agony, a debilitating weariness, a sickness that made her limbs too heavy for her even to lift. *Direct hit by antiaircraft fire. One parachute at low altitude. POW or MIA.* She simply sat on the sofa in the front room and shivered uncontrollably until dawn, too weak to walk, too upset even to cry. Mama Lesczynski had called the family and they came one by one, car doors slamming in the still black night, wet faces smothering her with embraces, sisters wailing and brothers silently fighting tears as they drank beer after beer.

Mama Lesczynski kept to herself in the kitchen, first stripping the wax off her small linoleum floor and then washing it again and again, scrubbing it a dozen times before sunrise brought the children from the upstairs rooms. They tried to make Mama come in and sit with them but her hurt and agitation worked her like a jumping bean. "I just need to keep moving. You'ns just go ahead and sit."

The old man scared them the most. He walked heavily out of the house by himself, shaking off their entreating grips on his massive shoulders, his eyes avoiding them, his thick, gnarled hands pushing them away, and disappeared in the dark. They found him late in the morning, crying as he sat alone near the railroad tracks, above the park where John Ford stared at his dead factory.

Ah, my Stasu, my Stasu. My life and my blood.

When the children came downstairs the whole family feigned strength and optimism, and then for the first time Sophie wept, embracing the three of them. They were too young to comprehend fully, even J.J. He calmed all of them, though, and at fourteen became a man in the time it took for him to read the telegram.

That night on the news they saw Navy footage of the flaming petroleum storage area outside of Hanoi, and then watched their own blood cling stoically to the bamboo rail of a truck with one hand as crowds of North Vietnamese threw their hate at him. The film clip switched to a shot of him marching up to a podium in some sort of newsroom, head bandaged, arm in a sling, and saluting. It was a small comfort, and for the rest of the evening they savored it. At least they knew he had survived the crash. Most families knew nothing, because the North Vietnamese never told.

*　*　*

She took the children back to their home in Arlington, and began the process of waiting. It was a rough business, dealing in the realm of the possible. There was no feedback from Hanoi, not even a note or another news picture. A faceless colonel from the Department of Defense wrote her a letter giving her the official news that "due to sufficient evidence," her husband was listed as a Prisoner of War rather than Missing in Action, and instructing her to speak to no one, "repeat no one," about it, lest she in some way harm "national security." There was nothing in the letter indicating what "evidence" had been considered "sufficient." She tried to call the Pentagon to talk with the colonel, and was informed by a curt major in the Casualty office that she would be told if anything new developed, but the most important thing for her to remember was to keep silent, "in the interest of the men." Every month the Department of Defense sent her a dry, mimeographed letter with information about pay and benefits. She called the major back one more time to ask if there were other wives in the area whose husbands were missing, and was told that it was not in the interest of national security for her to communicate with other wives.

She was alone, isolated in her little house with her children and all the odd things she and Red had collected over the years, those reminders, furniture and paintings, his clothes, their pictures, the small study area with his library of old military books and the deflated football the team had given him after the 1950 Army-Navy game, gathering dust on dark shelves. She wouldn't touch any of it. He was simply away, that was all, and he could straighten it out when he came back.

A trickle of visitors appeared, carrying condolences and hope over the months that followed. Jimmy and Louise Maxwell were among the first, Jimmy giving her the details through a face and voice that seemed appalled at having survived. She embraced them both, an act of reassurance rather than forgiveness. Jimmy Maxwell didn't need to be forgiven. It might have been the other way around.

Crane Howell called from Annapolis and drove down one Sunday, spending a dinner with the family, coughing and wheezing, spilling Bourbon and dropping pieces of pipe tobacco on her rug. He told her in graphic terms what Red would be undergoing. She had wanted to know. After Howell left and the children were in bed, she wept for hours, going through old picture albums, remembering, trying to imagine what was happening at that moment. *Don't die, Red.*

Judd Smith drove up so often that she sometimes wondered if the neighbors thought they had become lovers. He took the children to ball games and the movies. He answered hard adolescent questions for them, with a biting, almost irreverent humor. He told them funny stories about their father, from when he and Red were roommates. He had a way of embracing Sophie that was warm and yet almost antiseptic, as if she were his daughter. She needed so badly in that first year to hold onto someone who could walk that emotional tightrope.

And then one afternoon in the fall of 1967, the doorbell rang and Dorothy Dingenfelder was standing on a mat of leaves that extended from the front porch out into the yard, the red and golden tapestry thick and brilliant underneath her and behind her, making her look as if she were emerging from a Renoir painting. Her features had grown severe over the past three years. She wore little makeup. Her small face was drawn into a perpetual wariness, a look that indicated she was acting out of something just beyond dread, as if she had called herself on a dare. Her dark hair was short and straight, brushed back, unornamented by curls or dye, gray streaks mixing in it. Her hands were pushed deep inside a trench coat that covered her body like a tent.

"Dorothy?"

"How are you? I was—" She consciously began again. "I'm here in Washington for a few days, and I thought I'd come by and—" She was not faltering because she was unsure of herself. Rather, she seemed to be choosing her words with a lawyer's exactness. "I just thought I'd come and see you."

"Well, come on in." It was morning. The children were at school, and Sophie was still dressed in a terry cloth bathrobe. It had been a Christmas present from Red, just before he had deployed. She wore it too much, too often, not out of laziness but from loyalty, or perhaps superstition.

Dorothy followed her into the kitchen, an unspoken tension rebounding back and forth between them, carried like a tennis ball in their uneasy glances. Sophie gestured to the morning paper, which was still scattered on the breakfast table. "Funny. I was just reading about you in the *Post*. Has it only been three years? It seems like so long ago. The picnic, the Civil Rights Act, you and Judd arguing and the rest of us laughing." She smiled sweetly, her eyes seeing another vision in her little kitchen, far away but somehow more real. "Judd was right, you know. I've thought about that a lot."

"About what?"

"The Negro riots. They didn't happen in the South, did they? They happened in Los Angeles and Detroit and Newark and Boston. And Chicago was just picked as the most segregated city in the country. Isn't that something?" Sophie's eyes unfocused again as she forced another smile. "But that's not what I remember, really. I remember how much we laughed. Do you remember that? Laughing?"

Dorothy seated herself, and then seemed to gather in the chair, drawing in air as if she were going to spit. "I know what you must think. I'm sorry about that. I wanted you to know. It kind of bothered me to be in Washington and not come and talk to you face to face."

"Oh? What do I think?" Sophie automatically poured two cups of coffee, and sat one in front of Dorothy. "Do you still like it black?"

"Yes. You must have quite a memory."

"I do, I guess." Sophie gave a small, self-conscious shrug. "Untrained, of course." She sat down directly across from Dorothy, who had taken off her coat, revealing a formless dress, devoid of jewelry. They stared uncomfortably at each other, neither daring up a smile. "You said you know what I think. Is that why you came, Dorothy? To tell me what I think?"

"No, not exactly. You can think whatever you want. I came to tell you that it isn't directed at you, or at Red. I'm as sorry as anyone else that he was taken prisoner."

"Are you?" Sophie picked up the morning paper, deliberately folding the front section back to a continuation of a front-page story. "I just read something in here about Dorothy Dingenfelder saying that a communist system is probably better suited for the Vietnamese peasants, while a capitalist system only benefits American corporations. And something else about a war being bad if it pits rich American boys against poor Vietnamese boys, when the rich boys have airplanes that napalm and bomb the poor boys' families, and that it didn't matter if all of Asia went communist in the next ten years or so, because it's none of our business in the first place. Who *is* that directed at, Dorothy?"

"The government. Sophie, don't you realize that Red wouldn't even be a prisoner if our government hadn't gotten involved in the internal affairs of another country? We've been on an absolutely fascist bent ever since World War II! It's like a combination of the British white man's burden and the old crusades. Any government that claims to be communist, no matter how impotent or ridiculous, is the agent of Moscow and Peking, and becomes our enemy! Can't you see that it's the corporations who are getting fat over this? We're spending 30 billion dollars a year on Vietnam. That's why we're fighting this war!"

"Dorothy, that's silly."

"Do you really think so?" Dorothy was unloading, unburdening herself in the form of a confessional, not because she wished to pursue or even debate the issue, but because she wanted to feel Sophie's wrath, to allow Red Lesczynski's wife to come out with every ounce of vitriole she could summon. She suddenly realized that she *wanted* Sophie to hate her.

"Of course I do, because it is. The South Vietnamese have the chance to be free, just like the South Koreans and the West Germans are free. Do you really want to see South Vietnam living under communism?"

"This is a civil war, and—"

"Even I know that Vietnam has historically been three countries, Dorothy."

"We're in violation of the Geneva Accords, simply by being there!"

"Geneva Accords? Tell me about the Geneva Accords. The Geneva Accords say that you're supposed to notify each man's family when he's taken prisoner, and allow correspondence, Red Cross visits, packages to be sent. The North Vietnamese still haven't notified me that Red is shot down! The Red Cross isn't allowed near the prison! I haven't heard a word in fifteen months, Dorothy! Doesn't that bother you?"

"It does, but it's *our government's fault!* It wouldn't have happened if we hadn't gone into Vietnam. And every time I see pictures of our soldiers burning villages and making refugees out of civilians I can't help but think of Nazi troops pillaging their way through Poland!"

Sophie's eyebrows raised and her brown eyes filled her face. "You know a lot of things, Dorothy, but don't tell me about Poland. I'm a Polski, eh? And every time I see our troops in Vietnam, *I see what I wish had happened to keep Poland free from communism!*"

They stared silently into their coffee cups then, each dissipated by the emotion of the argument. Finally Sophie looked up, another smile on her smooth face. "So, how's Joe, and the kids?"

"He's fine. They're all fine. I've got to go." Dorothy stood suddenly, grabbing her coat and wrapping herself inside it. "I just wanted you to know that we're both hoping for the same thing: an end to the war, so people like Red can come home."

Sophie had kept maddeningly calm, infuriatingly gracious. "Well, you're not helping end the war by doing all of this marching in the streets, Dorothy. You're only encouraging the communists. Don't you see that?"

She wanted to hurt Sophie, to penetrate this veneer of kindness. "They're going to win, sooner or later. It may as well be sooner."

Sophie's brows furled. "Are you a communist?"

"Oh, Sophie, for God's sake. Why? Because I don't support a foolish war? That's exactly what we need to get beyond, isn't it?"

*   *   *

So what was I supposed to do, call Red Lesczynski a hero because he got what he deserved after blowing up poor peasants day after day?

She argued fretfully with herself as she drove back across the Memorial Bridge, toward the District. She hadn't been very good with Sophie, but she finally decided that it was better to have made a small fool of herself than to have made a large fool of both of them. Sophie was hurt enough by this war. There was no need to pull apart her wounds and make them bleed all over again. *But don't tell me about heroes.*

The Washington Monument pierced the stark blue sky in front of her. Nearer to her, at the edge of the river, was the Lincoln Memorial, where four years before she and hundreds of thousands of others had gathered to hear Martin Luther King's now famous speech, a speech that she herself had helped edit. Martin Luther King was now almost passé, that was how fast events were pushing people toward change. Stokely Carmichael, Rap Brown, Eldridge Cleaver, Bobby Seale— these were the new names, and they spoke not of civil rights but of

Black Power, not of nonviolent demonstration but of killing the Beast, having their revenge, putting whitey on his ass.

Heroes? The men who followed the government like sheep and ended up slaughtered by the undeniable, primeval power of an Asian revolution ten thousand miles away? Men who burned villages and pillaged poor peasants, who dropped millions of pounds of bombs on freedom fighters? *Those aren't heroes. At the best, they're mindless victims.*

Heroes?

Martin Luther King was a hero, something of a Moses, although he was no longer listened to that much. And so were the others, the Black Panthers, Carmichael and Seale and Cleaver. They were using violence toward constructive ends, putting the system on notice that it could not repress black people anymore, that it would either listen or be destroyed.

The Students for a Democratic Society were heroes. It enthralled her that these enlightened representatives of the coming generation, blessed with all that suburbia and postwar America could offer, could see the evils that their corporate fathers had created. Their Harvard chapter had shut down the university when Dow Chemical, the makers of napalm, had attempted to recruit on campus. Their Weathermen spin-off was taking to the streets, the same way that the Black Panthers were.

Levy and Cohen and O'Brien were heroes, test cases every one, who would soon be heard before the Supreme Court. Dorothy Dingenfelder was doing legal work for all three. Captain Levy had refused orders to train army medics for Vietnam, and had stood in an Army mess hall and exhorted the soldiers not to take part in a racist, immoral war. Cohen had worn a jacket with the words FUCK THE DRAFT to the county courthouse in California, upsetting several mothers who were present with their children, and had been arrested for disturbing the peace. O'Brien had burned his draft card on the steps of the Boston courthouse, in front of a potentially hostile mob. They were all exercising their First Amendment right of free speech, and should have been left alone.

Dr. Spock was a hero, as were Norman Mailer, Noam Chomsky, Robert Lowell, the Berrigans, and the other elders who had seen the insanity of the Vietnam War and decided to risk their reputations to try and stop it.

Dorothy allowed herself a small smile, thinking of the coming march on the Pentagon, an extravaganza that would likely draw a hundred thousand marchers. She had helped organize it. *Yes,* she thought. *Yes. And I am a hero, too.*

* * *

She was no longer young and she had given up on trying to be pretty and she had never been innocent, at least not since the moment she had last looked back on a doomed, churlish Vienna and whispered in her weeping child's voice that it wasn't right to have to leave, who were these people who could make you leave when you didn't want to? Her marriage was something that had once been important, a transient moment of focus, like college. Her children would manage. She had a theory, a defense mechanism actually, that said children had acquired their personalities and values by the time they were six, and the only thing left was management, school and diet and clothes, making sure that the right parts of their computer card were punched. *Management.* It drove Joe crazy, but that was too bad.

The only thing left of importance was fulfillment, making an impact, throwing her energy at the world and seeing the world move perceptibly, nudging it just a bit toward somewhere, it didn't matter really which direction. No, that wasn't totally true. It mattered, but the act of nudging was more important than the resultant direction.

She dressed quickly. The implements of femininity irritated her. When she wore them, panty hose and a brassiere pressed into her from all sides until she felt mildly claustrophobic, as if they were bonds, signals of repression. Hairdos and makeup were fetters also, time-consuming deferences to a male-dominated society, like a deep, waiting curtsy. She had given up all of them.

It was ironic for someone of her publicly egalitarian views to be sleeping at the Hay Adams Hotel and breakfasting in its lush, heavily wooded dining rooms, but she ignored the paradox as irrelevant. There were few enough rewards when you were perched on the edge of forty and could clearly see that life was never going to be fair or rational, anyway, so you may as well sleep where you want to, and eat what tastes good. And the Hay Adams was where the so-called notables stayed, the public figures who would lend credence to the march, as well as the media people who would be covering it. Staying at the Hay Adams was helpful, looking at the long run of things.

After breakfast she took a taxi to the Lincoln Memorial. As they drove past the White House she could see a crowd of protesters, young people mostly, milling around its outer fences, carrying signs and calling to pedestrians, warming up for the afternoon. The sight of them made her heart leap with excitement, as if she herself were soon going into battle. And in her mind she was.

* * *

Dorothy Dingenfelder surveyed her domain, her battleground, the area surrounding the Lincoln Memorial and the road behind it which led back across Memorial Bridge and eventually to the Pentagon itself. It gave her no small pleasure, having hated and feared the military all of her life and having spent long years as an officer's wife, an ornament, a prettied-up piece of protocol, that she now was something of a general. She had been a fierce negotiator with the National Park Service regarding the site location, the routes of the march, the parameters of dissent that would be allowed. She had trained her monitors and her crowd controllers, who themselves were graduates of detailed teach-ins on the Vietnam War and the dynamics of protest, sponsored the previous summer by the committee in conjunction with Students for a Democratic Society. Soon the Mall would fill up with a hundred thousand protesters, a people's army, and then they would all attack the Pentagon and its sorry minions of government policy.

The media was arriving. She watched the students greet them with exaggerated courtesy, directing their vehicles and helping them find the best spots for setting up cameras. The locations were vitally important, both here and at the Pentagon. It was, after all, a media war. Here, they would show the sweep of the crowd against a backdrop of monuments and tradition. It gave her another feeling of pleasure, of certainty. This was going to work. She was not the commander in chief of this army of dissent, but certainly she was a key general. Theirs was a battle of provocation, not unlike those mournful beatniks who had trudged slowly across the road toward the main gate at Vandenberg years before. It was a fight for national attention, a way to discredit the enemy. The enemy was the United States Government.

In May 1967 the National Mobilization Committee to End the War in Vietnam (which had nicknamed itself "the Mob") had met in Washington to discuss the possibility of holding a rally at the Lincoln Memorial and a march on the Congress in the fall. The Mobilization Committee's chairman, David Dellinger, a Yale-educated anarchist who was the editor of a small magazine called *Liberation*, was away on a visit to Hanoi, but the meeting was otherwise well attended. Representatives of the Women's Strike for Peace, the New York Peace Council, the Chicago Parade Committee, the Southern Christian Leadership Conference, the Ohio Area Peace Action Council, the Students for a Democratic Society, H. Rap Brown's SNCC, various pacifist, socialist, Maoist, communist, and Trotskyite fringe groups, and many others brought their views and suggestions to the conference. Opposition to the war in Vietnam was the first issue that the entire American left had been able to agree on in decades, and they were feasting on each other's enthusiasm.

Dorothy Dingenfelder had represented Californians in Search of Peace. She had made a motion at the meeting that Jerry Rubin be appointed project director of the march, and she in turn had been placed on the National Steering Committee, which planned the details of the demonstration. Rubin had organized Vietnam Day at Berkeley, the first successful mass protest of the war, and other disruptions, including attempts to block trainloads of soldiers heading from California bases to airports where they would be flown to Vietnam. He was wild-haired and loudmouthed, a leader of the Peking-oriented Progressive Labor Party, and he made no secret of his belief that America needed a new revolution. Rubin immediately declared that "we are now in the business of wholesale and widespread resistance, and dislocation of the American society." He decided that the protesters should march against the root of all American evil, the Pentagon, rather than the Congress. And now, after months of elaborate preparation, it was going to happen.

The pavilion around the Lincoln Memorial was roped off for special guests and media. Its edges fell down wide, terraced steps, ideal for placing layer after layer of demonstrators with their signs. Across a narrow road more steps led down to the Mall itself. On the Mall, long gardens and trees bordered the Reflecting Pool, which pointed like a narrow finger at the Washington Monument in the distance. Slowly they began to fill the green void of the Mall, languishing on the lawn, strolling next to the pool, not yet connected to one another in their purpose, merely occupying the same portentous piece of garden.

From the Memorial a trumpet sounded, and the loudspeakers beckoned them to gather, and they came. She watched exultantly from the steps of the Memorial, as this growing mix of people, of believers and the simply rebellious and the merely curious, soon took on its own ambience and became a crowd.

We can change the world.

Some came with signs proclaiming group affiliations, Students for a Democratic Society, Congress of Racial Equality, American Friends Service Committee, Christians for Peace, National Lawyers' Guild. Some waved other sorts of signs, "Che Guevara Lives," "Bloodfinger Johnson," "Where Is Oswald Now That We Need Him," "Babies Are Not for Burning." A rash of Viet Cong flags waved in front of the staid pillars of the Memorial.

Some wore silly costumes, as if this were going to be a masquerade ball, an evocation of a student schizophrenia that would allow a person to pretend, just for a weekend, that he or she was a cowboy or a pirate, a dropout, or, most often, a hippie, a protester, a *rebel*, a member of the *I Don't Care* community just for a day or so, so long as it did not damage grades or aspirations. *Isn't this fun?* Most were just themselves, though, out for a curious afternoon, down on the Mall to see the stars.

Rearrange the world.

A hundred thousand people had gathered on the Mall, not nearly the million the committee had knowingly misadvertised, not half the number that had come to the same spot to hear Martin Luther King four years before, but enough to fill the full screens of American televisions throughout the country, and that was the point, anyway. The speeches began and the crowd endured them, offerings from all compartments of the American left, featuring a harangue by Clive Jenkins, of the British Labor party.

Dr. Spock capped it off. "The enemy," he solemnly declared, "is Lyndon Johnson, who was elected as a peace candidate in 1964 and who betrayed us within three months."

It's dying.

Finally they gathered in front of the Memorial Bridge, Dorothy Dingenfelder's crowd controllers blaring out instructions from bullhorns, the celebrities at the front with their arms linked at the elbows, Norman Mailer, Robert Lowell, Dr. Spock, and others, a mass of media trucks just before them, in a way a replay of Martin Luther King's march into Selma of two years before.

Would it be like Selma? Would the thousands of Military Police and U.S. marshals put on alert at the Pentagon attack and harass them? It was a frequent topic at the front of the long, snaking column, the maddest fear of older men beyond their ability to endure a crack on the head and of the young students, boys and girls both, who had never felt a harsh hand on their face to begin with. Secretly, Dorothy

Dingenfelder prayed that it would be. The incidents on the bridge at Selma had caused a revulsion across America, a regurgitation of bilious dislike that had been invaluable to the Civil Rights movement. She knew that a large contingent from the Students for a Democratic Society planned to rush the guards, in hopes that the guards would retaliate on the crowd. Provocation, that was the name of the game, with the response recorded on film.

More than half of the people who had gathered at the Lincoln Memorial went home before the crowd began to march across the Memorial Bridge. Nonetheless, it took the marchers two hours to cross the bridge, and its constriction of their numbers had good media effect when captured on camera. They marched to the rock beat of a band called the Fugs. They sang "We Shall Overcome." They chanted.

"Hey, hey, LBJ, how many kids did you kill today?"

"Ho, Ho, Ho Chi Minh, the NLF is gonna win."

Army helicopters passed overhead, watching them, creating odious, quieting fear. Would the Army attack them? Would LBJ let some of them be killed? What were the depths of his hate and passion, what were the angers of his Army, which awaited them?

On the other side of the bridge they trudged across open fields toward the empty, vacuous north parking lot. They could see the Pentagon over a hill to their right, protected from the north parking lot by roads as if it were a medieval fort and the roads were a moat. They were supposed to gather in the lot, and then later proceed across to the Pentagon's mall for a vigil.

Suddenly, from the rear, the SDS contingent burst past the front of the crowd in a jog. In a burning moment that crossed the wires in her brain, Dorothy thought to herself how much they resembled Hitler's brown shirts of thirty years before. She had to stifle her repulsion consciously, to concentrate on the *reason*, the *reason* it was all happening. The SDS students carried ax handles and baseball bats. Some of them were helmeted. Several Viet Cong flags flew at their front. They formed a wedge and stormed a ramp that led up to the Pentagon's north parking entrance. The crowd, this creature unto itself, rippled with excitement, and surged forward. In an instant the hundred students retreated in panic down the curving ramp, away from an unseen chimera at its top. That small defeat vindicated Dorothy and the others, made the SDS troops callow youths again. The crowd lost its quiet restlessness. It surged again, and dislocated. People screamed with terror and lust for revenge. *Was the Army up there? What had it done to the students?*

The Army, the Army. Johnson's toy soldiers, Johnson's killers. It was an inanimate, ugly thing to them, a specter derived out of wisps of memories, themselves the product of color television footage of villages burning in Vietnam, and the subliminal fear that it might somehow turn on them in the cool autumn grass of the Pentagon. *The Army, the Army, it it it.*

The SDS contingent broke a hole through the fence that separated the north parking lot from the road next to it, and sprinted toward the mall entrance. The bulk of the crowd itself streamed forward, through the hole, having lost all sense of order or even mission, following the SDS troops with a mix of curiosity and hollow excitement. Dorothy followed, panting and enthralled. She no longer needed to worry about crowd control. The demonstration had taken on its own dynamics.

At the mall entrance the SDS had taken over a corner of the plaza itself. A man was standing at its heights with a bullhorn, calling to the demonstrators to join him. He was behind a rank of Military Policemen, separated from the crowd. They found themselves cheering him. He had beaten LBJ's soldiers! The marshals had tried once to dislodge him, and then left him alone. They, too, had learned from Selma, decided Dorothy Dingenfelder as she watched them consciously ignore him in front of a legion of photographers who had anticipated his forced removal.

The crowd gathered in front of a line of Military Police who were protecting the Pentagon's entrances. Johnson's Army, the great lurking dragon, the inanimate, collective *it* they had feared, was a wide line of nervous boys whose eyes betrayed their own fear and unease. They stood like statues in a park, ordered by their officers neither to look at nor talk to the demonstrators. They did their best to keep a numb parade rest, their rifles empty of ammunition at their sides, trying to ignore the insults that had begun to flow once the demonstrators realized their impotence.

It was provocation, a collective attempt to cause an incident for the sake of the cameras, the cameras themselves like a mother's skirt that the demonstrators hid behind as they taunted and screamed. Off at one entrance, a quick incident did occur, the protesters storming a door and being carried away. But as Dorothy watched, she comprehended that it quickly turned into something else. America's young peered back at itself through a warped mirror where the soldiers faced the students in front of the Pentagon, a stupefying twist that made the more restless and rebellious of them the stolid defenders and the more bookish and protected of them irascible and free.

"Hey, soldier, kill anybody today?"

"Hey, cannon fodder! Go kill a commie for LBJ!"

"Goddamn red-necks!"

"Hit them! They won't hit back!"

Dorothy caught the distinction, understood the tension, immediately. On the one side, holding the rifles, were the soul mates of the wild rebellious children of Vandenberg who had been free and easy at fourteen. Now taunting them were her own intellectual and social kin, people of ideas, people of fear, who could in these controlled surroundings, under the watchful eyes of the camera, for the first time appear courageous.

The students, the people of books and pep clubs and prom committees, who had from their childhood feared the simple power and brutality of the blue collar kids, the red-necks, the bowling alley kings, the hot-rodding, ducktailed greasers who once mocked their studies and their lack of manliness, who might attack them over the tiniest issue of honor, now found their scourges trapped as a result of those same aggressive instincts. The boys whose sense of danger and action had lured them into the Army instead of college wore their uniforms like straitjackets, becoming quiet, enduring objects, repositories for the insults of those they could have squashed in a microsecond if the odds were fair.

So the students unloaded on the soldiers, cursing them, daring them, under the accepted guise of hating Army, Pentagon, and War. The insults issued, and the soldiers did not move. Tomatoes and bottles smacked into them, and the soldiers did not move. Girls undid their blouses, dangling firm inviting breasts over tightly gripped rifles, and the soldiers did not move. Students spat on them, grew more hateful, megaphones telling them they were dupes, fools, *fuckheads,* that their war was sinful, immoral, *genocidal,* and the soldiers did not move.

Dorothy watched it, uneasy with the ugliness. It was the soldiers, the *Army* that was supposed to be hateful and brutal. That was the lesson of Selma, that was her view of the earth, that creatures of authority grew crueler as the symbols they protected decayed. The students were supposed to be the victims, not the soldiers. It was a fundamental flaw, a cancerous growth that grew by the minute, one that left her squinting with suppressed pain, even as she kept chanting to herself that it was for a reason, a *reason*, and that made it all right.

And the students continued, all through the afternoon, far into the night.

* * *

But the march, the reason behind the madness, worked. She had known it would. The real task was in the organization, in creating the conditions that would bring it into every American's living room. It was in the network news for two days. It made the front page of every major newspaper in the country. It received a feature story in *Newsweek*, and was the cover story for *Time*. Smaller demonstrations elsewhere, with Joan Baez seeking to block an induction center in Oakland and students gathering in Boston, Cincinnati, Chicago, at the University of Wisconsin and Brooklyn College, gave it a sweep, a largeness, that put all America on notice.

The media shots were wonderful: The Lincoln Memorial packed with people, draped with signs. Military Police at the Pentagon repulsing demonstrators who had penetrated the building. In the pictures the demonstrators were reeling back, faces filled with hurt and alarm, and the soldiers were stiff, helmeted, and armed. A wronged University of Wisconsin student screaming "fascist" at a policeman who had used tear gas.

Time summed it up on an upbeat, as "a reminder to the world of America's cherished right to dissent." And in a few days the world press was treated to a letter from Pham Van Dong, North Vietnam's Premier, to the Mobilization Committee:

"The Vietnamese people thank their friends in America and wish them great success in their mounting movement."

CHAPTER TWENTY-TWO

I

"You know, reverend, I remember when I was ten. Or maybe it was twelve. Let me see, now."

The sandy-haired young man lay back in his hospital bed and stared at the ceiling for a moment, his soft, freckled moon of a face almost swallowed by the pillow. "It was 1960. I guess I was twelve. And I was out on this lake fishing with my friend Woody Baker. It was a hot day and our worms started going all dry in the can, but we didn't care. We sat out on that lake and told the latest dirty jokes, trying to be like the men we saw in town. Maybe even smoked a few cigarettes. I guess we did."

The boy-man chuckled softly. In his mind, he was out on the lake again. "And every now and then we even fished. And we were drifting along the shoreline, kind of pushed by the wind, you understand, when out in front of us I saw this boy and his gal just about waist-deep in the water, standing absolutely still, pushed up so tight against each other that they seemed too close to actually be two people, and I guess really they weren't two people, not when they were like that. You understand what I'm saying, Reverend?"

"Sure I do, Joe Bob. I may be a preacher, but I've sure enough been in love."

"Well, that's right!" Joe Bob Holtzclaw, Specialist Fourth Class, United States Army (Ret.), returned to his memory, lost out on the lake again. "Well, that water just sort of kept kissing the girl's hips, little waves that moved against her. She had on a white bathing suit. I didn't see him, much. I saw his hands on the white cloth. They were still. I couldn't stop looking at them. I turned to Woody Baker and I said, 'What are they doing?'" Joe Bob chuckled again. "I was twelve."

He turned his head, staring up at Judd Smith. "Well, Woody was fourteen, so he knew all about those things. He said, 'They ain't doing a damn thing. They're in love.' And he was right, I guess, because they really didn't do anything, just stood there in the waves and held onto each other. We drifted by so close I might have caught them with my fishing line but all I could do was keep looking at them. That boy's hands moved once, just a little bit, and she said something that was drowned out by his face or a wave or something. I tried like hell to hear it, but I didn't. So I just watched them while we floated on by, and I felt an ache down in my belly and I knew I'd never live until I caught that feeling in my fingers. I mean, that was *life*, Brother Smith."

Judd Smith nodded, keeping his eyes off Joe Bob Holtzclaw's right side, which was mangled by war, armless and legless underneath the sheets. If Joe Bob was going to catch that feeling, he'd have to be doing it with five fingers and one leg.

"So, do you think I'll ever have that now, Reverend? That's what I been thinking about ever since I was wounded. Can a girl like that love me now?" In the first, evanescent pause after his question, the young man studied Judd Smith's face, as if he were afraid of delivering his final, crushing judgment. "I'll tell you, good sir, I been having my doubts about heaven."

"Joe Bob, they didn't blow away your balls, they didn't blow away your brain, and they didn't blow away your heart." Maybe it wasn't the sort of thing that a preacher was supposed to say, but it was honest, thought Judd Smith, and Joe Bob didn't need any sermon just then about life being a trial for heaven. "Now, maybe you'll have a hard time of it standing in the water and wrapping your arms around some girl's waist, but I never knew much worth doing that wasn't done laying down and with one arm, anyway."

Joe Bob Holtzclaw was laughing, staring back at Judd Smith with a new brightness in his eyes. "Reckon I can still drive an automatic, anyway, huh, Reverend?"

"Yeah, I believe you could burn up the tracks with an automatic."

"I never was much for stick shifts, anyway."

"Them clutches ain't nothing but a pain, Joe Bob."

"Maybe I'll get me a truck."

"Yeah, you could haul a lot of nice tail in a truck."

The young veteran howled gleefully, a modified rebel yell, causing the rest of the ward's patients and visitors to turn and stare curiously at him and his minister. Judd Smith worked hard to keep a straight face, but was unsuccessful.

"Preacher Smith, if my mother heard you say that, she'd likely quit your church."

"I doubt that."

"Well, so do I, more I think about it."

Judd Smith checked his watch, and stood, putting a hand on Holtzclaw's shoulder. "I'll come see you in a few days, and we'll check up on that truck, you hear?"

"That be fine, Reverend. Fact, you might bring one of them Turner girls along, and I'll start working on a load for it."

"They been waiting to hear that, Joe Bob. I'll just haul one of them up here next time I come. Take care, now."

He hated hospitals; the smell of them, the bland, boiled food, the bustle and dread in the hallways. Death's fear lurked in the eyes of relatives slumped in hardback chairs. Death itself peered out at him every time he saw a doctor or nurse walk past in turquoise garb, dressed for the operating room. His vocation was peering into people's souls, coaxing them toward their own best parts, but a doctor cut and probed into the body itself, sticking cold steel knives and clamps and pliers down into the goo, pulling out bloody bad things. Somehow that seemed worse, more intruding. God owned everybody's soul, so you could share it. But you owned your own body.

He would never get over knowing that strange doctors had frolicked in the secret depths of his own innards. He would never recover from having watched his large intestine empty thought a hole just underneath his ribs, for months, as his insides healed. Every time he entered a hospital he felt a sense of indignity, of violation, as if the operations that had saved his life had nonetheless been an intrusion into his private self, a rape, however justified. Or perhaps, having come so close, he merely knew how easy it was to die, and did not like to be reminded.

And try as he might to suppress the feeling, he especially hated Veterans Administration hospitals. There were no births, no children, few men of middle age. There were the old veterans, many of them charity cases now, who found their way back to die, like elephants returning to their graveyards. And there were the young, chewed and torn by battle, fresh from some sudden, hot explosion, a menopause event that in a moment left them forever changed, looking at life from the other side of youth's virility.

The wards were stacked deep with the young at Roanoke. It was the same in every war; indeed, it had been the same for at least two thousand years, since that British dawn when wiry, boasting Celts and Bretons painted their bodies with blue ink and roamed over black, craggy ridges covered with moss and purple flowers, looking for some prowling Roman invader to hit over the head with whatever new weapon they had invented. They would fight the Romans, they would fight the English, they would later fight the Indians and the British and the Yankees, the Spanish and the Germans and the Japanese. If things got boring, they would even fight each other. A mad impulse charged their blood, a fear that a battle might pass and others would have outdone them. It was the same, war after war, such a part of them that it approached synthesis. But that did not make it hurt any less to see them devoured and broken. They were only soldiers. They had never owned or determined the reasons for a war, and they had not asked for this one. They had merely yielded to their honor and tradition and agreed to fight it.

And they were not wrong, *not* wrong, mused Judd Smith as he reached the hospital lobby and headed for its front doorway. The frustration of the months he had spent along the outposts in Korea still haunted him in his unprotected moments; intimate, detailed memories leaping over a sixteen-year chasm as he watched the news reports from Vietnam. He knew what it was like to fight a war of attrition. He knew how much harder it would have been to have fought such a war without defined boundaries.

Outside the front doorway, a television crew was interviewing people for the Roanoke NBS network affiliate's evening news. A pudgy man with his hair frozen exactly into place approached Smith, squinting for a moment at his damaged ear.

"Excuse me, sir, I'm Earl Sherwood from WATV news. Have you been visiting a Vietnam casualty?"

Smith stopped, hesitantly eyeing the camera. It was rolling. "Yes."

"Is he a relative?"

"No, he's a parishioner. I'm his pastor."

The man's eyes brightened. "We're doing a special tonight on the effect of the war on our young men in southwest Virginia. As you must know, Robert Kennedy and others have called for an end to what they have termed 'the illusion of Vietnam,' and stated that it's time for the United States to disengage itself. The Tet Offensive of the last month has clearly taken our forces by surprise, and many now believe that we are on the brink of being defeated. Would you care to give us your views on this?"

"All right, I will." It had been brewing inside him for months. He straightened himself against the biting March wind, feeling somewhat shabby in his flannel shirt and heavy working coat. "I should first confess that I served for a number of years as a Marine Corps officer, including combat in Korea. I should also point out that my college roommate has been a prisoner of war in North Vietnam for almost two years. That seems to have a way of disqualifying people's opinions, these days."

"Not at all, sir. Not at all."

The microphone was just underneath his mouth, an inquiring, consuming gray trickster. He did not trust it, but there was no turning back. "All right. I cannot imagine how we can interpret this so-called 'Tet '68' offensive as an American defeat. We met the enemy's troops throughout the country, on their terms, and defeated every unit. What are we going to say, that the North Vietnamese Army is winning because it's capable of attacking? But the way this war has been fought, the strategy of it, has been shameful. Johnson and McNamara have blown it. At least everyone can agree on that. We've allowed the North Vietnamese to put fifteen of their sixteen combat divisions into the South, without fear of retaliation. We won't bomb their cities, but we're bombing the daylights out of the South Vietnamese cities, at least in the areas under dispute! McNamara continually played with numbers, numbers of enemy and friendly casualties, areas of control, as if this war is capable of being measured by corporate reporting techniques. The North Vietnamese could send troops into the South forever, at this rate. We're fighting a war of attrition, but we're letting the North Vietnamese control the tempo of the war, and the rate of casualties. They're masters at using the media. They're tying in their military operations to suit our reportage. It doesn't matter how well we're doing on the battlefield, or how many of their own men they're losing, if they can coordinate their attacks until the whole thing becomes a media event." He stopped suddenly, almost in mid-sentence, and shrugged. "I could go on, but I'm not sure you'd want me to."

Earl Sherwood was giving him a somber, studious look behind the microphone. He was obviously taken. "No, I wish you would." He considered it for another moment. "I didn't get your name."

"Judd Smith."

"And you're a minister, from—"

"Bear Mountain."

"A Bear Mountain County boy, eh?" Sherwood smiled easily, with grudging respect. He nodded again to his cameraman, and struck an official pose, renewing the interview. "Mr. Smith, the question that is on many people's minds right now, after almost three years of commitment to the war in South Vietnam, is how long we should continue to do another country's fighting for them. It didn't take us a whole lot longer than this to win World War II. Is there not a cost-benefit accounting that must be made? You're from Bear Mountain, which is known throughout the state for its pride in sending its boys off to war. Is there a time when you'll stop telling the Bear Mountain boys they should go off to fight, and possibly die, in a war halfway around the world that looks like it could drag on forever?"

"Mr. Sherwood, if you love somebody, you don't up and quit on them when they start having problems, and it's the same thing with a country. Now, I believe we had a reason to go into Vietnam, and if President Johnson's messed it up, the thing to do is try and get it right, not tell your sons to turn their backs on their country."

"But if you love someone, as you mentioned, isn't there a time that their life becomes more important than supporting a war that's gone wrong?"

"What does it mean when we say that the war has gone wrong, though? Does it mean we should *quit*, if the principle was worth fighting for in the first place? Our troops are good. We've just handed the enemy its greatest defeat. The American public still supports the war. In fact, support for the war has gone up to 74 percent, according to the Harris survey. Now, the problem is the way we've been going about it. That's not new, really. Every war we've ever fought has had major problems in its implementation. The thing to do is correct the mistakes, not quit. If our leaders plant the flag, you follow it." He grinned teasingly. "That doesn't mean we should keep following President *Johnson*, but that's a personal thing."

"How do you feel about the young men who are refusing the draft?"

"That's fine, as long as they're willing to face the legal consequences. I'm a minister, Mr. Sherwood. I understand the duty of conscience. But I'm also an American, and I believe in a nation of laws rather than specially privileged people. The by-product of civil disobedience has always been a willingness to pay the price. Thoreau went to jail for refusing to participate in the Mexican War, not to Canada."

The camera shut off. Sherwood looked mildly awed, as if he had gone out for coal and come back with a diamond. "You're really good. No, I mean it. Would you be available for some follow-up interviews?"

Smith wrote his address and telephone number on a piece of paper. "Be happy to oblige you. You know there's one thing a preacher will never turn down, and that's a chance to talk."

✿   ✿   ✿

"Hi, Judd."

She called almost languidly to him from across two hundred miles of telephone wire, her voice lazy and sad, as deep and hollow as if it were coming up from the bottom of a well. She was indeed reaching to him from a mournful, isolated hole, a cavernous pock in her spirit. Julie Clay Williams was drunk again.

"Hi, Julie. Are you all right?"

"I saw you on television tonight. Loretta was so excited. Why didn't you tell us you were going to be on?"

"I didn't know myself."

"They gave you a whole segment. You looked beautiful. You need a haircut. You made so much *sense*, Judd. Nobody makes sense anymore. They showed your ear, Judd. You should really get it fixed."

"Julie, Julie." Smith shook his head sadly, knowing she was paralyzed by a gentle fear, unhappy with her lieutenant governor husband and his St. Croix weekends, his continuous meetings, his unease with her daughter, but at the same time a child of the political process, keenly aware of what would happen if she pulled the plug on her unhappiness and ran. If she left, her misery might spread like a disease instead of disappear, covering all who were affected by her flight. He sensed that she wanted him to exhort her, to take charge of her life and make the decision for her. But that was the one thing he could not do. He couldn't quite figure out whether stealing his own wife back would be a sin in the eyes of God, but it did violate his own code of ethics. She was a free agent when she left him. She would have to freely decide to come back.

"I miss you so much, Judd."

"I miss you, too."

"When can I come see you?"

"Whenever you want." It was another ethical tangle, but he had decided that refusing her would be a form of pressure, a confusion of the problem, even. It was better to continue legal adultery than it was to use denial as a lever. Would his congregation understand that distinction? He doubted it, but he also doubted they would disapprove his judgment.

"When can I come live with you?"

"Whenever you want." She knew that also. It was almost a game that she played after a few drinks, a reassurance that she was capable of ending her misery if she only had the courage.

"I might, you know."

"I know, honey."

"I have to go."

"Kiss Loretta for me."

"I will. I love you, Judd. I was really proud of you."

"I love you, too."

Don't end up like your mother, he thought to himself as he hung up the receiver, almost angry at her fear. *Free yourself, Julie, before you kill yourself.*

II

Judd Smith watched from his mountain cloister as the year 1968 went through America like a chainsaw out of control, cutting and hacking indiscriminately until just about everyone had bled in one way or another.

The country was on its ass, there was no other way to say it. It was the worst year of the Vietnam War in terms of American casualties. The Tet Offensive made either liars or fools out of Johnson, Westmoreland, and McNamara, demonstrating that the North Vietnamese had the capacity to mount major military actions in spite of three years of optimistic reports to the American people about how well the war was being run, how soon it would be over, the end is near, folks, just around the corner. *I can finally see the light at the end of the tunnel,* went one political cartoon, showing Uncle Sam standing on the railroad tracks and holding a lantern, staring at a coming locomotive. If the train didn't knock Uncle Sam flat, it did take Johnson out, causing him to decline running for renomination.

Judd mourned the assassinations, Martin Luther King and Bobby Kennedy gunned down in cold blood. He fretted over the provocation and violence. The ghettos went up in flames, crumbling into their own ashes after King was killed. Martin Luther King's successors occupied a portion of the Mall in Washington, D.C., for months with tents and shacks, and called it Resurrection City. The Black Panther party was making a bid for control of the inner city, carrying weapons and using them. Student radicals directed by the Students for a Democratic Society were creating havoc on campus. The antiwar movement took its strategy of confrontation to Chicago, at the Democratic party's convention, causing mass arrests and the sort of police retaliation they had lusted for during the march on the Pentagon, brutal cops and screaming, youthful victims visiting American living rooms every night on the news.

And Judd finally decided, as he prepared for one Sunday sermon, that it was a time to decide whether or not you believed in America.

* * *

"I buried Frankie Pettigrew last Wednesday." The Reverend Judd Smith peered down from his pulpit at two hundred people who had packed into his little frame church. They were immediately silent, captured by the strong resonance of his voice and the intensity of his expression.

Judd Smith held up an American flag, folded into a neat triangle so that only white stars and their blue background showed. "This flag—" He paused for effect, holding the flag before them as if it were a sacrificial offering, or perhaps a mirror. "*Draped. His. Coffin.*" He let it sink in, wondering if they yet comprehended where he was headed. "The soldiers who helped give Frankie a military funeral folded it up like this, and gave it to his family. Now, why do you think they gave it to his family, brothers and sisters? *Why did they give his family this flag?*"

They were hushed, unmoving. He unraveled it, so that the American flag now hung from his pulpit, the stars up at the top and the stripes pointing toward the floor. He paused again, staring down at them with a power in his eyes, wanting them to consider the flag, perhaps for the first time. He spoke with an exaggerated slowness. "And let me ask you to think about something else. We have people in this country right now who are *spitting* on this flag, *burning* it, wearing it on their *jeans*, and blowing their *noses* on it. Does that bother you? If it does, and I can tell you it bothers me, ask yourself *why* it bothers you. *What is it about a flag,* anyway?"

He waited another moment, still staring at them, hoping the question would sink in. "Maybe while we're thinking about that, we can ask ourselves about some other symbols. Why do we have the cross, hanging above us in the church? I'll tell you why. Because it constantly reminds us that Jesus made the ultimate sacrifice for our sins, and we like to remember Him at that moment of sacrifice so that we can remember His teachings, and how far He went to show that He believed in them. And why do people all over the world react so strongly, even to this day, when they see a Nazi swastika? Some little piece of cloth with a symbol never hurt anybody, but what it stood for was so odious and terrifying that it can still cause our revulsion. And that's the same way a lot of people in the free world react when they see the communist symbol, the hammer and sickle and the red flag. Why? Because symbols speak to us in ways that go beyond words."

He delicately folded the flag in half, making them consider his movements. "Now, this flag represents every part of us. We think of a lot of things when we look at it, without having to say them out loud. At Annapolis and in the Marine Corps, they taught me to stand at attention when it went by, and to salute it. If the church represents the body of Christ, this flag represents the body of our country, all of our values, everything good and decent we stand for. *And when somebody burns it, they're burning me. When somebody spits on it, they're spitting on me. And you!"*

The congregation bristled with its agreement, commenting to each other and nodding. He allowed them to simmer, then began again. "And Frankie Pettigrew died in Vietnam for all of us, because he made a statement, with his body, that he believed in our way of life. He gave every one of us a gift, brothers and sisters, the same way that Christ gave us a gift, because Frankie Pettigrew showed us all that he believed in this country enough to place his life on the line in support of its policies. That's not as simple as dying because Japan came after us, or because Hitler was a madman. It took a lot more. *And they gave his family this flag because it represents the totality of that sacrifice."*

They were riled, some angry, many women moved to tears, Frankie Pettigrew's family sitting in the front row with an awesome, quiet dignity. They knew his point now, and agreed. He had finished refolding the flag. He stood erect in front of them, a commanding presence. "Well, let me tell you something. You and I and every other person in Bear Mountain County know full well that this flag hasn't flown from our courthouse since the Civil War began. That's more than a hundred years, and since then we've had Bear Mountain boys march off to fight for it in four wars! I bled for this flag in Korea! There probably isn't a person in this church today who hasn't been touched by this flag."

He took a deep breath. He had no idea what the reaction would be. He had gambled on them, or perhaps merely on himself, by calling

Earl Sherwood in Roanoke and predicting it, though. "The Civil War is *over*, brothers and sisters. There's a new Civil War being fought, a war of values. Now, I think it's time we had a little patriotic ceremony over at the courthouse, and put this flag up where it belongs."

The late summer sun beat down on a hazy cloud of dust as fifty cars sped into Bear Mountain Gap. It might have been a lynch mob following Judd Smith along the dirt roads in their cars and pickup trucks.

*   *   *

"Good evening, ladies and gentlemen, this is Larry Ocheltree with the KNZQ news. The fighting preacher strikes again, and America finally comes home to Bear Mountain County. Earl Sherwood, of our sister station, WATV in Roanoke, reports."

The television screen flashed to a small country courtyard, where hundreds of simple, unsmiling people in their Sunday best stood near the statue of a Confederate soldier, watching a man as he gave a speech from near the flagpole. A baritone voice narrated as the people on the screen watched the speaker intently.

"Virginia mountaineers have a tradition of not giving up in a fight. Perhaps that's why the Civil War still rankles in these hills. The American flag has not been flown in Bear Mountain County since Virginia seceded from the Union at the beginning of the Civil War. But the American flag has taken on a new significance in these days of protest, and the absence of the flag at the Bear Mountain courthouse might be misinterpreted by some as a statement of support for the various dissent movements who have so frequently defaced the flag. The Reverend Judd Smith, a Marine hero of the Korean War and an outspoken critic of the protest movements, decided that a statement had to be made."

Loretta's eyes went round and her mouth fell agape as she watched television in the living room. "Mama! Quick, it's Daddy again!"

Julie ran in from the kitchen in time to watch a camera do a close-up on Judd Smith's rugged, scarred face. His hair was going gray and his eyes had begun to bag and they showed the ear (how the camera loved his ear). She took him in like a lover, all the wrinkles and the scars. *Are you forty-one, Judd Smith? What happened to thirty and thirty-five?* But he was beautiful, beautiful, as he dropped heavy words of emotion without so much as raising his voice one decibel.

"The Civil War is *over*, brothers and sisters. We are in a new war, a war of values. This flag is the embodiment of all we believe in. It represents the body of our country, just as the church represents the body of Christ. It is not a simple piece of cloth. It is not an outmoded symbol of a decaying institution. It represents the values that have made us the greatest nation on earth. Anyone who doubts that statement might ask themselves how many people are trying to immigrate into Russia, or East Germany, or North Vietnam, or anywhere else. We are the hope of the world, and this flag represents that hope."

The screen widened again and showed the Reverend Judd Smith raising the flag on the courthouse flagpole, to the applause of the gathering. Then, spontaneously, the people put their right hands over their hearts and began singing "My Country 'Tis of Thee."

> *From every mountainside—*
> *Let freedom ring!*

The narrator came on, standing in front of the Confederate soldier, the singing voices a backdrop. He smiled, the camera just in front of his mouth. "County officials have indicated that the flag will continue to fly at the courthouse. This is Earl Sherwood, in Bear Mountain Gap, Virginia."

"Is Daddy in trouble again?" Loretta wore a knowing, pixie grin as she examined her mother's wet eyes.

"No. Your father is a very brave man, Loretta."

"You still love him, don't you, Mom?" She wasn't supposed to have those sorts of insights at twelve. She wasn't supposed to be even a discussant of life's cruelties. Julie smiled back at the round, maturing face and its frame of tousled curls.

"Yes."

"Can't we live with him?" The young girl's face was earnest, pleading, and her growing hands, almost the hands of a woman, were now on her mother's shoulders.

"It's not that simple, Loretta."

"Well, you've already been divorced once, Mom. So people are talking about you, anyway. And Daddy married you first. And you love him. I've *always* wanted to live with him. And we could live in the mountains and play with the dogs and walk in the woods! Oh, Mom!"

It wasn't even a conscious decision. *How I have hurt you,* she was thinking as she hugged Loretta, *How I have scarred you from my anger and my fear.* And she just heard herself saying it, as much to

comfort Loretta as to decide firmly the most terrifying move she had
ever made. "Go pack your suitcase. Just take your favorite clothes,
and one Sunday dress."

"Can't I bring my makeup? And my Teddies?" Ah, twelve, thought
Julie. To be confronted with dramatic change and worry about such
ornaments as lipstick and Teddy bears.

"Okay. Those, too. Oh, come on, I'll help you. But let's hurry!"

* * *

He heard tires coming downhill on the dirt road and then the dogs
barking. Headlights eased toward his cabin like a slow spotlight as the
car carefully negotiated the old wooden bridge over the stream. It was
three o'clock in the morning.

He threw on a pair of work pants, his boots, and a coat. Outside,
the crisp air greeted his face and lungs with the promise of autumn as
he strode toward the car. A full moon put a glow on both their faces
as they peered out of the car. She opened the door and walked slowly
toward him, dressed in jeans, the jeans themselves a statement, her
eyes tired and afraid. She said nothing at first. She simply buried her
head into his chest, not hard as if she were trying to hide, but gently,
her arms going around him, a surrender and a promise all in the same
slow embrace.

Loretta bounded out of the car carrying a Teddy bear, her bright
eyes electric in the moonlight as she grabbed him with the tight grip
of a wrestler.

"We ran away, Dad."

"You ran *away?*"

She spoke then, her voice just above a whisper, and her wet eyes
pressed against his neck.

"I'm always running away."

CHAPTER TWENTY-THREE

THE FOOTBALL GAMES WERE OVER. The dinner had been devoured; sauerkraut and kielbasa for Sophie's luck, black-eyed peas for Judd's and Julie's, ham and sweet potatoes, and three kinds of pie. Judd Smith and Joe Dingenfelder sat across from each other on two small couches in Sophie's living room, sated. A glass table was between them, cluttered with wine bottles and beer cans. An orchestra was playing symphonic versions of the Beatles' music on the radio. Downstairs, in the basement, the television blared and their children shouted occasionally to one another. Smith and Dingenfelder were pretending they could enjoy themselves in Red Lesczynski's home. It was the least they could do for Sophie.

"*The tiger springs in the New Year. Us it devours.*"

Smith raised a beer to Dingenfelder, toasting him. "Not that bad, Dingie. I always did say that every musician was in his heart a poet, and every poet was a minstrel."

"Oh, did you, now?" Dingenfelder raised a wineglass into the air, returning the toast. "And every hillbilly is in his heart a preacher, and every preacher is a philosopher."

"And the beat goes on." Smith watched carefully as Dingenfelder tossed down half of the wine in his full glass, noting the aura of forced gaiety, the hard, numb smile betrayed by his little boy's eyes. "And any man who drinks like that is choking back a tear."

Dingenfelder ignored Smith's concern. His face was very red. He was wearing an elegant, tan vicuña sportcoat, brown wool slacks, and a narrow silk tie. The tie was loose at the top, stylish, coming out of a button-down, blue Oxford-cloth shirt. He had been babying a pipe for a half-hour, tamping it and cleaning it. He looked like an Ivy League professor. He raised the wineglass again. "Let us drink to those less fortunate than we, for they will never know the stink of success. Ah, yes. We carve idols and then crave to become them. Welcome, 1969! I have gorged on ten of your brothers as I labored in the West, worshiping false gods. Now I will worship the sun."

Smith raised his beer glass. "On a cold Virginia night."

"On the far edge of the sea."

"The sea? As you wish. Give him the gull cry, and the sound of the hard surf on the reef." Smith frowned. "The sea? The mind of the man, I fear, is bewildered."

"But your eyes shall see the truth."

"Running away, are you, Dingie?"

"Back off, Boogaloo."

"Back off, Boogaloo?" Judd Smith frowned again. Julie and Sophie walked into the living room from the kitchen, having finished the dishes. Julie wore a green, Scottish-plaid kilt, and a dark green cashmere sweater. The kilt had a large safety pin holding it where the fabric joined. It was the style. Her long blond hair was pulled back and braided on top of her head, in the manner she had worn it when she and Judd had first dated. It resembled a crown, and made her look young. Perhaps, thought Smith as she walked toward him, the memories made her look young, rather than the hair. Smith put an arm around her as she joined him on the couch. He cocked his head, savoring the phrase again, as if it were from a foreign language. "Back off, Boogaloo. It must be some strange California dialect, wouldn't you say, Sophie?"

"No, my kids talk like that all the time. 'Oh, wow. Groovy. Bitchin'.' *Bitchin'!* Can you believe they use that to mean something is neat?"

"Well, yeah. But this man is a scientist, a musician, a poet! He's also forty years old." Smith waxed eloquent, waving his arm in the air. "Should such ribs be stuck in the sounds of surfer children? I say, he brings shame upon his intellect."

"No more beer for you, Judd Smith." Julie took the can from him, and replaced its emptiness with her hand.

"And she—" Smith watched her with heavy-lidded eyes. He felt content, almost unbelieving, as he stared at her face. "She is making me move into a real house. Can you imagine?"

Sophie smiled at them. Her eyes had grown tired, but her face had remained unwrinkled, smooth and high cheeked, even at thirty-nine. She wore a maroon sweater and skirt that illuminated her tawny skin. She crossed her legs and folded her arms underneath her breasts, so innocently inviting, so charged with unconscious sexuality, that Judd Smith pitied her as he watched. *So sad to be cheated of your man, year after year, your lush nest of a body waiting . . .*

She slowly shook her head, watching Judd and Julie coo like new, discovering lovers on her couch. "You guys are still in the papers almost every week, and it's been four months, hasn't it? I mean, when are they going to lay off?"

"Williams Tobacco buys a lot of newspaper ads. And the good lieutenant governor—" Judd Smith watched Julie wilt like a time exposure of a dying flower. Her head was on his shoulder, a silent plea. Julie was right. It was not a subject for jubilation. "Let them write, Sophie. They'll get tired of it, sooner or later."

"I don't think they will." Julie spoke in a whispering melody, sweet and yet sarcastic, staring into his shoulder. "Senator's daughter leaves lieutenant governor for ex-husband mountaineer preacher. It reads like a soap opera, doesn't it? The only thing left is for my two husbands to run against each other for governor. Wouldn't that be cute?"

"Are you going to run for governor, Judd?"

"Hardly, Sophie."

"Just wait. They're already after him to go for Congress. They tried to get him to run this time around." Julie held her small stomach, looking at Sophie and shaking her head as if it were inevitable. "Make way on Capitol Hill for the fighting preacher. Tony will fight it, though. It could be bloody. Oh, I'd just like to move to the Bahamas. Or maybe Australia." She touched Smith's arm, playing coy. "Wouldn't you like to move to Australia, Judd?"

Sophie poured herself and Joe more wine, her brown eyes captivated by the thought of it. "Can you imagine Dorothy and Judd both in Congress? Oh, my, think of the arguments they could have!"

"Dorothy doesn't need me to have an argument. I'd venture Dorothy could argue with a wall and get it to shout back, huh, Dingie?"

There was a flat calm in Joe Dingenfelder's voice that caught them all off guard, an edge that bordered on mendacity. "Well, she's gotten what she wanted. She's destroyed a family along the way, but that's all right. I hope she gets a lot of satisfaction out of it."

Sophie had developed an occasional shrill edge over the years of Red's captivity, her frail calm crumbling at odd times and a harsh voice taking over, flashing out of her like a bilious regurgitation. Her normally soft voice now leaped across the table at Dingenfelder, surprising him, as if it were a lance. "How much of that is envy, Joe? Can you be honest? I mean, you were the kingpin for so long, dragging her around the world with you, and now she's in control. I can't blame her, really!"

She caught their wondering looks. "I don't mean how she's gone about it. I mean the fact that she's done it." She straightened the hem on her skirt, avoiding their eyes, sensing that they might take it wrong. "You know, sometimes I get *mad* at Red! Can you believe it? I think about what he's going through, if he's still alive, and I think I can feel deep inside me that he *is* alive, because if he died I would feel it inside me, a dead space. And all right, I cry. But then I say, 'Red Lesczynski, you wanted to fly and I said okay. I left my family and my home for you and I followed you all over creation. I wrote you letters when you were gone. I learned to be alone, and to raise a family by myself. I learned how to do plumbing and to fix a car. I did all these things for you and I guess for me, and I wouldn't do it any other way, but I've spent more than half of my adult life *waiting!*' I feel so useless, sometimes. I guess I can just understand Dorothy, that's all."

"But you love Red." Joe Dingenfelder had packed his pipe, and was sucking on it.

"Oh, with all my heart! That doesn't mean I can't get mad at him, even when it doesn't make sense."

"And you're sticking by him. Three years he's been gone, and you're still sticking by him."

Sophie smiled. The edge was gone now, replaced with something that was almost embarrassment. "I told you. I love him with all my heart."

Dingenfelder leaned back on the couch. He pulled on the pipe, as if quietly debating whether to respond. He took a long time to answer. "She humiliated me, and it's true I resent it, Sophie. I think it was a conscious way to pay me back for the years she lost, to say, 'See Joe, you kept me on ice when I was really *better*.' But she stopped loving me, too. I hardly exist to her. I can't compete with her. I can't negotiate anything with her. I do it her way, or I leave." He raised his hands, a helpless gesture. "All right. I can't do it her way anymore. I'm leaving."

"You're leaving her, Joe? You really are?"

"Yeah, I really am. I'm sick of it. I just have to get away, to figure things out." He shrugged. "Now she can be the wounded party, and tell everyone I couldn't stand to play second fiddle to the congresslady. But she left me years ago. She just never made it official, that's all. She needed me around as a prop, a piece of furniture in her little stage play." He tossed down the rest of the wine in his glass. "I came back East to get the kids settled in at the new house, and I'm going away."

"Oh, my." Sophie clutched her wineglass with both hands, as if it were a rosary. "Joe, I'm so sorry."

"Don't be. She's got her friends. Where do you think she is right now? And listen to her talk, when you have the time. Dorothy Dingenfelder knew and loved Martin Luther King. Dorothy Dingenfelder was standing near Robert Kennedy when he was shot, and held his body in her arms. Dorothy Dingenfelder has argued the First Amendment before the Supreme Court. Dorothy Dingenfelder is going to end the Vietnam War and bring peace and justice to the world. Dorothy Dingenfelder does not need a husband who is jealous of her success." He shrugged calmly, as if helpless to decide anything else. "Fine. Dorothy Dingenfelder can enjoy it alone."

"So he will set up a tall mast, and sail into the glitter of sun rays as the porpoise snorts along the boatside."

Dingenfelder leaned over, his head down, looking between his legs. He wore wingtip shoes and Gold Cup socks. He did not belong in California. "Yeah, that's right. For the first time in my life, I'm doing something totally irresponsible." He looked over at Judd Smith and actually giggled with the expectation of it. "Don't worry about me, Judd."

"What about the moon shot?"

"It'll go. It's ready right now. Give it six months or so. And who cares, really? I'm tired of it, all of it. It's a game people are playing with each other, just like all the rest of this. A way to ignore death."

Judd Smith and Sophie looked quickly at each other. Smith frowned. "Ignore death? Where did that come from?"

"Let's face it." Dingenfelder peered up at them for a few seconds. "Once you become conscious of the fact that someday you're really going to die, life is nothing but surviving slow despair anyway. Success, meaning, the damn moon shot—they're lids on the truth! The truth is that we're all going to die. We are going to cease to exist, melt back into the earth, *disappear!* And rather than mindlessly waiting for the inevitable in an opium den, or killing ourselves quickly to end the suspense, we occupy ourselves with pretense."

He brought his eyes back up to them again. They were wide, adamant. "We're all in despair! Not the open, screaming despair of someone pushed over the edge, but the quiet despair of watching the cliff begin to crumble at our feet. The ground is shaking! We're going to fall into the pit of death! You, Sophie, what did you just say? You've spent half of your adult life waiting! You're getting bitter, don't try to fool me with your soft little voice! Despair! Judd and Julie! You lost ten years over an argument! Time is getting away from you! That's the story of middle age! We want it back and we despair."

He poured himself more wine. "It's like we're passengers on a train, unable to get off and unable to control the train, knowing that the end of the track is a huge stone wall and that the train is going to hit it at a hundred miles an hour, but also knowing that it won't happen for a while, maybe tomorrow, maybe next year, so we pretend that the train ride is *meaningful*, because we don't have any other way of dealing with it. Dorothy makes it to Congress, and that's meaningful. Joe helps put a man on the moon. But when the train hits the wall, is it really going to matter? The train hitting the wall is the most immutable part of the trip! It's the only reality. The rest is just a way to bide your time."

Judd Smith scrutinized his roommate of two decades before, peering past the bark of age that had wrinkled Joe Dingenfelder's face, ignoring the gray helmet of hair, seeing instead the soft eyes that had not changed, that still held his emotions with a warm fragility, like the tender center of a baby's skull. He could poke his finger through Joe Dingenfelder and hurt him deep. That was why he had always loved him, as if he were a younger brother to be fostered, defended from the town bully. Would Einstein have been able to survive a wife with the energy and power of Dorothy? Would Brahms have suffered well a woman who was in the news each day, on the train to every piece of chaos her country was experiencing? How would Picasso have fared, or Durant?

"What do you want back, Joe? Have you figured that out?"

"Oh, I don't want *anything* back. It's all beyond that, isn't it? I just feel like I've been walking somebody else's treadmill for twenty years. I want to do something stupid, okay? I want to ride the train from a different car for a while. Don't knock it, Judd. I'm going to have a ball."

"Doing *what?*"

Keys turned in the front door's lock and the door opened, bringing in a breath of icy air, new 1969 wind creeping across the floor to where they sat. The doorway itself filled with a tall, square figure, a gently smiling face framed by red hair that was cut and parted, worn above the ears. He quietly closed the door and faced them with his head slightly down, his hands inside his parka's pockets, so much like his father that the room filled with the emptiness until it was a presence just beside him, the vacuum of Red Lesczynski's absence as real as J.J. himself.

"Hi, Uncle Judd. Uncle Joe. Aunt Julie." He had huge, muscled hands, and size-twelve shoes. He leaned over and kissed Sophie on the cheek. "Hello, Mum. Everything okay?"

"Fine, hon. How was the party?"

"Not bad. Are the kids all right?"

The kids. The kids were fourteen and thirteen. J.J. was sixteen. He took off his parka. His deep, muscular torso pushed against his sweater. Thick arms and shoulders strained against the sleeves. His neck was like a tree trunk. His blue eyes held authority with the ease of a man twice his age. *Too soon old,* thought Judd Smith, watching Red Lesczynski's oldest son hang his coat in the front closet.

"Oh, they're fine. They're downstairs. Natasha and little Joe are here. So is Loretta. You should go say hello."

"I swear, J.J., you must go a hundred and ninety pounds."

J.J. smiled softly to Judd Smith. "Two hundred, Uncle Judd. I guess I should hit two ten by the time I graduate. Coach says maybe two fifteen." He glanced at Sophie, as if for reassurance. "Isn't that what Dad played at, Mom?"

"I don't think your dad ever made it past two hundred and ten pounds, J.J."

J.J. smiled, his calm blue eyes unfocused as they peered toward his mother. "I bet I wasn't a hundred and twenty pounds when he left. Boy, is he going to be surprised."

He gave them a small wave and walked toward the door that led to the basement. Sophie watched him with unmuted pride. "My baby. Red told him he was the man of the house until he got back. He takes it so seriously." She attempted a smile, staring at Joe Dingenfelder. "And that's why you're wrong, Joe. About the train. The train doesn't hit the wall. J.J. and the others, they'll be alive, and they'll have every part of me and Red in them, and then their own parts, too. I don't feel despair. I just get—oh, I don't know. Lonely. Angry. Sad." She wept now, openly but without sound. Her eyes became old when she cried.

"That's some boy, Sophie."

"I can't tell you what it does to me on Christmas Eve. Three Christmases now, and we set out two extra plates, one for Christ to come as a beggar and one for Red. The kids insist on filling up Red's plate.

And then my J.J. passes around the *oplatki,* taking Red's place, and
we take a bite and we all pray that this will be the year, and then we
break the walnut and every year the meat is sweet and we say that it's
going to be a good year, that this will be the year. And then the year
goes by and it isn't the year, and the only thing we get is our little
monthly form letter from the Department of Defense telling us how
much money we're going to make, and warning us not to communicate with the press or with the other wives, because it will hurt
our husbands. It isn't *right,* Judd! How is it going to hurt our husbands if the press finds out? The press knows all the other horrible
parts of this war. And why shouldn't we communicate with each
other? I don't understand. All I know is I've gotten one little letter
from him, four lines saying he's alive. And that was two years ago."

"Maybe this year, Sophie. Johnson's out, Nixon's in. It could be a
whole new ball game."

* * *

She was taunting Katherine as J.J. reached the bottom of the steps,
this small, dark-haired girl who carried the pinched intensity of her
mother in her face. Across the room, sitting on a couch, Johnny and
little Joe were trying to ignore the argument, immersed in a late night
movie. Katherine stood with her back to Red Lesczynski's study desk,
Blue Angel pictures on the wall, the mashed football from the 1950
Army-Navy game on a shelf among rows of military and historical
works. She was crying, her eyes bleary with the tears, resentful, but
confused by allegations that she lacked the sophistication to counter.
Loretta was standing between Natasha and Katherine, her arms
folded and her head shaking, her gaze telling J.J. immediately that it
had been going on for a long time and that it was neither humorous
nor tasteful.

At fourteen, Katherine was two years older than Natasha, and a
head taller. She had inherited Red Lesczynski's long limbs. She had
Sophie's smooth face, her ample body, and her quiet mannerisms. She
wore a Villager skirt and sweater, and Bass Wejun shoes. Across from
her, in the California casualness of blue jeans and a powder-blue
UCLA sweatshirt, Natasha was looking up at Katherine as if she
would soon bite off her nose.

Loretta sighed, the failed arbitrator, invoking J.J.'s wisdom. "*Natasha* says your dad's a war criminal, and that he should have told
them he wouldn't go to Vietnam. *Katherine* says Natasha's mom is the

criminal because she's on the side of the communists. *Natasha* says her mom hasn't murdered anybody, and that your dad did, with his bombs. *Katherine* says he did not. *Natasha* says he did, he did, he did, Bobby Kennedy said so, Martin Luther King said so—" She frowned, staring at the ceiling for a moment. "Some others said so. I can't remember."

"Eugene McCarthy. David Dellinger. Abbie Hoffman." Natasha spat it into Katherine's face. "And my mother. And my mother's a congresswoman, now."

J.J. watched them both, a quiet grieving washing over his face. Then he put a firm hand on his sister's shoulder. "Tell Natasha you feel sorry for her."

"*Sorry* for her?" Katherine sputtered through tears. "J.J.!"

"Yeah. *Tell her*, Katherine. Come on."

Katherine issued the words through grinding teeth, still crying. "I feel sorry for you."

Natasha cocked her head, smiling. "Why?"

"I don't know. *J.J.!*"

"Just because, Katherine. That's all you need to say." He looked at Natasha. "You'll find out yourself someday, and then maybe you'll understand."

"Oh, brother." Natasha examined J.J.'s gray wool sweater and his slacks. "Is this the way *everybody* out East dresses? For God's sake, how do I get back to California?"

Katherine spat the words through her tears. "Why don't we hope your mom gets beat in the next election, and you can all go home."

The two boys laughed from in front of the television. Little Joe called toward them, sprawled on the couch. He was small for his ten years, casually dressed also, but had the quick eyes and the fast voice of a young intellectual. "Don't mind Tasha. She just likes to argue. She thinks *she* just got elected to Congress."

"Oh, shut up, worthless!"

"Go play on the freeway, Tasha."

J.J. put a hand on Natasha's shoulder. She started to jerk away, her lips tight and her eyes combative, but he held firmly, then leaned over and gave her a gentle kiss on the cheek. "Happy New Year, Tasha. Can I get you a Coke?"

"Who are you kidding?"

"Calm down, okay? We don't bite. Do you want a Coke, or not?"

"What are you going to do, spike it with arsenic?"

"Whooo-eee." J.J. laughed softly, keeping his arm on her shoulder. "You really don't like us very much, do you, Tasha?"

Joe called from the couch again, not even bothering to look in their direction. "It's my mom."

"It is *not!*"

"Oh, come on, Tasha, give these people a break, will you? Just because Mom wouldn't come, you think they're the enemy, or something."

"She had a reception to go to. A very important party. For very important people."

"That wasn't the reason, and you know it. She thinks Uncle Judd is a racist and a fascist, and she thinks Uncle Red—"

"She does *not,* Joe Dingenfelder, you *shut up!*"

"She said it."

"She was mad at Dad! And that's private, Joe! You wait till you get home!"

"You scare me, Tasha. Can't you see I'm shivering?" Joe laughed, elbowing Johnny.

"Uncle *Judd?*" J.J. gave out a slow whistle. "Anyway, you're here, Tasha. Give us a try. Now, let me get you a Coke, okay?"

❊   ❊   ❊

"Congresswoman Dingenfelder?"

Oh, that sounded wonderful, beyond belief, as if it were two hundred years before and the man had inquired, *Princess?*

"Yes?"

She turned in the packed Georgetown dining room of former Ambassador Newman, confidant of Roosevelt, Truman, and Kennedy, bane to Lyndon Johnson, a friend of the movement, and one of her patrons. Despite her years of involvement, she had felt starstruck as she drifted alone across the room underneath the heavy crystal chandelier, tasting exquisite, catered food and exchanging empty wineglasses for full ones on the trays of omnipresent waiters. She had been recognized several times. *I'm here, I'm here, I've done it, I really have!* It was almost unbearably rewarding.

"I'm Sven Jorbati, of the Washington *Journal.*" The short man with his bulbous bald head waited tentatively, wishing to be recognized. They all wanted to be recognized. That was why many of them came in the first place.

"Oh, yes, *Sven Jorbati!* So nice to finally meet you. You're doing such a wonderful job!" It was too dangerous to tell him that she enjoyed his writing, because she had never heard of him. Who knew? He might be an editor. Saying the right innocuous affirmative thing, that was so important in politics.

He seemed gratified. "Why, thank you. As much as I admire you, I must say you've made my evening." He nestled up to her. He was shorter than she, and his large head made him look like a no-necked bulldog. His brown suit fit him as if it had been borrowed from a big brother. "Listen, you're quite a story, and I think you're important to the image of successful women these days. A former housewife and schoolteacher who has argued before the Supreme Court, and organized mass demonstrations. A family woman of varied talents. I'd like to do a feature, if you can find the time in the next week or so. You'd be one of perhaps a half dozen in my series called 'A Look At the New Congress.' Would that suit you?"

Would it suit me? she thought, almost unable to control her delight. *A feature in the* Journal *before I'm even sworn into the Congress?* "I'd be happy to give you some time, Sven. Call my appointments secretary day after tomorrow, and she'll book you in just about whenever you'd like."

"That would be wonderful." Jorbati searched around the packed room. "Is your husband nearby? I'd love to meet him. He must be a very unusual man, to successfully pursue his own career and be able to support yours, also. He's a scientist, is that correct?"

"Well, yes." She hesitated slightly, hoping Jorbati would not pick up on her tension. "Joe is many things. He's a musician and a poet, and of course he was a very fine Air Force officer, an Annapolis graduate. He couldn't make it tonight, though. Joe is a, uh, a very quiet man, and preferred to spend the night with the children and some friends."

"Why, that's absolutely touching!" Jorbati seemed to be scribbling the feature story in his brain as he talked, staring past Dorothy toward a far painting. "A man of humility, who prefers the company of family and friends to the bustle of the political and diplomatic scene."

"Yes, that's Joe, Sven. In fact, I doubt that he'd even consent to be part of an interview. He's a very private person."

"How fascinating, these days! I begin to understand the secret of your success." Jorbati raised a wineglass to her. "You've not only an abundance of talent, Dorothy, but you've married extremely well, also. To your long career in the Congress!"

* * *

Sophie drove him to the Dulles International Airport, in a cold sleet that was the precursor to a violent February storm. She spoiled him with her concern, almost as if he were her child. She even kissed him good-bye, a wet smack on the cheek. She did not ask him any questions. They closed the Chicago airport only hours after his connecting flight departed. The Frost Belt was going under, locked in a deep freeze.

On the flight from San Francisco they showed a movie about two college kids who fell in love and couldn't handle it. It made him want to write a letter to Dorothy, to apologize and plead, to ask her to remember that underneath all the resentment and mistakes, there had been a kernel of need and emotion that he at least had dared call love. In the hollow, droning darkness he remembered her from sixteen years before, on the other side of age and failure, standing naked and embracing him from behind as he drew rose petals of music from his Steinway,

Can you love me like you do that?

He couldn't write to her. She was too old for what they had dreamed of, yet too young in her new success to see beyond the wreckage of what they had become. He thought then, somewhat uncertainly, that he would always love her. He hadn't said that to himself for years. She was a paradox, brilliant and yet frail from the scars of her childhood, forever burrowed inside a fear that came back out as anger. She was consumed in her passion to make up lost years, years that she now blamed him for taking from her. Would it ever change? He did not know. He only knew that he was powerless to alter it.

And besides, to be honest, it was probably incurable. Human resilience was in overcoming pain, moving on. That didn't mean you could undo the anger and the scars, and make things innocent again.

In Honolulu the hot sun and the warm, stiff breeze smelled of promises. He boarded a small propellor-driven plane with five others, two lost, beaten men such as himself and three teenaged laborers. It was a loud flight, devoid of conversation.

On Kwajalein the air gave him a wet kiss as he climbed out of the plane. The rain did not matter; it was warm as a bathroom shower. The runway steamed from it. He was exhausted, disoriented from jet lag. New smells surrounded him, exciting his tension. The sandy earth was alive with yeasty surges, growth and decay. The sea offered a roaring greeting, pounding on a distant reef. At the far edge of the runway, a small community of tin-roofed shacks beckoned him with their quaintness. Palm trees and thick brush swayed gently in the heavy gray sky.

The irony was small, but inescapable. He had hocked his freedom, or perhaps merely his pride, to supervise a radar installation on Kwajalein. The radar would be "scoring" missile shots as they came into Kwajalein and Eniwetok from the mainland. The shots were Atlas and Minuteman and Titan II missiles. The missiles were launched from Vandenberg. He was overqualified for the job; in a sense, it was like a concert pianist deciding to become a piano tuner. And in another sense, he had come full circle since his Air Force years.

Once, in his moments of greatest joy, he had a waiting family, and he and Three Fingers Pattakos had pitched missiles toward Kwajalein from Vandenberg. Now, in his bewildered retreat, he would catch Vandenberg shots on the tiny desolation of Kwajalein. Alone.

Part Five

A COUNTRY SUCH AS THIS

CHAPTER TWENTY-FOUR

I

B. O. PLENTY WAS FISHING IN Lake Fester. The elfin guard stood at the edge of the cesspool, dressed in a faded khaki uniform and rubber sandals, his camouflaged pith helmet tilted slightly toward the back of his head.

He was staring intently into the odorous water. The prisoners dumped their waste buckets into Lake Fester every morning, gallons upon gallons of urine and feces, watery from dysentery. The water roaches were so thick on top of the cesspool that they appeared to be a black, knobby lid over the water. B. O. Plenty fished there almost every day, his crude pole held over the stench, the line lost in its depths, waiting for a whale. Red Lesczynski had never seen him catch anything, although B. O. Plenty would no doubt stroll the dark corridors outside the rooms after the guards' midday break was done, bragging in crude English of his success. Lesczynski secretly hoped the mindless North Vietnamese guard would someday catch a fish, a whopper, just to see what mélange of diseases he might suffer from if he ate his prize.

On the other side of Lake Fester, at the far corner of the square prison compound near the Quiz Rooms, Pox and Sweetpea were playing with a puppy. Lesczynski could not look toward the Quiz Rooms without wondering again when he might die. Their dark walls and floors were caked with blood, pus, and feces. The very concrete stank from it. Ropes and rubber hoses, those were its furniture.

Pox held the small, tan puppy. Its tail was wagging. Sweetpea poured gasoline over it. Pox let it go, and chased it with a match. The puppy exploded with fire, then howled with a piercing, terrified scream, almost human in its length and pitch. It ran from the flames, from itself, and in moments tumbled to one side, a dead hunk of blackened fur. Crispy critter. Pox and Sweetpea laughed, retrieving their prize. They would probably eat the puppy, but they burned dogs and rats regularly, for the sport of it.

In a clutch of trees near his cell, just in front of Lake Fester, Lesczynski could see Jawbone and Ashley Asthmatic napping together in the grass. They faced inward, their arms entwined. It looked like they were masturbating each other. It didn't surprise him. The North Vietnamese continually harangued him and the others during interrogations about how American troops had corrupted the South, turning the women into prostitutes or raping them. The North was pure, they reminded him. Promiscuity was not tolerated. But it was common to see men holding hands, embracing, playing with each other.

Some of them had wanted him. He could tell in those evanescent moments between his *bao cao* bow, the obligatory deference when a guard entered his cell, and the first word or blow that followed it. Lowered eyes examining his huge frame, which towered over them, even though it had become emaciated, boil-ridden, dripping from the scabs. Quick, grinding voices, turgid with repressed passion. An exploratory reaching of the hand near his groin met always with his one good fist and a steady stare. Then a scream and a punch over some other imagined slight—the crookedness of his bow, perhaps—to save face.

Red Lesczynski had not had an erection in three years.

Well, that wasn't entirely true.

In his first hot near-dead summer at the Zoo he was thrown into solitary confinement in a section of dark hovels called the Stable, inside a room so small that he could barely stand upright, and could only take three steps before he had to turn around. None of his wounds had been treated, and he had new infections on his wrists and arms from the ropes they had used during torture sessions. Two days after he arrived at the Stable, he had been locked into leg irons on the wooden planks of his bed. His wrists had been cuffed in front of him. He had been unable to lie down fully, or to turn over. They had left him in the leg irons for two weeks. His crime had been trying to talk to the man in the next cell.

Soon his infected ankles had swollen until they protruded around the "U" shaped manacles, as if they were pink balloons squeezed in the middle. Maggots found a home inside the long blisters of his shrapnel wounds. The shrapnel was still inside. His left arm was useless, almost dead. It had quickly atrophied. They ignored the injury. He could not reach his slop bucket. He was forced to lay in his own urine and feces the entire time. Guards had to leave his door open for several minutes to allow the stench to clear before they could deliver his twice-daily ration of pumpkin soup and rice.

His right leg had been the worst. It pulsed from the infection, swelling through the heat of the day, an angry red, the wounds black at the edges, crawling with maggots that disappeared inside. Then, every afternoon, it would seemingly burst, pus draining into the wet odorous boards of his bed. At night he would awaken from the rustling sounds of rats sweeping along the floor and then sitting next to his leg on the bed, drawn to the carrion, his own dead flesh. Just before his two weeks were up a female guard who told him she was a nurse examined the leg through a squinched, nauseated face, then reached inside the wound and pulled on something. A quart of green and red ooze leaked out, like air from a tire.

That afternoon an officer who said he was a doctor told Lesczynski that the leg would have to be cut off. Lesczynski refused, screaming at the surprised man, responding viscerally, the filth around him a warning that he would not survive an amputation, that an infection might enter his bloodstream and cause systemic damage, but that the trauma of amputation would kill him in the heat and stench of Hoa Lo prison. Surprisingly, they reacted to his insistence, taking him into a small, cluttered medic room and cutting away the infection, leaving deep troughs up both legs as they went after the shrapnel that had driven along the bone, several inches past the entry points. They packed the gouges with latex strips that were sprinkled with penicillin. They used no pain-killers as they worked, but he was too weak to scream, too pleased with saving his leg even to care.

He lost sixty pounds over the next five months. The leg continued to drain. His left arm wiggled like a wet noodle, dangling from the shoulder. Finally, they had taken him to a hospital somewhere in Hanoi, operating on both. They scoured and sterilized the leg. They hollowed out the two ends of his severed humerus bone, inserted a piece of bone taken from his pelvis, and sewed him back up with tobacco string. The arm had promptly separated again on his return to prison, and they had put him back into leg irons as punishment for his "bad attitude" that had allowed the operation to fail. Now, more than two years later, it still dangled at his side, more useless than before.

But when he was in the hospital they had fed him good food to strengthen him for the operations and when the dysentery stopped and his mind returned, he began seeing things. Like the two pretty North Vietnamese nurses who tended him. They were fascinated by his red hair and his size. They scrubbed him every day, until his boils disappeared. They flirted with him coyly, teasing each other in quiet giggles, as if fantasizing over some unmentionable, joyous scheme. He had teased back, dreamily watching small, soft breasts bulge against their clothes as they leaned over his bed, enjoying the smooth arms and warm features of a woman for the first time in a year, and the last time for maybe forever.

After several days of it, they walked quietly into his room during one of the seemingly universal afternoon breaks, the North Vietnamese siesta period, and stared excitedly at him, giggling to each other. Then one of the nurses stood in the doorway, as if on watch. The other one smiled brightly to Lesczynski and slowly opened up her blouse, displaying her rounded breasts. He felt himself grow huge underneath the sheets. He could not take his eyes off her breasts. She approached him, leaning over the bed, and he took first one breast and then the other into his mouth. She hummed softly, holding his head in one arm as if suckling him, then reached under the sheets and masturbated him. He came quickly, an explosive rush that made him choke from its intensity, then lay back on the bed, drained and somewhat embarrassed. She had caught his passion in the sheets. Continuing to hum, she redid her blouse, quickly changed the sheets, and touched him softly on the forehead with one finger as she and her friend departed. The next day, they were their same giggling, teasing selves. And in another day he was back inside the pit of Hoa Lo prison.

That had been more than two years ago. It sat in his memory, not quite real, as if it had been a morphine dream.

Lesczynski moved slowly away from the chink in the brick wall, the little peephole from which he had surveyed the midday antics of B. O. Plenty and the other guards. If he had been caught peering outside his cell, he would have been beaten and put into leg irons. His roommate, Ken Friedersdorf, was on his hands and knees, staring underneath the door down the dark hallway for guards. They were both dressed only in undershorts, the standard summer clothing. Perspiration was precious, to be avoided. They received less than a half gallon of water a day, for all uses. Friedersdorf, an Air Force captain much younger than Lesczynski, looked haggard and old. Thinking of Friedersdorf's aged features, Lesczynski was again glad that he had not seen himself in a mirror for three years. The shock might well have depressed him into slow, apathetic death.

He picked up his porcelain-covered tin cup, and held it against the wall, a makeshift ear horn. Then he began tapping furiously, using the tap code the prisoners had worked out years before. Lesczynski himself had been delivered the code on the end of a piece of wire during his first day at the Stable. The wire was shoved underneath his door by a prisoner in a room across the narrow aisle. On its end was a square of toilet paper. The other prisoner had written in ink made of cigarette ashes and water:

Tap Code: Memorize and eat this paper (FIRST TAP DOWN. SECOND TAP ACROSS).

	1	2	3	4	5
1	A	B	C	D	E
2	F	G	H	I	J
3	L	M	N	O	P
4	Q	R	S	T	U
5	V	W	X	Y	Z

His attempt to call across the hallway to the other prisoner was the reason he had ended up in leg irons. The prison authorities, many of whom had themselves survived Japanese or French prisons, knew that isolation was essential to destroying the human spirit, and forbade communication of any sort among the Americans. A simple "hello" if they happened to see another prisoner as they emptied waste buckets in Lake Fester or walked toward their weekly wash and shave was grounds for a smash in the jaw. Actively communicating, as Lesczynski was then doing by banging on his cell wall, called for torture and irons.

But there was work to be done. Over the years the prisoners had carefully constructed a command network based on rank, passing information from wall to wall, dropping notes into crevices near washing areas or waste dumpage spots. The "V," as they called their guards, had moved prisoners around through ten different camps, hopeful of breaking up the communications system, but in fact causing it to become universal. Policies were being articulated by Americans, to Americans. The word was spreading, from Dogpatch, near the Chinese border, to the brutal Briarpatch far west of Hanoi along the Red River, in the basement cells of Son Tay, and the shadowed dungeons of Faith, Skidrow, D-1, and Rockpile. It usually originated in the four Hanoi camps—the Zoo and its annex, the Hilton, Alcatraz where James Stockdale, Jeremiah Denton, and the other leaders had spent years in isolation, or in the Plantation, the showpiece camp for visitors on "peace missions," where the few collaborators dwelled among others who were treated less well. It might take weeks or even months for a message to circulate throughout the camps but in the afternoons, while the "V" took their siestas, the prisoners worked at it.

Under the covert command structure, Lesczynski was the senior officer in Building Four of the annex. It was his responsibility to help solve problems, to relay the policies of the senior officers, to keep a head count of prisoners in his building, and to keep a memory bank of names, injuries, and medical conditions, since prisoners were allowed no writing materials. He tried to keep the other prisoners aware of who was being interrogated by the "V," and what questions were being asked. It was also up to him to set the level of resistance to the "V"'s demands. Resistance was essential. Navy Captain James Bond Stockdale, the senior ranking officer and a prisoner since 1965, had set the parameters years before, in what was called a "BACK US" policy. Simply put, it meant that American prisoners gave nothing to the enemy without resisting to the point of personal harm. "US" stood for "unity over self."

Lesczynski knew that he and the others were not prisoners of war in the traditional sense. He had spent fifteen years in intense study of military and social history, and had seen the difference begin to evolve with the men taken prisoner by the North Koreans. He knew that, by tradition, war prisoners were simply men put on ice until the hostilities were finished. True, brutalities had been common, particularly in the Orient, and conditions inside prisoner of war camps had historically been cruel. But Vietnam was a political, rather than a military war, and Lesczynski and the others were political pawns. Far from being put on ice, they were in many ways the centerpiece.

Even Lesczynski's interrogators freely admitted that the United States could have defeated North Vietnam militarily, with one fierce rush of air power, if it had been willing to take the political risk in the world community. "Why won't your President bomb Hanoi with B-52s?" prodded Rabbit, again and again. "The war would be over in a few weeks." The limited use of American military force had been a political decision. And the enemy's campaigns in the South were political, tied to media and American political events. His guards often boasted that they had driven Lyndon Johnson out of office.

So the prisoners were political entities. It was the only reason, Lesczynski firmly believed, that many of them had been kept alive at all. On the one hand, they were hostages, bargaining chips at the conference table to be traded off for American concessions. On the other, they were the ultimate propaganda devices. "Confessions" of criminal acts, "reassurances" to visiting "peace" delegations of their "humane and lenient treatment," "revelations" regarding the politics of the war, all were priceless pieces of disinformation extracted from professional men, many of whom had distinguished reputations. The American public did not see the beatings and the disfigurement that preceded such statements. Visiting delegations most often were shown the weaker prisoners and the few collaborators who had displayed a "proper attitude." Others who attempted, carefully and subtly, to display scars from rope tortures and beatings or to speak of their maltreatment were chided by the peace delegations themselves as being "attitude cases."

The vitriole that was coming from the American peace movement at first stunned the American prisoners, ate away at their festering, worm-ridden intestines. There were loudspeakers in every cell and throughout the day the propaganda battered them, Hanoi Hannah in the morning and the evening with news of the war down South, her listing of American casualties by name, her music that was primarily antiwar songs. North Vietnamese news broadcasts about the war abounded in exaggerations. Lesczynski had been particularly amused at one report that proclaimed more F-4 Phantoms downed by North Vietnamese gunners than he knew had ever been manufactured. Fellow prisoners read news reports and American articles favorable to Hanoi over the air. Lesczynski was aware that most of the broadcasts had been "purchased" by the North Vietnamese guards. The price, worked out by the underground American command structure, was a week in leg irons before a prisoner would submit.

All of this they understood. But as the war lost its momentum, and particularly after the Tet Offensive of 1968, their loudspeakers were filled with statements from Americans at home, politicians and celebrities who were saying voluntarily what they themselves had refused under torture to broadcast or write. At first it hurt. Later, it became a victory, in some small way. *See,* they could say to their interrogators. *See what we have been fighting for? A system that allows the exchange of ideas, that encourages dissent.*

"What would happen to these people in your system, if they spoke against your government?" Lesczynski had carefully asked Rabbit one evening during a lengthy interrogation when the somber camp commander had thrown the antiwar movement in his face.

Rabbit had not hesitated. "We would take them out of this society and we would reeducate them. If they learned the proper attitude, we would allow them to reenter society."

Lesczynski had seen such prisoners in the shadows of Hoa Lo. The prison was a principal political reeducation center for all of North Vietnam. Those who could not conform spent their years inside its dark rooms, locked away for the crime of individuality.

The taps came back from the other side of the wall, as rapid as a teletype. Lesczynski spoke softly, relaying the information to Friedersdorf, so that they could later discuss it and commit it to memory.

"Rabbit quizzed Oglesby. Used the ropes. Wants cooperation for Japanese film crew doing Hanoi story on air war. Wants Oglesby to play downed pilot being captured for movie. Oglesby says no." That was good. It was one of the principal rules of resistance: no trips "out in town" that could be used for propaganda. Lesczynski felt a sliver of sadness, thinking of the Japanese watching such a film and at the same time wondering what his friend Kosaka thought of him, now that he had been taken prisoner. Would Kosaka hate him if he ever got out of this hell? Did *Bushido* still hold that power over the Japanese, that a man who had not fought until death had stained himself into eternity? Indeed, what did it mean to fight until death? Wasn't that exactly what he had been doing for the past three years? And did Kosaka even know he had been shot down? Lesczynski had not been allowed a letter from the outside during his entire captivity. The only personal news came from more recent shootdowns, and the tapping on his wall was doing that just now.

"New shootdown, Room Eight. Linkins, Roger C. Lieutenant. Navy. F-4's, off the *Essex*." Lesczynski recognized the name immediately. Linkins had been with him on the *Shiloh* three years before, as a young junior grade lieutenant on his first WESPAC deployment. "Says sideburns are 'in,' Johnny Cash has his own TV show, Sophie and kids fine, J.J. all-state linebacker."

The room grew completely silent. After a long moment, Friedersdorf whispered back, his voice intense as he continued to "clear the hallway" for guards. "Is that it?"

No answer. Finally he looked up, and saw Red Lesczynski leaning back against the wall, his good hand masking gaunt eyes. The cup was on the floor. Lesczynski was sobbing, squeezing his eyes, his thin, scarred body curled forward so that his right elbow was pushed into his stomach as the other arm dangled, like a piece of rope.

"Are you okay, Red?"

"I'm fine, I'm fine." Lesczynski looked over to his roommate, managing a smile. "Did you hear that? My boy made all-state!"

* * *

Then came the Summer of Horror.

In May two prisoners made an escape attempt. They had planned it for a year, secretly building up their strength through calisthenics and jogging inside their cell, saving iodine diarrhea pills and mixing them with brick dust and water to darken their skins, making conical hats from bamboo strips taken out of their sleeping mats, making knives from pieces of metal they found during cleanup details in the yard. They would try to make it to the Red River, and steal a succession of boats until they reached the South China Sea, where hopefully the U. S. Navy would find them before the North Vietnamese did.

Escape was encouraged by the U. S. Code of Conduct, so the other prisoners could not condemn the attempt. But many believed it would fail, and that the other prisoners would pay. So when the message was tapped to Red Lesczynski on May 10 that Dramesi and Atterbury had gone over the wall, escaping from a room under his responsibility as building SRO, he began waiting for the ropes and hoses, counting the hours, trying to put them out of his thoughts but dwelling on them, knowing he would soon be seeing Rat and Sweetpea, Soft Soap Fairy, and maybe even Fidel, the visiting interrogator on loan from Cuba, who delighted in his "hands-on" tour spent torturing Americans.

The North Vietnamese found the two escapees the next morning, huddled inside thick foliage against the wall of an old church a few miles away. Back at the prison, an infuriated and embarrassed Rabbit placed them on starvation rations and put them in isolation, across a courtyard from each other. Then for thirty-two days and nights the men were kept in leg irons and beaten continually, hung from the ceiling on ropes by their elbows, kept from even sleeping. Lesczynski and the others could hear the screams. They haunted the compound day and night, banshee wails in the still heat from men on the edge of death. Bug, whose enjoyment of his work was fully evil, was working on Atterbury. After several weeks, the screams ceased from his side of the compound. Atterbury had died from the torture.

On the night of June 12, Lesczynski heard Ashley Asthmatic

coughing as he made his way down the dank hallway toward his cell, and he nodded with resignation to Friedersdorf, feeling a certainty about what was to come.

"Just tell Sophie."

"Hang in there, Red. I'll pray for you."

Ashley Asthmatic opened the cell door, his face a mask. He coughed, avoiding Lesczynski's eyes, and pointed toward the floor. "Bring cup."

Lesczynski picked up his drinking cup. It was a signal that it would be a long night. Ashley Asthmatic's bayonet prodded him down the hallway, through the darkened courtyard and into one of the Quiz Rooms. Rat was waiting for him, standing underneath a dim light. The room stank of other people's sweat and feces. Two faceless guards stood in opposite corners, like prizefighters awaiting a bell. He could not see them clearly, but he saw the rubber whips they carried. Cut from automobile tires, the "fan belts" could slice a man's buttocks into hamburger.

Lesczynski bowed to Rat. This was no time for petty resistance. *"Bao cao."*

Rat's pointed, shrewish face measured him. "If you do not tell us what we want, you will be severely punished. Get on your knees."

They manacled his ankles. Rat paced slowly in front of him. "Who is the Escape Committee?"

There had been no Escape Committee. Dramesi and Atterbury had acted on their own. "There wasn't one."

A boot kicked him hard in the back of the head, flattening him. Two men yanked down his trousers, baring his middle from knees to shoulders. Suddenly one of the mystery guards jogged out of the shadows, growling and screaming, and hacked at Lescynski's back and buttocks with the fan belt, again and again, grunting with effort, as if he were delivering karate chops. As soon as he moved away, temporarily spent, the other guard moved forward, screaming and lunging, battering Lesczynski with his whip.

Tag team, thought Lesczynski, trying to withdraw from his body, to focus his pain somewhere on the dank boards that covered the window so that the pain would not be a part of it. He had learned to divide himself during interrogations, to separate his spirit and mental functions from the physical parts that they controlled. It had taken a year or so. After that, the only danger was that his body would be destroyed and the rest of him could not reenter it after they were finished. It had happened to Atterbury, only days before.

Lesczynski was bleeding. He could feel it trickling down his sides and gathering in the mat of dirt and cobwebs underneath him. A guard pulled him by his hair, back up to the kneeling position.

Rat sat wearily on a stool in front of him. "If you answer my questions correctly, you can go. If not, we stay here until the cows come home." The North Vietnamese liked to try American slang during their interrogations. Rat feigned patience, speaking softly. "Who is the Escape Committee?"

"There is no Escape Committee."

"*You* are Escape Committee! You are senior officer! You gave orders for escape!"

"I didn't give any orders for escape."

They lifted him onto a table. One of the mystery guards took a bamboo club and methodically began beating his shins, breaking the cartilage inch by inch. He slammed the club as if he were working an ax, feeling the shinbone as he worked, concentrating with the intensity of a doctor performing a precise medical service.

Lesczynski was out of his body now. He watched the guard work, reciting a poem he had learned as a boy, *It matters not how strait the gate, how charged with punishments the scroll, I am the master of my fate, I am the captain of my soul . . .*

Rat left the room, as if uninterested. They bound Lesczynski's arms behind him, mindless of the separated humerus bone, tightening the ropes until his elbows touched and his sternum felt in danger of coming apart. The guards were out of control. They had been unleashed during the weeks before, and in the wake of Dramesi's torture and Atterbury's death, they were like sharks gone crazy at the smell of blood. All of their hostilities, their repressed hatred toward Americans and their superiors and their sorry miserable lives, had spilled over into unremitting blows.

They hung Lesczynski upside down on a meat hook and beat him for hours, pulverizing his face with his own rubber sandals, slapping him again and again, unspeaking, trying to make him beg.

Toward dawn, Rat reentered the room. He sat behind the table. Lesczynski was dropped from the meat hook and made to kneel before him. Rat ordered the ropes untied. A guard gave Lesczynski a cigarette. His arms were too numb to smoke it. He could hear another

man screaming from torture nearby, in another Quiz Room. Rat gave
him a sip of water, his first since he had left his cell.

"Who are the senior prisoners in your communications network?"

Unity over self, unity over self . . . "I don't know about any communications network."

He knelt through the entire day. In the afternoon he lost control of
his bowels. Rat shook his head as Lesczynski shit onto the floor, as if
Lesczynski were a child who had fouled his diapers. The tag team
beat him again and again. His legs and buttocks were swollen, fibrous.

He spent the next night on a stool, holding his manacled hands over
his head. Every time they dropped even an inch a guard would
deliver a rabbit punch to his neck. Every few hours, Rat would reap-
pear and ask a few questions.

"Who is the Escape Committee? Who issued the orders to escape?
Who are the communicators?"

"I don't know."

He spent the next day on his knees again. They had swollen during
the night on the stool, and they split during the day. His buttocks
were purple. They oozed pus and blood when he was beaten again.

Over the next few days—he had lost track of them, he had been
without sleep for five or six days, now, it was unclear anymore—the
wounds on his knees began to leave narrow trails of pus every time
they moved him from his kneeling position. They were feeding him a
small piece of bread and a cup of water twice a day. He had fouled
himself so repeatedly that his feces simply mixed with the other viscous rivulets running onto the floor from his limbs and back and buttocks.

In the hours between interrogations, as he knelt before Rat's table,
he escaped inside his mind, treating himself to visions of railroad
tracks above the park in Ford City, his father heaving in the heat, a
heavy foundry worker's arm upon his shoulder, *we're so proud of you,
son. Come on down to the Falcon Club, we'll get a beer and I'll show
you your wall. There must be thirty guys waiting to meet you!* And to
Sophie, bright-faced and eighteen, huddled uncertainly against him
on the couch of his parents' home after the recruiter had left the house
twenty-three years before, *I'm going to be a pilot, Sophie! We'll see
the world, the whole world!* And to Baba, shawl around her, a gnarled
fist up in the air as she screamed to the whole neighborhood, was she

watching over him? *Hey, my Stasu, he go Annapolis, learn be boat captain, be REAL AMERICAN!*

There would be music, polkas with the resin rising in his memory until it tickled his nose. He saw his children, Katherine's delicate, inquiring eyes, Johnny working on a bicycle, J.J. running, always J.J. was running. *My boy made all-state, how about that, all-state!*

After eleven days—Rat had told him it was eleven days—they hooked him onto an electric current, a wire on each arm. The questions came and his body filled with whirring currents that pulsed him, lifted his knees up off the floor, and he slowly realized that he, too, might soon die, that they had killed Atterbury and would kill him, too, perhaps for the sake of discipline in the compound. And who would ever know, who outside of this grimy, stench-ridden hell would ever even believe? The screams from the other Quiz Rooms had been unremitting for days. He had to tell them something.

"*I am the Escape Committee!* Me! It was me!"

They took down all the information, as greedily as if he were giving them the secret to life, which in a way he was. He made it up as he went along, describing exactly how he was going to leave the compound—through the front door, naturally. He was going to break down the door, because he was so strong. He was going to float in the canals until they reached the Red River, and then float to the sea. He was a strong swimmer. He would use the side stroke and the back stroke. His bad arm would be a rudder. He would float on the sea until the Navy task force passed by and saw him. He figured he could float for a week or so.

They demanded that he make one last penance, a tape of apology. "We won't force you," stated Rabbit, the camp commander, as if the past three years of brutality had never occurred. "You must do it of your own free will. If we forced you, we would look bad in the eyes of the world."

Of course. Of course. So he wrote a "confession" for them, and read it into the tape recorder, of his own free will. His voice was a faded, husky monotone. "During the past eleven days, I have had many sleepless nights to contemplate my past behavior, and when I return to my room I will fully understand the meaning of the Democratic Republic of Vietnam's humane and lenient treatment. I do apologize to the camp commander."

And then they fed him and cleaned him up. Neither arm worked well enough to bring either soap or food to his face. They put him into a new cell. When he walked through the doorway, his two new roommates stared in awful disbelief at the skeletal frame, the puffed skin and the sagging eyes, and the dangling, useless arms of Red Lesczynski, Navy football hero, Blue Angel, instrument of propaganda.

So passed the summer of 1969.

II

Sophie Lesczynski waved good-bye to Katherine and Johnny as they headed down the sidewalk on their way to school. She watched them saunter along the street, until they turned a corner and disappeared. She closed the door and locked it, and then checked the lock and locked it again. In the kitchen, she stacked the breakfast dishes in the sink and ran hot water over them, leaving them to soak. Then, standing alone next to the kitchen table, she took off her bathrobe and flung it onto the floor, and began walking naked through the house.

Her full breasts bounced as she walked. She held them gently for a few moments, massaging the nipples that had nurtured three children and had been Red's perpetual playground. Fallow, they were, but not by choice. She pinched the nipples, rolling them in her fingertips. The mix of pain and sensuality stirred her memories, moistened her vagina.

He was everywhere around her. His quick laugh careened off darkened walls. His huge hands grasped skeins of his own hair as he studied at his desk. His deep voice muttered about long-dead wars as he prepared to disappear inside the vortex of a new one. She could see him on the couch, quizzing Katherine about decimals and fractions, and on the floor, wrestling with the boys. He beamed at her from a wall full of pictures in the basement alcove that was his study. A pencil and a pad still sat on the desk where he had left them before deploying, almost four years before. No one touched them. It had become a superstition.

In the bedroom he was with her, as real and yet as intangible as the air she breathed. She could feel him there. His presence was a sustenant, as vital as oxygen. But she could not see him or hold him, any more than she could see or touch the air. His clothes in the closet defined him, size and taste. She could still smell him in his pillow. The heavy manly odor from hot summer nights and from the afterwash of their passion had penetrated the fabric, a molecule at a time over the years until it smelled faintly of Red Lesczynski, needing a bath.

But that was all right. In fact, it was precious. She lay on the sheets and clutched the pillow to her nakedness, feeling faintly like a pubescent girl dreaming of adulthood. Then she walked to her dresser and squeezed a gob of body lotion into her hands, and began massaging it into her breasts. Her breasts glistened with it in the shadowed room. She squeezed another handful of it and rubbed it onto her stomach, and between her legs.

She hated the vibrator. It left her with an emptiness, a sense of guilt made acute by years of Catholic schools, the nuns admonishing her about the sinfulness of her body from the first months before puberty when her breasts had begun to swell and the boys had sat, awestricken, watching her movements. But she could never consider adultery. It would not be worth forty years of regret, a temporary convenience that would cause his own hands always to feel different on her body. And she would not let her passions atrophy and die, she was too young for that, *I'm forty, forty, I won't get dry and shrill.* The vibrator slid slowly along her breasts, then down past her stomach, and she breathed heavily, turning her head.

She and Red were running through the sea at Pensacola, half dressed, the passing cars honking at them and Red watching toward the western sky as the SNJ Texans buzzed and dove. Freedom was in his eyes, earthly passion, and he embraced her in the sand. And then that night she bounced on the bed as if it were a trampoline, calling to him, laughing, her breasts balloons in front of her, and soon he was on her, heavy and strong, in control. They were young and joyous and they would always be young, always joyous, they would always pass their strength into each other like this, yes, yes, that was life . . .

"Oh, Red! Red, Red, Red, where are you, Red?"

* * *

It wasn't enough to be a good citizen anymore. Good citizens got lost in the shuffle. That had been the great mistake of the wives whose husbands had been taken prisoner—unbounded loyalty. In the end, they had Sybil Stockdale to thank. And they could bless their luck that Richard Nixon cared.

He might indeed have been a racist and a sexist and a fascist and an imperialist, Sophie didn't really know. Newspaper and television reportage had become so shrill and irresponsible, so obsessed with defacing societal institutions while at the same time hero-worshiping every dissent movement imaginable, that she didn't believe anything they said, anymore, anyway. He might also have been using the POW wives as political symbols to rally the country behind the war effort, as Dorothy Dingenfelder maintained in a telephone call, the first and only telephone call that Dorothy had bothered to make since coming to Congress, but that was irrelevant in most aspects, and perfectly fine in others. Maybe the POW wives were using *Nixon,* Sophie responded to Dorothy, a lilt in her voice, asking the California Congresswoman what *she* had said or done lately to express concern over the men held captive or not yet accounted for by the North Vietnamese. And maybe the POW wives *wanted* the country to rally around the war effort.

All she knew was that Lyndon Johnson's administration had done everything in its power to keep the American people from knowing what her husband and the others were going through, while Richard Nixon had completely reversed the policy, and had even met personally with many of the wives to discuss it. Under Johnson, the wives were forbidden to communicate with each other, much less the press, ironically the same restriction that the North Vietnamese were forcing on their husbands in the torture camps. The Department of Defense continually admonished them not to discuss their husbands' captivity publicly, "in the interest of the men." It even refused to release the names of other POW wives who were living nearby, so that the women might share their burden of public silence. DOD went so far as requiring one wife who delivered a baby after her husband had become a prisoner to register in a military hospital under a vague rubric of "husband's whereabouts unknown." The woman had given birth to her son under the presumption that she had been deserted.

DOD justified its restrictions under the World War II rationale of aiding those who were still evading captivity. But no one had been able to evade captivity in the North for longer than a few weeks. It became clear, after a year or so, that it was a convenient way to play on the wives' loyalties and fears in order to suppress the issue. Lyndon Johnson had been inundated with enough problems without being faced with an organized group of POW wives offering comment on an indecisive war policy that was spending their husbands in a steady, incessant trickle for the honor of blowing away railroad tracks and trees.

It was possible, actually, that by the time Nixon assumed office, he had no choice but to recognize the women, and the only way for him to recognize them was to join them. They had slowly come together in spite of DOD, bridge clubs and Christmas cards and phone calls in the night identifying other wives who knew still other wives, the sharing of information actually enhancing the discontent, reinforcing the

belief that Lyndon Johnson was a broken, paralyzed man and McNamara an unapproachable technician, and that they would have to do
something themselves.

Their frustration had been compounded by the January 1968 capture of the U.S.S. *Pueblo* by the North Koreans. The wives of its crew
defied the Administration by immediately going public, demanding
humane treatment for their husbands, and the media responded with
such vehemence that in only eleven months the men were released.
And here in dutiful silence sat the loyal wives of the Vietnam warriors, some of them now having already waited for four years without
so much as Lyndon Johnson's public acknowledgment that their husbands were rotting in the hellholes of Hoa Lo and other prisons, the
only public information being the prisoners' "confessions" of complic-
ity in war crimes and the "praise" of their lenient treatment at the
hands of the North Vietnamese, vital propaganda that was used often
and intensively by the antiwar movement.

Sybil Stockdale had called from California one night in early 1968,
wanting to begin a "families" organization that could bring the wives
together, and organize a media campaign, a communications network.
A schoolteacher with four children, she was as tough and as perse-
vering as her imprisoned husband. Soon the wives were issuing a
monthly newsletter, calling themselves "The National League of Families," gaining new members by leaps and bounds. The Department
of Defense asked them to stop it. DOD organized a series of "receptions," seeking to quell the discontent with typical military slide shows
regarding the statistics of the war. The wives used the time to intro-
duce themselves, and to develop their own memory bank of names to
add to the league's mailing list. The league had become a movement.
The wives had stopped listening to the government after four years of
being isolated, without its support.

They wrote to members of Congress. They sent mailings to key
newspapers throughout the country, met with their editorial boards,
tried to make uninterested reporters understand the distinction between being a maltreated prisoner of war and being a tortured propaganda tool. The North Vietnamese had yet to give so much as an accounting of those shot down. *Are we wives or widows?* It became a
slogan, and it caught on.

The day after Richard Nixon took office, he received two thousand
telegrams from POW/MIA families, asking that he take public notice.
And he did. Soon Sophie Lesczynski found herself invited to the

White House, along with several dozen others. They waited in the press room just inside the Rose Garden, awed and stunned to see men so often reported on in the media walking casually by, Haldeman with his crew cut and boyish face finally ushering in the President himself. Nixon was smaller than she had imagined. He had a nice smile. He did not have shifty eyes. He shook hands with every wife. He had been briefed on each of their husbands. He told Sophie he had seen Red Lesczynski fly with the Blue Angels. It didn't matter if he really had or not. What a nice thing to say, after three years of nothing.

Every month or two after that, the wives were invited to the Roosevelt Room at the White House for an update on the war, and on the POW situation. Often Kissinger, fat and small, gave them the talk, caustically estimating the chances of their husbands' release over the next six months in percentages, 50 percent one month, 30 percent three months later, as if he were forecasting rain. Sometimes Defense Secretary Laird met with them, his bald square head scanning their midst continuously, like a radar antenna, and his cautious, flitting eyes making Sophie Lesczynski wonder if he feared violence from them. But it was a time of violence, of raw hate, and she thought, perhaps, that Laird was shell-shocked from his other battles. And she would feel guilty again for taking the man's time. Nixon, Kissinger, Laird— *What right do I have?* she would think, ever the good Navy wife. *I just want my husband back. They've got more important things to do than brief me on the war.*

* * *

"Mrs. Lesczynski?"

"Yes?"

She had answered the kitchen phone. It was July 1969. Things were falling apart. J.J. had attempted to enlist in the Marine Corps on June 10, having convinced her to give her permission, because his father would have wanted it that way. The Marine recruiter, who had learned during their conversation that his father was a prisoner, had taken J.J. into a back room and persuaded him to stay home. *You got a good kid, ma'am,* the Marine had told her when he dropped J.J. off at their house. *But I just couldn't do it to your family.*

Sophie looked out at the backyard. Under its heavy shade trees, Katherine sat on the grass, reading a book. She worried about Katherine. The doe-eyed girl was becoming more withdrawn every day, even as she grew into tall, delicate womanhood.

The voice on the phone interrupted her thoughts. "I'm Roscoe Mantle. You probably don't know me. I'm a member of Congress from Tennessee." He waited for some word of recognition, and received none. "I was with your husband in 1963 on the congressional trip to Saigon. A fine man, a truly great American."

He waited again. She had to say something. "Well, thank you, Congressman. But Red's not here."

"Dad blame it, I *know* that. I'm sorry for hitting you up like this, I know how much it must hurt you anyway, but I saw a little article they did on you and the other girls for the *Star* the other day, and I want you to know it hurt me, Mrs. Lesczynski. It *hurt* me. I saw the name and I recognized it. I knew it was the same Commander Lesczynski. How many Lesczynskis can there be who are Navy pilots, anyway? And I hadn't heard anything about him since our trip. I'd often thought I might be seeing him in the Pentagon as an admiral real soon. But here I've been raising such a fuss, making all these speeches supporting the war—I do continue to support the war, understand—but I've not done a thing to help these boys who are prisoners. If you can come see me, I've got an idea."

"An idea?" There had been no ideas, none. There had only been expressions of anger and helplessness, and percentage forecasts.

Roscoe Mantle had piled up twenty-three years in the Congress, having been elected from his middle Tennessee district as he lay in a hospital bed, recovering from World War II wounds. A heavily decorated infantry veteran, he had sought a seat on the Veterans Affairs Committee and by 1968 had become its chairman. He had helped author the GI Bill, and had been a sponsor of every important piece of veterans legislation of the post-World War II era.

Members of the organized veterans groups had nicknamed Roscoe Mantle "Mr. Veteran." His name was mentioned with reverence in veterans' posts throughout the country. He was a stocky, fiery man, given to flowery prose, who ruled his domain, which was responsible for the well-being of almost 30 million veterans, with a jealous firmness.

The American War Veterans, a group 2 million strong, was looking for its annual crusade project, to be unveiled shortly at its national convention, and Roscoe Mantle had just chosen it for them. The American War Veterans were going to crusade on behalf of the Vietnam prisoners of war. They were going to put Sophie Lesczynski and her fellow POW wives on the front page of every newspaper in the country. They were going to bring Sophie and a few others to Minneapolis for the national convention, where their leaders would make long speeches in praise of what the families were enduring. They were going to allocate a huge sum of money, in fact an unlimited sum, to help Sophie and the National League of Families in their efforts to bring the prisoners home. They were going to do it because Roscoe Mantle had decided they would, whether they yet knew it or not, and whether they even liked it or not.

And they ended up loving it.

Funny folk, these organized vets. They came to Minneapolis by the thousands, from places like Alma, Iowa, and Kensett, Arkansas, truck stops and back roads on the highways of American culture, to drink and relive the battles of their youth. Many were gray and flabby now, with slack jaws and thick glasses and wives who followed them as they walked, wearing new dresses and purple hair. They had purchased their right to congregate and debate American foreign policy by sailing off to places like Belleau Wood and Biak Island, to spend horror-filled moments contemplating their deaths as instruments of that same policy. It had made them fiercer, particularly as they grew older and their horror became safe, less real. They had the air of a crowd at Disneyland, walking through the lobby of the old Minneapolis Manor Hotel. Their ever-present blue caps jangled with ornaments; campaign ribbons, AWV buttons, "Longevity stars," "Trench Rat" emblems, the letterings of offices held and old war medals with battle stars.

They were confused by Vietnam. They longed for the simplicity of their own wars. By and large as they gathered over drinks at the hotel bar, and in the huge Convention Hall, they did not even want to *talk* about Vietnam. *For God's sake, let's talk about real war, the BIG one, Dub Dub II.* But when their new national commander solemnly invoked their past experience in his maiden speech, and then introduced Roscoe Mantle, Mr. Veteran, hero of Dub Dub II, guardian of freedom, who passionately railed and ranted about the antiwar movement and called on them to support a mission of patriotism, of mercy, of all that was good and loyal in America, they found themselves standing at their tables, cheering him, applauding, raising wrinkled fists into the air. *You tell 'em, Roscoe, by God!*

And when Sophie Lesczynski timidly approached the microphone, she and three other wives the only women in the Convention Hall during this evening business meeting, pristine images that recalled the veterans' youth, tugged at their memories, they melted into a hush, two thousand sets of eyes embracing her.

Why me, she thought, staring at the mass of men, the funny hats, the bright, mismatched suits and ties, the mix of covetous and fatherly faces awaiting her message. She had to stand on her toes to reach the microphone. "I think it's a wonderful thing that you're doing. Red's been gone three years, now. Three and a half, if you count his deployment time. That's as long as all of World War II, for Americans! And I haven't even been told by the North Vietnamese that he's a prisoner. So your support is the greatest lift I've had in the whole time. Thank you, so much."

Nicely said, safe and innocent, a sweet little speech by the essence of American womanhood. The new national commander put a protective arm around her and waved to his comrades, playing King for a Year, a high school coach who had been a World War II corporal and was now empowered, for the next twelve months, to comment on foreign policy as if he were Kissinger. "Mrs. Lesczynski, we think you gals are wonderful, wonderful. Whatever you want to do, you let the American War Veterans know. If you need us, you call us, you hear?"

When the new roars and applause died down, Sophie smiled brightly, awash in her innocent optimism, and tiptoed back to the microphone. *Whatever you want to do, that's what he said.* "Well, we'd like to go to Hanoi and see our husbands."

Boom. Bombshell. It hadn't been in the script. The room was silent as a morgue, and Roscoe Mantle shook his head, dumbfounded at her naïveté.

Mantle called her room at two in the morning.

"Mrs. Lesczynski, I want you girls down in my room, right now."

"Congressman, it's the middle of the night."

"Dad blame it, I know what the hell time it is, I've not been to bed yet. You don't know the trouble you've caused me. Now, get the other girls and come on down here. Come as you are, come as you are."

They shuffled into Mantle's room in robes and slippers, faces packed with eye cream, shaking off their sleepiness. One of the wives showed up with two small orange juice cans rolled into her hair, substitute rollers that were preserving her bouffant hairdo.

Mantle was pacing the room, thick arms behind his back, red suspenders holding up his white trousers, an undershirt covering his bulk. Cigar smoke lay like low fog, a four-foot stratum on the floor. Empty Scotch and beer bottles littered the table. He scowled at them, but Sophie could see the fire in his eyes. He was an idea man, and he had another idea.

"Why'd you say you wanted to go to Hanoi?"

They looked at each other for a moment, and then Sophie answered. "Well, we do."

"You won't do any good in Hanoi. They'd use you. They're masters at using people for propaganda, can't you see that?"

"We don't care, anymore, Congressman. It would be good just to see our husbands. Just to know they're alive!"

"You want to really do some good?"

They looked at each other again. "Of course we would."

"How about if we send you to meet with the North Vietnamese negotiators in Paris? Would you consider that?"

Sophie felt her jaw drop. "Congressman, I'm not a *negotiator*, I mean—" She saw the stares of the others. They wanted to do it. "Well, if you think it would do some good."

Mantle stopped pacing, his stockinged feet now bouncing with energy on the carpet. His thin lips were tight, pushing his jowls out like chipmunk pouches. His blue eyes were bright with determination. "Those bastards have the media bleeding and dying for them. The antiwar movement here is in the middle of a goddamn *love-in* with the media. Maybe *we* need a few media events."

❖ ❖ ❖

On their first trip to Paris, the wives stunned the world media. ARE WE WIVES OR WIDOWS made it onto the front pages of newspapers everywhere. Sophie Lesczynski, world traveler, international negotiator, was filmed in front of the North Vietnamese embassy, speaking plainly, without undue emotion, of how her husband had been paraded through downtown Hanoi on the back of a truck more than three years before, and had not been seen or heard from since. One letter. Four lines, Christmas 1966. The North Vietnamese began to claim that all prisoners had received humane and lenient treatment and Douglas Hegdahl, a Navy seaman recently released after two years' captivity, embarrassed them before the world by stating calmly that he had been a prisoner inside the camps, and that he knew the truth. Hegdahl was a ringer on the Paris trip. An enlisted man who had bamboozled his captors into releasing him by playing dumb, he was a man with a mission: to expose the North Vietnamese as liars.

The wives' second trip took place in November, at almost the same time the antiwar movement was staging its massive Vietnam Moratorium in Washington, D.C., and elsewhere. The day before Sophie left, the news was full of images that had the undeniable media impact of a Hitlerian rally: four columns of marchers, a quarter of a million of them descending on DuPont Circle in Washington from the four streets that fed into it, dozens of red and blue Viet Cong banners at their fronts, night torches, interminable chants, "HO, HO, HO CHI MINH, THE NLF IS GONNA WIN." So perfectly organized for television, so dramatic, so frightening to Sophie Lesczynski, who upon seeing it for some reason could think only of Poland, squashed by Nazis, counter-squashed by communists. It was all the same. Cruel ideology, people who wanted to control, produced chants and banners and people marching. *Were these Americans, AMERICANS? Who were they hurting by doing this? Who were they helping?*

The morning she left, news of the Paris trip was buried inside the front page. The lead story regarding Vietnam, mixed with news of the defeat of Clement Haynsworth's Supreme Court nomination and Indians taking over Alcatraz Island, perfectly and deliberately timed, was about Dorothy Dingenfelder.

CALIFORNIA CONGRESSWOMAN REVEALS
SOUTH VIET TORTURE PRISONS
Says Political Dissidents Kept in "Tiger Cages" Used
on Con Son Island

A California congresswoman with close ties to the National Mobilization Committee to End the War today charged the South Vietnamese government with operating a "concentration camp style" prison for political prisoners on an island off the coast of Vietnam. Dorothy Dingenfelder stated in a press conference held in the Cannon House Office Building that as many as seven thousand Vietnamese dissidents are being held on Con Son Island, many of them kept in so-called "tiger cages" and fed a ration of two bowls of rice a day. "It is unconscionable," noted Dingenfelder, "that we continue to support a government that denies its citizens the basic right to dissent . . ."

Dorothy, thought Sophie Lesczynski, reading the article and knowing that the revelation would be the focus of debate by the North

Vietnamese delegation when she reached Paris, a rejoinder to the wives, would be used as a piece of disinformation designed to rescue the communists from the sting of world opinion. *Dorothy, why'd you do that, Dorothy?*

CHAPTER TWENTY-FIVE

I

SPRING, 1970 CAME GENTLY, crawling week by week over the mountains to the south, a valley at a time, so that the grass was green in nearby Poor Valley and in Clinch while it stayed brown on the steep slope behind her house for ten more days. Along Smith Hollow the vegetable gardens went in and the tobacco seedbeds were sown and covered with plastic and in the mornings heavy fog poured over the mountaintops and curled, gray and wispy, in the low places. She became thankful for the slow thaw, watching Judd Smith crawl backward out of bed on dim gray mornings, hobbling on a bullet-scarred ankle in the cold house and through the fields outside, groaning and creaking, his memories back inside a Korean winter spent huddled over trash fires with a frostbitten face and lungs scorched from icy air. Judd Smith was forty-three, but the cold made him stiff and old.

He had built her a new home, or rather he had decreed that he would and then had quietly begun the task, sawing and hammering by himself. Soon groups of men showed up at odd hours, parishioners with varied skills who worked all day at their jobs for pay and then worked afterward for good old Preacher Smith, refusing so much as a cola in return. Judd insisted on buying the parts, lumber, and appliances. The labor was a gift, their most honest form of thanks. It was done within a month, every corner squared and finished, professionally wired, three bedrooms, two toilets, each with a bath, and a modern kitchen that even boasted of a dishwasher. The women wove more quilts and braided rugs, and when it was finished a dozen families showed up with pies and coffee. Judd Smith asked the Lord's blessing on them all, and on the house.

Other men kept coming. They had soft hands and uncreased faces and they wore suits. Sometimes they brought TV cameras and filmed Judd Smith in his living room as he spoke with quiet passion about the war, about the frail balance in a free society between dissent and loyalty, about racial hatred and drugs and the rights of criminals. He had a defensiveness about black people that had disarmed her, even fifteen years before, when he and her father had debated desegregation. Slowly, she came to realize that Judd Smith took it personally, that he felt nearer to the blacks than he did to many whites, first because he was part Indian, and secondly because he and the other mountain people had never been a part of a white hierarchy, anyway. There was nothing in Bear Mountain County for the blacks or anyone else to take away, except the land, and they would yield their land to no one, for no reason, not ever. No foreign fortune could lure away an acre of their rocks and ridges. The land passed down by family, or was sold quietly within the community for a perfunctory pittance.

Criminals and those who engaged in provocative dissent fared less well with Judd Smith. They tore at the heart of his values, and he attacked them before camera after camera. And still the soft men kept coming, and when the Republican party paid a visit, asking if he would run for Congress since the incumbent had decided to retire, she knew her quiet respite would soon be lost to the storms of politics. For almost two years she had sated herself with solitude as if it were ambrosia, feeling immortal in her contentment. Before that, she had spent a lifetime as something of a gilded ornament, smiling in public places, watching a father and then a husband speak boxy words before cameras and querying eyes that searched for flaws. She had had enough of it. Did Judd really understand politics? Did he know what treachery, what hate lay on the other side of those seductive sirens who sang promises of titles and pomp?

Every morning he prayed his thanks for their new life, and for his good fortune. And silently she begged his God to send him earwax.

And it almost happened, the refusal, not because he did not hear the voices but because he listened too well. The soft men had misread him and they began uttering their expectations as if they were demands, different positions to take on certain issues, none of them as important as the implication that they were crowding his freedom, trying to own his conscience. He had thanked them politely for having considered him, and then informed them that he did not like their thinking that they could tell him how to vote or what to say.

Then the newspapers and even the television stations began reporting that Judd Smith, the Fighting Preacher, had declined the invitation to run for Congress in the Eleventh District because he was afraid of exposing his wife and his vocation to the rigors of a nasty campaign. The reports had not been unkind and in fact had been protective, but that in itself aroused a feeling in him that now the media felt it owned him, and could shield him from the harshness of a world he had done battle with forever, and here it came again, Judd Smith stomping around his new house, his lips tight and his fists in balls, *Pride, get thee behind me . . .*

"*I will not have people think I'm afraid to defend my beliefs and my acts in public!*"

✿ ✿ ✿

Loretta pointed to the front as they drove slowly down a dusty back road in the early autumn heat. "Here you go, Dad." She nudged him, a teasing encouragement. "Shine, brother, shine. The Fighting Preacher strikes again."

"Loretta, that borders on sacrilege."

"Aw, come on, Dad." At fourteen, she had a grown woman's insight into human nature. "You're getting too stiff! *That* borders on hypocrisy."

"Shut your mouth. I ought to whack you." Judd Smith was smiling, though. She was right. You could only visit a few dozen stores and veterans' posts and farms on any given day before it made you numb to the very things you cared about.

MAXWELL'S GROCERY STORE. It was about as large as somebody's living room, and like so many other stores, it had been in the back country for perhaps a century. Such stores were gathering points for outlying farmers. The farmers and their families bought small staples at the stores, and mingled there on weekends. They were important campaign centers in rural districts.

The rear of the store stood precariously on wooden poles over a narrow, rushing stream. Its front bordered the dirt road. Steep green hills rose on the other side of the road from the store, and across a narrow field from the stream in back of it. The hills were shot with large gray ledges of rock, and bunches of hardwood trees. The road curved around through more hills, and disappeared among pastures and tobacco patches. White frame houses were scattered along the hills and narrow valleys, surrounded by unpainted outbuildings.

Smith halted the car. A curtain of dust blew past them from the rear. They let it go by, and then entered the store. A woman who was perhaps sixty sat behind the small counter, embroidering and listening to the radio. Paul Harvey was coming to her from Chicago, talking about American values.

Judd Smith smiled warmly. She tilted her head, studying his ear and his casual clothes, then gave him a cautious nod in return.

"Evening, ma'am. I'd like two RC Colas, and a Moon Pie, for my daughter, here." He had bought enough RC Colas and Moon Pies over the past few weeks to keep both companies in business for another year.

The woman rose and moved to the counter, taking out a Moon Pie. She pointed to the cooler. "That be fifty cents. You all can just fetch yourselves some RC from yonder, now."

He handed her the money. "These hills are mighty nigh straight up and down, here, ma'am. Or as the fellow said, perpendicular."

"Yes, sir. They been like that for years." She eyed him curiously, as if she were trying to place him. He had to wait until she asked. One thing you never did in the mountains was crowd somebody, or try to impress them with your importance.

He chuckled. "Well, they ain't changed since I can remember."

"So, you ain't lost, then."

"No." He and Loretta smiled to each other and then to her. "We live over in Bear Mountain."

"Well, now, that ain't far. How's your Moon Pie, baby?"

"It's great." Loretta grinned gamely. She claimed she had gained five pounds on Moon Pies in the past month. "My dad is Preacher Smith, from Bear Mountain? He's running for Congress."

"Well, I never!" The woman smiled widely, her eyes now transfixed by Judd Smith, studying his frame and then his face. "I seen you on the television, sure enough!" She held out a hand. "I'm right *proud* to meet you, Reverend!" As he took her hand she spoke, almost conspiratorially, her chin suddenly high and her lower lip out, as if in defiance. "I don't give one hang about all the things they been saying about your wife—that must be your mama, honey—and that Williams tobacco man! Sure enough, if them Williamses had some good in 'em they'd be paying more for our tobacco, anyway. And I been following this, good sir, I want you to know. Them talking about you going off to Annapolis by fraud, 'cause you once married that Alma Coulter and didn't put it on the form! Now, what's the sense in bringing up that? My husband and my boys was saying last night, 'What's the sense in trying to rub a man's face in a thing like that, twenty years later, after he come home a hero from Korea, and then been saved?' "

Judd Smith smiled softly, sippng his RC Cola. "I surely do appreciate that. We got some real problems in this country, and whether or not I was married for three months when I was eighteen hardly counts among them."

"Now, ain't that the truth! Now, Reverend, we got this Supreme Court running the country, telling us our childrens can't pray in their schools, busing them all over the countryside so they can sit next to a little colored child—I got nothing against the coloreds, Lord knows it ain't been any of their doings—telling women to abortion their babies, saying it's all right to go on flag spitting and antiwar marching! Lord knows, I been a-following it!"

"Well, you know I feel the way you do on it. Like this school prayer thing. Freedom *of* religion never was meant to be freedom *from* religion, was it? Why is our motto 'In God We Trust'?"

She nodded, her eyes embracing Judd Smith's words. "Amen to that."

"And I can't for the life of me see the sense in our government paying for women to abort their little babies. I have to tell you, ma'am, that I don't believe, as a Christian, that I have the right to force my religion on those who don't see God the way I do. But I don't believe those others should force their morals on the whole country, either, and a government that *pays* for an abortion morally *sanctions* it. That has to stop."

"It surely does. It surely does." The woman was quiet, overwhelmed. Loretta tapped Judd Smith on the shoulder.

"Dad, we've got to get on."

"That we do, honey." Judd Smith sat the RC Cola back on the counter, almost untouched. "I do appreciate, ma'am. It's been good talking with you."

"Well, Reverend, I'm just *proud* to know you. And I hope you win, I truly do."

"Well, I believe that means I can ask you to come out and vote, then."

"We all will, if I have to drag my boys in by the ears!"

"Would you like a picture, Dad?" Loretta held a Polaroid camera.

Judd Smith smiled to the woman. "Would you like a picture for your store window, ma'am?"

"Why, I'd lavish one, Reverend!"

So Loretta took a picture of the two of them standing together in front of the counter, arm in arm, smiling at each other. And from that point on, Judd Smith adorned the front window of Maxwell's Grocery Store, deep in the hollows where the farmers came in to talk and shop, just as he did in hundreds of other stores and veterans' posts and homes.

The Williams family and its money be damned. The Democratic party and its cries of Yankee Republicanism be damned. Judd Smith was doing it the hard way, true grass roots, a blade at a time.

* * *

Julie had stopped going with him the first week of the campaign. It was too much, the way they looked at her as if she were a *femme fatale*, a Cleopatra of the mountains who was bedeviled by options— Caesar or Marc Antony? But Loretta was an avid, natural campaigner. It amazed Julie and Judd both to watch their daughter, at fourteen, discuss complex political questions with farmers and newspapermen. She had her mother's beauty and her father's tenacity. It frightened Julie Clay Smith to watch Loretta. *Her, too? Will I ever be free from watching my blood on stage?*

Earl Sherwood, who liked to call himself the "Svengali of Judd Smith's political career," was an important media ally. The last week of the campaign, Sherwood did an interview with an ailing Jackson Clay. Julie's father had to that point stayed out of the race, still the titular head of the Virginia Democratic party, torn by mixed loyalties, pressured heavily not to abandon a lifetime of passion against Republicans merely because of personal wishes. But Julie's own situation had caused sensational stories throughout the East, as well as a blurb in *Time* magazine's "People" section: *Senator's Daughter Jumps Spouses and Political Parties*. Her father's dying breaths would be spent attempting to shield his daughter.

The old senator was now past eighty, chair-ridden and hang-jawed, but still adept with words. Sherwood reminded Clay of his frequent taunt while in office, that there were only two things he would never do in life: go to bed with another man and vote for a Republican.

"Senator," Sherwood gently asked Clay, "would you vote for Judd Smith in next week's election?"

Clay had snorted. "Well, of course I wouldn't. I live in the Third District, Sherwood, you know that. Judd's running down there in the Eleventh."

"Well, what if you lived in the Eleventh?"

Clay had snorted again, giving the most careful "nonendorsement" in the history of Virginia politics. "That's the sorriest, cheatingest campaign I ever saw the Democratic party run in my long life, Mr.

Sherwood. They had no call to go after Judd Smith with that sort of tripe! He's a man of honor and principle. Everybody in the Eleventh District knows that. I'd have been a lot happier with my party if they'd have stuck to the issues, and let the voters decide who's the better man for the district."

And a week later, the voters did just that, sending the first Republican ever to the Congress from their district, with a majority of 79 percent.

Julie cried again as she packed for the trip to Washington. Life was so funny, indeed so cruel. It famished your dreams until you let them wither and die, and then gave them to you after you had ceased your craving. Sixteen years before, this trip had been more than a wish; it had been an expectation. But now it was all too complicated, too nervously exhausting. It had cost too much, and in a way it had come too late.

II

"Well, top of the morning, *Congressman!*"

Donny Stuart was waiting in the doorway of Smith's office, grinning expectantly. Smith's friend from his first days in the Marine Corps had just retired as a lieutenant colonel after twenty years active duty, which included commanding an infantry battalion in Vietnam. His last tour had been at Headquarters, Marine Corps, near the Pentagon. Judd Smith had called him after the election, and asked him to become his administrative assistant. In less than a month, Stuart had put together an eight-person congressional staff that was now functioning smoothly, preparing legislative briefs and answering constituent mail, even though Smith would not officially be sworn in as a congressman until the Ninety-second Congress convened.

They shook hands, and Stuart gestured toward Smith's private office, which was just off the receiving room. "Your quarters, sir."

"Ah, knock it off, peon."

He entered his office. Stuart followed him, their jibing banter unchanged by the years. "They ought to make a movie about this. Mr. Smith comes to Washington."

"Yeah, I called my pa last night and he says, 'Judd boy, you been up there with them muck-a-mucks two days, now. Did they teach you how to *lie* yet?'"

"That's sure enough your pa. He make you another knife?"

"No, he says the last time he made me one, it liked to killed me."

In contrast to the cramped working spaces of the staff, his office was spacious, elegant. A huge wooden desk, ornate enough to have been a legacy of Jeffersonian times, sat in front of a window that looked out on the Capitol building and an adjacent park. Cars passed slowly below the window, on Independence Avenue. It had begun to drizzle and a flock of pigeons had gathered along the edges of the window's balcony.

"Get rid of those pigeons, Stuart."

"Right, sir. Should I use a machine gun, or a grenade?"

Judd Smith laughed warmly, delighted to be sharing all of this with a friend who had endured some of the miseries with him. "Dummy, this is the Congress! You'll have to *persuade* them to leave."

"Oh, I see. We'll *threaten* to use a grenade."

"No. Organize a protest, and the weight of public opinion will force them off the balcony."

"Cute. Hey, you'll go a long way up here, Judd." Stuart surveyed the rest of the office. The high-ceilinged walls were barren of the usual array of photographs and plaques that many members cultivated as symbols of the adoration of their constituency and their ability to mingle with power. The tall, glass-doored bookcase was empty. "We need some junk on these walls, and some books in there. 'Profound' books, like maybe *The Greening of America*."

"Give me a break, Stuart."

"Well, constituents and lobbyists *like* junk and profound books. It equates to power when they walk in here."

"So, go round up some junk. Leave the profound books to Dorothy Dingenfelder."

Stuart smiled whimsically. "That's right. You and she are, ah, old friends, aren't you, Judd?"

"My *esteemed and distinguished* colleague from California?" Smith chuckled, surveying the empty walls of his office.

"Man, you should hear the stories they tell about her on the staff level, Judd. She's a real nut-cutter, I mean it. She's shifted the roles around on her staff, so that the men answer the phones and the women run the legislation and the admin stuff. She's even sent men out to buy her panty hose. No fooling!"

"Ah, Dorothy." Smith seemed to be remembering. "Where's her office?"

"Over in the Longworth Building. I can get you the room number."

"No, that's okay. I can find it." Smith punched his old friend on the shoulder, a careful, shadowy gesture of middle age, empty of the ferocity of twenty years before. "Stow it, Stuart! A man gets elected to Congress and people think he can't even find the *bathroom* anymore."

* * *

Both of the kids were now in prep school. She saw them during the holidays. That was enough. She had never been a willing mother; not that she did not love them, because she often found herself insisting, quite honestly, to friends and colleagues about how important they were to her. But she had never known how to coo and nurture, anyway, so it had been futile, and even embarrassing, to attempt to play out that role. This way she was giving them more. Natasha sensed it. She was giving Natasha her very future, with every speech she made and every bill she helped pass. Little Joe was less sure. He still wrote to Joe. In fact, he was the only one who had Joe's address, and he guarded it as if it were the lost scrolls. Not that she had tried to talk him out of it.

Her main passion was work. She worked nights. She worked weekends. She worked when the Congress was out of session. She was always available for a speech. It was how you got ahead, being available. And besides, there was little else. She had turned into herself, becoming something of an onanist. Sex had always been overrated, that was her belief. And being with a man meant giving up control. She had never been able to develop the protective logic that said a woman was using a man when he was sweating and pumping on top of her body. Who needed it?

There was so much to do. *Always* there was so much to do.

They had to shut down Nixon, cut him off from power and box him up. And they had to grab back the power itself, after forty years of congressional docility. That was becoming her great passion as a congresswoman. The legislative branch of the federal system had taken a back seat to the executive and the judicial branches since the time of Roosevelt. All branches were supposed to be coequal under the Constitution. The real monster, in Dorothy Dingenfelder's mind, was the executive branch. Executive power was the octopus, while war and civil rights and in a sense Nixon himself were merely tentacles.

She worked her staffers almost as hard as she worked herself. She had quickly gained a reputation as a member who burned through people. Her administrative and legislative assistants were turning over at a rate of one every seven or eight months, leaving gratefully for the quieter pace of other jobs.

She didn't mind about the turnover. There were plenty of good people, and every time a woman who had performed well moved on, Dorothy Dingenfelder helped her find her next job. That way, the woman would always remember, always owe her. And people who thought like Dorothy Dingenfelder, who had been intellectually trained in her very office, were beginning to dot the halls of government and law firms throughout Washington, D.C. The Network. *What was it Kennedy had said? I'll bring in the best and the brightest, the most idealistic and the most innovative. I'll work them so hard that they'll be exhausted within a year. And then I'll bring in a new entourage of the best and the brightest, the most idealistic and the most innovative. I'll work them so hard . . .*

Sharon Zimmerle, who now sat across from Dorothy in her office, had been on the staff for only a month, and yet she was now briefing Dorothy on the legislative program for the 1971 session. She had graduated from Georgetown's Law Center three years before, clerked for a federal judge, and then worked as an associate at Hintz and Dingle, a litigation firm, after that. She was an accomplished constitutional scholar, and had worked on the Hill during law school. Dorothy already had a position in mind for Sharon when she was ready to leave the staff. She didn't have a friend in the Solicitor General's office yet. Sharon Zimmerle would be perfect. *Maybe a year from now.*

Sharon dressed casually on this morning when the House was out of session, wearing blue jeans and a pullover sweater, her large breasts hanging loose underneath. She had light brown hair and blue eyes. Her hair was pulled back in a tight bun. She wore no makeup. She studied a yellow legal pad as she spoke.

"We have the ERA in the bag. Your subcommittee hearings last May and then the discharge petition to pull it out of committee have blown the lid off. I'm not kidding, Dorothy. Since November, we've gotten everybody under the sun to sign on. I count fifty-three groups endorsing, now. We just added the United Auto Workers, the National Coalition of American Nuns, and the American Newspaper Guild."

Dorothy snorted, surprised. "The National Coalition of American *Nuns?*"

Sharon laughed, crossing her legs. "Don't knock it. Maybe they want to be priests."

"Well, why shouldn't they be?"

Sharon nodded, getting back to her notes. "Indeed? Well, I recommend pushing for new hearings immediately. Maybe March. I can talk to the committee staff this week, if you want me to. Tell them you'll raise hell on the House floor and in the press if they don't move as soon as the House goes into session. Let's take advantage of the momentum we had at the end of the Ninety-first Congress. Everybody's running scared, now."

Dorothy lit a cigarette. "What about the amendment the Senate put on it? The one that continued to exempt women from the draft?"

"Our Judiciary Committee will probably try to put the same amendment on it. I say, push it to a vote." Sharon smiled, revealing straight teeth. "The timing is just too good. I don't think it will carry on the House floor. That's what's important. Once we get it out of committee, we've won. You know how members get about these things once they have to speak on the floor. Chauvinism"—she waved her hands in the air—"evaporates."

They shared a quiet laugh. Dorothy checked her watch. "All right. Do we have any support for the War Powers Resolution? I really want that one. It will screw Nixon's ass to the wall."

"I think we can do it." Sharon flipped her notes onto the next page. "I had legislative counsel draft a resolution. We made it relate directly to Article One, Section Eight, of the Constitution, rather than to the U. S. Code. That way, we can be sure to keep it in the Judiciary Committee, where you can get hearings. Basically, we're saying that the President must consult with the Congress before introducing armed forces into any hostilities, or even where hostilities may be imminent, and continue to consult after introducing troops. We then give the President sixty days. If he doesn't get a declaration of war from the Congress, or a specific approval for further operations, he has to terminate the military action."

Dorothy stubbed out her cigarette, her small face lit with delight. "Nixon will go *crazy!* Oh, that's beautiful. I'm not sure it's constitutional, but it's beautiful!"

Sharon Zimmerle was smiling, also. "There will be a separation of powers argument from the Administration, no doubt. They'll start talking about the Federalist Papers and two hundred years of presidential prerogative in the protection of American security interests, the erection of technical barriers that redefine constitutional authority, the overkill due to a dissatisfaction with our Vietnam policy. They'll probably even sue. But that's all right. The point will be made."

"And you think we can win?"

Sharon shrugged. "Not this year. This one will take a couple years of hearings, and persistence in the media. I recommend you get off early on it. Draft a 'Dear Colleague' letter that will invite cosponsors, to see what kind of support we'll have from the start. I'd estimate maybe as many as eighty cosponsors, right off the bat. Then we'll get it to a few friends on the *Times* and the *Post*. We'll arrange a joint press conference when you reintroduce the resolution. Drum up some sympathy in the hinterlands. And the whole time, Nixon will be frothing at the mouth."

Dorothy nodded slowly. She played with a pen on her desk, eyeing Sharon with a warm embrace. "You're really good, Sharon. I think we can do with that. How about lunch?"

"I'd love to."

Dorothy's buzzer rang. She picked up her phone. "Yes?"

It was her receptionist, Tom Markley. "Congressman Judd Smith is here to see you, Mrs. Dingenfelder."

Oh, for God's sake. "Tell him to wait a minute." She turned to Sharon Zimmerle. "I'll meet you in the Longworth Cafeteria, in ten minutes." Sharon departed, her breasts bouncing underneath the sweater.

She didn't need this. She had no desire to speak casually with Joe's old roommate ever again. But now, in her outer office, like some ghoul that had ridden in with the ugly January rain, Judd Smith had come a-calling. *For God's sake,* she mused again, lighting a cigarette and composing herself, staring at walls filled with pictures of herself with all the icons of the left, King and Kennedys, Berrigans and Rubin. Why doesn't he go see *his* people?

She arranged a sheaf of papers on her desk, and picked up a pen. Then she pressed her intercom buzzer, and spoke to Tom Markley again. "All right, send him in."

"Well, hey there, Dorothy! Fancy you!"

He was talking hillbilly just to irritate her, she knew that, especially when she looked up and saw him striding toward her in an impeccably tailored Donegal tweed three-piece suit, with a red silk tie carefully knotted underneath his starched collar. Gone were the T-shirts and the boots. The eagle tattoo was submerged underneath layers of fine clothing. His ear was the same, though, like an ornament, a trophy of past violence that now blended with the clothing into a pastiche of power, at once raw and refined. Judd Smith was *in control* and she felt it, as if the wind outside had blown into her face when he entered her office.

"Well, Judd." She stood, as if reluctantly drawn away from important paperwork, and formally offered him her hand. "I suppose congratulations are in order."

He stared for a moment at her hand, measuring her formality, then took it. "I get the feeling this is like two fighters shaking hands before the bell rings."

"I'll be a dog at your heels, Judd, you know that."

"Dorothy, there ain't a dog in the world that can bite as hard as a man can shoot."

She let go of his hand with a jerk, as if further contact might give her leprosy. "Just what is *that* supposed to mean?"

"Oh, nothing." He laughed at her unease, folding his arms in front of his chest and standing in the middle of her office, dominating it. "Except you don't expect me to come all the way up here just to worry about whether Dorothy Dingenfelder will praise me on the House floor, do you?" He lifted his arms up in a shrug. "I just came by to say hi. Don't get hostile."

"I hardly need to be hostile. My side is winning. Your side is losing." She leaned back on her desk, her rear end over the edge as if she were a schoolgirl. "It's just hard to be a gracious winner, that's all."

"Now, Dorothy. Don't count your chickens before they hatch. One thing about American politics is that we'll all probably live to see our views in favor at one time or another. And out of favor, too."

"Well, right now you're *out*." She gave him a small, patronizing smile, daring to allow the edges of her lips to curl into a smirk. "Everybody hates Nixon. Everybody! And do you think *anyone* can fully support our Vietnam policy after My Lai and the Kent State massacre? That's done. You've lost."

"You think about something, Dorothy, at night just before you go to sleep. You think about who really caused Kent State, okay? The antiwar movement screams about fascism, but they've *created* the conditions of fascism, and I think you know it. If you provoke a government's institutions long enough and hard enough, they'll react. Then everyone points at the reaction and they say, 'See! See, we told you!'" She had riled him, she could tell. He was pacing in front of her. He stopped again, calm now, and smiled. "And I would hope you can see the distinction between My Lai, which was a failure of policy, a policy breakdown, and a policy that has deliberately killed civilians for years. Where were you when the communists were systematically executing almost three thousand people at Hue City, a month before My Lai?"

"I don't believe that happened."

"Of course you don't, Dorothy. We only comprehend what we can see. That's the flaw of the human species. The communists have appreciated that flaw for decades. That's why they keep their media as an organ of the state, rather than as a servant of the people. We see, and we believe. We do not see, therefore it did not exist."

"Even if it did happen, I fail to grasp your so-called distinction, in terms of evil. People have died unnecessarily, because of this war. And we are supporting a government that condones this conduct. *That* is an evil we can all see."

"Come on, Dorothy! I hope you *can* see the distinction, even if you won't admit it to me. Mushrooms and toadstools look the same, but failing to appreciate the distinction between them can kill you. And evil is always relative. That's why we supported Russia in order to defeat Germany."

"There are many issues, Congressman Smith. The war is merely one of them. I can tell we'll have a lot to debate." She had regained her formality, as if signaling the meeting's end. "In the meantime, I think you're going to learn that the Congress is a collection of 435 strongly opinionated people who deal continuously in words. Words, words words! Rhetoric is the blood of a politician. We all have our favorite speeches. If you save yours for the House floor, you'll be a lot more bearable."

He chuckled, standing again in the center of her office like a fighter controlling the ring. "Sorry. I didn't realize we'd frozen our intellects into speeches. Actually, I did just come by to say hello. And to ask about Joe. Where is he, Dorothy?"

She stared steadily at him, her eyes fixed and her features frozen. "He's in the Pacific."

"Yeah, I know, I know. But it's been two years. Where is he? Do you have an address where I can write him?"

"No."

CHAPTER TWENTY-SIX

THE SCAB OF LAND GREW larger as the aircraft neared, until finally it filled Joe Dingenfelder's window. An island stretched lonely below him, surrounded by an empty, unending desert of ocean. It was black, jungle black, blacker than the sky or even the sea. Now and then it was freckled with lights, groups of them indicating tiny towns. The aircraft turned into its final approach and he could see a string of other lights, blue jewels that ran down the spine of the long, thin island, marking the runway.

The island was gigantic compared to Kwajalein. Its 208 square miles loomed up at him as if it were Australia. *Eighty thousand people in one spot,* he wondered to himself. *Almost as many people as in all two thousand islands of Micronesia.*

Twenty times as many people, fifteen times as much land, as Joe Dingenfelder had seen in two years.

It seemed almost ritualistic in this part of the Pacific to land in the rain. The sudden storm had an intensity that seemed alive, angry, as if it wanted to swallow the island, or wash it back into the sea. He climbed quickly down the ladder and jogged past an ill-lit sign, his feet splashing through pools of water.

HAFA ADAI

WELCOME TO GUAM.

It was four in the morning. He had been flying for a full day, first to Hawaii and then four thousand miles across the sea to Guam. Bunny was supposed to meet his flight. He had never met Bunny, but had been told to look for a large, heavy-set American who spoke with a phony British accent. That seemed appropriate, actually. Guam was a half-hearted American imitation of a British colony, seized from the Spanish during the Spanish-American war and administered by the U.S. Navy until just after World War II. Except, that is, for three years during the war, when the Japanese had controlled Guam under a regime so cruel that Guamanians still celebrated the anniversary of the 1944 Marine invasion as "Liberation Day," complete with floats and a "Liberation Queen." After the war, Guam had been given a measure of self-government as an "Unincorporated U.S. Territory," a dependent status that seemed to Dingenfelder to be a euphemism for "American colony." Its importance was in its location, an almost equidistant nearness to Tokyo, Taiwan, and the Philippines. One third of the island was in Air Force and Navy bases.

He searched the small terminal and the bar and the parking area outside. No Bunny. Unsmiling Chamorro policemen followed his movements from behind hard brown eyes. An occasional car splashed through flooded streets. The rain had already stopped, and the ground was steaming. After he had given up hope (it seemed necessary in the islands first to give up hope), a man at the Micronesian Airways ticket counter awakened, waved lazily to him, and handed him a note. *Take cab to Asahi Hotel. I'll have a room for you. Bunny.*

Dingenfelder traveled for twenty minutes along steaming, empty roads, past drab buildings, through brush and vines so thick that they seemed to be in grotesque armlocks with each other, fighting for the dank air. Finally the Toyota taxi turned into a long driveway bordered by a manicured lawn and reaching palms. It stopped at a glorious and bright entranceway. The Asahi Hotel might have been in Beverly Hills. It did not belong.

Bunny was in his bed. Dingenfelder had known it even before he opened the door. The almond-eyed Japanese woman behind the registration counter had reminded him twice that she was giving him the extra key to the room and that she wanted both keys back. The room was pitch black when he opened the door, and he heard the indulgent, wheezing snores of a fat man. *Asshole.* Already he didn't like Bunny, and they had never even seen each other. It was violative, condescending, to rent a room for a man and then sleep in the bed.

Dingenfelder dropped his bags inside the door and slammed it. The wall shook and he smiled to himself as he walked back toward the elevator. He wasn't tired, anyway. His body's schedule was completely screwed up, from time differences and catnaps on the airplane.

For a half-hour, he was the only customer in the hotel restaurant. The waitress was Japanese. The menu was Japanese on one page, and English on the other. He drank coffee and waited for his omelet, idly studying the intricate Japanese symbols on the menu. They were as confusing as a differential equation. He wondered what it did to a person's mind to have to learn them and use them every day.

Dawn came quickly, the sun burning a sudden streak across the sea that lit the lawn and the pool outside as if God had turned on a light switch. Tourists followed the sun, filling the restaurant and the terrace so that in minutes Dingenfelder became surrounded, overwhelmed by their curious, focused energy. They were all Japanese. They moved in groups, like invading squads, never sitting or standing alone. They seemed sleek and prosperous, yet almost comical with their souvenir hats and Mickey Mouse shirts and their ubiquitous cameras.

He had heard about the recent Japanese tourist onslaught. They flew into Guam on Japan Air Lines. They owned the hotels. They toured the island on buses owned and operated by a Japanese company. They spent money on Guam, yes, but almost all of it went right back to Japan. It was a form of occupation, economic rather than military. Or maybe it was simply rapacious—the taking of pleasure without providing a reward.

He was thinking of the energy and blood it had cost to push them back to Japan only twenty-six years before. He was remembering Judd Smith lying near death on a scarred Korean battlefield following that, and Red Lesczynski still festering in a North Vietnamese hellhole. What had they suffered for? Over which principles had they undeniably shortened their lives? The protection of their country's former enemy as it reoccupied the Greater East Asian Co-Prosperity Sphere? Or had it all been an accident anyway, a momentary blunting of natural momentum? *We beat you and your fascist friends,* he thought, watching them frolic in the restaurant. *We battered you and shelled you. We killed you and sealed you off alive in caves. We sank your ships and firebombed your cities and dropped the Big One right on top of you. And what did it get us?*

He checked his tab, signing the room number on the check. *A ten-dollar breakfast.*

He wandered through the restaurant and then outside, making his way past the swimming pool and across the lawn. It ended at the edge of a stunning cliff. He sat in the grass, his feet dangling amid gnarled, wrist-thick little trees that clung to the cliff's edge. The Philippine Sea stretched before him. It was awesome, incomprehensibly empty. He held his head in his hands, rubbing red eyes and then the thick stubble of a two-day beard. His clothes steamed from last night's rain. Exhaustion descended on him like a muggy embrace that might suck him of his breath. Staring out into the unending sea, he felt as though he had indeed made the moon shot, and then been left behind to contemplate its unfathomable isolation.

That goddamn Bunny, he thought, rising to his feet. *I'm going to wake him up.*

*   *   *

"I came here to avoid the war, actually." Bunny smirked over at him, taking his eyes off the congested road for a quick moment. "Everybody who comes here seems to be avoiding something, at least at first. They stay for more complicated reasons."

It was an inquiry, cutely drawn, about Dingenfelder's own motives, and then an invitation for Dingenfelder to quiz Bunny on his ascent to power. Bunny was cute in many ways. *A real cutie,* thought Dingenfelder, declining to bite on either of Bunny's dangling topics. *I'll bet he gets off every morning by watching himself in the mirror, dreaming of being able to make love to himself.*

Bunny had indeed been admiring himself in the mirror when Dingenfelder returned to the hotel room, drying his fat, pink bulk after having taken a shower. He had given an uncaring, casual apology for having missed Dingenfelder's flight, and then dressed quickly, telling Dingenfelder he would wait for him in the lobby. Dingenfelder had taken his own quick shower, changed into dry slacks and a short sleeve shirt, and then discovered that Bunny had stuck him with a 147-dollar hotel bill, for one night spent by Bunny, one meal eaten by Bunny, and Dingenfelder's earlier breakfast. Cute.

"I was just finishing up my graduate studies at Oxford and I got notice of a change in my draft status." Bunny spoke it all as if he were a properly appalled Britisher, rather than a Coloradoan who had studied undergrad at Princeton. "I was twenty-four! And can you imagine *me* digging ditches and playing soldier? For God's sake!" He said 'for God's sake' just like Dorothy did. It startled Dingenfelder, who stared closely at his escort. "So I heard that, if one accepted a teaching job on Guam, he was draft exempt. Think of that! So I came here and taught for two years, and then the governor picked me up as an adviser." He chuckled, an assertion of his prestige. "I mean, teaching junior high school, with a degree from Oxford!"

The traffic was as heavy on Marine Drive during rush hour as it was anywhere in the United States. Virtually every car on the island was funneled through the only road that made a perimeter around Guam. Next to the two-lane rush hour traffic, thin, monkey-faced Filipino laborers worked on an expansion of the road, their clothes and bodies caked with dust and sweat. Passing cars continually flung dust on them, like winter snow.

Bunny watched a team preparing to lay concrete, then glanced over at Dingenfelder again. He seemed content to carry both ends of the conversation. "And actually, for a political scientist, Guam is a fascinating laboratory! A microcosm of the effects of imperialism." He nodded toward the Filipinos. "Consider these laborers. Filipinos, all of them. You'll never find a Guamanian working construction. It's absolutely beneath a Guamanian to do blue collar work. Most of them would starve first. They import these buggers on two-year visas, and treat them like slaves."

Dingenfelder swallowed his anger for a moment, yielding to his curiosity. "Why is that?"

"Why, they make them sleep in hovels. Actual hovels. I wouldn't put a horse in the stalls where they live. And they pay them almost nothing. But that's the Philippines for you. People are their most important export."

"No. Why won't Guamanians do this kind of work?"

Bunny seemed delighted at Dingenfelder's question, as if there might be some hope that his newest employee would become an eager student, after all. "It goes back to the Spanish, actually. The Spanish controlled every aspect of the island for three hundred years. If the natives didn't like it, they were killed—very effective way to control dissent, you know. In one year, when the natives got particularly restless, the Spanish killed eighty-five thousand of them, out of a population of eighty-eight thousand. But there was no money, and no industry of any sort. You bartered. So natives didn't get rich. Status was measured by how close a person was to the Spanish governor. Same with the American Navy government. No industry. Status was whether you were working for the Navy. Manual labor was something the slaves did. Even today, 40 percent of the work force is in civil service."

Bunny now beamed at Dingenfelder. "*Fascinating* microcosm. Here we are driving on Marine Drive. If the Americans hadn't needed to move troops and supplies across the island after the liberation, Guam wouldn't have a road that went in a straight line anywhere on the island! Did you know that there were two hundred thousand men on Guam during World War II?"

"Yes." Dingenfelder recoiled again, not concealing his irritation. The military was his business.

"And the Japanese were so very *hated*, so cruel with their behead-ings and slave labor, that the Guamanians actually rejoiced upon being recaptured by the Americans! *Recapture* was *liberation!* Think of that! Orwell would have loved it." Bunny chuckled. "Yet, the Japa-nese now make up about 70 percent of the tourists on the island, and the Guamanians think that's fine!"

In the distance, from the northern edge of the island fifteen miles to their front, greasy streaks of afterburner smoke drew a dozen black gashes in the stark blue morning sky. A flight of B-52 bombers was leaving Anderson Air Force Base for an Arclight mission inside Viet-nam, two thousand miles away. Bunny took them in with a nod. "And at the same time, they are fiercely patriotic. Truckloads of bombs pass along this road at all hours, every day, carrying them from Apra har-bor, where the ships unload, up to the air force base. They go right through Agana. Can you imagine what would happen if bombs passed through Washington or New York twenty-four hours a day? Do you know what their motto is? 'Guam, Where America's Day Begins.' They are fascinating, *fascinating!*" Bunny glanced at him again, a cute grin sitting on his round, fleshy face. "They have no identity."

"So what do you want out of them, Bunny?"

"Beg pardon?"

They drove along the edge of the island. Far from the shore, the reef drew a black line between a turquoise lagoon and the dark sea. Palms hung toward the water, as if reaching to caress it. Bunny turned from Marine Drive and followed a side street toward a group of gray stone buildings flavored with Spanish architecture. The American flag hung limp in the dank, windless air before one of the buildings.

"You heard me."

Bunny parallel parked the car. He smiled with grandiosity, just be-fore he worked his fat bulk out of the little Datsun. "You're going to be very useful to us, Joseph. We've not had a good time with the American military recently, and we need someone who can speak their language, don't you think? We'd like to develop a dialogue with the military. We'd also like to rework our political status with the United States. An island with one third of its precious land in military holdings, right here at the keystone of the Pacific, should think hard about whether it wants to be blown up in a war that benefits others more than its own people. The United States *does* have a way of fighting its wars on the periphery, does it not?"

He thought about telling Bunny to go to hell, but then he decided

that Bunny was already there, and loving it. He thought about telling
Bunny he didn't want the job, but he had already packed off Kwajalein, and it was about eight thousand miles back to the American
mainland, and his small parcel of belongings was already in transit to
Guam, anyway. He could take two years of anything; he had already
proved that on Kwajalein. Besides, he hadn't figured Bunny out yet,
not all the way.

He suddenly decided, staring at the fat, grinning megalomaniac,
that he would beat him. No, not merely beat him. *Destroy* him, drive
him away from Guam in humiliation. He liked that thought. He grew
comfortable with its splendorous fantasy. It gave context to his presence on Guam. He had discovered over the past two years that he was
very good at cutting people apart. It was like finding out, in middle
age, that you might have been the heavyweight champion of the
world, had you known thirty years before of your natural talents. It
was hardly more than a game to him, a way to pass the time. But he
would be doing Guam a favor. *Yes,* he thought. *Yes yes.*

"You remember one thing, Bunny. I don't like you. Keep your funny
ideas to yourself."

It rolled right off Bunny's ego. It wouldn't in a week or two. "Why,
of course! Come now, Joseph. Let's go meet the governor. He'll be
delighted to see you. He and I work very closely."

Of course, thought Dingenfelder, following Bunny through a crowd
of brown, beautiful people on their way to work inside the myriad of
government offices. *Of course.*

The governor seemed tired, only mildly interested. He was a shriveled little Chamorro gentleman, a veterinarian by trade, with Basset-
hound eyes that drooped immediately when Bunny and Dingenfelder
discussed intricate military details. It was clear to Dingenfelder that
Bunny was the governor's political brains, as if they were playing out
a colonial charade in India or West Africa.

By noon, Bunny had walked Dingenfelder's papers through process-
ing. By three o'clock, Bunny had personally introduced him to every
key member of the governor's staff. And at six o'clock, on his way to
one of his continual meetings, Bunny had handed him a pencil-drawn,
detailed map, filled with the necessary jags and detours of reaching
any point beyond the main roads of the island. His pink, unwrinkled
face beamed brightly. His massive, sweating body seemed to keep him

distant from Dingenfelder. He held out the map in his small hands as if it were a gift from royalty.

"We'll have quarters for you in about a week. In the meantime, I've arranged for you to stay with a man who works for me. He has a two-bedroom place, and I think he'd be glad for some company, actually." Bunny's bushy eyebrows raised slightly. "He's a bit, well, unusual, but he can be trusted."

He can be trusted. Now, what the hell does that mean, thought Joe Dingenfelder. Who trusts *you*, fat man?

* * *

"Are you Hendershot?"

Night had fallen with a suddenness that surprised Joe as he drove, as if the sea had snuffed out the sun. A mist had immediately begun to curl out of the dank earth like some malevolent, nocturnal being. It clung to grass and shrubs like cobwebs. The squat, bald man stood knee-deep in it when he stepped out of his battered Toyota. He had parked at the edge of the unpaved parking lot. Dingenfelder walked steadily toward him, studying his thick features and neckless frame. The man wore a flowered shirt, as if he were on vacation in Hawaii. It hung from him, untucked.

"Who are you?" The man reopened his car door and reached inside, as if for a weapon.

"Joe Dingenfelder. Dave Bunny told me I was invited by a man named Hendershot—Julius Hendershot—to stay in a spare bedroom. I tried the door and nobody answered. I've been waiting in my car."

The man hadn't moved. One arm was still inside his car. Dingenfelder shrugged and began to walk away. "Sorry to bother you." He reconsidered the complicated route he had driven in the dark. "Does a guy named Hendershot live here? Do you know that?"

"Yeah." The man slammed the car door and began walking toward the ugly square apartment building, speaking loudly, his face away from Dingenfelder. "Goddamn Bunny got it about half right, as usual." He looked absently over his shoulder when he reached the stairway. "Come on, then."

Hendershot climbed metal stairs and opened his apartment door, ignoring Dingenfelder. He left the door open and strode across a stark living room furnished only with a small Japanese television and a wicker couch. He did not stop until he reached the refrigerator. Dingenfelder stood self-consciously in the doorway, a damp wind now tickling his legs and neck, and watched Hendershot pull out a gallon bottle of Jim Beam from the refrigerator. The old man's hands shook as he reached for a filmy, unwashed glass next to the sink. The sink was stacked with dirty dishes. Hendershot filled the glass half full and drained it, then filled it again before turning back toward Dingenfelder.

"What the hell are you waiting for, a goddamn bellhop?"

"Sorry." He stepped quickly into the apartment, angry at himself for having said he was sorry. He had almost broken the old habit of apology. It had taken more than a year for him to realize that people who said they were sorry were taken for weaklings in the islands. "It's good of you to put me up, Hendershot." His feet stuck to the fungus growing on Hendershot's vinyl floor, as if they were mired in wet asphalt.

"I'll bet." Hendershot drained the second glass. His hands had stopped shaking. He sat down at his kitchen table, seeming to sigh into the chair. A stubby thumb and forefinger found his eyes and he pressed them shut, sitting motionless for a long moment, his head back as though he were asleep. Finally his hand moved slowly down to his nose, and he rubbed its veined and grainy surface, playing absently with it as if it were an ornament. Soft little curls grew on the edges of his mouth, his watery blue eyes now peering through the barren wall in front of him. The room was only faintly lit. It seemed to Dingenfelder that Hendershot had forgotten about him. Then the old man pulled a protruding hair out of one nostril, wiping it onto his trousers, and pointed with the same hand toward the far end of his apartment.

"You've got the bedroom on the left. I used to rent it out. How long are you staying?"

"Bunny says he'll have a place for me in about a week."

"Oh hell, in a week you should be running the island. Yes, sir, the Annapolis and MIT connection. Come out here with the peons." Hendershot sipped from his third glass of straight whiskey, peering at Dingenfelder with what appeared to be a mix of pity and disgust. He shook his permanently sunburned, bald head from side to side, conveying hopelessness. "The fucking military *expert*."

"I don't need to hear any bullshit, Hendershot. I just came out here—"

"Every time they have a goddamned problem they bring in an *expert* from the mainland, like nobody out here has the fucking sense to figure out how to even tie their shoes. We get Department of Interior experts, Department of Defense experts, family planning experts, Great Society experts, welfare experts, educational experts, how to wipe your ass experts—"

"I was hired to do a job, Hendershot. Like it or forget it."

"—and now we get a Guam military expert who's never been to fucking Guam." Hendershot barked at him. "Will you put your bags in your goddamn room? What, did they grow onto your arms at the airport, *sonny?*" He glared at Dingenfelder with a look that bordered on hate. "How old are you, anyway?"

"I'm no kid, Hendershot, I'm forty-two. Now, look—" He was about to tell Hendershot off and leave, then he remembered the maze of roads into the place, and the Asahi's Hotel bill. "Shit." He walked quickly along the gummy floor, past a bathroom whose rancid odors assaulted him in the hallway, and put his bags inside the bedroom door. It was clean enough, and was furnished with a double bed, a dresser, and a small fan. Two gecko lizards chased each other across the ceiling, barking when he entered the room, their loud clacks like angry squirrels. Two years before, he would have been alarmed. Now he knew they were normal, even welcome in the islands, a form of insect control.

He walked back toward the kitchen, his lips growing tight. Hendershot had not moved from his chair. His glass was again half filled with whiskey. Dingenfelder examined the ruins of the unkempt kitchen, his eyes resting at the sink piled with dirty dishes.

"Is there anything to eat?"

"*Kim chi.* A couple eggs. Help yourself."

"What's *kim chi?*"

"Oh, sweet Jesus, are you ever a babe in the woods." Hendershot shook his bulbous head in uncontained disgust. "A goddamned babe in the goddamned woods." He rose slowly and took a large jar from the refrigerator. The jar was half filled with a red mash that resembled relish. "You never been to Korea, I suppose?" Dingenfelder shook his head and Hendershot scowled ironically. "Figures." He unscrewed the lid and a harsh garlic odor filled the room. Hendershot ate from the jar, spooning out large gobs, deliberately savoring it. "I used to be married to a Korean." He considered it for a moment. "As far as I know, I still am." He held out the jar to Dingenfelder. "Go ahead, sonny. Try some."

Dingenfelder sat hesitantly at the table, his stomach rumbling a rebellious warning. "Maybe I'll just have an egg."

"Well, you'll have to wash some dishes if you want to cook."

He grabbed the bottle from Hendershot. "Maybe I'll just have a drink."

"Hah." Hendershot's red face lifted with its first hint at acceptance. "Welcome to Guam."

It was all right once he was drunk. Tolerable, anyway. The floor no longer stuck to the bottom of his feet and the hot air did not carry bad smells from nearby festers and his head was numb to those mad darts from his empty stomach. Even Hendershot was bearable, all blurred at the other end of the table, settled into his rickety chair like melted wax, his watery eyes afloat in a sea of memories. Dingenfelder smiled at Hendershot, leaning forward with both elbows on the table, his hands cradling his third glass of bourbon.

"Hendershot, you're an incredible asshole, did you know that?"

"Ilah." Hendershot addressed the wall, his permanent imaginary audience. "The expert has decided I'm an asshole." He turned back to Dingenfelder. "What do you even know about assholes? What do you know about *anything*? Forty-two. When I was forty-two I had fifteen years out here, sonny. Let me see." He counted carefully on his fingers, and finally nodded. "Korea. I was building roads for Ford, right behind the DMZ. Damn, we put some bases in! And Vietnam. I was there in '64, when the North Vietnamese moved in. Don't tell me about it, I was goddamn *there!* Had my own road gang. When the gooks came down we had just enough time to pack our trash and leave. Left them our equipment right there on the road, fifty miles from Saigon. Philippines after that. Put a new naval supply facility in at Subic." His voice trailed off as if he were suddenly bored or ashamed. "Now Guam. Yeah. Eight grand a year, living in a slum, kissing Bunny's ass." He grimaced over to Dingenfelder. "I'd eat a pound of dog turds to get off this island. A whole goddamn pound."

"What happened to your wife?"

"She left me." Hendershot said it as though she had gone to the corner store for groceries. "Who the hell cares? Bunny gets me a trip to Hong Kong twice a year, one to Manila every now and then. That's all I need. I'm too old to get it every night, anyway."

"Nothing here on Guam, huh?" Dingenfelder sounded almost conspiratorial in his curiosity.

"Stay away from Chamorro women, or you'll get your balls cut off. Unless you want to get married, that is."

"No, I've played that silly game already. Marriage is for Normals." Hendershot beamed approvingly. Dingenfelder measured him. "What's with Bunny? The son of a bitch stuck me with a hundred-and-fifty-dollar hotel bill this morning, and then gave me a speech that sounded like he believes he's the Lenin of Oceana."

Hendershot laughed with obscene delight. "Hah! Welcome to Bunny! You'll find out all about Bunny. There's a dozen of them out here, at least. He's on a power trip. He won't last long." Hendershot leaned forward, his bloodshot eyes intense. "We're the survivors, sonny! He's just a goddamn pretender, on a college field trip."

"He'll go. I'm going to stomp him into the coral." Hendershot did not yet believe him. That was all right. He'd find out. "Tell me about the *snails*." Dingenfelder leaned back in the kitchen chair, placing a thumb and finger over his eyes as he had seen Hendershot do earlier. His world swam when he shut his eyes, and he quickly opened them again. A gecko flitted by on the ceiling, chasing bugs. "It was like a bad movie driving in here through the mist. The road was wet and a million snails had crawled out on it. My tires popped snails like they were gravel."

"They come, they go, they leave something behind, and usually it fouls things up."

"The snails?"

"Jesus, are you dumb." Hendershot had been staring at his audience of a wall with a look of self-importance, giving a profound speech. "The Japs. Whoever. That's the key to the islands. Everybody leaves something behind. The Japs left the snails. They brought them in as food when they captured Guam in the war. Another kind, that is. And the Jap snails mated with the local snails and now they're poisonous. But goddamn, those snails like to screw. You can't walk across a field without stepping on a thousand goddamned half-Jap snails. You know what we ought to do?" Hendershot waved to his wall again, as if he were now announcing policy. "Every goddamn Jap tourist ought to be issued a bucket when he steps off the plane, and he shouldn't be allowed to leave the island until he picks up a bucket load of goddamn slimy snails. With all the Japs coming these days, we could solve the problem in a week."

Hendershot snorted, scratching a liver spot on the back of his hand. "You'd think they won the war. They own this goddamn island, boy."

"Except for the bases."

"Isn't that a joke?" Hendershot laughed heavily, as if it were hilarious, searching Dingenfelder's face for some sign that he shared the humor. "We kick their asses in the war for the privilege of defending their business interests! Oh, sweet Jesus." He seemed to remember something else. "And the dogs. Did you see the dogs? That's our own little present. Did you know there were more than two hundred thousand Americans on Guam at the end of the war? That's three times the population on the island today."

"I know, I know. And a hundred seventy-five thousand more on Tinian, with the largest airport in the world—"

Hendershot shouted to the wall. "The expert speaks, ladies and gentlemen!"

"—and now Tinian has eight hundred people—"

"Did you hear that?"

"—and they dropped the first atomic bomb on Japan from Tinian."

"Will you shut up?" Hendershot glanced over at Dingenfelder, then back to the wall, ready to continue his story. "So, Americans smuggled in dogs. Americans *love* dogs. Then the Americans won the war and went home to mom and apple pie and left the dogs. And the Guamanians hate the living *shit* out of dogs. So the dogs went wild. And now they run around the island in packs. Boonie dogs, they call them. So, when you start making your liaison with the great U.S. military, ask each one of them to take a dog home when they leave Guam."

Dingenfelder buried his head in his hands. It was ridiculous to be out here, doing this. For a moment, he remembered his expansive home in California. He chuckled dryly, considering himself. "What a shitbox you live in, Hendershot. This place sounds like a goddamn zoo."

Hendershot attacked him, rejuvenated. "No stomach! Another Bunny, *huh?* College prick. And what do you know about it, anyway? *Expert.* Hah!" His settled chin rose out of its thick folds around his neck. His eyes gazed steadily at Dingenfelder, a challenge. "I'll bet you don't even know the Chinese have Polaris submarines."

Dingenfelder felt immensely weary. He was beginning to believe that Bunny had put Hendershot up to the whole evening. And yet, there was such a striving for dignity in the old man, such a latent dislike for Bunny himself, that it did not seem probable. "Hendershot, look. One thing I do know is that the Chinese don't have Polaris subs. They hardly even have a Navy."

"Hah! That's what you know! How do you know that?"

Dingenfelder leaned back in his chair, rubbing his face again, feeling trapped in another mindless debate. "Everyone who works in military planning knows that, Hendershot. It's common knowledge."

"The Chinese have thirteen Polaris submarines." Hendershot weighed each word, addressing his wall again, as if making an official pronouncement. He turned back to Dingenfelder. "And you know where they got them?"

"No, Hendershot. Where did they get them?"

"Ellsberg." It was a profound revelation.

"*Ellsberg?*"

"Hah! You don't even know who Ellsberg is!"

"Goddamn it, of course I know who Ellsberg is! He stole the Pentagon Papers! What the hell does that—"

"You know where he stole them?" Hendershot's eyes were wide, conspiratorial. "Rand. He stole the plans for the Polaris from Rand, too." Hendershot nodded sagely, noting Dingenfelder's disbelieving grimace. "Sounds crazy, doesn't it? I know you don't believe me. You'll learn, though. And he gave them to the Russians. And the Russians gave them to the Chinese. And—"

Dingenfelder held up a hand, cutting off Hendershot. "—the Chinese built thirteen nuclear submarines."

"That's right!" Hendershot lifted his head again, this time in vindication.

"For the love of God, let me out of here! That's *bullshit*, Hendershot! Total *bullshit!*"

"You fucking experts, you're all the same! You know it all!"

Hendershot was raging above him. Dingenfelder decided not to argue further. It might go on all night. "All right. Thirteen subs. How did you find this out, Hendershot?"

Hendershot seemed incredulous. "The girl in Hong Kong!"

"The girl in Hong Kong?"

"*The girl in Hong Kong!* I'll bet you've never—"

"*I don't even want to hear it!*" Dingenfelder rose abruptly and stumbled toward his bedroom. He was too drunk and tired to drive. He would have to sleep at Hendershot's at least this once. The old man's voice chased him as he entered the bathroom to relieve himself. It echoed off the walls, a ragged, haunting rage that mingled with the foul bathroom odors and settled over him like unseen smoke. He wanted to throw up.

"She was there, goddamn it! She escaped from China. She saw them! Where the hell were you, expert?"

Dingenfelder turned on the fan and lay on the bed. His sheets smelled faintly of mildew. The geckoes chased across the ceiling, barking and eating bugs. The wind from the fan slowly lifted layers of anxiety from his body with his evaporating sweat, until he was simply angry and tired, afloat in a humid, sticky world of snails and dogs and ranting drunkards. Hendershot's voice rose and fell in the living room, careening off his audience of a wall. Dingenfelder slowly realized that the old man was giving a speech about the American military's role in the Pacific.

Dingenfelder thought again of earlier years, of his family and his friends, of a world that he had abandoned out of boredom and rejection. At that moment he wanted desperately to return. His problem was that he wanted to crawl back inside a world he had known ten or fifteen years before. The rest of it had rushed past him, changing the landscape until he was no longer a part of it. He could not go back, because it wasn't there.

Like it or not, it was here, at least for now. Right goddamn here in this fester of heat and mildew, he decided. He had to beat Bunny; that was the measure of his life.

Hendershot was in his doorway, staring into the room where Dingenfelder lay only in his undershorts, basking in the fan's faint breeze. It occurred to him that the old man wanted either to attack him or continue his half sane arguments. He thought to feign sleep, but suddenly became furious at his own tendency to seek the smoothest solution.

He jumped out of bed and stood in a crouch, screaming at the startled man. *"Get the fuck out of my room, you goddamn drunk! Just get out of here!"* Hands that once coaxed soft notes out of a Steinway now were balled in angry fists. "And I'll tell you what! You'll be washing my goddamn coffee cups within six weeks, Hendershot. You'd better get used to having my ass around. *Now get out of here!"*

He ran at Hendershot. The old man trotted back inside his own bedroom, terrified. And in a moment, Dingenfelder was asleep.

CHAPTER TWENTY-SEVEN

"I HATE THESE PEOPLE, Judd. I'm sorry. I can't control it anymore."

"Don't let it happen, Sophie. Once you let that happen, they've won. It's what a lot of them want. You can't let yourself get bitter. It'll destroy you."

"*Bitter?* Oh, let me tell you about being bitter."

She sat between Judd and Julie in the front seat of Judd's Buick. They were again halted in the dense traffic, and he examined the leavings of sorrow that had gathered the skin around her eyes and on her neck during five years of loneliness and tension. Those smooth Slavic features were breaking apart, and he feared that Sophie Lesczynski's insides were, as well.

Summer 1971 was on its way, and ushering it in were what Judd Smith had begun to call the Semiannual Temper Tantrum. He forced a chuckle, seeking to console Sophie.

"It's all Dr. Spock's fault. He wrote the book on spoiling kids, and now he's leading them. The Spoiled Baby Brigade, there they are. They did this in their living rooms for years, and now they think it's normal."

Sophie did not laugh. It wasn't funny after five years.

It had taken them more than two hours to travel from the Roosevelt Bridge, down Constitution Avenue to the Washington Monument. Usually it took ten minutes. The demonstration's leaders had claimed they were going to shut down Washington, close off the government for a day in order to prove some mad amorphous point about the nexus between Washington bureaucrats showing up for work and the continuation of the war. Protesters had sat in the streets and made garbage can blockades and rushed in swarms through the traffic. They had massed outside of government buildings, the Congress, and the Pentagon. A bomb had gone off in the Pentagon during the week, blowing up an empty bathroom and setting off a security scare. Another had been found in the Cannon House Office Building, near Judd Smith's office. Most of the people now in the street were simply curious or along for the ride, in the same way that others flocked annually to Fort Lauderdale, but the dominant mood had turned so ugly and irresponsible, so hateful, that even gentle Sophie had started hating them back, all of them, without discretion.

Police were arresting them in groups where they had been the most intransigent. Reporters and cameramen wandered the streets, recording the conflict. It was clear to Sophie as she watched from the car what would happen afterward, and that was another reason why she hated them. They were breaking the law, mocking those who did not, and yet there would be no accountability at the end. That was the maddening part to her. It all had become stacked. The camera was a mother's skirt, and they hid behind it.

Television news that night would feature the police rounding up innocent citizens (and there would be innocents among them) exercising their First Amendment rights. Film clips would show young kids choking on tear gas. Other shots would follow protesters on the Mall, college boys pulling pranks such as tipping over hot dog stands and girls walking naked in the Reflecting Pool, joyous as they turned Washington into their very own summer camp. The news broadcasts would inveigh heavily against the government, and talk about the youth movement, its depth and power, about the Younger Generation's rejection of the war and middle class values. Members of Congress would anguish on the House and Senate floors about the government's being out of touch with the sentiments of the country's sons and daughters, the children of wealth and privilege, the baby boom generation. And then those who were arrested would sue. The ACLU lawyers would win a class action giving them thousands of dollars in damages for their travail of "false imprisonment," since police were now having to choose between mass arrests and the total breakdown of order. *See America? Your cops are fascists.*

She could have written the script, it had become so predictable.

"I've had enough of it, Judd. I swear I'm about to go berserk."

No amount of rationalizing could soften Sophie's revulsion. She had developed her own routine over the years, including mornings spent in volunteer work at the National League of Families, which had incorporated in 1970 and kept its headquarters in downtown Washington, and a bowling league two nights a week, primarily with the wives of missing servicemen. Her torment was real. Theirs was imagined, fantastic, intellectual.

"I wonder if they care that this, this communist *government* they are helping out of whatever motivation—let's be kind and call it innocence—I wonder if they even care that the North Vietnamese haven't even told the wives of men shot down whether their husbands are dead or alive? Not one little note saying 'killed in crash,' or 'recovering from wounds,' or 'died in captivity,' nothing for five and six and seven years? They talk about human rights. What do they mean? How do they feel about prisoners of war being called 'pearls' by the communists, precious for bargaining chips and propaganda?"

Judd grunted. "If Nixon's for it, they're against it." He watched a tear gas canister explode near the Capitol. Hundreds of people scattered, jogging and holding clothing over their noses. "And if you don't see it, it hasn't happened. They see what the camera sees, and the camera shows our own imperfections. Injustice in the South, capitalist imperialism, fading morale. You know, I doubt 10 percent of these kids could really understand the cruelty of a communist system, and its utter disregard for human life. I doubt they've even considered it! The Russians lost 7 million soldiers in World War II, often because they'd rather lose people than tanks and trucks. The North Vietnamese have already lost six hundred thousand in South Vietnam, by their own count. That's the proportional equivalent of 6 million Americans." He shook his head. "They have never beaten us on the battlefield. Not in one major engagement. Not that it matters."

"I guess it doesn't matter, does it, Judd?" There was something sad in Sophie's voice, a capitulation. "But I still hate them. And why, of all days, today?" They were in an indirect way keeping Sophie from her husband, providing the North Vietnamese a soft American underbelly for their negotiating positions. And now, they were in a very direct way keeping Sophie from her son.

"Remember what you were telling me, Judd?" Julie leaned forward in the seat, and caught Judd Smith's eye. "That the Gallup Polls show that the strongest support for the war comes from those under the age of thirty?"

"That's right." The traffic began to move again, very slowly. They were near the National Gallery of Art, where they would cut up toward New York Avenue and head out to Annapolis. "I had my staff research it. It's been true for the whole war."

"But why haven't we seen that in the media? And where do these people come from?" A group was screaming and chanting in a small meadow near the Capitol. It was terrifying to Julie Clay Smith, a vision she had never imagined while growing up in Washington.

"They come from the most privileged homes in America." Judd

Smith said it without a trace of sarcasm. "They were raised on ideals and sent off to college with their bills all paid. They know a lot about ideals, and not much about the real world. They've been manipulated but they can't comprehend it. And besides, they're having fun. The rest of their age group, the ones who have supported the war, are at work today, making cars and digging coal and driving trucks. Or serving in the military. They aren't gathered in a way that a TV camera can catch them."

He glanced at his wife. "Scratch a hippie and you'll find a Porsche, that's what the Bear Mountain kids like to say. But the antiwar movement's leaders have been brilliant. You've got to hand that to them. They've mastered the use of the media, and they've known how to get to the idealism of the college kids. They know how to mass their people, and to get the issues into American living rooms. Americans don't agree with them much, but they've burned the rest of the country out."

They reached New York Avenue. In ten minutes they would be on the John Hanson Highway. Judd Smith could feel Sophie slowly relax against the seat. Finally, she sighed hopelessly. "It's just so vicious, Judd. And so wrong. How can they call themselves Americans?"

"We've always been this way. It's just gotten more out of hand this time, that's all. Lyndon Johnson tried to sneak a war past the American people, and whether it was a good war or not became irrelevant. Red understood that. He even wrote me about it before he was shot down. You don't fight a war when you haven't articulated what you're going to do, and expect people to go cheerfully off to bleed for years on end. And Nixon came in with the promise he was going to end it. Once he started pulling people out, that was it. The North Vietnamese have him cold, because the antiwar movement has taken away his negotiating leverage."

He felt awkward making his speeches. He knew it wasn't what Sophie wanted to hear. "I know I'm not consoling you, much, but I've been trying to put this in perspective. Did you know there were antidraft riots in World War I? And did you know that the Selective Service Act only passed by one vote in World War II—in 1940, with Europe already overrun by the Nazis?"

They passed by ugly, despairing neighborhoods along New York Avenue. Judd Smith watched black faces staring at his car, and thought some more. "No, here's a better example for you, Sophie. Did you know that during the Civil War, Lincoln had to deal with an antiwar movement? Imagine, the same people who created the abolition movement losing their stomach for the war. Robert E. Lee went north into Sharpsburg to try and defeat the Yankees on their own soil, so that the antiwar movement would force Lincoln to negotiate a settlement. There you have it, in a nutshell. The idealists didn't want slavery, but they didn't have the stomach for the bloody part of it. They wanted the world to be rational and sane, even when their very cause was the essence of the war!"

He shrugged. The traffic was thinning as they neared Maryland. "There's a lot of that same paradox in the antiwar movement today. Its leadership is more perverse, but the typical student in the street gets caught up in the same old rhetoric. The North Vietnamese, poor little fellows, are just trying to unite their country against the colonialist puppets in the South. We're the imperialist bad guys who are keeping it from happening. That's safely abstract. And it's rational if you don't have to look at the cruelty of a closed society. The communists will make sure that never happens. How many peeks do you get inside North Vietnam today?" Judd Smith thought of Red Lesczynski and the wound he had directly reopened, and finished quickly. "So, freedom is great, in the abstract, and communism is bad, but nobody should die over the issue, especially when it becomes confused with real world imperfections like napalm and the Thieu government. It should stay in the world of books and debate."

His pithy little speech had been beyond Sophie; not beyond her intellect but past her emotions, almost irrelevant. Judd Smith was talking like a congressman. Sophie herself was a wife and mother, trapped between her values and her desires. It had just gone on too *long*, that was all. She wanted with all her heart to remain loyal, principally because it represented her loyalty to Red, but she wanted even more to have him back alive. She grew livid watching the protesting students. On the one hand, they were denigrating all that Red and she and the children were undergoing, labeling travail with cheap Marxist names, *fascist imperialist warmonger colonialist baby killer*. She could not help feeling they were cheating her of his return, leeching it away for their pleasurable games.

On the other hand, every night she prayed that her eldest son might suddenly decide he did not want to be a pilot. It was a hollow prayer, and she knew it. J.J. was his father's son. It was her dread, not his, that he would suffer his father's fate.

"It's just got to end, Judd."

"It's going to. At least our part in it. This country may never live it down, but it's going to end the way these people want it to."

It was going very badly. Even the mood on Capitol Hill was turning against the war, against South Vietnam, and against the young soldiers who were fighting it. Judd Smith liked to scan the newspaper and magazine articles inserted into each day's *Congressional Record* by congressmen and women, for a quick indicator of their philosophical direction. The articles about Vietnam and the military were getting nasty. *Hooked on Skag in Vietnam. Last American Killed? Men at Arms: Changing Breed. Nation's Darkest Time. Draft Evaders Tell Why. Congress Rebelling at Size of Military. Unfair Military Discharges. Cambodia—Secret War. U.S. Role in Laos. Gloom in the Pentagon. Should We Have War Crimes Trials? Leave Vietnam and Leave It Now. Most Unhonored Combat Army Coming Home.*

They turned onto the John Hanson Highway and the Maryland countryside went lush green, dotted with little farms. Julie watched silently out the window, and then smiled to him, examining his scarred face and his arms and then his wide hands, which casually grasped the steering wheel. "Oh, Judd, I wish I'd known you when you were at Annapolis."

"No you don't." He chuckled. "Ask Sophie."

Sophie smiled too, remembering. "He was a *terror*, Julie. I'll bet they're still telling Judd Smith stories in Bancroft Hall."

❀   ❀   ❀

They could hear the screams and roars from three blocks away, pulsing, excited sounds that resembled a crowd at a football game. The crowd would go quiet for long moments at a time, and then its voices would surge together. They were mostly male voices. Judd Smith parked outside Gate Three and they walked quickly onto the Naval Academy grounds, Sophie's eyes searching, her neck forward and her small body stretching as she half jogged ahead of them. Julie took Judd's hand, pulling him back just a little and smiling to him, a secret, protective wish on her face telling him she wanted deeply for Sophie to have this small piece of satisfaction, this reward that stiffened her body with pride and excitement while it also filled her with a mother's fear.

The crowd lined the sidewalk in front of the Administration Building just inside the gate, and was dense with people underneath the chestnut trees across the street. They were on the plaza in front of the chapel, and in rows on the chapel steps. Midshipmen in their tropical white Alpha uniforms stood with pretty dates, tanned and wearing summer clothes. Officers and parents mixed among them. Hundreds of small black children from Annapolis town raced in and out, calling to each other.

In the center of the crowd, as if on stage, a thousand plebes surrounded the Herndon Monument, a twenty-foot phallus erected in honor of a ship once lost at sea. The monument and the small field around its base was slick with grease. Bags of grease dangled from its top, ready to pop when touched. The plebes in the grass were shin-deep in it, falling and laughing, covered with the ooze.

They were trying to build a human wall, in order to place a midshipman cap on top of the monument. Once they were able to do so, completing a ritual that dated back to Nimitz's and Halsey's midshipmen days, plebe year with all of its deprivations and humiliation would be over. They had been trying for more than an hour. Somewhere at the base of the monument, thick-legged and broad-backed, J.J. Lesczynski was providing a platform for that human wall.

She hadn't wanted him to go. He'd been offered twenty-seven scholarships, *twenty-seven*, she thought again, Duke and Princeton and even Penn State, a measure of the blood returning. But he would peer at his father's memorabilia, the pictures over the dust-ridden desk in their basement, the deflated football from those few hours long ago when all of Ford City had sat glued to their wooden boxes of radios, *tackle by Lesczynski*, and he would remember his father coming home to the gleeful shouts and praise of the home folks, *Hey, Stasu!* and other times when his father would wrestle, joke, and challenge him in the green grass of their own backyard, and his father was a god to him. It wasn't fair to either of them, and yet it was his greatest act of love. *I will walk with you, I will fly with you, I will follow you into the darkest pit of hell.* And what could she do about it? Go back on eighteen years of teaching a boy his value system, merely because she was afraid that any small piece of harm to him would be the ounce of negative energy that would drive her into irreversible depression, permanent madness? No. She would have to allow him to live out what he believed. That was the hardest, truest test of a mother's love.

The plebes were four layers high, now, a gluey ring around Herndon. A small midshipman was hiked up to the second layer, and crawled among his classmates as if they were boulders. A dixie cup hat was in his teeth. The crowd began to yell, a crescendo. He fell.

The noise died. Up he went again, covered with slime, dressed only in gym shorts, his wiry muscles shimmering from the oil and the sun. Slowly he climbed, aided by the shoves and shoulders of his classmates. The crowd followed him with increasing noise. At the third layer, a classmate hooked him by an arm, and then as he stepped onto another man's shoulder, the same classmate grabbed his bare heel and began lifting him up. The small plebe was straining, clawing at the greased walls, his face mashed into one side. He began to totter. He swayed, losing his grip, but as he fell he reached with his left arm and deposited the cap onto the peak of the monument. It stayed. The crowd roared with such volume that it echoed off the far bank of the Severn River, a mile away. The human wall erupted with joy. The small plebe fell to the grease and mud, breaking his collarbone.

But no matter. *THERE AIN'T NO MORE PLEBES!* The crowd applauded and the thousand plebes raised fists into the air, clasping friends and dancing in the muck around Herndon. Their joy was real, and infectious. A full year of pressure and discipline, of indoctrination and denial, was done. They had prevailed, earned their right to wear an upperclassman's stripe on their uniform, proved that they had the elements necessary to be trusted with leading American fighting men, if it ever came to it. The Class of 1974 had *arrived*.

She saw him then, and he seemed to notice her almost at the same time. He walked across the road to where they were standing, next to a large anchor in front of the chapel, and threw two fists into the air, smiling with accomplishment. He was wearing gym shorts and no shirt. He was covered with slime. It matted his hair and slicked his body, illuminating the ridges of his muscles. He had huge shoulders and a deep chest and his thighs were as big around as her waist. An electric memory danced between them as she thought of the hot Pensacola night when he was born, her water breaking in the stark dim bedroom, Red taking command, the lonely fear of labor and the searing pain, then the wailing mass of flesh who almost immediately sucked toothless at her breasts. The round little face, the wispy strands of hair. The eyes that needed her and the first amazing time he smiled. How could anyone so massive actually have come from inside her? *My little baby.* That was indeed the great mystery of life, and its most undeniable accomplishment. *He is me and Red. But mostly he is Red.*

He stood in the road, his fists still in the air, and roared like an elephant. They laughed. Judd Smith squinched up his face, feigning displeasure.

"What took you guys so long? I'll tell you, this place ain't what it used to be, J.J."

"Hi, Uncle Judd. Aunt Julie." J.J. raised his arms again, pretending that he would embrace Sophie. "Hey, Mum!"

"J.J., you get away from me until you take a shower!" She smiled and unconsciously arranged her hair with her hands, taken by his attention. "Go on, now! We'll wait for you in the Rotunda."

*　*　*

The harbor area in Annapolis had grown, taking on charm over the years. They walked its edges, surrounded by memories, quiet as their ghosts called them to different places in their pasts. J.J. was dating a girl he had known in high school, who had come down from the University of Maryland for June Week. She was one of those incurably fresh young women who looked better than a photograph. She had pink, sunburned skin, straight white-blond hair, and slim legs whose muscles stood out when she walked. She had green eyes. Her breasts seemed round and hard as tennis balls. Looking at her was like smelling peach blossoms. Her name was Shawna Hagstrom. Judd Smith marveled at her. At one point, as she and Sophie and Julie conferred on dinner, he pulled J.J. aside.

"Where'd you shop for her, son? *Seventeen* magazine?" J.J. had blushed and given him a confused smile, so he had backed off. A reaction like that meant something. *Maybe love,* thought Judd Smith. It had taken him a long time to figure out love, but it had almost been a birthright of Red and Sophie's. Nineteen wasn't all that young. Maybe it was even better.

The women decided that they wanted to eat at the Old Town Tavern, one of several restaurants that faced the harbor area itself. Judd Smith stared quietly at the restaurant's facade, his eyes narrowing in focus, and then widening. Established 1776, the sign said.

"Are you coming, Judd?"

Julie tugged at his arm. He had stopped walking, still staring at the sign. The waterfront area was now quaint, a tourist attraction that pulsed every weekend with Washingtonians out for a holiday. The Old Town Tavern had once been Mario's. It was where he and Joe Dingenfelder and Red Lesczynski had gotten drunk on Graduation Day.

Established 1776. He chuckled quietly.

"What's the matter, Judd? Do you want to eat somewhere else?"

"No. No, that's all right." He began to walk, and then stopped again. "You've got to know something, that's all. Twenty years ago, almost to the day, Red and Joe and I came into this place and celebrated graduation. It was called Mario's. We got drunk."

He noticed Shawna Hagstrom's fresh, pretty face watching him curiously and felt very old, as if her beauty were a referent. "It was a dive." He laughed, trying to shake off a melancholy that was swarming through him, numbing his ability to move. "We took a knife and became blood brothers and promised each other that we'd be brave. We said we'd meet back here in twenty-five years and do it again. I don't know why we said twenty-five years. We were going to see who was the happiest, stuff like that." He laughed again, dry and sad, shaking his head. His feet were heavy, reluctant. "I can't go in there, I'm sorry. I just can't do it."

They began to walk. They were all quiet now. The memories had become oppressive, stifling. He was too old, really, to think of his friends as blood brothers. Red Lesczynski had protested as much twenty years before. But he missed them, just as deeply as he cried for the joyous optimism of that beery afternoon. Loss, that was life. Unrelenting loss that you continually tried to wish away, like the very wrinkles that grew more deeply on your face.

"We're going to get him back, Sophie. I swear on the memory of this moment. I want both of them back."

CHAPTER TWENTY-EIGHT

TWENTY OLD MEN SAT in the bed of the creaking Russian truck, huddled forward as if watching a dice game on its hot, rusting floor. The truck jounced and rolled along parched roads, causing the old men to sway and lurch in unison. A box of rations and a fifty-five-gallon drum sat among them at the front of the truck bed, just behind the cab, stealing their precious space. The drum was scabbed with rust. It dribbled gasoline along its rim and down its sides when the truck stuttered and trembled. Greasy fumes permeated the truck bed, lingering sweet and heavy in the heat. The truck had five guards, North Vietnamese soldiers dressed in khaki, two in the cab and three in the bed with the old men. The guards seemed to alternate as they vomited from the odors, one and then another perfunctorily leaning over the side of the truck and throwing up onto the powder dry road.

The old men did not vomit. Occasionally they would pass a tin cup from one manacled hand to another, dropping their striped maroon and gray pajamas far enough to urinate into the cup. When the cup was full, it was emptied over the side, to mix with the dust and puke. All the smells, gasoline and urine and vomit, would soon be swallowed by the dank jungle festers of Vietnam summer.

They carried their possessions inside blanket rolls that lay on the truck's floor, between their feet. The rolls were wrapped in identical, soldierly fashion. Inside each roll was an enforced sameness: a tin cup with a porcelain finish, made in North Korea. A bar of lye soap made in Russia, which lasted each man three months, for washing clothes and skin and hair. A tube of Vietnamese toothpaste, to last three months. A Vietnamese toothbrush, issued yearly but ineffective soon after issue. A straw mat. Two thin blankets. An extra set of striped pajamas. Two pairs of undershorts. Two slipover shirts. A spoon, made in Vietnam from the aluminum of a downed American aircraft.

Six years of Red Lesczynski's life, boiled down to a bedroll.

There were ten other trucks in the convoy. Groups of curious villagers edged the dust roads as they passed, quietly watching them. They creaked northward from Hanoi toward the Chinese border, carrying 208 prisoners who would reopen the Dogpatch prisoner camp, near Cao Bang, six miles from China itself.

Since the American attempt in November 1970 to rescue prisoners held in the Son Tay camp west of Hanoi, the prisoners had been consolidated in large groups, for purposes of control. At the Hanoi Hilton, men were now crowded fifty at a time in rooms sixty feet long and twenty feet wide, rather than being isolated in solitary, or in groups of two and four and eight. The prisoners had named the new rooms Camp Unity. The most senior officers had even been transferred there, from the hellholes of Alcatraz. For the first time, the prisoners were all able to mingle freely. They held classes, where the most knowledgeable among them taught subjects ranging from intricate scientific principles to the works of the great philosophers. They had been allowed to put on their own versions of plays. But apparently, the "V" had become uneasy with so many prisoners in one spot, in case of another American rescue attempt, and decided to move Lesczynski and the others in order to decentralize. No one knew. No one even wondered anymore. When the "V" said pack, you packed.

The guards had not manacled Lesczynski's left arm when they put him into the truck. The forearm had completely atrophied and the hand was now a thin claw, curled toward the wrist and unable to function except in an inward, jerking motion. But the bones of his arm had been rejoined below the shoulder, and he was protective of its possibilities, to the point of angry protest with the guards. The guard had grabbed his wrist and held forth the manacle and Lesczynski had pulled back, scowling at the guard and yelling *"Dao! Dao!"* and the guard had finally strapped the bad arm against his leg with a rope.

Three years ago, before Ho Chi Minh's death and the Son Tay raid, he would have been beaten merely for complaining. But Uncle Ho's passing had been a blessed event for the prisoners. Tortures had ceased almost as soon as Ho was put into his mausoleum. Mail was allowed more frequently. Lesczynski had not been given a letter in his first three years of captivity, but had received seven carefully censored letters in the past three years, and one package, although the guards had stolen most of it, claiming "censorship." Interrogations were now either halfhearted attempts at obtaining propaganda, or something resembling English lessons for the interrogators. The same men who once beat him viciously now teased and smiled and asked him to identify objects in Sears catalogues. It was as if the "V" were consciously attempting to erase the torture from the prisoners' memories, so that they would not lose face when the prisoners someday returned home and told the world of their treatment.

He was playing a small game with the guards as the truck churned interminably along the narrow roads. He could pick the locks of the manacles with his claw. Secretly, he would undo his good arm, then the locks on the man next to him. That man would quietly undo the next man's chains. Soon, the prisoners would be sitting in the same huddled, leaning pose, with the manacles on the floor of the truck. The guards would notice it, and scream at the prisoners, relocking their chains. They couldn't catch the prisoners as they did it. The prisoners would chuckle quietly, winking to one another. It was hardly as if they might suddenly jump out of the truck bed and run across the countryside, chased by an army of guards through a whole country where they would be recognized on sight. Dumb guards. At least it kept them occupied for a while, so they forgot to throw up. *Ah, the games a forty-three-year-old man might play to convince himself he is alive.*

There had been good guards. They had not lasted long. A little man the prisoners called Cube used to sneak them candy and try to learn English. He was caught and beaten by the more senior guards, and then disappeared. Another man, a true soldier named Hai, who had fought in the battle for Hue City in 1968, had been Lesczynski's escort at the hospital when his arm was finally fixed in 1970. Hai had personally scrubbed Lesczynski before his operation, helped him through the wormy mess of an enema, and then seen to it that the arm was kept in ice afterward. He had even stolen a fan from the doctor's office every night when the doctors went home, and turned it onto Lesczynski's bed, then carefully sneaked the fan back into the office every morning before the doctors arrived. He seemed to regard Lesczynski and many others as comrades. Hai soon disappeared, too. The prisoners kidded each other, only half jokingly, that Hai had been sent back South for reeducation.

The "V" had announced to Lesczynski on the fourth anniversary of his shootdown that they would try again to repair his arm. It was almost too much, this obsession they had with days and anniversaries, four years of uselessness until the hand was almost completely paralyzed, now to be celebrated, supposedly, by a jubilant gush of thanks because they had decided to honor his ability to survive four years of their torture and deprivation by sending him to a real, live doctor. They prepped him for a week with vitamins and beef from Russian tins, then presented him to a doctor who spoke both French and English. A week after that, with Lesczynski still being pumped whole food for the first time, he was taken to downtown Hanoi to a large hospital, to meet with another doctor, introduced as a "specialist." The doctor spoke impeccable English. He asked Leszynski a series of questions about childhood diseases and family histories, as completely as if it were a preoperation physical in any American hospital. At one point, the doctor asked Lesczynski how his weight was, compared with his normal weight in the United States.

"Not really bad," Lesczynski answered. The food had improved since Ho's death, and besides, there had been the vitamins and the Russian beef. "I'd say I'm thirty pounds light. I guess I'd go a hundred eighty."

The doctor smiled sadly, and put him on a scale. He weighed one hundred thirty pounds.

The doctor gave him a spinal, and blocked off his shoulder with two shots of Novocain. He took several bone chips from Lesczynski's left pelvic blade. Then he sawed off the ruined ends of the humerus bone that had been hollowed out in the first primitive attempt to rejoin it, the attempt that had caused Lesczynski to be punished in 1966 because of his "bad attitude" that made the operation fail, placed the bone chips inside, and joined the humerus on the outside with a metal plate and four screws.

After the stitches were taken out, they sat Lesczynski up and stuck cotton all around him, then dripped plaster of Paris strips into water and bound him in a body cast, around his waist, up to his chest, over his left shoulder, and finally around the arm itself. They froze the arm away from his body and parallel to the ground, and propped it up until the plaster dried with a bamboo pole that ran from his waist to his elbow. Lesczynski looked as if he were a female dancing a waltz, with the left arm around the shoulder of an imaginary partner. After ten days in the hospital, under the watchful care of Hai, they then drove him back to Hoa Lo prison on the back of a bicycle. Half of Hanoi stared curiously at this huge American whose entire upper body was frozen in plaster, blindfolded and leaning back cautiously, almost majestic as he rode in a tiny pedicab seat with one arm dangling before his face.

They changed the cast every two months, and left it off after six and a half months. He had stunk unmercifully in the heat and dung, unable to bathe properly with the water buckets of Hoa Lo. When the

cast finally came off for good, his arm worked for the first time in almost five years. It was now three inches shorter than his right arm, the
elbow up near the armpit, and small, as if it belonged to a boy. The
hand was cupped and shriveled. But it worked, and he babied it as if
it were indeed a child.

They drove for thirty hours, the truck's gears grinding, the guards
continuing to vomit, the prisoners hunched forward, nodding in sleep
where they sat. They muttered quietly to each other when the guards
were distracted or asleep. Lesczynski pulled himself away from it all
as he lurched and bounced, closing his eyes and welcoming in the
sweetness of his past. The truck, the guards, the other men, the countryside around them, even the burning pit of worms and hunger in his
abdomen took on an unreality, an opaline distance, not to be examined in detail. It would someday pass, all of it, and then reality
would return. The important thing was not to lose touch with reality.

Inside his mind he walked every street of Ford City, waving to the
families on their front porches, watching the trains pull in at Pittsburgh Plate, greeting his brothers for their morning whiskey and beer
on the way home from the graveyard shift at the factory. He remembered every street, every store and bar. He could recall hundreds of
names and faces from the front porches. He could see the ridge behind the town and the children jumping from the bridge into the
river. He could feel his mother's arms around him and his father's
hand upon his shoulder. He did not know his father had died four
months before, a sagging, sighing expiration, victim of age, hard living, and unrelenting grief. His father had asked for him on his
deathbed, *Stasu, ah my Stasu,* but he had not answered.

And he would go through his house, every corner of every room,
watching Sophie and the children, carefully attempting to project the
changes. Yes, that was important, to anticipate the changes. Nothing
remained the same, and if you wanted that, it might destroy you.
Sophie would be older, beaten down by this, ready to leave the Navy
and go home to Ford City. Katherine would be a full-blown woman,
beyond his ability to help through adolescence. Johnny would be
young enough, if he could get home in time. Would Johnny remember
him, listen to him as a father? And J.J. was gone. That hurt beyond
pain at times, knowing he had lost the chance to see his eldest boy
charge like a young bull through the walls and fences of his teenage

years. J.J. had been thirteen when Lesczynski had deployed in the *Shiloh* an eternity ago. Now, incredibly, he was twenty.

He would think of childhood friends, others he had served with, still others such as Yukichi Kosaka in Japan. What were they doing with their lives? He wondered about Judd Smith and Joe Dingenfelder. He still had a hard time imagining Judd Smith as a preacher, and wondered if his old roommate had ever found the right woman and remarried. He thought about Dingenfelder's involvement with the missile program, and wondered about Dorothy's work with the civil rights movement. Was there still a civil rights movement? He could only guess. He did know, though, that the United States had put a man on the moon in 1969. He had first found out in late 1970. One of the prisoners had received a package from home and the censors had not checked the little pictures on the back of a dozen packets of sugar. One of the pictures showed Americans planting the flag on the moon with "July 20, 1969" inscribed underneath. The prisoner had let out a joyous scream and the walls had begun tapping as the word was passed from cell to cell, each message accompanied by a new scream. Had Dingenfelder been in the control room for that? It was possible. He was that good.

I wonder if they'll let me fly again?

That thought kept him going at times. It was like a reaching back, a negation of the years that had so altered him and his life. If he could fly again, then it would be like youth returning, a recapture of loss. *Hey, can you see me passing by, I was born to fly, I'm a bullet in the sky, the Polish Falcon, eh?*

The air grew cool and stiff as they neared the Chinese border. They passed through Cao Bang in the crisp night and churned into a valley. Each truck fired two shots as it entered the valley, a signal to the guards at Dogpatch. Eleven times the shots rang out. The prisoners were awake now, erect as they sat. Flat, long buildings appeared, silhouettes in the dark. Other guards scurried about in the compound. There were no lights anywhere. They were hurried off the trucks. The guards prodded them but they were old men, stiff in the joints, dead of muscle, and they mulled around the back end of the trucks for several minutes, working their arms and legs before they were able to comply.

They had been arranged in the trucks according to their date of captivity. In the dark buildings they were meticulously assigned eight-man rooms in the same manner. That was a good sign. They all knew that the fairest manner of release would be chronologically. Stockdale and their other leaders had insisted on it for years.

A long corridor ran through the center of their new prison building. A dozen rooms broke off the corridor. They filed in, now chattering despite the admonitions of the guards, and suddenly one of the prisoners screamed, a healthy roar, and refused to enter his room.

"There's a goddamn snake in there!"

The guards tried to push him into the room but he pushed back, overpowering them, and they all poured out of the building, an act of solidarity and mutual fear. Finally two guards went in with a lantern and several shots exploded and they came back out, carrying a six-foot king cobra. Lesczynski breathed heavily. He had not endured all of this madness, come so close to the end, to be killed off by a snake. And wasn't it nice to be afforded the luxury of protest, however small? Any act of freedom was precious, even when it was microscopic.

It was almost freezing at Dogpatch. He put on his extra pair of prison clothes and huddled underneath the two thin blankets on the stone ledge that was his bed. Later he awoke, his nose and ears numb, and pulled a pair of undershorts over his face to keep the cold away. No one in the room used the waste bucket or moved from his ledge in the dark. The ledges were safe. The floors were crawling with chimeras, unseen beasts and cobras. At first light all eight men rushed at the same time across an empty, dusty floor. They grinned sheepishly, laughing at each other, and urinated in groups of four into the bucket, by order of shootdown.

❋   ❋   ❋

"This is Jane Fonda, coming to you from Hanoi."

Even in the primitivity of Dogpatch, the "V" found a way to bring the propaganda into the cells. Stalin had once said that he could control the world if only he could control its films, and Uncle Ho had applied that principle in his own Vietnamese way. Gongs woke up his people as if the whole country were an Army camp. Gongs put them to bed. The loudspeakers blared in between, in the villages as well as in the stockades. The programs varied according to the audience, but always there were programs, chosen by the state for the benefit of the state and the control of the people.

Jane Fonda was praising the Vietnamese people for having liberated Quang Tri during the Easter Offensive. The 1972 invasion had been the heaviest attack of the war, a full-scale assault in the manner of more conventional wars. North Vietnamese troops had stormed across the DMZ accompanied by heavy armor. The American ground troops were gone. The South Vietnamese had lost most of Quang Tri, but finally stopped the invasion cold, far short of its objectives. Jane Fonda, introduced by the Vietnamese announcer in his nasal singsong, was an actress and "well-known American pacifist." She was praising the manner in which the people of Quang Tri had overthrown Thieu's puppets, all by their little selves.

". . . all the people in the province arose like birds breaking out of their cages! Why did the people arise? Why were they capable of defeating all the army units Thieu sent to Quang Tri? Because they are free. Because they are fighting for freedom and are protecting . . ."

Henry Gruber, an Air Force captain shot down the same month as Lesczynski, sat back on his concrete ledge of a bed and shook his head mournfully. His face was hollow and his eyes were emaciated. "Does she really believe that, do you think?"

Art Seratelli shrugged from an adjoining bunk. He was a Navy lieutenant at the time he had been bagged in early 1967. "Raise a girl in a pile of fame and money, send her off to Vassar, then turn her loose in the fairy-tale world of Hollywood. What's real and what isn't, and how could she ever be able to tell?"

"The question isn't whether she believes it, anyway." Lesczynski peered at his roommates. "The question is whether the rest of the world does. They beat propaganda out of us that we didn't believe. But what did the rest of the world think?"

"I think she's poison. I don't care what she believes and I can't do anything about what the rest of the world thinks." Steve Cherrington stared at a far wall, half asleep.

Jane Fonda was summarizing her views regarding the Vietnam War, based on two weeks of guided tours. ". . . I've met with students, with peasants, with workers and with American pilots—who are in extremely good health, I might add, and will I hope soon be returned to the United States. And when they are returned, I think and they think they will go back better citizens than when they left. They know the United States government has lied when it says they have been tortured. They have received humane and lenient treatment. There were seven prisoners that I talked to, and they all expressed regret about what they had done, and they said that they had come to recognize that the war is a terrible crime that must be ended immediately . . ."

Cherrington grunted, unimpressed. "*Seven people* she talked to. Let's see: that would be the PCs, and Miller and Wilber."

Cherrington was probably right. Lesczynski raged inwardly, trying to block the rest of Jane Fonda's harangue from his consciousness. The PCs were the Peace Committee, a half dozen enlisted men who had been curried by the "V" for propaganda purposes for years. They were given special rations, yard and athletic privileges, and encouraged to disobey any orders from American officers. They had become closer to the Vietnamese than they were to the Americans. When President Nixon had reinstituted the bombing of the North a few months before, the PCs had actually offered to join the North Vietnamese Army. Wilber and Miller were turncoat officers, who had refused to communicate with the other Americans. They had cooperated freely with the "V" from the beginning, and had never been maltreated. Their enthusiastic tapes against the war were often played over the prison speakers. They were allowed liberty in Hanoi and other favors. They could be counted on for whatever propaganda the "V" needed. The PC and the two officers knew they would be facing courts-martial for mutiny and aiding the enemy when they returned. They were looking for allies in the antiwar movement, to keep them from further jail in the United States.

Seven people, mused Lesczynski. One percent at best of the POWs. If Jane Fonda had wanted to know the truth, rather than simply making propaganda, why hadn't she insisted on walking through Hoa Lo, or into the courtyard of the Zoo and its annex, or on seeing the Quiz Rooms with their permanent, clinging stench drawn from the insides of bleeding, beaten men? Why hadn't she taken a chance, just *taken that chance?* Lesczynski did not know the exact number of prisoners still alive. The memory bank kept inside selected prisoners' heads had been working on that for years. But it was near a thousand, anyway. *Seven people.* In any grouping so large, seven pieces of propaganda could easily be found to serve another agent of propaganda.

Jane Fonda was talking to other pilots now, the ones still flying missions. ". . . How does it feel to be used as pawns? You may be shot down, you may perhaps even be killed, but for what, for whom? The people back home are crying for you. We are afraid of what must be happening to you as human beings. It isn't possible to destroy, to receive a salary for pushing buttons and pulling levers that are dropping illegal bombs on innocent people, without having that damage your own souls . . ."

You are damaging my soul, thought Lesczynski as he listened to the tight, strident voice of a beautiful woman gone either mad or evil from misplaced ideology, trying at the same time to imagine the feel, the actual feel rather than the memory, of Sophie's lips. He remembered the discussions he and Rabbit had gone through years before, regarding the American antiwar movement. *We would separate them from our society and reeducate them*, Rabbit had said.

The voice droned on, hurtful in its delusions, and Red Lesczynski decided that he would, in the deepest corner of his heart, always find a place that pitied its owner. She was committing the ultimate abuse in a free society—the direct collaboration with an enemy. Whether the war was declared or not and whether she could thus be tried for treason or not was irrelevant on that point, a legal technicality. Jane Fonda had sold out the society that nurtured her for some Yellow Brick Road vision of people breaking out of bird cages for the "freedom" that came from the North. *Poor, spoiled little girl*, he thought, *steeped in fairy tales*.

Gruber shook his head with exasperation. "I'll bet you didn't know that the whole world, except for the dirty, rotten U.S. imperialists, is made up of 3 billion little kittens."

"Sure I did." Lesczynski laughed softly, ready to mark another day off his captivity and his life. "Rabbit told me that six years ago."

CHAPTER TWENTY-NINE

THE REVOLVING DOOR SPUN hard from a sudden burst of energy and Judd Smith walked quickly out of the Cannon House Office Building. His mad rush on the outdoors startled three matronly women who were preparing to enter the building through the door, and he stopped for a microsecond, bowing slightly to them and apologizing. Then he rushed down the steps to the street. At the corner of South Capitol Street and Independence Avenue he waited for the light to change, jiggling on his toes. Finally he jogged across the avenue, passing through a curtain of shrubbery into a small park.

Judd Smith was running away. Sort of. Autumn's onslaught on Washington had slowed for a day or two, and a glorious Indian summer had come as an afternote to a wet rain. A warm wind chased leaves in the street and on the sidewalks. The trees in the park were bright umbrellas, mixed with tints of red and gold. Leaves and dry grass crunched underneath his feet as he walked. He carried a cardboard tray. A sandwich, a bag of potato chips, and a carton of milk bobbed on the tray as he walked. He found his favorite tree and removed his coat, folding it carefully inside out, and sat down, leaning back against the tree trunk as if it were a lounging chair.

The park was his frequent daytime hideaway, even in its openness. Inside the buildings the phones never stopped ringing and the people never stopped coming. On any given day he was invited to three or four constituent or association breakfasts, a half dozen lunches, two or three late afternoon receptions, and several dinners. At the same time there was usually at least one subcommittee hearing to attend in the morning, and legislation to debate on the House floor in the afternoon. He also participated in a perennial series of "oversight" meetings with officials from the Departments of Defense and Agriculture, because of his positions on the House Armed Services and Agriculture Committees. Recently, there had been detailed, time-consuming negotiations with the Atomic Energy Commission, since the government had proposed to dam up the Pootaw River and put a nuclear reactor in his district. He was frequently detained on the elevators, stopped on the way to the bathroom, bombarded with telephone calls, and pursued by lobbyists wandering into his office.

When it got to be too much, he simply picked up a carry-out lunch and escaped into the plain view of the park. It was funny how people stopped recognizing him as soon as he took off his coat and sat underneath a tree, joining the dozens of congressional staffers who were scattered on the green lawn. *Congressmen don't sit on their asses in the park. They eat in the congressional dining room with bankers and lobbyists.* His public cloister allowed contemplation, and took the edge off the false sense of importance brought on by so many meetings and appeals. Congress was a dog and pony show. He was doing vital things, at least part of the time, but it would end someday, just like everything else always had and always would. Watching those of his colleagues who had bought the flattery, believed the sycophants, and then become hooked on their status as if it were heroin, he frequently remembered what he had read of the papal ceremony: the cardinals waving a burning wisp of straw in front of the new Pope as he prayed, reminding him that the glory of his position was nothing more than a frail moment in eternity. *Sic transit gloria mundi.*

And the gnarled base of his favorite old tree was itself a throne, from which he could peer out on the Capitol, a few hundred feet away, and the House Office Buildings just across the street. Other Members of Congress bustled past on their way to the Capitol, dictating instructions to harried legislative aides, so caught up in the energy of the moment that they saw no one in the park. Television newsmen frequently stood only a few feet away, staring into the piercing brightness of aluminum sun deflectors toward the round, Daffy Duck eye of a camera, speaking with solemnity before mobile crews about the day's great events. The Capitol building was a wonderfully dramatic background, and Congressman Judd Smith was invisible on the grass.

The air of theatrical unreality in the Congress caused him to search for metaphors in the park. As he ate, a small squirrel carefully fed off a potato chip near his feet, rolling it expertly in little paws, eating it in circles, and he thought of the destructiveness of welfare programs. The squirrel had lost its ability to feed itself. Well-meaning people such as himself had tossed it scraps until it became dependent on their kindness, unable to survive without it. He had heard of animals in the national parks, alligators and bears, who had forgotten how to hunt and then exploded with violence, attacking the people who had fed them. *Do we do this to people, too?*

A lady bum, old and gray and toothless, searched trash cans behind him, along the sidewalk. She wore all of her clothes, more bundled than the warm October day required. She was pouring leftover drops of cola from several plastic cups into a larger one that she kept inside her shopping cart. The shopping cart was overflowing with bottles and small, mysterious boxes, her treasures. *All of the programs we vote inside the Capitol building, and what is the result? Women's lib hits the hoboes, a hundred feet outside its doors.*

During the previous summer, he had watched from his throne of bark and roots as a large, fat man with a frizz ball of Raggedy Andy hair sauntered through the park and sat on the other side of another tree, directly in front of him. The man had seemed agitated. He was carrying a duffel bag. The end of a barrel had then shown briefly from the left edge of the tree. The man was moving it, putting something together. Judd Smith's heart had begun to race and he had stood, mindful of the hundreds of members who walked across Independence Avenue several times a day to vote and debate inside the Capitol building, mindful also of the ugly decade he and other Americans had just endured, leaders gunned down for their views or simply because they were convenient targets. Presidential candidate George Wallace had just been shot in nearby Maryland, adding to a long list. Smith had crept slowly toward the man, keeping the tree between them. The barrel showed again, briefly. Smith thought to lunge, then crouched instead, just behind the tree, gathering himself.

Sad, sweet music had then emanated from the barrel, a hollow, haunting lament of the terror and the deaths, of the nine years that Americans had been torturing each other with words and guns. The barrel was a flute. The fat man with frizzy hair was really very good. His flute wept with his ode to lost innocence, slow notes filtered by the trees and drowned by traffic noise. *How far we've fallen,* thought Judd Smith as he shook his head and caught his breath, *that the first immediate fear should be of murder.* He had leaned for another moment against the tree, awash in the music, and then thanked God that he was now standing there foolishly, with ants crawling up his arm, rather than trying to wrestle a rifle out of a madman's hands.

He was unopposed for reelection. The prevailing belief among political commentators was that Judd Smith could represent the Eleventh District for as long as he wanted to, barring scandal or revolution. The only problem, really, was Julie, who ironically longed for the peaceful haven of Bear Mountain. She had no further need or use for the eighteen-hour days or the fishbowl life. She rarely went with him to official receptions, anymore. He had even taken Loretta in her place to a White House dinner earlier that year. Watching the military escorts jockey for position to escort his sixteen-year-old beauty of a daughter down the same corridors he had once guided Julie Clay conjured up a mix of memories in Judd Smith, too delicate and portentous to examine. *What was it Einstein had said when defining infinity? If you could see far enough in front of you, you'd be looking at the back of your head. Something like that.*

He had worried so long and hard about the possibility of Julie's falling into her mother's lonely furrow that he had not examined the prospect of himself falling into her father's.

He drained the last of his milk and checked his watch. Ten minutes to twelve. He stood, dusting off the back of his trousers and donning his coat. Then he threw his wrappers into the trash bin and gave a quick wave to the squinting female bum, who was too intent on measuring her cola to bother with such boring mundanities as congressmen, and walked toward the Capitol, rejoining the pretentious world of power.

❄   ❄   ❄

The House met at noon, and the chaplain offered a prayer, something from Paul's first letter to the Thessalonians admonishing them to "prove all things, and hold fast that which is good." Judd Smith nodded with professional approval at Chaplain Latch's selection. It was a well-placed wish in October 1972. Proof had too often given way to wild emotion, even in the halls of Congress. And holding fast to anything seemed almost anachronistic.

A scant few dozen members wandered across the thick carpets of the House floor, pausing at the brass railings along the back edge of the semicircular chamber, and among rows of wooden seats inside. The rows of seats curved around the elevated and crowded rostrum, which housed the Speaker's table, against the forward wall of the chamber. Democrats gathered and sat on the left, facing the Speaker's table, and Republicans were on the right.

The Speaker's rostrum was a three-tiered throne. Just beneath his chair sat the parliamentarian, and other aides. Below them, four scribes slaved in shorthand, taking down every word officially brought before the Congress, for later printing in the *Congressional Record*. Others, pages and members of the House doorkeeper's staff, gathered at the rostrum or roamed the floor, delivering messages to members.

In front of the rostrum were two microphones. Since they were below both the seats and the Speaker's table, their location was called the well. It was in the well, and from other microphones at counsel tables among the seats, that congressional speeches were made. Above the chamber, in the curved rows of balcony seats called the gallery, a hundred tourists and a half dozen members of the press watched, as if it were all a play.

The members greeted each other, paying no attention as Speaker Albert read through the formalities of the day in a rapid monotone. The *Journal* of the previous day's proceedings was accepted as read, and approved without objection. There was a long message from the Senate. The other body first agreed to the appointment of a conference committee on House Joint Resolution 1932, regarding further continuing appropriations for fiscal year 1973. It next announced to the House that the Senate had overridden the President's veto of S. 2110, which made major amendments to the Federal Water Pollution Control Act. Finally, the message affirmed that the Senate receded to the house on certain amendments to the Public Health Service Act, which would improve medical care to areas with health manpower shortages.

The floor was opened for "unanimous consent" requests, for the passage of legislation unopposed by any member. H. "Shug" Harley, a tall, frumpy Rhode Islander with a safe congressional seat, attempted to move recent Senate amendments to the Environmental Noise Control Act of 1972, a controversial bill opposed by many Republicans. The motion was immediately objected to by the minority party's procedural watchdog, Mathew Bund, an Iowan impeccable in both dress and speech. In the best tradition of parliamentary actions, Bund said nothing about the substance of the bill, but instead spoke grandly for the record of the need to preserve proper legislative procedures, even though the House was anxious to adjourn.

The Speaker announced the appointment of conferees for the consideration with the Senate of H.R. 18450, which would allow an increase in the national debt to 437 billion dollars. Bund, striking a Republican's obligatory blow for fiscal responsibility, solemnly reminded his colleagues that there had not even been a national debt until the twentieth century, and that it had grown by more than 100 billion dollars since Lyndon Johnson tried to create a Great Society and fight a war at the same time. No one on the House floor paid any attention to such a perfunctory objection. What was 100 billion dollars, anyway? It was intangible. With the country sundered by social chaos, the national debt was one of their lesser worries.

And then Bund, as he had done every day the House was in session for the past fourteen years, stood before the microphone in the almost empty chamber, smiling benignly at Speaker Albert.

"Mr. Speaker, it would appear that a quorum is not present."

The bells rang on the floor and downstairs in the members' dining room and back in the House Office Buildings, calling members from meetings and lunches and committee hearings. In minutes the House floor teemed with them, hundreds of minor emperors, each one of them on stage, wearing public faces and perfect haircuts and exact clothes, waving and smiling to each other, calling across rows of chairs to various colleagues. The clerk called the roll and many of them disappeared immediately, while others stayed on the floor to finish discussions. The future of the world was being passed casually back and forth a hundred times, punctuated by smiles and back slaps.

Judd Smith saw Dorothy Dingenfelder on the Democratic side of the aisle, speaking intently with two other members. She held a sheaf of papers, and was referring to them in their conversations. Smith recognized Chauncey O'Brien, chairman of the Congressional Black Caucus, and Leonard Malthus, an Oregonian, who, although he was a Republican, had assumed much of the House leadership in both the antiwar effort and the attempt to dump the President. Malthus had even campaigned against Nixon over the summer, making appearances supporting his opponent, Senator George McGovern.

Dorothy noticed Smith staring at her and consciously jerked her body away, so that her wide rear end faced him. He smiled softly, laughing to himself. *Ho hum. Got a little surprise for us today, Dorothy?*

The Speaker announced in his quick monotone that a "committee" had been appointed to notify the President that the two Houses had completed their business of the session and were ready to adjourn, unless the President had other communications to make to them. The "committee" was Majority Leader Tip O'Neill and Minority Leader

Gerald Ford. The notification was a formality that had been observed in the Congress since the days of George Washington.

All of this had been boiler plate, the perfunctory following of a historical script. Now the floor was open for the day's business, beginning with the "one-minute speeches," whereby any member could speak for one minute about anything at all, and insert an even longer speech into the *Congressional Record,* both for posterity and for immediate press releases. Often a member would make a rather mild one-minute statement, requesting permission to "revise and extend" the remarks for the *Record,* and then send a press release up to the gallery, stating that he or she had excoriated government policy before the Congress. Few other members objected. It saved them the tribulation of listening to their colleagues' rhetoric. Words, words, words. Dorothy had been right about that part of it, thought Judd Smith as the speeches began. Rhetoric, that was the blood of Congress. It got very wearing after a while. They all had their favorite speeches.

A dozen members gathered before the microphones in the well. One by one they marched forward and read their remarks. A string of them paid tribute to several senior colleagues who had decided to retire from the Congress. A Michigan congressman stated his fear that the new automobile safety standards would price American cars out of the market, and cost jobs. A Florida member blasted Castro. A Chicagoan spoke of Soviet repression in Czechoslovakia. A New Yorker went after new Egyptian encroachments along the Gaza strip. A Nebraskan honored the achievements of a high school football coach. Then Judd Smith watched Leonard Malthus wave to the Speaker, and gain permission to revise and extend his remarks.

Malthus was no slouch. He was an Army hero of World War II, as well decorated as Smith himself. Like many moderates and liberals, he carried a resentment of Nixon from his early days of politics, when Nixon, as a California congressman and then senator, had provoked liberal animus in his unrestrained zeal to rout communists from positions of power. Malthus also believed that the Vietnam War had gone from marginally supportable to totally insane during the Nixon years. To Malthus and a number of others, it was better to bring the whole house of cards crashing down than it was to attempt to negotiate with an unforgiving, uncompromising President.

Malthus wore a Brooks Brothers suit that accentuated his slimness. His prematurely white hair was worn in a manner that reminded many of Jack Kennedy. He seemed to cultivate that comparison. He spoke in clipped sentences, his face emotionless, accustomed to television cameras that magnified facial movements, drawing inferences from passionate words. "Mr. Speaker, it deeply pains me that we are going to adjourn at a time when the use of presidential power is at such an arrogant and tyrannical level. As you know, Mr. Speaker, the Congress will not reconvene until January. Are we doing our duty as responsible members of the legislative branch when we are totally abdicating to this President for three months, when we can expect the activities of the Committee to Reelect the President to time and again breach the bounds of lawfulness, and when Mr. Nixon has stated his intention to continue the most devastating bombing attacks in history on the people, villages, and culture of Vietnam? It pains me, Mr. Speaker, to have been so ineffective in convincing my colleagues of the importance of these issues. They are the greatest issues of our time. Until the President is willing to fully disclose the complete operations of the Committee to Reelect the President with respect to the Watergate burglary and the so-called Dirty Tricks operation, and until he comprehends the misplaced pride which associates 'Peace with Honor' with the carpet bombing by hundreds of B-52s on thatched-roof homes, on hundreds of thousands of women and children, this Congress should remain in session."

"The time of the gentleman has expired." Speaker Albert banged his gavel, seeming almost bored.

"Mr. Speaker! Mr. Speaker!" It was Dorothy, now. "I request permission to address the House for one minute, and to revise and extend my remarks."

"The gentlelady from California is recognized for one minute."

Smith watched Dorothy gather herself, standing in front of the microphone. She was smaller than many of the congressional pages who wandered across the floor as the members conducted their business. She had taken to dressing very conservatively, dark suits with the hem below the knee. She looked directly at Judd as she began, then spoke toward the Democratic side of the House, where perhaps twenty members were casually grouped, still for the most part ignoring the doings in the well. She spoke in a rush, trying to get it all out, her words falling over themselves.

"Mr. Speaker, I would like to associate myself with the remarks of my colleague from Oregon, and to add my own thoughts to them. First of all, I believe it imperative that the identity of the highest official associated with the Dirty Tricks operation, and the Watergate burglary, be made public. This official should either resign or be fired immediately, whether this is a White House aide, Attorney General Mitchell, or the President himself. We are adjourning at a time when the FBI and CIA are running rampant in their spying, with the knowledge of the Chief Executive! I must reiterate on this point that it is not out of the question for President Nixon, who has brought shame on the office of the presidency, to be impeached. Secondly, Mr. Speaker, I want to express my disappointment with the President's record on equal rights, particularly for women. Nineteen states have ratified the Equal Rights Amendment since March, when it finally cleared the Senate. President Nixon has, at the same time, made a mockery of the Equal Employment Opportunity Commission, and is only marginally pursuing equality. And finally, Mr. Speaker, my colleague Mr. Malthus has outlined far more eloquently than I the cruelty and genocide which the President is perpetrating in Southeast Asia. Vietnam, Laos, and Cambodia deserve to have peace. It is within our power to give them that peace, by ceasing our aggression. Mr. Speaker, the Executive Branch *must be controlled!* How many thousands will continue to suffer and die before the Congress and the country accept that fact? I—"

"The time of the gentlelady has expired." The gavel went down and Dorothy immediately stopped. It was a strictly enforced ritual.

"Mr. Speaker!"

"The gentleman from Illinois is recognized for one minute."

Chauncey O'Brien walked to the microphone, smoothly dressed and in control. A Chicago lawyer who had begun as an aide to Martin Luther King, he had been close to Dorothy Dingenfelder for more than a decade, working both as a fellow attorney and politician. O'Brien had litigated numerous desegregation and voting rights cases in the South, as well as having organized the most effective black boycott of white businesses in Mississippi history. He had become a master at using race as a weapon. In 1972, his blackness carried a two-edged sword: white guilt and black anger.

O'Brien wore a large Afro haircut. His hair was peppered with gray, as was the moustache that accented his long face and hollow cheeks. He reminded many people of Frederick Douglass, a black hero of a century before. He was a powerful orator. He had an unconcealed hatred for Richard Nixon and the U.S. military, which had forced him to serve humiliating duty as a stevedore in World War II. He stood rigidly erect as he spoke, and threw his words like knives, punctuated with ironic pauses.

"Mr. Speaker, I would like to fully associate myself with the comments of my two distinguished colleagues who preceded me. I agree with every word both of them have said. I would also like to announce that today I am inserting into the *Congressional Record* the Black Caucus' report on racism in the military. As you know, Mr. Speaker, the Black Caucus has toured many of the bases in this country and overseas, interviewing our black brothers and sisters who are serving in the military. The racial horrors they are undergoing are a *travesty*, Mr. Speaker, a national disgrace. Tell me why blacks, who have died in disproportionate numbers in Vietnam, should be subject to military discipline, jails, and bad discharges, in disproportionate numbers, too? Tell me what a black man should feel on patrol in Vietnam when he looks up and sees an American tank flying a Confederate flag from its antenna? I have come to believe after making these trips that it is wrong for *any* black man or woman in this country to go into the United States military under *any* circumstances."

O'Brien paused after having shouted his allegation. The House chambers were quiet as every member on the floor watched him. "Now, the military says it is introducing a 'Human Relations' program that's going to bring racial harmony. I say, Mr. Speaker, that no program is going to work until it recognizes the legitimacy and indeed the morality of teaching people to fight against militarism, and the first step in fighting against militarism is for the people of this country to *throw out* Richard Nixon from the presidency."

Speaker Albert yawned from his throne, pounding the gavel for the twentieth time that afternoon. "The gentleman's time has expired."

Judd Smith looked down at the brass railing just in front of him and saw that his right hand was gripping it so hard that his knuckles had gone white. Normally he did not listen, simply tuning such speakers out. That was the way most members dealt with rhetoric that cut against their values. If you couldn't either tune it out or fight it, you didn't belong in Congress, because the heart attacks from your anger would kill you off in one term. But he had been curious after watching Dorothy's furtiveness minutes before, and had made the mistake of listening.

He knew what would happen next. The press release was probably already in the press gallery: HOUSE ADJOURNS AS LIBERALS

DENOUNCE NIXON ON WAR, WATERGATE, CIVIL RIGHTS.
Media infatuation with those issues would probably propel the simple
one-minute speeches to the front pages of many major newspapers. It
would keep the issues before the public as elections neared, affecting
the races of members who had supported the President. But Judd
Smith knew Dorothy Dingenfelder well enough to know that she was
kicking off something bigger.

They wanted Nixon out. At the same time, Senator George McGovern had won the Democratic nomination for the presidency. They
knew as well as Judd Smith that McGovern was perceived by many
Americans to be a candy ass, who was running a preachy, self-righteous campaign, even offering to go on his knees and beg Hanoi for an
end to the war. McGovern had made Nixon's arrogance his only campaign tool. It was an oft-told joke in Congress that a spavined ox
could have beaten the whiny South Dakota senator. The average
American voter loathed him. So the only way to get Nixon out was to
allow his election and then hound him out, or impeach him. And
Dorothy Dingenfelder was an accomplished constitutional lawyer who
sat on the Judiciary Committee, the very body that would conduct
any investigations into executive impropriety, from White House
staffers all the way up to Nixon himself.

But never mind Nixon, these things they were saying were *wrong*.
He fretted, feeling like pounding on the railing. Half truths. One-
dimensional criticisms. Little hooks designed to shake the foundations
of belief in traditional views of the country as a wholesome and well-
intending nation. He began walking toward the well, unable to let
those comments pass without some response, some indication that
they were not accepted, even passively, by others in the House.

A Pennsylvania member was extolling the virtues of his hometown
priest, who had served the same church for fifty years, as if the previous three speeches had not even occurred. Later, he would clip the
page from the *Congressional Record* and frame it, sending it to the
priest. That was the way it was done, a symbiosis, the congressman
and the priest linked together on the wall of the priest's office, for
their mutual constituents to see. He finished, and Judd Smith waved a
hand to the Speaker.

"Mr. Speaker!"

"The gentleman from Virginia is recognized for one minute."

Dorothy was standing with Malthus and O'Brien just off the well,
near the doors that led to the Cloak Room. She stopped talking and

stared at Judd Smith, her head snapping as she locked him in her gaze. He narrowed his eyes and smiled thinly to her.

"Mr. Speaker, we have just witnessed here in the House a slander of the values of this country, and although these attacks seem to be happening with such frequency lately that many of us no longer even raise our eyebrows, I do not think I can keep my conscience without responding." He paused for a moment. He was winging it, speaking from memory to the main points the three had made. "First, I would hope that my Republican colleague from Oregon might consider that the enemy in this war can stop the bombing at *any moment*, simply by ceasing its aggression in the South and in Laos and Cambodia. This country has done nothing but respond to the instigations of North Vietnam. If they truly care about their people, let them cooperate in the peace talks in Paris. Second, while I do not condone the Watergate burglary and other indiscretions, I believe they are symptomatic of political abuses that have gone on throughout eternity, and I would ask my colleagues why they place such great weight on such a matter. I would wager, without intending any malice, that their own campaign people may have been guilty of similar acts at one time or another, without their knowledge. And finally, it deeply saddens me to hear my colleague from Illinois declare that no black man should serve his country. While it is demonstrably *untrue* that blacks suffered disproportionately in the Vietnam War—they sustained 12 percent of the casualties and had 12 percent of the troops—it is true that they did their full share, and this sort of hyperbole makes it difficult for those who admire that fact to say so. As for the disproportionate percentage of blacks in trouble in the military, I would ask my colleague to consider two points. First—"

Speaker Albert's gavel crashed behind him. "The time of the gentleman has expired."

Judd Smith left the microphone and walked immediately to Dorothy and the two others, his lips still in a forced smile and his fists clenched. He knew that even mentioning the issues would brand him as an "unthinking reactionary," particularly in the press, but he did want them to understand. There *were* two sides, even if only one side made it into the news anymore.

They followed him with arched, mocking eyes. He pointed at O'Brien and took up where he had left off. "First, that McNamara didn't have the guts to go after the college boys when he ran out of enlistees, so he created Project One Hundred Thousand, which eventually became Project Four Hundred Thousand, which brought in a mass of soldiers who hadn't been able to pass the tests for enlistment. A lot of them simply couldn't perform, Chauncey. And a lot of others didn't understand the difference between discipline and discrimination. And second, consider the mood in black America after Martin Luther King was killed. Blacks were taught to dissent—take a look at what you yourself just said—and you can't have a sit-down strike in the military, no matter what color you are."

They stared silently at him. The business of the House was continuing, the Speaker announcing that he had placed the Environmental Noise Control Act, as amended by the Senate, on the table for debate. Finally O'Brien shrugged, speaking slowly. "So, the military with its Confederate flags and jailed-up niggers is just fine, right?"

"The flags aren't aimed at the blacks, Chauncey, any more than a black man raising his fist, passing the Power to a buddy, is aimed at the whites. A lot of soldiers had ancestors who fought for the Confederacy. They're proud of the fighting spirit. That's what the flag is all about. Their ancestors didn't fight blacks, they fought Yankees. And no, the military isn't just fine. The point is, it isn't *corrupt*. It's a system with human failures. It's the first system in this country that was fully desegregated. Some of the very finest soldiers in the military are black, you know that! It's their way out of poverty, just like it was mine! Why on earth do you want to incite blacks and other Americans to hate it?"

The reasons sat on their faces with their little half smiles that asked him to leave their gathering. He shook his head, staring at Dorothy.

"You're a shameless little grig, did you know that? When Red Lesczynski gets back—and he'll be back, Dorothy, real soon—I want you to sit down and explain to him what's happened in this country."

❊   ❊   ❊

A shameless little grig. What the hell was a grig, anyway, and what right did he have to say that? She decided she would look the word up when she got back to her office, just to see in retrospect how badly she'd been insulted. It probably was some hillbilly term that had never made it into the dictionary. Or maybe he even made the word up. *Grig.* That was what happened when a man became a preacher and didn't swear anymore.

She took the elevator down to the Capitol basement and began winding through the underground tunnel that led to the House Office

Buildings. Narrow gray walls and overhead steam pipes marked her journey. She passed staffers and other members and policemen and they all knew her, nodding or calling to her as she walked, and it breathed contentment into her tensions. *Good afternoon, Congresswoman.* She was known. She made things happen. How dare he label her efforts defamation? Didn't he know all the wheels she had set in motion?

In the past year alone, Dorothy Dingenfelder had introduced more than a hundred bills, covering a mind-boggling spectrum of issues. She had sponsored legislation to recognize Bangladesh, to impose export quotas on cattle hides, to provide for education of the handicapped, to strengthen and expand the Head Start Program for economically disadvantaged children, to improve the efficiency of the highway system, to provide residential facilities for the mentally retarded, to strengthen safety standards on school buses, to increase Social Security benefits, to express sympathy for the Israeli Olympic Team after the killings in Munich by Arab terrorists, to eliminate restrictions on the emigration of Soviet Jewry, and to declare 1974 as America the Beautiful year. True, she had also introduced legislation that would establish a Department of Peace to counteract the Department of Defense, another that would require the President to cease the bombing of Vietnam immediately and promptly withdraw the remaining American troops there, another calling for blanket amnesty for all draft evaders, another that would establish a National Woman's Suffrage Day, and still another to establish a Woman's Rights Day. True, she had spoken out vehemently and often on the House floor and elsewhere as she had done today. But she did not view herself as a subversive or a rabble-rouser. Militarism, incipient fascism, a corporate society dominated by narrow-minded, rapacious males, those were the enemies, and if Judd Smith wished things would remain the same, he was either corrupted by all that, or their unwitting agent. *For God's sake, I even serve on the Select Committee on the House Beauty Shop.*

On the elevator two very young staffers, a woman and a man obviously just out of college, were discussing all the great, timeless issues with the simplicity of the newly initiated. The issues were as colorful and fresh to them as the new clothes they had bought with their first paychecks. Did welfare help or hurt? Was abortion murder or birth control? Was America the guardian of the free world, or its oppressor? Was the draft duty or slavery? They touched them all between the basement and the sixth floor, voting them casually up or down with quick summations of belief.

It reminded her of dormitory discussions during college. *Does God exist? How do we know? If He does, is He active or passive?* They were age-old, unanswerable wonderings, but the staffers' conversation troubled her, nagged at one of her greatest, lingering doubts. *Have the issues advanced during my eleven years of pushing against them, or have I myself simply moved along a power curve, changed in my perceptions of their complexity until I have convinced myself that they, too, have approached resolution?*

Judd Smith had said to her on his first day in Congress that the American system was such that everyone would live to see his or her views dominate at one time or another. If that was true, then they, all of them who were fighting these battles, were simply people washing back and forth over the unanswerable, deceiving themselves about their impact. What a tragedy that would be, what a waste of energy. What a diminution of the only things that gave her life true meaning.

She had thirty-two phone messages in her office, and seven calls from reporters. Their joint attack on Nixon had taken hold. Maybe they would run Nixon out, eventually. She didn't know that for sure, but the prospect of it was on the one hand scary and on the other the most exciting thing she had ever imagined. It was scary because she and some others were already so deeply committed to the attempt that, if Nixon survived, he would take revenge in a way that well might destroy them, all of them. It was exciting because it would prove Judd Smith wrong, and all those who thought the way he did. There *were* differences, lasting impacts, yes, and she was at the fulcrum of a tilt potentially as large as the American Revolution itself.

Well, World War II, anyway. America gone wild at home and in the world, crew cuts and atom bombs, conformity and coercion.

It would be revolution. That wasn't too strong a word. Revolution was permanent change, and the country would never again be the same, just as people were never the same after the last moments of innocence, whether it was the moment before they first rode a bike or lost their virginity or killed someone. There were some things that had never been done, and once they were done, the effect was inalterable, no matter what Judd Smith thought. And ousting a President had to be among them. To shut down Nixon, to kill off America's militaristic instincts through the slow, humiliating trauma of Vietnam, and with it the swaggering machismo of the country's dominant leadership, to keep the pressure on, always questioning, always dissenting—that would affect the country, and when America changed, the world would change. And if all that happened, Judd Smith and those of his ilk would never see a time when their views again predominated.

And Red Lesczynski would just have to blink his Rip Van Winkle eyes and step back into a new way of looking at things. *Sorry about that.*

CHAPTER THIRTY

I

ALL NIGHT HE LISTENED to the trucks as they passed through Cao Bang and then followed the road down steep hills into the valley. Each truck fired off two rifle shots as it crossed the valley's narrow floor, to warn the camp guards of its approach. The shots echoed in the still, icy darkness of Red Lesczynski's prison cell, high-pitched and portentous, like the crackling thunder of a coming electrical storm. The echoes and their promises were indeed electric. He and his cellmates sat wide-eyed on the edges of their beds, too convinced even to talk about it. *Another one. And another.*

The trucks came singly, one every half-hour or so, their churning engines faint at first and then growing louder, the drivers downshifting and the motors surging as they climbed the steep hills toward Dogpatch, working through gulleys in the road. By dawn he had counted eleven of them, the same number of trucks that had brought them to the camp nine months before. The guards did not speak to the prisoners during the day but the prisoners knew anyway, and at night they still sat on the edges of their beds with their bedrolls tightly done up, waiting to move.

It's over. It's over and I'm alive. Thank you, God. Thank you thank you thank you . . .

After midnight the guards put the prisoners in wrist irons and loaded them into the trucks. The guards were solemn, restrained. Lesczynski held his crippled arm away from the irons and the guard did not even make a symbolic effort to manacle it. On the far side of Cao Bang they stopped in a small clearing and waited for dawn. The guards removed the irons then, and gave the prisoners a meal of greasy pork sandwiches and water. The irons stayed off for the rest of the trip.

They lurched and bounced in the odorous, crowded truck beds all day and through the night. The next morning they reached Hanoi. Lesczynski and the other Dogpatch prisoners had heard the propaganda messages regarding the so-called Christmas bombing of the city a month before, exaggerated accounts of North Vietnamese missiles dropping aircraft after aircraft, other stories of hospitals and schools taken apart by the bombs, news reports of Ramsey Clark leading a campaign inside the United States focusing attention on the partial damage of the Bac Mai hospital. The prisoners nudged each other with professional acumen as the trucks passed along the outskirts of the city and through many of the damaged areas. Judging by the impact patterns in places that had once housed power plants, antiaircraft sites, communication centers, storage depots, and other facilities, it was evident that Nixon had for the first time in this long, foolish war unleashed B-52 bombers on Hanoi.

Lesczynski watched simple people as they pedaled bicycles or walked along the narrow roads. They were merely trying to survive life, he thought again, up against the obstacles of government, born into a travail that it was their sad fate to endure. It was the same in Poland, from which his grandparents had thankfully fled before two ugly wars killed off more than half the population and delivered the rest to an imprisonment of their souls. He remembered the soft little nurse of six years before, the only woman he had touched or felt since the Christmas of 1965. She had been the North Vietnamese people, not Bug and Rat and those others who had delivered him into dark days of beatings and solitary confinement. He did not hate these people; he pitied them. He was finally going to escape the oppression of a government bent on war and conquest. They would be left behind, to send their sons into the South and Laos and Cambodia. Did that little woman on the bicycle really want that?

But he could not conjure up a regret at seeing flattened sections of Hanoi. He remembered those despairing nights on the *Shiloh* seven years earlier, when he and other pilots had lived in fear and frustration because of Johnson's willingness to send them again and again in their tactical aircraft to perform a strategic mission. *If there was to be a war, and if I was to be sacrificed on its altar, could it not at least have been carried out with a clearness of purpose that matched the commitment of the men being sent to fight it?* He remembered Jimmy Maxwell's frequent analogy from those days, *You can't be a little bit at war, any more than you can be a little bit pregnant.* The North Vietnamese government reacted to strength, not reason. Those carefully pinpointed rolls of rubble, product of ten days of terror that for the first time matched what had been happening in the South for ten years, had finally bought him his freedom.

At Hoa Lo prison the shutters were off the windows. The prisoners from Dogpatch crawled stiffly out of the trucks, and men who for years had not even been allowed to tap on a wall or peer out of a window without punishment were yelling into the courtyard at them, their voices filled with glee. Even as the guards were filing them into new rooms, by order of shootdown, Red Lesczynski was communicating to the senior ranking officers in their covert military structure. *Commanding Officer of Dogpatch, reporting return of 208, awaiting further orders.* And the word came back, official for the first time. They were going home.

Rabbit brought him into interrogation the next morning. With the promise of release so sweetly floating inside his spirit, Lesczynski could only look at the menacing interrogator with contempt, as if he were a memory, a nightmare. Rabbit held the confessions Lesczynski had signed in 1966 and 1969 in one hand. He teased Lesczynski that if he spoke of his torture, the world would not believe him. He threatened also to release the confessions to the American government. He seemed convinced that the confessions would cause Lesczynski to be court-martialed.

But there was something else in Rabbit's sleek stare, a fear. Was he worried about more B-52s once the prisoners were released, an American victory, and a trial as a war criminal? Or was he worried that he would be disciplined by his own people for having embarrassed them if this all got out? Anything was possible inside Hanoi's controlled regime, Lesczynski thought, remembering being disciplined in 1966 for the failure of the first operation on his arm. They could be on the verge of punishing Rabbit for not being cruel enough, for being too cruel, or for being just properly cruel but letting the cat out of the bag. Or, for nothing. They didn't need a reason.

Lesczynski had dared a smile. "You do whatever you want. And I'll do whatever I want."

Ashley Asthmatic ushered him back to his cell. It was almost like Old Home week as the consumptive guard stumbled and hacked and coughed. *But I'm getting out of here,* thought Lesczynski, remembering the night three years before when Ashley Asthmatic had shuffled into his room and shown him to endless days and nights of torture. *He's got to stay.*

Ashley Asthmatic was actually currying his favor as they walked across the courtyard toward his cell. He even called Lesczynski by his rank. "Hey, Commander. When United States bomb Hanoi one more time, win war, you come back province chief, huh?" He laughed, his chest rumbling. "What province you take?"

"Whichever one Rabbit lives in." And they both had laughed, a knowing camaraderie in the unspoken promise.

* * *

February 12, 1973.

Six years, seven months, and eight days of dreaming for this wakeup call. It was wet and gray, Hanoi's winter chill seeping into scars and cracked bones. He went through the morning ritual for the last time, trying to summon up all the emotions and say good-bye to slop buckets and cold water and monkey-faced guards, to all the odors and the permeating noise of the loudspeakers and the gongs. It was still too inundating, too filled with fear and disbelief to be done away with. *Have I really grown from thirty-seven to forty-four inside this hell?*

The guards took them out in groups of ten. Inside a stark gray prison room they shed their striped pajamas for the last time and dressed in identical drab slacks and shirts, made in Czechoslovakia. They were given a breakfast of sweet bread and hot, sweet milk. It was so rich that it almost curdled in Red Lesczynski's stomach, leaving him dizzy from the sugar. They began to load into the buses, the injured "combat ineffectives" first, and then the others, by exact order of shootdown. The North Vietnamese insisted that the two turncoat officers would be among the first to leave, and the senior American officers at first refused, holding up the departure for more than an hour, embarrassing the communists before giving in to the inevitable. The PCs, the enlisted men who had earlier offered to join the North Vietnamese Army, had applied for asylum, believing they would be tried for treason if they returned. The North Vietnamese had turned them down, urging them to help the "revolution" in the United States instead.

They rode inside a shabby little bus to Gia Lam airport. An exchange area had been marked out on the dull bricks at the edge of the runway, three rows of chairs, two tables covered with white cloth. A crude tarp had been erected over the tables on four bamboo poles, to keep the drizzle off. American and North Vietnamese officials sat at one table. At the other, was a microphone. Several dozen North Vietnamese stood in the drizzle, watching, most of them in uniform. A small group of reporters were gathered in a fenced area, waiting to record the moment.

The buses halted one by one in front of a tattered, corrugated tin hangar filled with military trucks. Guards were meeting the buses. Rat stood in front of his bus, and ordered the men out. It occurred to Lesczynski that he was the senior officer of the group. He climbed from the bus, his left arm now strapped to a brace for the first time, and towered over the brutal interrogator who had tortured him for those unending days during the Summer of Horror. The eyes of the world were finally his protector. He smiled at Rat. It was a mean, threatening smile, one that redeemed his manhood, one that he wanted Rat to remember.

"We don't need you anymore."

"You must line up! We will march you to exchange stand."

"Go fuck yourself, Rat."

Lesczynski turned to the twenty men from his small bus. "Form up. Column of twos. Right, *face*. Forward, *march*."

Rat and the other guards fell away, disoriented and impotent. And the prisoners delivered themselves to freedom.

Rabbit and Spot read their names from the microphone at the second table, one by one, and they stepped over the line to waiting Americans, real unfettered Americans whose faces reflected their own pride and joy. Somebody gave him a beer and he sipped it, the bubbles burning his tongue, and then three huge C-141 "Freedom Birds" approached from the distance and roared onto the runway. As the aircraft taxied toward the release point he could see the large American flag on the tail and the crew waving and he wanted to do everything at once; laugh, weep, dance, pray. On the aircraft three nurses smiled and joked. He had forgotten how wonderful perfume smelled. One of the prisoners grabbed a nurse and kissed her full on the mouth, long and unhurried. They all cheered.

The aircraft taxied out and then put on the power and they were silent, inside their memories and fears, the last gossamer of their captivity, that final stretch of Hanoi earth, rumbling underneath them. The C-141 "broke ground" and was airborne and they cheered, but only once, before falling back into silence. Then a few minutes later the pilot came onto the intercom and announced, "Gentlemen, we have just cleared North Vietnam. For you Navy pilots, we are now 'feet wet.' For all of you, welcome to freedom." Then they finally laughed and wept, dancing in the aisles and shaking hands, throwing off the ugliness of their captivity with a tumultuous cheer.

He read his first newspaper since 1966. He read every magazine he could get his hands on, from *Time* to *Playboy*. The woman on the *Playboy* centerfold was completely nude. It was a shock. A man looking over his shoulder remarked that things had certainly changed. He stared closely at the picture, his loins shivering and aching from what he saw.

"Looks pretty much the same to me."

The nurses made them drinks, and tried to warn them of what was awaiting them at Clark Air Force Base in the Philippines. They drank the liquor and sucked in their freedom like a diver up for air, not yet appreciating its permanence. And they had no comprehension of the rest of it.

They climbed from the aircraft at Clark, somber and hesitant. A few cameramen were at the bottom of the ladder. Nearby, a color guard saluted them. Nice. In fact, wonderful. And then they saw the crowd, thousands of Americans who suddenly screamed and applauded, waving signs and jumping up and down. He saw children and a deep pain rushed from somewhere he had sealed off for nearly seven years and he could not control his tears. Television cameras were everywhere and Jeremiah Denton, the senior officer on the first plane, was speaking, *"We are honored to have had the opportunity to serve our country under difficult circumstances,"* and the children were running in and out of the crowd, touching the returnees, and he was standing at his best attention, still quietly weeping. *It's over. It's really over.*

* * *

They kept him for three days at the hospital in Clark. As his freedom sank deeper into his consciousness, he grew more joyous, more exuberant. He did not sleep for one minute. He wanted to soak it all up, every bit of it. At one point the doctors tried a knockout pill to slow him down, but it didn't even slur his speech, much less put him to sleep. Red Lesczynski was on a roll, a natural high.

As soon as he reached his hospital room, he stripped off the drab communist clothing and raced into the shower. He used an entire bar of soap as he stood and scrubbed for an hour, carefully going over every inch of his skin and hair, every tiny crease of every scar. Stench and fear gurgled down his shower drain, along with loneliness and humiliation. Then he put on clean hospital pajamas and a robe, and began to prowl the corridors, moving without restriction for the first time since 1966.

They had done up the hospital cafeteria for the returnees, covering the walls with thousands of posters and letters from all over the world. Many of them were Valentines. He and the other former prisoners walked along the walls, reading them, and then he had to stop reading them because he could not stop crying.

We never forgot you guys when you were gone and we never will, at least I won't. We have bracelets with POW and MIA names on them. My POW on my bracelet has not been on any of the lists but I have my hopes up. Thanks for fighting for us. You make me proud to say I am an American.

Dear POWs: Yesterday, was a lucky, lucky day. The President said you were coming home and I found five dollars on the sidewalk. My father is trying to take it. I'm glad you're all home safe. Don't get sick on American food.

I did not know the magnificence of life, nor the freedom I have had, until the wonder of your return. God Bless You.

He craved dairy products and meat, mounds of both. His first dinner in the hospital consisted of a slab of cheese, half a fried chicken, a porterhouse steak, broiled lobster, vegetables, milk, and a whole pint of chocolate ice cream. Periodically he would pass the cafeteria on the way to somewhere, anywhere, and eat another pint. A whole pint.

Lieutenant Dave Toumanoff knew everything about him. The naval intelligence officer had been Lesczynski's case officer for months. It was Toumanoff's job to help ease Lesczynski's transition back to the United States, and to garner any intelligence of value from Lesczynski during the process. He debriefed Lesczynski about the prison camps, their conditions, the names and whereabouts of every man he had seen alive. Lesczynski was one of the "memory bank" prisoners. He had mentally recorded the names of every man any prisoner had actually communicated with. Since they had been allowed no writing materials, it was all done from memory. Lesczynski would announce the letter of the alphabet, and then give each man's last name, first name, and branch of service, so quickly that it sounded like an auctioneer's chant. *"There are forty-seven 'K's: Kari, Paul Anthony, Air Force, Kasler, James Helms, Air Force, Kavanaugh, Abel L., Marine Corps . . ."* Toumanoff was astounded at Lesczynski's ability to rattle off hundreds of names in a few minutes.

Toumanoff delicately passed the word that Lesczynski's father had died. He knew that Sophie had saved ten thousand dollars during Lesczynski's captivity. He knew that Sophie had worked for the National League of Families. He knew that J.J. was playing first-string linebacker at Navy, and was in the 22nd Company. He knew that Katherine was studying at George Washington University, majoring in history, and that Johnny was working at a motorcycle repair shop while finishing high school. He knew that Lesczynski had won the Silver Star the day he was shot down.

Every returnee had such a case officer. Some of the former prisoners were getting bitter news. Word of divorces and other disappointments floated quickly across the hospital cafeteria, each time Lesczynski visited it for food. Dreams that had kept men alive were crashing to the floor like precious, irreplaceable china. Everyone had been secretly afraid, even Red Lesczynski. There were no certainties in life, that was the one thing he had learned through almost seven years of watching strong men give up hope and die.

Toumanoff arranged for him to call home during the evening of his first day at Clark. He was to be allowed twenty minutes. *Twenty minutes to catch up on seven years!* He fretted over it. He could not get too emotional. He could not start weeping or talking about unanswerable pains from eight thousand miles away. He wrote a series of reminders onto a notepad, deciding that it would be best to talk about facts; his injuries, when he would be home, the kids. He was scared. *Sophie, Sophie, all my dreams for almost thirty years, what do you look like, how have we changed?*

"Hi, Red. Welcome home."

Welcome home? No, everyone had been saying that. Why was she in such control? She was supposed to be weeping and dancing (he could always see her dancing, her full breasts bouncing in her childish glee) and he was supposed to be in control. Was there something wrong?

"Hi, Sophie." He checked his notes. "I have a badly damaged arm."

"I know. I saw it on television. It isn't paralyzed, is it? It doesn't matter to me if it is, I'm just wondering."

"No, I talked to the doctor and he told me I could have an operation. He said they can do it at Bethesda. They can hook it up and if I can make it work I can even fly again."

"I knew you would want to do that."

Oh, you did, did you? Well, I suppose you would. But can't you say anything else besides you know, you know, you know?

"I'll be home in a few days."

"Three days, they say."

It wasn't on his list, but it just came out, a penetration of both their careful facades. "Will you marry me again, Sophie? We could do it in Ford City and have a reception at the Falcon Club."

"Oh, Red!" She was suddenly sobbing, near hysteria. "Oh, it's been so terrible, Red, I've missed you so much! I wrote down a list of everything I was going to say but I can't *do* it anymore, Red! I saw you come off the airplane and I just wanted to jump through the television and grab you! Can we go away, Red? Will they let you just go away for a while?"

"Yeah, Sophie." Here he was, crying again and yet laughing, too. Now, there was Sophie, that little wonder woman who could cut through anybody's false formality. Oh yes, he was back, he was finally back. "We'll sneak off as soon as I get home."

After the C-141 took off from Clark he eased his way forward and talked the copilot out of his seat, and he rode in the copilot seat all the way to Hawaii. It was such an astoundingly good feeling to be sitting with a headset on again, staring down at a mass of gauges and then through the window at the blue sky and the sea below, listening to the antiseptic roar of the engines and the crew's chatter on the earphones. *This is me, oh, how I love it.*

They picked up a new crew at Hickam and he kept the copilot seat, the crew good-naturedly kidding him about his little-boy fascination with the aircraft. They droned for hours across the ocean, and then entered the continent over southern California. He watched dawn illuminate his country, cities blanketed in smog, the mountains casting long shadows into brown valleys, mist and haze below him like a pastel watercolor painting. From thirty-five thousand feet America was awakening in a mingling of gray and pink and orange. It extended forever to his front, to his future, and he wanted to somehow wrap it up in his arms, embrace it with his soul.

I have been long at sea.

At Shepherd Air Force Base in Texas, they put him and three others on a small T-39 jet, and within hours he was on his way to Andrews Air Force Base, just outside of Washington. *Perhaps a person has to know despair*, he thought as the aircraft bounded off the runway with the light quickness of a gnat, *before he is allowed to experience un-mitigated joy.*

* * *

The psychologists had talked with her and the children, interviewing them and also uttering weird warnings. *He may want to hunker down in the corner of the room every now and then. He isn't used to sitting on chairs. He might go off in a rage without warning, or sink into a deep funk.* They had prepared a suite for him, right at the Andrews hospital. It was on the fifth floor, in a private place at the end of the hallway. They had put bars over the windows, in case he tried to commit suicide. It was so stupid, and she knew immediately, with an absolute certainty, that he would refuse to stay in a room with bars on the windows. And why would anyone survive seven years of brutality and then want to commit suicide, anyway? Besides, he could always take the elevator up to the sixth floor, and jump off the roof. The bars weren't a very smart idea.

It had happened too quickly. That was a stupid thing to say after having waited for seven years, but somehow it was the truth. She was so used to his being gone that she needed a few days to adjust to his *not* being gone.

I haven't even had time to buy a new dress.

"It's a T-39. That must be it, Mum." J.J. scanned the approaching aircraft with the expert eye of an aspiring aviator. He was wearing his midshipman uniform, the diagonal stripes of a second classman on his shoulderboards. She couldn't even see his shoulderboards, that was how tall he had grown.

She unconsciously ran her hands over her hair. She had been to the beauty shop that morning. She had thought about getting a dye put on it, to wash out the gray, but had then decided that he must see what it all had done to her, as well. He was scarred and broken, she was gray, and the children were grown. They had all suffered, all experienced his captivity in different ways. Katherine huddled near her, her eyes already wet, and took her hand as the aircraft touched down. Johnny stood behind them. He had grown dark and muscular and square. He was short, like Sophie's father. His hair was too long, Sophie knew it. He was the most uncertain of them, having last seen his own father when he was ten. He had said nothing, but had been moody from the time they learned that Red was to be released. He was worried that his father would not approve of him.

The T-39 taxied quickly from the runway to the terminal area. Several hundred people had gathered behind a nearby railing. Many of them carried signs. In a moment, the crowd cheered and the signs waved and Red Lesczynski popped out of the little doorway, waving, smiling brightly, and Sophie had not been prepared for him to come out so quickly. J.J. and Katherine pulled her forward at a trot and they were all running and she could not even think, it was happening so fast, she could only run with them, swept along by their exuberance.

J.J. stopped six paces from his father and gave him a slow, sharp salute and Red faced him, returning it just as slowly, their saluting hands identically wide and thick, their eyes inspecting each other through age windows, memories on one side of the glass, promises on the other. Both of them were taut and somber, their faces glowing, and Sophie was crying, watching this symbolic moment, the passing of a warrior's torch with all of its terrifying, glorious, prideful symbolism, and then all three of them were in his arms, too full of Red's return even to talk.

Johnny lurked behind them and then Red saw him and stepped forward and grabbed him with a crushing hug and he smiled slowly, and finally hugged his father back. They brought Red to a microphone and asked him, as the senior returnee on the flight, to address the crowd that had come to greet him and the others. He stood for an awkward moment, watching them and their signs and the cold February landscape of Maryland. He was not an orator, he knew it. Jeremiah Denton had said it all, a few days before.

"I thank God that there is a country such as this."

In a moment he was shaking hands with the people who had come to greet him. Crane Howell hobbled up and hugged him, muttering through his pipe that they must have a visit soon. Jimmy Maxwell came from the Pentagon, where he was a military aide to the Chief of Naval Operations. Teammates from the Blue Angels, classmates from the academy, friends from the neighborhood in Arlington clasped his hand and patted his back.

Judd Smith lingered at the back of the crowd. Lesczynski was surprised to see him in a three-piece suit. He ran over to Smith and they embraced.

"Where'd you steal the suit, redneck?"

"Well, it's about time you decided to come home, you dumb Polack!"

Julie and Loretta walked up from behind them. Judd Smith turned then, and brought them forward. "You remember Julie, and Loretta? This isn't any time to tease you, Red, so let me just tell you that we're all back together."

"Judd, that's great." They both kissed him on the cheek, welcoming him home. Lesczynski examined Judd Smith's clothes again. "What are you doing these days?"

"I'm a congressman. Come on, quit laughing. It's the truth."

Lesczynski grabbed Sophie, shaking his head and continuing to laugh. "Judd's back with Julie and he's a congressman."

Sophie nodded her head slightly, scrutinizing Red for any of the problems the psychologists had warned her of. "Yes."

"Did you arrange this, Sophie?"

"No, it's the truth."

Lesczynski eyed Judd with true amazement. "You really are?" Then he laughed some more, enjoying the thought. "What about Dingie? Let me guess. He's president of MIT."

"No, he's out in the Pacific."

"Doing what?"

Smith shrugged. "Nobody knows, really. Hey, listen, I know you want some time with your family. Call me up in a few days, and we'll catch up. We live in Mclean, not too far from you."

Lesczynski messed Judd Smith's hair. "Congressman. That's hot, Judd. And you know something? I'm not really even surprised."

"See you in a few days, Red." Judd Smith was grinning ironically. "We'll fill you in on a few little odds and ends to be surprised about!"

The doctor met Red at the hospital and showed him to his suite. President Nixon had sent a note welcoming him home, and an orchid to Sophie. The doctor wanted to admit him, and do some tests. Red Lesczynski opened up his medical records and showed the doctor a twenty-page computer printout from three days of tests at Clark Air Force Base, which contained everything from a proctoscopy to a report that he had fungus growing between his toes. He watched the bars on the window with his first feeling of claustrophobia in years as the doctor went on about how he needed another few days of tests and observation.

Finally Lesczynski raised a hand, cutting the doctor off. "Let me put it this way, Doctor. You don't have enough guards on this base to keep me in that room."

He took Sophie's arm, and began to walk out. The kids were waiting in the car. The doctor called to him down the hallway. "When
will I see you?"

"I've got a lot of leave time coming, Doctor. I'll give you a call on
Tuesday."

* * *

He wasn't supposed to drive yet but all day he drove, up from
Washington to Breezewood, across central Pennsylvania on the turnpike, then over fifty miles of winding roads through gritty little mill
towns. All five of them chattered in the car, trading small jokes, pushing the heavy issues into the background for a while, until the bedrock
had been reestablished. J.J. was a straight arrow, filled with force
and drive, playing the role of junior officer as well as son. He brought
Red Lesczynski up to date on seven lost football seasons, and on new
Navy weapons systems. Katherine fawned over him, her voice satin,
hinting of a boyfriend she wanted him to meet. Johnny was the quiet
observer, the jokester. And Sophie sat against her door and watched, a
dreamy smile on her face. She was thinking of the car trip to Pensacola twenty-two years before. How frightened she had been, how
lonely for her family and her home, and yet how small that fear now
appeared, compared with the real dread and loneliness of the past
seven years.

He crossed the ridge behind Ford City just after dusk. He could
have painted the picture in his cell, he had remembered it so exactly.
The bulbs and spires of the churches, German Catholic and Polish
Catholic and Russian Orthodox and Slovak, rose up from the tawdry
little rows of homes, symbols of a reaching for freedom that had
created the most unusual country on earth. The factory was black and
silent on the far side of the narrow town, bordered by railroad tracks
and river. Images still lingered—Baba, his father, his childhood—
rushing from pocks of memory and embracing him with a prideful silence that his family shared in the car. *Ah, my Stasu, he go be REAL
AMERICAN!*

He drove down Main Street. It was a ghost town. The store that had
once sold baby toys and carriages now catered to geriatric needs, portable pots, and prosthetics. He followed the road to the Falcon Club.
It was run down, unpainted. No music blared from inside.

"What's happened, Sophie?"

"They've just about shut the factory down, Red. There's only four hundred people working there, now. The young people have gone off. They've had to. Some of the older men have been able to get work over at the pottery. Some others are working in the mill in Cadogan. Pete's driving a beer truck in Pittsburgh."

Four hundred people. When he had come back to Ford City to be married, the factory had employed more than four thousand. At the time of the strike, just after Kennedy's election, three thousand men had still been working. *Four hundred?*

"Why?" It was as if he had lost a portion of himself, all the things that defined him.

"Union and management tearing each other apart. Modernization. I don't know, Red. I'm not an economist." She watched the bleakness of February as it rubbed Ford City's streets and homes in soot and sludge. "It makes me feel so sad."

His mother was working at the sink in her small kitchen. He watched her for several seconds through the windowpanes of the back door, standing on the porch where he had played as a boy. She was thick and very gray. She moved slowly, washing her dishes. He pushed the door open. He knew it would be unlocked. She turned and stared at him through the cobwebs of age, her fleshy face considering him as if he were an image, as if she had dreamed of the moment so many times that she refused to believe it was real. He walked into the house and hugged her tightly. She began rocking him, stroking his withered hand.

"Oh, my baby, my baby."

"Take it easy, Mum. Everything's going to be all right."

They left the kids with his mother, and drove up on the ridge past Kittanning, to the Coach and Four Motel. The motel was almost unoccupied. They were able to get the same room where they had spent their wedding night. All night they lay naked on the bed, touching and laughing and weeping. Sophie went over all his scars, the gash marks on his legs, the primitive incisions over both his pelvic blades, wide marks with dots from the tobacco string stitchings, the similar mark along his bicep, the roughened skin on his upper arms where the torture ropes had been applied, the long scars on his buttocks from the rubber whips that Rat had directed during the Summer of Horror. He ran his fingers along her eyes and neck and mouth, measured the hurt inside her eyes, feeling the painful cost of being left behind.

They talked, for hours on end. And then in the dawn of his fifth day of freedom, they made love.

II

"Johnny, I think we need to have a talk."

"Okay. So, talk, Pop."

Sophie had just placed dinner in front of them. Red had been home almost a month, and had been in a leave status, although he had participated in several debriefings, including special sessions with the Joint Chiefs of Staff and the Chief of Naval Operations. In two days, he would return to the Bethesda Naval Hospital for intricate surgery on his arm. He had been interviewed several times on local television, having dryly assessed the measure of his captivity as "the amount of time it took America to eat 11 billion McDonald's hamburgers, if the signs on the Golden Arches are accurate." Judd Smith had caught him up on the chaos of American politics. But he hadn't been able to make much headway with the thing that counted most.

I am the head of this family, by God.

Katherine's boyfriend was a nice enough fellow, but he had this *hair* that went down to his shoulders. And Katherine was smoking at home. There had been a few battles on both those points. Lesczynski had won, although he was beginning to feel they were Pyrrhic victories. The boy could still date her, but he wasn't allowed in the Lesczynski house unlesss he got a haircut. The cigarettes were to be smoked in her room. She still embraced him every morning and when she came home from school, but she seemed to view him as a Neanderthal who needed to be indulged but not respected.

And this Johnny. He was a little wild man, built like a fire plug, totally undisciplined. He had always been fascinated with mechanics. Red Lesczynski had helped him before, spending Saturdays directing his skills. But now it seemed that he had given up everything else, just to work on motorcycles.

Johnny stared at him with a mix of mild tolerance and irritation, awaiting his words. Red Lesczynski took a bite of potatoes, chewed slowly, and began. "It has occurred to me over the past few weeks that you haven't been going to school like you're supposed to."

Johnny eyed him evenly. "I quit."

"You *quit?*"

"That's right. I quit. I've got a good job, and I don't need it."

"Now, hold on, son. Nobody in this family quits before they finish high school. You can take this talent and do a lot with it, did you know that?"

Johnny scratched his neck and grabbed a hunk of his thick hair. The hair was almost down the back of his neck. Sophie and Katherine watched, their faces trying to conceal true dread. The confrontation had been brewing since the moment Red Lesczynski had stepped off the airplane.

"I don't want to do anything else with it. I like what I'm doing, and I'm making good money."

Lesczynski chewed slowly. "Well, tomorrow morning you and I are going down to school and reenrolling you. That's all there is to it."

"I'm not going back. And *that's* all there is to it."

"Maybe you didn't hear me—"

"Maybe you didn't hear *me!* You can't come back in here and try to run my life anymore! I'm almost eighteen! I know what I want. *I'm not J.J., Dad!* Leave me the hell alone!"

Lesczynski bit into a piece of pork and chewed very, very slowly, watching his son with steady eyes. Johnny met his stare. Old bull, young bull. Heads butted across the table. Lesczynski turned to Sophie. "Sophie, you and Katherine go for a ride. A *long* ride. I'll turn on the porch light when you can come back inside the house."

"Red, you've—"

"Get out of here."

He stared into Johnny's eyes, waiting. The front door closed. Lesczynski rose from the table and shut both doors that led into the kitchen, locking himself and his son into the pit.

"Stand up, son." Johnny stood slowly, watching him. He walked over until he was only inches from his son. His left arm dangled useless at his side. The boy could tear him apart in his present condition, Red knew that. He just didn't care.

"Let me put it this way. Either you're going back to school, or only one of us is walking out of this room alive."

Johnny watched him through unbelieving eyes. He was breathing fast. "I don't want to hit you, Dad."

"Are you going back to school, or not?"

"You *can't* tell me what—"

Lesczynski growled, crashing into the boy, sending dishes from the table onto the floor. He swung and missed. The boy's face was hollow with fear. He fended off his father's blows. Lesczynski chased him

around the kitchen, swinging and missing. He fell, slipping on a pile
of potatoes. His head smacked against the edge of the table, opening
up a cut that trickled down his cheek.

"Dad, you've got to stop this! *Dad—*"

He kept coming. He grabbed Johnny's hair with his one good arm
and shook the boy as if he were a rag doll. Johnny yelled with pain
and embarrassment, finally pulling loose. Red backed him into a
corner, where the refrigerator joined the wall. The boy breathed rag-
gedly. His father's blood was on his shirt. His father was in a half
crouch, coming after him again, blood trickling down his neck from
his forehead. The kitchen was almost demolished. Chairs were scattered everywhere. Most of the dishes were broken.

Red Lesczynski growled again, and grabbed Johnny's hair once
more, starting to pound his head against the wall. *He'll kill himself,*
thought Johnny Lesczynski. *He'll kill himself just to get me to sit
through three months of school.*

"All right, Dad! All right! Stop it, will you? *Stop it!* I'll go back and
finish. I promise, Dad! I'll go back tomorrow."

Red Lesczynski immediately ceased. He was a mess, all sweating
and bloody, his lined face smeared with it. He viewed his son with a
small smile as he caught his breath. "Good, son. Good. You'll never
regret it, I promise you." He viewed the mess in the kitchen. "Now,
start cleaning this up."

Lesczynski turned on the porch light. Sophie and Katherine were
huddled outside in the crisp March air, their eyes filled with unbelieving dread. They walked back inside the house and hurried into the
kitchen, where Johnny was busily cleaning up broken plates.

Lesczynski nodded, speaking without a trace of victory. "Everything's fine."

Sophie shook her head, taking Katherine's hand and staring up at
the mess of blood, food, and sweat that was her husband. She slowly
smiled.

"Yes, sir. Big Red is definitely *back.*"

Part Six

BLOOD BROTHER

CHAPTER THIRTY-ONE

THE AIRCRAFT TREMBLED AND shuddered. Its wheels ripped away a barbed-wire fence as it broke ground, and then knocked over a truck as if it were a cardboard toy. The plane rose through a haze of dust. The people inside were packed tightly, filthy and sweaty and screaming, hollow-eyed in terror, and the aircraft climbed higher. Below it and behind it the other people, the ones who had clung to the outsides of the plane, were falling. They skimmed the wind currents, descending through the blue sky, back toward the dank angry exploding earth that they had fled.

Like sycamore seeds they were falling, spinning gently on bursts of air. Like snowflakes they were falling, each one a little different, no two alike. Like helicopter rotors they were falling, spun loose from the main parts, faint military memories in their descent. Like bloated dead men they were falling, arms and legs stretched outward in the wind as if they were afloat in the sea and stinking already.

Like their country they were falling, ripped loose from the cold metal embrace of American power, sinking inside a terrifying vacuum, certain within moments to die.

Before the eyes of the world they were falling, as a television camera captured their last gory incomprehensible moments in living color, from the rear door of the aircraft as it droned out of Da Nang, carrying its cargo of fear to Saigon.

The world was ending with a disgraceful whimper. The sky was dotted with dozens of people who had clung to impossible rails of hope on the last flight, the final Freedom Bird. And Red Lesczynski was watching it in his living room, in between commercials that showed beautiful women drinking the right soft drinks or sensually stroking the interior fabric of the proper cars.

They were uncaring, the people in the commercials. They had no knowledge of the greatness of this tragedy, and no need for it. It did not exist for them, and it never had, really, except as a piece of translucent film that held the same unreality as the commercials themselves, that was a space between commercials, filler to allow advertisements. Lesczynski tried to forgive them for their years of conscious ignorance as they broke the stream of agony in order to sell a Coke.

Welcome to the death of Vietnam, brought to you tonight by Coca-Cola. Have a Coke, folks. It's the REAL thing! Now, back to tonight's show.

"Are we that sick in this country, that we should just sit here and watch it?"

Sophie searched his face, a bit apprehensive. "There's nothing we can do, Red. You're just going to have to get used to it."

"Get *used* to it? Sophie, I got used to the antiwar movement being the experts on Vietnam, and the Indochina Peace Coalition lobbying the media and the Congress. I got used to the media making everyone who served their country look and sound like sickos. I got used to policemen being called pigs, and the attacks on the FBI and the CIA. I got used to seeing Dorothy Dingenfelder sitting on the House Judiciary Committee, pontificating about ethics during the Watergate hearings. I almost even got used to seeing the presidency disgraced. But this isn't something you get used to! We *caused* it! We cut off support to them—this so-called Watergate Congress chucked them out the window, for the sake of 800 million dollars of equipment! What do you think would have happened if the Russians and the Chinese had said to the North Vietnamese, 'Hey, guys, you've been trying for thirty years and you still haven't taken over the South. We're cutting off your aid'? The North Vietnamese would have had to regroup, and if we'd sent in a rush of aid, the South might have caught the North with their pants down, and this whole thing could have been the other way around. No, I'll *never* get used to it. It's the most deplorable thing this country has ever done. Our country did this, Sophie!"

"Red, nobody cares anymore. We can't undo it. You've got to let go, Red. It's over."

"The hell it's over. In two years, there'll be Russians using those bases. And then it will be someplace else. And if we don't have the guts to stand up to it now, we'll be in it again, only it will be worse. Do you want J.J. to have to go through what I did, Sophie?"

It knocked her silent, like a belly blow that pushed out all her air. J.J. was in flight school, hoping to pilot F-14s. He loved it. He was a natural. He had a moustache and he talked with his hands.

Red took Sophie's hand. A South Vietnamese helicopter pilot had made it to an American aircraft carrier out in the South China Sea.

Sailors nonchalantly pushed the helicopter over the side after the pilot climbed out. The television showed an instant replay, as if the fall of Saigon were a sporting match. Red Lesczynski winced, watching the helicopter roll over the side. People were falling from the sky. Aircraft were sinking into the sea. A country was ceasing to exist, and Americans were responding by taking pictures and throwing helicopters overboard like trash.

The television program broke for another commercial. A middle-aged woman was holding her head as the announcer offered her an aspirin, promising FAST FAST FAST RELIEF. Yes, thought Red. That was America. The aspirin society. Fix any headache with a pill. And if the pill doesn't work, you toss it away and find another brand. He felt incurably sad. "I don't either, Sophie. But you don't stop it by running away from it."

"So what *do* you do, Red?"

He did not know. He sat holding Sophie's hand and contemplated a quarter century of daily effort to prevent the very moment that was occurring before his eyes. He could remember almost every day of it. That was one legacy of the prison camps, those long months of solitary where he had conjured up and analyzed every moment of his life. Flight school, the bombing runs in Korea, his fascination with the Japanese, the months of shipboard life in Asian waters and the port calls. His passion for study, which still continued. He was an instructor at the Naval War College now, and had written a paper a year before on Asia after Vietnam. He had not foreseen the disaster that at that moment confronted him on the television screen.

He thought then that it was too late in his own lifetime to undo it, if it ever got undone, and an anger welled up in him. There was a weakness in his country, in its leaders or maybe its system, that had botched this thing badly, called on citizens to sacrifice and then rebuked their efforts, fading again and again in the clutch. He felt a pulse of fear, and for a moment thought he would contact his son and warn him to leave the military, to flee from these cowards and madmen who would ask him to bleed and then whisper that he should be ashamed of his scars. But that passed. The answer was not on the screen before him. It was in the years that would follow, and it was above all not a time to cry "foul."

"I'm going back out there, Sophie. I need to see it."

* * *

Judd Smith sat at his desk in the Cannon House Office Building and picked up the telephone and here was Red Lesczynski telling him that he wanted to go back.

"Go *back?* Son, there ain't anything to go back *to*. Have you been reading the same newspapers I have?"

Red chuckled on the other end. "We all know the media lies. Hey, come on, Judd, I didn't get my bell rung *that* bad. Not to Vietnam, dummy. To WESPAC. They're putting the South Vietnamese who've been able to get out in temporary camps on Guam. You're on the Armed Services Committee. There's a military hook in there, somewhere. Figure out something you need to look at. How about the conditions of the refugee camps? And bring me along as your military liaison. You can pull that off."

"Why, Red?"

"Damage control."

"Damage control? The damage is done, buddy. The ship just sank."

"I've given my whole life to this, Judd. Not Vietnam, but the use of force and its place in world politics. These are the most important moments of the decade, at least. They're not happy moments, but, goddamn it, why is everyone lying around like cowed puppies, peeing on their own tummies? Let's get out there and see what's going on. We could go up to Japan, or maybe get my friend Kosaka to come down to Guam. He's pretty honest. Let's see what he's thinking. And Dingie's out on Guam. We could have a reunion, anyway." Joe had written Red two years before, when he had been released from the prison camps.

Red taunted Judd from the other end of the phone. "That is, if you don't have a speech to give at the Rotary Club, or something."

Judd sighed, knowing that he would do it. It would not be terribly productive, but neither would it be hard to arrange. And Red Lesczynski was right. Almost everyone but Red was sick of it, weary and frustrated and embarrassed. It was supposed to have been the other way around. Red would be drained from his imprisonment, old and beaten, and they would welcome him back and comfort him. But he had won, and they had not. He had prevailed, simply by surviving the worst part of it, while they had let their end of it slip away, debate by debate, media event after media event, until the horrors that Red had overcome were now being delivered to the country they had grown weary of helping.

Red had earned the trip. And his vision was clearer than theirs anyway, at least at that moment. "All right, Lesczynski. But I want you to
know you're causing me to miss the hog competition at the Bear
Mountain county fair. I was going to crown Miss Piggy of 1975."

Lesczynski laughed, delighted and suddenly exuberant. "I'll make it
up to you, Smith. Come out to Ford City this summer and you can
crown Miss Kielbasa."

* * *

The aircraft taxied to the small terminal building and Joe Dingenfelder watched from an observation deck as the passengers unloaded.
Here they came, dressed in flowered shirts they had bought during
their two-day layover in Hawaii. What a pair they made as they
laughed and jibed each other. They were beat up by a quarter century
of violence, both of them scarred and graying. Judd Smith limped
slightly on the ankle-shot leg. Smith had steel-gray hair, still darker
than Dingenfelder's own, but it surprised Joe. Smith's face was going
fleshy. His tattered ear was visible from the observation deck. Red
Lesczynski's shortened arm gave Dingenfelder a start. Lesczynski remained thin, even two years after being released from the camps.
Watching them made Joe feel vaguely guilty for having survived his
young manhood in one piece. *Hey, blood brothers.*

Hendershot leaned over to Dingenfelder as the passengers approached the terminal. "Which one's your big shot friend, college
boy?"

"Shut the fuck up."

He and Hendershot walked down concrete steps and waited just inside the gate. Smith saw him first, and called to him.

"Hey, Dingie! Where'd you find that white wig?"

He grinned self-consciously, greeting them. His hair was indeed
white, bleached by the sun that had deeply tanned the rest of him. Joe
Dingenfelder looked like a rich Miami developer, dressed in his own
flowered shirt, open at the waist, gold chain around his neck, solid
gold Rolex watch on his wrist.

Lesczynski fawned over him, turning him in a circle as if he were a
model. "Goddamn, Dingie, has it really been eleven years? Let me get
a look at you!"

He had to get Hendershot out of the way for a while, so he could
talk to them. No one on the island even knew about Dorothy, and he

wanted to keep it that way. The bald old alcoholic had a machine gun for a personality, and would tell tales all over the island. "Go get the car, Hendershot."

"Sure, *Dingie*. Anything you say."

He grabbed Hendershot roughly by the collar, squeezing his throat. "If I hear one person call me that, I'm shipping you off the island, scumbag. You got it?"

Hendershot straightened his shirt, immediately repentant, eyeing Dingenfelder and the others through red eyes and a veiny face. "Yeah. Sorry, *Mr.* Dingenfelder."

They watched the warted, veiny-faced old minion shuffle away. Judd Smith emitted a low whistle. "Whooee. I'd say Mr. Dingenfelder is in *charge* out here."

Dingenfelder laughed softly. He felt immediately comfortable with them. He was glad for that. "I told you I was going to have fun, Judd. I'm having fun! Hey, don't mention Dorothy. They don't know about that."

"Sure, Dingie."

"And call me Joe. It's no big deal, but what the hell." He shrugged. "I guess I grew up."

Joe Dingenfelder had his finger into everything on the island. He worked right behind the governor. He was the governor's principal liaison with the military, which owned one third of the island. He entertained visiting dignitaries. He was a silent partner in several businesses with government connections, from real estate to oil refining. He admitted to writing the governor's speeches and policy statements, and it was clear by the twinkle in Dingenfelder's eyes that he did more than write about policy.

Judd Smith had read the smile and nodded with certainty. "Lord Joe, off running his very own island."

Joe Dingenfelder smiled comfortably at that, enthroned in a lawn chair on his elegant veranda, which looked out onto the jungle and the sea near Tamuning. Hendershot now served them drinks and Joe stroked the leg of a sultry Chamorro woman half his age. She had deep eyes and wonderful breasts. "Lord Joe. Ha!" His head went back and his woman smiled demurely to Judd Smith and Red Lesczynski, and Joe Dingenfelder laughed again. "Ha! Could you ever have imagined me doing this? God, life's a bitch, isn't it?"

The next morning the three of them drove along the mountainous spine of Guam, the sea visible on both sides of them, toward the refugee camps. Soon they were out of the car, standing on a bluff near Tumon Bay. They peered down toward two old World War II airfields, unused for thirty years. Along the flat gray runways, camped on the ruins of America's greatest surge of power, was a tent city of devastated and suddenly impoverished South Vietnamese, fresh from the demolition of their country.

Dingenfelder presented the Vietnamese to Smith and Lesczynski with a ceremonial wave of his hand, as if they were his personal possessions. "There you have it. Do you want to go down there?"

Red Lesczynski stood motionless, looking at the tents and the people squatting or walking slowly. He thought of the hundreds of flights he had made over Korea and North Vietnam. He thought of the thousands of days he had rotted in captivity. Had that been an expiation? Was this? Or would the expiation come in future years from the people below? He spoke to himself. "Maybe this sounds stupid. But we dropped bombs on people from those airstrips and now, after two more wars, people have been dropped back on us."

They walked through clutches of vines and entered the camp. Pleading, hollow-eyed South Vietnamese children clung to them as they strode along acrid rows of tents. And then Red Lesczynski wanted to leave, because he could not watch it anymore.

* * *

Yukichi Kosaka flew down from Tokyo the next day, arriving on Japan Airlines and staying at the Dai Ichi Hotel, entertaining them all at a Japanese *sushi* restaurant. Kosaka seemed as fascinated with Americans as Lesczynski was with the Japanese, and that was another part of it, thought Judd Smith as he watched the two of them talk about defense policy and economics. They were the same, really, the same! They had to go into things, to examine and study, to delve into them beyond the ability to do anything about them, even beyond the sake of understanding, off the edge to some undefined, shared emotion.

It wasn't the political conversation, which was interesting and which Judd followed easily. Kosaka was now a senior executive at Toyota, and Red Lesczynski chided him for Japan's trade relations with North Korea, at a time when Americans were still serving in South Korea. A division of American troops stabilized the Korean peninsula, protecting Japan and South Korea from North Korean aggression. At the same time, Japan had become North Korea's principal free world trading partner.

It wasn't even the economic debates, which revolved around defense responsibilities, using Toyota and Pittsburgh Plate Glass for examples. Toyota had increased its annual production from ten thousand cars and trucks to 3 million, just in the time Lesczynski and Kosaka had been friends. Pittsburgh Plate's plant at Ford City had gone from four thousand employees to four hundred. Lesczynski argued that American defense had made much of it possible, by the dedication of American dollars to the defense of Japan, in effect subsidizing Japanese industry.

It wasn't even the history. Judd Smith himself was as fascinated with the World War II battlefields as they, and had researched the Saipan battle before leaving Washington. He, too, wanted to fly up and see the battlefield.

It was the *going into things*. Red had asked Kosaka what the Japanese thought about the fall of South Vietnam. Kosaka had at first demurred, and then given some polite and evasive answer about it being sad for such a great country as the United States to have not been allowed to defeat such a small adversary. It was clear that Kosaka viewed the whole matter as a horrendous loss of face, best addressed by silence. But Lesczynski had pushed and probed, and finally Kosaka had nodded his head vigorously, again and again, carefully eyeing Judd Smith, who he knew was a United States congressman.

"Yes, yes! Even great countries can lose a war!" Judd Smith immediately sensed that Kosaka was speaking also of Japan. "But a truly great country must overcome such things! It will be harder for the United States than for Japan because it has wounded itself! But your people must come together again. They must first honor their soldiers. Then they must learn that all wars have sad endings! This was the lesson of the Japanese. On Saipan, you will see it. And then you will understand."

Kosaka had lost a brother in the Saipan battle. Red had invested his soul in the *meaning* of war, whatever that meant. They didn't want merely to see the battlefield; they wanted to rub their fingers on old bones, to sit inside the wreckage and meditate. Yes, they really were so much the same! When Red Lesczynski pulled out the little square of Yasukuni scroll that Kosaka had given him in 1963, both of their faces had lit up with the conviction that the piece of paper had some-how helped Lesczynski through the prison camps.

Judd Smith and Joe Dingenfelder had arched their eyebrows to each other, sitting across the table of the *sushi* bar. Big Red was in-deed the All-American Boy. But part of his soul was Japanese.

CHAPTER THIRTY-TWO

TWENTY MINUTES INTO THE flight from Guam to Saipan, after they had
passed Rota and just before they reached Tinian, the pilot suddenly
dove toward tiny Aguijan Island and chased a herd of goats. The fourteen passengers oohed and laughed and took pictures of the wild herd
and the craggy rocks. The aircraft then regained its altitude, and flew
over the southern corner of Tinian. Tinian was thirty square miles of
jungle vines and ridges, twin to Saipan in size, but flatter and almost
empty of people. During World War II the island had housed nearly
two hundred thousand Americans. Its runways and hangars had held
more aircraft than La Guardia. The first atomic bomb had been
dropped from a B-29 that had taken off from the island. The runways
remained, dark straight ribbons of concrete that looked like a trellis
laid over the island, built so well that they still kept back the undergrowth, even after thirty years. *American Can-do, Runways Built to
Last.*

From Tinian they crossed a three-mile stretch of sea and landed at
the Saipan Airport. The Japanese had built the airstrip, using Chamorro slave labor. When they controlled Saipan it was known as
Aslito Airfield. For decades after that, the airport was called Isely
Airfield, in honor of a Navy pilot shot down during the Battle of the
Philippine Sea. General Curtis LeMay had led the 21st Bomber Command from Isely Field in March 1945, to fire bomb Tokyo, a raid that
killed more Japanese than did either atomic bomb. Abandoned shells
of hangars and mysterious pieces of runway disappeared into the wall
of tangantangan that edged the airstrip. An old red fire truck chased
after them as they landed.

They were rebuilding the runway, and the small shack that served
as a terminal would soon be replaced by a modern, multimillion-dollar
complex. Hotels were springing up on Saipan. One of them, already
half built and operational, would offer three hundred air conditioned
rooms, and had its own 4-million-dollar desalinization plant, to make
drinking water from the sea. When the runway was finished, two tourist flights would arrive each day from Tokyo.

A bus picked them up at the airport. They drove along a narrow road that bordered the western edge of the island. It was hot and there was no wind. It was Sunday. The little town nearest the airport advertised cockfights for that night. There were very few cars on the road. To their right, jungle growth and sharp hills crowded the road. They passed through tiny villages with tin-roofed homes that had screens instead of glass for windows. Chickens strutted freely. Laundry hung limp in the blistering sun.

They could see Tapotchau, the craggy green mountain that sliced fifteen hundred feet into the air, dominating Saipan. The 2nd Marine Division had assaulted straight up Tapotchau in 1944. To their left, beaches fell into a starkly beautiful lagoon. An occasional islander waded in the lagoon, staring intently into the water, pulling a small boat with one hand and carrying a fishing spear with the other. Japanese pillboxes still lined the lagoon, half buried in sand. Rusted junk from landing craft freckled the water and the beaches. For decades after the war, scrap iron had been Micronesia's most valuable export.

At Chalan Kanoa they passed the JoeTen Shopping Center, a few drab buildings next to the road. It was the only shopping center on the island. Beyond that was a Catholic mission. Its Spanish architecture was a vestige of other colonial days. The bus passed the John F. Kennedy High School. A life-sized statue of the martyred President overlooked a large lawn.

They turned off the main road and followed a tree-lined driveway to the Royal Taga. It had been the American headquarters after the battle, and for years after that was the only hotel on the island. Built at the centerpoint of the American invasion, it overlooked a portion of the lagoon that had hosted the bitterest fighting of D-Day on Saipan.

* * *

On Saipan you will see it. And then you will understand.

What, wondered Judd Smith, sitting at the window of the restaurant at the Royal Taga Hotel. *What is it I am supposed to see, and what is it I will then understand? What does Kosaka mean, and why is he so sure?*

Outside the window were two American tanks, mired in the lagoon at the place where they had been hit by Japanese artillery during the invasion of the island. The water had turned pink on June 15, 1944, the day the Marines had stormed ashore and suffered thousands of casualties in the lagoon and on the beach. The water was emerald green now, and the tanks were barnacled artifacts, half buried in the white sand. They were a conversation piece for the room full of Japanese tourists. One short generation after the slaughter, Saipan had become a honeymoon haven for the former enemy. *What was it that the men in the tanks died for, and how long did it last? Was that what I am supposed to understand?*

They had toured the island during the afternoon. Japanese remembrances were everywhere: narrow intersections choked with Shinto prayer sticks, a peace monument erected atop Suicide Cliffs, where thousands of Japanese soldiers and families had jumped to their deaths rather than surrender, another monument at Banzai Cliffs, where thousands more had jumped into the sea. Underneath Suicide Cliffs, Judd Smith had watched a team of Japanese women patiently sifting through the dirt, culling out small pieces of bone to be returned to Japan and given a proper Shinto burial.

Is this what he wanted me to see? And how should I presume to understand?

The only American monument, other than the accidental ones, the pieces of battle wreckage that yet littered the island, was a small cross with a helmet on it, which stood in front of the local Toyota dealership.

There was indeed something graphic in the contrast, a way of dealing not simply with defeat but with war itself, and Judd Smith struggled with it as he sipped his coffee and watched the pink sun dive into the distant sea. A generation later, the reasons were irrelevant, and the duty to culture was paramount. Forget the reasons for the war, that was what the Japanese were saying on Saipan as Judd Smith watched. They had fought to the death, almost every one of the thirty thousand soldiers who had defended the island, and then the country had blessed each death, absorbing the souls of their lost soldiers into the spirit of the nation. He could see it in the faces of every Japanese who visited the shrines. It was eerie. It was powerful. He was uncertain if it was good.

And what is it that I am to understand? That no political rationale is absolute, and therefore that conduct is more important than philosophy? That loyalty to culture overrides loyalty to some rationale that may eventually be proved wrong, even if the victor in a war holds that logic? The right and wrong of a war is determined by who wins, that was what a North Vietnamese official had proclaimed in Paris not two weeks before, gleaming with the victory that had been gained by a massive violation of the 1973 cease-fire.

But how had Japan become strengthened by its defeat while the United States became spiritually weakened by a victory? Or was that even true? Judd Smith thought it was. And he finally decided that the Japanese knew, as a nation, what every mountaineer knew without ever having to articulate it: that loyalty to people and culture were the key to life. And that the rest of it might change a million times, be called wrong or right or anything else, but that you must never violate your loyalty if you wished to survive the judgment of the ages.

Dingenfelder was teasing Kosaka. He had been indirectly baiting the squat, gray businessman all day, believing he could penetrate the calm, overly polite exterior and surface all the other emotions. Kosaka had approached the monuments as if he were indeed in the presence of deities. So many Japanese soldiers remained lost on Saipan that the islanders referred to the battle areas as "hills of skeletons," and avoided them, afraid of ghosts. But they were not ghosts to Kosaka.

It had continued over dinner, not pugnacious, simply a series of small probes, trying to unearth Kosaka. Now Dingenfelder was asking him about his brother.

"So your brother's remains were never found?"

"That is right."

"And he's never had a proper Shinto burial?"

"No. We put up a shrine for him in our village. But now we have search teams who go all over the islands and bring back our soldiers. Twice a year, they come to Saipan." Kosaka nodded gently toward Dingenfelder, impervious to his acidity. "Maybe soon."

"Maybe we'll find him tomorrow."

Red Lesczynski intervened, protective of Kosaka, ever the mediator. He spoke gently, his face filled with questions. In the Saipan sunset, looking out on a lagoon full of ghosts, there were lessons to be learned. "How does this make you feel, Yukichi? What do you think of when you see the pillboxes where Japanese and Americans killed each other?"

Kosaka drew on a Japanese cigarette and surveyed them as they awaited an answer. They were sitting at a large, rectangular table. They watched him draw on the cigarette again, all of them having spent their adult lives on the rebound from the terror and destruction of a generation before. Kosaka was still very muscled. His eyebrows had grown thick and gray. He normally spoke with the quick, firm tones of his profession, but now he uttered poetry.

"I look at this small island and I remember my brother. I can see him when he went away to the Army. I think of him watching the American attack from the hills and then fighting until he knew he must die. I try to see his face on the moment he died. I wish him peace. I wish all of us peace. It is so difficult, and so precious."

Then they all went to a *tapanyaki* restaurant, right on the beach. The lagoon lapped at sand twenty feet from them. Just down the beach, a Japanese pillbox still sat, buried in the sand, its firing apertures barely above ground level. Out in the water, two American tanks made knobby silhouettes above the flat lagoon. The silent aura of dead young men haunted all of them. The Japanese cook was very good. They drank Kirin beer. And Judd Smith ate Japanese food with chopsticks, enjoying the smiling approval of a Japanese businessman and his friend Red Lesczynski.

* * *

"Well, get a load of this!"

Joe Dingenfelder sucked on an orange. The juice dripped off his chin. It mixed with the dirt on his hands, until it appeared that his palms were covered with a black glue. He slowly spat seeds onto the matted floor of Death Valley. They bounced off rotted undergrowth and snail shells.

"You find something, Joe?" Judd Smith moved toward him. Smith was soaked with sweat. It ran in tiny rivulets down the end of his fingers. Smith's cheeks had gone bright underneath the eyes, from the sun and heat. The heat was getting to him, Dingenfelder could tell. But Smith would never admit it. Several hermit crabs rustled underneath Smith's feet as he walked. His shoes smashed snail shells as if they were autumn leaves.

Dingenfelder's hands had already begun to wash themselves, with sweat. The heat did not bother him, as it did the others, nor did the sweat. You were always wet in the islands. If you weren't wet from sweat it was raining on you. He casually tossed the remainder of his orange into the mat of weeds that surrounded them. The orange rousted out a spider as large as his hand. It was a brilliant blue, and silky. It looked more like a crab than a spider. It disappeared back inside the weeds.

"This must have been a night position. Probably Army."

Before them, underneath the canopy of a clump of flame trees, was a pile of rocks and a wide, waist-deep hole. The rocks had been placed in a semicircle at the forward edge of the hole, making a protective wall. It was almost a park setting a generation later, with the massive, scarlet blooms of the flame trees overhead.

Smith eased himself into the fighting hole. Lesczynski and Kosaka walked slowly over, bent from the heat. Their clothes were soaked with sweat, and heavy. Lesczynski was limping slightly. Kosaka began to stare intently as he watched Judd Smith play inside the sacred artifacts of the past. He might have been frowning, or simply watching with a consuming curiosity. You never knew what a Japanese was thinking.

"K-rations, anyone?" Smith tossed out an unopened coffee tin. The lettering was still clear, and the olive-drab coloring remained, unrusted. He probed the floor of the fighting hole, and came up with a boot heel. He handed Lesczynski the boot heel. Lesczynski passed it to Dingenfelder, who offered it to Kosaka. Kosaka declined.

Smith peered toward the front, where the Japanese had been, as if he were standing watch. Jungle foliage obscured his view; frail pandanus trees, thick stands of tangantangan, tall weeds where the spiders made their nests. Hermit crabs rustled, making eerie, rattling sounds. To his left, ascending ever upward, was Tapotchau. To his right was a high, long ridgeline. He spoke, entranced by the moment, by the time warp they had passed through when they entered the unoccupied jungle.

"The 2nd Marine Division was on the left. They were moving forward, assaulting Tapotchau. The 4th Marine Division was on the right. They were pushing hard down the ridge. The Army's 27th Division was here. It could not advance. Soon, the Japanese held an interior position. They could fire on the flanks of both the 2nd and 4th Divisions, and could hold the 27th. The ridge became Purple Heart Ridge. The valley became Death Valley."

"Let me have some of that Coke, Dingie."

Dingenfelder tossed a full can to Lesczynski. He was the only one who had brought a knapsack.

Lesczynski took a long drink, and passed it to Kosaka. Kosaka drank a few sips, and gave it back. "Want some, Judd?"

"No, that's okay." Smith stared to the front again, consumed by the moment. "It happened. Right here. And we're probably the first people to see it again."

"Do you want to keep the coffee tin?" Lesczynski held it out.

"Yeah." Smith took it. He could feel the wind beginning to move. The eastern sky was going white, like the edges of feathers pushing against the blue. "It's going to rain, huh, Joe?"

"Soon."

"Then we'd better get moving."

"We'll have to quit before too long. We've been gone five hours. I'm about to run out of steam, Judd." Joe smiled gamely. "One more stop, okay?"

Smith watched the others. Kosaka smiled thinly, agreeable to anything.

Red Lesczynski stared through the weeds, entranced by the battlefield. "We'll never get another chance to see this. It'll be gone in a few years, the way the island is being developed."

Smith shook his head, flinging sweat from his face. The rest of him was too wet to wipe it. "All right. Let's go up to Marpi Point. That was the last defense line."

They drove along narrow roads, toward the far edge of the island. Musty undergrowth surrounded them, and high trees kept the sky away. They passed ridges filled with pocks of caves. Scars from naval gunfire still marked the ridges, light crags in the stone like starbursts. The jungle floor itself seemed musty and alive. It was not hard to imagine Japanese stragglers still crawling among the steep, hidden hills.

The road turned into dirt. The car crawled a ridge, and passed a concrete bunker that sat alone in the wilderness. Kosaka watched it for a long time as the rental car descended the ridge into the jungle once again. On the eastern side of the island they paralleled the beach. There was no lagoon on that side of the island. The sea fell straight down for seven miles off Saipan, into what biologists called the Mariana Trench.

To their left the ridgelines continued, high, steep bluffs overgrown with foliage. Smith peered into them as Dingenfelder drove. "The Americans had tanks. The battle continued on the ridges. They pushed the Japanese north, until the ridgeline ended and they ran out of jungle. That's why so many killed themselves on Suicide Cliffs and Banzai Cliffs. There was nowhere left to hide."

Smith carried a map. He studied it as they drove. The rain began suddenly, a heavy wall of water that blew in off the sea. It beat against the car. Dingenfelder could barely see the road. Finally, he stopped the car. The small Toyota rocked from the sheets of rain. He had to shout to be heard over the rain. "It's raining too hard, Judd."

"There should be a trail up here. It's on the map."

Dingenfelder began to drive again, very slowly. Smith watched the ridge. It fell abruptly, just off the road. Finally he saw it, just the slightest crease in the thick press of foliage. "There it is! Stop the car!"

They sat silently in the car, watching the mat of jungle. The rain had a life of its own. It pulsed against the car, like a small child's angry screams.

Smith studied the map, and then Red Lesczynski's washed, creased face. They grinned at each other, emitting an unspoken challenge. Finally, Red opened the car door, stepping into rain so heavy that it knocked him backward for a moment.

"I'm game. Who's coming?"

He slammed the car door and began walking the trail. Smith watched him for a moment and then jumped out of the car. The rain was cold. He was drenched in a second, and then he forgot about it. He heard the other doors shut and they called to him. He grinned, the water running off his face as if he were taking a shower.

Red laughed, his arms outstretched, embracing the rain. "I thought you all would come."

Judd Smith waved him onward. It was fun, like being kids again. "I just couldn't stand the thought of a sea story about what we missed."

They followed the trail for twenty minutes. It curved along a stream bed, and then finally began to cut upward toward the top of the ridge. A shadowed rise of rock and jungle bordered each side of it. Judd studied the terrain, and then stopped in the narrow corridor, shouting to them over the rain. "Right here! It had to be! The Americans would have come down from the ridge through this draw, sweeping toward the northern edge of the island! The Japanese would wait for them in caves dug into the sides of these fingers!"

They left the trail, wading a small, rushing stream, and poked through the undergrowth along the finger. Dud American rocket rounds and artillery shells lay in the foliage, half buried, noses into the ground where they had impacted. They avoided them, pointing them out to each other. The detonators of such explosives corroded after a few years, and made them dangerous if even touched.

Suddenly Judd shouted. "Over here!" It was a cave, large enough for a machine gun team. A canteen and a half-dozen bottles lay on the floor of the cave, behind cobwebs and leaves. They nodded to each other and spoke quietly, fingering the items with an almost eerie respect.

They had found a battlefield, a point of major contact between Americans and Japanese. For an hour they crawled along the ridge, finding more small caves and other military oddments, their hushed voices and hollow eyes sure indications of awe. The past had come to them in a rain-beaten jungle, offering up its painful secrets. This was what Americans and Japanese had died for. This was the embryo of the decades of their own adulthoods: wet jungle, men cowering in pockets of stone as other men killed them off like bugs. And why? Because back home, the politicians—people like me, thought Judd Smith —had failed to keep the world in balance.

Then Judd found it. He had crossed the stream again, outpacing the others. Just off the trail, where it shot upward toward the ridge, was a huge pile of brown earth. At its top was a small hole, now large enough after a generation of erosion for a man to crawl through. It was a mammoth cave, the kind Judd had read about when studying the battle. The Americans had blown the entrance shut three decades before, sealing it off while sweeping through the last Japanese defenses.

He climbed the loose earth and peered into the darkness of the cave.

"It's *humongous!*"

He dug at the opening as if he were a dog, throwing dirt between his legs. Soon he was sitting on the mound, peering easily inside.

Dingenfelder climbed the dirt. "Is there anything in there?"

"Look at it. Just look at it!"

Smith slid carefully inside. The cave had the odor of a wet basement. A narrow stream of water trickled down an air shaft to his left. In the gray darkness he could see pickaxes up against one wall, and down to his right, in another room, was a large concrete cistern that had once held drinking water. The cave had at least three rooms. Hundreds of old grenades were stacked against another wall. And lying just at his feet, as if guarding the entranceway to a shrine that marked Japan's brutal past, was the fully uniformed skeleton of a Japanese soldier, carrying a rifle.

Dingenfelder called to him. "Are you all right, Judd?"

"*There's bodies in here!*"

"Oh, my God."

One by one the others slid down the loose earth and entered the cave. Smith eased their entrance, his eyes having adjusted to the darkness.

"Don't step there! Be careful, now. Watch out for the grenades."

They stared silently at the skeleton and then around the cave. Shelves were dug into the walls. Bottles and dishes were neatly arranged on them. Kosaka knelt next to the skeleton, and was fingering it. He was trembling with emotion. Dingenfelder walked into the darkness. Spiders and hermit crabs swept across his feet. He peered up the air shaft. It twisted, elbow-shaped, and opened up on the ridge above. It seemed big enough for a man. Dingenfelder hefted himself on a ledge, and wiggled up the shaft. Furry live things tickled his arms and neck. Rocks scratched him. He pushed on, oblivious.

His head popped through the moss-covered ground of the high ridge, as if he were a mole breaking the earth. The shaft's opening was too small for him to climb out, so he rotated his head around, as it were a periscope. To his right, a foot away from him on the jungle floor, splattered by the heavy rain, was a helmet.

An American helmet, still perfectly formed, sitting lonely on top of a ridge that led to nowhere. Now, here was an artifact, the true symbol of the past thirty years. His eyes went wet, and anger burned his throat. *What did you die for, who remembers you?* Dingenfelder lowered a shoulder, and struggled mightily, finally freeing one arm from the hole, his head back inside the shaft. He wanted the helmet. They could have their Jap souvenirs. This needed remembering.

He reached for it, and it disintegrated in his hand, a frail shell of rust that crumbled as if it were sand.

He cursed silently, thinking of the moment that had left the helmet rusting on the earth, a dead Marine dropped by a waiting Japanese who had then sneaked back down the air shaft. He was disgusted with it, all of it. He wanted to leave. It solved nothing, and the anger complicated things.

He slid back down the air shaft, blinking his eyes to readjust to the darkness. Smith was exploring another room. Lesczynski and Kosaka were kneeling over a second body they had found, searching for identification.

"Let's get out of here. I'm getting sick."

Lesczynski was animated, enraptured. "Are you kidding? Do you realize what we've found?"

"Yeah. A tomb, Red! That's all! It's like we're inside a grave! That's what we've found! Come on, let's get back. I'm ready to throw up."

"We'll never get another chance to see something like this."

"I hope not! I mean that! Let the dead lay, Red!"

Dingenfelder watched Kosaka, who was even more entranced than Lesczynski. The squat Japanese was now choking back sobs, peering deeper inside the large room at other pieces of bone and uniform. He moved toward the artifacts, oblivious to the pile of grenades near his feet.

Joe screamed, watching the grenades. "Don't move, Kosaka! Stop!"

Red looked up to Joe, ever Kosaka's protector. "Joe, leave him alone, will you?"

Joe's eyes were terrified. "No! No, it's his feet! The—"

"Yukichi! No!" Red Lesczynski saw Kosaka edge the mass of old explosives and lunged forward, an attempt to tackle him and roll him away. Kosaka growled, surprised, fighting to get free. The two men rolled in the darkness, Red pleading faintly, his voice now frightened.

"No, Yukichi, no!"

Joe Dingenfelder knew what was going to happen. He lunged away, trying to get out of the cave. Behind him, the cave erupted with hollow blasts. Another, and another. He pressed his face helplessly into the dirt and listened to them screaming and then Judd Smith's voice joined them, calling loud and guttural, a piercing wail.

And then it was silent, except for Judd's babbling. The clinging smell of blood and powder emanated from the cave, and finally Joe Dingenfelder moved down the mound of earth, back inside. Lesczynski and Kosaka lay twisted and sprawled, on the altar of a past they had fought to understand and overcome. Smith was next to them, on his knees, weeping and vomiting from the odor.

"Red." Judd was moving his hands along the pulpy body, but it was no use. Red Lesczynski stared out in the darkness through opaque, empty eyes, and Judd had seen that look too many times, in too many places. "Oh, Red. Why, Lord, why?"

Dingenfelder watched silently, leaning against the mound of earth that had sealed the Japanese soldiers inside a generation before. The skeleton lay in pieces at his feet. The rain still fell heavily outside the cave, and it trickled down the air shaft. The dripping of the water was now the only sound, light gurgles, nature slowly reclaiming what man had in his arrogance defiled. Dingenfelder caught his breath, then put a hand on Judd Smith's shoulder.

"I wanted to leave. It all made me sick."

Judd Smith still ran his fingers over Red's body as if he might caress it back to life. The smell of old war and new death permeated the cave. A dreadful ache filled his stomach like a heavy, knifing weight. "It's over, now. It's over. Not you, Red. It wasn't supposed to be you."

CHAPTER THIRTY-THREE

So JUDD SMITH SAT BY HIMSELF in the Old Town Tavern, Established 1776, which those years before had been Mario's Bar.

Big Red had come back, and then he was gone. And Joe Dingenfelder had never come back, and never would. Red Lesczynski was dead. Joe Dingenfelder was pretending death, or maybe committing suicide, or perhaps simply having too much fun. *There are a lot of ways to die,* that was what Dingenfelder had said to Judd Smith two days after they made their way out of the dank, bloody dead-man cave on Saipan. *Red is all the way dead. He can't come back. And I won't come back, so I am dead, too. At least as far as all that goes.*

He had said it while sitting in the same lawn chair on his veranda, where they had first laughed and drank upon their arrival in Guam. He had said it with a serene, unrepentant face, so deeply tanned that it looked like a chunk of polished teak, his hair a white thatch above it, the brown eyes no longer a puppy dog's but instead certain, and yet at the same time resigned, as if the certainty was of the resignation itself, the withdrawal from the person Judd Smith had known.

Joe had consciously shed his former self, like a snake crawling out of its dry old skin on the hot rocks of a new spring. That wrenched, apologetic mass of uncertainty which was in so many ways the legacy of the sixties had been left behind at Dulles International Airport with the cold winter snow of 1969. And the new Joe Dingenfelder was doing what Kipling had believed to be impossible; he was hustling the East.

But Red Lesczynski had been hustled by the East, drawn into the labyrinth, unable to resist the lure of its contrived corridors and unlit rooms. He couldn't let go. He had followed Asia all of his adult life, studied its people and its wars, pondered their complexities. Lesczynski had an insatiable need to keep turning the kaleidoscope; it was in many ways the measure of his being alive. And in the end, it had killed him.

Judd Smith twirled the admiral's stars on the restaurant table as if they were tiny spinning tops. There they were, Red Lesczynski's dreams. He looked at the poem again. It was a good poem. Joe Dingenfelder had known twenty-five years ago that it would be the right one. Such sensitivity was almost uncanny. *When youth, the dream, departs, it takes something from our hearts* . . . And he sipped from the Scotch bottle, his own gift to the Time Machine. The least thoughtful inclusion, and yet he had survived in the manner that they all had dreamed. He reached inside his suit pocket and dropped a fourth memento onto the table top: the green and rusty K-ration coffee tin he had found on Saipan, the day Lesczynski died. It bracketed their experiences. Somehow, it belonged.

At the bottom of Judd Smith's melancholy was the belief that he should have been where either of them were, and either of them should have been sitting at this table in a three-piece suit, drinking Scotch, and remembering. He did not deserve to have survived. He firmly believed that. He had been the wild one, uncultured and unkept, the midnight baby whose touch could turn anything to chaos. He was the one who would more logically have either died or ended up off on a tropical island, having divorced the world.

In his mind they were with him. Their laughter reflected off the bare walls of Mario's, walls that now were covered with pictures of Revolutionary War battles and softened by burlap wallpaper. They were young, uncertain but happy, and as he remembered them they grew older, taking on wrinkles and scars. And finally they were together again, in the late spring of 1975, all three of them drinking and laughing in the scorching, humid heat of Joe Dingenfelder's veranda. And then in an instant they were gone.

And now he sat in the bar, the one who was not supposed to have survived, sucking on Scotch and peering too deeply into all of it himself.

The Scotch bottle was a third gone. He had been nipping at it steadily for two hours. The young waitress with her funny costume and Revolutionary War hat was becoming less and less thankful for the five-dollar tip. The dinner crowd was beginning to fill the restaurant. The waitress hovered over his table, pressuring him. He laid another five dollars on the corner of the table and nodded to it the next time she flashed her bright young eyes his way and then she smiled sweetly, picking it up, and gave him a menu.

He took the Ben Franklin grilled steak, the Lexington and Concord

mixed salad, and Independence peas. Later, he would let her coax
him into a piece of George Washington cherry pie. He glanced around
him, at waitresses in Revolutionary War costumes and tourists wearing Bicentennial T-shirts. The country was attempting to reach over
more than a decade of pain, to ignore it, and to celebrate its two hundredth birthday with the pie-eyed innocence that it once reserved for
Davy Crockett tales. It seemed hokey, contrived, rooted in a longing
to avoid the unmanageable rawness of the present. The country was
too jaded for a Ben Franklin grilled steak, just as an adult stops chewing bubble gum. But here it was, right on his plate.

Or perhaps it's simply me, thought Judd Smith, pulling on the
Scotch bottle and savoring some Independence peas.

He would call Sophie later on. She would be remembering today. In
a few days it would be her silver anniversary. She did well with her
memories, and had taken easily to widowhood, perhaps because she
had been forced to rehearse it for seven years before. She was back in
Ford City. J.J. was flying F-14s, which Judd knew terrified her beyond
words. Katherine was married, and had borne her a grandson, Stanislaus McClinton, named after Red. Judd chuckled, thinking of how
Red would have appreciated that. Anyone who could name his first
son after a Jew and a redneck could only love a Stanislaus McClinton.
And Johnny had just finished his third year of college, another item
that would have made Big Red burst with pride.

His own Loretta was in Washington for the summer, working as an
intern with the House Foreign Affairs Committee. In her first ten
days, she had put together a position paper on precious minerals and
their impact on policy toward South Africa that had been so incisive
that the ranking Republican had sent it to the White House. She was
a jewel, Loretta, a charmer with a brain. He had breakfast with her
twice a week at the Capitol Hill Club, and dinner at least once a
week. But you didn't get in the middle of all that. She had an apartment with three other girls, and, after all, she was twenty years old.

And Julie was back in Bear Mountain. Red's death had been the last
straw. She was not running away anymore, but rather grabbing life on
her own terms for the first time, milking the good parts. She hated
politics. *When you get tired of it, Judd, come on home*, that's what she
had said. He saw her almost every weekend, but it was a lesson he
had learned about himself, that he simply was not tired of it. He loved
it.

He picked at his Independence peas and sipped Scotch. The world had gone sour and blurry. Wind blew from a ceiling fan in front of him and perfume slowly gathered in its currents, the steady warm breeze stealing a woman's odors and delivering them to him. He thought it was the waitress again and he looked up from his plate to tell her he would order the George Washington cherry pie and he was staring into an amused smile that sat on the face of Dorothy Dingenfelder.

Her arms were crossed in front of her. Her face held a mix of discovery and disbelief, as if she were a wife who had caught her husband with another woman.

"Drinking it straight out of the bottle, are you? What would your congregation think, Reverend Smith? Or your constituents?"

"My constituents would probably figure it's normal behavior for Washington politicians. My congregation would understand spiritual duty."

"Spiritual duty?"

"I cannot leave this table until the bottle is finished. It was a promise I made, consecrated by blood. Don't you understand duty, Dorothy? Go ahead, sit down. What are you doing here, anyway?"

"Yes, I think I do." She sat, carefully. The wind from the fan wore Chanel. "Joe asked me to come. I had to walk into four restaurants before I found you. It wasn't the way he described it. But I did it, didn't I? For Joe. Isn't that a little bit of duty, that I would? And anyway, that's why I'm here."

"So when did you start listening to Joe, all of a sudden?"

They stared at each other, their faces frozen in identical, taut smiles. Everything was a power play between them. It had been that way for more than twenty years, from the first moment that Joe Dingenfelder had introduced them over a drink. Even the stares and the smiles reeked of it. Each was waiting for the other to go belly up in some small way, to show the greater weakness, the greater need for communication or reassurance or even debate.

She measured her words, leaning into the table, still smiling, still meeting his eyes. "He hasn't been very easy to listen to, has he? It's the first time he's written in seven years."

"Now, who's fault is that?" Judd Smith mimicked the press stories. "Congresswoman Dingenfelder's husband is a scientist who avoids publicity. Currently, he is working in the Pacific, on highly sensitive government projects." He reverted to his normal voice. "You could have found him. Hell, you could have gotten his address from me, Dorothy, at least for the last three years."

"I knew he would write when he was ready. There wasn't any use pushing it, and I didn't need the hassle." She was tough, Dorothy, her words bitten, with the clipped edge of a good lawyer. She raised her eyebrows. "And I don't think I need to be lectured to by you. Where's your wife today, Congressman Smith? Down home, slopping hogs?"

"She's keeping the house in Bear Mountain."

"She couldn't take it. She ran away."

"She's found some peace. That isn't exactly running away." He shrugged. "She'll be waiting for me when I'm done with Congress."

"So might Joe be waiting for me. When I'm done. And besides," she leaned back, taking out a cigarette and lighting it, as if resting her case before an unseen jury, "who says you'll ever be done, Congressman Smith? They *do* seem interested in getting you to run for the Senate, now, don't they?"

He smiled then, a bit sadly, knowing she was right. The men with the soft hands and the film crews were indeed pressuring him again. He would probably go for the Senate, and if he did he would probably win, because he would do it only if the polls showed he was very strong, and then he would plan it like a military campaign, thoroughly and aggressively. Yes, that was his flaw, that he could get such things done. And there was a chance that it would hurt Julie, make it all seem so unending that she would decide they didn't really have a marriage anymore. It was a risk, one to be considered, but only one among many. He had learned that about himself. Not that he liked it.

And he and Julie had never really resolved the balance between love and duty, not all the way. Only Red and Sophie had, and only they approached what might have been labeled happiness, compatibility, symbiosis. He with Julie and Dorothy with Joe had failed in a similar way, although he hated to admit it. Was there an inverse relationship brewing, a law of physics that had not yet been articulated? Could it be that there was only so much joy available in one life, and if it was soaked up in professional success it had to come from somewhere else, somewhere more fragile and less durable, somewhere like love? Sensing that, or at least viscerally grasping it, made him for the first time feel comfortable with Dorothy Dingenfelder.

He pushed the bottle across the table, leaning forward with it, his hand still grasping it and his eyes fixing her in an electric stare.

"All right, lady Dingenfelder. Duty, honor, country. Drink."

* * *

She had moved around the table, so that she was sitting on one side of it rather than across from him. She was sprawled in her seat, eyeing him with the first relaxed smile she had ever issued in his direction. She was not unattractive, Dorothy. She exuded a mix of wicked matronliness. She almost giggled. The bottle had perhaps two inches of Scotch remaining.

"I am quite drunk."

Smith laughed. The world was moving very slowly. "What are we going to do when we finish this bottle?"

She focused in on him, her small face intense. "You undress a woman faster with your eyes than anyone I've ever met."

"You're not hard to picture nude."

"Is that an insult, or an invitation?"

He leaned his head back and laughed again, toward the ceiling. The room full of diners watched them closely for a few seconds, then returned to their meals. The first waitress had gone off duty, and he had immediately bribed her relief with another five-dollar tip. "Neither. I know better than to pick up on that. If it was an insult, you'd want to fight, and if it was an invitation, you'd be throwing some feminist garbage back at me."

She watched him closely. Her voice had lost its biting edge. "Not necessarily. I've never had a preacher before, you know."

"Well, I've never had a congresslady, either."

"This is going very fast, Reverend Smith." She sipped from the bottle. "And not at all in the direction I had imagined."

"We were hypothesizing."

She giggled, deep in her throat. Her eyes enveloped him. She had a power in her, there was no doubt. "Maybe *you* were."

"You know, Dorothy, I find you impossible to hate." He took the bottle from her. "I mean, Christian duty aside, even."

She faked a southern drawl. "Why, that had to have been the most *charmin'* compliment a man has ever given me, I do declare!" She reached for the bottle again. Their hands briefly touched, and lingered. "And Mr. Smith, I must say that, although you are a complete fool in your politics, you do have a *way* about you, otherwise."

"Let's not talk politics."

"How can we talk about anything else? All of life is politics, you know that."

"We'll get into a fight, lawyer lady. I've never been too drunk to fight."

She was no longer giddy. Her voice was normal now, although thick with Scotch and humming with invitation. "Well, don't you see how wonderful that is, and how unusual? That we live in a country where we can fight so loudly and still be so creative?"

"You might not think so when things turn around. There are two rules in life, Dorothy. One, things never work out all the way. And two, they always turn around. Always."

"Perhaps." She lit a cigarette, her tenth, watching him. She did not believe they would turn around this time, not completely. But she would give him the point, for the sake of discussion. "Even so, that's better than a system hell-bent for destruction. I lived through that, once."

"Yeah, and you wear it like a crown. That was in another country, forty years ago. And besides, Hitler is dead."

"Is he? Is Lenin?"

"Ask your communist friends in Hanoi."

She shook her head hopelessly, smiling at him with amusement. Judd Smith would never make a lawyer. He dealt too much from emotions, and not enough through logic. It was the exact answer she had wanted from him. "Well, if Lenin still survives, can't Hitler? Come now, Judd. And what do you wear like a crown? Your wars. Your friends who died in battle. Red Lesczynski."

Smith tipped the bottle up. It was almost gone. "People. And pride. And proud people are loyal. Think of this, okay? If nothing ever works out all the way, and if all things change, what's left? Your family and your friends and your values, that's what's left. And your duty to them. So they aren't the most important things in life, Dorothy. They're the *only* important things in life."

"So why do you keep wasting all of that on wars?"

"Nobody hates that worse than somebody who's seen it happen. But some things are worth dying for. Do you believe that? Huh?" Her eyebrows were raised, as if he were being melodramatic. He leaned forward, intense. "If you don't believe that, you deserve to live as a slave. I'm not kidding. You know what you're missing, Dorothy? The understanding of how fragile this country is."

"Don't tell me about fragile countries. I watched a whole continent fall apart."

"Here we go again. Look, Dorothy. This time it's different. This isn't a murderous state. It never could be. The people who made this country are too strong, as individuals! I'd think you'd be the first to understand that. How did this country start? We didn't simply stumble on this, you know. At least my culture. The old Scotch-Irish. The people you call the red-necks. We came over here and suffered and took it and made it what it is. We *made* this, from nothing. When we got here, there weren't any libraries or schools or police, no rat-infested tenements to hate, even. There was *nothing*. Those first boat-loads from Ulster—two thirds of the people were dying on the boats! Now, why did they take a chance like that? *Because they wanted people and government to leave them the hell alone, to let them pursue life according to their own values!* They created a government that would leave them alone, that wouldn't substitute somebody else's values for theirs and shove them down their throats. Now, you came over here after it was working and saw this great monster society, strong and fearful. Give us a break, will you? All this litigation and weeping and marching is okay. I don't like it, but all right, I don't like what it would take to stop it, either. And you're helping to refine us. Maybe you're even giving us a better conscience. But don't overdo it."

"And how does one overdo it?"

"We're not the source of evil in this world. We should start with that premise."

He fingered the admiral's stars that Red Lesczynski had put into the Time Machine twenty-five years before. Lesczynski would have worn them. He had earned them in a thousand ways. They all would have been so elated back in Ford City. They understood in Hunky Town, where the spires that were transplanted from Eastern European soil reached above homes and factories and the kids now wore T-shirts— everything was done with T-shirts in 1976—*PROUD AMERICAN, POLISH ROOTS.*

"Freedom isn't free. You've got to pay the price, Dorothy. I am very drunk."

"So, what is freedom, if you don't use it?"

"What does that mean?"

She smiled coyly. She was actually cute, Dorothy, especially through the din of Scotch that whirred inside his ears and blurred his vision. "It means everything! It's the whole ball game. Have you ever read the Preamble to the Constitution, the part about 'securing the blessings of liberty to ourselves and our posterity'? Well, what are the blessings of liberty? What can we do that few other countries can?"

"I know what you're going to say, Dorothy. Some cute little speech about dissent and free speech, and how wonderful the last fifteen years have been because they've proved we can hold the outer fabric together while we adjust to change. *What* changes, though? That's the question! It's not the adjustment part that's wrong, it's the changes! But one thing about changes, Dorothy. They just keep changing." He laughed, noting what appeared to be a scowl growing on her face. "Words, words, words. We all have our speeches, right?"

"But it's true, Judd. Don't you realize what a precious thing it is to be able to speak your mind without fear? Liberty is more than owning corporations, you know." She seemed irritated at him now, as if he had rained on her little parade, and then she smiled gamely again. "Well, I'll take what I can get. At least you accept that the system is served by change. I'd say that's how it has survived for two hundred years."

He grunted, holding back a grin. "Two hundred years wouldn't make a pimple on the ass of Time, Dorothy. But, all right. The system is served by change, and change is caused by debate. So, aren't we clever? Even you and I can agree, if we drink enough Scotch."

"Of course we can! And isn't this supposed to be a reaching for compromise, anyway? Isn't that what we're doing here? Why are we here?"

He laughed then, unable to restrain it. "*We* are here because *I* came to honor a promise, and *you* crashed the party and drank my Scotch."

"Under orders on both counts."

"Let the record show that Congresswoman Dingenfelder has learned how to obey orders."

"Sir? Ma'am?" It was the waitress. "Would you all like to order anything, or should I bring you the bill?"

"I would like a razor blade." Judd Smith stared steadily at Dorothy Dingenfelder. "Or in the alternative, a very sharp steak knife."

"Mister, are you all right?" The waitress examined his swooning eyes and sprawled frame, going over the wrinkled face and torn ear.

"My dear, I am fine." Twenty-five years ago, he would have sweet-talked her. Instead, he handed her a ten-dollar bill. He had lost count, but that made it about fifty dollars left. "Now, get us a good steak knife, would you?"

"What are you going to do with a steak knife?" Dorothy's eyes had enlarged, and she viewed him with sudden fear.

"We're going to cut our wrists, Dorothy! How about that, huh? We're going to be blood brothers." He laughed at that. "Or whatever."

"Oh, for God's sake, Judd Smith. Blood and violence! You are a manifestation of what's gone wrong in this country! You are the goddamned *problem!* How can we talk responsibly and have you come up with such a thing?" She wrinkled up her nose as if nauseated. "That's so *childish.*"

"It isn't blood and violence, it's loyalty! Can't you understand that? It's a bond of pain! You see, I'm part Indian, remember? And the Indians and the pioneers agreed this way. But that was before we had eighty-seven-page contracts and three years of litigation whenever somebody wanted to know whether they had to honor their own word. You want loyalty? Come on, Dorothy. You bleed with me, I'll die for you."

The waitress brought the knife. She had an uncertain look on her face. Her Revolutionary hat was lopsided and silly. Smith thanked her with elaborate grandiosity.

"Wonderful job, my dear. Exactly what I desired. All right, now, Dorothy, this won't hurt. Just lay your little arm on the table, like this." He placed his own, palm up, onto the table. "Go ahead, right next to mine, now."

"You're out of your mind." She slowly stood, and left the restaurant, teetering from the whiskey.

* * *

He sat for another five minutes, playing with the knife, reading Dingie's poem, flicking Red Lesczynski's stars like tiny spinning tops on the table. He decided he would spend the rest of the night on the telephone. He would start by calling Sophie in Ford City. She had been a mother to them through all of those early, ugly years. It would be so good to talk with her. Then he would call Julie, and remind her how much he loved her. He might even call Guam, and tell Joe he had been to Mario's, and that actually Mario's had never even existed because underneath its greasy facade the bar really had been the Old Town Tavern, Established 1776.

He repacked the cloth bag with his treasures, including the coffee tin, and left all the money for the waitress. He didn't know how much his dinner had been, but he felt a need to be done with it, all of it. Outside the restaurant the tourists flocked in twos and fours, arms entwined, enjoying the warm, odorous June evening along the waterfront. A black man on roller skates discoed among the slowly moving cars, shirtless and powerful, grooving on music that came from deep within his soul. A policewoman whistled at the skater to get off the street and he waved happily, heedless of her orders.

Dorothy was standing at the edge of the water, leaning on a large bollard, looking out into the bay. She seemed so alone and vulnerable, so small and sad. Or was he reading his own interpretations into the long stare and the emptiness of the sea? On the far side of her gaze, around the corner of the world, sat Europe, her creator and tormentor. Would she ever be free of its ugly scars? Or was even that a creature of his imagination?

He called to her as he walked past, a gentle attempt at humor. "Don't jump in now, Dorothy."

She turned to face him in the dark. He could tell she had been crying. She gave him a fierce smile. "And let people like you run the country, Judd Smith? Not on your life."